HOUSE OF CARDS

and the sequel

TO PLAY THE KING

MICHAEL DOBBS
HOUSE OF CARDS
and the sequel
TO PLAY THE KING

BCA
LONDON · NEW YORK · SYDNEY · TORONTO

This omnibus edition published 1992
by BCA
by arrangement with Harper Collins Ltd.

House of Cards © Michael Dobbs 1989
To Play The King © Michael Dobbs 1992

CN 1428

Printed and bound in Great Britain by
Mackays of Chatham PLC,
Chatham, Kent.

CONTENTS

DEDICATIONS

House of Cards

For Amanda
And For William

To Play The King

Lucy and Andrei.
For Medford 1971. For Fiskardon 1981. For Villars 1991.
For everything.

HOUSE OF CARDS

PART ONE
THE SHUFFLE

THURSDAY 10TH JUNE

It seemed scarcely a moment since she had closed her eyes,
yet already the morning sun was waking her as it crept
around the curtain and began to shine on her pillow. She
turned over irritably, resenting the unwanted intrusion.
The past few weeks had been hard, with days of poorly
digested snacks washed down by nights of too little sleep,
and her body ached from being stretched too tightly
between her editor's deadlines.

She pulled the duvet more closely around her, for even
in the glare of the early summer sun she felt a chill. It had
been like that ever since she had left Yorkshire almost a
year before. She had hoped she could leave the pain
behind her but it cast a long, cold shadow which seemed
to follow her everywhere, particularly into her bed. She
shivered, and buried her face in the lumpy pillow.

She tried to be philosophical. After all, she no longer
had any emotional distractions to delay or divert her, just
the challenge of discovering whether she really did have
what it took to become the best political correspondent in
a fiercely masculine world. But it was bloody difficult to be
philosophical when your feet were freezing.

Still, she reflected, sex as a single girl had proved to be
excellent basic training for politics – the constant danger of
being seduced by a smile or a whispered confidence, the
unending protestations of loyalty and devotion which
covered, just for a while, the bravado, the exaggeration,
the tiny deceits which grew and left behind only reproach
and eventually bitterness.

And in the last few weeks she had heard more outrageous and empty promises than at any time since – well,
since Yorkshire. The painful memories came flooding back
and the chill in her bed closed unbearably around her.

With a sigh Mattie Storin threw back the duvet and clambered out of bed.

As the first suggestion of dusk settled across the June skies, four sets of HMI mercury oxide lamps clicked on with a dull thud, illuminating the entire building with 10,000 watts of high intensity power. The brilliant beams of light pierced deep behind the mock Georgian facade, seeking out and attacking those inside. A curtain fluttered at a third floor window as someone took a quick glance at the scene outside before retreating quickly.

The moth also saw the lamps. It was resting in a crevice in the mortar of the building, waiting for the approaching dusk. As the shafts of light began to pierce through its drowsiness, the moth began to tingle with excitement.

The lamps glowed deep and inviting, like nothing it had ever known. It stretched its wings as the light began to warm the early evening air, sending a tremor throughout its entire body. The moth was drawn as if by a magnet and, as it approached, the glow of the lamps became more intense and hypnotic. The moth had never felt like this before. The light was as brilliant as the sun yet much, much more approachable.

Its wings strained still harder in the early evening air, forcing its body along the golden river of light. It was a source of unimaginable power which seemed to be dragging the willing moth ever deeper into its grasp. Nearer and nearer it flew – until, with one final triumphant thrust, it was there!

There was a bright flash and crackle as the moth's body hit the lens a millisecond before its wings wrapped around the searing glass and vaporised. A charred and blackened carcass fell back from the lamp towards the ground. The night had gained the first of its victims.

A police sergeant cursed as she tripped over one of the heavy cables. The electrician looked the other way. After all, where the hell was he supposed to hide the miles of wiring which now ran around the square. The graceful Wren church of St John peered down darkly in disapproval. You could almost feel it wanting to shake itself free of the growing crowds of technicians and watchers who now clung tenaciously around its footings. The ancient steeple clock had long since stopped at twelve, as if the church was willing time to stand still and trying to hold back the encroachment and pressures of the modern age. But like looting heathens they swarmed over and around it more vigorously with every passing minute.

Above the church's four soaring limestone towers, the dusk was slowly spreading red streaks through the skies over Westminster. Yet the day was far from over, and it would be many hours before the normal gentility of Smith Square crept back over the piles of discarded rubbish and empty bottles.

The few local residents who had remained in the square throughout the devastation of the campaign gave up a silent prayer to St John and his Creator that at last it was almost over. Thank God elections only happen every three or four years.

High above the square, in a portable cabin perched temporarily on the flat roof of party headquarters, the Special Branch detectives in their election base were taking advantage of the relative lull while the senior politicians were out of London making one last effort in their constituencies. A poker school was in full session in one corner, but the detective inspector had declined to join in. He had better ways of losing his money. All afternoon he had been thinking of the WPC who worked on traffic control at Scotland Yard, all starched efficiency on duty and unrestrained passion off. He hadn't seen his wife since the start of the campaign nearly a month before, but he hadn't seen the WPC either. Now his first free weekend beckoned, and he would have to choose between the open pleasures of his mistress and the increasing suspicions of his wife. He knew that his wife would not believe him if he told her he was on protection duty again this weekend, and he had spent all afternoon trying to decide whether he cared.

He cursed silently to himself as he listened once more to the raised voices inside him, tearing him in different directions as they argued between themselves. It was no damned good; the decisiveness which he had displayed to all of his police promotion boards had simply deserted him. He would have to do what he always did in such situations – let the cards decide.

Ignoring the jibes of the poker school, he took out a pack of cards and slowly began building the base of a house of cards. He had never got above six levels before; if he got up to seven now, he would spend the weekend with the WPC and to hell with the consequences.

He decided to give Fate a helping hand and reinforced the base with a double layer of cards. It was cheating, of course, but wasn't that what it was all about? He lit a cigarette to calm his nerves, but the smoke only got in his eyes, so he decided on a cup of coffee instead. It was a mistake. As the strong dose of caffeine hit his stomach, he felt the little knot give an extra twist of tension and the cards began to tremble in his hand.

Slowly, carefully so as not to disturb the rising construction of cards, he got up from the table and walked to the cabin door, taking in the view as he gulped down the fresh evening air. The roof tops of London were bathed in the red glow of the setting sun, and he imagined himself on some Pacific island, stranded alone with the incandescent WPC and a magical supply of ice cold lager. He felt better now, and with fresh determination returned to the cards.

The cards seemed to rise effortlessly in front of him. He had now reached the sixth level, as high as his card houses had ever gone before, and he started quickly on the seventh level so as not to destroy his rhythm. Two more cards to go – he was nearly there! But as the penultimate card got to within half an inch of the top of the tower, his hand began to shake again. Damn the caffeine!

He cracked his knuckles to relax his fingers, and picked up the card once more. With his left hand clamped firmly around his right wrist for extra support, he guided the card slowly upwards and sighed in relief as he watched it come to rest gently on top of the others. One more to go, but try as hard as he could he was unable to stop the tremble. The tower had become a great phallic symbol, his mind could see nothing but her body, and the harder he tried to control it the more his hand shook. He could no longer feel the card, his fingers had gone numb. He cursed Fate and implored it for just one last favour. He sucked in another lungful of breath, positioned the shaking card a half inch above the tower and, scarcely daring to look, let the card fall. It dropped precisely into its appointed place.

Fate, however, had other ideas. Just as the inspector watched the final card complete his masterpiece, the first cool breeze of evening passed across the top of Smith Square, lightly kissed the tall towers of St John's, and wafted through the door of the cabin which the inspector had left open. It nudged gently into the house of cards, which first trembled, then twisted, and finally crashed to the table top with a roar which cut dead the inspector's inner cry of triumph and echoed inside his head as loudly as if the house had been built of brick and steel.

For several long moments he stared at the ruins of his weekend, trying in desperation to convince himself that he had after all succeeded, if only for an instant, before his house of dreams had crumbled. Perhaps he had, but he knew now he would have to make up his own mind. He felt more miserable than ever.

His private misery and the poker game were cut short by the crackling of the radio in the corner. The Party Chairman was on his way back from visiting the troops at the front line, and soon other senior politicians would be joining him in party headquarters. The work of the long night was about to begin for the Special Branch protection officers. Just time for the inspector's colleagues to lay a few final bets as to which Ministers they would still be protecting next week, and which would by then have been dumped in the great waste bin of history.

The Right Honourable Francis Ewan Urquhart was not enjoying himself. Ministerial office brought many pleasures, but this was not one of them. He was squashed into the corner of a small and stuffy living room pressed hard up against a hideous 1950s standard lamp, which showed every sign of wanting to topple over. Try as he could, he had been unable to escape the devoted attentions of the

17

posse of matrons who doubled as his constituency workers and who now surrounded him, chattering proudly about their canvass returns and pinched shoes. He wondered why they bothered. This was suburban Surrey, where Range Rovers stood in the driveways and only got mud on their tyres when being driven carelessly over the lawns late on a Friday night. They didn't count votes here, they weighed them.

He had never felt at home in his constituency, but then he never felt at home anywhere any more, not even in his native Scotland. As a child he had loved to wander through the bracing, crystal air of the Perthshire moors, accompanying the old gillie on a shoot, lying for hours in the damp peat and sweetly scented bracken waiting for the right buck to appear, just as he had imagined his older brother was waiting even at that same moment for German tanks in the hedgerows outside Dunkirk. But the Scottish moors and ancestral estates had never completely satisfied him and, as his appetite for politics and power grew, so he had come steadily to resent the enforced family responsibilities which had been thrust at him when his brother failed to return.

So amidst much family bitterness he had sold the estates, which could no longer provide him with an adequate lifestyle and would never provide him with a secure majority, and at the age of thirty-nine had exchanged them for the safer political fields of Westminster and Surrey. His aged father, who had expected no more of his only surviving son than that he devote himself to the family duties as he and his own father had done, had never spoken to him again. To have sold his heritage for the whole of Scotland would have been unforgivable, but for Surrey?

Urquhart had never disciplined himself to enjoy the small talk of constituency circles, and his mood had begun to sour as the day drew on. This was the eighteenth committee room he had visited today, and the early morning smile had long since been transfixed into a rigid grimace. It was now only forty minutes before the close of the polling booths, and his shirt was wringing wet under the Savile Row suit. He knew he should have worn one of his older suits: no amount of pressing would get it back into shape again. He was tired, uncomfortable and losing patience.

He spent little time in his constituency nowadays, and the less time he spent the less congenial his demanding constituents seemed. The journey to the leafy suburbs, which had seemed so short and attractive when he had gone for his first adoption meeting, seemed to grow longer as he climbed the political ladder from backbencher through Junior Ministerial jobs and now attending Cabinet as Chief Whip, one of the two dozen most powerful posts in the Government, with its splendid offices at 12 Downing Street just yards from the Prime Minister's own.

Yet his power did not come directly from his public office. The role of Chief Whip does not carry with it full Cabinet rank. Urquhart had no great Department of State or massive civil service machine to command; his was a faceless task, toiling ceaselessly behind the scenes, making no public speeches and giving no television interviews. Less than 1 per cent of the Gallup Poll gave him instant name recognition.

His was a task which had to be pursued out of the lime-light for, as Chief Whip, he was responsible for discipline within the Parliamentary Party, for delivering a full turnout on every vote. Which meant he was not only the Minister with the most acute political antennae, knowing all the secrets of Government before almost any of his colleagues, but in order to deliver the vote day after day, night after night, he also needed to know where every one of his Members of Parliament was likely to be found, with whom they were conspiring, with whom they might be sleeping, whether they would be sober enough to vote or had any personal crisis which could disrupt their work and the smooth management of parliamentary business.

And in Westminster, such information is power. More than one of his senior colleagues and many more junior members of the Parliamentary Party owed their continuing position to the ability of the Whips Office to sort out and occasionally cover up their personal problems. And many disaffected backbenchers had found themselves suddenly supporting the Government when reminded of some earlier indiscretion which had been forgiven by the Party and Whips Office, but never forgotten. Scarcely any scandal in Government strikes without the Whips Office knowing about it first, and because they know about it first, many scandals simply never strike – unless the Chief Whip and his ten Junior Whips wish it to.

Urquhart was brought up sharply by one of his ladies whose coyness and discretion had been overcome by the heat and excitement of the day.

'Will you still stand at the next election, Mr Urquhart?' she enquired brashly.

'What do you mean?' he spluttered, taken aback.

'Are you thinking of retiring? You are sixty-one years old now, aren't you? Sixty-five or more at the next election,' she persisted.

He bent his tall and angular figure low in order to look her directly in the face. 'Mrs Bailey, I still have my wits about me and in many societies I would just be entering my political prime,' he responded defensively. 'I still have a lot of work to do and things I want to achieve.'

But deep down he knew she was right. Instead of the strong red hues of his youth, he was now left with but a dirty smear of colour in his thinning hair, which he wore over-long and straggly as if to compensate. His spare frame no longer filled the traditionally cut suits as amply as in earlier years, and his blue eyes had grown colder with the passage of time. While his height and upright bearing presented a distinguished image in the crowded room, those closest to him got no warmth from his carefully rationed smile, which revealed only uneven teeth badly stained by nicotine from his forty-a-day habit. He was not ageing with the elegance or the authority for which he would have wished.

Time was not on his side. Like most of his colleagues he had first entered Parliament harbouring unspoken ambitions to make it all the way to the top, yet during his career he had watched as younger and less gifted men had found more rapid advancement. The bitter experience had tempered his ambition while not being able to extinguish it completely. If not Downing Street, then at least a major

Department of State would allow him to become an acknowledged national leader, repaying his father's scorn with greater prominence than the old man could ever have dreamed of. He still had time to make his mark. He believed in his destiny, but it seemed to be taking an unholy long time to arrive.

Yet now was surely the time. One of the most important responsibilities of a Chief Whip is to advise the Prime Minister on any Ministerial reshuffle – which Ministers should be preferred, which backbenchers deserved elevation, which colleagues were dispensable and should make way. Not all the suggestions were accepted, of course, but the majority usually were. He had given the post-election reshuffle a lot of thought, and he had in his pocket a handwritten note to the Prime Minister covering all his recommendations. They would not only mean a stronger and more effective Government, and God knew they needed that after the last couple of years, but also one in which his close colleagues and allies would be in the strongest positions of influence. And he, of course, would have that prominent position which he had so long deserved. Yes, at last his time had come.

He tapped his pocket to reassure himself that the envelope was still there, just as Mrs Bailey switched her attention to the proposed one-way system for the High Street shopping centre. He raised his eyes in supplication and managed to catch the attention of his wife who was busily engaged in conversation on the far side of the room. One glance told her that his rescue was long overdue, and she hurried to his side.

'Ladies, you will have to excuse us, but we have to go back to the hotel and change before the count. I can't thank you enough for all your help, you know how indispensable you are to Francis.'

Urquhart made quickly for the door, but as he tried to complete his escape he was waved to a halt by his election agent, who was busily scribbling down notes while talking into the telephone.

'Just getting the final canvass returns together,' she explained.

'That could have been done an hour ago,' snapped Urquhart.

The agent blushed. Not for the first time she resented Urquhart's sharp tongue and lack of gratitude, and promised herself that this would be her last election for him. She would swap this safe seat for a marginal seat as soon as she could. The pay would be even poorer and the hours longer, but at least she would be appreciated and not treated as another piece of constituency furniture. Or maybe she would give up politics altogether and go and get a proper job.

'It doesn't look quite as cheerful as last time,' she said. 'Turnout is poor, and a lot of our supporters seem to be simply staying at home. It's very difficult to read, but I suspect the majority will be down. I can't tell how much.'

'Damn them. They deserve a dose of the Opposition for a few years. Maybe that would get them off their complacent rumps.'

'Darling,' his wife soothed as she had done on countless previous occasions, 'that's scarcely generous. With a majority of 22,000 you could allow for just a little dip.'

'Miranda, I'm not feeling generous. I'm feeling hot, tired and I've had as much chatter about doorstep opinion as I can take. For God's sake get me out of here.'

As she turned round to wave thanks and farewell to the packed room, she was just in time to see the standard lamp go crashing to the floor.

The air of controlled chaos which usually filled the editor's office had gone, to be replaced by a sense of panic which was getting out of hand. The first edition had long since gone to press, complete with a bold front page headline proclaiming: 'Home and Dry!'

But that had been at 6 p.m., four hours before the polls closed. The editor of the *Daily Telegraph*, like all other editors, had taken his chance on the election result in order to make his first edition of even marginal interest by the time it hit the streets. If he was right, he would be first with the news. If he got it wrong, he would be covered in it and would not be allowed to forget.

This was Greville Preston's first election as an editor. He was not feeling comfortable as he constantly changed the front page and demanded rewrites and updates from his political staff. He had been brought in just a few months earlier by the new owner of Telegraph Newspapers, and he had been given only one instruction: 'Succeed'. Failure was not an option if he wished to continue as editor, and he knew he would not be given a second chance – any more than would his staff. The demands of the accountants for instant financial gratification had required ruthless pruning, and a large number of senior staff had found themselves being 'rationalised' – as the accountants put it – and replaced by less experienced but equally less expensive substitutes. It was great for the bottom line but quite dreadful for morale. The purge left the remaining staff insecure, the loyal readers confused and Preston with a perpetual sense of impending doom, a condition which his proprietor was determined to do nothing to dispel.

Preston's efforts at increasing the circulation by taking the paper down-market had yet to show the promised results, and the smooth and dapper appearance which he effected was spoilt by the beads of perspiration and concern which constantly appeared on his brow and made his heavy rimmed glasses slip down his nose. The carefully manufactured attempt at outward authority had never fully hidden the insecurity within.

He turned away from the bank of television monitors which had been piled up against one wall of his office to face the member of staff who had been giving him such a hard time.

'How the hell do you know it's going wrong?' he shouted.

Mattie Storin did not flinch. At twenty-eight she was the youngest recruit to the paper's political staff, having only recently replaced one of the senior correspondents who had fallen foul of the accountants for his habit of conducting interviews over extended lunches at the Savoy. Yet Mattie had a confidence about her judgement which belied the nine hectic months she had spent in the job. Anyway, she was as tall as Preston, 'and almost as beautiful' as she often quipped at his expense. She did not care for this new style of editor whose job was not so much to produce a prime quality newspaper but foremost to return a good profit. Preston came from the 'management school' of editing, where they teach readership audits and costs per thousand rather than what makes a good story and when to ignore the lawyers' advice; and it stuck in Mattie's gullet. Preston knew it, and resented Mattie and her obvious if raw and unfashioned talent, but he knew in many ways that he needed her more than she needed him. Even in the management school of journalism, a newspaper still requires a sharp journalistic nose to reach its circulation target, as Preston was slowly beginning to discover.

She turned to face him with her hands thrust defensively into the pockets of her fashionably baggy trousers, which in spite of the flowing lines somehow still managed to emphasise her willowy elegance. Mattie Storin very much wanted to succeed as a journalist and to develop the skills which she knew she possessed. But she was also a woman, a very attractive one, and was determined not to sacrifice her identity simply to conform to the typecasting expected of young women working their way up in journalism. She saw no reason why she should attempt either to grow a beard in order to have her talent recognised, or to play the simpering lovely lady to satisfy the chauvinistic demands of her male colleagues, particularly so inadequate an example as Preston.

She began slowly, hoping he would get the full flavour of her logic. 'Every single Government MP I've been able to talk to in the last two hours is downgrading his forecast, and every Opposition spokesman I have talked to is smiling. I've telephoned the returning officer in the Prime Minister's constituency, who says the poll looks as if it's going to be down by 5 per cent. That's scarcely an overwhelming vote of confidence. Something is going on out there. You can feel it. The Government are not yet home and are certainly not dry, and our story is too strong.'

'Crap. Every poll taken during the election suggests a strong Government win, yet you want me to change the front page on the basis of feminine instinct?'

Mattie could sense her editor's nervousness. All editors live on their nerves, but the secret is not to show it. Preston showed it.

'OK,' he demanded, 'they had a majority of 102 at the last election. Tell me what you think it's going to be tomorrow. All the opinion polls are predicting around 70 seats.'

'You trust the polls if you want, Grev,' she warned, 'but I'd rather trust the feel I get out on the streets. There's no enthusiasm amongst Government supporters. They won't turn out and it will drag the majority down.'

'Come on,' he bullied. 'How much?'

She shook her head slowly to emphasise her caution, her short blonde hair brushing around her shoulders. 'A week ago I would have said it would be about 50. Now it could be even less,' she responded.

'Jesus, it can't be less. We've backed those bastards all the way and they've got to deliver.'

And you've got to deliver, too, she mused. She knew that the editor's only firm political view was that his newspaper couldn't afford to be on the losing side. The new cockney proprietor, Benjamin Landless, had told him so and editors didn't argue with Landless. As the country's most recent newspaper magnate constantly reminded his already insecure staff, it was easier to buy ten new editors than one new newspaper, thanks to the Government's competition policy, 'so we don't piss off the Government by supporting the other bloody side'.

He had delivered his growing army of newspapers into the Government camp, and he expected his newspapers to deliver the proper election result. It wasn't reasonable, of course, but Landless had never found that being reasonable helped get the best out of his employees. Over lunch a few weeks earlier the proprietor had explained to Preston that a change of Government could be difficult for Landless, but for Preston such a result would be fatal.

Mattie tried again. She sat herself on the corner of the editor's vast and far too tidy desk and marshalled her case, hoping that for a change he would concentrate on her arguments rather than her legs.

'Look, Grev, forget the opinion polls for a minute. Put it in perspective. When Margaret Thatcher at last decided to retire, they concluded in their wisdom that it was time for a change of style. They wanted a new fashion. Something less abrasive, less domineering; they'd had enough of trial by ordeal and being shown up by a woman.'

You of all people should understand that, she thought.

'So in their wisdom they chose Collingridge, for no better reason than he was confident on TV, smooth with little old ladies and was likely to be uncontroversial.' She shrugged her shoulders dismissively. 'But they've lost their cutting edge. It's rice pudding politics and there's no energy or enthusiasm left. He's campaigned with as much vigour as a Sunday school teacher. Another seven days of listening to him mouthing platitudes and I think even his wife would have voted for the other lot. Anything for a change.'

For the tenth time that evening Mattie wondered if her editor used lacquer to keep his carefully coiffured hair so immaculate. She suspected he had an aerosol and hairbrush in his drawer, and she was certain he used eyebrow tweezers.

'Let's dispense with the analysis and mysticism and stick to hard numbers, shall we?' challenged Preston. 'What's the majority going to be? Are they going to get back in, or not?'

'It would be a rash man who said they wouldn't,' she replied.

'And I have no intention of being rash. Any majority will be good enough for me. In the circumstances it would be quite an achievement. Historic, in fact. Four straight wins, never been done before. So the front page stays.'

Preston quickly brought his instructions to an end by finding solace in his glass of champagne, but Mattie was not to be so easily put off. Her grandfather had been a modern Viking who in the stormy early months of 1941 had sailed across the North Sea in a waterlogged fishing boat to escape from Nazi-occupied Norway and join the RAF. He had handed down to Mattie not only her natural Scandinavian looks but also a strength and independence of spirit which she needed to survive in the masculine worlds of politics and newspapers. Her old editor on the *Yorkshire Post* who had given Mattie her first real job had always encouraged her to fight her own corner. 'You're no good to me, lass, if I end up writing all of your stories for you. Be a seeker, not just another scribbler.' It was an attitude which did not always commend itself to her new masters, but what the hell.

'Just stop for a moment and ask yourself what we could expect from another four years of Collingridge. Maybe he's too nice to be Prime Minister. His manifesto was so lightweight it got blown away in the first week of campaigning. He has developed no new ideas and his only philosophy is to cross his fingers and hope that neither the Russians nor the trade unions break wind too loudly. Is that really what the country wants?'

'Daintily put, as always, Mattie,' he taunted, reverting, as was his custom, to being patronising whenever he was confronted by an argumentative woman. 'But you're wrong,' he continued, sounding none too certain. 'The punters want consolation, not upheaval. They don't want the toys being thrown out of the pram all the time.' He stabbed his finger in the air to indicate that the discussion was almost over and this was now official company policy. 'So a quiet couple of years will be no bad thing. And Collingridge back in Downing Street will be a great thing!'

'It'll be murder,' she muttered.

It was the Number 88 bus thundering past and rattling the apartment windows which eventually caused Charles Collingridge to wake up. The small one-bedroom flat above the travel agency in Clapham was not what most people would have expected of the Prime Minister's brother, but a messy divorce and an indulgent lifestyle had a nasty habit of making the money disappear much faster than it came in. He lay slumped in the armchair, still in his crumpled suit which had got him through lunch and which still carried some of it on the lapel.

He cursed when he saw the time. He must have been

27

asleep for five hours yet he still felt exhausted. He needed a drink to pick himself up, and he poured himself a large measure of vodka. Not even Smirnoff any more, just the local supermarket brand. Still, it didn't hang on the breath or smell when you spilled it.

He took his glass to the bathroom and soaked in the tub, giving the hot water time to work its wonders on those tired limbs. Nowadays they often seemed to belong to an entirely different person. He must be getting old, he told himself.

He stood in front of the mirror, trying to repair the damage of his latest binge. He saw his father's face, reproachful as ever, urging him on to goals which were always just beyond him, demanding to know why he never managed to do things quite like his elder brother Henry. They both had the same advantages, went to the same school. But somehow Henry always had the edge, and gradually had overshadowed him in his career and his marriage. He did not feel bitter. Or at least he tried not to be. Henry had always been there to help when he needed it, to offer advice and to give him a shoulder to cry on when Mary had left him. Particularly when Mary had left him. But hadn't even she thrown Henry's success in his face? 'You're not up to it. Not up to anything!' And Henry had much less time to worry about other people's problems since he had gone to Downing Street.

As young boys they had shared everything together, as young men they had shared much, even a few girlfriends. But these days there was little room left in Henry's life for his younger brother, and Charles felt angry – not with Henry, but with life. It had not worked out for him, and he did not understand why.

He guided the razor past the old cuts on his baggy face, and began putting the pieces back together. The hair brushed over the balding pate, the fresh shirt and clean tie. He would be ready soon for the election night festivities to which his family links still ensured he was invited. A tea towel over his shoes gave them back a little shine, and he was almost ready. Just time for one more drink.

North of the river, a taxi was stuck in a traffic jam on the outskirts of Soho. It was always a bottleneck, and election night seemed to have brought an additional throng of revellers onto the streets. In the back of the taxi Roger O'Neill drummed his fingers impatiently, watching helplessly as the bikes and pedestrians flashed past. He did not have much time.

'Get over here quick, Rog,' they had said. 'We can't wait all bleedin' night, not even for you. And we ain't back till Tuesday.'

He neither expected nor received preferential treatment, even as the Party's Director of Publicity and one of its best-known members of staff. But then he doubted whether they voted at all, let alone for the Government. What did politics matter when there was a lot of loose tax-free money to make?

The taxi at last managed to make it across Shaftesbury Avenue and into Wardour Street, only to be met by another wall of solid traffic. Christ, he would miss them. He flung open the door.

'I'll walk,' he shouted at the driver.

'Sorry, mate. It's not my fault. Costs me a fortune stuck in jams like this,' replied the driver, indicating that O'Neill's impatience should not lead him to forget a tip.

O'Neill jumped out into the road, jammed a note into the driver's hand and dodged another motorcyclist as he made his way past peep shows and Chinese restaurants into a narrow, Dickensian alley piled high with rubbish. He squeezed past the plastic bin liners and cardboard boxes and broke into a run. He was not fit and it hurt, but he did not have far to go. As he reached Dean Street he turned left, and a hundred yards further down ducked into the narrow opening to one of those Soho mews which most people miss as they concentrate on trying either to find the whores or to avoid them. Off the main street, the mews opened out into a small yard, surrounded on all sides by workshops and garages which had been carved out of the old Victorian warehouses. The yard was empty and his footsteps rang out on the cobbles as he hurried towards a small green door set in the far, dark corner of

29

the yard. He stopped only to look around once before entering. He did not knock.

Less than three minutes later he had re-emerged, and without glancing to either side hurried back into the crowds of Dean Street. Whatever he had come for, it clearly was not sex.

Inside party headquarters the atmosphere was strangely quiet. After the weeks of ceaseless activity during the general election campaign, most of the officers and troops had disappeared on election day itself to carry the combat into the far outposts of the constituencies, drumming up the last few and possibly crucial converts for the cause. Most of those who remained were by now taking an early supper at nearby restaurants or clubs, trying to sound confident and relaxed but lapsing repeatedly into insecure discussion of the latest rumours about voter turnout and exit polls. Few of them enjoyed the break, and they soon began drifting back, pushing their way through the ever-growing crowds of spectators and cordons of police. They found great comfort in their overcrowded and cluttered offices which for the last month had become their home, and they settled in for what would seem an interminable wait.

As Big Ben struck 10 o'clock and dusk at last began to take a firm hold, an audible sigh of relief went up from around the building. The polling booths had closed and no further appeal, explanation, attack, insinuation or – more predictably – almighty cock-up could now affect the result. It was over. One or two of them shook each other's hand in silent reassurance and respect for the job done. Just how well done they would shortly discover.

As on so many previous evenings, like a religious ritual they turned their attention to the familiar voice of Sir Alastair Burnet. He appeared for every purpose like a latter-day Gabriel, with his reassuring tones and flowing silver hair which had just enough back lighting to give him a halo effect. For the next few hours God would have to take second place.

'Good evening. The election campaign is now over. Just seconds ago thousands of polling booths across the country closed their doors, and the first result is expected in just forty-five minutes. We shall shortly be going over live for interviews with the Prime Minister, Henry Collingridge, in his Warwickshire constituency, and the Opposition leader in South Wales.

'But first ITN's exclusive exit poll conducted by Harris Research International outside 153 polling booths across the country during today's voting. It gives the following prediction . . .'

The country's most senior newsreader opened a large envelope in front of him, as reverently as if the A4 Manila contained his own death certificate. He extracted a large card from within the envelope, and glanced at it. Not too quickly, not too slowly he raised his eyes once more to the cameras, and the venerable broadcaster held 30 million viewers in the palm of his hand, teasing them gently. He was entitled to his moment. After twenty-eight years and nine general elections as a television broadcaster, he had already announced that this was to be his last.

'ITN's exclusive exit poll forecast – and I emphasise this is a forecast, not a result – is . . .'

He glanced once more at the card, just to check he had not misread it. His professional, emotionless eyes betrayed not a hint of his own views on the matter. From somewhere within Smith Square a sound of the prematurely loosened champagne cork broke the straining silence, but they ignored the cold and sticky froth as it splashed over the desk top.

'. . . that the Government will be re-elected with a majority of 34.'

The building itself seemed to tremble as a roar of triumph mixed with relief came from deep within. It was winning and only winning that mattered to the professionals, not how they played the game or how close the result. Time enough later for sober reflection as to whether they would be deemed to have had a 'good' war or not.

The whoops of joy drowned out the protesting tones of Sir Alastair as he continued to remind his audience that this was a forecast and definitely not a result, and in any event was much closer than the opinion polls had been predicting. The screen briefly divided between mute shots of the party leaders taking in the prediction, Collingridge displaying a thin humourless smile which indicated no pleasure, while the broad grin and shake of his opponent's head left viewers in no doubt that the Opposition had yet to concede. 'Wait and see,' he was mouthing, 'wait and see', but the producer did not wait to see and cut back to Burnet as he proceeded to report on the rest of the election night news.

'Bollocks,' Preston was shouting, his hair falling into his eyes. 'What have they done?' He looked at the ruins of his first edition, and began furiously scribbling on his note pad. 'Government Majority Slashed!' he tried. 'It's Too Close To Call'. 'Collingridge Squeaks In'. They all ended up in the bin.

He looked around desperately for some help and inspiration.

'Let's wait,' Mattie advised. 'It's only thirty minutes to the first result.'

Even without the first result, celebrations were already well under way at the Party's advertising agency. With the confidence that is shown by all positive thinkers, the staff of Merrill Grant & Jones Company PLC had been squashed for nearly three hours in the agency's reception area to witness history in the making projected on two vast TV screens. Not that history would be made for at least another seventeen minutes or so, but like all positive thinkers they prided themselves in being ahead of the game, and the champagne was already flowing to wash down an endless supply of deep pan pizzas and Big Macs. Indeed, the predictions of a drastically reduced majority had only served to spur those present on to greater efforts. Even at this early hour it was clear that two ornamental fig trees which had graced the reception area for several years would not survive the night, and it seemed probable that several young secretaries wouldn't either. Most of the wiser heads were pacing themselves much better, but there seemed to be little reason to exercise excessive restraint.

32

Particularly as the client was setting a fearsome example.

Like so many expatriate Dublin adventurers, Roger O'Neill was renowned for his quick wit, exaggeration and determination to be involved in everything. So many and varied had been his involvements and so wittily had he exaggerated them that no one could be quite certain precisely what he had done before he joined the Party – it was something in public relations or television, they thought, and there was rumour about a problem with the Inland Revenue – but he had been available when the post of Publicity Director had become vacant and he had filled it with great energy, fuelled by a ceaseless supply of Gauloises and vodka-tonics.

As a young man he had shown great promise as a fly-half on the rugby field, but had never fulfilled it, his highly individualistic style making him ill-suited for team games. 'With him on the field,' complained his coach, 'I've got two teams out there, Roger and fourteen other players.'

At the age of forty his unruly shock of dark hair was now perceptibly greying and his muscle tone long since gone, but O'Neill refused stubbornly to acknowledge the evidence of middle age, hiding it beneath a carefully selected wardrobe worn with a deliberate casualness which displayed the designers' labels to their best advantage. His non-conformist approach and the lingering traces of an Irish accent had not always endeared him to the Party's grandees – 'all bullshit and no bottom' one of them had loudly observed – but others were simply overwhelmed by his unusual energy and charm.

And then there was his secretary. Penelope – 'Hi, I'm Penny' – Guy. Five foot ten, an exciting choice of clothes, a devastating figure on which to hang them. And she was black. Not just dusky or dark but a polished hue of black that made her eyes twinkle and her smile fill the entire room. She had a university degree in the History of Art, 120 wpm shorthand, and was ruthlessly efficient and practical. Of course there had been much gossip when she had first arrived with O'Neill, but her sheer efficiency had silenced, if not won over, the Doubting Thomases, of which there were many.

33

And she was totally discreet. 'I have a private life,' she explained. 'And that's just how it's going to stay.'

Right now at Merrill Grant & Jones – Grunt & Groans as Penny preferred to call them – she was effortlessly providing the centre of attention for several red-blooded media buyers plus the deputy creative director while at the same time carefully ensuring that O'Neill's glass and cigarettes were always available but closely rationed. She didn't want him going over the top tonight of all nights.

He was deep in conversation with the agency's managing director.

'I want you to complete the analysis as soon as possible, Jeremy. It's got to show just how effective our marketing and advertising have been in the election. It needs to be divided into the usual age and social groups so that we can show how we hit our target voters. If we win, I want everyone to know that they owe it to us. If we lose, God help us . . .' He sneezed violently. '. . . I want to be able to show the press that we beat them hands down at communications and it was only the politics which blew it. We shall have to live off this for the next few years, so don't screw it up. You know what we need, and it's got to be ready by Saturday morning at the latest if we're to get it in the Sunday papers as prominently as possible.'

He spoke a little more quietly. 'If you can't get the figures, make the bloody things up. They will all be too exhausted to look at them closely, and if we get in there first and loudest we'll be fine.'

He paused only to blow his nose, which did nothing to ease the other man's visible discomfort.

'And remember that I want you to send the most enormous bunch of flowers around to the PM's wife first thing in the morning. In the shape of a gigantic letter 'C'. She must get them as soon as she wakes up. She'll get into a twist if they don't arrive because I've already told her they are coming. And I want the TV cameras to film them going in and to know who's sent them, so make sure they are bigger and more eye-catching than anything they've ever seen before. Even better, send them round in the back of

34

one of your company vans. That should look good pulled up outside Number Ten.'

The advertising executive was used to his client's breathless monologues by now, and even to some of the extraordinary instructions and accounting procedures issued by O'Neill. But a political party was unlike any other client he had ever encountered, and the last two years working on the account had given him and his youthful agency more than enough publicity to stifle most of the lingering doubts.

Now the election was over, however, and he was waiting nervously for the results, a silent fear struck him as he thought of what would happen if they lost; to have supported the losing side, probably to be made the scapegoat for failure. It had all looked rather different when they had started the work, with the opinion polls predicting a comfortable win. But his confidence had begun to evaporate with the exit polls. In an industry of images, he realised that his business could wither as rapidly as the flowers which O'Neill was making such a fuss about.

He sucked his lip nervously as O'Neill rattled on, until their attention was grabbed by the six-foot image of Sir Alastair, who was now holding his ear with his head cocked to one side. Something was coming through his earpiece.

'And now I believe we are ready for the first result of the evening, which looks likely to be in Torbay once again. Breaking all records. It is just forty-three minutes after the polls have closed, and already the candidates are gathering behind the returning officer and it's time to go over live . . .'

In Torbay Town Hall, amidst the banks of hyacinths and spider plants, rosettes and mayoral regalia, the first result was being announced. The scene resembled more a village pantomime than an election, as the promise of nationwide television coverage had attracted more than the usual number of crank candidates who were now doing their best to capture the moment by waving balloons and brightly coloured hats to attract the cameras' attention.

The Sunshine Candidate, dressed from head to toe in a

bright yellow leotard and waving the most enormous plastic sunflower, stood firmly in front of the sober suited Tory, who tried to move to his left to escape from the embarrassment but only succeeded in bumping into the National Front candidate, who was inciting a minor riot in the crowd by displaying a clenched fist and an armful of tattoos. Not quite sure what his candidates manual would prescribe in such circumstances, he reluctantly retreated back behind the sunflower.

Sir Alastair came to his rescue. 'So there we have it from colourful Torbay. The Government hold the first seat of the night but with a reduced majority and a swing against them of, the computer says, nearly 8 per cent. What does that mean, Peter?' asked Burnet, as the screen cut to ITN's tame academic commentator, a bespectacled and rather ragged figure in Oxford tweeds.

'It means the exit poll is just about right, Alastair.'

'Great show, Roger, isn't it? After all, it looks like another majority. I can't tell you how absolutely relieved and delighted I am. Well done indeed,' enthused the chairman of one of Grunt & Groans major clients, thoroughly enjoying what was turning into a fully-fledged victory party irrespective of the fact that the Government had just lost its first two seats of the night. He was standing crushed together along with two other invited clients and the agency's chairman in a corner which gave some slight relief from the pressure of celebration going on all around.

'That's very kind of you, Harold. Yes, I think a 30 or 40-seat majority will be enough. But you must take some of the credit.' O'Neill was gushing. 'I was reminding the Prime Minister just the other day how your support goes way beyond the corporate donation. I remember the speech you gave at the Industrial Society lunch last March. You know, it was extremely good, you really got the message home well. Surely you've had professional training?'

Without waiting for an answer, O'Neill rushed on. 'You've pushed home the message about gaining co-operation from all sides by showing leadership from the top and I told Henry – I'm sorry, the PM! – that we need to find more platforms for captains of industry like you to express these views.'

'There was no need for that,' replied the captain without the slightest trace of sincerity. The champagne had already overcome his natural caution and images of ermine and the House of Lords began to materialise in front of his eyes. 'But that was very kind of you. Look, when this is all over perhaps we could have lunch together. Somewhere a little quieter, eh? I have several other ideas on which I would very much welcome your views.'

O'Neill's response was a series of enormous sneezes which bent him almost double, leaving his eyes tearful and rendering any hope of continued conversation impossible.

'Sorry,' he spluttered. 'Hay fever. I always seem to get it early.' As if to emphasise the point he blew his nose forcefully and wiped his eyes.

The TV screen promptly announced the loss of another Government seat, a Junior Minister with responsibility for Transport who had spent the last four years earnestly visiting every motorway crash scene in the country and who had quite convinced himself of the human race's unquenchable capacity for violent self-sacrifice. It did not help him, however, to accept their demand for his own self-sacrifice, and he was finding it very difficult to put on a brave face.

'More bad news for the Government,' commented Burnet, 'and we shall see how the Prime Minister is taking it when we go over live for his result in just a few minutes. In the meantime, what is the computer predicting now?'

He punched a button and turned to look at a large screen behind his shoulder. 'Still around 30 by the look of it.'

A studio discussion then began as to whether a majority of 30 was enough to see a Government through a full term of office, but the discussion was interrupted by more results which now began to flood in. O'Neill excused himself from the group of businessmen and fought his way through a growing and steadily more voluble group of admirers which had gathered around Penny. In spite of their protests he drew her quickly to one side and whispered briefly in her ear, as the ruddy face of Sir Alastair intruded once more into the celebrations to announce that the Prime Minister's own result was just about to be declared.

A respectful if not total silence grew over the revellers, and O'Neill returned to the industrial captains. All eyes were fixed on the screen. No one noticed Penny gathering her bag and slipping quietly out.

The screen announced another Government win, but yet again with a reduced majority. While the commentators analysed and sought to be the first to get in with their view that the Government were indeed having a less than splendid night of it, a loyal roar of approval arose from all the agency staff present, most of whom had by now totally forgotten their own political convictions and were ready to celebrate at the slightest excuse. After all, it was only an election.

The Prime Minister waved back from the screen, his stretched smile indicating that he was taking the result rather more seriously than was his audience. The festive mood began to drown out his speech of thanks to the returning officer and local police, and by the time he had left the platform to begin his long drive back to London two agency art directors were pronouncing the official demise of the battered fig trees.

A shout from across the room reached through to O'Neill's group.

'Mr O'Neill. Mr O'Neill. Telephone for you.' The security guard held the telephone up in the air and pointed dramatically to the mouthpiece.

'Who is it?' mouthed O'Neill back across the room.

'What?' queried the guard, looking nervous.

'Who is it?' he mouthed again.

'Can't hear you,' the guard yelled above the hubbub, gesticulating wildly.

O'Neill cupped his hands around his mouth and once more demanded to know who it was.

'It's the Prime Minister's Office!' screamed the frustrated guard, unable to restrain himself and not quite knowing whether he should be standing to attention.

His words had an immediate effect, and the noise of

celebration subsided into an expectant hush. An avenue to the telephone suddenly opened up in front of O'Neill, and he slowly and obediently made his way over to the phone, trying to look modest and matter of fact.

'It's one of his secretaries. She will put you through,' said the guard, obviously grateful to hand over the awesome responsibility.

'Hello. Hello. Yes, this is Roger.' A brief pause. 'Prime Minister! How are you? Many, many congratulations. The result is really very good in the circumstances. A victory is sweet whether you win 5–0 or 5–4 . . . Yes, yes. Oh, that's so kind. I'm at the advertising agency as it happens.'

The room was now so hushed they could almost hear the fig trees crying. 'I think they have performed marvellously, and I certainly couldn't have done it without their support . . . May I tell them that?'

He put his hand over the mouthpiece and turned to the totally enraptured audience. 'The Prime Minister just wants me to thank you all on his behalf for helping run such a fantastic campaign. He says it made all the difference.' He went back to the phone and listened for a few seconds more. 'And he's not going to demand the money back!'

With that the room erupted into a great roar of applause and cheers, and O'Neill held the phone aloft to catch every last sound.

'Yes, Prime Minister. I am totally thrilled and honoured to receive your first telephone call after your own election . . . I look forward to seeing you, too. Yes, I shall be at Smith Square later . . . Of course, of course. I will see you then, and congratulations once again. Good night.'

He replaced the telephone gently in its cradle, and turned to face the whole room. Suddenly his face burst into a broad smile, and as he did so the entire gathering broke out into a series of ringing cheers. They pummelled him forcefully on the back as he tried to shake all their hands at once. He was still trying to force his way back to the beaming captains as, in the next street, Penny carefully put down the car phone and began to adjust her lipstick in the car mirror.

FRIDAY 11TH JUNE

The onlookers in Smith Square had increased dramatically in number as they waited for the Prime Minister's arrival. Midnight had long since tolled but tonight biological clocks would be stretched to the limit. They could see from the TV technicians' monitors that his convoy, escorted by police outriders and pursued by camera cars, had long since left the M1 and was now approaching Marble Arch. It would be less than ten minutes before they arrived, and three youthful cheerleaders were encouraging the crowd to warm up with a mixture of patriotic songs and shouts.

They were having to work harder than at previous elections. While some people were waving enormous Union Jacks, the members of the crowd seemed to be less keen on brandishing the large mounted photographs of Henry Collingridge with which they had been supplied. Several of them were wearing personal radios, and informing those around them of the results. Even the cheerleaders would stop occasionally to discuss the latest information.

They also had competition, because several Opposition supporters had decided to infiltrate the crowd and were now proceeding to wave their own banners and chant their own slogans. Half a dozen policemen moved in to ensure that high spirits on both sides were kept under control, but they did not interfere.

Reports began to circulate that the computers were now forecasting a majority of 28, and two of the cheerleaders broke off to indulge in an earnest discussion as to whether this constituted an adequate working majority. They concluded that it probably was, and returned to their task. But the crowd had turned into an unresponsive audience, the early enthusiasm increasingly deflated with concern, and

40

they decided to save their effort until Henry Collingridge arrived.

Inside the building, Charles Collingridge was getting increasingly drunk. His ruddy and capillaried face was covered in perspiration, and his eyes were liquid and bloodshot.

'A good man, brother Henry. A great Prime Minister,' he was babbling. Those around him who were still listening could detect the alcoholic lisp which had begun to creep into his voice as he repeated the familiar family history. 'I always thought he would have been an even better manager of the family business, could have made it one of the country's truly great companies, but he always preferred politics. Mind you, manufacturing bath fittings was never my cup of tea, either, but it kept father happy. Henry could have grown the business, made something of it, I'm sure. Do you know they even import the stuff from Poland nowadays? Or is it Romania . . . ?'

He interrupted his monologue by knocking what was left of his glass of whisky over his already stained trousers and, amidst the fluster of apologies and appeals for help, the Party Chairman Lord Williams took the opportunity to move well out of range. His wise old eyes revealed none of it, but he resented having to extend hospitality to the Prime Minister's brother. Although Charles was not a bad man, he was a weak man who was becoming a bloody nuisance on a regular basis, and the Party's ageing and most senior *apparatchik* liked to run a very tight ship. Yet as experienced as he was, he was only the navigator and knew there was little point in trying to throw the admiral's brother overboard.

He had once raised the problem directly with the Prime Minister of the increasing rumours and the growing number of snide references to his brother in the gossip columns. As one of the few men left who had been a prominent player even in the pre-Thatcher days, he had the seniority and some would argue even the responsibility to do so. But it had been to no avail.

'I spend half my time having to spill blood,' the Prime

Minister had pleaded. 'Please don't ask me to spill my own brother's.'

Henry had agreed to ensure that Charles would watch his behaviour, or rather that he would watch Charles's behaviour himself. But he never really had the time, and he knew that Charles would promise anything even while he became increasingly incapable of delivering. He couldn't moralise or be angry, because he knew it was always the other members of the family who suffered most from the pressures of politics. And Williams understood that, too, for hadn't he gone through three marriages since he first entered politics nearly forty years ago?

It was not a matter of lack of love, more a lack of time for loving, with lonely women and neglected families stuck at home and suffering much more from the unkind barbs of politics than the politicians themselves. Politics left a trail of pain and tortured families in its wake, all the more hurtful because it was incidental and unintended. Even the hardened Party Chairman felt a twinge of sorrow as he watched Collingridge stumble from the room. But such feelings were not a sound basis on which to run a Party, and he resolved to have another discussion with the Prime Minister now that the election was over.

Michael Samuel, the Secretary of State for the Environment and one of the newest and certainly most telegenic members of the Cabinet, came over to greet him. He was young enough to be the Chairman's son, and he was something of a protégé for the elderly statesman. He had been given his first major step up the greasy Ministerial pole by Williams when, as a young Member of Parliament, on Williams' recommendation he had been made a Parliamentary Private Secretary, the unpaid skivvy to a senior Minister who is meant to fetch and carry, to do so without complaint and to offer his support without question on any issue – qualities designed to impress Prime Ministers when selecting candidates for promotion. Williams' help had ignited a spectacular rise through Ministerial ranks for Samuel, and the two men remained firm friends.

'Problem, Teddy?' Samuel enquired.

'Michael. A Prime Minister can choose his friends and his Cabinet, but unfortunately not his relatives.'

'Any more than we can select our colleagues.'

Samuel nodded towards Urquhart, who had just entered with his wife after driving up from his constituency. Samuel's glance was cold. He did not care for Urquhart, who had not supported his promotion to Cabinet and who on more than one occasion had been heard to describe Samuel as 'a latter day Disraeli, too good looking and too clever for his own good.'

The veneer over the traditional and still lingering anti-Semitism wore very thin at times, but Williams had offered the brilliant young lawyer good counsel. 'Don't be too intellectual,' Williams had advised, 'and don't look too successful. Don't be too liberal on social matters or too prominent on financial matters. And for God's sake watch your back. Many more politicians have been betrayed by their colleagues than have ever been destroyed by their opponents. Remember it.'

Samuel watched unenthusiastically as Urquhart and his wife were forced by the crush of people towards him. 'Good evening, Francis. Miranda.' Samuel forced his practised smile. 'Congratulations. A 17,000 majority. I know about 600 MPs who are going to be very jealous of you in the morning with a majority like that.'

'Michael! Well, I'm sure you managed to hypnotise the female voters of Surbiton once more. If only you could pick up their husbands' votes as well, you too could have a majority like mine!'

They laughed gently at the banter, accustomed in public to hiding the fact that they did not enjoy each other's company, but there was an embarrassed silence as neither of them could think of a suitable means of disengaging rapidly from the conversation.

They were rescued by Williams, who had just put down the phone. 'Don't let me interrupt, but Henry will be here any minute.'

'I'll come down with you,' volunteered Urquhart immediately.

'And you, Michael?' asked Williams.

'I'll wait here. There will be quite a rush when he arrives. I don't want to get trampled.'

Urquhart wondered whether Samuel was having a gentle dig at him, but chose to ignore it and accompanied Williams down the stairs, which had become crowded with excited office staff as the word had spread of the Prime Minister's imminent arrival. The appearance of the Party Chairman and Chief Whip outside on the pavement galvanised the cheerleaders, who resumed their attempts to raise the spirits of the crowd. An organised cheer went up as the armoured black Daimler with its battalion of escorts swung around the square, to be greeted by the brilliance of the television lights and a thousand flaring flashguns as both professional and amateur cameramen tried to capture the scene.

As the car drew to a halt, Collingridge emerged from the rear seat and turned to wave to the crowd and the cameras. Urquhart tried just a little too hard to get to him to shake his hand, and instead managed to get in the way. He retreated apologetically while on the other side of the car Lord Williams, with the chivalry and familiarity which comes of many years, carefully assisted the Prime Minister's wife out of the car and planted an avuncular kiss on her cheek. A bouquet appeared from somewhere along with two dozen party officials and dignitaries who all wished to get in on the act, and the whole heaving throng somehow managed to squeeze through the swing doors and into the building.

Similar scenes of confusion and congestion were repeated inside as the Prime Minister's party tried to push its way upstairs through the workers, pausing only for a traditional word of thanks to the staff from the stairs, which had to be repeated because the press photographers had not managed to assemble themselves quickly enough.

Once upstairs in the relative safety of Lord Williams' suite, the signs of strain which had been so well hidden all evening began to appear for the first time on the Prime Minister's face. The television set in the corner was just announcing that the computer was predicting a still lower majority, and Collingridge let out a long, low sigh. His eyes wandered slowly round the room.

'Has Charles been around this evening?' he asked quietly. Charles Collingridge was nowhere to be seen. The Prime Minister's eyes met those of the Chairman.

'I'm sorry,' the older man replied.

Sorry for what?, thought Collingridge. The fact that my brother's a drunk? Sorry that I seem almost to have thrown away our parliamentary majority? Sorry that you will have to carry the can along with me? But anyway, thanks for caring.

He was suddenly feeling desperately tired as the adrenalin ceased to flow. After weeks of being hemmed in on all sides by people and without a single private moment to himself, he felt an overwhelming need to be on his own and he turned away to find somewhere a little quieter and a little more private. Instead he found his way blocked by Urquhart who was standing right by his shoulder. The Chief Whip was thrusting an envelope at him.

'I've been giving some thought to the reshuffle,' he said. 'While this is hardly the time, I know you will be thinking about it over the weekend so I have prepared some suggestions. I know you prefer some positive ideas rather than a blank sheet of paper, so I hope you find this of use.'

Collingridge looked at the envelope and raised his exhausted eyes to Urquhart. 'You're right. This is scarcely the time. Perhaps we should be thinking about securing our majority before we start sacking our colleagues.'

The sarcasm cut deep into Urquhart, deeper than the Prime Minister had intended, and he realised he had gone too far.

'I'm sorry, Francis. I'm afraid I am a little tired. Of course you're quite right to think ahead. Look, I would like you and Teddy to come round on Sunday afternoon to discuss it. Perhaps you would be kind enough to let Teddy have a copy of your letter now, and send one round to me at Downing Street tomorrow – rather, later this morning.'

Urquhart stood rigid with embarrassment at the semi-public rebuke he had received. He realised that he had been all too anxious about the reshuffle, and cursed himself for his folly. His natural assurance seemed to desert him when it came to Collingridge, a grammar school product who in social terms would have had trouble gaining membership of his club. The role reversal in Government unnerved him, unsettled him, and he found himself acting out of character when he was in the other man's presence. He was frustrated with his inadequacy, and quietly loathed Collingridge and all his kind for undermining his position. But now was not the time, and he retreated into affability.

'Of course, Prime Minister. I will let Teddy have a copy straight away.'

'Better copy it yourself. Wouldn't do to have that list getting around here tonight,' smiled Collingridge as he tried to bring Urquhart back into the conspiracy of power which always hovers around Downing Street. 'In any event, I think it's time for me to depart. The BBC will want me bright and sparkling in four hours' time, so I shall wait for the rest of the results in Downing Street.'

He turned to Williams. 'By the way, what is the computer predicting now?'

'It's been stuck on 24 for about half an hour now. I think that's it.' There was no sign of pleasure or sense of victory in his voice. He had just presided over the Party's worst election result in nearly two decades.

'Never mind, Teddy. A majority is a majority. And it will give the Chief Whip something to do instead of sitting idly around with a majority of over a hundred. Eh, Francis?' And with that he strode out of the room, leaving Urquhart clutching his envelope.

With the Prime Minister's departure the crowds both inside and outside the building began perceptibly to melt, and Urquhart made his way to the back of the first floor where he knew the nearest photocopier could be found.

Room 132A was not an office at all, but a windowless closet barely six feet across which was kept for supplies and confidential photocopying. As Urquhart opened the door the smell hit him before he had time to find the light switch. Slumped on the floor by the narrow metal storage shelves was Charles Collingridge, who had soiled his clothes even as he slept. There was no glass or bottle anywhere to be seen, but the smell of whisky was heavy in the air. He had crawled away to find the least embarrassing place to collapse.

Urquhart coughed as his nostrils rebelled at the stench, and he reached for his handkerchief and held it to his face. He stepped over to the body and turned it on its back. A shake of the shoulders did little other than disrupt still further the fitful heavy breathing. A firmer shake gave nothing more, and a gentle slap across the cheeks produced equally little result.

He gazed with disgust at what he saw. Suddenly Urquhart's body stiffened as his contempt mingled with the lingering humiliation he had suffered at the Prime Minister's hands and welded into a craving for revenge. He turned cold and the hairs on the nape of his neck tingled as he stood over the stupefied body. Slowly, powerfully, Urquhart's hand swung down and began to slap Collingridge's face and, as his signet ring began to rake across the flesh of the cheeks, the whole head whipped from side to side until blood began to seep from the mouth and the body coughed and retched. Urquhart bent over the other man, staring closely as if to see that the body still breathed. He remained motionless for several minutes, like a cat at its prey, his muscles tense and expression contorted until he straightened with a start, towering over the drunk.

'And your brother's no damned better,' he hissed.

He turned to the photocopier, took the letter out of his pocket, made one copy and left without looking back.

SUNDAY 13TH JUNE

It was the Sunday after the election. At 3.50 p.m. Urquhart's official car turned from Whitehall into Downing Street to be greeted by a policeman's starched salute and a hundred exploding flashguns. The press were gathered behind the barriers which cordoned them off across the road from the world's most famous front door. It stood wide open as the car drew up – like a political black hole, Urquhart thought, into which new Prime Ministers disappeared and rarely if ever emerged without being surrounded and suffocated by the protective hordes of civil servants. Somehow the building seemed to suck all political vitality out of some leaders.

He had made sure to travel on the left-hand side of the car's rear seat that day in order that his exit in front of Number Ten would provide an unimpeded view of himself for the TV and press cameras, and as he climbed out and stretched himself to his full height he was greeted by a chorus of shouted questions from across the road, providing him with a good excuse to walk over for a few quick words amidst the jungle of notepads and microphones. He spotted Charles Goodman, the legendary Press Association figure, firmly planted under his battered trilby and conveniently wedged between ITN and BBC news camera crews.

'Hello, Charles. Did you have any money on the result?' he enquired, but Goodman was already into his first question as his colleagues pressed around him.

'Are you here to advise the Prime Minister with the reshuffle, Mr Urquhart, or has he called you to give you a new job?'

'Well, I'm here to discuss a number of things, but I

48

suppose the reshuffle might come into it,' Urquhart responded coyly.

'It's rumoured that you are expecting a major new post.'

'Can't comment on rumours, Charles, and anyway you know that's one for the PM to decide. I'm here at this stage solely to give him some moral support.'

'You'll be going to advise the PM along with Lord Williams, will you then?'

'Lord Williams, has he arrived yet?' Urquhart tried to hide any suggestion of surprise.

'About 2.30. We were wondering whether someone else was going to turn up.'

Urquhart hoped that they hadn't noticed the steel which he felt entering his eyes as he realised that the Prime Minister and Party Chairman had been working on the reshuffle without him for an hour and a half. 'Then I must go. Can't keep them waiting,' he smiled. He turned smartly and strode back across the road and over the threshold. He was annoyed, and it smothered the sense of excitement which he still felt whenever he passed that way.

The Prime Minister's youthful political secretary was waiting at the end of the corridor which led away from the front door towards the Cabinet Room at the rear of the building. As Urquhart approached, he sensed that the young man was uneasy.

'The PM is expecting you, Chief Whip,' he said quite unnecessarily. 'He's in the study upstairs. I'll let him know you have arrived,' and bounded off up the stairs.

It was a full twelve minutes before he reappeared, leaving Urquhart to stare for the hundredth time at the portraits of previous Prime Ministers which adorned the famous staircase. He could never get over the feeling of how inconsequential so many of the recent holders of the office had been. Uninspiring and unfitted for the task. Times had changed, and for the worse. The likes of Lloyd George and Churchill had been magnificent natural leaders, but one had been promiscuous and the other arrogant and often drunk, and neither would have been tolerated by the modern media in the search for sensationalism.

The media's prying and lack of charity had cast a blanket of mediocrity over most holders of the office since the war, stifling individualism and those with real inspiration. Collingridge, chosen largely for his television manner, typified how superficial much of modern politics had become, he thought. He yearned for the grand old days when politicians made their own rules rather than cowering before the rules laid down by the media.

The return of the political secretary interrupted his thoughts. 'Sorry to keep you waiting, Chief Whip. He's ready for you now.'

As Urquhart entered the room traditionally used by modern Prime Ministers as their study he could see that, in spite of efforts to tidy up the desk, there had been much shuffling of paper and scribbling of notes in the previous hour and a half. An empty bottle of claret stared out of the waste paper bin, and plates covered with crumbs and a withered leaf of lettuce lurked on the windowsill. The Party Chairman sat to the right of the Prime Minister's desk, his notes spilled over the green leather top. Beside them stood a large pile of MPs' biographies supplied by party headquarters.

Urquhart brought up a chair and sat in front of the other two, who were silhouetted against the sun as it shone in through the windows overlooking Horse Guards Parade. He squinted into the light, balancing his own folder of notes uneasily on his knee.

Without ceremony, Collingridge got straight down to business. 'Francis, you were kind enough to let me have some thoughts on the reshuffle. I am very grateful; you know how useful such suggestions are in stimulating my own thoughts, and you have obviously put a lot of work into them. Now before we get down to the specific details, I thought it would be sensible just to chat about the broad objectives first. You've suggested – well, what shall I call it? – a rather radical reshuffle with six new members being brought into the Cabinet and some extensive swapping of portfolios amongst the rest. Tell me why you would prefer an extensive reshuffle and what you think it would achieve.'

Urquhart did not care for this. He had expected some inevitable discussion of individual appointments, but he was being asked to justify the strategy behind the reshuffle proposals before he had any chance to sniff out the Prime Minister's own views. He knew that it was not healthy for a Chief Whip to fail to read his Prime Minister's mind correctly, and he wondered whether he was being set up.

As he peered into the sunlight streaming in from behind the Prime Minister, he could read nothing of the expression on Collingridge's face. He desperately wished now that he had not committed all his thoughts to paper instead of talking them through, but it was too late for regrets.

'Of course, they are only suggestions, indications really of what you might be able to do. I thought in general that it might be better to undertake more rather than fewer changes, simply to indicate that you are firmly in charge of the Government and that you are expecting a lot of new ideas and new thinking from your Ministers. And a chance to retire just a few of our older colleagues; regrettable, but necessary if you are to bring in some new blood and bring on those Junior Ministers who have shown most promise.'

Dammit, he thought suddenly, that was a stupid thing to say with that ancient bastard Williams sitting on the PM's right hand. He knew he should have been more careful, and now he had a knot in the pit of his stomach. Collingridge had never seemed to be a Prime Minister with grip, one who enjoyed making decisions, and Urquhart had felt sure that most if not all of his proposals would be favourably received. All of his suggested promotions were men of talent which few would deny. He hoped that even fewer would realise that most were also men who owed him. Ministers whom he had helped out of trouble, whose weaknesses he knew, whose sins he had covered up and whose wives and electors would never find out.

Williams was staring at him with his old, cunning eyes. Did he know, had he figured it out? The room was silent as the Prime Minister tapped his pencil on the desk, clearly having trouble with the argument Urquhart had put forward.

51

'We've been in power for longer than any Party since the war, which presents a new challenge. Boredom. We need to ensure we have a fresh image for the Government team,' Urquhart continued. 'We must guard against going stale.'

'That's very interesting, Francis, and I agree with you to a large extent. Teddy and I have been discussing just that sort of problem. We must bring on a new generation of talent, find new impetus by putting new men in new places. And I find many of your suggestions for changes at the lower Ministerial levels below Cabinet very persuasive.'

'But they are not the ones that matter,' Urquhart muttered beneath his breath.

'The trouble is that too much change at the top can be very disruptive. It takes most Cabinet Ministers a year simply to find their feet in a new Department, and a year is a long time to struggle through without being able to show positive signs of progress. Rather than Cabinet changes helping to implement our new programme, Teddy's view is that on balance it would more likely delay the programme.'

What new programme?, Urquhart screamed inside his skull. We deliberately published the most flaccid and uncontroversial manifesto we could get away with! He calmed himself before responding.

'Don't you think by cutting our majority the electorate was telling us of its desire for some degree of change?'

'An interesting point. But as you yourself said, no Government in our lifetimes has been in office as long as we have. Without in any way being complacent, Francis, I don't think we could have rewritten the history books if the voters believed we had run out of steam. On balance, I think it suggests that they are content with what we offer, and there is no great sign of them demanding upheaval or change. There's another vital point,' he continued. 'Just because our majority has been cut, we must avoid giving the impression that we are panicking. That would send entirely the wrong signal to the Party and the country, and could bring about just that demand for change which you are so nervous of. Remember that Macmillan destroyed his own Government by panicking and sacking a third of his Cabinet. "The Night of the Long Knives" they called it, and he was out of office the following year. That was a mistake I am not anxious to repeat. So I'm thinking of a much more controlled approach myself.'

Collingridge slipped a piece of paper across the desk towards Urquhart, who picked it up. On it was printed a list of Cabinet positions, twenty-two in all, with names alongside them.

'As you see, Francis, I am suggesting no Cabinet changes at all. I hope it will be seen as a sign of great determination and strength. We have a job to do, and I think we should show we want to get straight on with it.'

Urquhart quickly replaced the paper onto the desk, anxious that the tremble in his hand might betray his inner feelings.

'If that is what you want, Prime Minister,' he said, slipping into a formal tone. 'I have to say that I am not sure how the Parliamentary Party will react. I've not had sufficient chance to take soundings since the election.'

'I'm sure they will accept it. After all, we are proposing a substantial number of changes below Cabinet level to keep them happy.' There was the slightest pause. 'And of course I assume I have your full support?' he asked quizzically.

There was another pause, slightly longer this time, until Urquhart heard himself responding.

'Of course, Prime Minister.'

His own voice sounded strangely distant. He knew he had no choice: it was either support or suicide through instant resignation. The words of acceptance came out automatically, but without conviction. He felt the Whips Office closing around him like the walls of the condemned cell. Once again Urquhart felt uneasy in Collingridge's presence, not knowing how to read him or how to respond to him. But he could not leave it there. His words faltered as he found his mouth suddenly dry.

'I have to say that I . . . was rather looking for a change myself. A bit of new experience . . . a new challenge.'

53

'Francis,' the Prime Minister said in his most reassuring manner, 'if I move you, I have to move others. The whole pile of dominoes begins to fall over. And I need you where you are. You are an excellent Chief Whip. You have devoted yourself to burrowing right into the heart and soul of the Parliamentary Party. You know them so well, and we have to face it that with such a small majority there might be one or two sticky patches over the next few years. I need to have a Chief Whip who is strong enough to handle them. I need *you*, Francis. You are so good behind the scenes. We can leave it to others to do the job out front.'

'You appear to have made up your mind,' Urquhart said, hoping that it sounded like a statement of fact rather than the accusation which he felt.

'I have,' replied the Prime Minister. 'And I am deeply grateful that I can rely on your understanding and support.'

Urquhart felt the cell door slam shut. He thanked them, cast a dark eye at the Party Chairman, and took his farewell. Williams hadn't uttered a single word.

He left through the basement of Number Ten which led him past the ruins of the old Tudor tennis court to the Cabinet Office, which faces onto Whitehall. He was well out of sight of the waiting press. He couldn't face them. He had been with the Prime Minister less than half an hour, and he did not trust his face to back up the lies he would have to tell them. He got a security guard at the Cabinet Office to telephone for his car to be brought round.

The battered BMW had been standing outside the house in Cambridge Street, Pimlico for almost a quarter of an hour. Amidst the chaos of discarded newspapers and granary bar wrappers which covered the vacant seats, Mattie Storin sat biting her lip. Ever since the reshuffle announcement from Downing Street late that afternoon, fevered discussions had been undertaken in editorial offices trying to decide whether the Prime Minister had been brilliant and audacious or simply lost his nerve; they needed the views of the men who had helped shape the decisions. Williams had been persuasive and supportive as usual, but Urquhart's phone had only rung and rung.

Without knowing quite why, after work Mattie had decided to drive past Urquhart's London home, just ten minutes away from the House of Commons. She expected to find it dark and empty but instead she discovered that the lights were burning and there were signs of movement around the house, yet still the telephone rang unanswered.

She knew it was not the done thing in Westminster circles for political correspondents to pursue their quarry back to their homes; indeed, it was a practice which was darkly frowned upon not only by politicians but also by other correspondents. The world of Westminster is a club which has many unwritten rules, and those rules are guarded jealously by both politicians and press – particularly the press, the so-called Westminster 'lobby' of correspondents which quietly and privately regulates all media activity in the Palace of Westminster. The lobby system sets the rules of conduct which permit briefings and interviews to take place without their ever being reported, which encourage politicians to be indiscreet and to break confidences without ever being quoted, which allow the press to get round the Official Secrets Act and the oaths of collective Ministerial responsibility without ever giving their sources away. It was the lobby correspondent's passport, without which he – or she – would find all doors closed and all mouths firmly shut.

Mattie gave the inside of her cheek another bite. She was nervous. She did not lightly bend the rules, but why was the bloody man not answering his phone? What on earth was he up to?

A thick Northern voice whispered in her ear, the voice she had so often missed since leaving the *Yorkshire Post* and its old, wise editor. What had he said? 'Rules, my girl, are meant for the guidance of the wise and the emasculation of the foolish. Don't ever tell me you haven't got a good story because of somebody else's sodding rules.'

'OK, OK, you miserable bugger,' Mattie said out loud. She didn't feel good about breaking lobby rules, but she knew she would feel even worse missing a valuable opportunity. She checked her hair in the mirror, running a hand through it to restore some life, and opened the car door wishing that she were somewhere else. Twenty seconds later the house echoed with the heavy thumping of the ornate brass knocker on the front door.

Urquhart was alone, and not expecting visitors. His wife had returned to the country, and the maid didn't work weekends. He opened the door impatiently, and he did not immediately recognise the caller.

'Mr Urquhart, I've been trying to contact you all afternoon. I hope it's not inconvenient but I need some help. Downing Street has announced that there will be no Cabinet changes, and I'd appreciate your help in trying to understand the thinking behind it.'

How do these damned journalists always find where you are? thought Urquhart.

'I'm sorry but I have nothing to say,' he responded and began to close the door. He saw the journalist throw her hands up in exasperation and take a step forward. Surely the silly girl wasn't going to put her foot in the door, it would be too comic for words. But Mattie spoke calmly and quietly.

'Mr Urquhart. That's a great story. But I don't think you mean it.'

Intrigued, Urquhart paused. What on earth did she mean? Mattie saw the hesitation, and threw a little more bait into the water. 'The story would read: "There were signs last night of deep Cabinet divisions over the non-shuffle. The Chief Whip, long believed to have harboured ambitions for a move to a new post, refused to comment on or to defend the Prime Minister's decision." How would you care for that?'

Only now did Urquhart recognise the *Telegraph* correspondent away from her usual surroundings. He knew Mattie Storin only slightly as she was relatively new to the Westminster circuit, but Urquhart had seen her in action often enough to suspect she was no fool. He was therefore astonished that she was now on his doorstep trying to intimidate the Chief Whip.

'You cannot be serious,' Urquhart said slowly.

Mattie broke into a broad smile. 'Actually, no, sir. Although you won't answer your telephone or talk face-to-face, even I wouldn't go that far to get a story. But it does raise some very interesting questions in my mind, and frankly I would prefer to get the truth rather than having to concoct something out of thin air. And that's all you are leaving me at the moment, thin air.'

Urquhart was disarmed by the young journalist's candour. He ought to be furious and on the phone to her editor, demanding an apology for such blatant harassment. But Mattie had already sensed there might be a much deeper story behind the formal announcement from Downing Street. Now she stood in a pool of light at his front door, highlights glinting in her short, blonde hair. What had he got to lose?

'Perhaps you had better come in after all – Miss Storin, isn't it?'

'Please call me Mattie.'

He led the way upstairs to a tasteful, if very traditional, sitting room, covered in oil paintings of horses and country scenes, and crammed with ancient but comfortable furniture. He poured himself a large Scotch and, without asking her, a glass of white wine for his guest before settling into an overstuffed armchair. Mattie sat opposite, nervously perching on the edge of the sofa. She got out a small notebook, but Urquhart waved it away.

'I'm tired, Miss Storin – Mattie. It's been an arduous campaign, and I am not sure I would express myself particularly well. So no notes and no quotations, if you don't mind.' Urquhart knew he had to be careful.

'OK, Mr Urquhart. Let's do this entirely on a lobby basis. I can use what you tell me, but I can't attribute it to you in any way and absolutely no quotations.'

'Precisely.'

He took a cigarette from a silver cigarette box and relaxed back in his chair, inhaling deeply. He did not wait for Mattie's questions before starting his defence.

'So what if I tell you that the Prime Minister sees this as being the best way of getting on with the job? Not letting Ministers get confused with new responsibilities and new civil service teams, but allowing us to continue full steam ahead?'

'I would say, Mr Urquhart, that we would scarcely have to go off the record and on to a lobby basis for that!'

Urquhart chuckled at the young journalist's bluntness. Yes, he would have to be very careful.

'I would also say that the election result showed the need for some new blood and some new thinking,' she continued. 'You lost a lot of seats, and your endorsement by the voters wasn't exactly gushing, was it?'

'Steady on, steady on. We've got a clear majority and won many more seats than the main opposition party. Not too bad after so many years in office . . .' He rehearsed the official creed.

'But not really full of promise for the next election, is it? Even some of your own supporters have described your programme for the next five years as being "more of the same". "Steady as she sinks", I think one of your opponents called it. And you may remember I came to one of your election rallies. You were speaking a great deal about new energy, new ideas and new enterprise. The whole thrust of what you were saying was that there would be change – and some new players.'

She paused, but Urquhart didn't seem keen to respond. 'Your own election address – I have it here . . .' She fished a glossy folded leaflet from a wad of papers which were stuffed into her shoulder bag. Urquhart stared at her intently. 'It speaks about "the exciting years ahead". All this is about as exciting as last week's newspapers.'

'I think that's a little harsh,' protested Urquhart, knowing he should be protesting more. He had no enthusiasm for inventing excuses, and he suspected that it showed.

'Let me ask you bluntly, Mr Urquhart. Do you really think that this is the best the Prime Minister could do?'

Urquhart did not answer directly but raised his glass slowly to his lips, without for a moment taking his eyes off her. They both knew that they were role playing, but neither was yet clear quite how this theatre piece would finish.

Urquhart savoured the fine Islay malt around his tongue,

and let it warm him inside before replying. 'Mattie, how on earth do you expect me to reply to a question like that? You know as Chief Whip I am totally loyal to the Prime Minister and his shuffle – or rather non-shuffle.' There was an edge of sarcasm in his voice.

'Yes, but what about Francis Urquhart, a man who is very ambitious for his party and is desperately anxious for its success. Does *he* support it?'

There was no reply.

'Mr Urquhart, in my piece tomorrow I shall faithfully record your public loyalty to the reshuffle and your justification of it. I know you would not wish to see anything appear in the press which even remotely hinted that you were not happy with events. But I remind you we are speaking on lobby terms. I sense that you are not content with what is happening. I want to know. You want to ensure that it doesn't get back to my colleagues, or to your colleagues, or become common Westminster gossip. I give you my word on that. This is just for me, because it might be important in the months ahead. And by the way, no one else knows I came to see you tonight.'

Mattie was offering a deal. In exchange for Urquhart's real views she would ensure that nothing she wrote could ever be traced back to its source.

Urquhart toyed in his mind with a variety of stilettos, wondering which one to throw first. 'Very well, Mattie, let me explain the real story to you. It's really very simple. The Prime Minister has to keep the lid firmly closed on the pressure cooker in order to contain the ambition of some of his colleagues. Those ambitions have grown since the poor election result and, if he were to release the pressure now, there would be the danger of the entire Government getting plastered all over the kitchen ceiling.'

'Are you telling me that there is a lot of rivalry and dissent within the Cabinet?'

'Let me put it this way.' He paused to consider his words carefully before continuing in a slow, deliberate voice. 'Some elements of the Party are deeply distressed. They believed the PM came dangerously close to throwing away the last election, and they don't see him as having the stamina or authority to last all the way through for another four or five years. So they are thinking of what life might be like in another eighteen months or two years, and what position they want to be in if there happened to be a leadership race. The game has suddenly become a very different one since Thursday, and Henry Collingridge is no longer playing with a full team behind him. It could get very unsettling.'

'So why doesn't he get rid of the troublesome ones?'

'Because he can't risk having several former Cabinet Ministers rampaging all over the backbenches when he has got a majority of only 24 which could disappear at the first parliamentary cock-up. He has to keep everything as quiet and as low key as possible. He can't even move the Awkward Brigade to new Cabinet posts because every time you get a new Minister in a new Department they get a rush of enthusiasm and want to make their mark, while you gentlefolk of the press give them a honeymoon period and plenty of personal publicity. Their views suddenly take on a renewed importance for the leader writers, and all of a sudden we find that they are not simply doing their Ministerial jobs but also promoting themselves for a leadership race. The whole of Government business is thrown into chaos because everyone is looking over their shoulders at their colleagues rather than training their sights on the Opposition. Government becomes confused, the Prime Minister becomes even more unpopular – and suddenly we are confronted with a real leadership race.'

'So everyone simply has to remain where they are. Do you think that's a sound strategy?'

He took a deep mouthful of whisky. 'If I were the captain of the *Titanic* and I saw a bloody great iceberg dead ahead, I don't think I would be saying "steady as she goes". I'd want a change of course.'

'Did you tell this to the Prime Minister this afternoon?'

'Mattie, you take me too far!' he chuckled in protest. 'While I respect your professional integrity and I am thoroughly enjoying our conversation, I think I would be offering you too much temptation if I started divulging the details of private discussions. That's a shooting offence!'

Mattie had not moved from the edge of her chair. She understood very clearly the significance of his words, and was determined to gather more. 'Well, let me ask you about Lord Williams. He was with the PM an extraordinarily long time this afternoon if all they were deciding was to do nothing.'

Urquhart had been toying with this specific stiletto for several minutes. Now he threw it with deadly accuracy. 'Have you heard the phrase, "Beware of an old man in a hurry"?'

'You surely can't imagine that he believes he could become Party Leader. Not from the Lords!'

'No, even he's not that egotistical. But he still has a couple of years left, and like so many elder statesmen would like to make sure that the leadership found its way into suitable hands.'

'Whose hands?'

'If not him, then one of his acolytes.'

'Like who?'

'Do you have no thoughts of your own?'

'You mean Michael Samuel.'

Urquhart smiled as he heard the stiletto thud home. 'I think I've said enough. We must call this conversation to a halt.'

Mattie nodded reluctantly, and remained silent, pondering the pieces of the political jigsaw which now lay in front of her. Without further discussion Urquhart guided his guest downstairs, and they were shaking hands by the front door before she spoke again.

'You've been very helpful, Mr Urquhart. But one last question. If there were a leadership election, would you be part of it?'

'Good night, Mattie,' Urquhart said, and closed the front door firmly behind her.

Daily Telegraph. Monday 14th June. Page 1.

In a move which startled most observers, the Prime Minister yesterday announced that there were to be no immediate Cabinet changes following the election.

After conferring for several hours with his Party Chairman, Lord Williams, and also with the Chief Whip Francis Urquhart, Mr Collingridge issued a 'steady as she goes' message to his Party.

Downing Street sources said it was intended that the Government would be able to pursue their programme as quickly and as effectively as possible by leaving all Cabinet Ministers in place. However, senior Westminster sources last night expressed astonishment at the decision. It was seen in some quarters as betraying the weakness of the Prime Minister's position after the decimation of his parliamentary majority and criticisms of what was seen as a lacklustre campaign, for which both he and the Party Chairman are being blamed.

There was speculation last night that the Prime Minister was unlikely to fight another election, and that some senior Ministers were already manoeuvring for position in the event of an early leadership contest. One Cabinet Minister compared the Prime Minister to 'the captain of the *Titanic* as it was entering the ice pack'.

The decision not to make any Cabinet changes, the first time since the war that an election has not been followed by some senior reshuffle, was interpreted as being the most effective way for Collingridge to keep the simmering rivalries of some of his Cabinet colleagues under control.

Last night, the Chief Whip defended the decision as being 'the best means of getting on with the job'. However, speculation is already beginning as to who might be the likely contenders in the event of a leadership race.

Lord Williams described any suggestion of an imminent leadership election as 'nonsense'. He said, 'The Prime Minister has gained for the Party an historic fourth election victory, and we are in excellent shape.' However, the position of the Party Chairman would be crucial during a leadership race, and Williams is known to be very close to Michael Samuel, the Environment Secretary, who could be one of the contenders.

Opposition spokesmen were quick to pounce on what they saw as indecisiveness on the part of the Prime Minister. Claiming that he had been greatly heartened by the gains his Party had made last Thursday, the Opposition Leader said: 'The fires of discontent are glowing within the Government. I don't think Mr Collingridge has the strength or the support to put them out. I am already looking forward to the next election . . .'

TUESDAY 22ND JUNE

Roger O'Neill sat back comfortably in the arms of one of the large leather armchairs which surround the snooker tables in the back room at White's Club. When the tables are not in use, the seats which are spread around the games room offer a quiet and confidential spot for members to take their guests. He had been delighted, and not a little astonished, to receive the invitation from the Chief Whip to dine at his prestigious club in St James's. Urquhart had never shown much warmth towards O'Neill in the past, and O'Neill had been more used to a cold and condescending gaze down Urquhart's aquiline nose, rather like a well-fed bird eyeing future prey, than an invitation 'to celebrate the splendid work which you have done for us all throughout the campaign'.

O'Neill, hypertense as always, had tried to calm his nerves with a couple of mighty vodka-tonics before he arrived, but they had not been necessary. Urquhart's cosy manner, two bottles of Château Talbot '78 and the large cognacs which Urquhart was even now ordering from the bar suggested that O'Neill had at last been able to break through the barriers which some traditionalists within the party leadership still erected against the likes of O'Neill and his 'marketing johnnies with their vulgar cars'. Even as O'Neill derided the traditionalists and their narrow jealousies, he desperately wanted their acceptance, and now he felt guilty for having misjudged Urquhart so badly. He beamed broadly as his host returned from the bar with two crystal glasses on a silver tray. O'Neill stubbed out his cigarette in preparation for the Havana which he hoped would be following.

'Tell me, Roger, what are your plans now the election is

over? Are you going to stay on with the Party? We can't afford to lose good men like you.'

O'Neill flashed yet another winning smile and assured his host that he would stay on as long as the Prime Minister wanted him.

'But how can you afford to, Roger? May I be brutally honest with you? I know just how little the Party pays its employees, and money is always so short after an election. It's going to be tough for the next couple of years. Your salary will probably get frozen and your budget cut. Aren't you tempted by some of the more handsome offers you must be getting from outside?'

'Well, it's not always easy, Francis, as you've already guessed. It's not so much the salary, you understand. I work in politics because I'm fascinated by it and love to play a part. But it would be a tragedy if the budget gets cut.'

His smile faded as he contemplated the prospect and began to fidget nervously with his glass. 'We should start working for the next election now, not in three years' time when it may be too late. Particularly with all these rumours flooding around about splits within the Party and who is to blame for the loss of seats. We need some strong and positive publicity, and I need a budget to create it.'

'The Chairman receptive to all this?' Urquhart raised an enquiring eyebrow.

'Are Chairmen ever?'

'Perhaps, Roger, there is something I can do about that. I would like to be able to help you very much, because I think you've done such excellent work. I'll go in to bat with the Chairman about your budget, if you want. But there is something I must ask you first. And I must be blunt.'

The older man's blue eyes looked directly into O'Neill's, taking in their habitual flicker. He paused while O'Neill blew his nose loudly. Another habit, Urquhart knew. He examined O'Neill closely. It was as if there were another life going on within O'Neill which was quite separate from the rest of the world, and which communicated itself only through O'Neill's hyperactive mannerisms and twitching eyes.

'I had a visit the other day from an old colleague I used to know from the days when I held directorships in the City,' Urquhart continued. 'He's one of the financial people at the Party's advertising agency. And he was very troubled. Very discreet, but very troubled. He said you were in the habit of asking them for considerable sums of cash to cover your expenses.'

The twitching stopped for a moment, and Urquhart noticed just how rarely he had ever seen O'Neill stop moving.

'Roger, let me assure you I am not trying to trap you or trick you. This is strictly between us. But if I am to help you, I must be sure of the facts.'

The face and the eyes started up again, and O'Neill's ready laugh made a nervous reappearance. 'Francis, let me assure you that there's nothing wrong at all. It's silly, of course, but I am grateful that you raised it with me. It's simply that there are times when I incur expenses on the publicity side which are easier and more convenient for the agency to meet rather than putting them through the Party machine. Like buying a drink for a journalist or taking a Party contributor out for a meal.'

O'Neill was speeding on with his explanation, which showed signs of having been practised. 'You see, if I pay for them myself I have to claim back from the Party. We have a pretty laborious accounts department which takes its own sweet time paying those invoices – two months or more. Frankly, with the way I get paid, I can't afford it. Yet if I charge them through the agency, I get the money back immediately while they have to put them through their own accounts before invoicing us at headquarters. That takes another month or so, which simply means that the Party gets an even longer holiday on repaying those expenses. It's like an interest-free loan for the Party. And in the meantime I can get on with my job. The amounts are really very small.'

O'Neill reached for his glass.

'Like £22,300 in the last ten months small?'

O'Neill nearly choked. He put his glass down quickly and his face contorted as he struggled simultaneously to gulp down air and blurt out a denial.

'It's nothing like that amount,' he protested. His jaw dropped as he debated what to say next. This explanation he hadn't practised.

Urquhart turned away from him to signal for another two cognacs. His eyes returned calmly to O'Neill, whose twitching now resembled a fly caught in a spider's web. Urquhart spun more silken threads.

'Roger, you have been charging regular expenses to the agency without clearly accounting for those amounts to the tune of precisely £22,300 since the beginning of September last year. What began as relatively small amounts have in recent months grown up to £4,000 a month. You don't get through that many drinks and dinners even during an election campaign.'

'I assure you, Francis, that any expenses I've charged have all been entirely legitimate!' The choking had begun to subside. As the steward placed the fresh drinks on the table, Urquhart moved in to bind his prey with a lethal touch.

'And let me assure you, Roger, that I know precisely what you have been spending the money on,' he said quietly.

He took a sip from his cognac as his victim remained motionless, transfixed. 'Roger, as Chief Whip I have to become familiar with every problem known to man. Do you know, in the last two years I have had to deal with cases of wife beating, adultery, fraud, mental illness. I've even had a case of incest. We didn't let him stand for re-election, of course, but there was nothing to be gained by making a public fuss about such things. That's why you almost never hear about them. Incest I draw the line at but in general we don't moralise, Roger. Every man is allowed one weakness or indulgence – so long as it remains a private one.'

He paused. 'In fact, one of my Junior Whips is a doctor who was appointed specifically to help me spot the signs of strain, and we get quite practised at it. After all, we have well over 300 MPs to look after, all of whom are living on the edge and under immense pressure. You'd be surprised, too, how many cases of drug abuse we get at Westminster. The specialists say there is something like 10 per cent of the population, including MPs, who are physiologically or psychologically vulnerable to chemical addiction of one sort or another. Not their fault, it's something in their makeup, and they have much more trouble than the rest of us in resisting drink, pills and the rest. There's a charming and utterly private drying-out farm just outside Dover where we send them, sometimes for a couple of months. Most of them recover completely and return to a full political life.'

He paused yet again to swill the cognac around his glass and sip it gently, but continued to watch O'Neill closely. The other man did not stir. He sat there as if petrified.

'But it helps to catch them early,' Urquhart continued, 'which is why we are so sensitive to the signs of drug abuse. Like cocaine. It's become a real problem recently. They tell me it's fashionable – whatever that means – and too damned easy to obtain. Do you know it can rot your nasal membranes clean away if you let it? Funny drug. Gives people an instant high and persuades them that their brain and senses can complete five hours' work in just five minutes. Makes a good man brilliant, so they say. Pity it's so addictive.'

There was another pause. 'And expensive.'

Urquhart had not taken his eyes off O'Neill for a second during his narrative, and had witnessed the exquisite agony which had racked O'Neill inside. Any doubt about his diagnosis that he had started with had been brushed aside with the whimpering which began slowly to emerge from the other man. Now his words were tortured and pleading.

'What are you saying? I am not a drug addict. I don't do drugs!'

'No, of course not, Roger.' Urquhart adopted his most reassuring tone. 'But I think you must accept that there are some people who could jump to the most unfortunate conclusions about you. And the Prime Minister, you know, is not a man to take chances. It's not a matter of condemning a man without trial, simply opting for a quiet life without unnecessary risks.'

'The Prime Minister can't believe this!' O'Neill gasped as if he had been butted by a charging bull.

'I'm afraid that the Chairman was a little less than helpful with the PM the other day – he knows nothing, of course, but I don't think the dear Lord Williams is one of your greatest fans. Don't worry, I reassured the Prime Minister about you, and you have nothing to fear. As long as you have my support.'

Urquhart knew full well of the paranoia which dominates the minds of cocaine addicts, and the impact which his totally invented story about the Chairman's disaffection would leave on O'Neill's helter-skelter emotions. He also knew that the paranoia was matched by a lust for notoriety, which O'Neill could only achieve through his political connections and the continued patronage of the Prime Minister, and this he could not bear to lose. 'As long as you have my support,' rang in O'Neill's ears. 'One slip and you are dead,' it was saying. The web around O'Neill was complete, and now Urquhart offered him the way out.

'You see, Roger, I have seen gossip destroy so many men. Gossip founded on no more than circumstantial evidence or even naked jealousy, perhaps, but you know that the corridors around Westminster have been killing fields for less fortunate people than you or me. It would be a tragedy if you were pilloried either because of Lord Williams' hostility towards you or because people misunderstood your arrangement about expenses and your – hay fever.'

'What should I do?' The voice was plaintive.

'Your position is a delicate one, particularly at a time when the political currents within the Government are ebbing and flowing. I would suggest that you trust me. You need a strong supporter in the inner circles of the Party, particularly as the Prime Minister appears to be getting into more difficult waters and will be concentrating on rescuing himself rather than spending his time rescuing others.'

He paused to watch O'Neill writhe in his chair. 'I would

suggest the following. I shall tell the agency I have fully established that your expenses are legitimate. I shall ask them to continue with the arrangement, on the basis that we are doing it this way to avoid unhelpful jealousy from some of your colleagues within party headquarters who do not support extensive advertising budgets and who might use your high but perfectly legitimate expenses to attack the whole communications set-up. The agency can regard it as a sensible insurance policy. Also, I shall ensure that the Prime Minister continues to be fully informed of the good work you are doing for the Party. I shall certainly try to persuade him of the need to continue a high level publicity campaign to get him through the difficult months ahead, so that your budget is not cut to shreds by the Chairman.'

'You know I would be most grateful. . .' O'Neill mumbled.

'In return, you will keep me informed of everything that is going on at party headquarters and in particular what the Chairman is up to. He's a very ambitious and dangerous man, you know. Playing his own game while professing loyalty to the Prime Minister. Between us, though, I think we can ensure that no harm is done to the Prime Minister's – or to your – interests. You must be my eyes and ears, Roger, and you will have to let me know immediately of anything you hear of the Chairman's plans. Your future could depend upon it.' He punched home the words to let O'Neill be in no doubt that he meant it.

'We must work together on this. You will have to help me. I know how much you love politics and the Party, and I think the two of us together can help steer the Party through some difficult times ahead.'

'Thank you,' O'Neill whispered.

WEDNESDAY 30TH JUNE

The Strangers Bar in the House of Commons is a small, dark room overlooking the Thames where Members of Parliament may take their 'Stranger' or non-Member guests. As a result it is usually crowded and noisy with rumour and gossip. Tonight was no exception as O'Neill propped up the bar with one elbow and struggled valiantly with the other to avoid knocking the drink out of his host's hand.

'Another one, Steve?' he asked of his immaculately dressed companion.

Stephen Kendrick looked somewhat out of place in his light grey Armani mohair suit, pearl white cuffs and immaculately manicured hands clasped around a glass of Federation bitter, a draught beer for which the bars of the Palace of Westminster afford a warm home.

'Now you know better than me that Strangers can't buy drinks here. And anyway, I've only been here two weeks and I wouldn't want to ruin my career by having anyone see the Prime Minister's pet Irish wolfhound forcing drinks down the Opposition's newest and fastest rising backbencher. Some of my more dogmatic colleagues would treat that as treachery!'

He grinned and winked at the barmaid to attract her attention. Another pint of dark bitter and a double vodka-tonic were quick in coming.

'You know, Rog, I'm still pinching myself. I never really expected to get here, and I still can't decide whether it's a dream or just a bloody awful nightmare. When we worked together at the same little PR shop seven years ago, who would have guessed you would now be the chief grunter for the Prime Minister and I would be a humble if wonderfully talented Opposition MP?'

71

'Certainly not that little blonde telephonist we used to take turns with,' ribbed O'Neill. They both chuckled at the memory of younger and more frivolous days.

'Dear little Annie,' mused Kendrick.

'I thought her name was Jennie,' protested O'Neill.

'Rog, in those days I never remember you being fussy about what they were called.'

The banter finally broke the ice between the two men which had been slowly thawing with the drink. When O'Neill had telephoned the new MP to suggest a drink for old times' sake, they had both found it difficult to revive the easy familiarity which they had known in earlier years. They had been careful, perhaps too careful, to avoid the subject of politics which now dominated both their lives and it had forced their conversation along artificial lines. Now O'Neill decided to take the plunge.

'Steve, I don't mind you buying the drinks all night as far as I'm concerned. The way my masters are going at the moment, I think a saint would be driven to drink.'

Kendrick accepted the opening. 'Your lot do seem to be getting their robes of office in something of a twist. There are all sorts of weird rumours going round this place about how Samuel is furious with Williams for putting his head on the block with the PM, Williams is furious with Collingridge for screwing up the election campaign, and Collingridge is furious with just about everyone.'

'Maybe it's simply that they are all tired after the election and can't wait to get away on holiday,' O'Neill responded. 'Like an irritable family squabbling about how the car is packed before taking a long trip.'

'If you don't mind me saying, old chum, I think your leader is going to have to put an end to all the bickering very quickly, or else he'll go into the Summer Recess with the family looking more like a pack of Westminster alley cats. No Prime Minister can afford to let those sort of rumours run away from him, otherwise they begin to gain a life of their own. They become reality. Still, that's where you and your vast publicity budgets come to the rescue, like the Seventh Cavalry over the hill.'

'More like Custer's last bloody stand,' O'Neill said with some bitterness.

'What's the matter, Rog, Uncle Teddy run off with all your toy soldiers or something?' Kendrick asked with genuine curiosity.

O'Neill emptied his glass and Kendrick ordered another round.

'Between you and me, just as old chums, Steve, he's run off with almost all of them. Hell, we need to find new friends more than ever, but instead of going onto the offensive the Chairman seems content to retreat behind the barricades.'

'Ah, do I detect the cries of a frustrated Publicity Director who has been told to shut up shop for a while?'

O'Neill banged the bar in exasperation. 'I shouldn't tell you this, I suppose, but as it's not going to happen there's no harm. The new hospital expansion programme which we promised at the election giving matching Government funds for any money raised locally. We had a wonderful promotional campaign, all ready to go throughout the summer while all you bastards were off on the Costa del Cuba or wherever it is you go.'

Kendrick held his silence, not responding to the jibe.

'By the time you all came back in October, we would have won the hearts and minds of voters in every marginal seat in the country. We had the campaign all set! Advertising, a party political broadcast, ten million leaflets, direct mail. "Nursing Hospitals Back To Health." It would have made a wonderful build-up to the party conference as "The Party Which Delivers". But . . . he's pulled the plug. Just like that.'

'Why?' asked Kendrick consolingly. 'Money problems after the election?'

'That's the damnable thing about it, Steve. The money's in the budget and the leaflets have already been printed, but he won't even let us deliver them. He just came back from Number Ten this morning and said the thing was off. Then he had the nerve to ask whether the leaflets would be out of date by next year. It's so bloody amateurish!'

He tried to sound morose as he took another large

mouthful of spirits, and hoped that he had followed Urquhart's instructions properly, not showing too much disloyalty or too much frankness, just professional pique. He had no idea why Urquhart had told him to concoct an entirely spurious story about a non-existent publicity campaign to pass on in the Strangers Bar. But it seemed a small thing to do for a man on whom he knew he depended.

As he gazed into the bottom of his glass, he saw Kendrick give him a long and deliberate glance. With the air of camaraderie squeezed from his voice, the MP asked 'Why, Rog, why?'

'If only I knew, old chum. Complete bloody mystery to me.'

Thursday 1st July

The Chamber of the House of Commons is of relatively modern construction, rebuilt following the war after one of the Luftwaffe's bombs had missed the docks and carelessly scored a direct hit on the Mother of Parliaments instead. Yet in spite of its relative youth the Chamber has an atmosphere centuries old. If you sit quietly in the corner of the empty Chamber, the freshness of the leather on the narrow green benches fades and the ghosts of Chatham, Walpole, Fox and Disraeli pace the gangways once again.

It is a place of character rather than convenience. There are seats for only around 400 of the 650 Members, who cannot listen to the rudimentary loudspeakers built into the back of the benches without slumping to one side and giving the appearance of being sound asleep. Which sometimes they are.

The Chamber places Members in face to face confrontation with their antagonists in opposition parties, separated only by the distance of one sword's length, lulling the unwary into complacency and into forgetting that the greatest danger is always but a dagger's length away, on the benches behind.

Least of all can a Prime Minister forget that well over half the members of his own Parliamentary Party usually believe they can do his job far better, with a firmer grip of detail, or diplomacy, or both. Prime Ministers are called to account twice a week when Parliament is sitting through the time honoured institution of Prime Minister's Question Time. In principle it gives Members of Parliament the opportunity to seek information from the leader of Her Majesty's Government; in pratice it is an exercise in survival which owes more to the Roman arena of Nero and

Claudius than to the ideals of the constitutionalists who developed the system.

The questions from Opposition Members usually do not seek information, they seek to criticise and to inflict damage. The answers rarely seek to give information, but to retaliate. Prime Ministers always have the last word, and it is that which gives them the advantage in combat, like the gladiator allowed the final thrust.

But Prime Ministers also know that they are expected to win, and it is the manner rather than the fact of their victory which will decide the level of vocal support and encouragement from the troops behind. Woe betide the Prime Minister who does not dispatch the Opposition's questions quickly but who allows them to return once again to the attack. The noisy enthusiasm of the Government backbenches can soon turn to sullen resentment and silent condemnation, for a Prime Minister who cannot dominate the floor of the House of Commons soon finds that he can count on the support of few of his colleagues. Then the Prime Minister must watch not only the opposition in front, but also the competition behind.

It was this constant challenge which made Macmillan sometimes sick with tension before Question Time, which caused Wilson to lose sleep and Thatcher to lose her temper. And Henry Collingridge was not quite up to any of their standards.

The day following O'Neill's evening foray into the Strangers Bar had not been going smoothly for the Prime Minister. The Downing Street press secretary had been laid low by his children's chicken pox, so the normal daily press briefing was of inferior quality and, even worse to the impatient Collingridge, was late. So was Cabinet, which had gathered at its accustomed time of 10 a.m. on Thursday to resolve Government policy. It had dragged on, embarrassed and confused by the explanation from the Chancellor of the Exchequer of how the Government's reduced majority had taken the edge off the financial markets, making it impossible in this financial year to implement the hospital expansion programme which they had promised so enthusiastically during the election campaign. The Prime Minister should have kept a grip on the discussion, but it rambled on and ended amidst acrimony.

'A great pity the Chancellor wasn't a little more cautious before allowing us to run off and make rash commitments,' the Education Secretary commented, dripping acid.

The Chancellor muttered defiantly that it wasn't his fault the election results were worse than even the cynical Stock Market had expected, a comment he had instantly regretted making although he knew it was precisely what all his colleagues were thinking. Collingridge had knocked their heads together and instructed the Secretary of State for Health to prepare a suitable explanation for the change of plans, which would be announced in a fortnight's time during the last week before the August recess.

'Let us hope,' said the septuagenarian Lord Chancellor, 'that everybody's minds will by then be on the lighter follies of summer rather than the more depressing follies of their political masters.'

Cabinet overran by twenty-five minutes, which meant that in turn the Prime Minister's briefing meeting with officials for Question Time was also late, and his ill-temper ensured that he took in very little of what they were saying. When he strode into a packed Chamber just before the appointed time of 3.15 p.m., he was not as well armed or as alert as usual.

This did not seem to matter for the first thirteen minutes fifty seconds of combat, as he batted back questions from the Opposition and accepted plaudits from his own party with adequate if not inspired ease. The Speaker of the House, in charge of parliamentary proceedings, decided that with just over a minute left there would be time for just one more quick question to round off the session.

'Stephen Kendrick,' he called across the Chamber to summon the Member whose question was next on the Order Paper. It was the first occasion that the new Member had been involved at Question Time, and many older Members were nudging their colleagues to find out who this new man was.

'Number Six, sir.' Kendrick rose briefly to his feet to

indicate the question from the Order Paper he wished the Prime Minister to answer: 'To ask the Prime Minister if he will list his official engagements for the day'. It was a hollow question, identical in form to Questions One, Two and Four which had already preceded it, and designed not to elicit information but to hide from the Prime Minister the nature of the following supplementary thrust. Such is the nature of the combat.

The Prime Minister rose ponderously to his feet and glanced at the red briefing folder already open on the Despatch Box in front of him. He read in a monotone.

'I refer the Honourable Member to the reply I gave some moments ago to Questions One, Two and Four.' Since his earlier reply had said no more than that he would spend the day holding meetings with ministerial colleagues and hosting a dinner for the visiting Belgian Prime Minister, no one had yet learned anything of interest about the Prime Minister's activities – which was precisely his intention.

Collingridge resumed his seat, and the Speaker summoned Kendrick once more to place his supplementary question. The gladiatorial courtesies were now over, and battle was about to commence. Kendrick rose to his feet from the rear row of the Opposition benches.

Kendrick was a gambler, a man who had found professional success in an industry which emphasised ostentatious reward, yet who had decided to risk his expense account and sports car by fighting a marginal parliamentary seat. Not that he had really expected or indeed wanted to win; after all, the Government had been sitting on a pretty reasonable majority. Fighting the seat, he reasoned, would give him a platform and a prominence which would help him both socially and professionally, and would certainly give him a higher profile in the public relations trade magazines. 'The man with the social conscience' always made good copy in an aggressively commercial industry, and the ability to be able to drop a name or two usually helped.

His majority of 76, after three recounts, at first had come as an unpleasant shock as suddenly he was forced to contemplate the reduced income and additional hours of a parliamentary career. It would not be much of a career at that, either, since he knew the odds were that after the next election he would probably be looking for a new seat or a new job. In either case he knew that the plodding progress of a loyal and patient backbencher was not for him. He would have to make his mark, and make it quickly.

Kendrick had spent all of the previous evening and much of that morning turning over O'Neill's remarks in his mind. Why cancel a publicity campaign promoting a vote-winning policy which had been sold heavily during the election, when the campaign was all set to go? Whichever way he looked at it, the pieces would only fit together into a pattern suggesting that it was the policy rather than the publicity campaign which was in trouble. But should he enquire or accuse? To question or condemn? Or simply take the course expected of new Members and be completely anodyne? He knew that if he got it wrong, the first and lasting impression he made would be that of the House fool.

His momentary uncertainty caused the general commotion of the House to die away as MPs sensed indecision and surprise. Had the new Member frozen? But Kendrick felt calm and at ease. He remembered his small majority, and he knew he must gamble. What had he got to lose, except his dignity, which in any event was a commodity of little practical value in the modern House of Commons? He took a deep breath.

'Will the Prime Minister explain to the House why he is not implementing the promised hospital expansion programme?'

No criticism. No elaboration. No added phrase or rambling comment which would allow the Prime Minister to dodge or divert the question. Kendrick had thrown his grenade and he knew that if his gamble were wrong the grenade would be picked up by a grateful Prime Minister and thrown directly back to explode in his own lap.

A murmur went up as he resumed his seat. The sport had taken an interesting new turn, and the 300-odd spectators turned as one to look towards Collingridge. He rose

79

aware that there was nothing in his red briefing folder from which to draw inspiration. The whole House could see the broad smile with which Collingridge accepted the challenge; only those sitting very close to him could see the whites of his knuckles as he gripped the Despatch Box.

'I hope that the Honourable Gentleman will be careful to avoid being carried away by the summer silly season, at least before August arrives. As he is a new Member, may I remind him that in the last four years under this Government the health service has enjoyed a substantial real increase in spending of some 6 to 8 per cent?' Collingridge knew he was being inexcusably patronising, but he could not find the right words. 'The health service has gained more than any Government service from our success and continuing determination in defeating inflation, which compares . . .'

'Answer the bloody question,' came the irreverent growl from below the gangway on the Opposition benches, which was immediately echoed by several Members around the interrupter. Kendrick was no longer alone.

'I shall answer the question in my own way and in my own time,' snapped the Prime Minister. 'It is a pathetic sham for the Opposition to whine on about such matters when they know that electors have reached their own conclusions and only recently voted with their feet for this Government. They support us and I can repeat our determination to protect them and their hospital service.'

Increasingly rude shouts of disapproval began to rise from the Opposition benches, most of which would go unrecorded by Hansard but which were clearly audible to the Prime Minister. His own backbenchers began to shift uneasily, uncertain as to why Collingridge did not simply reaffirm often stated party policy.

'The House will be aware that it is not the custom of Governments to discuss the specifics of new spending plans in advance, and we shall make an announcement about our intentions at the appropriate time.'

'You have. You've bloody dropped it, haven't you?' the Honourable and usually disrespectful Member for Newcastle West shouted, so loudly that even Hansard could not claim to have missed it.

The Opposition Front Bench smiled and chuckled, beginning to appreciate that the Prime Minister's increasingly taut smile hid inner turmoil. The Leader of the Opposition, not six feet from where Collingridge stood, turned to his nearest colleague and whispered loudly. 'Do you know I think he's fluffed it. He's running away!'

Opposition Members began taunting him from all around, slapping their thighs and chortling like old hags around a guillotine.

The tension and pain of a thousand such encounters in the House welled up inside Collingridge. He was unprepared for this. He could not bring himself to admit the truth, yet neither could he lie to the House, and he could find no form of words which would tread that delicate line between honesty and outright deceit. As he observed the sneers and smugness on the faces in front of him and listened to their jeers, he remembered all the many lies they had told about him in the past, the cruelty they had shown and the tears they had caused his wife to shed. As he gazed at the sea of waving Order Papers and contorted faces just a few feet in front of him, his patience vanished. He had to bring it to an end, and he no longer cared how. He threw his hands in the air.

'I don't have to take comments like that from a pack of dogs,' he snarled, and sat down.

Even before the shout of triumph and rage had a chance to rise from the Opposition benches, Kendrick was back on his feet.

'On a point of order, Mr Speaker. The Prime Minister's remarks are an absolute disgrace. I asked a perfectly straightforward question about why the Prime Minister had reneged on his election promise to patients and nurses, and all I have got are insults and evasion. While I understand the Prime Minister's reluctance to admit to the House that he has perpetrated a gigantic and disgraceful fraud, is there nothing you can do to protect the right of Members of this House to get a straight answer to a straight question?'

A roar of approval grew from Opposition members as the Speaker struggled to be heard above the commotion. 'The Honourable Member, although he is new, seems already to have developed a sharp eye for parliamentary procedure, in which case he will know that I am no more responsible for the content or tone of the Prime Minister's replies than I am for the questions which are put to him. Next business!'

As the Speaker tried to move matters on, a red-faced Collingridge rose and strode angrily out of the Chamber, gesticulating for the Chief Whip to follow him. The very unparliamentary taunt of 'Coward!' rang after him across the floor. From the Government benches there was an uncertain silence.

'How in Christ's name did he know? How did that son-of-a-bitch know?'

The door had barely closed upon the Prime Minister's office just off the rear of the Chamber when the screaming began. The normally suave exterior of Her Majesty's First Minister had been drawn back to reveal a wild Warwickshire ferret.

'Francis, it's simply not good enough. It's not bloody good enough I tell you. We get the Chancellor's report in Cabinet Committee yesterday, the full Cabinet discusses it for the first time today, and by this afternoon it's known to every snivelling creep in the Opposition. Less than two dozen Cabinet Ministers knew, only a handful of civil servants knew, but now every single Member of the Opposition knows. Who leaked it, Francis, who? I'm damned if I know, but you're Chief Whip and I want you to find out who the hell it was.'

Urquhart breathed a huge sigh of relief. Until the Prime Minister's outburst he had no idea if the finger of blame was already pointing at him, and the last couple of minutes had been distinctly uncomfortable.

'It simply astonishes me that one of our Cabinet colleagues would want deliberately to leak something like this,' Urquhart began, implicitly ruling out the possibility of a civil service leak and narrowing the circle of suspicion to include each and every one of his Cabinet colleagues.

'They've got us by the balls now, and it's going to hurt. Whoever is responsible has humiliated me, and I want him out, Francis. I want – I insist – that you find the worm. And then I want him fed to the crows.'

'I'm afraid there's been too much bickering amongst our colleagues since the election. Too many of them seem to want someone else's job.'

'I know they all want *my* job, damn them, but who would be so – cretinous . . .' – the words were spat out – 'as to deliberately leak something like that?'

'I can't say for sure, Prime Minister.'

'Can't you even give me an educated guess, for Chrissake?'

'That would not be fair.'

'Life's not fair, Francis. Tell me about it.'

'But . . .'

'No "buts", Francis. If it's happened once it can and almost certainly will happen again. Accuse, imply, whatever you damned well like. There are no minutes being taken here. But I want some names!' Collingridge kicked a chair in frustration.

'If you insist, I'll speculate. But I hope I'll not live to regret anything I'm going to say. I know nothing for sure, you understand . . . let's work from deduction. Given the time scale involved, it seems more likely to have leaked from yesterday's Cabinet Committee rather than from today's full Cabinet. Agreed?'

Collingridge nodded his assent.

'And apart from you and me, who is on that Committee?'

'Chancellor of the Exchequer, Financial Secretary, Health, Education, Environment, Trade and Industry.' The Prime Minister reeled off those Cabinet Ministers who had attended.

Urquhart remained silent, forcing Collingridge to finish off the logic himself. 'Well, the two Treasury Ministers were scarcely likely to leak the fact that they had screwed it up. But Health bitterly opposed it, so Peter McKenzie had a reason to leak it. Harold Earle at Education has always had a loose lip. And Michael Samuel has a habit of

83

enjoying the company of the media rather too much for my liking.'

The shadowy suspicions which lurk in a Prime Minister's mind were being brought into the light, and Urquhart relished the spectacle as he watched the seed of accusation grow alongside Collingridge's insecurity.

'There are other possibilities, but I think them unlikely,' Urquhart joined in. 'As you know Michael is very close to Teddy Williams. They discuss everything together. It could have come out of party headquarters. Not from Teddy, I mean, but one of the officials there. They can be as tight-lipped as drunken Glaswegians on a Friday night.'

Collingridge pondered this possibility for some moments in silence. 'Could it really have been Teddy?' he mused. '*Et tu, Brute*? Could that really be, Francis? He was never my greatest supporter – we're from different generations – but I made him one of the team. Now surely not this?'

Urquhart was delighted at the effect his words were having on his battered leader, who sat grey and tired in his chair, staring ahead, lost in surmise and suspicion.

'Perhaps I have relied on him too much recently. I thought he had no axe to grind, no real ambition in the House of Lords. One of the loyal old guard. Was I wrong, Francis?'

'I simply don't know. You asked me to speculate. I can do no more at this stage.'

'Make sure, Francis. I want him, whoever he is.'

With that the Prime Minister announced open season, and Urquhart felt himself back on the heather moors of his childhood, gun in hand, waiting for the bucks to appear.

Friday 16th July –
Thursday 22nd July

The life of the House of Commons is arduous and little appreciated. Long hours, heavy workloads, too much entertaining and too little respite ensure that the long summer break beckons to all Members like an oasis in a desert. As they approach closer to the oasis during the dog days of July, their thirst and their irritability increase, particularly after the exhaustion of an early summer election campaign.

During the next couple of weeks, Urquhart was prominent in moving steadily around the corridors and bars of the House, trying to bolster morale and calm the doubts of many Government backbenchers about Collingridge's increasingly scratchy performance. Morale is easier to shatter than to rebuild, and some old hands thought that Urquhart was trying perhaps a little too hard, his high profile serving to remind many that the Prime Minister was in especial need of support at a time when he should have been dominating events. But if it were a fault, it was one they recognised as aggressive loyalty in the Chief Whip. In any event, the end of the Session was only a week hence and the grapes of the South of France would soon be washing away much of the parliamentary cares.

It was because of this safety valve of August that Governments have developed the knack of making difficult announcements on the last day of the Session by means of Written Answers published in Hansard, the voluminous official report of parliamentary proceedings. Statements of Government intent can be placed openly and clearly on the public record, but at a time when most Members are packing up their desks rather than poring over the endless

85

pages of Hansard, and when in any event there is little time or opportunity to make a fuss. The truth, the whole truth and nothing but the truth – so long as you read the fine print.

Which is why it was most unfortunate that a photocopy of a draft Written Answer from the Secretary of State for Defence informing the House of substantial cuts in the Territorial Army on the grounds that they were increasingly less relevant in the nuclear era should have been found, a full ten days before it was due to be published, lying under a chair in Annie's Bar where Members and journalists congregate to exchange views and gossip. It was still more unfortunate that it was found by the lobby correspondent of the *Independent*, because everybody liked and respected him, and he knew how to check the story out. When the story was reported as the lead item in the *Independent* four days later at the start of the final full week of the Parliamentary Session, people knew that it was reliable.

Stories of 'cuts' are nothing new for Governments to deal with. If they maintain spending at existing levels while new and inevitably more expensive techniques for performing the task are discovered, they are accused of 'cuts'. If they increase expenditure in vital areas, but not as much as the self-appointed 'experts' require, they are still accused of 'cuts'. If they shift resources from one area to another, once again the accusations of 'cuts' fly. But should they dare make actual 'cuts' in any area other than their own salary levels, retribution is swift.

Retribution on this occasion came from unusual sources. While Territorial Army pay is not large, their numbers are great and they represent important votes to Government Members of Parliament. Moreover, throughout the higher echelons of the Government's constituency parties up and down the country could be found prominent figures with the initials 'TD' after their names – 'Territorial Decoration' – someone who has served in, respects and will defend The Terrors to their last drop of writing ink.

Thus it was that, when the House gathered next to discuss forthcoming Parliamentary Business with the Leader of the House, the air was heavy with the mid-summer heat, made more oppressive by the accusations of betrayal and emotional appeals for a change of course which on this occasion were coming from the Government benches, while the Opposition sat back like enthusiastic and very contented Roman lions watching the Christians do all the work for them.

The Right Honourable Sir Jasper Grainger, OBE, JP, TD, was on his feet. The old man proudly sported a carefully ironed regimental tie along with a heavy three piece tweed suit, refusing to compromise his personal standards in spite of the inadequate air-conditioning. And as the elected Chairman of the Backbench Defence Committee, his words carried enormous weight.

'May I return to the point raised by several of my Honourable Friends about the unnecessary and deeply damaging cuts in our Territorial Army establishment? Will the Leader of the House be in no doubt about the depth of feeling amongst his own supporters on this matter? Have he and the Prime Minister yet fully understood the damage that will be done to the Government's support over the coming months? Will he even now allow the House time to debate and reverse this decision, because I must ask him not to leave his colleagues defenceless to the accusations of bad faith which will follow if this goes through?'

The Leader of the House, Simon Lloyd, straightened and readied himself once again to come to the Despatch Box, which he was beginning to feel should have been constructed with sandbags. It had been a torrid twenty minutes of trying to defend the Government's position, and he had grown increasingly tetchy as he found the response he had prepared earlier with the Prime Minister and Defence Secretary affording increasingly less protection from the grenades being thrown by his own side. He was glad Collingridge and the Defence Secretary were sitting beside him on the Front Bench. Why should he suffer on his own?

'My Right Honourable Friend misses the point. The document which found its way into the newspapers was stolen Government property. These are issues which rise high above the details of the document itself. If there is to be a debate, it should be about such flagrant breaches of honesty. Will he not join me in wholeheartedly condemning the theft of important Government documents as being the major issue at stake here? He must realise that by coming back to the details of expenditure he is as good as condoning the activity of common theft and assisting those who are responsible for it.'

Sir Jasper rose to seek permission to pursue the point and, amidst waving of Order Papers throughout the Chamber, the Speaker consented. The old soldier gathered himself up to his full height, back as straight as a ramrod, moustache bristling and face flushed with genuine anger.

'Does my Right Honourable Friend not realise that it is he who is missing the point,' he thundered, 'that I would rather live alongside a common British thief than a common Russian soldier, which is precisely the fate this policy is threatening us with?'

The uproar which followed took the Speaker a full minute to calm sufficiently for any chance of a response to be heard. During that time, the Leader of the House turned and offered a look of sheer desperation to the Prime Minister and the Defence Secretary, huddled together on the Front Bench. Collingridge muttered briefly in the ear of his colleague, and then gave a curt nod to the Leader of the House.

'Mr Speaker,' the Leader of the House began, and paused to let the clamour subside and to clear his throat, which was by now parched with tension. 'Mr Speaker, I and my Right Honourable Friends have listened carefully to the mood of the House. I have the permission of the Prime Minister and the Secretary of State for Defence to say that, in light of the representations put from all sides today, the Government will look once again at this important matter to see whether any alternative solution can be found.'

He had run up the white flag, and he didn't know whether to feel sick or relieved.

The cries of victory and relief reached far outside the Chamber as the parliamentary correspondents drank in an emotional scene and recorded it in their notebooks. Amidst the hubbub and confusion on all sides, the lonely figure of Henry Collingridge sat small and shrunken, staring straight ahead.

Some minutes later, a breathless Mattie Storin had pushed her way through the crowd of politicians and correspondents who were jostling in the lobby outside the entrance to the Chamber, as Opposition Members claimed victory for themselves while Government supporters with considerably less conviction tried to claim victory for common sense. Few were in any doubt that they had witnessed a Prime Minister on the rack. Above the mêlée Mattie saw the tall figure of Urquhart edging his way around the out side of the crowd, avoiding the questions of several agitated backbenchers. He disappeared through a convenient door, and Mattie pursued him. By the time she had almost caught up with her quarry, Urquhart was striding two at a time up the stairs which led to the upper galleries surrounding the Chamber.

'Mr Urquhart,' she shouted breathlessly after the fleeing Minister, promising herself once again that she would give up late nights and resume jogging. 'I need your view.'

'I'm not sure I have one today, Miss Storin.' Urquhart did not stop.

'Surely we're not back on the "Chief Whip refuses to endorse Prime Minister" game again?'

Urquhart stopped and turned to face the still panting Mattie. He smiled in amusement at the young correspondent's cheek. 'Yes, Mattie, I suppose you have a right to expect something. Well, what do you think?'

'If the PM had trouble in controlling his Cabinet before this, his task now is going to be – what, a nightmare? Impossible?'

'It is not unusual for Prime Ministers to change their minds. But to be forced to change your mind publicly, simply because you are unable to defend your own decision, is . . .'

Mattie waited in vain for Urquhart to finish, but realised he would not do so. He would not condemn his Prime

Minister, not openly on the stairs, but it was clear there would be no justification either. She prompted the Chief Whip yet again. 'Isn't the Government getting accident prone – the second major leak in a matter of weeks? Where are these leaks coming from?'

'As Chief Whip I am responsible only for discipline on the Government backbenches. You can scarcely expect me to play headmaster to my own Cabinet colleagues as well.'

'But if it's coming from Cabinet – who, and why?'

'I simply don't know, Mattie. But doubtless the Prime Minister will instruct me to find out who and why.'

'Formally or informally?'

'I can't comment on that,' muttered Urquhart, and continued up the stairs pursued by Mattie.

'So we have got to the point where the Prime Minister is about to launch an inquiry into which of his own Cabinet colleagues is leaking sensitive information. Is that what you are saying?'

'Oh, Mattie. It seems I have already said too much. You're a damn sight quicker on the uptake than most of your colleagues. It seems to me that your logic rather than my words has led you to your conclusions, eh? And I trust that you will be keeping my name out of this.'

'Usual lobby terms, Mr Urquhart,' she assured him. 'Just let me get this perfectly clear. You are not denying, indeed you are confirming that the Prime Minister will order an investigation into his Cabinet members' conduct?'

'If you keep my name out of it – yes.'

'Jesus, this will set them all flapping,' Mattie gasped. She could already see her front page lead taking shape.

'June 10th does seem a long time ago, doesn't it, Mattie?'

Urquhart continued up the stairs which led to the Strangers Gallery, where members of the public perched on rows of cramped, narrow benches to view the proceedings of the House, usually with a considerable degree of discomfort and a still larger degree of astonishment. He caught the eye of a small and impeccably dressed Indian for whom he had previously obtained a seat in the Gallery, and signalled to him. The man struggled past the outstretched knees of other visitors packed into the benches, and emerged with obvious embarrassment past two extremely buxom middle-aged ladies. Before he had any opportunity to speak Urquhart motioned to him for silence and led him towards the small hallway behind the gallery.

'Mr Urquhart, sir, it has been a most exciting and highly educational ninety minutes. I am deeply indebted to you for assisting me to obtain such a comfortable position.'

Urquhart, who knew that even small Indian gentlemen such as Firdaus Jhabwala found the seats acutely uncomfortable, smiled knowingly. 'I know you are being very polite in not complaining about the discomfort of the seating. I only wish I could have found you some more comfortable position.'

They chatted politely while Jhabwala secured the release of his black hide attaché case from the attendant. When he had arrived he had firmly refused to hand it over until he discovered that his entry to the Gallery would be forbidden unless he lodged it with the security desk.

'I am so glad that we British can still trust ordinary working chaps with our possessions,' he stated very seriously, patting the case for comfort.

'Quite,' replied Urquhart, who trusted neither the ordinary working chap nor Jhabwala. Still, he was a constituent who seemed to have various flourishing local businesses, and had provided a £500 donation towards his election campaign expenses and had asked for nothing in return except, shortly afterwards, a personal interview and private meeting in the House of Commons.

'Not in the constituency,' he had explained to Urquhart's secretary on the phone. 'It's a matter of national rather than local attention.'

Urquhart led the way under the great vaulted oak ceiling of Westminster Hall, at which point Jhabwala asked to stand for a while. 'I would be grateful for a silent moment in this great hall in which Charles I was tried and condemned and Winston Churchill lay in state.'

He noticed the condescending smile appearing at the corner of Urquhart's mouth.

'Mr Urquhart. Please do not think me pretentious. My

91

own family associations with British institutions go back nearly 250 years to the days of the Honourable East India Company and Lord Clive, whom my ancestors advised and to whom they loaned considerable funds. Both before and since my family has occupied prestigious positions in the judicial and administrative branches of Indian Government.'

Jhabwala's eyes lowered, and a strong sense of sadness filled his voice. 'But since Independence, Mr Urquhart, that once great subcontinent has slowly crumbled into a new dark age. Muslim has been set against Hindu, worker against employer, pupil against teacher. You may not agree, but the modern Gandhi dynasty is less inspired and far more corrupt than any my family ever served in colonial days. I am a Parsee, a cultural minority which has found little comfort under the new Raj, and the fortunes of my family have declined. So I moved to Great Britain, where my father and grandfather were educated. I can tell you without a trace of insincerity, Mr Urquhart, that I feel more at home and more attached to this country and its culture than ever I could back in modern India. I wake up grateful every day that I can call myself a British citizen and educate my children in British universities.'

Urquhart saw his opportunity to interrupt this impassioned and obviously heartfelt monologue. 'Where are your children educated?'

'I have a son just finishing a law degree at Jesus College, Cambridge, and an elder son who is undertaking an MBA at the Wharton Business School in Philadelphia. It is my earnest hope that my younger son will soon qualify to read medicine at Cambridge.'

They were now walking towards the interview rooms beneath the Great Hall, their shoes clipping across the worn flagstoned floor where Henry VIII had played tennis and which now was splattered with shafts of bright sunlight slanting through the ancient windows. It was a scene centuries old, and the Indian was clearly in great awe.

'And what precisely do you do?' asked Urquhart.

'I, sir, am a trader, not an educated man. I left behind any hope of that during the great turmoil of Indian

Independence. I have therefore had to find my way not with my brain but by diligence and hard work. I am happy to say that I have been moderately successful.'

'What sort of trade?'

'I have several business interests, Mr Urquhart. Property. Wholesaling. A little local finance. But I am no narrow minded capitalist. I am well aware of my duty to the community. It is about that I wished to speak with you.'

By now they had arrived at the interview room and at Urquhart's invitation Jhabwala seated himself in one of the green leather chairs, fingering with delight the gold embossed portcullis which embellished the upright back of this and all the other chairs in the room.

'Mr Urquhart. I was not born in this country, and I know that of necessity I must work particularly hard to gain respectability in the community. That is important, not so much for me but for my children. I wish them to have the advantages which my father could not secure for me at a time of civil war. So I try to participate. I assist the local Rotary Club. I help with many local charities. And as you know, I am an ardent supporter of the Prime Minister.'

'I am afraid that you did not see him to best advantage this afternoon.'

'Then I suspect he needs his friends and supporters more than ever.'

There was a short silence. Urquhart struggled to find the meaning and direction behind his guest's remarks, but it eluded him, although meaning and direction he knew there must be. Jhabwala began again, a little more slowly.

'Mr Urquhart. You know that I have great admiration for you. I was happy to assist in a modest way with your election appeal and would be happy to do so again. I am also a fervent admirer of the entire Government. I would wish to help you all.'

'May I know how?'

'I know election campaigns are expensive, and perhaps I could make a small donation to Party coffers. I imagine that funds must be short at times like these.'

'Indeed, indeed,' said Urquhart. 'Could I ask how much you were thinking of giving?'

Jhabwala lifted his case onto the table top, twirled the combination and flipped the two brass catches. The lid sprang open and he slid the black leather case around to Urquhart.

'I would be delighted if the Party could accept £50,000 as a gesture of my support.'

Urquhart resisted the ferocious temptation to pick up one of the bundles of notes and start counting. He noticed that all the wads were of used £20 notes and were tied with rubber bands rather than bank cashiers' wrappers.

'This is . . . most generous, Mr Jhabwala.' He found himself using his guest's name for the first time since they had met earlier in the afternoon. 'But it is a little unusual for me to accept such a large donation on behalf of the Party, particularly in cash.'

'You will understand that during the civil war in India my family lost everything. Our house and business were destroyed, and we narrowly escaped with our lives. In 1947 a Muslim mob burned my local bank to the ground – with all its deposits and records. The bank's head office apologised, of course, but without any records could only provide my father with their regrets rather than the funds he had deposited with them. It may seem a little old fashioned of me, but I still prefer to trust cash rather than cashiers.'

The businessman's smile shone reassuringly from beneath his dark features. Urquhart did not trust him or his story.

'I see.' Urquhart took a deep breath. 'May I be blunt, Mr Jhabwala, and ask if there is anything you wish from us in exchange for your support? It is sometimes the case with first-time donors that they believe there is something the Party can do for them, when in reality our powers are very limited . . .'

Jhabwala beamed and shook his head to halt Urquhart's question. 'There is nothing I wish to do other than to be a firm supporter of the Prime Minister and yourself, Mr Urquhart. You will understand as a local MP that my business interests often bring me into friendly contact with local authorities for planning permission or tendering for contracts and so forth. I cannot guarantee that you will never find my name in the local press or that I will not ask at some point to seek your guidance through the maze of local decision makers, but I assure you I am looking for no favours. I want nothing in exchange, other than to request that I and my wife have the honour of meeting with the Prime Minister at some suitable time, particularly if he should ever come to the constituency. It would mean a great deal to my wife, as you will appreciate.'

And the photographs of Jhabwala closeted with the Prime Minister would go down remarkably well in the local and ethnic press, as Urquhart well knew. He didn't care for the hint about local planning or contract decisions, but he was an experienced hand at dealing with such requests when they arose. Urquhart began to relax and to return the Indian's smile.

'I am sure that could be arranged. Perhaps you and your wife would like to attend a reception at Downing Street?'

The Indian was nodding. 'It would be an honour, of course, to be able to have just a few private words with him, simply to express my great personal enthusiasm.'

'That might be possible, too, but you will understand that the Prime Minister himself could not accept the money. It would not be – how should I put it? – delicate for him to be involved with such matters.'

'Of course, of course, Mr Urquhart. Which is why I would be delighted if you would accept the money on his behalf.'

'I'm afraid I can only give you a rudimentary receipt. Perhaps you would prefer to deliver the money directly to the party treasurers.'

Jhabwala threw up his hands in horror. 'Sir, I do not require a receipt from you. You have my fullest trust. It was you as my local Member of Parliament I wished to see, not a party official. I have even taken the liberty of engraving your initials on the hide case, Mr Urquhart, a small gesture which I hope you will accept for all your dutiful work in Surrey.'

You crafty, ingratiating little sod, thought Urquhart, all the while smiling broadly at Jhabwala and wondering how long it would be before he got the first call about planning permission. Perhaps he should have thrown the Indian out, but an idea was already forming in his mind. He reached across the table and shook Jhabwala's hand warmly.

'It has been a great pleasure meeting you at last, Mr Jhabwala.'

The night was hot and humid, even for late July. Mattie had taken a long, cool shower and thrown the windows wide open, but she could get no relief from the still and heavy air. She lay in the darkness upon her bed, feeling her hair stick clammily to the nape of her neck. She could not sleep while the scenes of parliamentary turmoil she had witnessed earlier in the day kept tumbling through her thoughts. But there was something else, too, something not of the mind but in her body that was disturbing her, making her restless.

She lay back on her lonely, cold bed and felt the dampness trickling between her shoulder blades. She could not forget that it was the first time since Yorkshire she had sweated in bed, for any reason . . .

FRIDAY 23RD JULY

The following morning a young black woman walked into a scruffy newsagents just off Praed Street in Paddington and enquired after the cost of accommodation address facilities advertised on the card in the shop window. She explained that she was working in the area and needed a local address to which she could direct her mail. It was a brilliant summer's day in London, but behind the thick shutters and dirty windows the shop was dark and musty. At first the fleshy, balding assistant behind the counter scarcely lifted his eyes from his copy of *Playboy*. This was one of London's notorious red light areas, and young women or seedy men asking to open an accommodation address was one of the less surprising requests he had to deal with. This girl was particularly attractive, though, and he wondered where she did business. His wife was staying with her mother over the weekend, and a little distraction would be better than the long list of household jobs she was threatening to leave behind.

He brushed away the cigarette ash he had spilled over the counter and smiled encouragingly at her. He got no response, however. With scarcely another word, the young woman paid the fee for the minimum three months, carefully put away the receipt which would be needed for identification, and left.

The assistant had time only for one last look at the retreating and beautifully curved backside before he was engaged by the complaints of an old age pensioner who had not yet received her morning newspaper, and he did not see the young woman get into the taxi outside.

'All right, Pen?' asked the man waiting inside.

'No problem, Roger,' his secretary answered. 'But why couldn't he do it himself?'

'Look, I told you that he has some delicate personal problems to sort out and needs some privacy for his mail. Dirty magazines for all I know. So no questions, and not a word to anyone. OK?'

Urquhart had sworn him to secrecy, and he suspected that the Chief Whip would be furious if he discovered that O'Neill had got Penny Guy to carry out his dirty work. But he knew he could trust Penny with such chores. After all, what were secretaries for?

As the taxi drew away, Penny once again remarked to herself how strangely O'Neill was beginning to act nowadays.

The day was growing ever hotter by the time the man in the sports jacket and trilby hat ventured into the North London branch of the Union Bank of Turkey on the Seven Sisters Road. The Cypriot counter clerk often swore that Englishmen only ever had one set of clothes which they wore throughout the winter or summer, irrespective of the temperature. And this one obviously had money since he wanted to open an account. In a slight but perceptible regional accent which the clerk could not quite place, he explained that he lived in Kenya but was visiting the United Kingdom for a few months to develop the holiday business which he ran. He was interested in investing in a hotel which was being built just outside the Turkish resort of Antalya, on the southern Mediterranean coast.

The clerk responded that he did not know Antalya personally, but had heard that it was a beautiful spot, and of course the bank would be delighted to help him in whatever way possible. He offered the prospective customer a simple registration form, requiring details of his name, address, previous banking reference and other details.

Five minutes later, the customer had returned to the clerk's window with the completed form. He apologised for being able to provide a banking reference only from Kenya, but this was his first trip to London in nearly twenty years. The clerk assured the older man that the bank was very accustomed to dealing with overseas enquiries, and the banking reference in Kenya would be no problem.

That's what you think, the other thought. He knew it would take at least four weeks for the reference to be checked, and probably another four before it could be clearly established that the reference was false. By that time the account would have been closed with all bank charges paid, so no one would care or question.

The clerk sought no further verification of any of the other items on the form. 'How would you like to open your account, sir?'

'I would like to make an initial deposit of £50,000 – in cash.'

The man pulled open a brown corduroy holdall and passed the bundles of notes across the counter. He was glad he did not have to count them. It had been years since he had last worn these glasses, and in the meantime he had changed his contact lens prescription twice. His eyes were not focusing properly and they ached, but Urquhart knew that his simple disguise would be more than enough to avoid recognition by any but his closest colleagues. There was after all some benefit in being the most faceless senior member of Her Majesty's Government, he told himself sarcastically. He delighted at long last in being able to take advantage of his enforced anonymity.

The clerk had finished counting the money, with a colleague double checking the total, and was already filling out a receipt. Banks are like plumbers, Urquhart thought, cash in hand and no questions asked.

'Rather than have the cash just sitting idle in a current account, I would like you to purchase some shares for me. Can you arrange that?' he requested.

It took only another five minutes for Urquhart to fill out two further forms placing an order for 20,000 ordinary shares in the Renox Chemical Company PLC, currently trading at just over 240p per share. He was assured that the order would be completed by 4 p.m. that afternoon, at a cost of £49,288 including stamp duties and brokers' fees, leaving him exactly £712 in his new account. Urquhart signed the forms with a flourish and a signature that was illegible.

The clerk smiled as he pushed the receipt across the counter. 'A great pleasure doing business with you, Mr Collingridge.'

Monday 26th July – Wednesday 28th July

Seventy-two hours later MPs gathered in the House to begin the final week of bickering before the summer recess. There were relatively few Members present, as many of their colleagues had tried to take their leave of London early. There had been little attempt to dissuade them, since there was already enough tetchiness around Westminster without piling on needless aggravation. There was very much an end-of-term mood amongst the parliamentarians and little business was done. However, the Hansard record of parliamentary proceedings for that day would be thick, fleshed out with a remarkable number of Written Answers to MPs' questions which the Government were anxious to deal with while attention was diverted elsewhere and before Ministers and their civil servants left for their own recuperation. Ministers from the Department of Health were particularly careful not to be seen around the corridors of Westminster that day, because one of the many Written Answers they had issued concerned the long awaited postponement of the hospital expansion programme. They did not expect to get much comfort from MPs of any party on that subject.

It was not surprising, therefore, that few noted another announcement from the Department concerning a list of three drugs which the Government, on the advice of their Chief Medical Officer and the Committee on the Safety of Medicines, were now licensing for general use. One of the drugs was Cybernox, a new medication developed by the Renox Chemical Company PLC which had proved startlingly effective in controlling the craving for nicotine when fed in small doses to addicted rats and beagles. The same excellent results had been obtained during extensive test programmes with humans, and now the drug had been approved for general use under doctor's prescription.

The announcement caused a flurry of activity at Renox Chemicals. A press conference for the medical and scientific press was called for the following day, the Marketing Director pressed the button on a pre-planned mail shot to every single general practitioner throughout the country, and the company's broker informed the Stock Exchange of the new licence.

The response was immediate. Shares in the Renox Chemical Company PLC jumped from 244p to 295p. The 20,000 ordinary shares purchased two days before by the Union Bank of Turkey's brokers were now worth exactly £59,000.

Shortly before noon the next day, a telephone call instructed the bank to sell the shares and credit the amount to the appropriate account. The caller also explained that regrettably the hotel venture in Antalya was not proceeding, and the account holder was returning to Kenya. Would the bank be kind enough to close the account, and expect a visit from the account holder later that afternoon?

Just before the bank closed at 3 p.m. the same bespectacled man in the hat and sports jacket walked into the branch on Seven Sisters Road and collected £58,962 which he placed in bundles of £20 notes in the bottom of his brown corduroy bag. He bridled at the £750 in charges which the bank had levied on his short-lived and simple account but, as the deputy manager had suspected, he chose not to make a fuss. He asked for a closing statement to be sent to him at his address in Paddington, and thanked the clerk for his courtesy.

The following morning and less than one week after Firdaus Jhabwala had met with Urquhart, the Chief Whip delivered £50,000 in cash to the party treasurers. Substantial payments in cash were not unique, and the treasurers expressed delight at discovering a new source of funds. Urquhart suggested that the treasurers office make the usual arrangements to ensure that the donor and his wife were invited to a charity reception or two at Downing

Street, and asked to be informed when this happened so that he could make a specific arrangement with the Prime Minister's political secretary to ensure that Mr and Mrs Jhabwala had ten minutes alone with the Prime Minister beforehand. One of the party treasurers made a careful note of the donor's address, said that he would write an immediate cryptic letter of thanks, and locked the money in a safe.

Probably uniquely amongst Cabinet Ministers, Urquhart left for holiday that night feeling utterly relaxed.

PART TWO

THE CUT

AUGUST

The newspapers during August were dreadful. With politicians and the main political correspondents all away, second string lobby correspondents struggled to fill the vacuum and develop any story they could which would get their by-line on the front page. So they clutched at whispers and rumour. What was on Tuesday only a minor piece of speculation on page five of the *Guardian* had become by Friday a hard news story on the front page of the *Daily Mail*. This was the chance for the junior correspondents to make their mark, and the mark they chose to make was all too frequently on the reputation of Henry Collingridge. Minor backbenchers who were too self-promoting even to take a break during the holiday season were honoured with significant pieces quoting 'senior party spokesmen', putting forward their views as to where the Government was going wrong and how a new sense of direction had to be imposed. Rumours about the Prime Minister's dissatisfaction with and distrust of his Cabinet colleagues abounded, and since there was no one around authoritatively to deny the rumours, the silence was taken as authoritative consent. So the speculation fed on itself and ran riot. The early August rumours about an 'official inquisition' into Cabinet leaks had, by later in the month, grown into predictions that there would after all be a reshuffle in the autumn. The word around Westminster had it that Henry Collingridge's temper was getting increasingly erratic, even though he was in fact enjoying a secluded holiday on a private estate many hundreds of miles away near Cannes.

The Prime Minister's brother also became the subject of a spate of press stories, mostly in the gossip columns, and the Downing Street press office was repeatedly called upon to comment on suggestions that the Prime Minister was bailing out 'dear old Charlie' from the increasingly close attentions of his creditors, including the Inland Revenue. But Downing Street would not comment – it was personal, not official – so the formal 'no comment' which was given to the most fanciful of accusations was recorded in the news coverage, usually in the most damaging light.

As August drew on, with only the lightest of nudges down the telephone from Urquhart, the press tied the Prime Minister ever more closely to his impecunious brother. Not that Charlie was saying anything stupid. He had the common sense to keep well out of the way, but an anonymous telephone call to one of the sensationalist Sunday newspapers enabled them to track him down to a cheap hotel in rural Bordeaux. A reporter was despatched to pour enough wine down him to encourage a few vintage 'Charlie-isms', but instead succeeded only in making Charlie violently sick over the reporter and his notebook before passing out. The reporter promptly paid £50 to a big busted girl with a low-cut dress to lean over the slumbering form, while a photographer captured the tender moment for posterity and the newspaper's 11 million readers.

'"I'm broke and busted" says Charlie' screamed the headline, while the copy reported for the umpteenth time the fact that the Prime Minister's brother was nearly destitute and cracking under the pressure of a failed marriage and a famous brother. Downing Street's 'absolutely no comment' seemed in the circumstances even more uncaring than usual.

The next weekend the same photograph was run alongside one of the Prime Minister holidaying in considerable comfort in the South of France – to English eyes a mere stone's throw from his ailing brother – and seemingly unwilling to leave his poolside to help. The fact that the same newspaper a week earlier had been reporting how deeply Henry was involved in sorting out Charlie's financial affairs seemed to have been forgotten – until the Downing Street press office called the editor to complain.

'What do you want?' came the reply. 'We give both sides of the story. We backed him warts and all throughout the election campaign. Now it's time to restore the balance a bit.'

Yes, the newspapers during August were dreadful.

SEPTEMBER – OCTOBER

September was even worse. As the new month opened, the Leader of the Opposition announced that he was resigning to make way for 'a stronger arm with which to hold our banner aloft'. He had always been a little too verbose for his own good.

Like most political leaders he was pushed by the younger men around him who had more energy and more ambition, who made their move quietly and secretly almost without his knowing until it was too late and he had announced his intention to resign in an emotional late night interview. For a moment he seemed to have changed his mind under pressure from his still intensely ambitious wife, until he discovered that he could no longer rely on a single vote in his Shadow Cabinet. Yet they were warm in their praise of their fallen leader. As so often happens, the faithful were far more effusively united by his death than by anything he had achieved in office.

The news electrified the media, and Mattie was summoned back from her beach in Zakynthos, much to her silent relief. Eight days of lying in the sun watching couples grow increasingly tender and uninhibited in the Ionian sun had made her feel utterly miserable. She was lonely, very lonely, and the loving couples around her only served to rub the point home. When the telephone call came instructing her to return to cover the breaking story, she packed her bags without complaint and found a seat on the next flight home.

She returned to discover an Opposition Party which had been galvanised. Their seemingly endless internal divisions were now being played down as they stepped up the attack on a lacklustre Government, most of whose members were still away on holiday. The real prospect of power at the next election, even one which was still perhaps four years away, was helping to focus Opposition minds and encourage fraternal thoughts. Better as one of twenty senior Cabinet Ministers in Government than the sole Party Leader in endless Opposition, one explained.

So by the time the new leader was elected just a week before the Party's annual conference in early October, the Opposition had dominated the news for several weeks and the conference turned into a united salute to the new leader. Under an enormous slogan of 'VICTORY', the conference was unrecognisable as the assembly of a party which had lost the election only a few months before.

By contrast, just a week later the representatives gathered for the Government Party's conference in a spirit of trepidation and complaint. The conference centre at Bournemouth could be uplifting if filled with 4,000 enthusiastic supporters, but now its bare brick walls and chromium-plated fitments served only to emphasise the sullenness of those who gathered.

As Publicity Director, it was Roger O'Neill's task to present and package the conference, but as the task of raising spirits became increasingly daunting, so he could be seen talking more and more feverishly to journalists – apologising, justifying, explaining, and blaming. And particularly he blamed Lord Williams. The Chairman had cut the budget, he explained, delayed making decisions, not got a grip on things. There were rumours circulating within party headquarters that he deliberately wanted the conference to be low key because he thought the Prime Minister was likely to get a rough ride from the faithful. 'Party doubts about Collingridge leadership' was the first *Guardian* report to come out of Bournemouth.

In the conference hall, the debates proceeded according to the rigid pre-set schedule. An enormous sign hung above the platform – 'FINDING THE RIGHT WAY'. The speeches struggled to obey its command beneath glaring television lights and an annoying buzz from the hall which the stewards were quite incapable of quelling. On the fringes of the hall the representatives, journalists and politicians gathered in little huddles to exchange views, a

111

regular part of any political gathering, and a fertile breeding ground for idle gossip.

The 'buzz' around the conference was one of discontent. Everywhere they listened, the men from the media were able to hear criticism. Former MPs who had recently lost their seats were critical, but asked not to be quoted for fear of endangering their chances of being selected for safer seats at the next election. Their constituency chairmen showed no such reticence. They had not only lost their MP, but also faced several years of the Opposition Party ruling their local councils, nominating the mayor and committee chairmen, and disposing of the fruits of local office.

There was also growing concern that the parliamentary by-election, due on Thursday, would give a poor result. The Member for Dorset East, Sir Anthony Jenkins, had suffered a stroke four days before the general election. Elected while in intensive care, he had died only three weeks later.

His seat, just a few miles from Bournemouth, was a safe one with a majority of nearly 20,000, so the Prime Minister had decided to hold the by-election during conference week. He had been advised strongly against it, but he argued that on balance it was worth the risk. The conference publicity would provide good campaigning material for the by-election, there would still be a strong sympathy vote for the fallen MP, conference representatives could take a few hours off to undertake some much-needed canvassing, and the Prime Minister would be able to welcome the victorious candidate during his own conference speech – a good publicity stunt.

Now the busloads of conference-goers returning from a morning's canvassing were reporting a lack of sympathy on the doorstep. The seat would be held, of course, it had been in the Party since the War, but the thumping victory which Collingridge had demanded was beginning to look more distant with every day's canvass returns.

It was going to be a difficult week, not quite the victory celebration the party managers had planned.

WEDNESDAY 13TH OCTOBER

A cold wet wind was blowing off the sea when Mattie Storin was woken by a pounding headache early on Wednesday morning. As the representative of a major national newspaper she was one of the fortunate few journalists offered accommodation in the headquarters hotel where she could mix freely with the key politicians and party officials. She had mixed a little too freely the previous evening, and she began her regular morning calisthenics with heavy limbs and a distinct lack of enthusiasm. Her whole body shouted at her that this was a rotten way to cure a hangover, so she quickly changed her mind and opted for an open window – a move which she immediately recognised as the second bad decision of the day. The small hotel was perched high on the cliff tops, ideal for catching the summer sun but exposed and unprotected on such grey and swirling autumn mornings. Her overheated hotel room turned into an icebox in seconds, and Mattie decided that she would make no more decisions until after a gentle breakfast.

She heard the scuffling of something being delivered outside in the corridor and pulled the blanket protectively around her shoulders, stumping her way across to the door. Work, in the form of the morning newspapers, was piled outside on the hallway carpet. She picked them up and threw them carelessly towards the bed. As they spread chaotically over the rumpled bedclothes, a sheet of paper fluttered from between the pages and fell to the floor. With a tired grunt she bent down to retrieve it, and through the morning mist which seemed completely to have enveloped her head read the words: 'Opinion Research Survey No. 40, 6 October – SECRET', emblazoned across the top.

She rubbed her eyes to open them properly. They've

113

surely not started giving them away with the *Mirror*, she thought. Mattie knew the Party conducted weekly surveys to track the nationwide movement of public opinion on political issues, but these had a highly restricted distribution to Cabinet Ministers and only a handful of top Party officials. She had been shown copies rarely and only when they had good news to convey which the Party wished to publicise; otherwise they were kept under strictest security. She wondered what good news could possibly have been found in the latest survey, and why it had been delivered wrapped up like fried fish and chips.

The contents of the note made her rub her eyes once more. The Party, which had won the election with 41 per cent of the vote, now had only 31 per cent support, 14 per cent behind the main Opposition Party. Even more damaging were the figures on the Prime Minister's popularity. Less than one in four now preferred him while the new Leader of the Opposition stood at well over 50 per cent. It made Collingridge more disliked than any Prime Minister she could remember.

Mattie squatted on her bed. She no longer needed to ask why she had been sent the information. It was dynamite, and she felt the paper almost burning in her hand. 'Government crashes in opinion polls', it seemed to say as she composed her own introduction. And someone wanted her to throw this explosive news right into the middle of the party conference. It was a deliberate act of sabotage which would be an excellent story – her story, as long as she got it in first.

She grabbed for the telephone. 'Hello, Mrs Preston? It's Mattie Storin. Is Grev there, please?'

There was a short pause before her editor came on the phone, and his husky tones announced that he had just been woken up.

'Who's died?'

'What?'

'Who's bloody died? Why else would you call me at such a bloody stupid time?'

'Oh, nobody. I mean . . . I'm sorry. I forgot what time it was.'

114

'Shit.'

'Sorry, Grev.'

'Well, something must have happened, for pity's sake.'

'Yes, it came with my morning newspapers.'

'Well, that's a relief. We're now only a day behind the rest.'

'No, Grev. Listen will you? I've got hold of the Party's latest polling figures. They're sensational!'

'How did you get them?'

'They were left outside my door.'

'Gift wrapped, were they?' The editor was clearly having great difficulty controlling his sarcasm.

'But they're really sensational, Grev.'

'And who left them outside the door, Santa Claus?'

'Er, I don't know.' For the first time a hint of doubt crept into the young journalist's voice. She was waking up very rapidly now.

'Well, I don't suppose Henry Collingridge left them there. So who do you think wanted to leak them to you?'

Mattie's silence could not hide her confusion.

'Were you out on the town with any of your colleagues last night?'

'Grev, what the hell's that got to do with it?'

'Have you never heard of being set up by your so-called friends?' The editor sounded almost despairing.

'But how do you know?'

'I don't bloody know. But the point is, Wonder Girl, neither do bloody you!'

There was another embarrassed silence from Mattie before she decided to have a last, despairing attempt to restore her confidence and persuade her editor. 'Don't you even want to know what they say?'

'No. Not if you don't know where they come from or can't be certain they are not a stupid hoax. And remember, the more sensational they look, the more certain it is that you're being set up.'

The crash of the telephone being slammed down exploded in her ear. It would have hurt even had she not been hung over. What a mug. As her headline dissolved back into the grey morning mists of her mind, her headache returned, more insistent and painful than ever. She needed a cup of black coffee badly.

Twenty minutes later Mattie eased gently down the broad stairs of the hotel and slipped into the breakfast room. It was still early and there was only a handful of early morning enthusiasts yet about. She sat down at a table on her own and prayed she would not be disturbed. She hid herself in a copy of the *Express* and hoped people would conclude that she was working rather than fixing a hangover.

The first cup of coffee made no impact, but the second helped a little. Slowly her headache began to loosen its grip and she began to take some interest in the rest of the world. Perhaps she could even stand an early morning gossip.

She looked around the intimate Victorian room and noted another political correspondent who was deeply engrossed in conversation with a Minister, and would not want to be disturbed. Two other people she thought she recognised but could not be sure. The young man on the next table she did not know and Mattie had just decided to finish a solo breakfast when she noticed the pile of papers and folders on the chair next to her neighbour. The papers and the rather academic scruffiness with which he was dressed suggested that the breakfaster was one of the many party officials Mattie had not yet got to know. The name scribbled on top of the folder was K. J. Spence.

The journalist's professional instincts had by now begun gradually to reassert themselves under the steady bombardment of caffeine, and she reached inside her everpresent shoulder bag for a copy of the internal party telephone list that at some point she had begged or stolen – she couldn't remember which.

'Spence. Kevin. Extension 371. Opinion Research.'

Mattie checked again the name on top of the folder, feeling that mistakes on opinion research had caused her enough trouble already that morning, but there was no confusion. Her editor's sarcasm had already demolished her faith in the leaked poll's statistics but she thought there would be no harm in trying to find out what the real figures were. She caught his eye.

'Kevin Spence, isn't it? From party headquarters? I'm Mattie Storin of the *Telegraph*. I haven't been on the paper long, but one of my jobs is to get to know all the party officials. Can I join you for a cup of coffee?'

Kevin Spence, aged thirty-two but looking older, unmarried and a life-long headquarters bureaucrat with a salary of £10,200 (no perks), nodded obligingly, and they were soon in conversation. Spence was rather shy and deeply flattered to be recognised by someone from a newspaper, and he was soon explaining with enthusiasm and in detail the regular reports he had given during the election on the state of public opinion to the Prime Minister and the Party's War Committee. Yes, he admitted, they did take opinion polls seriously in spite of what they always said on television. He ventured the thought that some even took opinion polls too seriously.

'What do you mean, too seriously? That's your job, isn't it?'

Somewhat donnishly Spence explained the foibles of opinion polling, the margin of error you should always remember, the rogue polls which in spite of all the pollsters' efforts still sneaked through and simply got it wrong.

'Like the one I've just seen,' Mattie remarked with a twinge, still tender from her earlier embarrassment.

'What do you mean?' Spence enquired sharply.

Mattie looked at him and saw that the affable official had now developed a flush which even as she looked was spreading from the collar up to the eyes. The eyes themselves had lost their eagerness. Spence was not a trained politician and was not adept at hiding his feelings, and the confusion was flowing through. Why was he so flustered? Mattie mentally kicked herself. Surely the damned figures couldn't be right after all? The dynamic young reporter of the year had already jumped several somersaults that morning, and feeling rather sour with herself decided that one more leap could scarcely dent her professional pride any further.

'I understand, Kevin, that your latest figures are quite

disappointing. In fact, somebody mentioned a figure of 31 per cent.'

Spence, whose cheeks had been getting even redder as Mattie spoke, reached for his tea to give himself time to think, but his hand was trembling.

'And the PM personally is down to 24 per cent,' she ventured. 'I can't remember any Prime Minister being as unpopular as that.'

At this point the tea began to spill from the cup, and Spence returned it quickly to the saucer.

'I don't know what you're talking about,' he muttered, addressing the napkin which he was using to mop up the tea.

'Aren't these your latest figures?' Mattie reached once more inside her bag and pulled out the mysterious sheet of paper which she proceeded to smooth on the table cloth. As she did so, she noticed for the first time the initials KJS typed along the bottom.

Spence reached out and tried to push the paper away from him, seemingly afraid to get too near to it. 'Where on earth did you get that?' He looked around desperately to see whether anyone had noticed the exchange.

Mattie picked up the piece of paper and began reading it out loud. '"Opinion Research Survey Number 40" – this is yours, isn't it?'

'Yes, but . . . Please, Miss Storin!'

He was not used to dissembling. Spence was clearly deeply upset, and seeing no way of escape decided to throw himself on the mercy of his breakfast companion. In a hushed voice, and still looking nervously around the room, he pleaded with her.

'I'm not supposed to talk to you about any opinion research. It's strictly confidential.'

'But Kevin, it's only one piece of paper.'

'You don't know what it's like. If these figures get out, and I'm the one thought to have given them to you, I'd be out on my ear. Everyone's looking for scapegoats. There are so many rumours flooding around. The PM doesn't trust the Chairman. The Chairman doesn't trust us. Everybody says that heads are going to roll. I like my job, Miss

Storin. I can't afford to be blamed for leaking confidential figures to you.'

'I didn't realise morale was so bad.'

Spence looked utterly miserable. 'I've never known it worse. Everyone was exhausted after the election, and there was a lot of bad feeling flying around because the result wasn't as good as we expected. Then all those leaks and reports that the Cabinet were at each other's throats, so instead of a long break during the summer Lord Williams kept us all hard at it. Frankly, all most of us are trying to do is to keep our heads down so that when it hits the fan we get as little of it as possible.'

He looked at Mattie eye-to-eye for the first time. 'Please don't drag me into this.'

'Kevin, you did not leak this report to me and I shall confirm that to anyone who wants to know. But if I'm to help you I shall need a little help myself. This is your latest polling report, right?'

She slipped the paper back across the table. Spence took another anguished look at it and nodded in confirmation.

'They are prepared by you and circulated on a tightly restricted basis?'

Another nod.

'All I need to know from you, Kevin, is who gets them. That can't be a state secret, can it?'

There was no more fight left in Spence. He seemed to hold his breath for a long time before replying.

'Numbered copies are circulated in double-sealed envelopes solely to Cabinet Ministers and five senior headquarters personnel: the Deputy Chairman and four senior directors.'

He tried to moisten his mouth with another drink of tea, but discovered he had already spilt most of it. 'How on earth did you get hold of it?'

'Let's just say someone got a little careless, shall we?'

'Not my office?' he gasped, his insecurity flooding out.

'No, Kevin. You've just given me the names of over two dozen people who receive the figures, and with their secretaries it would bring the possible number of sources to well over fifty.' She gave him one of her most reassuring, warm smiles. 'Don't worry, I won't involve you. But let's keep in touch.'

Mattie left the breakfast room. She should have been feeling elated about the front page story she was now able to write but she was wondering too hard how the devil she was ever going to identify the turncoat.

Room 561 in the hotel could not be described as five star. It was one of the smallest rooms, far away from the main entrance and at the end of the top floor corridor under the eaves. The party hierarchy did not stay here, it was definitely a room for the workers.

Penny Guy hadn't heard the steps outside in the corridor before the door burst open. She sat bolt upright in bed, startled and exposing two perfectly formed breasts.

'Shit, Roger, don't you ever bloody knock?' She threw a pillow at the intruder. 'And what the hell are you doing up so early? You don't normally surface until lunchtime.'

She did not bother to cover herself as O'Neill sat down at the end of the bed. There was an ease between them suggesting an absence of any sexual threat which would have startled most people. O'Neill constantly flirted with her, particularly in public, but on the two occasions when Penny had offered, O'Neill had been very affectionate and warm but had complained of being too exhausted. She guessed he had a deep streak of sexual insecurity running through him, which he hid beneath flattery and innuendo. Penny had heard from other women who had spent time with O'Neill that he was frequently too exhausted – attentive, very forward, suggestive, but rarely able to commit himself fully. She was very fond of him, and longed to ease the insecurities out of him with her long, electric fingers, but she knew he would not drop his guard long enough to let her weave her magic. She had worked for O'Neill for nearly three years and had seen him slowly change as he found the pressures of political and public life increasingly infatuating, yet steadily more difficult to cope with.

To those who did not know him well he was extrovert, amusing, full of charm, ideas and energy. But Penny had watched him become increasingly erratic. He rarely came into the office nowadays before noon; he had started making many private phone calls, getting agitated, disappearing suddenly. His constant hay fever and sneezing were unpleasant, but Penny was devoted to him. She did not understand many of the odd ways he had developed – particularly why he would not sleep with her. She had that strange blindness for him which comes with daily familiarity and strong affections. But she knew he depended on her. If he didn't need her in bed, he needed her practically every other moment of his day. It wasn't the same as love, but her warm heart responded anyway. She would do almost anything for him.

'You got up this early just to come and woo me, didn't you? You can't resist me after all,' she teased.

'Shut up, you little tart, and cover up those gorgeous tits. That's not fair.'

Smiling wickedly, she lifted her breasts up towards him, goading him. 'Can't resist them after all. Well, who am I to refuse an order from the boss?'

Playfully she threw the bedclothes off her naked body and moved over on the mattress to make room for him. O'Neill's eyes couldn't help but follow the line of her long legs, and for the first time since Penny had known him he began to blush. She giggled as she noticed him staring hypnotically at her body, and he made a grab for the bedclothes to try and cover her up but instead succeeded only in losing his balance and getting tangled up in her long brown arms. As he lifted his head off the mattress, he found a rigid dark nipple staring at him from less than three inches away, and he had to use all of his strength to tear himself free. He retreated to the other side of the small room, visibly shaking.

'Pen, please! You know I'm not at my best this early in the morning.'

'OK, Roger. Don't worry. I'm not going to rape you.' She was laughing playfully as she pulled the sheets loosely around her. 'But what are you doing up so early?'

'I've just left this incredibly beautiful Brazilian gymnast who has spent all night teaching me a whole series of new exercises. We didn't have any gymnastic rings, so we used the chandelier. OK?'

She shook her head firmly.

'How could one so young and beautiful be so cynical?' he protested. 'All right. I had to make a delivery in the vicinity and I thought I'd come and say good morning.'

He didn't bother to add that Mattie Storin had nearly caught him as he was placing the document amongst the newspapers, and he welcomed the chance to lie low in his secretary's room for a while. He was still elated at the trouble which the leaked poll would cause the Party Chairman, who had been openly hostile to him in the last few weeks. Through his paranoia, worked on by Urquhart, he had failed to notice that the hard-pressed Williams had been short with most of his colleagues as well.

Penny tried to bring him back down to earth. 'Yeah, but next time you come to say good morning, try knocking first. And make it after 8.30.'

'Don't give me a hard time. You know I can't live without you.'

'Enough passion, Roger. What do you want? You have to want something, don't you, even if not my body?'

'Actually, I did come to ask you something. It's a bit delicate really . . .'

'Go ahead, Roger. You can be frank. You've already seen there's no one else in the bed!' She started laughing again.

O'Neill began to recover his salesman's charms, and started upon the story which Urquhart had drummed into him the previous evening.

'Pen, you remember Patrick Woolton, the Foreign Secretary. You typed a couple of his speeches during the election, and he certainly remembers you. He asked after you when I saw him last night and I think he's rather smitten with you. Anyway, he wondered if you would be interested in dinner with him but he didn't want to upset or offend you by asking direct, so I sort of offered to have a quiet word as it might be easier for you to say no to me rather than to him personally, you see.'

'OK, Roger.'

'OK what, Pen?'

'OK. I'll have dinner with him. What's the big deal?'

'Nothing. Except . . . Woolton's got a bit of a reputation with the ladies. He might just want more than – dinner.'

'Roger, every man I've ever been out with since the age of fourteen has always wanted more than dinner. I can handle it. Might be interesting. He could improve my French!' She burst into fits of giggles once again, and threw her last pillow at him. O'Neill retreated through the door as Penny was looking around for something else to throw.

Five minutes later he was back in his own room and on the phone to Urquhart.

'Delivery made and dinner fixed.'

'Splendid, Roger. You've been most helpful. I hope the Foreign Secretary will be grateful too.'

'But I still don't see how you are going to get him to invite Penny to dinner. What's the point of all this?'

'The point, dear Roger, is that he will not have to invite her to dinner at all. He is coming to my reception this evening. You will bring Penny, who you have established is more than willing to meet and spend some time with him. I shall introduce them over a glass of champagne or two, and see what develops. If I know Patrick Woolton – which as Chief Whip I do – it won't take more than twenty minutes before he's suggesting that they go to his room to discuss – how does *Private Eye* put it – Ugandan affairs?'

'Or French lessons,' muttered O'Neill. 'But I still don't see where that gets us.'

'Whatever happens, Roger, you and I will know about it. And knowledge is always useful.'

'I still don't see how.'

'Trust me, Roger. You must trust me.'

'I do. I have to: I don't really get much choice, do I?'

'That's right, Roger. Now you are beginning to see. Knowledge is power.'

The phone went dead. O'Neill thought he understood but wasn't absolutely sure. He still often struggled to figure out whether he was Urquhart's partner or prisoner, but could never really decide. He rummaged in his bedside cabinet and took out a small carton. He swallowed a couple of sleeping pills and collapsed fully clothed on the bed.

'Patrick. Thanks for the time.'

'You sounded quite serious on the phone. When Chief Whips say they want an urgent private word with you, they usually mean they've got the photographs under lock and key but unfortunately the *News of the World* has got the negatives!'

Urquhart smiled and slipped through the open door into the Foreign Secretary's room. He had not come far, indeed only a few yards from his own bungalow next door in what the local constabulary had named 'Overtime Alley', the row of luxury private bungalows in the grounds of the conference hotel which housed leading Ministers, all of whom had a 24-hour rota of police guards running up huge overtime bills for the hapless local ratepayers.

'Drink?' the genial Lancastrian offered.

'Thanks, Patrick. Scotch.'

The Right Honourable Patrick Woolton, Her Majesty's Principal Secretary for Foreign and Commonwealth Affairs and one of Merseyside's many successful *emigrés*, busied himself at a small drinks cabinet which quite obviously had already been used that afternoon, while Urquhart placed the Ministerial red box he was carrying in the corner of the room beside the four belonging to his overworked host. The brightly coloured leather-clad boxes are provided to all Ministers to house their official papers, speeches and other items which they require to keep secure. Red boxes go wherever Ministers go, even on holiday, and the Foreign Secretary was habitually followed around by a host of the small suitcase-sized containers carrying telexes and despatches, briefing papers and the other paraphernalia of diplomacy. The Chief Whip, with no conference speech to make and no foreign crises to handle, had arrived in Bournemouth with his box filled with three bottles of twelve-year-old malt whisky. Hotel drink prices are always staggering, he explained to his wife, even when you can find the brand you want.

He faced Woolton across a paper-strewn coffee table, and dispensed with the small talk.

'Patrick, I need to take your mind. In the strictest confidence. As far as I am concerned, this has to be one of those meetings which never took place.'

'Christ, you do have some photographs!' exclaimed Woolton, now only half joking. His eye for attractive young women was much discussed, but he was usually highly discreet, especially when he travelled abroad. Ten years earlier when he was just starting his Ministerial career, he had spent several painful hours answering questions from the Louisiana State Police about a weekend he had spent in a New Orleans motel with a young American girl who looked twenty, acted as if she were thirty and turned out to be just a few days over sixteen. The incident had been brushed over, but Woolton had never forgotten the tiny difference between a glittering political future and a charge of statutory rape.

'Something which could be rather more serious. I've been picking up some unhealthy vibrations in the last few weeks about Henry. You've sensed some of the irritation with him around the Cabinet table, and the media seem to be falling out of love with him in a very big way. There was no reason to expect an extended honeymoon after the election, but it's in danger of getting out of hand. I have just been approached by two of the most influential grass-roots party members saying that feeling at local level is getting very bad. We lost two more important local council by-elections last week in what should have been very safe seats, and we are going to lose quite a few more in the weeks ahead. Our majority in the Dorset by-election tomorrow is likely to be hit badly. To put no finer point on it, Patrick, the PM's unpopularity is dragging the whole Party down and we would have trouble winning an election for local dogcatcher at the moment. We seem to have blown it rather badly.' Urquhart paused for a sip of whisky.

'The problem is,' he continued, 'there's a view around that this is not just a passing phase. If we are to win yet another election, we will have to show plenty of vigour and life otherwise the electorate will want a change simply

125

out of boredom. Quite a few of our backbenchers in marginal seats are already beginning to get nervous, and with a majority of just 24 we may not have as much time as we would like. A few lost by-elections and we could be forced into an early election.'

He took another sip of whisky, cupping his hands around the tumbler as if to draw reassurance for his difficult task from the warm, peaty liquid.

'I'll come to the point, Patrick. I've been asked as Chief Whip . . .' – notice the formality, nothing personal in this, old chap – '. . . by one or two of our senior colleagues to take some gentle soundings about how deep the problem actually goes. In short, Patrick, and you will appreciate this is *not* easy . . .' – it never is, but it never seems to stop or even slow the inevitable thrust – '. . . I've been asked to find out how much trouble you personally think we are in. Is Henry any longer the right leader for us?' He took a deep draught and settled back in his chair.

The silence settled around the Foreign Secretary, impaling him on the point of the question. It took him more than a minute to respond. A pipe appeared out of his pocket, followed by a tobacco pouch and a box of Swan Vestas. He patiently filled the bowl, tamping down the fresh tobacco with his thumb, and took out a match. The striking of the match seemed very loud in the silence, and Urquhart shifted uneasily in his chair. Smoke began to rise from around Woolton as he drew on the pipe stem, until the sweet smelling tobacco was well alight and his face was almost hidden from view by a clinging blue fog. He waved his hand to disperse it and through the clearing air he looked directly at Urquhart, and chuckled.

'You'll have to forgive me, Francis. Four years in the Foreign Office has not prepared me particularly well for handling direct questions like that. Maybe I'm not used any more to people coming straight to the point. I hope you will forgive me if I struggle a little to match your bluntness.'

This was nonsense, of course. Woolton was renowned for his direct, often combative political style which had found an uneasy home in the Foreign Office. He was simply playing for time, collecting his thoughts.

'Let's try to put aside any subjective views . . .' – he blew another enormous cloud of smoke to hide the patent insincerity of the remark – '. . . and analyse the problem like a civil service position paper.'

Urquhart continued to look strained and nervous, but smiled inwardly. He knew Woolton's personal views, and so he already knew the conclusion at which their hypothetical civil servant was going to arrive.

'First, have we really got a problem? Yes, and it's a serious one. My lads back in Lancashire are hopping mad, we have a couple of local by-elections coming up which we are going to lose, and the polls are looking awful. I think it's right that you should be taking soundings.

'Second, is there a painless solution to the problem? Don't let us forget that Henry has led us successfully through our fourth election victory. He is the leader of the party which the voters supported. So it's not easy so soon after an election to contemplate a radical alteration to either the policies or the personalities with which we were elected.'

Woolton was by now obviously beginning to relish the analysis.

'Think it through. If there were any move to replace him – which is essentially what we are discussing . . .' – Urquhart contrived to look pained at Woolton's bluntness and once more examined the drink in his glass – '. . . it would be highly unsettling for the Party, while the Opposition would be rampant. It would look like a messy palace coup and an act of desperation. What do they say? "Greater love hath no politician than he lay down the life of his friends to save his own"! We could never make it look like the response of a mature and confident political party, no matter how we tried to dress it up. It would take a new leader at least a year to repair the damage and glue together the cracks. So we should not fool ourselves that replacing Henry represents an easy option.

'Third, when all is said and done, can Henry find the solution to the problem himself? Well, you know my views on that. I stood against him for the leadership when

Margaret retired, and I have not changed my mind that his selection was a mistake.'

Urquhart now knew that he had read his man well. While Woolton had never expressed any open dissatisfaction after the waves of the leadership election had settled, public loyalty is rarely more than a necessary cover for private ambition, and the Foreign Secretary had never done more than was strictly necessary to maintain that cover.

Woolton was now refilling their glasses while continuing his analysis. 'Margaret managed an extraordinary balance of personal toughness and sense of direction. She was ruthless when she had to be – and often when she didn't have to be as well. She always seemed to be in such a hurry to get where she was going that she had no time to take prisoners and didn't mind trampling on a few friends either. It didn't matter so much because she led from in front. Yet Henry doesn't have any sense of direction, only a love of office. And without that sense of direction, when he tries to be tough it simply comes across as arrogance and harshness. He tries to mimic Margaret but he hasn't got the balls.

'So there we have it. If we try to get rid of him we're in deep trouble. If we keep him, to use an old Lancashire expression, we're stuffed.'

He returned to his pipe, puffing furiously to rekindle its embers until he disappeared once more behind the haze.

Urquhart hadn't spoken for nearly ten minutes, but now moved to the edge of his chair once again. 'Yes, I see. But I don't see. What is it you are saying, Patrick?'

Woolton roared with laughter. 'I'm sorry, Francis. Too much bloody diplomatic claptrap. I can't even ask the wife to pass the cornflakes nowadays without confusing her. You want a direct answer? OK. A majority of 24 simply isn't enough, and at the rate we are going we shall get wiped out next time around. We cannot go on as we are.'

'So what is the solution? We have to find one.'

'We wait. We need time, a few months, to prepare the public perception and pressure for the PM to stand down, so that when he does we shall be seen to be responding to a positive public demand rather than indulging in private squabbles. Perceptions are crucial, Francis, and we shall need a little time to get them right.'

And you need a little time to prepare your own pitch for the job, thought Urquhart. You old fraud. You want the job just as badly as ever.

He knew Woolton would need the time to spend as many evenings as possible in the corridors and bars of the House of Commons strengthening relationships with his colleagues, increasing the number of his speaking engagements in the constituencies of influential MPs, broadening his reputation with newspaper editors and columnists, building up his credentials. His official diary would get cleared very rapidly. He would spend less time travelling abroad and much, much more time travelling around Britain making speeches about the challenges facing the country in the year 2000.

'You have a particularly difficult and delicate task, Francis. You are in a central position for judging whether there is any chance of Henry staging some sort of recovery or, failing that, when the time is right to move. Too early and we shall all look like assassins. Too late and the Party will be in pieces. You will have to keep your ear very close to the ground, and decide if and when the time has come to move. I assume you are taking soundings elsewhere?'

Urquhart nodded carefully in silent assent. He's nominated me as Cassius, he thought, put the dagger in my hand and left it to me to nominate the Ides of March. Urquhart was exhilarated to discover that he did not mind the sensation at all.

'Patrick, I'm very grateful that you feel able to be so frank with me. The next few months are going to be difficult for all of us, and if I may I will continue to take your counsel. And you may be sure that not a word of this will pass outside this room.' He rose to finish the meeting.

'My Special Branch team are all going on at me about how walls have ears. I'm damned glad you have the next door bungalow!' Woolton exclaimed, thumping Urquhart playfully between the shoulder blades as his visitor strode over to retrieve his red box.

'I hope you will be joining me there for my reception this evening, Patrick. You won't forget, will you?'

'Course not. Always enjoy your parties. Be rude of me to refuse your champagne!'

'I'll see you in a few hours then,' replied Urquhart, picking up a red box.

As Woolton closed the door behind his visitor, he poured himself another drink. He would skip the afternoon's conference debates and have a bath and a short sleep to prepare himself for the evening's heavy schedule. As he reflected on the conversation he had just had, he began to wonder whether the whisky had dulled his senses. He was trying to remember how Urquhart had voiced his own opposition to Collingridge, but couldn't. 'Crafty sod. Let me do all the talking.'

As he sat there wondering whether he had been just a little too frank with his guest, he totally failed to notice that Urquhart had walked off with the wrong red box.

Mattie had been in high spirits ever since sending through her copy shortly after lunch and had spent much of the afternoon thinking of the new doors which were slowly beginning to open for her. She had just celebrated her first anniversary at the *Telegraph*, and her abilities were getting recognition. Although she was one of the youngest members of staff, her stories had begun to get on the front page on a frequent basis – and they were good stories, too, she knew that. Another year of this sort of progress and she would be ready to make the next step, perhaps move up as an assistant editor or find a role with more room to write serious political analysis and not just daily pot boilers. Mind you, she had no complaints today. It would take an outbreak of war to stop the copy she had just filed from making the splash headline on the front page. It was a strong story about a Government which had lost their way; it was well written and would certainly help to get her noticed by other editors and publishers.

But it was not enough. In spite of it all, she was beginning to realise that something was missing. Even as her career developed, she was gradually discovering an emptiness which hit her every time she left the office and got worse as she walked past her front door into her cold, silent apartment. There was a pit somewhere deep inside her which had begun to ache, an ache she hoped had been left way behind in Yorkshire. Damn men! Why couldn't they leave her alone? But she knew no one else was to blame; her own needs were gnawing away inside her, and they were becoming increasingly difficult to ignore.

Neither could she ignore the urgent message to call her office which she received shortly before 5 o'clock. She had just finished taking tea on the terrace with the Home Secretary, who was anxious to get the *Telegraph* to puff his speech the following day and who in any event wanted an excuse to avoid sitting through another afternoon of his colleagues' speeches. The hotel lobby was crowded as people began to desert the conference hall early in search of refreshment and relaxation, but one of the public telephones was free and she decided to put up with the noise. When she got through, Preston's secretary explained that he was engaged on the phone and connected her with the deputy editor, John Krajewski, a gentle giant of a man she had begun to spend a little time with during the long summer months, spurred on by a shared enjoyment of good wine and the fact that his father, like her grandfather, had been a wartime refugee from Europe. She greeted him warmly, but his response left her feeling like ice.

'Hello, Mattie. Look, let me not cover everything in three feet of bullshit but come straight to the point. We're not – he's not – running your story. I really am sorry.'

There was a stunned silence over the phone as she turned over the words in her own mind to make sure that she had understood correctly.

'What the hell do you mean you're not running it?'

'Just what I say, Mattie.' Krajewski was clearly having grave difficulty with the conversation. 'I'm sorry I can't give you all the details because Grev has been dealing with it personally – I haven't touched it myself – but apparently it's such a hot story that he feels he cannot run it without being absolutely sure of our ground. He says that we have always supported this Government loyally and he's not

131

about to throw editorial policy out of the window on the basis of an anonymous piece of paper. He says we have to be absolutely certain before we move, and we can't be if we don't know where this piece of paper came from.'

'For God's sake, it doesn't matter where the bloody paper came from. Whoever sent it to me wouldn't have done so if he thought his identity was going to be spread all over our news room. All that matters is that it's genuine, and I've confirmed that.'

'Look, I know how you must feel about this, Mattie, and I wish I were a million miles away from this one. Believe me I've argued this one hard and long for you, but Grev is adamant. It's not running.'

Mattie wanted to scream. She suddenly regretted making the call from a crowded lobby, where she could not argue the case for fear that a rival journalist would hear, and neither could she use the sort of language she felt like using with dozens of constituency wives crowding around her.

'Let me talk to Grev.'

'Sorry. I think he's busy on the phone.'

'I'll hold!'

'In fact,' said the deputy editor in a voice heaped with embarrassment, 'I know he's going to be busy for a long time and insisted that I had to be the one to explain it to you. I know he wants to talk to you, Mattie – but tomorrow. There's no point in trying to scream him into submission tonight.'

'So he's not running the story, he hasn't got the balls to tell me why, and he's told you to do his dirty work for him!' Mattie spat out her contempt. 'What sort of newspaper are we running, Johnnie?'

She could hear the deputy editor clearing his throat, unable to find suitable words to respond. Krajewski appreciated just how tearingly frustrated Mattie felt, not only with the story but with Preston's decision to use him as a buffer. He wondered if he should have made more of a fight of it on her behalf, but in recent weeks he had become increasingly distracted by Mattie's obvious if unpromoted sexuality and he was no longer certain just how professionally objective he was.

'Sorry, Mattie.'

'And screw you, Johnnie!' was all she was able to hiss down the line before slamming the phone back into its cradle.

She was consumed with anger, not only with Preston and politics but also with herself for being unable to find a more convincing argument to fight her cause or a more coherent way of expressing it.

Ignoring the tart look flashed at her by the conference steward on the next phone, she stalked across the foyer. 'I need a drink,' she explained loudly to herself and every-one else within earshot, and made straight for the bar.

The steward was just raising the grille over the counter when Mattie arrived and slapped her bag and a £5 note down on the bar. As she did so she knocked the arm of another patron who was already lined up at the varnished counter and clearly intent on being served with the first drink of the night.

'Sorry,' apologised Mattie huffily, without sounding entirely as if she meant it. The other drinker turned to face her.

'Young lady, you look as if you need a drink. My doctor tells me there is no such thing as needing a drink, but what does he know? Would you mind if a man old enough to be your father joins you? By the way, the name's Collingridge, Charles Collingridge.'

'So long as we don't talk politics, Mr Collingridge, it will be my pleasure. Allow my editor to buy you a large one!'

The room was spacious, but it had a low ceiling and it was packed with people. The heat from the mass of bodies had combined with the central heating to make the atmosphere distinctly muggy, and many of the guests were quietly cursing the insulation and double glazing which the archi-tects had so carefully installed throughout 'Overtime Alley'. As a consequence the chilled champagne being dis-pensed by Urquhart's constituency secretary was in great demand, and it was already on its way to being one of his more relaxed conference receptions.

Urquhart, however, was not in a position to circulate and accept his guests' thanks. He was effectively pinned in one corner by the enormous bulk of Benjamin Landless. The newspaper magnate was sweating heavily and he had his jacket off and collar undone, displaying his thick green braces like parachute webbing which were holding up his vast, flowing trousers. Landless refused to take any notice of his discomfort, for his full attention was concentrated on his trapped prey.

'But that's all bloody Horlicks, Frankie, and you know it. I put my whole newspaper chain behind your lot at the last election and I've moved my entire worldwide headquarters to London. I've invested millions in the country. And if you lot don't pull your fingers out, the whole bloody performance is going down the drain at the next election. Those buggers in the Opposition will crucify me if they get in because I've been so good to you, but you lot seem to be falling over yourselves to open the damned door for them.'

He paused to produce a large silk handkerchief from within the folds of his trousers and wipe his brow, while Urquhart goaded him on.

'Surely it's not as bad as that, Ben. All Governments go through sticky patches. We've been through this all before – we'll pull out of it!'

'Horlicks, Horlicks, bloody Horlicks.' That's complacent crap, and you know it, Frankie. Haven't you seen your own latest poll? They phoned it through to me earlier this afternoon. You're down another 3 per cent, that's 10 per cent since the election. If you held it today, you'd get thrashed. Bloody annihilated!'

Urquhart relished the thought of the *Telegraph* headline tomorrow, but could not afford to show it. 'Damn. How on earth did you get hold of that? That will really hurt us at the by-election tomorrow.'

'Don't worry. I've told Preston to pull it. It'll leak, of course, and we'll probably get some flak in *Private Eye* about a politically inspired cover-up, but it'll be after the by-election and it will save your conference being turned into a bear pit.' He sighed deeply. 'It's more than you bloody deserve,' he said more quietly, and Urquhart knew he meant it.

'I know the PM will be grateful, Ben,' said Urquhart, feeling sick with disappointment.

'Course he will, but the gratitude of the most unpopular Prime Minister since polls began isn't something you can put in the bank.'

'What do you mean?'

'Political popularity is cash. While you lot are in, I should be able to get on with my business and do what I do best – make money. That's why I've supported you. But as soon as your popularity begins to fade, the whole thing begins to clam up. The Stock Market sinks. People don't want to invest. Unions get bolshy. I can't look ahead. And it's been happening ever since June. The PM couldn't organise a farting contest in a baked bean factory. His unpopularity is dragging the whole Party down, and my business with it. Unless you do something about it, we're all going to disappear down a bloody great hole.'

'Do you really feel like that?'

Landless paused, just to let Urquhart know it wasn't the champagne speaking. 'Passionately,' he growled.

'Then it looks as if we have a problem.'

'You do so long as he goes on like he is.'

'But if he won't change . . .'

'Then get rid of him!'

Urquhart raised his eyebrows sharply, but Landless was not to be deflected. 'Life's too short to spend it propping up losers. I haven't spent the last twenty years working my guts out just to watch your boss piss it all away.'

Urquhart found his arm gripped painfully by his guest's huge fingers. There was real strength behind the enormous girth, and Urquhart began to realise how Landless always seemed to get his way. Those he could not dominate with his wealth or commercial muscle he would trap with his physical strength and sharp tongue. Urquhart had always hated being called Frankie, and this was the only man in the world who insisted on using it. But tonight of all nights

135

he did not think he would object. This was one argument he was going to enjoy losing.

'Let me give you one example, in confidence. OK, Frankie?' He pinned Urquhart still tighter in the corner. 'Very shortly I expect that United Newspapers will be up for sale. If it is, I want to buy it. In fact, I've already had some serious discussions with them. But the lawyers are telling me that I already own one newspaper group and that the Government isn't going to allow me to buy another. I said to them, you are telling me that I can't become the biggest newspaper owner in the country, even if I commit all of the titles to supporting the Government!'

Perspiration was slipping freely from his face, but he ignored it. 'You know what they said, Frankie? It's precisely because I *do* support the Government that I'm in trouble. If I moved to take over United Newspapers the Opposition would kick up the most godawful stink. No one would have the guts to stand up and defend me. The takeover would be referred to the Monopolies and Mergers Commission where it would get bogged down for months with a herd of expensive lawyers stuck in a bloody committee-room, with me having to listen to a bunch of closet queen bureaucrats lecturing me on how to run my own business. And whatever arguments I use, in the end the Government will bow to pressure and refuse to allow the deal to go through, because they haven't got the stomach for a public fight.'

He blew cigar smoke in Urquhart's face.

'In other words, Mr Chief Whip, because your Government doesn't have the balls, my company is going to go through the wringer. Because you're buggering up your own business, you're going to bugger up mine as well!'

The point had been forcefully made and the pressure applied. It was not a subtle way to lobby a Minister, but he had always found the direct approach to be far more effective than complicated minuets. Politicians could be bullied like any other men. He paused to refresh himself from his glass, waiting for a reply.

Urquhart framed his response slowly, to emphasise that he too, like Landless, was speaking in earnest.

'That would be a tremendous pity, Ben. You have been a great friend of the Party, and it would be a great shame if we were unable to repay that friendship. I cannot speak for the Prime Minister. In fact, I find myself increasingly unable to speak for him nowadays. But from my point of view, I would do everything I could to support you when you needed it.'

'That's good to know, Frankie. I appreciate it, very much. If only Henry could be so decisive, but I know that's simply not his nature. If it were up to me, he'd be out.'

'But isn't it up to you?'

'Me?'

'You have your newspapers. They are tremendously influential, and you control them. One headline can make news and break politicians. You were saying that the polls show the public's dislike for the PM is undermining the whole Party. It's personal, not political.'

Landless nodded his assent.

'Yet you say you are not going to publish because it will turn the conference into a bear fight. Do you really think you are going to be able to sort this out without one hell of a fight?'

The bullying Landless of a few moments ago had disappeared, to be replaced by a subtle man who understood every nuance of what was being suggested to him.

'I think I see your point, Frankie. And I think we understand each other.'

'I think we do.'

They shook hands. Urquhart almost winced as his hand disappeared inside the vice-like grip of Landless. He knew the other's handshake was distinctly ambiguous – an expression of friendship, by all means, but also a promise to crush anyone who reneged on a deal.

'Then I have some work to do, Frankie. The *Telegraph* first edition is closing in less than thirty minutes and I shall have to make a telephone call.' He grabbed his jacket and draped it over his arm.

'Thanks for the party. It's been most stimulating.'

Urquhart watched silently as the industrialist, damp

shirt sticking closely to his broad back, shuffled across the crowded room and disappeared through the door.

Across the other side of the room beyond the dignitaries, journalists and hangers-on who were squashed together, Roger O'Neill was huddled on a small sofa with a young and attractive conference-goer. O'Neill was in an excited and very nervous state. He fidgeted incessantly and his words rattled out at an alarming pace. The young girl from Rotherham had already been overwhelmed with the names O'Neill had skilfully dropped and the passion of his words, and she looked on with wide-eyed astonishment, an innocent bystander in a one-way conversation.

'The Prime Minister's under constant surveillance by our security men. There's always a threat. Irish. Arabs. Black Militants. One of them's trying to get me, too. They've been trying for months, and the Special Branch boys insisted on giving me protection throughout the election. Apparently, they'd found a hit list; if the PM were too well protected they might turn to targets close to the PM like me. So they gave me twenty-four-hour cover. It's not public knowledge, of course, but all the journos know.'

He dragged furiously at a cigarette and started coughing. He took out a soiled handkerchief and blew his nose loudly, inspecting it before returning it to his pocket.

'But why you, Roger?' his companion ventured.

'Soft target. Easy access. High publicity hit,' he rattled. 'If they can't get the PM, they'll go for someone like me.'

He looked around nervously, his eyes fluttering wildly.

'Can you keep a confidence? A real secret?' He took another deep drag. 'They think I've been followed all week. And this morning I found my car had been tampered with, so the Bomb Squad boys went over it with a fine tooth comb. They found the wheel nuts on one of the front wheels had been all but removed. Straight home on the motorway, the wheel comes off at eighty miles an hour and – more work for the road sweepers! They think it was deliberate. The Murder Squad are on their way over to interview me right now.'

'Roger, that's awful,' she gasped.

138

'Mustn't tell anyone. The SB don't want to frighten them off if there's a chance of catching them unawares.'

'I hadn't realised you were so close to the Prime Minister,' she said with growing awe. 'What a terrible time for . . .' She suddenly gasped. 'Are you all right, Roger? You are looking very upset. Your, your eyes . . .' she stammered.

O'Neill's eyes were flickering wildly, flashing still further lurid hallucinations into his brain. His attention seemed to have strayed elsewhere; he was no longer with her but in some other world, with some other conversation. His eyes wavered back to her, but they were gone again in an instant. They were bloodshot and watering, and were having difficulty in finding something on which to focus. His nose was dribbling like an old man in winter, and he gave it a cursory and unsuccessful wipe with the back of his hand.

As she watched, his face turned to an ashen grey, his body twitched and he stood up sharply. He appeared terrified, as if the walls were falling in on him. She looked round helplessly, unsure what he needed, too embarrassed to make a public scene. She moved to take his arm and support him, but as she did so he turned on her and lost his balance. He grabbed at her to steady himself, caught her blouse and a button popped.

'Get out of my way, get out of my way,' he snarled.

He thrust her violently backwards, and she fell heavily into a table laden with glasses before sprawling back onto the sofa. The crash of glass onto the floor stopped all conversation in the room as everyone looked round. Three more buttons had gone, and her left breast stood exposed amidst the torn silk.

There was absolute silence as O'Neill stumbled towards the door, pushing still more people out of the way as he tumbled into the night. The young girl clutched at her tattered clothing and was fighting back the tears of humiliation as he disappeared. An elderly guest was helping her rearrange herself and shepherding her towards the bathroom and, as the bathroom door shut behind the two women, a ripple of speculation began which quickly grew

into a broad sea of gossip, washing backwards and forwards over the gathering. It would go on all evening.

Penny Guy did not join in the gossip. A moment before
she had been laughing merrily, thoroughly enjoying the
engaging wit and Merseyside charm of Patrick Woolton.
Urquhart had introduced them more than an hour earlier,
and had ensured that the champagne flowed as easily as
their conversation. But the magic had been smashed with
the uproar. As Penny had taken in O'Neill's stumbling
departure, the sobbing girl's dishevelled clothing and the
ensuing speculation and chatter, her face had dissolved
into a picture of misery. She fought a losing battle to control the tears which had welled up and spilled down her
cheeks and, although Woolton provided a large handkerchief and considerable support, the pain in Penny's face
was all too real.

'He really is *kind*. Very considerate,' she explained. 'But
sometimes it all seems to get too much for him and he goes
a little crazy. It's so out of character.' She pleaded for him,
and the tears flowed still faster.

'Penny. I'm so sorry, dear. Look, you need to get out of
this party. My bungalow's next door. Let's go and dry you
off there, OK?'

She nodded in gratitude, and the couple squeezed their
way through the crowd. No one seemed to notice as they
eased their way out of the room, except Urquhart. His cold
blue eyes followed them through the door where Landless
and O'Neill had gone before. This was certainly going to
be a party to remember, he told himself.

THURSDAY 14TH OCTOBER

'You're not going to make a bloody habit of getting me out of bed every morning, are you?' Even down the telephone line, Preston made it clear that this was an instruction, not a question.

Mattie felt even worse than she had the previous morning after several hours of alcoholic flagellation with Charles Collingridge who was clearly determined to prove his doctor hopelessly wrong. Now she was having great difficulty grasping what on earth was going on.

'Hell, Grev. I go to bed thinking I want to kill you because you won't run the story, and I wake up this morning and find a bastardised version all over the front page with a by-line by someone called "Our Political Staff". Now I *know* I want to kill you, but first I want to find out why you are screwing around with my story. Why did you change your mind? Who's rewritten my story, and who the hell is "Our Political Staff" if it's not me?'

'Steady on, Mattie. Just take a breath and let me explain. If only you had been around when I tried to call you last night and not flashing your eyes at some eligible peer or whatever it is you were doing, then you would have known all about it before it happened.'

Mattie began vaguely to recall the events of last night through the haze, and her pause to persuade her memory to catch up with itself gave Preston time to continue. He began to search for his words carefully.

'As I think Krajewski may have told you, last night some of the editorial staff here didn't believe there was enough substantiation of your piece on the opinion polls for it to run today.'

He heard Mattie snort at the clumsy twisting of the tale,

141

but knew he must press on or he would never get the chance to finish the justification.

'Frankly, I liked the piece and wanted to make it work, but I thought we needed more corroboration before we tore the country's Prime Minister apart on the day of an important by-election. A single anonymous piece of paper wasn't enough.'

'I didn't tear the Prime Minister apart, you did!' Mattie wanted to interject, but Preston rode through her objections.

'So I had a chat with some of my senior contacts in the Party, and late last night we got the corroboration we wanted just before our deadline. The copy needed to be adapted to take account of the new material and I tried to reach you but couldn't, so I rewrote it myself. I refused to let anyone else touch it, your material is too good. So "Our Political Staff" in this instance is me.'

'But that's not the story I sent in. I wrote a piece about a terrible opinion poll and the difficult days the Party was facing. You've turned it into the outright crucifixion of Collingridge. These quotes from "leading party sources", these criticisms and condemnations. Who else do you have working in Bournemouth apart from me?'

'My sources are my own business,' snapped Preston.

'Bullshit, Grev. I'm supposed to be your political correspondent at this bloody conference, you can't keep me in the dark like this. The paper's done a complete somersault over my story and another complete somersault over Collingridge. A few weeks ago he was the saviour of the nation as far as you were concerned, now he's – what does it say? – "a catastrophe threatening to engulf the Government at any moment". I shall be about as popular as a witch's armpit around the conference hall this morning. You've got to tell me what's going on!'

Preston, his carefully prepared explanation already in tatters, retreated into aggression and pomposity.

'As editor I am not in the dubious position of having to justify myself to every cub reporter stuck out in the provinces. You do as you're told, I do as I'm told, and we both get on with the job. All right?'

Mattie was just about to ask him who the hell it was who could tell the editor what to do when she heard the line go dead. She shook her head in amazement and fury. She couldn't and wouldn't take much more of this. Far from having new doors open up to her, she was finding her fingers getting caught as her editor kept slamming the doors shut. And who else had he got ferreting away at the conference?

It was a good thirty minutes later as she was trying to clear her thoughts and calm her temper with yet another cup of coffee in the breakfast room when she saw the vast bulk of Benjamin Landless lumbering across to a window table for a chat with Lord Peterson, the party treasurer. As the proprietor settled his girth into a completely inadequate chair, Mattie wrinkled her nose. She didn't care for what she smelt.

The Prime Minister's political secretary winced. For the third time the press secretary had thrust the morning newspaper across the table at him, for the third time he tried to thrust it away. He knew how St Peter must have felt.

'For God's sake, Grahame.' The press secretary was raising his voice now; the game of ping-pong with the newspaper was irritating him. 'We can't hide every damned copy of the *Telegraph* in Bournemouth. He's got to know, and you've got to show it to him. Now!'

'Why did it have to be today?' he groaned. 'A by-election just down the road, and we've been up all night finishing his speech for tomorrow. Now he'll want to rewrite the whole thing and where are we going to find the time? He'll blow a bloody gasket, and that won't help the by-election or the speech either.'

He slammed his briefcase shut in uncharacteristic frustration. 'All the pressure of the last few weeks, and now this. There just doesn't seem to be any break, does there?'

His companion chose not to answer, preferring to study the view out of the hotel window across the bay. It was raining again.

The political secretary picked up the newspaper, rolled

it up tight, and threw it across the room. It landed with a crash in the waste bin, overturning it and strewing the contents across the carpet. The discarded pages of speech draft mixed with cigarette ash and several empty cans of beer and tomato juice.

'I'll tell him after breakfast.'

It was not to be his best decision.

Henry Collingridge was in a good mood and enjoying his eggs. He had finished his conference speech in the early hours of the morning, and had left his staff to tidy it up and have it typed while he went to bed. He had slept soundly if briefly for the first time during conference week.

The end-of-conference speech always hung over his head like a dark cloud. He disliked conferences and the small talk, the week away from home, the over-indulgence around the dinner tables – and the speech. Most of all the speech. Long hours of anguished discussion in a smoke-filled hotel room, breaking off just when progress seemed in sight in order to attend some ball-breaking function or reception, resuming a considerable time later and trying to pick up where they had left off, only more tired and less inspired. If the speech was good, it was only what they expected and required. If it was poor, they still applauded but said the strain of office was beginning to show. Sod's Law.

But it was now almost over, bar the delivery. The Prime Minister was enjoying breakfast with his wife, watched carefully from surrounding tables by his personal Special Branch detectives. He was discussing the merits of a winter holiday in Antigua or Sri Lanka.

'I would recommend Sri Lanka this year,' he said. 'You can stay on the beach if you want, Sarah, but I would rather like to take a couple of trips into the mountains. They have some ancient Buddhist monasteries and some nearby wildlife reserves which are supposed to be quite spectacular. The Sri Lankan President was describing them to me last year, and they sounded really . . . Darling, you're not listening!'

144

'Sorry, Henry. I was . . . just looking at that gentleman's newspaper.'

'More interesting than me, is it? What's it got to say, then?'

He began to feel ill at ease, remembering that no one had yet given him his daily press cuttings. Someone would surely have told him had there been anything that important.

Come to think of it, he had never felt comfortable since his staff had persuaded him that he didn't need to spend his time reading the daily newspapers, that an edited summary of press clippings prepared by them would be more efficient. But were they? Civil servants had their own narrow views on what was important for a Prime Minister's day, and he found increasingly that their briefing on party political matters was scant. Particularly when there was bad news, the controversy and the in-fighting, he often had to find out from others, sometimes days or weeks after the event. He began to wonder if eventually he would never find out at all, and some great political crisis would burst upon the Party about which he was kept blissfully unaware. They were trying to protect him, of course, but the cocoon they spun around him would, he feared, eventually stifle him.

He remembered the first time he had stepped inside 10 Downing Street as Prime Minister. He had left the crowds and the television crews outside and, as the great black door closed behind him, he had discovered an extraordinary sight.

On one side of the great hallway leading away from the door had gathered some 200 civil servants, *his* civil servants now, who were applauding him loudly – just as they had done Thatcher, Callaghan, Wilson and Heath, and just as they would his successor. On the other side of the hallway facing the host of civil servants stood his political staff, the team of loyal supporters he had hurriedly assembled around him as his campaign to succeed Margaret Thatcher had begun to take off, and whom he had invited to Downing Street to enjoy this historic moment. There were just seven of them, four assistants and three secretaries, dwarfed in their new surroundings.

He told his wife afterwards that it was rather like the Eton Wall Game, with two hugely unequal sides lined up to do battle, with no clear rules and with him cast as both the ball and the prize. He had felt almost relieved when three senior civil servants called an end to the proceedings by physically surrounding him and guiding him off to the Cabinet Room for his first Prime Ministerial briefing. One of the party officials present had described it more as an Assumption, with the Prime Minister disappearing into a different world surrounded by a band of guardian angels – Civil Service, Grade 1, Prime Ministers, for the Protection and Guidance Thereof: Exclusive. His party officials had scarcely seen him for the next six months as they were effectively squeezed out by the official machine, and none of the original band was still left.

Collingridge's attention returned to the newspaper being read at the far-off breakfast table. At such a distance he had great difficulty in bringing it fully into focus, and he fumbled for his glasses, perching them on the end of his nose and trying not to stare too hard. He found his air of studied indifference difficult to maintain as the large headline print came into focus.

'Poll crisis hits Government', it screamed. 'PM's future in doubt as personal slump hits party'. 'By-election disaster feared'. And this in what was supposed to be the most loyal of newspapers.

Collingridge threw his napkin down on the table and kicked back his chair. He left the table even as his wife was still discussing the finer advantages of January in Antigua.

It did not improve the Prime Minister's temper when he had to retrieve the copy of the *Telegraph* from among the cigarette ash in the waste bin.

'Over the bloody breakfast table, Grahame. May I, just occasionally, not be the last to know?'

'I am sorry, Prime Minister. We were going to show it to you just as soon as you had finished,' came the meek response.

'It's just not good enough, not good eno . . . What the hell's this rubbish?'

He had arrived at the point in the *Telegraph* report when the hard news – if opinion polls can ever be considered to qualify as 'hard' news – had been superseded by sheer speculation and hype.

The latest slump revealed in the Party's own private opinion polls is bound to put intense pressure on the Prime Minister, whose conference speech tomorrow is awaited anxiously by party representatives in Bournemouth. Rumblings about the style and effectiveness of the Prime Minister's leadership have increased in intensity since the election, when his performance disappointed many of his colleagues.

These doubts are certain to be fuelled by the latest poll, which gives him the lowest personal rating any Prime Minister has achieved since these polls began nearly forty years ago.

Last night, a leading Minister commented, 'There is a lack of grip around the Cabinet table and in the House of Commons. The Party is restive. Our basically excellent position is being undermined by the leader's lack of appeal.'

Harsher views were being expressed in some Government quarters. Senior party sources were speculating that the Party was fast coming to a crossroad. 'We have to decide between making a new start or sliding gently into decline and defeat,' one source said. 'We have had too many unnecessary setbacks since the election. We cannot afford any more.'

A less sanguine view was that Collingridge was 'like a catastrophe threatening to engulf the Government at any moment'.

The result of today's parliamentary by-election in Dorset East, reckoned to be a safe Government seat, is now being seen as crucial to the Prime Minister's future.

Collingridge was by now almost consumed with fury.

147

His face had flushed and he gripped the newspaper like a drowning man, yet his years of experience in the political trenches kept him in control.

'I want to find out who's behind this, Grahame. I want to know who wrote it. Who spoke to them. Who leaked the poll. And for breakfast tomorrow I want their balls on toast!'

'Shall I give Lord Williams a call?' the political secretary offered as a tentative suggestion.

'Lord Williams!' Collingridge exploded. 'It's his bloody poll that's leaked! I don't want apologies, I want answers. Get me the Chief Whip. Find him, and whatever he is doing get him here right now.'

The secretary summoned his courage for the next hurdle. 'Before he arrives, Prime Minister, could I suggest that we have another look at your speech. There may be various things you want to change as a result of the morning press, and we don't have too much time . . .'

'Grahame, the speech stays, just as it is. I'm not ripping up a perfectly good speech just in order to run in front of a pack of bloody news hounds. That's just what they want, and that is just what will make us most vulnerable. Maybe we can have another look at it later, but what is top priority at the moment is that we stop the leaks right now, otherwise they will turn into a flood. So find Mr Urquhart, and get him here immediately!'

With a look of resignation, the political secretary reached for the phone.

Urquhart was sitting in his bungalow waiting for a telephone call, which came not from the Prime Minister but from the Foreign Secretary. When Woolton got through, much to Urquhart's relief he was chuckling.

'Damned fool. I must put more water in your whisky next time. You walked off with one of my boxes yesterday and left your own behind. I've got your sandwiches and you've got a copy of the latest secret plans to invade Papua New Guinea, or whatever other damn fool thing they are trying to convince me of this week. I suggest we swap before I get arrested for losing confidential Government property. I'll be round in twenty seconds.'

Less than a minute later Urquhart was smiling his way through an apology to his Ministerial colleague, who was still in high spirits as he left, having thanked Urquhart for – as he put it – 'an exceptionally stimulating evening'.

As soon as Woolton had stepped outside, Urquhart's mood changed. His brow furrowed with concern as he locked the door from the inside, testing the handle to make absolutely certain it was closed. He wasted no time in pulling the blinds down over the windows, and only when he was certain that he could not be observed did he place the red box gingerly on the desk.

He examined the box carefully for any signs of tampering, and then selected a key from the large bunch which he produced from his pocket, sliding it carefully into the lock. As the lid came up, it exposed a thick slab of polystyrene packing which entirely filled the box. He extracted the polystyrene and laid it to one side before turning the box on its end. Delicately he eased up the corner of a strip of four-inch surgical tape which had been stuck across most of the side wall of the box, gently peeling it back until it revealed a small recess carved right through the wooden wall until only the rough red leather covering stood between the recess and the outside world.

Externally there was no sign that the leather covered anything other than a solid piece of wood, and he complimented himself that he had not forgotten the art of using a wood chisel which he had learned at school nearly fifty years before. The recess measured no more than two inches square, and snuggling neatly in its middle was a radio transmitter complete with its own miniaturised mercury power pack, compliments of its Japanese manufacturer.

The manager of the security shop just off the Tottenham Court Road which he had visited two weeks earlier had displayed a carefully practised mask of indifference as Urquhart had explained his need to check up on a dishonest employee, yet had shown great enthusiasm in describing the full capabilities of the equipment he could

149

supply. This was one of the simplest yet most sensitive transmitters on the market, he had explained, which was guaranteed to pick up almost any unobstructed sound within a distance of fifty metres and relay it back to the custom-built receiver and voice-activated tape recorder, which he also highly recommended.

'Just make sure the microphone is pointing generally towards the source of the sound, sir, and I guarantee it will sound like a Mahler Symphony.'

Urquhart went over to his wardrobe and from the back pulled out another Ministerial red box. Like all such boxes, this one was secured with a precision-made, high-security tungsten lock for which he alone had the keys. Inside, nestling in another protective wrapping of polystyrene, sat a modified FM portable radio with inbuilt cassette recorder which was tuned to the wavelength of the transmitter. Urquhart noticed with satisfaction that the long-playing tape he had installed was all but exhausted. He had left the radio transmitter in Woolton's room pointing towards the bed.

'I hope it's not simply because he snores,' Urquhart joked with himself. As he did so, the equipment clicked once more into action, ran for ten seconds, and stopped.

He pressed the rewind button and was watching the twin reels spin round when the telephone rang, summoning him to the Prime Minister for yet another 'plumbing lesson', as he called it.

'Never mind, you'll wait,' he whispered, and relocked both boxes before concealing them in the back of his wardrobe. He was reliving the explosion of excitement he had felt when he had set his first rabbit trap on his father's estate with the help of the gillie. They had gone out into the warm evening air to lay the trap together, but Urquhart could not contain his impatience and had returned alone before dawn the following morning, to find the creature swinging helplessly from the snare.

'Got you!' he exclaimed in triumph.

SATURDAY 16TH OCTOBER

It was not just the *Telegraph* which, the day after the Prime Minister's speech, declared it to be a disaster. It was joined in varying degrees by all the other newspapers, several Government backbenchers, and the Leader of the Opposition. Particularly the Leader of the Opposition, whose animated braying appeared for all the world like a hound which had just scented the first sign of real vulnerability in its prey.

The loss of the Dorset East by-election, when the news had burst on the conference in the early hours of Friday morning, had at first numbed the party faithful. It had taken them until breakfast time before they began to vent their frustration and disillusionment, and there had been only one target – Henry Collingridge.

Correspondents in Bournemouth seemed to have been inundated with nameless senior Party officials, each of whom claimed personally to have warned the Prime Minister not to hold the by-election in conference week and who were now absolving themselves of responsibility for the disastrous defeat. In turn, the Prime Minister's office retaliated – unattributably, of course – that the blame was really in the organisational deficiencies of the party headquarters for which, of course, Lord Williams was responsible. The explanation, however, fell on deaf ears. The pack instinct had taken hold of the press as well as the Leader of the Opposition, as the scarcely restrained phrases of one normally pro Government newspaper indicated.

The Prime Minister yesterday failed to quell growing doubts being expressed within his Party about his leadership with a closing speech to his party conference in Bournemouth which one Cabinet colleague

151

described as 'inept and inappropriate'. Following this week's leaking of disastrous internal opinion polls and the humiliating by-election defeat in one of the Party's safest seats, conference representatives were looking for a realistic acknowledgement of the problems which have caused the collapse of voter support for the Government.

Instead, in the words of one representative, 'we got a stale rehash of an old election speech'.

The open disenchantment with the Prime Minister is no longer being voiced with traditional caution within Government circles, particularly amongst anxious backbenchers with marginal seats. Peter Bearstead, MP for Leicester North, said last night: 'The electorate gave us a warning slap across the knuckles at the election, and we should be responding with fresh initiatives and a much clearer statement of our policies. But all we got was more of the same, clichés and suffocating complacency. It may be time for the Prime Minister to think about handing over.'

In an office tower on the South Bank of the Thames, near the spot where Wat Tyler 600 years before had gathered disenchanted rebels to launch his attempt at overthrowing the Establishment, the editor of *Weekend Watch*, the leading current affairs programme, studied the newspapers and called a hurried conference of all his staff. Twenty minutes later, the programme planned for the following day on racketeering landlords had been shelved and the entire sixty-minute slot had been recast. Bearstead was going to be invited to participate, as were several opinion pollsters and pundits, in a new programme entitled 'Collingridge – Time To Go?'

From his home in the leafy suburbs near Epsom, the senior manager of market makers Barclays de Zoete Wedd telephoned two colleagues. They agreed to be in the office very early on Monday. 'All this political nonsense is going to upset the markets, and we mustn't be caught holding on to stock when every other bastard is selling.'

The Chief Whip, at his magnificent Palladian country home in the New Forest of Hampshire, received several calls from worried Cabinet colleagues and senior back-benchers, none wishing to make a break from cover but all of them expressing concern. The chairman of the Party's grass-roots executive committee also called him from York-shire reporting similar worries. 'I would normally pass these on to the Party Chairman,' the bluff Yorkshireman explained, 'but with relations between Downing Street and party headquarters so poor, I just don't want to get caught in the middle of that particular battle.'

The defeated candidate in Thursday's by-election was contacted by the *Mail on Sunday* just after a lunch spent drowning his sorrows, and showed no reticence in his broadside against Collingridge. 'He cost me my seat. Can he feel safe in his?'

At Chequers, the Prime Minister's official country residence set amidst rolling lawns and massive security in rural Buckinghamshire, Collingridge just sat, ignoring his official papers and devoid of inspiration. The rock had begun to roll down hill, and he had no idea how to stop it.

When it hit later that afternoon, the news caught almost everyone by surprise. Even Urquhart. He had expected the *Observer* to take at least a couple more weeks checking the bundle of papers and photostats he had sent them and obtaining their lawyers' clearance. Clearly, however, they had felt pressured by the growing political clamour and feared that a competitor might also be on the trail. 'Damned if we don't publish, damned if we do. So let's go!' the editor had shouted at his investigative reporters.

Urquhart was adjusting the triple carburettors on his 1933 Rover Speed Pilot, which he kept for touring around the lanes of the New Forest, when Miranda called from inside the house.

'Francis! Chequers on the phone!' He picked up the extension on the garage wall, wiping his hands carefully on a greasy rag.

'Urquhart here.'

153

'Chief Whip, please hold on. I have the Prime Minister for you,' a female voice instructed.

The voice which now came on the end of the phone was almost unrecognisable. It had no more vitality than a voice from the grave.

'Francis, I am afraid I have some bad news. The *Observer* have just called up the Downing Street press office to let us know of a story they will be running tomorrow. I can't explain it all, but apparently my brother Charles has been buying shares in companies just before they benefit from Government decisions, and making a killing on them. They say they've got documentary evidence – bank statements, brokers' receipts, the lot. He bought nearly £50,000 worth of Renox, they say, a couple of days before we are supposed to have approved a new drug of theirs for general use, and sold them a day later for a substantial profit. They say he used a false address in Paddington. It's going to be the lead story.'

There was an exhausted pause, as if he no longer had the energy to continue. 'Francis, everyone's going to assume I'm involved with this. What on earth do I do?'

Urquhart settled himself comfortably in the front seat of the car before replying. It was a seat from which he was used to taking risks and making split-second decisions.

'Have you said anything to the *Observer*?'

'No. I don't think they were expecting a comment from me. They were really trying to find Charlie.'

'Where is he?'

'Gone to ground, I hope. I managed to get hold of him. He . . . was drunk. I just told him to take the phone off the hook and not to answer the door.'

Urquhart gripped the steering wheel, staring ahead. He felt strangely detached. He realised for the first time that he had set in motion a machine which was far more powerful than his ability to control it. He had manipulated, analysed and considered, but in spite of weeks of planning he knew that events were no longer under his command. He imagined that he was speeding down a country lane, the Rover ready to respond to his every command as he slammed it through its four gears and accelerated around

154

the curve of the road, knowing now that he was lost in the exhilaration of its speed. He thrilled to its performance and the scent of danger in his nostrils, pressing ever more firmly down on the accelerator, oblivious of what lay around the next blind corner. It was already too late for second thoughts. It was instinct, not intellect, which would take over now.

'Where is he?'

'At home in London.'

'Yes, I know it. You must get someone down there to take care of him. Look, I know it must be painful as he's your brother, but there's a drying-out clinic outside Dover which the Whips Office has used for the occasional back-bencher. Very confidential, very kind. Dr Christian, the head of the clinic, is excellent. I'll give him a call and get him to Charles immediately. You must arrange for someone else from the family to be there, too, in case your brother proves to be difficult. Your wife, Sarah, perhaps? I will find someone from the Whips Office to get there and keep a careful eye on it all. But we must move fast, because in four hours' time when the *Observer* hits the streets your brother's home is going to be besieged by journalists. We have to beat them to the punch. With Charles in his present state there is no knowing what he might say or do.'

'But what do we do then? I can't hide Charlie for ever. He's got to face up to it sooner or later, hasn't he?'

'Is he guilty?'

'I simply don't know,' the words said, but the tone conceded doubt and probable defeat. 'The office checked after they got the phone call. Apparently we did license a new Renox drug a couple of months ago, and their shares jumped sharply. Anyone holding any of their shares would have made a handsome profit. But Charlie hasn't got any money to splash around on shares. And how would he know about Renox?'

Urquhart came back in a tone which did not imply any argument. 'Let's worry about that when we have taken care of him. He must be put away somewhere quiet, somewhere the press can't get to him. He needs help, whether he wants it or not, and you must get some breathing space.

You must be very careful how you decide to respond.'

There was a short pause for the words to sink in. 'You cannot afford to get this one wrong.'

Collingridge's wearied assent was mumbled down the phone. His Chief Whip's sudden authoritativeness had stripped away piece by piece both his family pride and the dignity of his office. He had neither the will nor the capacity to argue. He looked through the leaded windows across the fields surrounding Chequers to an ancient beech wood. He tried to draw strength and confidence from the magnificent trees glowing golden in the evening sunshine of autumn. They had always been an inspiration to him, a constant reminder that all problems eventually pass, yet this evening, no matter how he tried, they left him feeling empty and hollow.

'What else do I do?'

'Nothing. Let us see precisely what the *Observer* says, then we shall have a better idea. In the meantime, instruct your press office to say nothing while we sort out your brother.'

'Thank you, Francis. May I call you later when we see what they print? In the meantime, I would be grateful if you would contact Dr Christian. Sarah will be at my brother's home in just under two hours if she leaves right now. I'll instruct her immediately.'

Collingridge had adopted a formal tone in an attempt to stifle the tension inside him, but Urquhart could hear the emotion trembling in his voice.

'Don't worry, Henry. Everything will work out. Trust me.'

Charles Collingridge did not object when his sister-in-law let herself into the flat with the spare key. In fact, he was snoring soundly in an armchair, the clutter of an afternoon's heavy indulgence spread around him. He only began to object when Sarah had spent five frustrating minutes trying to shake him awake, and had resorted to ice wrapped in a tea towel. His objections became more vigorous when he began to understand what Sarah was saying, persuading him to 'come away for a few days', but the dialogue became totally incoherent when she began to question him about shares. She could get no sense out of him, and neither could she persuade him to move.

It took the arrival of Dr Christian and a Junior Whip almost an hour later before the situation progressed any further. An overnight bag was rapidly packed, and the three of them bundled the still-protesting brother into the back of Dr Christian's car, which was parked out of sight at the back of the building. Fortunately for them, he had lost the physical coordination to take his objections further.

Unfortunately, however, the whole matter had taken some considerable time, so that when the doctor's Granada swept out from behind the building into the High Street with Sarah and Charles in the back, the whole scene was witnessed by an ITN camera crew, the first to arrive on the scene.

The video tape of a fleeing Charles apparently hiding in the back seat of the car and accompanied by the Prime Minister's wife was played on the late evening news, together with details of the *Observer*'s allegations. The night duty editor at ITN had phoned the managing editor to get approval to play the tape before putting it on air. He wanted his arse covered by senior management on this one. As he had explained, 'Once this gets out, there's no way the Prime Minister can argue he's not involved right up to his neck.'

Sunday 17th October

The scenes of the fugitive Charles Collingridge were still being played at midday on Sunday as *Weekend Watch* came on the air. The programme had been thrown together in frantic haste, and there were many untidy ends. The control room reeked of sweat and tension as the programme started. It had not been rehearsed fully, much of it was being done live, and the autocue for the latter stages of the programme was still being typed as the presenter welcomed his viewers.

It had been impossible to find any Minister who would agree to appear on the programme, and one of the invited pundits had not yet arrived. A special overnight opinion poll had been commissioned through Gallup and the polling company's chief executive, Gordon Heald, was presenting the results himself. He had been kicking his computer all morning and was sitting slightly flushed under the hot lights. The computer analysis did nothing to help his sense of ease for his polling agents had uncovered still further disenchantment with the Prime Minister.

Yes, admitted Heald, it was a significant fall. No, he acknowledged, no Prime Minister had ever won an election after being so low in the polls.

The gloomy prognostications were supported by two senior newspaper commentators and an economist forecasting turmoil in the financial markets in the days ahead, before the presenter switched his attention to Peter Bearstead. Normally the garrulous East Midlands MP would have been videotaped beforehand, but there had been no time for recording. The Honourable and diminutive Member for Leicester North was on live. He was scheduled on the director's log for only two minutes fifty

158

seconds, but the presenter soon discovered that it was the politician who had taken charge of proceedings.

'Yes, Mr Bearstead, but how much trouble do you think the Party is in?'

'That depends.'

'On what?'

'On how long we have to go with the present Prime Minister.'

'So you are standing by your comment of earlier in the week that perhaps the Prime Minister should be considering his position?'

'Not exactly. I'm saying that the Prime Minister should resign. His present unpopularity is destroying the Party, and now he has become enmeshed in what looks like a family scandal. It cannot go on. It must not go on!'

'But do you think that the Prime Minister is likely to resign? After all, there are almost another five years before an election is necessary, and that must leave enormous scope for recovering lost ground.'

'We will not survive another five years with this Prime Minister!' The MP was clearly agitated, rocking back and forth in his studio chair. 'It is time for clear heads, not faint hearts; and I am determined that the Party must come to a decision on the matter. If he does not resign, then I shall stand against him for election as Leader of the Party.'

'You will challenge him for the Party leadership?' the presenter spluttered in surprise. He was nervous, trying to follow the voluble MP while at the same time listening to instructions in his earpiece which were getting rapidly more heated. 'But surely you can't win?'

'Of course I can't win. But it's up to the senior figures within the Party to grasp the initiative and sort the problem out. They are all constantly griping about it, but none of them has the guts to do anything. If they won't take a stand or won't act, then I will. Flush it into the open. We can't let this continue to fester behind closed doors.'

'I want to be absolutely clear about this, Mr Bearstead. You are demanding that the Prime Minister resigns, or else you will stand against him for leadership of the Party . . . ?'

'There has to be a leadership election no later than Christmas: it's Party rules after an election. Instead of a mere formality I shall make it into a real contest where my colleagues will have to make up their minds.'

There was a pained expression on the presenter's face. He was holding his earpiece, through which a shouting match was under way. The director was demanding that the dramatic interview should continue and to hell with the schedule; the editor was shouting that they should get away from it before the bloody fool changed his mind and ruined a sensational story.

'We shall be going for a short commercial break,' announced the presenter.

Monday 18th October – Friday 22nd October

Shortly before midnight in London as the Tokyo financial markets opened, sterling began to be marked down heavily. By 9 a.m. and with all the Monday newspapers leading on the public challenge to Collingridge's leadership, the FT All Share Index was down 63 points, and down a further 44 points by 1 p.m. when it became clear that Bearstead intended to proceed. The money men don't like surprises.

The Prime Minister wasn't feeling on top form, either. He hadn't slept and had scarcely talked since Saturday evening. His wife had kept him at Chequers rather than allowing him to return to Downing Street, and had called the doctor. Dr Wynne-Jones, Collingridge's loyal and highly experienced physician, had immediately recognised the signs of strain and had prescribed a sedative and rest. The sedative gave some immediate release in the form of the first lengthy spell of sleep he had had since the start of the party conference a week earlier, but his wife could still detect the tension which fluttered beneath his closed eyelids and which kept his fingers firmly clamped onto the bedclothes.

Late on Monday afternoon when he had come out of his drugged sleep, he instructed the besieged Downing Street press office to make it known that of course he would contest the leadership election and was confident of victory. He was too busy getting on with official Government business to give any interviews, but undoubtedly he would have something to say later in the week. He effected to give a display of total authority and Prime Ministerial stature, but unfortunately no one had yet been able to get

161

any sense out of Charles and there was not a word to be said to refute the allegations of illegal share dealing.

While Downing Street tried to give the impression of business as usual, over at party headquarters Lord Williams ordered additional opinion research to be rushed through. He wanted to know what the country really thought.

The rest of the party machinery moved less quickly. For a further forty-eight hours it was stunned into silence by events which had suddenly sprung off in a totally unexpected direction. The rules for a contested leadership election following a general election were dusted off both in party headquarters and in the media, with many discovering for the first time that the process was under the control of the Chairman of the Parliamentary Party's Backbench Committee, Sir Humphrey Newlands, although the choice of timing was left in the hands of the Party Leader. This proved to be a wise decision since Sir Humphrey, displaying an acutely poor sense of timing, had left the previous weekend for a ten-day holiday on a private island in the West Indies, and was proving extraordinarily difficult to contact. Some speculated that he was deliberately keeping his head low while the awesome but invisible powers of the party hierarchy were mobilised to persuade Bearstead to withdraw. It would be only weeks rather than months, they thought, before Bearstead found himself preoccupied with a senior directorship in industry, in Government as a Junior Minister, or silenced in some other lucrative fashion.

By Wednesday, however, the *Sun* had discovered Sir Humphrey on a silver stretch of beach somewhere near St Lucia along with several friends, including at least three scantily clad young women who were obviously nearly half a century younger than him. It was announced that he would be returning to London as soon as flights could be arranged, for consultation about the election with the Prime Minister.

Collingridge was back in Downing Street, but not in better spirits. Every day brought racy new headlines about turmoil in the Party as newspapers fought to find some new angle on the story. As still further reports began to circulate of growing disaffection between Downing Street and party headquarters, Collingridge began to find himself drifting, cut off from the information and advice which he had previously gained so freely from his wise and wily Party Chairman.

He had no specific reason to distrust Williams, of course, but the constant media discussion of a growing gulf between the two began to make a reality of what previously had been only irresponsible and inventive gossip. Distrust is a matter of mind, not fact, and the press had created strong and virulent perceptions. In the circumstances the ageing and proud Party Chairman felt he couldn't offer advice without being asked, while Collingridge took his silence as probable evidence of disloyalty. Anyway, rationalised Collingridge, party headquarters had let him down badly if not deliberately, and who was responsible for that?

Sarah went for the first visit to Charles, and came back late and very depressed. They were in bed before she could bring herself to talk about it. 'He looks awful, Henry. I never realised quite how ill he was making himself, but it all seems to have caught up with him in a few days. The doctors are still trying to detoxify him, get all the alcohol out of his system. They said he was close to killing himself.' She buried her head in his arms.

'I blame myself. I could have stopped him. If only I hadn't been so preoccupied . . . Did he say anything about the shares?'

'He's scarcely coherent yet; he just kept saying "£50,000? What £50,000?" He swore he'd never been anywhere near a Turkish bank.'

She sat bolt upright in bed, looking deep into her husband's eyes. 'Is he guilty?'

'I simply don't know, darling. But what choice do I have? He has to be innocent. If he did buy those shares, then who on earth is going to believe that I didn't tell him to do so. If Charles is guilty, then I shall be judged guilty with him.'

She gripped his arm in alarm.

Collingridge smiled to reassure her. 'Don't worry, my

163

love, I am sure it will never come to that.' But his voice was tired, unconvincing.

'Couldn't you say that Charles was ill, he didn't know what he was doing, he somehow . . . found the information without your knowing . . .' Her voice faded away as she began to realise how transparent the argument was.

He took her gently in his arms, surrounding her with warmth and comfort. He kissed her forehead and felt a warm tear fall on his chest. He knew he was close to tears, too, and felt no shame.

'No, Sarah, I shall not be the one to finish off Charlie. God knows he's been trying hard enough to do that himself, but I am still his brother. On this one we will survive, or sink if we must, as a family. Together.'

Mattie's original intention had been to take the whole week off recovering from the after-effects of the media circus which had spent the best part of six weeks travelling around some of the country's less splendid bars and boarding houses following the various political parties' annual conferences. It was an exhausting schedule, and most of the following weekend she had intended to devote to sampling some exotic Chilean wines and soaking in the bath. But the relaxation she sought proved to be elusive. Her indignation at the way Preston had not only trampled on her story but also abused her sense of journalistic pride seemed to make the wine taste acidic and the bathwater turn cold.

So she tried burning off her anger with strenuous physical work, but after three days of taking it out on the woodwork of her Victorian apartment with sandpaper and paint, she could stand her frustration no longer. On Tuesday morning at 9.30, Mattie was planted firmly in the leather armchair in front of the editor's desk, determined not to move until she had confronted Preston. He would not be able to put the phone down on her this time.

She had been there nearly an hour before his secretary peered apologetically round the door. 'Sorry, Mattie. He's just called in to say he's got an outside appointment. He won't be in until after lunch.'

Mattie felt as if the world was conspiring against her. She wanted to scream or smash something or put chewing gum in his hair brush – anything to get her own back. It was therefore unfortunate timing that John Krajewski decided at that moment to see whether the editor was in his office, only to discover an incandescent Mattie.

'I didn't know you were in!'

'I'm not,' she said between clenched teeth. 'At least, not for much longer.' She stood up to go.

Krajewski was ill at ease and awkward, glancing around the room to make sure they were alone.

'Look, Mattie, I've picked up the phone a dozen times to call you since last week, but . . .'

'But what?' she snapped.

'I was afraid I couldn't find the words to stop you biting my head off,' he said softly.

'Then you were right!' But Mattie's voice had changed, growing gentler as she realised how totally she had lost her sense of humour. It wasn't Johnnie's fault, so why take it out on him, just because he was the only man around to kick? He was worth more than that.

Since his wife had died two years earlier, Krajewski had lost much of his self-confidence, both about women and his professional abilities. He had survived in his demanding job on the strength of his undoubted journalistic talents, but his confidence with women was only slowly returning, penetrating and gradually cracking the shell which his pain had built around him. Many women had tried, attracted by his tall frame, dark hair and deep, sad eyes. But he wanted more than their sympathy, and slowly he had begun to realise that he wanted Mattie. At first he had allowed himself to show no special interest in her, just the respect of a professional colleague which had only slowly developed into something more relaxed during their shared moments in the office and over countless cups of machine coffee. The thrill of the chase was at last beginning to return to his empty life, helping him tolerate the lash of Mattie's tongue. And now he sensed the softening in her mood.

'Mattie, let's talk about it. But not here, not in the office.

165

Over dinner where we can get away from all this.' He made an irritated gesture in the direction of the editor's desk.

'Is this an excuse for a pick up?' The slightest trace of a smile began to appear at the corners of her mouth.

'Do I need an excuse . . . ?'

She grabbed her bag and swung it over her shoulder. 'Eight o'clock,' she instructed, trying in vain to look severe as she walked past him and out of the office.

'I'll be there,' he shouted after her. 'I must be a masochist, but I'll be there.'

And indeed at eight o'clock prompt, he was. They hadn't gone very far, just around the corner from Mattie's flat in Notting Hill to The Ganges, a little Bangladeshi restaurant with a big clay oven and a proprietor who ran an excellent kitchen during the time he allowed himself away from his passionate preoccupation with trying to overthrow the Government back home.

They were waiting for the chicken tikka to arrive when Mattie told him. 'Johnnie, I've been burning up with anger all afternoon. I think I've made a terrible mistake. With all my heart I want to be a journalist, a good journalist. Deep down I always thought I could be a great journalist, but it will never happen working for a man like that. Grev Preston is not what I left everything behind and came to London for, and I'm not taking any more of his crap. I'm quitting.'

He looked at her sharply and took his time in responding. She was trying to smile defiantly, but he could see the sense of bitter failure tearing at her inside.

'Don't rush it. And don't leave until you have something else to go to. You would regret it if you were out of action right now, just when the political world seems to be falling apart.'

She looked at him quizzically. 'Frankly, Johnnie, you surprise me. That's not the impassioned plea to stay on as part of the team that I was expecting from my deputy editor.'

'I'm not speaking as the deputy editor, Mattie. You mean more to me than that.' There was a short, embarrassed, very English silence which he covered by elaborately breaking a large hunk of nan bread in two. 'I understand why you feel like that. I feel exactly the same way.' There was an edge of bitterness in his words.

'You are thinking of leaving, too?' said Mattie with astonishment.

His eyes were dark and sad once more, but with anger rather than self pity.

'I've been with the paper over eight years. It used to be a quality paper, one I was proud to work for – before the takeover. But what they have done to you, and what they are doing to everyone there, is not my idea of journalism.' He bit into the warm, spicy bread as he considered carefully what he would say next.

'As deputy editor I bear some responsibility for what appears in the paper. Perhaps I shouldn't tell you the story of what happened the other night, but I'm going to because I can't tolerate any more being stuck with the responsibility for the things that are happening now. Mattie, do you want to know what happened to your story?'

There was no need to answer the question. The chicken tikka and vegetable curry had arrived, with the strongly flavoured dishes crowded onto the tiny table, but neither of them showed any interest in the food.

'That night a few of us were standing around in the news room shortly before the first edition deadline. It was a quiet night, not much late breaking news. Then Grev's secretary shouted across the floor that there was a phone call for him and he disappeared to take it in his own office. Ten minutes later he reappeared, very flustered. Someone had really lit a fire under him. "Hold everything," he shouted. "We're going to change the front page." I thought, Jesus, they must have shot the President. He was in a real state, very nervous. Then he asked for your story to be put up on one of the screens. He announced we were going to lead with it, but first we had to beef it up.'

'But the reason he spiked it in the first place was because he said it was too strong!' she protested.

'Of course. But wait, it gets better. So there he was, looking over the shoulder of one of our general reporters

167

who was sitting at the screen, dictating changes directly to him. Twisting it, hyping it, turning everything into a personal attack on the Prime Minister. And you remember the quotations from senior Cabinet sources on which the whole rewrite was based? He made them up, on the spot. Every single one of them. It was fiction from beginning to end. You should have been delighted that your name wasn't on it.'

'But why? Why on earth invent a story like that? Changing the whole editorial stance of the newspaper by dumping Collingridge. What made him change his mind in such a hurry?' She paused for a second, biting her lip with impatience. 'Wait a minute. Who was he talking to on the phone? Who was this so-called source in Bournemouth?' she demanded. 'Of course, I see it now.' She let out a low sigh of understanding. 'Mr Benny Bunter Landless.'

He nodded confirmation.

'So that's why Grev was jumping through the hoops and screwing around with my story. I should have realised it earlier. The ringmaster was cracking the whip.'

'And that's why I feel I can't go on either, Mattie. We are no longer a newspaper, we're beginning to act as the proprietor's own personal edition of *Pravda*.'

But Mattie's curiosity had already begun to overhaul her own anger and disappointment. There was a story lurking somewhere, and the excitement of the chase began to take a hold on her. 'So Landless has suddenly turned against Collingridge. All his newspapers were craven sycophants during the election, yet now we are running a lynch party. Why, Johnnie, why?'

'That's an excellent question, Mattie, but I don't know the answer. It can't be politics, Landless has never given a damn about that. He has politicians of every party in his pocket. I can only think it's personal in some way.'

'If it's personal it must be business. That's the only thing which really rattles his cage.'

'But I can't figure out why he should have fallen out with Collingridge over business.'

'And I would love to know who he's got on the inside.'

'What do you mean?' asked Krajewski.

'Grev couldn't have concocted that article without the material on the opinion poll. Without my copy on which to work he had nothing, and without the leaked statistics I had nothing either. And at the same time as this occurs, Landless decides to ditch Collingridge. It's too much of a coincidence for that all to have come together by chance.' She banged her hand on the table with a renewed passion. 'But it can't be Landless on his own. There's somebody on the inside of the Party leaking polls and pulling strings.'

'The same person who's supposed to have been leaking all the material since the election?'

'The one the Chief Whip was trying to sort out? That's a fascinating thought. He found nothing definite and before tonight I was never convinced that it was a deliberate campaign of leaks rather than a series of cock-ups . . .'

'But now . . . ?'

'Now I've got just two questions, Johnnie – who, and why?'

The adrenalin was pouring into her veins, replacing her earlier despondency with electric urges which tingled throughout her body and brain. She felt exhilarated. Something had touched her deep down, an almost animal lust to pursue her prey until she had found and trapped it. This is what she had come south for. This made it all worthwhile.

'Johnnie, you sweet man. How wise you are! Something smells and I want to find out what – I knew it when I saw Landless prowling around at Bournemouth. You're right. Now is definitely not the time to throw in the towel and resign. I'm going to get to the bottom of this even if I have to kill someone. Will you help me?'

'If that's what you want – of course.'

'There's another thing I want, Johnnie.' She felt alive, charged with excitement and a feeling burning deep inside her which she thought she had long ago forgotten. 'Let's pass on the bloody biryani and go back to my place. I've got a bottle of vintage Sauterne in the fridge, and I need some company tonight. All night. Would you mind?'

'Mattie, it's been a long time . . .'

'Me, too, Johnnie. Too long.'

169

*   *   *

The statement – or briefing, in fact, because it was not issued in the form of a quotable press release – was made available on Wednesday and was simple. As the Downing Street press secretary told the gathered lobby correspondents, 'The Prime Minister has never provided his brother with any form of commercially sensitive Government information, and has never discussed any aspect of Renox Chemicals with him. The Prime Minister's brother is extremely ill, and is currently under medical supervision. His doctors have stated that he is not in a fit state to give interviews or answer questions. However, I can assure you that he categorically denies purchasing any Renox shares, having a false address in Paddington, or being involved in this matter in any way whatsoever. That's all I can tell you at the moment.'

'Come on, Freddie,' one of the correspondents carped, 'you can't get away with just that. How on earth do you explain the *Observer* story if the Collingridges are innocent?'

'I can't. Perhaps they were getting confused with another Charles Collingridge, how do I know? But I've known Henry Collingridge for many years, just as you've known me, and all of my experience tells me he is incapable of stooping to such ridiculous and sordid depths. My man is innocent, and you have my word on that!'

He spoke with the vehemence of a professional placing his own reputation on the line along with that of his boss, and the lobby's respect for one of their old time colleagues swung the day for Collingridge – just.

'We're innocent!' bawled the front page of the *Daily Mail* the following day, with most of the other newspapers following on cue. Finding no more incriminating information with which to play, the media and the Party together sat back exhausted, relishing the opportunity to concentrate for just a moment on other disasters.

Urquhart once again had stepped from the Chief Whip's office at Number 12 Downing Street along to Number 10 at the request of Collingridge. 'You're the only smiling face I see at the moment, Francis, and I need you to keep my spirits up!' They were sitting together in the Cabinet Room reviewing the newspapers, with Collingridge at last managing a smile of his own. For the first time in days he felt he could see the mists beginning to clear.

'What do you think, Francis?'

'Perhaps we are through the worst.'

'No, not necessarily. But at least we have a breathing space and I can tell you, I need that more than anything. The pressure . . .' He shook his head slowly. 'Well, you understand, I'm sure.'

Collingridge took a deep breath to summon up fresh resources from within. 'But it is only a breathing space, Francis.' He waved to the empty seats around the Cabinet table. 'I don't know how much firm support I still have amongst colleagues, but I have to give them something to hold on to. I can't afford to run away. I have to show I've nothing to hide, to take the initiative once again.'

'What do you intend to do?'

The Prime Minister sat quietly, beneath the towering oil painting of Robert Walpole, his longest-serving predecessor who had survived countless scandals and crises and whose magnificent portrait had inspired many leaders during times of trial. As Collingridge gazed in contemplation across St James's Park, the sun burst through the grey autumn skies, flooding the room with light. The sound of children playing rose up from the park. Life would go on.

He turned to face Urquhart. 'I have an invitation from *Weekend Watch* to appear this Sunday and put my own case – to restore the balance. I think I must do it – and I think I must do it damned well! They've promised no more than ten minutes on the *Observer* nonsense, the rest on broad policy and our ambitions for the fourth term. What do you think?'

Urquhart chose not to express any opinion. He was more than content to let Collingridge use him as a sounding board while he made up his own mind, bouncing ideas and arguments off him to see how they sounded, letting Urquhart know of every move along the way.

'At times like these, men must make up their own minds.'

'Good!' Collingridge exclaimed with a chuckle. 'I'm glad you think that way. Because I've already accepted.' He took a deep breath and exhaled fiercely through flared nostrils. 'The stakes are high, Francis, and I know there are no easy options. But for once I feel lucky!'

It was Urquhart's turn to gaze out through the window and think hard. As he did so, the sun disappeared once more behind the clouds, and the rain began to beat down on the pane.

Penny put the call from the Chief Whip through to O'Neill in his office. A few seconds later the door was carefully closed. Penny heard the sound of O'Neill's raised voice some minutes later, but could not decipher what he was shouting about.

When the red light on the extension phone flashed off to indicate the call was finished, there was no sound at all from O'Neill's office. Pressed forward by a mixture of curiosity and concern, she knocked gently on his door, and opened it cautiously. O'Neill was sitting at his desk with his head in his hands. He looked up as he heard Penny come in, and confronted her with wild, staring eyes.

His voice croaked and his speech was disjointed.

'He . . . threatened me, Pen. He said if I don't he would . . . tell everyone. I said I wouldn't but . . . I've got to alter the file . . .'

'What file, Roger? What have you got to do?' She had never seen him like this. 'Can I help?'

'No, Pen, you can't help. Not on this . . . Damned computers!' He seemed to regain a little self-control. 'Penny. I want you to forget all about it. I want you to go home. Have the rest of the day off. I'm . . . going out shortly. Please, don't hang around waiting for me, go home now.'

'But, Roger, I . . .'

'No questions, Pen, no questions. Just leave!'

She gathered her things in tearful confusion as O'Neill slammed his door shut once again and she heard it locking from the inside.

SUNDAY 24TH OCTOBER

Collingridge began to relax as the programme unfolded. He had rehearsed hard for the previous two days, and the questions were much as expected, giving him an excellent opportunity to talk with genuine vigour about the next few years. He had insisted that the questions concerning the *Observer* allegations be kept until the end, partly so that *Weekend Watch* could not renege on its promise to restrict the section to ten minutes, and partly because he wanted to be into his stride and in command before grappling with them. He hoped that after forty-five minutes of him talking about the bright future for the country the questions would look mean and irrelevant.

Sarah was smiling encouragingly from the edge of the studio as they went into the final commercial break. He gave her a thumbs-up sign as the floor manager waved his arms to let them know that they were about to go back on air.

'Mr Collingridge, for the final few minutes of this programme, I would like to turn to the allegations printed in the *Observer* last week about Charles Collingridge and possible improper share dealing.'

Collingridge nodded seriously into the camera to show that he had nothing to fear from such questions.

'I understand that earlier this week Downing Street issued a statement denying any connection of your family with the matter, and suggesting that there may have been a case of mistaken identity. Is that correct?'

'There may have been some confusion with another Charles Collingridge for all I know, but I am really not in a position to explain the extraordinary *Observer* story. All I can tell you is that none of my family have anything whatsoever to do with this matter. You have my word

173

of honour on that.' He spoke the words slowly, leaning forward, looking directly at the presenter to give added dramatic emphasis.

'I understand that your brother denies ever having opened an accommodation address in a Paddington tobacconists.'

'Absolutely,' Collingridge confirmed.

'Prime Minister, earlier this week one of our reporters addressed an envelope to himself, care of Charles Collingridge, at the Paddington address used to open the bank account. He used a vivid red envelope to make sure it stood out clearly. I would like you to look at this video tape which we took at that address yesterday when he went to reclaim it. I apologise for the poor quality, but I am afraid we had to use a concealed camera, as the proprietor of the shop concerned seemed very reluctant to cooperate.'

The presenter swivelled his chair so that he could see the dark and fuzzy but still discernible video which was being projected onto the large screen behind him. Collingridge flashed a concerned look at Sarah, and cautiously swivelled his own chair around. He watched as the reporter approached the counter, pulled out various pieces of plastic and paper from his wallet to identify himself, and explained to the counter assistant that a letter was waiting for him in the care of Charles Collingridge, who used this address for his own post. The assistant, the same overweight and balding man who had served Penny several months before, explained that he could not release letters except to someone who could produce a proper receipt. 'Lots of important letters come here,' he sniffed. 'Can't go handing them out to just anyone.'

'But look, it's there. The red envelope. I can see it from here.'

A little uncertain as to what he should do, the assistant turned and extracted the envelopes from a numbered pigeon hole behind him. There were three of them. He placed the red envelope on the counter in front of the reporter, with the other two envelopes to one side. He was trying to confirm that the name on the envelope, c/o

174

Charles Collingridge, matched that of the reporter's identity cards while the camera zoomed in closely on the other two envelopes. It took a few seconds for the operator to focus the concealed equipment properly, but as he did so, the markings on the envelopes came clearly into view. Both were addressed to Charles Collingridge. One bore the imprint of the Union Bank of Turkey. The other had been sent from the Party's Sales and Literature Office at Smith Square.

The presenter turned once more to confront Collingridge – and there was no doubt left in Collingridge's mind that the triumphant interview had now turned into open confrontation.

'The first envelope would seem to confirm that the address was indeed used to buy and sell shares in the Renox Chemical Company through the Union Bank of Turkey. But we were puzzled about the letter from your own party headquarters. So we called your Sales and Literature Office, pretending to be a supplier with an order from Charles Collingridge but with an indecipherable address.'

Collingridge was just about to shout an angry denunciation of the immoral and underhand methods adopted by the programme when the studio was filled with the recorded sound of the telephone call.

'. . . so could you just confirm what address we should have for Mr Collingridge and then we can get the goods off to him straight away.'

'Just one minute, please,' said an eager young man's voice. 'I'll call it up on the screen.'

There was the sound of a keyboard being tapped. 'Ah, here it is. Charles Collingridge, 216 Praed Street, Paddington, London W2.'

'Thank you very much indeed. You have been most helpful.'

The presenter turned once again to Collingridge. 'Do you wish to comment, Prime Minister?'

He shook his head, uncertain of what to say, or whether he should walk off the set. He was astonished that Charles was registered with the Sales and Literature Office, because he had only ever shown interest in the social side of politics. But he suspected that this was likely to be the least of his surprises.

'Of course, we took seriously your explanation that it might be a case of mistaken identity, of confusion with another Charles Collingridge.'

Collingridge wanted to shout in protest that it was not 'his' explanation, that it was simply an off-hand and speculative remark made without prejudice by his press secretary. But he knew it would be a waste of time, so he remained silent.

'Do you know how many other Charles Collingridges there are listed in the London telephone directory, Prime Minister?'

Collingridge offered no response, but sat there looking grim and ashen faced.

The presenter came to the assistance of his silent guest. 'There are no other Charles Collingridges listed in the London telephone directory. Indeed, sources at British Telecom tell us that there is only one Charles Collingridge listed throughout the United Kingdom. Your brother, Prime Minister.'

Again a pause, inviting a response, but none was offered.

'Since a Mr Charles Collingridge seems to have acted on inside information concerning the Renox Chemical Company and decisions of the Department of Health relating to it, we asked both organisations if they had any knowledge of a Charles Collingridge. Renox tells us that neither they, nor their subsidiaries, have any Collingridge amongst their employees. The Department of Health's press office was rather more cagey, promising to get back to us but never did. However, their trade union office was much more cooperative. They, too, confirmed that there is no Collingridge listed as working at any of the Department's 508 offices throughout the country.'

The presenter shuffled his notes. 'Apparently they did have a Minnie Collingridge who worked at their Coventry office until two years ago, but she went back to Jamaica.'

'They're laughing at me,' screamed Collingridge to

176

himself. 'They have convicted, sentenced and now are executing me!' In the background he could see Sarah, and the tears which were running like rivers of blood down her cheeks.

'Prime Minister. We have almost come to the end of our programme. Is there anything you wish to say?'

Collingridge sat there, staring ahead at Sarah, wanting to run to her and embrace her and lie to her that there was no need for tears, everything would be all right. He was still sitting motionless in his chair a full minute later, as the eerie studio silence was broken by the programme's theme music. While the lights dimmed and the credits rolled, the viewers saw him rise from his seat, walk slowly over to embrace his sobbing wife, and start whispering all those lies.

When they arrived back at Downing Street, Collingridge went straight to the Cabinet Room. He entered almost like a visitor, looking slowly and with a new eye around the room, at its elegant furnishings, fine classical architecture and historic paintings. Yet his gaze kept coming back to the Cabinet table itself, symbol of the uniquely British form of collective Government. He walked slowly around it, trailing his hand on the green baize cloth, stopping at the far end at the seat he had first occupied ten years ago as the Cabinet's most junior member. He raised his eyes to meet those of Robert Walpole, who seemed to be looking directly at him.

'What would you have done, old fellow?' he whispered. 'Fight, I suppose. And if you didn't win that one then fight and fight again. Well, we'll see.'

He reached his own chair and settled slowly into it, feeling physically lost as he sat alone at the middle of the great table. He reached for the single telephone which stood beside his blotter. There was a duty telephonist on call every hour of the day and night.

'Get me the Chancellor of the Exchequer, please.'

It took less than a minute before the receiver buzzed, with the Chancellor on the line.

'Colin, did you see it? How badly will the markets react tomorrow?'

The Chancellor gave an embarrassed but honest opinion.

'Bloody, eh? We shall have to see what can be done about it. We shall be in touch.'

He then spoke to the Foreign Secretary. 'What damage, Patrick?'

Woolton told him bluntly that with the Government's reputation so weak it would now be impossible to achieve the reforms of the Common Market's budgetary system which the United Kingdom Government had long been demanding and which had been made a clear priority during the election. 'A month ago it was there, within our grasp, after all these years. Now we carry about as much political clout around the negotiating table as O'Reilly's donkey. Sorry, Henry, you asked me to be brutally frank.'

Then it was the turn of the Party Chairman. Williams could hear the formal tone being used by Collingridge on the end of the phone, and responded in kind.

'Prime Minister, within the last hour I have had calls from seven of our eleven Regional Party Chairmen. Without exception, I am sorry to say, they think the situation is quite disastrous for the Party. They feel that we are beyond the point of no return.'

'No, Teddy,' contradicted Collingridge. 'They feel that *I* am beyond the point of no return. There's a difference.'

He made one more phone call, to his private secretary asking him to seek an appointment at the Palace around lunchtime the following day. The secretary rang back four minutes later to say Her Majesty looked forward to seeing him at 1 o'clock.

He felt suddenly relieved, as if the tremendous weight had already shifted from his shoulders. He looked up one last time to face Walpole.

'Oh, yes. You would have fought. You would probably have won. But this office has already ruined my brother and now it is ruining me. I will not let it ruin Sarah's happiness, too. If you will excuse me, I had better let her know.'

178

Walpole's forty-ninth successor as Prime Minister strode towards the Cabinet Room door for almost the last time and, with his hand on the brass handle, turned once more.

'By the way, it already feels better.'

PART THREE
THE DEAL

Monday 25th October

Shortly before 10 o'clock the following morning, the members of the Cabinet assembled around the Cabinet table. They had been called individually to Downing Street rather than as a formal Cabinet, and most had been surprised to discover their colleagues also gathered. There was an air of expectation and great curiosity, and the conversation around the table while they waited for their Prime Minister was unusually muffled.

As the tones of Big Ben striking the hour reached into the room, the door opened and Collingridge walked in.

'Good morning, gentlemen.' His voice was unusually soft. 'I am grateful to see you all here. I shall not detain you long.'

He took his seat, and extracted a single sheet of paper from the leather bound file he was carrying. He laid it carefully on the table in front of him, and then looked slowly around at his colleagues. There was not a sound to be heard in the room.

'I am sorry I was unable to inform you that this morning's meeting was to be one of the full Cabinet. As you will shortly see, it was necessary to ensure that you could all be assembled without creating undue attention and speculation amongst the press.'

He let out a long sigh, a mixture of pain and relief.

'I am going to read to you a short statement that I shall be issuing later today. At 1 o'clock I shall be going to the Palace to convey the contents to Her Majesty. I must ask all of you, on your oaths of office, not to divulge the contents of this message to anyone before it is officially released. I must ensure Her Majesty hears it from me and not through the press. I would also ask it of each one of you as a personal favour to me.'

He looked slowly around the table to catch the eye of those present, all of whom nodded their assent as he did so. He picked up the sheet of paper and began to read in a slow, matter-of-fact voice. He squeezed out any trace of regret he might have felt.

'Recently there has been a spate of allegations in the media about the business affairs of both me and my family, which shows no sign of abating.

'I have consistently stated, and repeat today, that I have done nothing of which I should be ashamed. I have adhered strictly to the rules and conventions relating to the conduct of the Prime Minister.

'The implied allegation made against me is one of the most serious kind for any holder of public office, that I have used that office and the confidential information available to me from it to enrich my family. I cannot explain the extraordinary circumstances referred to by the media which have given rise to these allegations, and I have asked the Cabinet Secretary to undertake a formal independent investigation into them.

'The nature of these allegations makes it impossible for me to prove my innocence of the charge of misconduct, but I am confident that the official investigation by the Cabinet Secretary will eventually establish the full facts of the matter and my complete exoneration.'

He swallowed hard; his mouth was dry and increasingly he was struggling with some of the words.

'However, this investigation will inevitably take some time to complete, and in the meantime the spread of doubts and insinuations is doing real harm to the normal business of Government, and also to my Party. While the time and attention of the Government should be devoted to implementing the programme on which we were so recently re-elected, this is not proving possible in present circumstances.

'The integrity of the office of Prime Minister has been brought into question, and it is my first duty to protect that office. Therefore, to re-establish and preserve that unquestioned integrity, I have today asked the permission of Her Majesty the Queen to relinquish the office of Prime Minister as soon as a successor can be chosen.'

There was a sharp intake of breath from somewhere around the table, but otherwise there was absolute silence throughout the room. Hearts had momentarily stopped beating.

Collingridge cleared his throat and continued.

'I have devoted my entire adult life to the pursuit of my political ideals, and it goes against every bone in my body to leave office in this fashion. I am not running away from the allegations, but rather ensuring that they may be cleared up as quickly and expeditiously as possible, and striving to bring a little peace back to my family. I believe history will show that I have made the right judgement.'

Collingridge replaced the piece of paper in his folder. 'Gentlemen, thank you,' he said curtly, and in an instant strode out of the door and was gone.

Urquhart sat at the end of the Cabinet table transfixed. As the murmuring and gasps of surprise broke out around him he would not, could not, join in. He gazed for a long time at the Prime Minister's empty chair, exulting in his own immense power.

He had done this. Alone he had destroyed the most influential man in the country, wielding might beyond the dreams of the petty men who sat with him around that table. And he knew he was the only one of them who could truly justify filling that empty seat. The others were pygmies, ants.

He was seized by the same exhilarating perspective which had gripped him forty years earlier when as a raw military recruit he had prepared to make his first parachute jump 2,500 feet above the fields of Lincolnshire. All the instruction in the world could not have prepared him for the chilling excitement as he sat in the open hatchway of a twin engine Islander, his feet dangling in the fierce slipstream, gazing down at the green and yellow landscape far below.

He was attached to a parachute which in turn was fastened to a static line and this, so the instructors had assured him, would guarantee a safe landing. But this was no matter of mere logic. It was an act of faith, of trust in one's destiny, a willingness to accept the danger if that were the only way of finding the fulfilment which every real man sought. Despite the logic of the static line, sometimes even the most courageous of men froze in the open hatchway as his faith deserted him and his self-respect was ripped away in the slipstream. Yet Urquhart had felt omnipotent, God-like, viewing His Kingdom from on high, disdaining the logic and fears which beset the ordinary mortals around him.

As he gazed now at the empty chair, he knew there was no time for doubt. He must have faith in himself and his destiny. He had launched himself and was rushing through the air until he reached that point on the very edge of discovery where he would find what Destiny had decided for him. He gave an inner smile of anticipation, while contriving outwardly to look as shocked as those around him.

Still shivering from the excitement, Urquhart walked the few yards back to the Chief Whip's office in Downing Street. He locked himself in his private room and by 10.20 a.m. he had made two phone calls.

Shortly after 10.30, Roger O'Neill called a meeting of the entire press office at party headquarters.

'I'm afraid I am going to have to ask you to cancel all your lunch arrangements today. I've had the word that shortly after 1 o'clock this afternoon we are to expect a very important statement from Downing Street. It's absolutely confidential, I cannot tell you what it is about, but we have to be ready to handle it. It's a real blockbuster.'

By 11 a.m., five journalists had been contacted by various press officers in party headquarters to apologise for not being able to make lunch. All of them were sworn to secrecy and told with various shades of detail and speculation that 'something big was going on in Downing Street'.

Charles Goodman of the Press Association, using the formidable range of contacts and favours he had built up over the years, quickly discovered that there had been a meeting of all Cabinet Ministers at Downing Street that morning, although the Number Ten press office had nothing to say on the matter. Too many official schedules for 10 a.m. had been hastily altered for anyone to be able to hide the fact. On a hunch he then phoned the Buckingham Palace press office, which also had nothing to say – at least officially. But the deputy press secretary there had worked with Goodman many years before on the *Manchester Evening News*, and confirmed entirely off the record and totally unattributably that Collingridge had asked for an audience at 1 p.m.

By 11.25 a.m. the PA tape was carrying the story of the secret Cabinet meeting and the unscheduled audience expected soon to take place between the Prime Minister and the Queen, an entirely factual report.

By midday IRN local radio was running a sensationalised lead item on their news programmes.

'The news at noon is that Henry Collingridge will soon be on his way for a secret meeting with Her Majesty the Queen. Speculation has exploded in Westminster during the last hour that either he is going to sack several of his leading Ministers and inform the Queen of a major Cabinet reshuffle, or he is going to admit his guilt to recent charges of insider trading with his brother. There are even rumours that she is going to sack him. Whatever the outcome, it seems certain that in just over an hour's time somebody in Government is going to be very unhappy.'

In fact it took less than a couple of minutes to infuriate Henry Collingridge for, when the Prime Minister looked out of his front window, the other side of the street was obscured in a forest of television cameras around which was camped an army of reporters and press photographers.

He was purple with rage as he slammed the door of his office shut with a noise which echoed along the corridor. Two passing messengers witnessed his fury. 'What was that he was muttering?' asked one.

'Didn't quite get it, Jim. Something about "oaths of office".'

When Collingridge walked out through the front door and into his car at 12.45, he ignored the screams of the press corps from the other side of the road. He drove off into Whitehall, where he was pursued by a camera car which in its eagerness to chase him nearly crashed into the rear of the Prime Minister's police escort. There was another crowd of photographers outside the gates of Buckingham Palace. His attempt at a dignified resignation had turned into a three-ring circus.

As he watched these frenzied scenes on live television, Benjamin Landless, alerted more than two hours earlier by Urquhart, contented himself with a broad smile and a second bottle of champagne.

The Prime Minister had asked not to be disturbed unless it was absolutely necessary. After returning from the Palace, he had retired to the private apartment above Downing Street, wanting to be alone with his wife for a few hours. Somehow, those official papers no longer seemed so pressing.

The private secretary apologised. 'I'm terribly sorry, Prime Minister, but it's Dr Christian. He said it was important.'

The phone buzzed gently as the call was put through.

'Dr Christian. How can I help you? And how is Charles?'

'It's about Charles I'm calling, Mr Collingridge. As we have discussed before, I have been keeping him very isolated and away from the newspapers so that he wasn't disturbed by all the allegations. But we have a problem. Normally we switch his television off and find something to divert him during news programmes, but we weren't expecting the unscheduled programme about your resignation – I'm deeply sorry you've had to resign, by the way, but it's about Charles I am most worried. I have to put his interests first, you understand.'

'I do understand, Dr Christian, and you have your priorities absolutely right.'

'He heard of the allegations about you and himself for the very first time, and how they had helped bring about your resignation. He is deeply upset and disturbed, Mr

Collingridge; it's come as a great shock. He believes he is to blame for all that's happened, and I'm afraid is talking about doing harm to himself. I thought we were just on the verge of making real progress in his case, and now I fear this will not only set him right back but in his present delicate emotional state could bring about a real crisis for him. I don't wish to alarm you unduly, but he needs your help. Very badly.'

Sarah saw the look of anguish on her husband's face, and came over to sit beside him and hold his hand. It was trembling.

'Doctor, what can I do? I'll do anything, anything you want.'

'We need to find some way of reassuring him. He's desperately confused.'

There was a pause as Collingridge bit deep into his lip, hoping it would distract from the pain burning inside.

'May I talk to him, doctor?'

There was a wait of several minutes as Charles was brought to the telephone.

'Charlie, how are you old boy?' he said softly.

'Henry, what have I done to you? I've ruined you, destroyed you!' The voice sounded old, touched by hysteria.

'Charlie, Charlie. You've done nothing. It's not you who has hurt me, you have nothing to feel guilty about.'

'But I've seen it on the television. You going off to the Queen to resign. They said it was because of me and some shares. I don't understand it, Henry, I've screwed it all up. Not only my life, but you and Sarah too. I don't deserve to be your brother. There's no point in anything any more.'

There was a huge, gulping sob on the end of the phone.

'Charlie, I want you to listen to me very carefully. Are you listening? It's not you who should be asking for pardon, but me who should be down on my knees begging for forgiveness from you.'

He cut through the protest beginning to emerge from his brother.

'No, listen, Charlie! We've always got through our problems together, as family. Remember when I was running

189

the business – the year we nearly went bust? We were going down, Charlie, and it was my fault. And who brought in that new client, that order which saved us? I know it wasn't the biggest order the company ever had, but it couldn't have come at a more vital time. You saved the company, Charlie, and you saved me. Just like you did when I was a bloody fool and got caught driving over the limit that Christmas. The local police sergeant was a rugger playing friend of *yours*, not mine, and it was you who somehow managed to persuade him to fix the breath test at the station. If I had lost my licence then, I would never have been selected by the constituency for the seat. Don't you see, Charlie, far from ruining it for me, you made it all possible. We've always faced things together, and that's just how it's going to stay.'

'But now I've ruined everything for you, Henry . . .'

'No, it's me that's ruined things. I got too high and bloody mighty, and forgot that the only thing that matters in the end is those you love. You were always around when I needed help, all the time. But I got too busy. When Mary left, I knew how much you were hurting. I should have been there. You needed me, but there always seemed other things to do. I was always going to come and see you tomorrow, or the next day. Always tomorrow, Charlie, always tomorrow.'

The emotion was cracking Collingridge's voice.

'I've had my moment of glory, I've been selfish, I've done the things that *I* wanted to do. While I watched you become an alcoholic and practically kill yourself.'

It was the first time that either of them had spoken that truth. Charles had always been under the weather, or over-tired, or suffering from nerves – never uncontrollably, alcoholically drunk. They both knew there were no secrets now, no going back.

'I will walk out of Downing Street and will be able to say good bloody riddance – if only I know I still have my brother. I'm just terrified, Charlie, that it's too late, that I've neglected you too much to be able to ask for your forgiveness, that you've been alone too long for you to want to get better.'

190

The tears of genuine anguish were flowing down his cheeks. Sarah was hugging him tightly.

'Charlie, without your forgiveness, all this will have been for nothing.'

There was silence from the other end of the phone.

'Say something, Charlie!' he said in desperation.

'I love you, big brother.'

He let out a sigh of release and total joy.

'I love you too, old boy. I'll come and see you tomorrow. We'll both have a lot more time for each other now, eh?'

They were both laughing through the tears, with Sarah joining in. Henry Collingridge hadn't felt so whole for years.

She was sipping a drink, admiring the night view of London from his penthouse apartment when he came up behind her and embraced her warmly.

'Hey, I thought we came here to discuss business,' she said, not resisting.

'There are some things I don't have the words for,' he said, burying his face in her blonde hair and rejoicing at its freshness.

She turned round in his arms to face him and look directly into his eyes.

'You talk too much,' she said, and kissed him passionately. She was glad he had made the first move; she was not competing tonight, she wanted to be free, uncomplicated, just a woman.

She made no sound of protest as he slipped her silk blouse over her shoulders and it fell away, revealing a smooth and unblemished skin which could have been a model's. Her breasts were immaculate, small but very feminine and sensitive. She gasped as his fingers gently ran over her nipples, which responded instantly. She undid her own belt and let her trousers fall straight to the floor, stepping out of them and out of her shoes in one graceful movement. She stood tall and unashamed against the glittering lights of London behind her.

He marvelled for a moment at what he saw. He couldn't

remember when he last had felt like this, so excited and so much a man.

'Mattie, you look lovely.'

'I hope you are not just going to look, Johnnie,' she said.

He took her to the fireplace where the flames flickered invitingly, held her close against him and prayed that the moment would last for ever.

When they were spent, for some while they lay silently on the rug, lost in their thoughts and each other's arms. It was Mattie who broke the spell.

'Is it all coincidence, Johnnie?'

'Let's try again and see.'

'Not this, you fool,' she laughed. 'It's time to talk now!'

'Oh, I wondered how long it would take you to get back to that,' he said with an air of resignation. He got them both blankets to wrap themselves in.

'We find a plan, effort, plot – call it what you will – in which our paper is involved, to chop the legs off Collingridge. For all we know it has been going on for months. Now Collingridge resigns. Is it all part of the same operation?'

'How can it be, Mattie? In the end Collingridge hasn't been forced out by his opponents but by his brother's apparent fiddling of share purchases. You're surely not suggesting all that was part of the plan.'

'You have to admit it's a hell of a coincidence, Johnnie. I've met Charles Collingridge, spent several hours drinking and chatting with him at the party conference, as it happens. He struck me as being a pleasant and straightforward drunk, who certainly didn't seem as if he had two hundred pounds to put together, let alone being able to raise tens of thousands of pounds to start speculating in shares.'

Her face was screwed up in concentration as she grappled with her still confused thoughts. 'It may seem silly, I know he's an alcoholic and they often aren't responsible for their actions, but I don't believe he would have jeopardised his brother's whole career for a few thousand pounds' profit on the Stock Market. And do you really think it's likely that Henry Collingridge, the Prime Minister of this country, was feeding his drunk brother insider share tips to finance his boozing?'

'Is it any more credible to believe there is some form of high-level plot involving senior party figures, the publisher of our newspaper and God knows who else to kill off the Prime Minister? Surely the easiest explanation is the simple one – that Charles Collingridge is a drunk who is not responsible for his actions and who has done something so overwhelmingly stupid that his brother's had to resign.'

'There's only one person who can tell us, I suppose. Charles Collingridge.'

'But he's locked away in some clinic or other, isn't he? I thought his whereabouts were a closely guarded family secret.'

'True, but he's the only one who could help us get to the bottom of this.'

'And how does our Reporter of the Year propose to do that?' he teased.

She was concentrating too intently to rise to the bait. Instead, she sat on the hearth rug wrapped deep in thought and an enormous yellow blanket while he refreshed their drinks. As he returned with two glasses, she spun round to face him.

'When was the last time anyone saw Charles Collingridge?' she demanded.

'Why, er . . . When he was driven away from his home over a week ago.'

'Who was he with?'

'Sarah Collingridge.'

'And . . . ?'

'A driver.'

'Who was the driver, Johnnie?'

'Damned if I know. Never seen him before. Hang on, being a dutiful deputy editor I keep all the nightly news on tape for a fortnight, so I should have it here somewhere.'

He rummaged around by his video player for a few moments before slotting a tape into the chamber and winding it forward. In a few seconds, through the blizzard produced by the fast replay button, appeared the scenes of Charles Collingridge huddled in the back of the fleeing car.

'Go back!' she ordered. 'To the start.'

And there, for less than a second at the front of the report, as the car swept from behind the building into the main road, they could clearly see the face of the driver through the windscreen.

Krajewski punched the freeze frame button. They both sat there entranced, staring at the balding and bespectacled face.

'And who the hell is he?' muttered Krajewski.

'Let's figure out who he's *not*,' said Mattie. 'He's not a Government driver – it's not a Government car and the drivers pool is very gossipy, so we would have heard something. He's not a political figure or we would have recognised him . . .'

She clapped her hands in inspiration. 'Johnnie, where were they going?'

'Not to Downing Street, not to some hotel or other public place.' He pondered the options. 'To the clinic, I suppose.'

'Precisely! That man is from the clinic. If we can find out who he is, we shall know where Charles is!'

'OK, Clark Kent. Seems fair enough. Look, I can get a hard copy of the face off the video tape and show it around. We could try old Freddie, one of our staff photographers. Not only does he have an excellent memory for faces, he is also an alcoholic who dried out a couple of years ago. He still goes religiously every week to Alcoholics Anonymous, and he might well be able to put us on the right track. There aren't that many treatment centres, we should be able to make some progress – but I still don't accept your conspiracy theory, Mattie. It's still all much more likely to be circumstance and coincidence.'

'You cynical bastard, what do I have to do to convince you?'

'Come here and show me a little more of that feminine intuition of yours,' he growled.

At almost exactly the same time in the private booth of a fashionable and overpriced restaurant in the West End of London, Landless and Urquhart were also locked together, in an embrace of an entirely mercenary kind.

'Interesting times, Frankie, interesting times,' mused Landless.

'In China, I believe, it is a curse to live in interesting times.'

'I'm sure Collingridge agrees!' said Landless, bursting into gruff laughter.

He tapped the ash off his thick Havana cigar and savoured the large cognac before returning to his guest.

'Frankie, I invited you here this evening to ask just one question. I shan't beat around the bush, and I shall thank you to be absolutely blunt with me. Are you going to stand for the leadership?' He glared directly at Urquhart, trying to intimidate him into total frankness.

'I can't tell yet. The situation is very unclear, and I shall have to wait for the dust to settle a little . . .'

'OK, Frankie, let me put it this way. Do you want it? Because if you do, old son, I can be very helpful to you.'

Urquhart returned his host's direct stare, looking deep into the protruding, bloodshot eyes.

'I want it very, very much.'

It was the first time he admitted to anyone other than himself his burning desire to hold the reins of Prime Ministerial power, yet with Landless, who wore his naked ambition on his sleeve, he felt no embarrassment in the confession.

'That's good. Let's start from there. Let me tell you what the *Telegraph* will be running tomorrow. It's an analysis piece by our political correspondent, Mattie Storin. Pretty blonde girl with long legs and big blue eyes – d'you know her, Frankie?'

'Yes,' mused Urquhart. 'Only professionally, of course,' he hastened to add as he saw the fleshy lips of his companion preparing a lewd comment. 'Bright, too. I'm interested to discover how she sees things.'

'Says it is an open race for the leadership, that Collingridge's resignation has come so quickly and unexpectedly that no potential successor has got his public case prepared very well. So almost anything could happen.'

'I believe she is right,' nodded Urquhart. 'Which worries

me. The whole election process could be over in less than three weeks, and it's the slick, flashy television performers who will gain the best start. The tide is everything in winning these contests; if it's with you, it will sweep you home; flowing against you, then no matter how good a swimmer you are, you'll still drown.'

'Which slick, flashy television performers in particular?'

'Try Michael Samuel.'

'Mmmm, young, impressive, principled, seems intelligent – not at all to my liking. He wants to interfere in everything, rebuild the world. Got too much of a conscience for my liking, and not enough experience in taking hard, sound decisions.'

'So what do we do?' asked Urquhart.

Landless cupped the crystal goblet in his huge hands, swirled the dark liquor and chuckled quietly.

'Frankie, tides turn. You can be swimming strongly for the shore one minute, and the next be swept out to sea . . .'

He took a huge gulp of cognac, raised his finger to order another round, and settled his bulk as comfortably as he could into his chair before resuming the conversation.

'Frankie, this afternoon I instructed a small and extremely confidential team at the *Telegraph* to start contacting as many of the Government's Members of Parliament as they can get hold of in the next twenty-four hours to ask which way they are going to vote. In the next edition of the *Telegraph*, they will publish the results – which I confidently predict will show Mr Samuel with a small but clear lead over the rest of the field.'

'What?' exclaimed Urquhart in horror. 'How do you know this? The poll hasn't even been finished yet . . .'

'Frankie, I know what the poll is going to say because I am the publisher of the bloody newspaper.'

'You mean you've fixed it? But why are you pushing Samuel?'

'Because although the poll will show a very reasonable level of support for you, at the moment you can't win the contest. You're the Chief Whip, you don't have any great public platform from which to preach, and if it becomes a free-for-all you're going to get trampled in the rush.'

Urquhart had to acknowledge the weakness of his position as the faceless man of Government.

'So we push Mr Samuel, get him off to a roaring start, which means instead of a free-for-all we have a target at which everyone is going to shoot. In a couple of weeks' time, he's going to be amazed at the number of bad friends he's got within the Party, all trying to do him down. He'll be on the defensive. Fighting the tide.'

Urquhart was astonished at the clarity of the Landless analysis, and began to understand why the East-Ender had become such a striking success in the business world.

'So where do I come into this great plan?'

'You've got to develop a unique selling proposition for yourself, something which will be attractive to your fellow MPs and set you apart from your rivals.'

'Such as?' asked the bewildered Urquhart.

'Frankie, you become the archetypal compromise candidate. While all those other bastards are shooting and stabbing each other in public, you slip quietly through as the man they all hate least.'

'That's what the Social Democrats used to pin their hopes on. Remember them? And frankly I'm not sure I have much of a reputation as being the obvious compromise candidate.'

'But the Social Democrats didn't have my help or my bunch of newspapers behind them. You will. High risks, I know, Frankie. But then they are high rewards.'

'What do I have to do?'

'To catch the tide, your timing has to be right. Frankly, I would be happier if there were a little time – perhaps a month – between now and when the voting starts to give the other contenders time to tire, for their campaigns to ship a little water and to get everyone bored with the choice of candidates on offer. Then you discover a large press campaign promoting your late and unexpected entry into the race, which brings back an element of excitement and relief. The tide starts running with *you*, Francis.'

Urquhart noted that Landless had called him by his

proper name for the first time. The man was absolutely serious about his proposal.

'So you want me to see if I can slow the election procedure down a little.'

'Can you do it?'

'Although Humphrey Newlands runs the election, according to the Party's constitution the timing of the ballot is entirely in the hands of the Prime Minister, and he would do nothing to help Teddy Williams' favoured candidate. So I think there's a damned good chance . . .'

TUESDAY 26TH OCTOBER

'Prime Minister, I haven't had a chance to speak with you since your announcement yesterday. I can't tell you how shocked and – devastated I was.'

'Francis, that's very kind of you. But no sympathy, please. I feel absolutely content with the situation. In any event, I have little time today for second thoughts. Humphrey Newlands is coming in twenty minutes so we can get the leadership election process under way, then I'm off to spend the rest of the day with my brother Charles. It's marvellous to have time for such things!' he exclaimed.

Urquhart was astonished to see he meant every word of it.

'Prime Minister, you don't appear to be in a mood for maudlin sentiments, so I shan't spend any time adding to them. But you must know how deeply saddened I am. As I listened to you yesterday I felt as if I . . . were falling out of the sky, quite literally. But enough. Let's look forward, not back. It seems to me that some of our colleagues have served you rather badly in recent months, not showing the support you deserved. Now while you have already said you will not support any particular candidate in the election, I suspect you have some clear views as to whom you do *not* wish to get his hands on the leadership. As things stand at the moment I have no intention of becoming a candidate myself, so I thought you might like me to keep you informed of what's going on and give you some feedback from the Parliamentary Party on the state of play. I know you are not going to interfere, but perhaps that won't stop you taking a close interest . . .'

They both knew that even a failed Party Leader in his last days still has enough influence to sway a crucial body

199

of opinion within the Parliamentary Party. It is not only the favours he has accumulated from placemen over time, but also the not inconsiderable matter of his nominations for the Resignation Honours List, which every retiring Prime Minister is allowed to make. For many senior members of the Party, this would be their last chance to rise above the mob of ordinary parliamentarians and achieve the social status to which their wives had so long aspired.

'Francis, that's most understanding.' Collingridge was clearly in a relaxed and very trusting mood. 'You know, the Prime Minister is expected to be aware of everything that's going on but, as I have discovered to my cost, it's so easy to get isolated, to have events just slip past you without making any contact with them. I suspect dear old Sir Humphrey is past giving the best intelligence on the state of parliamentary opinion, so I would very much welcome your advice. As you so delicately put it, I shall certainly take a close interest in the matter of who is to succeed me. So tell me, how do things look?'

'Early days yet, very difficult to tell. I think most of the press are right to suggest it's an open race. But I would expect things to develop quickly once they get going.'

'No front runners yet, then?'

'Well, one perhaps who seems to have something of a head start. Michael Samuel.'

'Michael! Why so?'

'Simply that it's going to be a short and furious race, with little room for developing solid arguments or issues. In those circumstances, the ones who use television well are going to have a strong advantage. And, of course, he's going to have the strong if subtle support of Teddy and party headquarters.'

Collingridge's face clouded. 'Yes. I see what you mean.' He drummed his fingers loudly on the arm of his chair, weighing his words carefully.

'Francis, I shall be absolutely scrupulous in not favouring any candidate in this race. My only concern is to let the Party have a fair and free leadership election so they can make their own choice. But you make it sound as if the election won't be as open as it perhaps should be, with party headquarters playing too influential a role.'

He chose his words carefully, and uttered them slowly and softly. 'I would not welcome that. I don't think Teddy's bunch of merry men has distinguished itself recently. A poor election campaign, then all those infuriating bloody leaks. Now I'm told that the news of my visit to the Palace yesterday also leaked out of the backdoor at Smith Square.'

His tone hardened. 'I can't forgive that, Francis. The Cabinet swore on their oaths of office to keep it confidential, to let me offer my resignation with some dignity instead of being the clown in a damned media circus. I will not stand for it. I will not have party headquarters interfering in this election!'

He leaned towards Urquhart. 'I suspect you have no great love for Teddy Williams, particularly after he did such an effective demolition job on your reshuffle proposals – I'm sure you guessed that at the time.'

Urquhart was glad to have his suspicions confirmed. On Judgement Day it might help to justify a lot of his recent actions.

'So what can I do, Francis, to make sure this election is run properly?'

Urquhart smiled to himself. A 'proper' election was now defined as one in which Michael Samuel felt the full force of the Prime Minister's revenge.

'My interests, like yours, are simply to ensure fair play. I know that neither you nor I wish to interfere in any way – let party democracy have its way, of course. My only concern is that the process is likely to go ahead in such a rush that there will be no proper time for mature reflection or consideration. In the past, leadership elections have taken place only a week to ten days after they were announced – Ted Heath was elected just five days after Alec Douglas-Home resigned – but on those occasions the resignations were expected. People had time to think, to make a proper and balanced judgement. That won't be the case this time. I'm afraid it will all be over in a breathless rush, and become just another part of the media circus.'

'So?'

'So give them just a little longer to make their choice. Slow the pace down. Enjoy your last few weeks in office, and hand over to a successor who has been chosen by the Party, not the media.'

'What you say makes sense. I've no wish to extend the period of uncertainty while the campaign is fought, but I'm sure an extra week or so could do no great harm.'

He extended his hand towards Urquhart. 'Francis, I'm sorry to cut this short; Humphrey will be waiting outside. I shall have to consult him as Chairman of the Backbench Committee, but the final choice on timing is entirely in my hands. I'm going to think very carefully overnight about what you have said, and let you know in the morning what I decide.'

He led the Chief Whip towards the door. 'I'm so grateful, Francis. It's really comforting to have a source of advice with no axe to grind.'

Daily Telegraph. Wednesday 27th October. Page 1.

Samuel is favoured candidate – takes early lead in party soundings

Michael Samuel, the youthful Environment Secretary, was last night emerging as the early front runner to succeed Henry Collingridge as Party Leader and Prime Minister.

In a poll conducted during the last two days by the *Telegraph* amongst 212 of the 337 Government MPs eligible to vote, 24 per cent nominated him as their first choice in the forthcoming party leadership election, well ahead of other potential candidates.

While Samuel has yet to announce his candidature, he is expected to do so soon. Moreover, he is expected to get the backing of influential party figures such as Lord Williams, the Party Chairman, whose influence as the Party's elder statesman could be crucial.

No other name attracted more than 18 per cent. Five potential candidates obtained between 12 per cent and 18 per cent, including Patrick Woolton the Foreign Secretary, Arnold Dollis the Home Secretary, Harold Earle the Education Secretary, Peter McKenzie the Health Secretary, and Francis Urquhart the Chief Whip.

The inclusion of Urquhart's name in the list at 14 per cent caused something of a surprise last night at Westminster, as he is not even a full member of the Cabinet. As Chief Whip he has a strong base in the Parliamentary Party and could be a strong outside candidate. However, sources close to Urquhart last night emphasised he had made no decision to enter the contest, and he would clarify his position sometime today.'

'Mattie, I think I've got it!'

Krajewski was striding across the room as if he had discovered a blazing fire in his pocket. He was breathless with excitement. As he reached Mattie's desk in the *Telegraph* news room, he pulled a 10×12 colour photograph out of the large manila envelope he was clutching, and threw it on her desk. The face of the driver stared at her, slightly blurred and distorted from the lines of the video screen, but nonetheless clearly recognisable.

'Freddie came up trumps. He took this along to his meeting of AA last night, and the group leader recognised it immediately. It's a Dr Robert Christian, who's a well known authority on the treatment of drug and alcohol addiction. Runs a treatment centre in a large private house near the south coast in Kent. That's where our Charlie is bound to be.' He was flushed with triumph.

'Johnnie, I could kiss you – but not in the office!'

His face contorted into a picture of mock misery.

'And there I was hoping you would want to sleep your way to the top . . .' he said mournfully.

The Prime Minister read all the newspapers that morning. He smiled ruefully as he read the commentaries which a week before had been excoriating him and for the most part were now, in their fickle and inconstant fashion, lauding him for his statesmanlike and responsible action in allowing the Government to make a fresh start – 'although he must still resolve many outstanding personal and family issues to the public's satisfaction', thundered *The Times*. As always, the press had no shame in playing both sides.

He read the *Telegraph* particularly carefully, and twice. Their prompt polling of Government MPs had given them a lead over the other journals, many of which were forced to refer to the poll findings in their later editions. The consensus seemed to be emerging: it was an open race but Samuel was clearly the front runner.

He summoned his political secretary.

'Grahame. I want you to send an instruction to Lord Williams, with a copy to Sir Humphrey Newlands. Party headquarters are to issue a press release at 12.30 this afternoon for the lunchtime news that nominations for election as Leader of the Party will close in three weeks' time, on Thursday November 18, with the first ballot to take place on the following Tuesday November 23. If a second ballot is required it will be held as prescribed by the Party's rules on the following Tuesday, November 30, with any final run-off ballot two days later. Have you got that?'

He noticed his secretary's obvious anguish. It was the first time since his resignation announcement that they had been able to talk.

'That means in exactly six weeks and one day, Grahame, you and I will be out of a job. Don't worry. You've been an excellent aide to me. I haven't always found time as I should to thank you properly in the past, but I want you to know I'm very grateful.'

The aide shuffled with embarrassment.

'You must start thinking about your own future. I'm certain that there are several newly knighted gentlemen in the City or any other part of industry who would be happy to make you a generous offer. Think about it for a few days and let me know what interests you. I still have a few favours to cash in.'

The secretary mumbled his thanks, looking much relieved, and made to depart.

'By the way, Grahame. It's possible that the Party

204

Chairman might seek to get hold of me and encourage me to shorten the period of the election process. I shall not be available, and you are to ensure he realises that these are instructions, not terms for negotiation, and they are to be issued without fail by 12.30.'

There was a short pause.

'Otherwise, tell him, I shall be forced to leak them myself.'

It is often written that time and tide wait for no man. They certainly did not wait that day for Michael Samuel. He had been as openly astounded and as privately elated by Collingridge's bombshell as the rest of his colleagues. His natural enthusiasm had quickly turned to the positive aspect of events, and the opportunities which they afforded him. He recognised that no one started the race as favourite, and that he had as good a chance as any, if he played his cards right.

He had consulted the redoubtable Lord Williams, who agreed on his assessment of his chances. 'Patience, Michael,' he had advised. 'You will almost certainly be the youngest candidate, and they will try to say you are too youthful, too inexperienced and too ambitious. So don't look too much as if you want the job. Show a little restraint, and let them come to you.'

Which was to prove excellent advice, but entirely irrelevant to the circumstances. The media had been having a busy day. No sooner had the *Telegraph* hit the streets promoting Samuel's name than Urquhart appeared in front of television cameras to confirm that he had no intention of standing, because he felt it was in the Party's best interests that the Chief Whip should be entirely impartial in this contest. These two events had the instant effect of getting the media hunt firmly under way for those candidates who would be standing, and promoting a wide degree of praise for Urquhart's unselfishness and loyalty. The release later that morning of the detailed timetable for nomination and election only added fuel to the flames. None of which helped the front runner.

By the time the television cameras had tracked him down

to the Intercontinental Hotel off Hyde Park, which he was just about to enter for an early lunch meeting, they were in no mood to accept conditional answers. He couldn't say no, they wouldn't accept maybe, and after some considerable harassment he was forced into making a reluctant announcement that he would indeed be running.

The one o'clock news offered a clear contrast between Urquhart, in a dignified and elder party statesman role declining to run, and the youthful and apparently eager Samuel, holding an impromptu press conference on the street and launching himself as the first official candidate, nearly a month before the first ballot was to be held.

As Urquhart watched the proceedings with considerable satisfaction, the telephone rang. A gruff voice which he recognised instantly as Landless said simply, 'Moses parted the Red Sea. We shall see whether Michael can catch the tide.'

They both laughed before the voice rang off.

Saturday 30th October

The following Saturday, Mattie had a clear day. She climbed into her BMW, filled it with petrol, and pointed it in the direction of Dover. Having barged her way through the shopping crowds of Greenwich, she emerged with great relief onto the A2, the old Roman road which for nearly two thousand years had pointed the way from London into the heart of Kent. It took her past the cathedral town of Canterbury, and a few miles beyond she turned off at the picturesque little village of Barham. Her road map was not very helpful in finding the even smaller village of Norbington nearby, but with the help of several locals she found herself some while later outside a large Victorian house, bearing a subdued sign in the shrubbery which announced, 'Fellowship Treatment Centre'.

There were several cars in the driveway and the front door was open. She was surprised to see people wandering around with apparent freedom, and no sign of the formidable white coated nurses she had expected to find patrolling the grounds for potential escapees. She parked her car on the road and walked cautiously up the drive towards the door.

A large, tweed-suited gentleman with a white military moustache approached and her heart sank. This was surely the security patrol, and she had clearly been spotted as an intruder.

'Excuse me, my dear,' he said in a clipped accent as he intercepted her by the front door. 'Have you seen any member of staff about? They like to keep out of the way on family visiting days, but you can never find one when you want them.'

Mattie offered her apologies and smiled warmly in relief. She realised that by good fortune she had struck the best possible day to look around, and could lose herself amidst the other visitors.

She picked up one of the brochures which were piled on the hall table, and found a quiet chair on which to sit while she inspected it. A brief glance at the literature told her that the treatment centre was run on very different lines than she had imagined. No straitjackets, no locks on the doors, just twenty-three well-trained people waiting to give guidance, encouragement and their medical experience to addicts who sought help in an atmosphere resembling more a fashionable country retreat than an institution. Even more encouragingly for Mattie, the brochure had a plan of the thirty-two-bed house, which Mattie used to guide herself around the premises in search of her quarry.

She found him outside on a garden bench, enjoying the view across the valley and the last of the October sun. She wasn't going to enjoy the deception, but that is what she had come for.

'Why, Charles!' she exclaimed. 'What a surprise to find you here.'

He looked at her with a total lack of comprehension.

'I . . . I'm sorry,' he ventured. 'I don't recognise . . .'

'Mattie Storin. Don't you remember? We spent a most enjoyable evening together in Bournemouth a couple of weeks ago.'

'Oh, I'm sorry, Miss Storin. I don't remember. You see, I'm an alcoholic, that's why I'm here, and I'm afraid I was in no condition a few weeks ago to remember very much at all.'

She was taken aback by his frankness, and he smiled serenely.

'Please don't be embarrassed. The biggest single step I've had to make in curing myself of addiction is to admit that I am an addict. I had a million ways of hiding it, particularly from myself, and it was only when I was able to face myself that I began being able to face the outside world again. That's what this treatment centre is all about.'

Mattie suddenly blushed deeply. She realised that she

had intruded into the private world of a sick man, and she felt ashamed.

'Charles, if you don't remember who I am, then you will not remember that I am a journalist.'

The smile disappeared, to be replaced by a look of resignation.

'I suppose it had to happen at some time, although Henry was hoping that I could be left alone here quietly . . .'

'Charles, please let me explain. I've not come here to make life difficult for you, and when I leave here your privacy will continue to be respected so far as I am concerned. I think the press owe you that.'

'I think they probably do . . .'

'But I would like your help. Don't say anything for the moment, just let me talk a little.'

He nodded in encouragement.

'Your brother, the Prime Minister, has been forced to resign because of allegations that he helped you to speculate in shares and make a quick profit.'

He started to wave his hand to bring her to a halt but she pressed on.

'Charles, none of those allegations make any sense to me. You and your brother risking the office of Prime Minister for a measly few thousand pounds – it doesn't add up. What's more, I also know that someone has deliberately been trying to undermine your brother for some time by leaking damaging material to the press. But I only have suspicions. I came to see if you could point me towards something more tangible.'

'Miss Storin – Mattie, as we seem to be old friends – I am a drunk. I cannot even remember meeting you. How can I, of all people, be of help? My word carries no weight whatsoever.'

'I'm neither a judge nor a prosecutor, Charles. I'm just trying to piece together a puzzle from a thousand scattered shards.'

He looked far over the hills towards Dover and the Channel beyond, searching in the distance.

'Mattie, I've tried so hard to remember, believe me. The

thought that I have disgraced Henry and forced him into resignation is almost more than I can stand. But I know nothing about buying and selling shares, nothing at all. I don't know what the truth is. I can't help you, I'm afraid.'

'Wouldn't you have remembered something about buying the shares, if you had indeed bought them?'

'For the last month I have been a very sick . . .' – he laughed gently – '. . . a very drunk man. There are many things I have absolutely no recollection of.'

'Wouldn't you have remembered where you got the money to buy the shares, or what you did with the proceeds?'

'I admit that it's hugely unlikely I would have had a small fortune lying around without my remembering it or, more likely, spending it on alcohol. I have no idea where the money could have gone. Even I can't drink away £50,000 in just a few weeks.'

'What about the false address in Paddington?'

'A complete mystery. I don't even know where Praed Street in Paddington is when I'm sober, so it is preposterous to suppose I would have found my way there drunk. It's the other side of London from where I live.'

'But you used it – so they say – for your bank and subscription to the Party's literature service.'

Charles Collingridge roared with laughter. 'Mattie, you're beginning to restore my faith in myself. No matter how drunk I was, I cannot conceive I could possibly have shown any interest in the Party's literature service. I object when political propaganda is pushed through my letter box at election time; having to pay for it every month would be an insult!'

'Have you ever contributed to the Party's literature service?'

'Never!'

The sun was setting and a warm, red glow filled the sky, lighting up his face. He seemed visibly to be returning to health, and to be content.

'I can't prove it, but I don't believe I am guilty of the things they say I have done. It would mean a lot to me if you believed that, too.'

210

'I do, Charles, very much. And I'm going to try to prove it for you.'

She rose to leave.

'I've enjoyed your visit, Mattie. Now that we are such old friends, please come again.'

'I shall. But in the meantime, I've got a lot of digging to do.'

It was late by the time she got back to London that evening. The first editions of the Sunday newspapers were already on the streets. She bought a heavy pile of them and, with magazines and inserts slipping from her laden arms, she threw them on the back seat of her car. It was then she noticed the *Sunday Times* headline.

'Now why is Harold Earle making such a fuss about environmental matters?' she asked herself. The Education Secretary, not a noted Greenpeace lover, had just announced his intention to stand for the leadership and simultaneously had made a speech entitled 'Clean Up Our Country.'

'We have talked and talked endlessly about the problems of our inner cities, while those who live in them have been forced to watch their neighbourhoods continue to decline. In the meantime, the impoverished state of our inner cities has been matched by the deplorable degeneration of far too much of our rural countryside,' the *Sunday Times* reported him as saying. 'For too long we have neglected such issues, to our cost. Recycled expressions of concern are no substitute for positive action, and it is time we backed our fine words with finer deeds. The opinion polls show that the environment is the most important non-economic issue on which the voters say we have failed. After more than twelve years in office, this is unacceptable, and we must wake up to these concerns.'

'Silly me,' said Mattie. 'I'm getting slow in my old age. Can't decipher the code. Which Cabinet Minister is supposed to be responsible for environmental matters, and therefore responsible for this mess?'

The public fight to eliminate Michael Samuel had begun.

211

WEDNESDAY 3RD NOVEMBER

Mattie tried many times during the following week to get hold of Kevin Spence, but he was never available. In spite of the repeated assurances of his gushingly polite secretary, Mattie knew that he was deliberately avoiding her. He was therefore not at all pleased when, in some desperation, she called very late on Wednesday evening and was put straight through to his extension by the night security guard.

'No, of course I haven't been avoiding you,' he assured her, 'but I have been very busy. Working very late.'

'Kevin, I need your help again.'

'I remember the last time I gave you my help. You said you were going to write a piece on opinion polls and then you wrote a story slandering the Prime Minister. Now he's gone.' He spoke with a quiet sadness. 'He was always very decent to me, very kind, and I think the press have been unspeakably cruel.'

'Kevin, I give you my word that I was not responsible for that story. You may have noticed that my name was not on the article, and I was even more displeased about it than you. It's about Mr Collingridge's resignation that I'm calling. Personally, I don't believe the allegations which are being made against him and his brother. I would like to be able to clear his name.'

'I can't see how I could assist you,' he said in a distrusting tone. 'Anyway, I'm afraid that nobody outside the press office is allowed to have contact with the media during the leadership campaign. Chairman's strictest orders.'

'Kevin, there's a lot at stake here. Not only the leadership of the Party, and whether you are going to win the next election or not, but also whether history is going to regard Henry Collingridge as a crook and a cheat or

212

whether he is going to have a chance to put the record straight. Don't we owe him that?'

He thought about it for a second, and she heard his hostility slowly melting.

'If I could help, what would you want?'

'Very simply, do you understand the computer system at party headquarters?'

'Yes, of course. I use it all the time to help analyse opinion research. I've got a screen in front of me which is linked directly to our main frame.'

'I think your computer system has been tampered with. Will you let me see it?'

'Tampered with? That's impossible. We have the highest security. Nobody from outside can access it.'

'Not outside, Kevin. Inside.'

There was a stunned silence from the other end of the phone.

'I'm working at the House of Commons. I can be with you in less than ten minutes, and I suspect at this time of night the building is very quiet. No one will notice. Kevin, I'm on my way over.'

Before he could mutter a flustered few words of protest, the phone went dead as he held it. Mattie was with him less than seven minutes later.

They sat in his small garret office, dominated by the mountains of files which tumbled over every available flat surface and onto the floor, with their attention fixed rigidly on the glowing green screen in front of them.

'Kevin, Charles Collingridge ordered material from the Party's sales and literature service and asked them to be delivered to an address in Paddington. Right?'

'Correct. I checked it as soon as I heard, but it's there all right. Look.'

He tapped a few characters on the keyboard, and up came the incriminating evidence on the screen. 'Chas Collingridge Esq 216 Praed St Paddington London W2 — 001A/01.0091.'

'What do these other hieroglyphics mean?'

'The first set simply means that he subscribes to our comprehensive literature service and the second that his subscription has been fully paid from the beginning of the year. If he wanted to receive only the main publications, or was a member of our specialist book club or one of our other marketing programmes, that would be shown by a different set of reference numbers. Also if he were behind with his subscription payments.'

'And this information is shown on all the monitors throughout the building?'

'Yes. It's not information we regard as particularly confidential.'

'And if you felt like bending the rules a little and wanted to make me a subscriber to your comprehensive literature service, could you do that, enter my details from this terminal?'

'Without making the proper payments through the accounts department, you mean? Why . . . yes.'

Spence was beginning to follow her line of enquiry.

'You think that Charles Collingridge's details were falsely entered from a terminal within this building, Miss Storin? Yes, it could be done. Look.'

Within a few seconds the screen was showing a comprehensive literature subscription in the name of 'M Mouse Esq, 99 Disneyland Miami.'

'But you couldn't get away with backdating it to the beginning of the year because . . . What a stupid fool I am! Of course!' he exploded, and started thrashing away at the keyboard. 'If you really know what you're doing, which very few people in this building do, you can tap into the main frame subdirectory . . .'

His words were almost drowned in the clattering of the keys.

'That gives access to the more restricted financial data. So I can check the exact date when the account was paid, whether it was paid by cheque or credit card, when the subscription was first started . . .'

The monitor screen started glowing.

'And those financial details can only be entered or altered by accounts department staff with their security passwords.'

He sat back to consider the details on the screen. He

tapped a few more characters into the computer, and then turned to Mattie.

'Miss Storin. According to this, Mr Collingridge has never paid for the literature service, this month or any month. His details only appear on the distribution file, not the payment file.'

'Can you tell me when his name first appeared on the distribution file?'

A few more keystrokes.

'Jesus. Exactly two weeks ago today.'

'So someone in this building, not the accounts staff or anyone who understood computers very well, two weeks ago altered the file to include Charles Collingridge's name for the first time.'

'This is terrible, Miss Storin . . .' Spence's face had gone white.

'Kevin, can you by any chance tell me who might have altered the file, or from which terminal it was altered?'

'Sadly, no. It could have been done from any terminal in this building. The computer programme trusts us . . .' He shook his head as if he had totally failed the most crucial test of his life.

'Don't worry, Kevin. We're on the trail. But I must ask you not to utter a word of this to anyone. I want to catch whoever did this, and if he knows we're looking he will cover his trail. Will you help me once more, and keep quiet until I have something more to go on?'

'Who on earth would believe me, anyway?' he murmured.

215

SUNDAY 7TH NOVEMBER

The newspapers that weekend were irritable. In the convention of leadership elections, candidates were discouraged from outright electioneering or making personal attacks on their rivals; the right leader was supposed somehow still to 'emerge' without any apparent effort on his part from a process of consensus rather than combat. So all the press had been left with for ten days was a series of coded messages which failed to inspire the public or ignite the hoped-for forest of press headlines. The campaign had not so much run out of steam; it had simply never generated any effective heat.

So the press took it out on the candidates – they had no alternative. 'A disappointing and uninspiring campaign so far, still waiting for one of the candidates to breathe life back into the Party and Government', pronounced the *Observer*. 'Irrelevant and irritating', complained the *Sunday Mirror*. Not to be outdone, the *Sun* in characteristic style described it all as 'flatulent, a passing breeze in the night'.

Far from allowing a thorough airing of the issues, as Urquhart had predicted to the Prime Minister, the lengthy campaign was suffering from a severe dose of boredom, as all along he had secretly hoped.

This came as little comfort to Mattie, who was finding her growing conviction that skulduggery was afoot matched only by her inability to find the opportunity to proceed with her investigations. Journalists have to work much harder when there is no news to report, and the flaccid leadership campaign was causing more than a few nightmares amongst the political lobby in their collective efforts to find new angles with which to fill their column inches.

'You have to face it, Mattie, you still don't have a case,'

Johnnie told her. 'Fascinating circumstantial evidence about computers, perhaps, but what about the shares, what about the bank account, what about Paddington?'

She unwrapped herself from his arms where she had been dozing for most of Sunday afternoon. The weather was appalling, the scudding grey skies hurling angry bursts of rain against the windows. They hadn't needed much encouragement to decide to spend the whole afternoon in bed.

'Those shares were bought by whoever had the bank account and arranged the false address in Paddington,' Mattie began, marshalling her arguments. 'That's the only conclusion you can reasonably reach. But the trail is very difficult to follow. Apart from telling us that the account was opened for less than a fortnight, the bank will tell us nothing, and have point-blank refused to let us see the signatures on the documents relating to the bank account. And the Paddington tobacconists is even less helpful. I think all the attention and notoriety has put paid to some of the more profitable sidelines which he seems to have run out of his back room.'

Johnnie was not finished. 'But what is it you are trying to prove? The documentation is scarcely going to tell you any more than you know already. What you need to establish is not so much whether it was Charles Collingridge, but whether it could have been anyone other than him. If it could, along with your computer tampering you might have the beginnings of a circumstantial story.'

She rolled out of his arms to look him directly in the face.

'You still don't believe it was a frame-up, do you?'

'You haven't even yet proved that a crime was committed, let alone having any idea as to who might have done it,' he argued, but his voice softened as he recognised the growing impatience in her eyes. 'You have to be realistic, Mattie. If you are going to launch yourself publicly into this great conspiracy theory, you will have a very sceptical audience who will want more than a few 'maybes'. If you turn out to be wrong, you will do yourself and your career a lot of harm. And should you turn out to be right, you're

217

going to have some very powerful enemies out there, who could do you even more harm. If they can nobble the Prime Minister, what could they do to you?'

He stroked her hair tenderly.

'It's not a matter of whether I believe your theory, Mattie. It's a matter of caring about you, of not wanting you to get caught in something which could be bigger than both of us and could cause you a great deal of pain. Frankly I'm scared you might be taking this one a bit too far. Is it really worth it?'

Instantly he knew he had said something wrong. He didn't know why, but he sensed her body go rigid, unresponsive, enveloped by a cold shell that had suddenly divided the bed in two.

'Hell, Johnnie, I would be even more scared if it turned out to be true and nobody did anything about it,' she snapped. 'And damn it, it was you who encouraged me to go after the story.'

'But that was before . . . well, before you got into my bed and into my life. This isn't just another story for me, Mattie, this is personal. I really care about you.'

'So that's it. Drop the bloody story and concentrate on getting laid. Thanks, but no thanks! I asked you to go to bed with me, Johnnie, not own me.'

She rolled away from him so that he could no longer see her face. She could sense his bewilderment and pain, but how could she tell him. The feeling of panic which had come over her as he confronted her with a choice between her career and his caring. God, it was going to happen all over again.

'Look, Johnnie . . .' She was having tremendous difficulty finding the right words. 'I am fond of you – very fond, you know that. But my career is most important to me. This story is most important to me. I can't let anything else get in its way.' She paused for a painful moment. 'Perhaps we made a mistake.'

'What are you saying? Goodbye? Just like that? You drag me into bed as if I'm the last caveman left on earth for a couple of hot nights and then – bugger off? What is it? Just adding to your collection of notches on the bedpost?'

The sarcasm bit deep and rattled her. 'I needed you, Johnnie. I needed a man, not a lifelong commitment. I needed to feel like a woman again, it had been so long . . .'

'Great. A million pricks out there and you had to pick this one. I didn't realise it was just that, Mattie. I really wish you hadn't bothered,' he said with evident bitterness and anger.

'Johnnie, stop! This isn't right. Don't make me say something I don't mean. I like you, very much. That's the problem.'

'That's a problem? Well, I'm glad you have managed to put it behind you.' He gave a dry, humourless laugh and stared straight at the ceiling.

Mattie buried her head in the pillow. She hadn't intended to hurt him, but how could she make him understand. She hadn't told anyone in London before, but maybe now was the time.

'There was someone else,' she began, her voice faltering. 'In Yorkshire. Someone I was very close to. We had known each other since we were children and everyone assumed that our relationship was . . . sort of permanent. That was the trouble. No one asked me, they just assumed. But I wanted something more, and when he forced me to choose between him and my career, I chose my career. It was the only way for me to live with myself, Johnnie!' she exclaimed, as if fearing that he would neither understand nor accept. His cold expression told her she was right.

'But . . . he went to pieces. There were begging letters, midnight telephone calls. I would see him just standing at the end of my street, waiting for hours, sometimes all through the night.'

She drew a deep breath as if the memory were exhausting her. 'Then, there was a car crash. A long, straight piece of road with no other traffic, and his car hit a tree. They had to cut him out. When I heard, it was as if it were all my fault, as if I had been the one who had crashed the car. I felt so guilty, do you see, yet I felt so angry with myself for feeling that way. I hadn't done anything wrong!'

She desperately wanted to justify herself and convince him that she deserved no blame but tears of anguish and self-recrimination were filling her eyes and starting to roll, one by one, down her cheeks.

'It took every piece of willpower that I had to go to the hospital, and the hours I spent in the waiting room were the loneliest I have ever known. Then the nurse came to tell me that he wouldn't see me. Never wanted to see me again. Left me standing in the middle of that hospital feeling completely and utterly worthless.'

She was struggling hard to keep hold of her emotions now, as the recollections stirred deep within her. 'It was all or nothing for him, Johnnie. I really did care for him, yet all I did was cause him pain and turn his love to hatred. It . . . it nearly killed him. That's why I left Yorkshire, Johnnie, to bury that feeling of worthlessness and guilt through my work. And for what it's worth, I'm beginning to like you too much to risk all that again.'

As she spoke, his eyes once more met hers. The sarcasm and anger had left him as he listened, but there was still a hard, determined edge to his voice when he spoke.

'Believe me, I know what it's like to lose the one you love and have your world pulled apart around you. I know how much pain and loneliness it's possible to feel when it happens. But you weren't driving that car and you can't change the facts simply by running away from them. And that's precisely what you are doing – running away!'

She shook her head in denial but he cut her short. 'When you came to London, you may have been chasing your future – but you were also hiding from everything which hurt you in the past. Yet it's not going to work, Mattie, don't you see? You can't hide away in journalism – investigating, exposing, pulling people's worlds apart in search of the truth – unless you are willing to face those people afterwards and live with their pain.'

'That's unfair . . .' she protested.

'Is it? I hope so for your sake, because if you can't accept the fact that your work may cause a lot of innocent people great hurt, then you'll never be a good journalist. Look for the truth, Mattie, by all means, but only if you're willing to recognise and share the pain it may cause. If you think it's enough just to float like a butterfly from one story to another, never hanging around long enough to see the damage that your version of the truth might inflict on other people, how the devil can you put any real value on your work? It's your job to criticise self-important politicians, but how dare you criticise the commitment of others if you are afraid to commit yourself? You say you are afraid of commitment. But commitment is what it is all about, Mattie. You can't run away from it for ever!'

But she was already running, sobbing into the bathroom and into her clothes. In a minute she had fled out of the front door, and all he could hear was the echo of her tears.

MONDAY 8TH NOVEMBER – FRIDAY 12TH NOVEMBER

The criticisms of the weekend press kicked the campaign to life early on Monday morning. Encouraged by the media view that the right contender still had not emerged, two further Cabinet Ministers announced their candidatures – Peter McKenzie, the Secretary of State for Health, and Patrick Woolton, the bluff Foreign Secretary.

Both were reckoned to have a reasonable chance of success. McKenzie had been prominent in selling the popular hospital scheme, and had managed to ensure that blame for its postponement had been heaped entirely on the Treasury and the Prime Minister's Office.

Woolton had been running hard behind the scenes ever since his conversation with Urquhart at the party conference, having lunched almost every editor in Fleet Street in the previous month. By emphasising his Northern origins he was hoping to establish himself as the 'One Nation' candidate in contrast to the strong Home Counties bias of most of the other major contenders – not that this had impressed the Scots, who tended to view the whole affair as if it were an entirely foreign escapade. Woolton had been hoping to delay his formal entry into the race, wishing to see how the various rival campaigns developed, but the weekend press had been like a call to arms and he decided he should delay no longer. He called a press conference at Manchester Airport to make the announcement on what he termed his 'home ground', hoping that no one would notice he had flown up from London in order to be there.

The weekend press also incited into action those candidates who had already declared themselves. It was becoming clear to the likes of Michael Samuel and Harold Earle that their gentlemanly campaigns with their obscure, coded messages were rapidly running into the sand. With the advent of new candidates, their appeals needed to be freshened up and their cutting edges toughened.

Under the pressures of an extended campaign, the candidates were becoming increasingly nervous – so the press at last got what they wanted. When Harold Earle repeated his environmentalist criticisms, but this time choosing to attack the record of Michael Samuel by name, the gloves came off.

Samuel retorted that Earle's conduct was reprehensible and incompatible with his status as a Cabinet colleague, as well as being a rotten example for an Education Secretary to set for young people. In the meantime, Woolton's loose language at Manchester concerning the need to 'restore English values with an English candidate' was vigorously attacked by McKenzie, who was desperately trying to rediscover his lost Gaelic roots and claiming it was an insult to five million Scots. Trying to find a unique line as always, the *Sun* interpreted Woolton's words as a vicious anti-Semitic attack on Samuel, which had Jewish activists swamping the air waves and letter columns with complaints. A rabbi in Samuel's home constituency called on the Race Relations Board to investigate what he called 'the most atrocious outburst by a senior political figure since Mosley'. Woolton was not entirely unhappy with this over-reaction; 'for the next two weeks everyone will be looking at the shape of Samuel's ears rather than listening to what he's saying,' he told one close supporter.

By Wednesday afternoon, Urquhart felt the situation had developed sufficiently well for him to issue a public call for 'a return to the standards of personal conduct for which our Party is renowned and without which collective Government becomes impossible'. It was echoed loudly in the editorial columns, even as the front pages were splashing the latest outburst of internecine bickering.

When, therefore, on Friday afternoon Mattie walked in to Preston's office asking him if he wanted a fresh angle on the contest, his response was generally unenthusiastic.

'Christ, I shall be glad when we can get back to real news,' he blustered. 'I'm not sure we can afford to devote any more space than we're already doing to the back-stabbing.'

'This bit of back-stabbing,' she said defiantly, 'is different.'

He was still looking at a mock-up of the following day's front page rather than showing any interest in Mattie, but she was not deterred.

'The leadership election was caused by Collingridge's resignation, which in turn was caused in the end by allegations that he or his brother had been fiddling share deals through a Paddington tobacconist and a Turkish secondary bank. I think we can prove that he was almost certainly set up.'

Preston at last looked up. 'What the hell are you talking about?'

'He was framed, and I think we can prove it.'

Preston could find no words to express his astonishment; his jaw dropped so low that with his large glasses Mattie felt she was talking to a goldfish.

'Here's what we have, Grev.' Patiently she explained how she had checked the computer file at party headquarters and discovered the distribution file had been tampered with.

'It was deliberately altered to ensure that the false address in Paddington could be tied in directly to Charles Collingridge. But anyone could have opened that accommodation address. I don't think Charles Collingridge ever went anywhere near Paddington. Somebody else did it in his name – somebody who was trying to frame him!'

Preston was listening intently now.

'I went to Paddington myself this morning. I opened up an accommodation address at the same tobacconist shop in an entirely fictional name. I then got a taxi to Seven Sisters Road and the Union Bank of Turkey, where I opened up an account in the same fictional name – not with £50,000 but with just £100. The whole thing took less than three hours from start to finish. So I can now start ordering pornographic magazines, paid for out of the new bank account and delivered to the Paddington address, which could do a lot of damage to the reputation of one completely innocent politician.'

'Er, who?' asked Preston, still having difficulty catching up.

She laughed and threw down a bank book and the tobacconist's receipt onto the editor's desk. He looked at them eagerly.

'The Leader of the Opposition!' he shouted in alarm. 'What the hell have you done?'

'Nothing,' she said with a smile suggesting victory. 'Except to show that Charles Collingridge was almost certainly framed; that he probably never went near the tobacconist shop or the Union Bank of Turkey, and therefore that he could not have bought those shares.'

Preston was holding the documents at arm's length as if they might catch fire.

'Which means that Henry Collingridge did not tell his brother about Renox Chemicals. . .' Her inflexion indicated that there was more.

'And? And?' Preston demanded.

'He didn't have to resign.'

Preston sagged back in his chair. The beads of perspiration had begun to trickle down his brow, plastering his hair to his forehead. He was looking exceedingly uncomfortable. He felt as if he were being torn in two. With one eye he could see the makings of a superb story, which, when promoted vigorously by his advertising agency, could bring with it the substantial boost in circulation he was finding so elusive. Whether the story was accurate or not hardly bothered him; the lawyers could ensure that it libelled no one and it would make a splendid read.

With his other eye, however, he could discern the enormous impact that such a story would make on the leadership race itself, the uncontrollable shock waves which would stretch out and swamp various innocent bystanders – possibly including himself. And Landless had just told him on the telephone that he had other fish to fry. He brushed back the lick of hair which was stuck clammily above his glasses, but it did not seem to help his vision.

He could not focus on which decision would be the right one to take, the one which would be acceptable to Landless. He had been instructed that all major pieces affecting the leadership race were to be cleared with Landless before publication, and he had feared being confronted with an unexpected decision like this. He needed to play for time.

'Mattie, I scarcely know what to say. You've obviously been very . . . busy.' His mind was charging through his Thesaurus of flannel, words which were meaningless and noncommittal but which left their audience with an appropriately warm feeling of encouragement. It was a well thumbed volume. But then it hit him, and the book closed shut with a snap.

'You've illustrated very well that it might have been someone else who was charging round London opening accounts in Collingridge's name, but you haven't proved that it wasn't Collingridge himself. Surely that is the easiest explanation to accept?'

'But the computer file, Grev. It was tampered with. And that wouldn't have happened if Charles Collingridge were guilty.'

'Haven't you considered the possibility that the computer file was altered, not to incriminate Collingridge, but by Collingridge or one of his friends to offer him an alibi, to muddy the waters after he had been found out? For all we know it was not the distribution file but the accounts file which was altered, possibly only minutes before you saw it, just to throw you off the trail.'

'But only a handful of people have access to the accounts file,' Mattie protested with considerable vigour. 'And how could Charles Collingridge have done that? He's been drying out in a treatment centre.'

'But his brother?'

Mattie was incredulous. 'You can't seriously believe that the Prime Minister took the incredible risk of ordering the party headquarters' computer file to be altered just to falsify the evidence – after he had already announced his resignation.'

'Mattie, think back. Watergate. Files were burnt and tapes erased – by the President. During Irangate, incriminating material was shredded and smuggled out of the White House by a secretary in her underwear. Scores of presidential aides and US Cabinet ministers have gone to prison in recent years. And in this country, Jeremy Thorpe was put on trial for attempted murder, John Stonehouse went to gaol after faking his own suicide and Lloyd George sold peerages from Downing Street while he screwed his secretary on the Cabinet table. Things much stranger than fiction have happened in politics.' Preston was warming to his theme now. 'Power is a drug, like a candle to a moth. They are drawn towards it, no matter what the dangers. They would rather risk everything, including their lives and careers, than do without it. So it's still easier to believe that the Collingridges got caught with their hands in the till and are trying to cover up than to accept there was a great con spiracy against the Prime Minister.'

'So you won't run it!' she accused sharply.

'No, I'm not saying that,' Preston continued, smiling in a manner which betrayed not a shred of sympathy. 'I'm saying you haven't yet got enough for the story to stand up. We have to be careful not to make ourselves look ridiculous. You need to do some more work on it.'

He meant it as a dismissal, but Mattie had been at the receiving end of too many of his dismissals. She had spent every waking hour since running out on Johnnie working on this story, chasing the details and trying to drown her private pain, knowing that only by uncovering the truth would she find any release from the emotions which were twisted in a state of perpetual warfare deep inside her. She would not leave it there. She felt like screaming at him, but she was determined not to lose her self-control. She took a deep breath, lowered her eyes for a moment to help herself relax, and was almost smiling when she looked at him once again.

'Grev. Just explain it to me so I can understand. Either somebody set the Collingridges up, or the Prime Minister of this country has established his guilt by falsifying evidence. One way or the other, we have enough to lead the paper for a week.'

'Er, yes. But which is it? We have to be sure. Particularly

in the middle of a leadership contest we cannot afford to make a mistake on something so important.'

'Doesn't Collingridge deserve the chance to establish his innocence? Are you telling me that the story has to be left until after the contest has finished – until after the damage has been done?'

Preston had run out of logic. Once again he was discovering that this inexperienced woman, one of his most junior members of staff, was slipping every argument he could throw at her. As she suspected he would, he sought refuge in bluster and bullying.

'Look!' he snapped, pointing an accusatory finger in her direction. 'You burst into my office with a story so fantastic, demanding that I scrap the front page for it . . . But you haven't written any copy yet! How the devil can I tell whether you've got a good story or simply had a good lunch?'

Her blue eyes glinted like polar ice, her mind tumbling with the many slights she wanted to throw back at him. Instead, a frosty calm settled over her.

'You will have your copy in thirty minutes,' she said as she walked out, barely able to resist the temptation to slam the door off its hinges.

It was actually nearer forty minutes when she walked back in, without knocking, six pages of double-spaced copy clutched in her hand. Without comment she dropped them on the desk, standing directly in front of Preston to make it clear that she would not budge until she had her answer.

He left her standing while slowly he read through the pages, trying to look as if he were struggling with an important decision. But it was a sham. The decision had already been made just a few minutes after Mattie had left his office and seconds after he had managed to reach the newspaper's owner on the phone.

'She's determined, Mr Landless. She knows she's got the makings of a good story and she won't take no for an answer. What the hell do I do?'

'Persuade her she's wrong. Put her on the cookery page.

228

Send her on holiday. Promote her to editor, for all I care. But keep her quiet!'

'It's not that simple. She's not only stubborn as hell, she's one of the best political brains we've got.'

'Preston, you already have the best political brains in the business. Mine! All I am asking you to do is to control your staff. Are you telling me you can't do even that?' Landless asked in a tone full of menace. 'There are scarcely two weeks before the leadership race is over,' he continued. 'There are great things at stake, the whole future of the country, my business – your job. Do whatever you have to do to keep her quiet. Just don't screw up!'

The proprietor's words were still ringing in Preston's ears as he continued to shuffle the pieces of paper, no longer reading them, concentrating instead on what he was about to say. Normally he enjoyed his power as editorial executioner, but he knew she would never fit the typecast role of whimpering victim. He was unsure how he should handle her.

Finally he put Mattie's story down, and pushed himself back into his chair. He felt more comfortable with the support of the chair behind his back.

'We can't run it. It's too risky, and I'm not willing to blow the leadership contest apart on the basis of speculation.'

It was what she had expected all along. She replied in a whisper, but her soft words hit Preston like a boxing glove.

'I will not take no for an answer.'

Dammit. Why didn't she just accept it, shrug it off or just burst into tears like the others? The quiet insolence behind her words and his inability to handle it made him feel nervous. He started to sweat; he knew that she had noticed this sign of tension, and he began to stumble over his carefully prepared words.

'I . . . cannot run the story. I am the editor, and that's my decision.' He wasn't even convincing himself. 'You have to accept it, or . . .'

'Or what, Grev?'

'. . . or realise that you have no future on our political staff.'

'You're firing me?' This did surprise her. How could

229

he afford to let her go, particularly in the middle of the leadership contest?

'No. I'm moving you to women's features, starting right now. Frankly, I don't think you have developed the judgement for our political columns.'

'Who has nobbled you, Grev?'

'What the hell do you mean . . . ?'

'You normally have trouble making up your mind whether you want tea or coffee. Deciding to fire me from this story is somebody else's decision, isn't it?'

'I'm not firing you! You're being transferred . . .'

He was losing control now, eyes bulging in anger and with a complexion which looked as if he had been holding his breath for three minutes.

'Then, dear editor, I have some disappointing news for you. I quit!'

God, he hadn't expected this. He was scrambling now to regain his authority and the initiative. He had to keep her at the *Telegraph*, it was the only way to control her. But what the hell was he to do? He forced a smile, and spread his hands wide in an attempt to imitate a gesture of generosity.

'Look, Mattie. Let's not be hasty. Let's be mature about this – friends! I want you to get wider experience on the paper, you've got talent, even if I think you haven't quite fitted in on the political side. We want to keep you here, so think over the weekend what other part of the paper you might like to work on.' He saw her steely, determined eyes and knew it wasn't working. 'But if you really feel you must go, don't rush into anything. Sort out what you want to do, let me know, we'll try to assist you and give you six months' salary to help you on your way. I don't want any hard feelings. Think about it.'

'I've thought about it. And if you are not printing my story, I'm resigning. Here and now.'

She had never seen him so apoplectic. His words came spitting out. 'In which case I must remind you that your contract of employment stipulates that you must give me three months' notice of departure, and that until that time has elapsed we retain exclusive rights over all your journalistic work. If you insist, we shall rigidly enforce that provision, in the courts if necessary which would ruin your career once and for all. Face it, your copy isn't going to get printed here or anywhere else. Wise up, Mattie, accept the offer. It's the best one you are going to get!'

She knew now what her grandfather must have felt as he set out from his fishing village on the Norwegian fjord, knowing that once he had started he could never turn back even though ahead of him lay enemy patrol boats, mine fields, and nearly a thousand miles of hostile, stormy seas. She would need some of his courage, and his good fortune.

She gathered up the papers on Preston's desk and ripped them slowly in half before letting them flutter back into his lap.

'You can keep the words. But you don't own the truth. I'm not sure you would even recognise it. I still quit.'

This time she slammed the door.

Sunday 14th November –
Monday 15th November

Some two weeks earlier, immediately after the *Telegraph* had published the Landless opinion poll, Urquhart in his capacity as Chief Whip had written to all of his parliamentary colleagues on the weekly Whips' circular which is sent to party MPs.

> During the course of the leadership election, newspapers and opinion pollsters will undoubtedly be trying to obtain your view as to whom you are likely to support. I would encourage you not to cooperate, since at best the results of these surveys can only serve to disrupt the proper conduct of what is supposed to be a confidential ballot, and at worst will be used by the less responsible press to make mischief and subject our affairs to lurid headlines and comment. The best interests of the Party can only be served by discouraging such activity.

The majority of the Parliamentary Party was more than happy to cooperate, although it is a well established fact that at least a third of MPs are constitutionally incapable of keeping anything quiet, even state secrets.

As a result, the two opinion polls which appeared in the Sunday press following Mattie's abrupt departure from Preston's office were profoundly incomplete, leaving the pollsters scratching their heads at the *Telegraph*'s earlier persuasiveness. Less than 40 per cent of the 337 Government MPs who constituted the electorate for the ballot had responded to the polling companies' pestering telephone calls, which gave the impression that the Parliamentary

Party was still a long way from making up its mind. Moreover, the small sample of those who had agreed to respond gave no clear indication as to the likely result. Samuel was ahead, but only narrowly and to a degree which the pollsters emphasised was 'not statistically significant'. Woolton, McKenzie and Earle followed in close order, with the four other declared candidates a little further behind.

The conclusions to be drawn from such insubstantial evidence were flimsy, but made excellent headlines, just four days before the close of nominations.

'Samuel slipping – early lead lost', roared the *Mail on Sunday*, while the *Observer* was scarcely less restrained in declaring 'Party in turmoil as poll reveals great uncertainty'.

The inevitable result was a flurry of editorials hostile to the Party, criticising both the quality of the candidates and their campaigns. 'This country has a right to expect more of the governing Party than the undignified squabbling we have been subjected to in recent days and the lacklustre and uninspired manner in which it is deciding its fate,' the *Sunday Express* intoned. 'We may be witnessing a governing Party which is finally running out of steam, ideas and leadership after too long in power.'

The following day's edition of the *Daily Telegraph* was intended to resolve all that. Just three days before the close of nominations, it put aside convention and for the first time in its history ran its editorial on the front page. Its print run was increased and a copy was hand delivered to the London addresses of all Government MPs. No punches were pulled in its determination to make its views heard throughout the corridors of Westminster.

This paper has consistently supported the Government, not through blind prejudice but because we felt that they served the interests of the nation better than the alternatives. Throughout the Thatcher years our convictions were well supported by the progress which was made in restoring the economy to health and the inroads which began to be made in some of the more pressing social problems.

233

In recent months we began to feel that Henry Collingridge was not the best leader to write the next chapter, and we supported his decision to resign. However, there is now a grave danger that the lack of judgement being shown by all the present contenders for his job will threaten a return to the bad old ways of weakness and indecisiveness which we hoped had been left behind for good.

Instead of the steadying hand which we need on the tiller in order to consolidate the economic and social advances of recent years, we have so far been offered a choice between youthful inexperience, environmental upheaval and injudicious outbursts bordering on racial intolerance.

This choice is insufficient. The Government and the country need a leader who has maturity, who has a sense of discretion, who has a proven capacity for working with all his colleagues in the Parliamentary Party.

There is at least one senior figure in the Party who not only enjoys all of these attributes, but who in recent weeks has been almost unique in remembering the need to uphold the dignity of Government and who, so rare in present day politics, has shown himself capable of putting aside his own personal ambition for what he perceives as being the wider interests of his Party.

He has announced that it is not his intention to seek election as Leader of the Party, but he still has time to reconsider before nominations close on Thursday. We believe it would be in the best interests of all concerned if the Chief Whip, Francis Urquhart, were to stand and to be elected.

There were forty press, television and radio men waiting outside Urquhart's home in Cambridge Street when he emerged at 8.10 that morning. He had been waiting rather nervously inside, wanting to ensure that the timing of his exit enabled BBC radio's *Today* programme and all breakfast television channels to take it live. Attracted by the scramble of newsmen, a host of passers-by and commuters from nearby Victoria Station had gathered to discover the cause for the commotion, and the live television pictures suggested a crowd showing considerable interest in the man who now emerged onto the doorstep, looking down on the throng.

The shouted questions from the journalists were identical, and he waved a hand to quieten them so that his answer could be heard. The hand also contained a copy of that morning's *Telegraph*, and for a moment it looked as if he were giving a victory salute which only encouraged the scramble still further, but eventually he managed to bring a degree of calm to the proceedings.

'Ladies and Gentlemen, as Chief Whip I would like to think you had gathered here because of your interest in the details of the Government's forthcoming legislative programme, but I suspect you have other things on your mind.'

The gentle quip brought a chuckle from the journalists and put Urquhart firmly in control.

'I have read with considerable surprise and obvious interest this morning's edition of the *Telegraph*.' He held it up again so that the cameras could get a clear shot. 'I am honoured that such a significant and authoritative newspaper should hold a high opinion of my personal capabilities – one which goes far beyond my own judgement of the matter. As you know, I had made it clear that I had no intention of standing, that I thought it was in the Party's best interest that the Chief Whip should stand above this particular contest.'

He cleared his throat. 'Generally that is still my view. However, the *Telegraph* raises some important points which should be considered carefully. You will forgive me if I don't come to an instant or snap judgement out here on the pavement. I want to spend a little time consulting with a few colleagues to obtain their opinions, and also to have a long and serious discussion with my wife, whose views will be most important of all. I shall then sleep upon it, and let you all know tomorrow what decision I have reached. In the meantime, I hope you will allow me and my family a few hours of peace to think about things. I shall have nothing more to say until tomorrow.'

With one final wave of his hand, still clutching the newspaper and held for many seconds to satisfy the screaming photographers, Urquhart withdrew into his house and shut the door firmly.

By Monday evening, Mattie was beginning to wonder whether she had been too hasty. After storming out of Preston's office she had persuaded herself that she had resolved all her personal and professional problems in one grand gesture – no more Krajewski, certainly no more Preston, just the story to concentrate on. Yet now she was not so sure. She had spent a lonely weekend identifying the newspapers for which she would like to work, but as she did so she quickly realised that none of them had any obvious gaps in their political reporting teams which she could hope to fill. The newspaper world is highly competitive, and although she could offer youthful energy and talent in abundance, she had just thrown away the track record of experience on which most editors hire their staff.

She had made many telephone calls but they had led to few appointments; she began to discover that somebody was spreading a story that she had stormed out in tears when Preston had questioned her judgement, and sensitive feminine outbursts do not generally commend themselves to the heavily male-dominated club of newspaper editors. It did not help her mood that the Bank of England had pushed up interest rates sharply to protect sterling from speculators while a new Prime Minister was selected, leading the building societies that morning to threaten a rise in the mortgage rate. It made her realise that she would have no apparent means of paying for it. It was difficult enough with a salary. Without one, her affairs could very soon become impossible.

And she was also lonely. Her bed was once more an Arctic outpost fit only for penguins, and gave her no comfort from her other problems.

Yet the story kept taking over and pushing to one side any thoughts of dismay in her mind, while the *Telegraph*'s editorial intervention had given it a totally new twist. Throughout the early evening she had watched the various television news programmes, all of which were dominated by speculation as to whether Urquhart would stand, and informing a generally unaware audience about what a Chief Whip actually does and who Urquhart was.

She needed to talk, and without wishing to question too deeply the conflicting emotions which were tangling in her mind she found herself waiting on a wooden platform which bobbed in the Thames tide alongside Charing Cross pier. Just a few minutes later she could see the approach of the *Telegraph*'s private river taxi which shuttled employees between the newspaper's dockland plant downstream and the rather more central and civilised reaches of the capital.

As she had hoped, Krajewski was on board. He said nothing as he found her standing on the pier, but accepted her silent invitation to walk.

It was a dry and clear November night, so they wrapped up warm and without speaking strolled along the Embankment, tracing the sharp curves of the river bank and with it the floodlit vistas of the Festival Hall and the Houses of Parliament beyond, with the tower of Big Ben looking down from high above. It was some time before he broke the silence. No questions about the other night, he decided. He knew what was foremost in her mind.

'So what do you make of it all?'

She smiled shyly in gratitude for the lifeline, for not demanding an explanation of her motives which she would not – or was it could not? – give.

'It's extraordinary. They're building him up like a Messiah on a white charger galloping to the rescue. Why did Grev do it?'

'I don't know. He just came in late yesterday, not a word to anyone, turned the paper inside out and produced his front page editorial from out of his pocket. No warning, no explanation. Still, seems to have caused quite a story. Perhaps he got it right after all.'

Mattie shook her head. 'It wasn't Grev. He's not capable of making a decision like that. It took balls to position' – she almost used the word 'commit' but stopped herself just in time – 'to position the paper in that way, and it could only have come from one place: the desk of our – your! – beloved proprietor, Mr Landless. Last time he interfered he was dethroning Collingridge, now he's trying to hand the crown to someone else.'

As they traced their way along the winding river bank, they kicked through the windswept piles of leaves and passed by the pale, massive bulk of the Ministry of Defence.

'But why? Why Urquhart?'

'No idea,' Mattie responded. 'Urquhart is very low profile, although he's been in the House for many years. He comes across as being vaguely aristocratic, patrician, old school tie. He's something of a loner, certainly not one of the boys, which means he's got no great fan club but also no one hates him enough to campaign against him as they are doing with Samuel. Nobody knows what his views really are, he's never had to express them as Chief Whip.'

She turned to face him. 'You know, he might just slip through the middle as the man the others dislike least. Landless could have picked a winner.'

'You think he'll stand, then?'

'Certain of it. He told me way back in June that there was going to be a leadership race, and he flatly refused then to rule himself out. He wants it all right, and he'll stand.'

'That sounds like a great feature – "The Man Who Saw It Coming".'

'If only I had a paper to write it for,' she said with a wistful smile.

He stopped and looked at Mattie, her fair hair glowing in the lights which bounced back from the soft yellow stone of the Houses of Parliament behind her, wondering if he detected a hint of regret in her voice.

'Grev refuses to print your story and then announces the paper's support for Urquhart. Defusing one bomb and then launching another. Isn't that a bit of a coincidence?'

'I've been thinking about that all day,' she said. 'The simple explanations are always the easiest to accept, and the simple fact is that Grev Preston is a pathetic excuse for an editor who is terrified of getting anything wrong. Knowing that Landless was going to throw Urquhart's hat into the ring, he didn't have the nerve to upset his proprietor's plans and I suspect he found my story simply too hot to handle.'

'So you think Landless may be at the bottom of it all?'

'It's possible. He certainly welcomed the leadership contest, but then so did many others. Urquhart told me the weekend after the election of all the internal rivalry and bitterness inside the Government. Whoever is stirring it behind the scenes, we have the entire Cabinet to choose from, as well as Landless. And I am going to find out who.'

'But how, without a newspaper?'

'Preston has been stupid enough to insist that I shall remain employed by the *Telegraph* for another three months. OK. They may not print it, but I'm still a journalist and I can still ask questions. If the truth is half as devious as I suspect it is, the story will still be worth printing in three months' or even three years' time. They can't lock up the truth for ever. I may have lost my job, Johnnie, but I haven't lost my curiosity.'

And what about your commitment? he asked silently.

'And will you be my spy on the inside, keeping an eye on what that bastard Landless is up to?'

He nodded, wondering just how much she was using him.

'Thanks, Johnnie,' she whispered. She squeezed his hand, and disappeared into the night.

Tuesday 16th November

The following day's news was still being dominated by intense speculation as to whether Urquhart would run. It was clear that the media had excited itself to the point where they would feel badly let down if he didn't, yet at 3 p.m. he was still keeping his own counsel. By this time, Mattie was feeling irked, not by Urquhart but by O'Neill. She had been waiting in his office with growing impatience for a full half hour.

When she had telephoned party headquarters the previous day wanting to get an official view about computers, literature sales, accounting procedures, Charles Collingridge and all the other things which were bothering her, she discovered that Spence had been absolutely right about the ban on staff contact with the media for the duration of the campaign. She could only deal with the press office, and no press officer seemed capable or willing to talk to her about computers or accounts.

'Sounds as if you are investigating our expenses,' a voice only half-jokingly had said down the telephone.

So she had asked for the Director of Publicity's office, and had been put through to Penny Guy. Mattie asked to come and talk the following morning with O'Neill, whom she had met a couple of times at receptions.

'I'm sorry, Miss Storin, but Mr O'Neill likes to keep his mornings free to clear his paper work and for internal meetings.' It was a lie, and one she was increasingly forced to use as O'Neill's time keeping had become spectacularly erratic. He rarely came into the office before 1 p.m. nowadays. 'How about 2.30 in the afternoon?' she had suggested, playing safe.

She did not comprehend the mind-pulverising effects of cocaine, which kept O'Neill hyperactive and awake well

240

into the small hours, unable to sleep until a cascade of depressant drugs had gradually overwhelmed the cocaine and forced him into an oblivion from which he did not return before midday or later. She did not comprehend this, but she suffered deeply from it nonetheless.

Now she was getting increasingly embarrassed as Mattie sat waiting for O'Neill. He had promised his secretary faithfully he would be on time, but as the wall clock ticked remorselessly on, her ability to invent new excuses disappeared completely. Her faith in O'Neill, with his public bravado and his private remorse, his inexplicable behaviour and his irrational outbursts, was slowly and painfully fading.

She brought Mattie yet another cup of coffee.

'Let me give him a call at home. Perhaps he's had to go back there. Something he forgot, or not feeling too well . . .'

She sat on the corner of his desk, picked up the direct line and punched the numbers. With some embarrassment she greeted Roger on the phone, explaining that Mattie had been waiting for more than half an hour and . . . Her face became gradually more concerned, then anguished and finally horrified before she dropped the phone and fled from the office as if pursued by demons.

Mattie watched these happenings with complete astonishment, rooted to her chair, clutching her saucer, unable to speak or move. As the door banged shut behind the fleeing secretary she rose and moved over to the phone, picking the dangling receiver up from where it was swinging beside the desk and putting it to her ear.

The voice coming out of the phone was unrecognisable as that of O'Neill, or indeed anyone. The words were incoherent, indecipherable, slowed and slurred to the point where it sounded like a doll with the batteries almost dead. There were gasps, moans, long pauses, the sound of tears falling, and of a man falling apart. She replaced the receiver gently in the cradle.

Mattie went in search of the secretary, and found her washing her face in the cloakroom. Her eyes were red and swollen. Mattie put a consoling arm around her shoulders.

241

'How long has he been like that, Penny?'

'I can't say anything!' she blurted, and started weeping once more.

'Look, Penny, he's obviously in a very bad way. I'm not going to print any of this, for goodness sake. I would like to help.'

The other girl turned towards Mattie, fell into her arms, let the pain and worry of the last few months gush out, and sobbed until there were no more tears left.

When she had recovered sufficiently to escape from the cloakroom, Mattie took her gently by the arm and they went for a walk in nearby Victoria Gardens, where they could refresh themselves in the cold, vigorous air blowing off the Thames and talk without interruption. Penny told her how the Prime Minister's resignation had deeply upset O'Neill, how he had always been a little 'emotionally extravagant', as she put it, and the recent internal party turmoil and Prime Minister's resignation had really brought him close to a breakdown.

'But why, Penny? Surely they weren't that close?'

'He liked to think he was close to the whole Collingridge family. He was always arranging for flowers and special photographs to be sent to Mrs Collingridge, doing little favours whenever he could. He loved it all.'

Mattie shrugged her shoulders, as if she were shrugging off O'Neill's reputation once and for all. 'It's a great pity, of course, that he should be so weak and go to pieces just when the Party needs him most. But we both heard him this afternoon, Penny. Something has really got to Roger, something which is eating away at him from the inside.'

Mattie threw down the challenge. It wasn't fair, of course, but she gambled that Penny would not stand by and see O'Neill accused of weakness. She would loyally try to defend her boss – and would not lie in order to do so.

'I . . . I don't know for sure. But I think he blamed himself so badly over the shares.'

'The shares? You mean the Renox shares?' said Mattie in alarm.

'Charles Collingridge asked him to open the

accommodation address because he wanted somewhere for his private mail. Roger and I went to Paddington in a taxi, and he sent me in to do the paper work. I knew he felt uneasy at the time, I think he sensed there was something wrong. And when he realised what it had been used for and how much trouble it had caused, he just began going to pieces.'

'Why did Mr Collingridge ask Roger to open the address and not do it himself?'

'I've no idea, really. Perhaps he felt guilty because of what he was going to use it for. Roger just breezed into the office one day during the summer and said he'd got a favour to do for Charles Collingridge, that it was terribly confidential and I was to breathe a word to no one.'

Her words reminded her that she had broken her promise of silence and more tears began to flow, but Mattie soon reassured her, and they continued their walk.

'So you never saw Charles Collingridge yourself?'

'No. I've never really met him at all. Roger likes to handle all the important people himself, and as far as I'm aware Mr Collingridge has never come into the office.'

'But you are sure it was Charles Collingridge?'

'Of course, Roger said so. And who else could it have been?' The dampness began to appear again at the corner of her eyes. She shivered violently as a burst of cold November air from across the river sent the dead autumnal leaves cascading around them. 'Oh, God, it's all such an awful mess.'

'Penny, relax! It will be all right. Why don't you take a couple of days off and let Roger take care of himself? He can survive without you for a little while. He knows how to use the office computer, doesn't he?'

'He can struggle through on the basics reasonably well if I'm not around, but even he wouldn't pretend he's a keyboard magician. No, I'll be all right.'

So it was O'Neill who had 'struggled through' with the computer file. Another piece fell into place in Mattie's mind. She didn't feel comfortable squeezing information out of a vulnerable and trusting secretary, but there was no alternative.

'Look, how can I put this . . . Roger sounds as if he is

243

very unwell. He's obviously been under a lot of strain, and he might be having a breakdown. Perhaps he's drinking too much. I'm not a doctor, but I do know one who's very good at that sort of thing. If you need any help, please give me a call.'

They had arrived back in Smith Square by now, and prepared to part.

'Mattie, thank you. You've been a great help.'

'No, Penny. I'm the one who is grateful. Take care of yourself.'

Mattie walked the few hundred yards back to the House of Commons, oblivious of the chill and wondering why on earth Roger O'Neill had framed Charles and Henry Collingridge.

TUESDAY 16TH NOVEMBER –
WEDNESDAY 17TH NOVEMBER

Urquhart declared his intention to seek the leadership of
the Party at a press conference held in the House of Commons at 5 p.m., timed to catch the early evening TV news
and the first editions of the following day's press. The
surroundings afforded by the meeting room in the Palace
of Westminster, with its noble carved stone fireplace, its
dark oak panelling and its traditional atmosphere of authority gave the proceedings a dignity which the announcements of Samuel, Woolton and others had lacked.
Urquhart succeeded in establishing the impression of a
man who was being dragged reluctantly towards the seat
of power, placing his duty to his colleagues and country
above his own, modest personal interests.

It was seventeen hours later, on Wednesday morning,
that Landless held his own press conference. He sat in one
of the palatial reception rooms of the Ritz Hotel at a long
table covered with microphones, facing the cameras and
questions of the financial press. Alongside him and almost
dwarfed by his bulging girth sat Marcus Frobisher, the
Chairman of the United Newspapers Group who, although
an industrial magnate in his own right, was clearly cast to
play a secondary role on this occasion. Behind them for
the benefit of the cameras had been erected a vast backdrop
with the colourful logo 'TEN' carefully crafted upon it and
highlighted with lasers. To one side was a large video
screen, on which was playing a corporate video featuring
some of the *Telegraph*'s better advertising material inter-
spersed with cuts of Landless being greeted by workers,
pulling levers to start the printing presses and generally
running his empire in a warm and personal manner. The

245

press conference, for all its immediacy, had clearly been carefully planned.

'Good morning, ladies and gentlemen.'

Landless called the throng to order in a voice which was considerably less cockney than the one he adopted on private occasions. 'Thank you for coming at such short notice. We have invited you here to tell you about one of the most exciting steps forward for the British communications industry since Julius Reuter established his telegraph service in London more than a hundred years ago.'

He shifted one of the microphones a little closer to stop himself craning his neck. 'Today we wish to announce the creation of the largest newspaper group in the United Kingdom, which will provide a platform for making this country once again the worldwide leader in the rapidly expanding industry of providing information services.

'Telegraph Newspapers has made an offer to purchase the full issued share capital of the United Newspapers Group at a price which values them at £1.4 billion, a premium of 40 per cent above the current market price. I am delighted to say that the board of the United Newspapers Group has unanimously accepted the bid, and also agreed the terms for the future management of the combined group. I shall become Chairman and Chief Executive of the new company, and my good friend and former competitor, now colleague . . .' – he stretched a huge paw to grasp the arm of Frobisher, as menacingly as if he were grasping him around the neck – '. . . is to be the President.'

Several nodding heads around the room indicated that they clearly understood which of the men would be in sole charge of the new operation. Frobisher sat there trying hard to put on a good face.

'This is an important step for the British newspaper industry. The combined operation will control more national and major regional titles than any other newspaper group in this country, and the amalgamation of our international subsidiaries will make us the third largest newspaper group in the world. To mark this new departure we are renaming the company, and as you can see, our new corporate title will be Telegraph Express Newspapers

Company PLC – TEN.' He at last released his grip on Frobisher and waved at the logo behind.

'Do you like my new corporate design?' he asked jovially. He hoped they did. His daughter's two-woman partnership had been given the contract – its first – for devising the company's new name and corporate design, and he was determined that she be given almost as much attention as himself.

'You will find waiting for you at the door a document which gives the full details of the offer and agreement. So, questions please!'

There was an excited hum from the audience, and a forest of hands shot up to catch his eye.

'I suppose to be fair I ought to take the first question from someone who will not be working for the group,' jested Landless. 'Now, can we find anyone here who won't be part of the new team?' With theatrical exaggeration he shielded his eyes from the bright lights and searched the audience for a suitable victim, and they all laughed at his cheek.

'Mr Landless,' shouted the business editor of the *Sunday Times*. 'The Government have made it very clear in recent years that they feel the British newspaper industry is already concentrated into too few hands, and that they would use their powers under the monopolies and mergers legislation to prevent any further consolidation. How on earth do you expect to get the necessary Government approval for this deal?'

There was a strong murmur of assent to the question from around the room. The Government had made loud if imprecise noises during the election about their commitment to increasing industrial competition.

'An excellent point.' Landless spread his arms wide as if to hug the question to his chest and slowly throttle it to death.

'You are right, the Government will need to take a view on the matter. And I hope they will be sufficiently wise and visionary to realise that the operation we are putting together, far from jeopardising the British newspaper industry, is vital to its continuing success. Newspapers are just part of the worldwide information industry, which is growing and changing every day. You all know that. Five years ago you all worked in Fleet Street with old type-writers and printing presses which should have been scrapped when the Kaiser surrendered. Today the industry is modernised, decentralised, computerised. Yet still it must keep changing. It has more competition, from satel-lite television, local radio, breakfast TV and the rest.'

'Shame!' cried a voice within the audience, and they laughed nostalgically about the cosy days of Fleet Street and El Vino's wine bar, and the prolonged printers' strikes and disputes which allowed them weeks or even months off to write books or build boats and dream dreams while still on full pay. But they all recognised the inescapable truth in what Landless was saying.

'In ten years' time more and more people will be demanding information twenty-four hours a day, from all parts of the world. Fewer and fewer of them will be getting that information from newspapers which arrive hours after the news has occurred and which covers them in filthy printing ink. If we are to survive in business we must no longer think of ourselves as parochial newspaper men, but as suppliers of information on a worldwide basis. So our new group, "TEN", will not just be a traditional news-paper business but will be grown into the world's leading supplier of information to business and homes around the world, whether they want that information printed, tele-vised, computerised or sung by canaries. And to do that we need the size, the muscle and the resources which only a large group such as "TEN" can provide.'

He gestured generously towards the questioner.

'And as you so rightly point out, we also need the Government's permission. So the Government have a choice. They can take the narrow view, prohibit the merger and preside over the decline of the British newspaper industry, which will be dead within ten years as the Ameri-cans, Japanese and even Australians take over. Or they can be responsible and visionary, and care about the jobs which exist and which can be created in the industry, and think not about narrow British competition but about the much broader international competition which we need to take on and beat if we are to survive. If they do that, they will allow us to build the biggest and finest information service in the world, based right here in Britain.'

A blitz of flash guns greeted him as he sat back in his chair, the carefully rehearsed appeal finished while the journalists who still took shorthand scribbled furiously to catch up with him. The questioner turned to his neighbour.

'What do you think? Will he get away with it?'

'If I know our Ben, he won't be relying just on industrial logic or compelling rhetoric. He will have prepared the ground very carefully beforehand. We'll soon see how many politicians owe him favours.'

The answer seemed to be that many politicians owed Landless, at least on the Government side. With nominations closing the following day and the first ballot due in just a week, few contenders seemed willing to risk antagonising the combined might of the Telegraph and United groups and their substantial number of national newspapers. Within hours the endorsements for Landless grew into a stampede of support amongst contenders as they struggled not to be left behind in finding airtime to praise his 'enlightened and patriotic industrial leadership' By teatime, Landless was well pleased with his day's work and the careful planning which had gone into it. Once again, it seemed that his sense of timing and understanding of politicians had been just right.

The *Independent* could not resist the temptation to have a dig at the proceedings. 'The Landless announcement burst like a grenade in the middle of the leadership race – which presumably was his intention. The sight of so many senior politicians falling over themselves to kiss his hand was reminiscent of Tammany Hall at its worst. It is salutary to reflect that these very same politicians, just a few months ago at the time when Landless bought out Telegraph Newspapers, were insisting that he sign a public declaration of non-interference with the editorial policies of his newspapers. Only on the basis of that solemn and binding undertaking did they allow the purchase to proceed. Today, in their craven attempts to placate Land-less, they are acting as if they automatically assume that alongside his personal support goes the editorial support of his many newspapers. They seem to prefer to swim with sharks rather than honour their own undertakings.'

Not all the aspirants joined the stampede, however. Samuel was cautious and non committal – he had too many knife wounds in his back from the previous weeks to wish to stick his head above the parapet yet again, and he said he wished to consult the workforce of the two groups before reaching his decision. Immediately the union representatives issued their vigorous denunciation of the scheme. They had noted that there were no guarantees about job security in the published document, and they had plenty of experience of Landless's quite ruthless 'industrial rationalisation programmes'. In a careless moment Landless had once joked that he had fired 10,000 people for every million he had made, and he was an exceedingly wealthy man. Samuel realised after his brief consultation with the unions that it would be absurd in the face of their public opposition for him now to endorse the deal, so sought refuge in silence.

Urquhart also stood out from the crowd. Within an hour of the announcement he was on television and radio giving a thoroughly polished and well informed analysis of the global information market and its likely trends, all of which seemed to support the Landless proposal. His technical expertise far outshone his rivals, yet he was cautious.

'While I have the highest respect for Benjamin Landless I think it would be wrong of me to jump to immediate conclusions before I have had an opportunity to consider all the details of the proposal. I think politicians should be careful; it gives politics a bad name if they are perceived as dashing around trying to buy the support of the editorial columns. So to avoid any possible misinterpretation, I shall not be announcing my own views until the leadership contest is over. By which time, of course,' he said modestly, 'they may be of no interest anyway.'

'If only all his colleagues could have taken the dignified and principled stand of the Chief Whip', praised the

Independent. 'Urquhart is establishing a statesmanlike tone for his campaign which marks him out from the pack and will certainly improve his chances.'

Other editorials echoed the line, not least of all the *Telegraph.*

> We encouraged Francis Urquhart to stand for the leadership because of our respect for his independence of mind and his integrity. We were delighted when he accepted the challenge, and we are still convinced that our recommendation was correct. His refusal to rush to judgement over the Telegraph-United newspaper merger and his determination to consider his views carefully is no less than we would expect from someone with the qualities to lead this country.
>
> We still hope and believe that after due deliberation he will wholeheartedly endorse the merger plans, but our judgement of Urquhart is based on much more than commercial interest. He is the only candidate who so far has demonstrated that he is also a man of principle.

There was the sound around the corridors of Westminster of doors being slammed shut in frustration as ambitious politicians realised that Urquhart had once again stolen a march on them.

'How the heck does that fart-artist do it?' barked Woolton, discarding any vestige of diplomatic restraint.

In a Mayfair penthouse overlooking Hyde Park, Landless and Urquhart smiled serenely and toasted each other's health and good fortune as they reviewed the success of each other's campaign.

'To the next Prime Minister,' saluted Landless.

'And to his impartial endorsement of the merger,' responded his companion.

Thursday 18th November

When nominations closed at noon on Thursday, the only surprise was the last minute withdrawal of Peter Bearstead, who had been the first to announce his intention to stand.

'I've done what I set out to do, which was to get a proper election going,' he announced punchily. 'I'm not going to win and I don't want a consolation prize of a Ministerial job, so now let the others get on with it.'

He immediately signed up with the *Daily Express* to write personal and indiscreet profiles of the candidates for the duration of the campaign.

That left nine declared candidates, an unprecedentedly large field. However, the general view was that only five of them were in with a serious chance – Samuel, Woolton, Earle, McKenzie and Urquhart. With a completed list of contestants, pollsters redoubled their efforts to contact Government MPs and decipher which way the tide was running.

The starter's flag had now officially fallen, and Peter McKenzie was determined to make an immediate showing. The Secretary of State for Health was a frustrated man. Having been in charge of the health service for more than five years, he had hoped as ardently as Urquhart for a new challenge and new responsibility after the June general election. The long years in charge of an unresponsive bureaucracy, watching almost helplessly as the remorselessly expensive progress of medical science grew faster than the taxpayers' ability or willingness to keep pace, had left him deeply scarred. A few years previously he had been regarded as the rising star of the Party, the man who could combine a tough intellectual approach with an obvious deep sense of caring, and many said he would go all the way. But the health service had been utterly unresponsive to his attempts to reform and improve it, and his repeated encounters with picket lines of protesting nurses and ambulance men had left his image as a man of conscience and humanity in tatters. The postponement of his much touted hospital expansion plan had been the last straw. He had become deeply dispirited, and had talked with his wife about quitting politics at the next election if his lot did not improve.

He greeted Collingridge's downfall like a drowning man discovers a life raft. It was the only thing that mattered to him, and drew all his concentration and effort. Of course he had made mistakes during the initial stages of the campaign, as had most of his rivals, but he entered the final five days before the first ballot full of enthusiasm and energy. He had planned from the start to make an impact on Nomination Day itself, determined to get his head above the crowd. So he had asked his staff to find a suitable visit for him to make which would provide some powerful photo-opportunities for the cameramen and a chance to revive his tarnished image as a humane and caring politician.

But no hospitals, he instructed. He had spent the first three years in the Ministry visiting hospitals and trying to learn about patient care, only to be met on bad days by massed picket lines of boisterous nurses complaining about pay and on worse days by violent demonstrations from ancillary staff protesting about 'savage cuts'. Even the doctors seemed to have embraced the philosophy that health budgets were now set by the level of noise rather than the level of need. He almost never got to see the patients, and even when he tried to sneak into a hospital by a side or back entrance, the demonstrators always seemed to know beforehand precisely where he would be, ready to throw their personal and deeply hurtful abuse at him just when the television camera crews had arrived. No Minister had ever found an effective way of dealing with protesting nurses; the public will always side with the angels of mercy, leaving the politician in the role of perpetual villain. So McKenzie had simply stopped visiting hospitals. Rather than running an inevitable and image-denting gauntlet of abuse, he opted out and stuck to safer venues.

Just a couple of hours after nominations closed, the Secretary of State's car was approaching the Humanifit Laboratories just off the M4 where he would spend a couple of hours in front of cameras opening the new factory and examining the wide range of equipment which they manufactured for handicapped people. They had just developed a revolutionary new wheelchair which would operate to the voice commands of paraplegic patients unable to move their limbs. The combination of new British technology and enhanced care for the disabled was just what he had hoped his office would find for him, and he was looking forward to his afternoon and the media coverage it would generate.

McKenzie had been careful, however, not taking the success of the visit for granted. He had been ambushed by protesters too many times to take chances that the television camera crews would bring a demonstration with them in order to enhance the vividness of their pictures. 'One good demo is worth a thousand new factory openings to us,' a friendly television executive had once advised him, and he had taken care to ensure that the media had been informed only three hours before his impending arrival, soon enough to get their camera crews there, but not sufficient time for anyone to arrange a welcoming demonstration. Yes, he thought as the factory came into view, his office had been very efficient and he had been sensibly cautious. It should all work very well.

Unfortunately for McKenzie, his office had been too efficient. Governments need to know where their Ministers and supporters are at all times, in case of emergency or in case of a sudden vote in the House of Commons for which they will need to be called in at short notice. And the office accorded the responsibility for maintaining and updating the information on the whereabouts of Ministers is, of course, that of the Chief Whip. On the previous Friday, following her standing instructions to the letter, McKenzie's diary secretary had sent a full list of his forthcoming week's engagements over to Urquhart's office in

12 Downing Street. Thereafter, one telephone call was all it took.

As they drove the last few hundred yards down the country road to the factory's green-field site, McKenzie combed his hair and prepared himself for the cameras. They drew alongside the red brick wall which curved around the site and, as the Minister in the rear seat made sure his tie was straight, the car swept in through the front gates.

No sooner was it through than the driver jammed on all the brakes, throwing McKenzie against the front seat, spilling papers on the floor and ruining his careful preparations. Before he had a chance to curse the driver and demand an explanation, the cause of the problem immediately confronted and swirled around him. It was a sight beyond his wildest nightmare.

The tiny car park in front of the factory's reception office was jammed with a throng of seething protesters, all dressed in nurse's uniform and hurling abuse, with every angry word and action recorded by three television cameras which had been dutifully summoned by McKenzie's press officer and placed in an ideal viewing position on top of the administration block. No sooner was the official car inside the gates than the crowd surged around, kicking the bodywork and banging placards on the roof. In a couple of seconds the aerial had gone and the windscreen wipers had also been wrenched off. The driver had the sense to press the panic button fitted to all Ministerial cars which automatically closed the windows and locked the doors, but not before someone had managed to spit directly into McKenzie's face. Fists and contorted faces were pressed hard up against the glass, all threatening violence on him; the car rocked as the crowd pressed hard against it, until he could see no sky, no trees, no help, nothing but hatred at close distance.

'Get out! Get out!' he screamed, but the driver raised his hands in helplessness. The crowd had surrounded the car, blocking off any hope of retreat.

'Get out!' he continued to scream, overcome by the claustrophobia of the crowd, but to no avail. In desperation the Minister leaned forward and grabbed the automatic gear stick, throwing it into reverse. The car gave a judder and moved back barely a foot before the driver's foot hit the brake, but the closely penned crowd had felt the impact. The protesters quickly withdrew to leave an exit for the car, taking with them a young woman in nurse's uniform who appeared to be in great pain after having been struck by the retreating car. Seeing his opening, the driver smoothly reversed his vehicle out of the gates and onto the road, pulling off a spectacular hand-brake turn to bring the nose of the car round and effect a rapid escape. He sped away leaving large black rubber scars on the road surface. The cameras continued to record every panic-stricken moment.

McKenzie's political career was also left on the road alongside the ugly burnt tyre marks. It did not matter that the woman was not badly injured, or that she was not indeed a nurse at all but a fulltime union convenor and an experienced hand at turning a picket line drama into a newsworthy crisis. No one bothered to enquire. No man who could antagonise so many nurses and act in such a cowardly fashion in seeking to evade their protest could possibly occupy 10 Downing Street. For McKenzie, the tide had turned again and he watched helplessly as his life raft drifted back over the horizon.

FRIDAY 19TH NOVEMBER

It had been a difficult week for Mattie, and a lonely one too, and she was having to work hard to keep her spirits up. While the pace of activity in the leadership race had picked up sharply, she found herself treading water, feeling as if she were being left behind by events. Nothing had come of her few job interviews, it had become clear to her that she had been blacked by all the newspapers in the expanding Landless empire, and none of his remaining competitors seemed particularly keen to antagonise him unnecessarily. And on Friday morning the mortgage rate had gone up.

Even worse, while she had more pieces of the jigsaw, still she could find no pattern in them. And it hurt. Inside her head the few facts she had gathered collided with her own speculative thoughts, but nothing seemed to fit. The collision left a dull, throbbing ache in her temples which had been with her incessantly for days. So she had hauled her running gear out of the wardrobe and was soon pounding her way around the leaf-covered tracks and pathways of Holland Park, hoping that the much needed physical exercise would purge both body and mind. But the throbbing in her head only combined with the new and growing pains in her lungs and legs to make it all hurt even more. She was running out of ideas, stamina and time. The first ballot was just four days away.

In the fading evening light she ran along the sweeping avenue of chestnut trees which towered magnificent and leafless above her like a living tunnel inhabited by half-seen, ghostly apparitions; down Lime Tree Walk where in daylight the squirrels and sparrows were as tame as house pets; past the red bricked ruins of old Holland House, burned to the ground half a century before along with its books, beauty and secrets, leaving just its brooding memories of past glories. In the days before what was left of Elizabethan London had grown into a voracious urban sprawl, Holland House had been the country seat of Charles James Fox, the legendary 18th century radical who had spent a lifetime pursuing revolutionary causes and who had used his ancestral home to gather all his conspiratorial colleagues and plot the downfall of the Prime Minister. It had always been in vain. Yet who had succeeded now where he had failed?

She went over the ground again, the field of battle on which Collingridge had fallen. It had started with the general election campaign which had gone badly wrong, with Collingridge and Williams left to blame each other and argue whose fault it all was.

Then came the fiasco of the hospital scheme, courtesy of Stephen Kendrick. There were no leads on the leak of Territorial Army cuts to the *Independent*; the document had been discovered floating around Annie's Bar, and they could scarcely blame Annie . . . The opinion poll, too, had been leaked – just another part of Collingridge's death by a thousand cuts – but she had no idea whom to thank for that. O'Neill, she knew, was involved in the extraordinary episode of share purchases through the Paddington address, and Landless had taken a sudden and uncharacteristic interest in high politics, with motive unclear.

That was it. That was all she had. So where did she go from here? As she climbed up the slope towards the highest part of the wooded park, she pounded away at the alternatives.

'Collingridge isn't giving interviews. Williams will only talk through his press office. O'Neill doesn't seem capable of answering questions, and Landless wouldn't stop for me on a pedestrian crossing. Which leaves only you, Mr Kendrick!'

With one final spurt she reached the top of the hill and began stretching out on the long downhill slope which led towards her home. Now she felt better. She had got her second wind.

SATURDAY 20TH NOVEMBER

It had not been too bad a week for Harold Earle. The media had nominated him as one of the five candidates most likely to succeed; he had watched Samuel's bandwagon fail to roll and McKenzie's become derailed. And in spite of the Chief Whip's creditable showing, Earle could not believe that Urquhart would succeed because he had no senior Cabinet experience of running any great Department of State, and at the end of the day experience really counted for the top job. Particularly experience like Earle's.

He had started his climb many years before as the Prime Minister's Parliamentary Private Secretary, a post in which he joked that he held more power than anyone below Chancellor. His promotion to the Cabinet had been rapid, and he had held several important portfolios, including, for the last two years under Collingridge, responsibility for the Government's extensive school reforms as Secretary of State for Education. Unlike some of his predecessors, he had managed to find common ground with the teaching profession, although some accused him of being unable to take really tough decisions and being a conciliator.

But didn't the Party in its present mood need a touch of conciliation? The infighting around Collingridge had left its scars, and the growing abrasiveness of the campaign was only rubbing salt in the wounds. In particular, Woolton's attempt to shed his diplomatic veneer and rekindle memories of his early rough and tumble North Country political style was antagonising some of the more traditional spirits in the Party. Perhaps the time was exactly right for Earle.

On Saturday, he planned a rally amongst the party faithful in his constituency to wave the flag. A brightly decked hall packed with supporters whom he could greet on first-name terms – in front of the cameras, of course – seemed an ideal location for a major pronouncement on schools policy. He and his officials had been working on it for some time, and with just a little hurrying forward they would have it ready for announcement on Saturday – a Government-sponsored plan offering school leavers who could not find a job not only a guaranteed place on a training course, but now the opportunity to complete that training in another Common Market country, providing practical skills and language training as well.

Earle was confident it would be well received. The speech would glow with rapture about the new horizons and job opportunities which would open up for young people, and the mortal blow he was delivering to the British businessman's traditionally apathetic approach to dealing with foreign customers in their own language.

And then the *coup de grâce*. He had got the Common Market bureaucrats in Brussels to agree to pay for the whole thing. He could already feel the tumultuous applause washing over him, carrying him on to Downing Street.

There was a large crowd of cheering supporters outside the Essex village hall to greet him when he arrived at midday. They were waving little Union Jacks and old election posters which had been brought out to give the occasion all the atmosphere of the campaign trail. The village band struck up as he came through the doors at the rear of the hall, proceeding down the aisle shaking hands on all sides. The local mayor led him up onto the low wooden platform as the cameramen and lighting crews scurried around to find the best angle. He gazed out over the crowd, shielding his eyes from the lights, waving to their applause even as the mayor tried to introduce him. He felt as if he was on the brink of the greatest personal triumph of his life.

Then he saw him. Standing in the front row, squashed between the other cheering supporters, waving and applauding with the rest of them. Simon. The one person in the world he had hoped he would never see or hear from again. He remembered how they had first met – how could he ever forget? It was in the railway carriage as Earle had been coming back from the late night rally in the North West. They had been alone, Earle had been drunk, and Simon had been very, very friendly. And handsome. As the train thundered through the night they had entered a different, dark world cut off from the bright lights and responsibilities they had just left, and Earle had discovered himself committing an act which would have made him liable to a prison sentence several years before, and which was still only legal between consenting adults in private. And a British Rail carriage twenty minutes out of Birmingham is not the most private of locations.

Earle had staggered out of the carriage at Euston, thrust two £20 notes into Simon's hand, and spent the night at his club. He couldn't face going back to the home he shared with his ailing mother.

He hadn't seen Simon for another six months, but suddenly he had turned up in the Central Lobby of the Houses of Parliament asking the police attendants if he could see him. When the Minister arrived the youth didn't make a fuss, explaining how he had recognised Earle from the recent party political broadcast, asking for the money in a very delicate and gentle fashion. Earle had paid him some 'expenses' for his trip to London, but on Simon's second visit a few weeks later he knew there would be no respite. He had instructed Simon to wait, and had sought sanctuary in the corner of the Chamber. He spent ten minutes looking over the scene which he had grown to love so dearly, knowing that the youth outside threatened everything he had.

He could find no answer himself, so he had gone straight along to the Chief Whip's Office and spilled the lot. There was a youth sitting in the Central Lobby blackmailing him for a brief and stupid fling they had had many months before, he had confessed. He was finished.

Never mind, don't worry, he had been assured. Worse things had happened on the retreat from Dunkirk. Point him out and leave it all to the Chief Whip.

Urquhart had been as good as his word. He had introduced himself to the boy, and assured him that if he were not off the premises in five minutes the police would be called and he would be arrested for blackmail. The boy was further assured that in such cases the arrest and subsequent trial were held with little publicity, no one would discover the name of the Member concerned, and few people would even hear how long he had been sent down for. Little more pressure was needed to persuade the youth he had made a terrible mistake and should depart as quickly as possible, but Urquhart had taken the precaution of taking down the details from Simon's driving licence, just in case he were to continue to cause trouble and needed to be tracked down.

And now he was back there, in the front row, ready to make unknown demands about which Earle's fevered imagination could only torment itself. The torment went on throughout the speech, which ended as a considerable disappointment to his followers. The content was there, printed in large type on his small pages of recycled paper, but the fire was gone. The faithful had come to listen to him, not his officials' tired prose, yet he seemed to be elsewhere even as he was delivering the lines.

They still clapped and applauded enthusiastically when he was finished, but it didn't help. The mayor had almost to drag him into the pit of the hall to satisfy the clamour of the crowd for one last handshake and the chance personally to wish their favourite son well. As they shouted at him and kissed his cheeks and pummelled him on the back, he was drawn ever closer to the youthful eyes staring benevolently at him, as if he were being dragged towards the gates of Hell itself.

But Simon caused no scene, did nothing but shake his hand warmly and smile prettily, one hand toying nervously with the gold medallion which swung ostentatiously around his neck. Then he was gone, just another face left behind in the crowd, and Earle was in his car speeding back towards London and safety.

When he arrived back at home, two men were standing outside in the cold street waiting for him.

'Evening, Mr Earle. Simmonds and Peters from the *Mirror*. Interesting rally you had. We've got the press handout, the words, but we need a bit of colour for our readers. Like how the audience reacted. Got anything to say about your audience, Mr Earle?'

He rushed inside without saying anything, slamming the door behind him. He watched through a curtained window as they shrugged their shoulders and retreated to the estate car parked on the other side of the street. They pulled out a book and a thermos flask, and settled in for the long night ahead.

SUNDAY 21ST NOVEMBER

They were still there the following morning just after dawn when Earle looked out. One was asleep, napping under a trilby hat pulled down over his eyes. The other was reading the Sunday newspapers, which bore little resemblance to the previous week's editions. A leadership campaign which then had been dead in the water had now, with Urquhart's intervention and McKenzie's catastrophe, sprung to life. And the pollsters were beginning to wear down the MPs' resistance to their probing.

'All square!' declared the *Observer*, announcing that the 60 per cent of the Parliamentary Party they had managed to cajole into giving a view were now evenly split between the three leading candidates – Samuel, Earle and Woolton, with Urquhart close behind and McKenzie now clearly out of it. The small lead to which Samuel had previously clung had entirely disappeared.

But the news gave no joy to Earle. He had spent a ruinous and totally sleepless night, pacing the floors but being able to find no solace. Everywhere he had looked for comfort, he could see only Simon's face. The presence of the two journalists had kept nagging at him. How much did they know? Why were they squatting on his doorstep? The long wait through the night until the first fingers of dawn spread cold and grey in the November sky had drained him of hope and resistance. He had to know for certain.

Peters nudged Simmonds awake as the unshaven figure of Earle, his silk dressing gown dragged tightly around him, appeared at the front door of the house and made towards them.

'Works like a dream every time,' Peters said. 'They simply can't resist trying to investigate, like a mouse after cheese. Let's see what he has to say for himself, Alf – and turn that bloody tape machine on.'

'Good morning, Mr Earle,' Peters shouted as Earle approached. 'Don't stand out there in the cold, sit inside. Care for a cup of coffee?'

'What do you want? Why are you spying on me?'

'Spying, Mr Earle? Don't be silly, we're just looking for a bit of colour. You're a leading candidate in an important election campaign. Seen the newspapers yet? People are bound to take more interest in you – about your hobbies, what you do, who your friends are.'

'I have nothing to say!'

'Could we interview your wife, perhaps?' asked Simmonds 'Silly me, you're not married, of course, are you Mr Earle?'

'What are you implying?' Earle demanded in a contorted, high pitched voice.

'My goodness me nothing at all, sir. By the way, have you seen the photos of your rally yesterday? They're very good, really clear. We're thinking of using one on our front page tomorrow. Here, have a look.'

A hand thrust a large glossy photograph out of the window and waved it under Earle's nose. He grabbed it, and gasped. It clearly showed him gripping the hand and looking straight into the eyes of a smiling Simon. The details were awesomely clear, perhaps too clear. It almost looked as if some hidden hand had added a trace of eyeliner around Simon's large eyes, and his fleshy, petulant lips appeared to have been made darker, more prominent. As his manicured fingers played with the gold medallion around his neck, he looked very, very effeminate.

'Know him well, do you, sir?'

Earle threw the photograph back through the car window.

'What are you trying to do? I deny everything. I shall report your harassment to your editor!'

Earle rushed back towards his front door.

'Editor, sir? Why, bless me, it was him what sent us,' Simmonds shouted at the Minister's retreating back.

As the door slammed shut behind the fleeing figure,

Peters turned to his colleague. 'There goes one very worried man, Alf.'

They settled back to their newspapers.

MONDAY 22ND NOVEMBER

Kendrick had accepted Mattie's request for a chat with alacrity. He wasn't sure he had been so keen simply because as an Opposition backbencher he was flattered to be in demand, or simply because his eyes flared and his knees tingled every time he saw her. In any event, it didn't really matter to Kendrick what his real motives were, he was delighted to meet with her. He was making their tea himself in his single room office in Norman Shaw North, the red brick building made famous in countless ageing black and white films as New Scotland Yard, the head-quarters of the Metropolitan Police. The forces of law and order had long since moved to a more modern and efficient base in Victoria Street, but the parliamentary authorities had been delighted to snap up the vacant, albeit dilapidated, space just across the road from the Houses of Parliament to provide much needed additional working room for the horrendously overcrowded Members of Parliament.

As he gazed out over the Thames towards the South Bank arts complex, Kendrick poured tea and opened his heart.

'I have to say I never really expected all this,' he said. 'But I've grown to like it very much indeed.'

'You've also managed to make your mark very quickly,' Mattie smiled her most winning of smiles and recrossed her legs. She had been careful to discard her favoured trousers for a fashionable blouse and skirt which showed off her legs and slender ankles to their best effect. She needed some information, and would buy it with a little flirting if needs be.

'I'm doing a feature piece on the decline and fall of the Prime Minister, trying to get behind the basic news stories and talk to those who played a part in it, whether they had intended to or not. It won't be an unsympathetic piece, I'm not trying to moralise or lay blame. I'm trying rather to offer an insight into how Parliament works and how politics can be so full of surprises. And when it comes to surprises, yours was one of the biggest.'

Kendrick chuckled. 'I'm still amazed at how my parliamentary reputation was built on such a – well, what would you call it? Stroke of luck? Throw of the dice? Guess work?'

'Are you saying you didn't actually know that the hospital scheme had been shelved, that you were guessing?'

'Put it this way. I wasn't absolutely certain. I took a risk.'

'So what did you know?'

'Well, Mattie, I've never really told the full story before to anyone . . .' He glanced down to where Mattie was rubbing her ankles, as if to relieve sore shins. 'But I suppose there's no harm in telling you a little of the background.'

He pondered a second to decide how far he should go. 'I discovered that the Government – or rather their party headquarters – had planned a massive publicity campaign to promote the new plan for expanding hospitals. They had worked hard at it, spent a lot of money on the preparations, yet at the last minute they cancelled the whole thing. Just pulled the plug on it. I thought about this for a long while, and the only explanation I could reach was that they were actually pulling the plug, not just on the publicity campaign but on the policy itself. So I challenged the Prime Minister – and he fell for it! I couldn't have been more surprised myself.'

'I don't remember any discussion at the time about a publicity campaign. It must have been kept very quiet.'

'Of course, they wanted to keep the element of surprise. I believe all the planning of it was highly confidential.'

'You obviously have excellent confidential sources.'

'Yes. And they are staying confidential, even from you, I'm afraid!'

Mattie knew that she would need to offer much more than a flashing pair of ankles to get that sort of information out of him, and she was unwilling to pay so high a price.

'Of course, Stephen. I know how valuable sources are.

But can you give me a little guidance? The leak could only have come from one of two sources, Party or Government, yes . . . ?'

He nodded.

'And there has been a tremendous amount of publicity about the rift between party headquarters and Downing Street in recent months. Particularly as it was to be a party publicity drive, it would be logical to suspect that the information came out of party headquarters.'

She raised an enquiring eyebrow, and puckered her lips.

'You're very good, very good, Mattie. But you didn't get that from me, OK? And I'm not saying any more about my source. You're too hot by half!'

He was beginning to chuckle merrily when Mattie played her own hunch.

'No need to worry. I want to write a feature piece, not conduct an inquisition. Roger's secret is safe with me.'

Kendrick spat out the mouthful of tea he was trying to drink and started choking.

'I never . . . said anything about . . . Roger!' he spluttered. But he knew he had betrayed his familiarity with O'Neill, and the calm face he was trying to restore simply eluded him. He decided to surrender.

'Jesus. How did you know? Look, Mattie. Big favour time. I didn't say anything about Roger. We're old friends and I don't want to land him in any sort of hot water. He's got enough at Smith Square as it is, eh?'

Mattie laughed loudly, teasing the politician for his discomfort.

'Your sordid secret is safe with me,' she assured him. 'But when you have risen to become a senior member of Government some time in the future, perhaps even Prime Minister, I hope you will remember you owe me!'

They both laughed loudly at the banter but, inside, Mattie's stomach churned. Another piece of the jigsaw had just fallen into place.

They were there at lunchtime and still there in the evening, just reading, picking their teeth, and watching. Like avenging angels they had waited for Earle in their sordid little car from over forty-eight hours, witnessing every flicker of the curtain, photographing everyone who called including the postman and the milkman.

'What do they want with me?' he screamed to himself inside his head. 'Why are they persecuting me like this?'

He had no one to turn to, no one with whom to share his misery and offer consolation. He was a lonely figure, a sincere and even devout man who had made one mistake, and he knew sooner or later he must pay for it. His mother had always drilled into him the need to pay for one's sins or be consumed by hell fire, and he felt the flames licking at him now with growing ferocity.

He had been home half an hour on Monday evening when they knocked on the door.

'Sorry to bother you, Mr Earle. Simmonds and Peters again. Just a quick question our editor wanted us to ask. How long have you known him?'

Into his face was thrust another photograph, still of Simon, but this time taken not at a public rally but in a photographer's studio, and dressed from head to foot in black leather slashed by zip fasteners. The jacket was open to the waist, exposing a slender, tapering body, while from his right hand there trailed a long bullwhip.

'Go away. Go away. Please – go away!' he screamed, so loudly that neighbours came to the window to investigate.

'If it's inconvenient, we'll come back some other time, sir.'

Silently they filed back to their car, and resumed the watch.

TUESDAY 23RD NOVEMBER

They were still there the following morning. After yet another sleepless night, Earle knew he had no emotional resources left. With red eyes and husky voice, he sat weeping gently in an armchair in the study. He had worked so hard, deserved so much, yet it had all come to this. He had tried so desperately to deserve his mother's love and commendation, to achieve something with which to illumi nate her final years, but once again he had failed her, as she always said he would.

He knew he must finish it. There was no point in going on. He no longer believed in himself, and knew he had forfeited the right to have others believe in him. Through misty eyes he reached down into the drawer of his desk, and fumbled as he took out his private phone book. He punched the numbers on the phone as if they were nails being driven through his soul. He fought hard to control his voice throughout the brief conversation, but then it was finished, and he could weep again.

The news that Earle had pulled out of the race left everyone aghast as it flashed round Westminster later on Tuesday morning. It had happened so unexpectedly that there was no time to alter the printed ballot papers except with an ignominious scratching through of the name with a biro. Sir Humphrey was not best pleased that his carefully laid preparations should have been thrown into chaos at the last minute, and had some rough words to use for anyone who was willing to listen. But on the stroke of ten Committee Room Number 14, which had been set aside in the House of Commons for the ballot, opened its doors and the first of the 335 Government MPs who were going to vote began to file through. There would be two prominent

271

absentees – the Prime Minister, who had announced he would not vote, and Harold Earle.

Mattie had intended to spend the whole day at the House of Commons chatting to MPs and gauging their sentiment. Most appeared to think that Earle's withdrawal would tend to help Samuel as much as anyone: 'the conciliators tend to stick with the conscience merchants,' one old buffer had explained, 'so Earle's supporters will drift towards young Disraeli. They haven't got the sense to make any more positive decision.' Behind the scenes and in private conversations with colleagues who could be trusted, the campaign was taking a more unpleasant personal edge.

She was in the press gallery cafeteria drinking coffee with other correspondents when the tannoy system announced there was a telephone call for her. She took it at the nearest extension. The sense of shock which hit her when she heard the voice was even greater than the news of Earle's withdrawal.

'Hello, Mattie. I understand you were looking for me last week. Sorry you missed me, I was out of the office. Touch of gastric 'flu. Do you still want to get together?'

Roger O'Neill sounded so friendly and enthusiastic that she had trouble connecting it with the voice she had heard a few days earlier. Could it really have been O'Neill she had listened to drivelling down the phone? She remembered the reports about his outrageous performance at Urquhart's reception in Bournemouth, and realised the man must be riding an emotional helter skelter, careering between highs and lows like a demented circus ride.

'If you are still interested, perhaps you would like to come across to Smith Square later today,' he offered.

He showed no signs of the verbal bruising he had received from Urquhart, which had been particularly merciless. Urquhart had telephoned to instruct O'Neill to make the appropriate arrangements for Simon to attend Earle's weekend meeting, and to ensure that the *Mirror* was anonymously informed of the connections between the two men. Instead he had discovered that O'Neill was sliding steadily into his cocaine-induced oblivion and losing

272

touch with events outside his increasingly narrow, kaleido-
scopic world. There had been a confrontation. Urquhart
could not afford to lose O'Neill's services inside party
headquarters, or have loose ends unravelling at this point.

'One week, Roger, one more week and you can take a
break, forget about all of this for a while if you want, and
come back to that knighthood you've always wanted. Yes,
Roger, with a "K" they will never be able to look down
their noses at you again. And I can arrange everything for
you. But you let me down now, you lose control and I will
make sure you regret it for the rest of your life. Damn you,
get a grip on yourself. You've got nothing to fear. Just hold
on for a few more days!'

O'Neill wasn't absolutely sure what Urquhart was going
on about; to be sure he had been a little unwell but his
befuddled brain still refused to accept there was a major
problem which he couldn't handle. Why fill one's life with
doubts, especially about oneself? He could cope with it,
particularly with a little help . . . Still, a few days more to
realise all his ambitions, to get the public recognition he
deserved, to wipe the condescending smiles off their faces,
would be worth a little extra effort.

He had got back into the office to be told that Mattie had
been looking for him, that she was asking questions about
the Paddington accommodation address.

'Don't worry, Pen. I'll deal with it.' He fell back on the
swaggering confidence of years of salesmanship, of persuading people to buy ideas and arguments, not because
they were all particularly good but because his audiences
found themselves captivated by his energy and enthusiasm. In a world full of cynicism, they wanted to put their
trust in a man who seemed to believe so passionately in
what he was offering.

When Mattie arrived in his office after lunch, he was
bright, alert, those strange eyes of his still amazingly animated but seeming very anxious to help.

'Just a stomach upset,' he explained. 'Sorry I had to
stand you up.'

Mattie acknowledged that his smile was full of charm; it
was difficult not to want to believe him.

273

'I understand you were asking about Mr Collingridge's accommodation address?'

'Sounds as if you are admitting that it *was* Charles Collingridge's address?' she enquired.

'Well, if you want something on the record, you know I have to say that Mr Collingridge's personal affairs are his own, and no one here is going to comment one way or the other on any speculation.' He trotted out the Downing Street line with accomplished ease. 'But may I talk to you off the record, not for reporting?'

He made strong eye contact with her as if to establish his sincerity, rising from behind his desk to come and sit alongside Mattie in one of the informal chairs which littered his office.

'Even off the record, Mattie, there's a limit to how much I can say, but you know how unwell Charles has been. He's not been fully responsible for his actions, and it would be a terrible pity if we were to go out of our way to punish him still further. His life is in ruins. Whatever he has done wrong, hasn't he suffered enough already?'

Mattie felt angry as she watched the loading of guilt onto the shoulders of the absent Charles. The whole world is to blame, Roger, except for you.

'Are you denying that Charles Collingridge himself asked you to open that address?'

'So long as this is not for reporting but for your background information, I'm not going to deny it, but what good will it do anyone to re-open such old wounds? Give him a chance to rebuild his life,' he pleaded.

'OK, Roger. I see no point in trying to subject him to further harassment. So let me turn to a different point. There have been lots of accusations about how party headquarters has been very careless in allowing damaging material to leak out in recent months. The Prime Minister is supposed to blame Smith Square very directly for much of his troubles.'

'I doubt whether that is fair, but it is no secret that relations between him and the Party Chairman have been very strained.'

'Strained enough for that opinion poll we published

during party conference week to have been leaked deliberately from party headquarters?'

Mattie had to look very hard to detect the faint glimmer of surprise behind his flashing eyes before he sped into his explanation.

'I think that assumption is very difficult to justify. There are only – what, five people in this building who are circulated with copies of that material apart from the Party Chairman. I'm one of those five, and I can tell you how seriously we take the confidentiality of such material.' He lit a Gauloise. Time to think. 'But it also gets sent to every Cabinet Minister, all twenty-two of them, either at the House of Commons where it would be opened by one of those gossipy secretaries, or to their Departments where it would be opened by a civil servant, many of whom have no love for this Government. Any leak is much more likely to have come from there.'

'But the papers were leaked at the headquarters hotel in Bournemouth. House of Commons secretaries or unfriendly civil servants don't go to the party conference or roam around the headquarters hotel.'

'Who knows, Mattie. It's still much more likely to have come from a source like that. Can you imagine Lord Williams scurrying around on his hands and knees outside hotel room doors?'

He laughed loudly to show how ridiculous it was, and Mattie joined in, realising that O'Neill had just admitted he knew the manner in which the opinion poll had been handed over, and he could only have known that for one reason. His overconfidence was tightening the noose around his neck even as he laughed.

'Let me turn to another leak then, on the hospital expansion scheme. Now I am told that party headquarters was planning a major publicity drive during last summer, which had to be scrapped because of the change of plan.'

'Really? Who on earth told you that?' asked O'Neill, knowing full well that it could only have been Kendrick, probably egged on by his weakness for a pretty woman. 'Never mind, I know you won't reveal your sources. But they sound exaggerated to me. The Publicity Department

275

here is always ready to sell Government policy, and had the scheme gone ahead then certainly we would have wanted to help promote it, but we had no specific campaign in mind.'

'I was told you had to scrap a campaign which had been carefully planned and which was ready to go.'

The limp ash from his cigarette gave up its struggle to defy the laws of gravity and cascaded like an avalanche down his tie, but O'Neill ignored it. He was concentrating hard now.

'You've been misinformed. Sounds to me like someone wanting to dig up the story again and trying to show the Party in much greater confusion than it actually was. Your source sounds a bit dubious to me. Are you sure he's in a position to know all the facts, or has he got his own angle to sell?'

With a broad grin, O'Neill tried to smother Kendrick as a reliable source, and the smile which Mattie returned betrayed none of her own wonderment at his impromptu yet superbly crafted explanations. But she was asking far too many leading questions, and even a polished performer such as O'Neill was beginning to feel distinctly uncomfortable. He felt a gut-wrenching need for greater stimulation and support than his Gauloise could give him, no matter what Urquhart had said.

'Mattie, I'm afraid I've got a busy day, and I have to make sure we are ready to handle the result of the ballot later this evening. Could we finish it here?'

'Thanks for your time, Roger. I have found it immensely helpful in clearing up a few things.'

'Any time I can help,' he said as he guided her towards the door. As they did so, they passed by the computer terminal stationed in the corner of his crowded office. She bent down to inspect it more closely.

'I'm an absolute moron with these things,' she commented, turning to look straight into his flickering eyes. 'I'm impressed to see your Party is well ahead of the others in using new technology. Are all the terminals in this building linked through the central computer?'

'I. . . believe so,' he said, pressing her more firmly towards the door.

'I never knew you had such high-tech skills, Roger,' she complimented.

'Oh, I don't,' he said in a surprisingly defensive mood. 'We all get put through a training course, but I'm not even sure how to switch the wretched things on, actually. Never use it myself.' His smile had tightened, and his eyes were flickering ever more violently. He propelled Mattie through the door with some force, and bade her a hasty farewell.

At 5 p.m. the doors to the Commons Committee Room were ceremoniously shut to bar any further attempts to lodge votes in the leadership election. The gesture was an empty one, because the last of the 335 votes had been cast ten minutes earlier. Behind the doors gathered Sir Humphrey and his small team of scrutineers, happy that the day had gone smoothly in spite of the appalling start given to their preparations by Earle. A bottle of whisky did the rounds while they fortified themselves for the count. In different rooms around the Palace of Westminster, the candidates waited in various states of excitement for the summons which would tell them that the counting had finished and the result was ready to be announced.

Big Ben had struck the quarter after six before the eight candidates received the call, and at half past the hour more than 120 active supporters and interested MPs accompanied them as the Committee Room doors swung open to allow them back in. There was much good humour mixed with the tension as they filed in and stood around in loose groups, with substantial sums being wagered as Members made last-minute calculations as to the likely result and gambled their judgement against the inconclusive opinion polls which had been filling the press. Outside the room, excluded from what was technically a private party meeting, the men from the media did their own speculating and made their own odds.

Sir Humphrey was enjoying his little moment of history. He was in the twilight of his career, long since past his parliamentary heyday, and even the little misunderstanding over his holiday in the West Indies had helped bring him greater recognition and attention around the Westminster circuit than he had enjoyed for many years. Who knows, if he handled this correctly, his secret longing for a seat in the House of Lords might yet be fulfilled. He sat on the raised dais of the Committee Room, flanked by his lieutenants, and called the meeting to order.

'Since there has been such an unprecedentedly large number of names on the ballot paper, I propose to read the results out in alphabetical order.'

This was unwelcome news for David Adams, the former Leader of the House who had been banished to discontented exile on the backbenches by Collingridge's first reshuffle. Having spent the last two years criticising all the major economic decisions which he had supported whilst in Government, he had hoped for a good showing in order to establish his claim for a return to Cabinet. He stood there stoically, hiding his grief as Newlands announced he had received only twelve votes. He was left to wonder what had happened to all those firm promises of support he had received while Sir Humphrey continued with his roll call. None of the next four names, including McKenzie's, could muster the support of more than twenty of their colleagues with Paul Goddard, the maverick Catholic who had stood on the single issue of banning all forms of legalised abortion, receiving only three. He shook his head defiantly; his rewards were not to be of the earthly kind.

Sir Humphrey had only three more names to announce – Samuel, Urquhart and Woolton – and a total of 281 votes to distribute. The level of tension soared as those present recalled that a minimum of 169 votes was required for success on the first ballot. A couple of huge side bets were instantly concluded in one corner as two Honourable Members wagered that there would, after all, be a result on the first round.

'The Right Honourable Michael Samuel,' intoned the chairman, '99 votes.'

In the dead silence of the Committee Room, the sound

of a tug blowing its klaxon three times as it passed on its way up the Thames could be clearly heard. A ripple of amusement covered the tension, and Samuel muttered that it was a pity tug masters didn't have a vote. He was clearly disappointed to be such a long way from the necessary winning total, particularly after Earle's withdrawal.

'The Right Honourable Francis Urquhart – 91 votes.'

Two of the gamblers in the corner looked crestfallen as they calculated the final figure.

'The Right Honourable Patrick Woolton – 91 votes.'

There was general commotion as the tension ebbed, congratulations and condolences were exchanged, and one Member leaned around the door to give the highlights to the anxious press.

'Accordingly,' Sir Humphrey continued, 'no candidate has been elected and there will be a second round of balloting a week today. I would remind everyone that those wishing to offer themselves as candidates for the second ballot must resubmit their nominations to me by Thursday. I declare this meeting closed!'

Urquhart was giving some celebratory drinks to colleagues in his room. It was one of the finest offices available to a Member, located on the premises rather than in one of the various annexes spotted around the periphery of the Palace of Westminster, large and airy with a gracious bow window offering a fine view across the river to the Arch bishop of Canterbury's ancient Gothic home at Lambeth Palace. The room was now crowded with several dozen Members, all offering their best wishes for the Chief Whip's success. Wryly he noted that it was the first time during the campaign that he had seen some of these faces, but he did not mind. Votes were votes, wherever they came from.

'Quite splendid, Francis. Absolutely excellent result. Do you think you can go on to win?' enquired one of his senior parliamentary colleagues.

'I believe so,' Urquhart responded with quiet confidence. 'I suspect I have as good a chance as anyone.'

'I think you're right, you know,' his colleague said.

'Young Samuel may be ahead, but his campaign is going backwards. It's between the experienced heads of you and Patrick now. And, Francis, I want you to know that you have my wholehearted support.'

Which, of course, you will want me to remember when I have my hands on all that Prime Ministerial patronage, he thought to himself while he offered his gratitude and a fresh drink to his guest.

New faces were still pouring into the room as word spread that the Chief Whip was entertaining. Urquhart's secretary was pouring a large whisky for Stephen Dunway, the most ambitious of the new intake of MPs who had already that evening made brief but prominent appearances at both Samuel's and Woolton's receptions on the basis that you can never be too sure. The secretary excused herself to answer the telephone, which had been ringing all evening with calls of congratulations and press enquiries.

'It's for you,' she whispered gently into Urquhart's ear. 'Roger O'Neill.'

'Tell him I'm busy and that I will call him later,' he instructed.

'He called earlier and sounds very anxious. Asked me to tell you it was "very bloody hot", to quote his exact words,' she said primly.

With an impatient curse he withdrew from his guests and sought shelter in the corner of the bay window from the noise of celebration.

'Roger,' he spoke sharply into the phone. 'Is this really necessary? I've got a room full of people.'

'She's on to us, Francis. That bloody bitch – she knows, I'm sure. She knows it's me and she'll be on to you next, the cow. I haven't told her a thing but she's got hold of it and God knows how but . . .'

'Roger! Pull yourself together!' snapped Urquhart. O'Neill was gabbling and the conversation was running away like a driverless express. It was clear he had been unable to stick to Urquhart's orders, and was not fully in control.

There was a moment of silence and Urquhart tried to

re-establish his authority. 'Tell me slowly and clearly what all this is about.'

Immediately the gabbling began again, and Urquhart was forced to listen, trying to make some sort of sense of the garbled mixture of words, splutters and sneezes.

'She came over to see me, the cow from the press lobby. I don't know how, Francis, it's not me and I told her nothing. I fobbed her off – think she went away happy. But somehow she had got onto it. Everything, Francis. The Paddington address; the computer; she even suspects that someone from headquarters leaked the opinion poll I put under her door. And that bastard Kendrick must have told her about the hospital campaign you told me to concoct. Jesus, Francis. I mean, what if she doesn't believe me and decides to print something?'

'Hold your tongue for a second,' he seethed down the phone, anxious that none of his guests should overhear him. 'Just tell me this. Who came to see you from the lobby?'

'Storin. Mattie Storin. And she said . . .'

'Did she have any firm evidence?' Urquhart interrupted. 'Or is she just guessing?'

O'Neill paused for the briefest of moments to consider the question.

'Nothing firm, I think. Just guesswork. Except . . .'

'Except what?'

'She's been told I opened the Paddington address.'

'How on earth did she find that out?' Urquhart's fury poured like molten lava down the phone.

'My secretary told her, but there is no need to worry because she thinks I did it for Collingridge.'

'Your secretary knew?'

'I . . . took her with me. I thought she would be more inconspicuous and she's utterly trustworthy. You know that.'

'Roger I could happily . . .'

'Look, it's me who's done all your dirty jobs for you, taken all the risks. You've got nothing to worry about while I'm in it up to my neck if this breaks. I need help, Francis. I'm scared! I've done too many things for you which I shouldn't have touched, but I didn't ask questions and just did what you said. You've got to get me out of this, I can't take much more and I *won't* take much more. You've got to protect me, Francis. Do you hear? You've got to help me!' O'Neill broke down into uncontrollable sobbing.

'Roger, calm yourself,' he said quietly into the receiver. 'She has absolutely no proof and you have nothing to fear. We are in this *together*, you understand? And we shall get through it together, to Downing Street. I shan't let you down. Look, I want you to do two things. I want you to keep remembering that knighthood. It's just a few days away now, Roger.'

A stumbling expression of gratitude came spluttering down the phone.

'And in the meantime, Roger – for God's sake keep well away from Mattie Storin!'

After he had put the phone down Urquhart sat there for a moment, letting his emotions wash over him. From behind him came the hubbub of the powerful men who would project him into 10 Downing Street, fulfilling the dream which had burned inside him all these years. To the front he gazed across the centuries old view of the river which had inspired generations of great national leaders whose ranks he was now surely to join. And he had just put the phone down on the only man who could ruin it all for him.

Trying to sort out the implications of the leadership ballot had left Mattie feeling drained. She needed to assess opinions as they were being formed and while the excitement of the race still gripped the participants, rather than waiting until the morning by which time they would simply be reiterating the non committal party line. Even the powerful elder statesmen of the Party would be caught up with the passion of the moment and find themselves offering delphic but expressive signs. Around Westminster a raised eyebrow or a knowing wink can speak as loudly to some ears as a sentence of political death, and it was vital that she knew in which direction the tumbrils were headed.

There was also the complicated election procedure to fathom. The Party's balloting rules made sense to nobody other than those who had devised them; they prescribed that the first ballot should now be set aside and new nominations made. It was even permissible, although not likely, that individuals who had not even stood in the original ballot could now enter the race for the first time. If from the confusion no victor emerged with more than half the votes, a third and final round of voting would be held between the leading three candidates, with the winner being selected by a system of proportional representation which the Government would rather die than allow to be used at a general election. It was clearly a case of one rule for the Party, an entirely different rule for the public. It was all enough to make for furrowed brows and wearied pens amongst the parliamentary correspondents that evening.

She had called Krajewski. It had been more than a week since they had seen or talked to each other, and in spite of herself she felt an inner desire to be with him. She seemed to be surrounded on all sides by doubts and unresolved questions, and she was finding it difficult on her own to pierce through the confusion. She hated to admit it, but she needed to share.

Krajewski was unsure how to respond to the call. He had spent the week debating whether she was important to him or simply using him, or both. When she had asked to see him he had offered a lavish dinner at the Ritz, which he instantly knew was a mistake. She wasn't in a mood for romance, with or without violins. Instead they had settled for a drink at the Reform Club in Pall Mall, where Johnnie was a member. She had walked the half mile from the press gallery in the House of Commons, only to discover that he was exercising the privileges of a deputy editor and was late. Or was this simply his way of expressing frustration with her? She waited in the club's vaulted reception area with its magnificent columns and smoke-laden atmosphere. It was a time capsule, which Gladstone could have re-entered to find scarcely a single significant change since he had enjoyed its hospitality a century earlier. She always felt it was ironic that this great bastion of Liberalism and Reform had taken 150 years to accept women and she had often twisted the noses of its members about their sexual chauvinism until one had reminded her that there never had been a female editor of the *Telegraph*.

When Johnnie arrived they took their drinks and sat amongst the shadows of the upper gallery in the deep, cracked leather chairs which were so easy to relax in and so difficult to leave. As Mattie drank in the cloistered atmosphere and thick veneer of generations long departed, she desperately wanted to give herself over to the tired will of the flesh and float gently into oblivion. In those chairs, she felt as if she could sleep for a year and wake to find herself transported back several lifetimes. Yet the nagging in her head allowed her no relief.

'What is it?' he asked, although he didn't need to. One glance had been enough to reveal that she was tired, anxious, quite lacking in her usual spark.

'The usual,' she responded grimly. 'Lots of questions, too few answers, and the pieces I do have don't make sense. Somehow I know it has to be tied in with the leadership election, but I simply don't know how.'

'Tell me about it.'

She brought him up to date, how she could with more or less certainty hang most of the identifiable bits of the puzzle around O'Neill's neck.

'He almost certainly leaked the poll to me, he as good as admits he opened the accommodation address in Paddington, he caused the hospitals fiasco by leaking the promotional plans to Kendrick, and I'm sure he altered the headquarters' computer file to incriminate Charles Collingridge. Which means he's mixed up in some way with the share purchase and the bank account as well. But why?'

'To get rid of Collingridge,' prompted Krajewski.

'But what good does that do him? He's not going to take over the Party. What motive does he have for undermining Collingridge?'

He offered no suggestion, but gazed along the gallery at the grand oil portraits of Victorian statesmen to whom conspiracy and cunning had come as second nature, wondering what they would have thought. Mattie could not share his wry amusement.

'He must be acting together with someone else who does have something to gain – someone more important, more powerful, who could benefit from the change of leadership. There has to be another figure in there somewhere, pulling O'Neill's strings.'

'So you are looking for a mystery man with the means and the motive. Well, he has to be in a position to control O'Neill, and have access to sensitive political information. It would also help if he had been engaged in a much publicised and bitter battle with the Prime Minister. Surely you don't have to look too far for candidates.'

'Give me one.'

He took a deep breath and savoured the dark, conspiratorial atmosphere of the evening air.

'It's easy. Teddy Williams.'

It was late that evening when Urquhart returned to his room in the Commons. The celebrations and congratulations had followed him all the way from his office to the Harcourt Room beneath the House of Lords where he had dined, being interrupted frequently by colleagues eager to shake him by the hand and wish him well. He had proceeded on to the Members' Smoking Room, a private place much loved by MPs who gather there away from the prying eyes of the press not so much to smoke as to exchange views and gossip and to twist a few arms. The Whips know the Smoking Room well, and Urquhart had used his hour there to good effect before once more climbing the twisting stairs to his office.

His secretary had emptied the ashtrays, cleared the glasses and straightened the cushions, and his room was once again quiet and welcoming. He closed the door behind him, locking it carefully. He crossed to the four-drawer filing cabinet with its stout security bar and combination lock which the Government provide for all Ministers to secure their confidential papers while out of their departmental offices. He twirled the combination four times, until there was a gentle click and the security bar fell away into his hands. He removed it and bent down to open the bottom drawer.

The drawer creaked as it came open. It was stuffed full of files and papers, each one with the name of a different MP on it, each one containing the personal and incriminating material he had carefully winnowed out of the safe in the Whips Office where all the best kept parliamentary secrets are stored to await Judgement Day, or some other parliamentary emergency. It had taken him nearly three years to amass this material, and he knew it was more valuable than a drawer crammed full with gold bars.

He knelt down and sorted carefully through the files. He quickly found what he was looking for, a padded envelope, already addressed and sealed. After extracting it he closed the drawer and secured the filing cabinet, testing as he always did to make sure the lock and security bar had caught properly.

It was nearly midnight as he drove out of the entrance gates to the House of Commons, a police officer stopping the late night traffic around Parliament Square to enable him to ease out into the busy road and speed on his way. However, he did not head the car in the direction of his Pimlico home. He first drove to one of the twenty-four-hour motorcycle messenger services which flourish amongst the seedier basements of Soho, where he dropped the envelope off and paid in cash for delivery early the following morning. It would have been easier to post it in the House of Commons, where they have one of the most efficient post offices in the country. But he did not want a House of Commons postmark on this envelope.

WEDNESDAY 24TH NOVEMBER

The letters and newspapers arrived almost simultaneously with a dull thud on Woolton's Chelsea doormat early the following morning. Hearing the clatter, he came downstairs and gathered them up, spreading the newspapers out on the kitchen table while he left the post on a small table in the hallway for his wife. He received over 300 letters a week from his constituents and other correspondents, and he had long since given up trying to read them all. So he left them for his wife, who was also his constituency secretary and for whom he got a generous secretarial allowance from the parliamentary authorities to supplement his Cabinet Minister's stipend.

The newspapers were dominated by news and analysis of the leadership election. The headlines all seemed to have been written by moonlighting journalists from the *Sporting Life*, and phrases such as 'Neck And Neck', 'Three Horse Race' or 'Photo Finish' dominated the front pages. Inside, the more sanguine commentaries explained that it was difficult to predict which of the three leading contenders was now better placed, while most concluded that, in spite of his first place, Samuel was probably the most disappointed of the contestants since he had failed to live up to his early promise.

'The Party is now presented with a clear choice,' intoned the *Guardian*.

Michael Samuel is by far the most popular and polished of the three, with a clear record of being able to combine a political career with the retention of a well defined social conscience. The fact that he has been attacked by some elements of the Party as being 'too liberal by half' is a badge he should wear with

287

considerable pride. He would undoubtedly provide a firm lead for the Party and would continue to confront the leading social issues head on – a laudable characteristic which has, however, not always commended itself to his colleagues.

Patrick Woolton is an altogether different politician. Immensely proud of his Northern origins, he poses as a man who could unite the two halves of the country. Whether his robust style of politics could unite the two halves of his own Party is altogether more debatable. He plays his politics as if he were still hooking for his old rugby league club, although his recent experience at the Foreign Office has done much to knock some of the sharper edges off his style. Unlike Samuel he would not attempt to lead the Party in any particular philosophical direction, setting great store on a pragmatic approach. But robustness combined with pragmatism has occasionally been an unhappy combination. The Leader of the Opposition has described him as a man wandering the streets of Westminster in search of a fight for any available reason.

Francis Urquhart is more difficult to assess. The least experienced and least well known of the three, nevertheless his performance in the first round ballot was truly remarkable, far outstripping many of his better fancied senior colleagues. Three reasons seem to explain his success. First, as Chief Whip he knows the Parliamentary Party extremely well, and they him. Since it is his colleagues in the Parliamentary Party and not the electorate at large who will decide this election, his low public profile is less of a disadvantage than many perhaps assumed.

Second, he has conducted his campaign in a dignified style which sets him apart from the verbal fisticuffs and misfortunes of the other contenders. What is known of his politics suggests he holds firm to the traditionalist line, somewhat patrician and authoritarian perhaps, but sufficiently ill-defined for him not to have antagonised either wing of the Party.

Finally, perhaps his greatest asset is that he is neither of the other two. Many MPs have certainly supported him in the first round rather than commit themselves to one of the better fancied but more contentious candidates. He is the obvious choice for those who wish to sit on the fence. But it is that which could ultimately derail his campaign, because as the pressure for a clear decision forces Government MPs off the fence, Urquhart is the candidate who could suffer most.

So the choice is clear. Those who wish to air their social consciences will support Samuel. Those who thirst for blood-and-thunder politics will support Woolton. Those who cannot make up their minds have an obvious choice in Urquhart. Whichever way they decide, they will inevitably deserve what they get.

Woolton chuckled as he munched his breakfast toast. He knew it was most unlikely at the end of the day that his colleagues would support a call to conscience – it was so difficult to explain in the pub or over the garden fence, and popular politics shouldn't be too complicated. If Urquhart's support was going to be squeezed, he decided, then the majority of switchers would come to him, and the bleeding hearts could go hang. Margaret Thatcher had shown how it could be done, and she was a woman. Take away her feminine shrillness and the dogmatic inflexibility, he mused, and you had the ideal political leader – Patrick Woolton.

As his wife replenished his tea he debated with himself whether he should rile another prominent rabbi in the next few days just to remind his colleagues of the Jewish issue. He decided against it; it wasn't necessary, the Party's old guard would see to that without his interfering.

'Darling, I have this feeling it is going to be an excellent day,' he proclaimed as he kissed his wife goodbye at their doorstep. A couple of photographers were outside on the pavement, and they asked him to repeat the kiss before he was allowed to get into his official car and drive off for a day's campaigning in the House.

His wife went through her daily routine of clearing the breakfast table before settling down to handle the correspondence. The volume had increased dramatically in the last few years, she noted with a sigh of resignation. Gone were the days when there was any hope of a personal answer to them all; it was now up to the word processor and its carefully programmed series of standard responses. She wondered whether anybody really noticed or cared that most of her husband's constituency letters were written by computer and signed by a little autograph machine he had brought back from the States on a recent trip. The majority of the letters were from lobby groups, professional critics or downright political opponents who weren't the least bit interested in the content of the replies. But they all needed answering nonetheless, she told herself as she began the monotonous daily task of opening the thick bundle of envelopes. She would never risk losing her husband a single vote by failing to offer some form of reply even to the most abusive of letters.

She left the padded brown envelope until last. It had clearly been hand-delivered and was firmly stapled down, and she had to struggle to extract the infuriating metal clips before getting at the contents. As she pulled out the last tenacious staple, a cassette tape fell out into her lap. There was nothing else in the envelope, no letter, no compliments slip, no label on the tape to indicate where it had come from or what it contained.

'Fools. How on earth do they expect me to reply to that!' She put the tape to one side before switching on the word processor.

It took her three hours of solid work to go through the letters, persuade the word processor to churn out a reply which had some chance of persuading the recipient that they were receiving personalised attention, watch them being signed by machine, then fold and seal them. The tape she left on the desk. Her mouth was gummed up from licking too many envelopes, and she needed a cup of coffee. The silly tape could wait.

It was very much later that evening when she remembered the cassette. Woolton had come back from a hectic day canvassing at the House, and was feeling tired as the adrenalin of the first ballot began to wear off. He had heeded the advice of his close colleagues not to overdo the canvassing, and to get a couple of good nights' rest. He was planning later in the week to make three major speeches, and he would need to conserve his energy.

He was sitting in his favourite armchair sketching out some preliminary speech notes when his wife remembered the tape on the desk.

'By the way, darling, a tape cassette was dropped off for you today without any form of identification. Do you know what it is? A recording of last weekend's speech or a tape of a recent interview, perhaps?'

'Haven't a clue. Pour me another drink and let's listen to it.' He waved broadly in the direction of the stereo unit.

His wife, dutiful as ever, did as he bade. He was just savouring his freshened gin and tonic when the tape deck ate up the last segment of blank tape and with a burst of red light the playback meter on the equipment began to show that the tape heads were reading something. There was a series of low hisses and crackles, it was clearly not a professional recording, and she turned the volume up.

The sound of a girl's laughter filled the room, followed by her low, deep gasp. The noise hypnotised the Wooltons, rooting them to the spot. For several minutes, the speakers gave out the sound of a series of shorter, higher breaths as the unmistakable sounds of sex were accompanied by the rhythmic banging of a bedhead against a wall. The tape left little to the imagination. The woman's sighs became shorter and more shrill, as the two bodies climbed ever higher, pausing occasionally for breath before pressing on remorselessly until with a shrieking crescendo they had burst through to reach the summit of their mountain. They shared gasps of pleasure and satisfaction before descending gently together, accompanied once more by the sound of the woman's laughter mixed with the deep bass chuckling of her companion.

The laughter stopped for an instant, until the turning tape found the next distinctive sound.

'That was great, Patrick. Can we do it again?' The woman's voice laughed.

'Not if you're going to wake up the whole of bloody Bournemouth!' the unmistakable Lancashire accent said.

Neither Woolton nor his wife had moved since the tape had begun, but now she stepped slowly across the room and switched it off. A soft, gentle tear fell down one cheek as she turned to look at her husband. He could not return her gaze.

'What can I say? I'm sorry, love,' he whispered. 'I'll not lie and tell you it's bogus. But I am sorry, truly. I never meant to hurt you.'

She made no reply. The look of reproach and sorrow on her face cut into him far more deeply than any angry words could have done.

'What do you want me to do?' he asked gently.

She turned on him with real anger flaring in her eyes. 'Pat, I've turned many a blind eye over the last twenty-three years, and I'm not so much of a silly little housewife to think this is the only time. You could at least have had the decency to keep it away from me and not rub my face in it. You owed me that.'

He hung his head, and she let her words sink deep into him before she continued. 'But one thing my pride will not tolerate is having a little tart like that trying to break up my marriage and make a fool of me. I'll not stand for it. Find out whatever the blackmailing little whore wants, buy her off or go to the police if necessary, but get rid of her. And get rid of this!' She flung the tape at him. 'It doesn't belong in my house. And neither will you if I have to listen to that filth again!'

He looked at her with tears in his own eyes now. 'I'll sort it out first thing in the morning. You'll hear no more about it.'

Thursday 25th November

Penny cast an unwelcoming frown in the direction of the steel grey November sky, and stepped carefully onto the pavement from the Earl's Court mansion block in which she lived. The weather men had been talking for days about the possibility of a sudden cold snap, and now it had arrived with a vengeance. As she tried to pick her way over frozen puddles, she regretted her decision to wear high heels instead of boots. She was moving slowly along the edge of the pavement when a car door swung open in front of her, blocking her path.

She bent low to tell the driver to be more bloody careful when she saw Woolton at the wheel. She beamed at him but he did not return her warmth. He was looking straight ahead, not at her as she obeyed his clipped instruction and slipped into the passenger seat.

'What is it you want?' he demanded in a voice which was as frozen as the morning air.

'What are you offering,' she smiled, but there was an edge of uncertainty creeping in as she began to discern the ice in his words. She had never seen him so soulless.

He turned to look at her for the first time. He cursed quietly at his folly when he saw how attractive she still seemed to him.

'Did you have to send that tape to me at home? It was a particularly cruel thing to do, because my wife heard it. It was also extremely stupid, because it means she knows about it and so you can't blackmail me. No newspaper or radio station will touch it, the potential libel damages will frighten them off, so there's not much use you can make of it.'

He hoped she would be too stupid to see how much damage the tape could do to him in the wrong hands, and

293

his bluff seemed to have worked as he watched the sparkle drain out of her eyes and the lustre fade from her cheeks.

'Patrick, what on earth are you talking about?'

'The tape you sent me, you silly trollop. Don't go bloody coy on me!'

'I sent you no tape. I haven't the slightest idea what you are talking about.'

The unexpected assault on her feelings and the unfathomable questions he was throwing at her had come as a considerable shock, and she began to sob and gasp for breath. He grabbed her arm ferociously and tears of real pain began to flow.

'The tape! The tape! You sent me the tape!'

'What tape, Patrick? Why are you hurting me . . . ?'

The trickle had become a flood and now a torrent and, as the outside world began to disappear behind misted windows, he began to realise he had misunderstood. He began to spit out his words, staccato-like, so there could be no doubt about their seriousness.

'Look at me and tell me you did not send me a tape of us in Bournemouth.'

'No. No. I sent no tape. I don't know . . .' She suddenly gasped and stopped crying, his words at last piercing through her confusion. 'There's a tape of us in Bournemouth? God, Patrick, that's horrid. But who?'

Her bottom lip quivered in surprise and horror. He released her arm, and his head sank slowly onto the steering wheel.

'Yesterday a cassette tape arrived at my home address. The tape was of us in bed at the party conference.'

'And you thought that I had sent it and was trying to blackmail you? Why, you miserable bastard!'

'I . . . I didn't know what to think. I hoped it was you, Penny.'

'Why? Why me?' she shouted in disgust.

He took his head off the wheel to look once more at her. He had suddenly aged, his skin stretched like old parchment across his cheeks, his eyes red and tired.

'I hoped it was you, Penny, because if it's not you then I haven't the faintest idea who did manage to record us.

And it can be no coincidence that it has arrived now, so many weeks after it was made. It means they're not trying to blackmail me for money, but over the leadership race.'

His voice faded to a whisper. 'As far as next Tuesday goes, I'm dead.'

Woolton spent the rest of the morning trying to think constructively. He had no doubt it was the leadership race which had caused the sudden appearance of the tape; a blackmailer simply wanting money would have had no reason to wait so long before striking. It was the leadership and its power, not money, they were interested in, and he knew their price would be too high. He suspected it was the Russians, who would not be as understanding as the New Orleans police. No, he could not stand

Faced with such a problem, some might have decided to fade gently from the scene and pray that their quiet retirement would not be disturbed. That was not Woolton's style. He would rather go down fighting, and try to salvage whatever he could from the wreckage of his dreams.

He was in a determined mood by the time the press conference he had called gathered shortly after lunch. With no time to make more formal arrangements he had summoned the media to meet him on the other side of the river directly opposite the Houses of Parliament and under the shade of St Thomas's Hospital, where the Thames and the tower of Big Ben would provide a suitably dramatic backdrop. As soon as the cameramen were ready, he began.

'Good afternoon. I've got a short statement to make, and I'm sorry that I will not have time afterwards for questions. But I hope you will not be disappointed.

'Following the ballot on Tuesday, it seems as if only three candidates have any realistic chance of success. Indeed, I understand that all the other candidates have already announced that they do not intend to stand in the second round next week. So, as you gentlemen have put it, this is a three-horse race.

'Of course, I'm delighted and honoured to be one of

those three, but three can be an unlucky number. There are not three real alternatives in this election, only two. Either the Party can stick to the practical approach to politics which has proved so successful and kept us in power for over a decade. Or it can develop a new raft of policies, sometimes called conscience politics, which will get Government much more deeply involved – some would say entrapped – in trying to sort out the everyday problems of individual people and families.'

There was a stir amongst the reporters at this sharp public acknowledgement of the division between the two wings of the Party which politicians habitually denied existed.

'I don't believe that a new emphasis on conscience politics would be appropriate – indeed, I think that however well intentioned that emphasis may be, it would in reality be a disaster for the Party and the country. I think that is also the view of the clear majority within the Party.

'Yet paradoxically that is just the way we could end up drifting if that majority support for a pragmatic approach to politics is divided between two candidates, Mr Urquhart and myself. I am a practical man. I don't deal in personalities but in hard-nosed politics. Because of that I believe it would be wrong for my personal ambitions to stand in the way of achieving those policies in which I believe.'

The cold air was condensing his breath and setting fire to his words.

'So I have decided to ensure that the support for those general policies is not divided. I am withdrawing from the race. I shall be casting my own personal vote for Francis Urquhart, who I sincerely hope will be our next Prime Minister. I have nothing more to say.'

His last words were almost lost in the clatter of a hundred camera shutters, which continued to click as they captured the sight of Woolton striding so fast up the riverside steps towards his waiting car that he was almost running. A few gave chase, but were unable to catch him before he reached the car and was driven off across Westminster Bridge in the direction of the Foreign Office. The rest simply stood in a state of considerable bewilderment, trying to ensure that they had not only accurately recorded but also understood what Woolton had said. He had given them no time for questions, no opportunity to develop theories or surmise any hidden meaning behind his words. They had only what he had given them, and they would have to report it straight – which is precisely what Woolton intended.

His wife was no less confused when he returned home later that evening and they watched his dramatic announcement lead off the *Nine O'Clock News*.

'I understand why you had to back out, Patrick, and I suppose that ought to be punishment enough. I shall go on supporting you, as I always have. But why did you decide to support Urquhart, for Heaven's sake? I never knew you were that close.'

'That superior bugger? I'm not close to him. Don't even like him!'

'Then why?'

'Because I'm fifty-five and Michael Samuel is forty-eight, which means that he could be in Downing Street for twenty years until I'm dead and buried as a politician. Francis Urquhart is sixty-two, and is likely to be in office for no more than five years. So with Urquhart, there's a chance that there will be another leadership race before I retire. In the meantime, if I can find out who is behind that tape, or they fall under a bus or get driven over by a Ministerial limousine, then I'm in with a second chance.'

His pipe was hurling thick blue smoke into the air as he worked on his logic.

'In any event, I had nothing to gain from remaining neutral. Samuel would never have tolerated me in his Cabinet. So instead I've handed the election to Urquhart on a plate, and he will have to show some public gratitude for that.'

He smiled at his wife for the first time since they had heard the tape. 'How do you fancy being the Chancellor of the Exchequer's wife for the next couple of years?'

Friday 26th November

The following morning's weather was still well below freezing, but a new front had passed over London bringing with it crystal blue skies to replace the leaden cloud cover of the previous day. As Urquhart looked out from his Commons office across the Thames, the riverscape glowed brightly in the clear winter sunshine like a brilliant symbol of what lay ahead for him. As he gazed at the press reports of Woolton's endorsement, he felt invulnerable, almost home.

Then the door burst open. It was O'Neill. Even before Urquhart could demand to know what on earth he thought he was doing, the babbling commenced. The words were fired like bullets in a battle, being hurled at Urquhart as if to overwhelm and force his submission.

'They know, Francis. They've discovered that the file is missing. The locks were bent and one of the secretaries noticed and the Chairman's called us all in. I'm sure he suspects me. What are we going to do? What are we going to *do*?'

Urquhart was shaking him to stop the incomprehensible gabble, and he was surprised at how much physical force was needed before the man was brought under some sort of control.

'Roger, for God's sake shut up!' He pushed him bodily into a chair and the shock caused O'Neill to pause for breath. 'Now slowly, Roger. What are you trying to say?'

'The files. The confidential party files on Samuel you asked me to send to the Sunday newspapers.' He was panting for breath from physical and nervous exhaustion. 'Well, I was able to use my pass key to get into the basement storage room without any trouble, but the files are all in locked cabinets. I had to force the lock, Francis. I'm sorry but I had no choice. Not very much but it bent a little. There's so much dust and cobwebs around that it looked as if no one had been in there since the Boer War, but yesterday some bitch of a secretary decided to go in there and noticed the bent lock. Now they've gone through the whole lot and discovered that Samuel's file is missing.'

'You sent them the original file? You didn't just copy the interesting bits as I told you?'

'Francis, the file was very thick, it would have taken hours to copy. I didn't know which bits they would be most interested in, so – I sent them the lot. It could have been years before anyone noticed the file was missing, and then they would have thought it was simply misplaced.'

'You bloody fool, you . . .'

'Francis, don't shout at me!' O'Neill screamed 'It's me who's taken all the risks, not you. The Chairman's personally interrogating everyone with a pass key and there are only nine of us. He's asked to see me this afternoon. I'm sure he suspects me. And I'm not going to take the blame all on my own. Why should I? I only did what you told me . . . Francis, I can't go on lying. I simply can't stand it any more. I'll go to pieces!'

Urquhart froze as he realised the truth behind O'Neill's desperate words. This quivering man in front of him had no resistance or judgement left; he was beginning to crumble and flake like some old, brittle newspaper. The eyes were flickering furiously once more as the words tumbled out, and Urquhart realised that not even for a week, not even for *this* week, could O'Neill control himself. He was on the very edge. The slightest wind could send him hurtling down towards destruction. And he would take Urquhart with him.

'Roger, you are over-anxious. You have nothing to fear, no one can prove anything and you must remember that I'm on your side. You are not alone in this. Look, don't go back to the office, call in sick and go home. The Chairman can wait till Monday. And tomorrow I would like you to come and be my house guest in Hampshire. Come for lunch and stay overnight while we talk the whole thing through – together, just the two of us.'

O'Neill gripped Urquhart's hand in delight and relief, like a cripple clinging to his crutch.

'But don't tell anyone that you are coming to visit me. It would be very embarrassing if the press were to find out that a senior party official is my house guest just before the final leadership ballot – it wouldn't look right for either of us – so this must be strictly between the two of us. Not even your secretary must know.'

O'Neill tried to mutter a word of thanks but was cut short by three enormous sneezes which had Urquhart reeling in disgust. O'Neill didn't seem to notice as he wiped his face and smiled with the new found eagerness of a spaniel.

'I'll be there, Francis. I'll be there.'

SATURDAY 27TH NOVEMBER

Urquhart got up before dawn. He hadn't slept, but was not in the least tired. He knew this was to be a very special day. Well before the early light of morning was breaking above the New Forest moors, he dressed in his favourite hunting jacket, pulled on his boots and strode out into the freezing morning air along the bridle path which led across Emery Down towards Lyndhurst. The ground mist clung closely to the hedgerows, discouraging the birds and damping down all sound. It pressed around him like a cocoon and he was utterly alone, a man on an empty planet who must make his own decisions and decide his own fate.

He had walked nearly three miles before he began a long, slow climb up the southern face of a hill, and slowly the fog began to clear as the rising sun cut through the damp air. He had just emerged from a bank of swirling mist when he saw the stag across the patch of sun-cleared hillside, browsing amongst the damp gorse. He slipped gently behind a low bush, waiting, like a hunter for his prey. But he was not a complete hunter. He had never hunted a man. He had been too young for Hitler, too busy at university for Korea, too late for Suez. He had never known what it was like to exchange another man's life for his own, to condemn someone before they had the chance to do the same to you.

He wondered how his brother had died. He imagined him in a shallow dugout underneath a Dunkirk hedgerow, waiting for the barrel of the first German tank to appear over the brow of the hill. As he lay there ready to kill, to destroy as many other lives as possible, had he felt exhilarated like some savage animal by the chance to shed blood? Had he been immobilised by terror, a man turned rabbit by panic in spite of his training and sense of duty? Or had he felt a calming certainty about the need for self-preservation which had overcome all apprehension and a lifetime of Sunday School morality – just as Urquhart felt now?

The stag edged closer towards him as it continued to browse, oblivious of his presence. Suddenly, Urquhart stood bolt upright, not twenty yards in front of the deer which froze in confusion. Neither breathed as they stood in confrontation, until Urquhart let forth a peal of almighty laughter, racking his body with the sound which bounced off the surrounding banks of mist. The stag, sensing that it should already have been dead, leapt to one side and in an instant was gone.

Urquhart spent all morning walking through the woodlands and across the downs, not returning home until almost noon. When he did so, he walked straight into his study without changing, and picked up the phone.

He first called the editors of the four leading Sunday newspapers. He discovered that two of them were writing editorials supporting him, one was supporting Samuel and the other was noncommittal. However, all four were confident in varying degrees that he had a clear advantage, a conclusion confirmed by the *Observer*'s pollsters who by now had succeeded in contacting a substantial majority of the Parliamentary Party. The survey predicted that Urquhart would win comfortably with 60 per cent of the vote.

'It seems it would take an earthquake to stop you winning now, Francis,' the editor had said.

He then called a Kent number, and asked to be put through to Dr Christian.

'Good afternoon, Chief Whip. Nice of you to take time out of your weekend to enquire about Charles. He is progressing very well indeed, I'm delighted to say. His brother the Prime Minister is down here almost every other day to see him, and it's been like a tonic to both of them.'

'There's something else I wanted to ask you, doctor. I need your advice. We have a Member of Parliament who has a real problem. He's a cocaine addict, and recently his

behaviour has deteriorated rapidly. His physical mannerisms – the nasal problems, exaggerated eye movements –
have become much worse. His speech varies between a
chaotic cavalry charge and a slow, incomprehensible drool.
He has become very agitated and disturbed and has caused
several public scenes. He has grown utterly paranoid,
making wild accusations and threats. The man is clearly
very ill, and I am trying to persuade him to take treatment
but, as you keep telling me, addicts are often the last
people to face up to their problems.

'In the meantime, he occupies a very sensitive position
of considerable trust. It could inflict untold damage if he
were to break that trust and be indiscreet. The question I
have for you, doctor, is to what extent a man in that situation is able to keep his word and any sense of perspective.
Is there any chance we can trust him?'

'You sound as if you have a very sick man on your
hands, Mr Urquhart. By the time he is unable to keep his
behaviour private but makes a public exhibition of himself
on a regular basis, showing those sort of physical symp-
toms, then he is in the final stages of collapse. He is probably taking the drug several times every day, which means
he's not only unable to do his work but – much more
seriously from your point of view – has lost all self
restraint. The habit is very expensive and he will do anything to continue his supply of drugs. Lie, steal, cheat,
sometimes kill. He will sell anything he can lay his hands
on in exchange for drugs, which includes any information
he may have. He will also be getting very paranoid, and if
you try to persuade him too hard to seek treatment against
his will, he may turn on you as a vicious enemy and do
anything to destroy you. I have seen it tear husbands from
their wives and mothers from their children. They are
driven by a need which stretches far beyond all others.'

'He's already threatened to break the deepest confidences. Are you saying he might be serious about that?'

'Deadly serious.'

'Then we have a problem.'

'A very considerable one, by the sounds of it. I'm sorry.
Please let me know if I can help.'

'You already have, doctor. Thank you.'

Urquhart was still sitting in his study when he heard O'Neill's car draw up in the driveway outside.

As the Irishman stepped into the hallway, Urquhart could not help but note that the man who now stood in front of him was almost unrecognisable as the man he had taken to dinner in his club less than six months before. The casual elegance which O'Neill used to effect had now turned into outright scruffiness. His hair was unkempt, the clothes were badly creased as if he had found them at the bottom of a laundry bag, the tie hung loosely round the unbuttoned and crumpled collar. Trying to look at O'Neill as if meeting him for the first time, Urquhart was shocked. The gradual decline over several months had become part of O'Neill's pattern for those colleagues who saw him frequently, and had largely hidden the true extent to which he had deteriorated. The once suave and fashionable communicator now looked like a common tramp. And those deep, twinkling eyes, the features which women had found so captivating and clients so enthusing, had sunk without trace, to be replaced by two wild, staring orbs which flashed around the room in constant pursuit of something they could never find. This was a man possessed.

Urquhart led O'Neill to one of the second floor guest rooms, saying little as they wound their way through the mansion's long corridors while O'Neill babbled away about whatever came into his mind. Increasingly in recent days his conversation had turned to others and their opinion of him; in O'Neill's mind the whole world seemed slowly and unjustly to be turning on him, betraying him. His Chairman, his Prime Minister, his secretary now. Even his local policeman seemingly patrolled the street for no other purpose than to spy on O'Neill, waiting to pounce on him.

O'Neill threw his overnight bag carelessly on the bed, showing little interest in the room and its fine views across the New Forest scenery. They returned the way they had come down two flights of stairs until Urquhart led him through the heavy oak doors into his book-lined study. He suggested O'Neill help himself to a drink, and watched

304

with clinical concentration as O'Neill filled the entire tumbler with whisky and began draining it. Soon the alcohol had begun to do battle with the cocaine, and the raging in O'Neill's eyes became just a touch less frenetic even as his tongue became thicker and his conversation began increasingly to lose its coherence. Depressant fought stimulant inside him, never achieving peace or balance, always leaving him on the point of toppling backwards or forwards into the abyss.

'Roger,' began Urquhart, 'it looks as if we shall be in Downing Street by the end of the week. I've been doing some thinking about what I shall need, and I thought we might talk about what you wanted.'

O'Neill took another gulp before answering.

'Francis, I'm bowled over that you should be thinking of me. You're going to be a class act as Prime Minister, really you are. As it happens, I've also been giving some thought to it all, and I was wondering whether you could use someone like me in Downing Street – you know, as a special adviser or even your press spokesman. You're going to need a lot of help and we seem to have worked so well together that I thought . . .'

Urquhart waved his hand for silence. 'Roger, there are scores of civil servants to take on those responsibilities, people who are already doing that work. What I need is someone like you in charge of the political propaganda, who can supplement the civil service properly and can be trusted to avoid all those mistakes which the party organisation has been making in recent months. I would very much like you to stay at party headquarters – under a new Chairman, of course.'

A look of concern furrowed O'Neill's brow. The same meaningless job, watching from the sidelines as the civil service ran the show, as aloof as he thought they were incompetent? What the devil was in it for him?

'But to do something like that effectively, Francis, I shall need support, some special status. I . . . thought we had mentioned a knighthood.'

'Yes, indeed, Roger. That would be no more than you deserve. You've been absolutely indispensable to me, and you must understand how grateful I am. But I've been making enquiries. That sort of honour may not be possible, at least in the short term. There are so many who are already in line to be honoured when a Prime Minister retires and a new Government comes in, and as you know there is a limit on the number of honours even a Prime Minister can hand out. I'm afraid it could take a while . . .'

Urquhart was determined to test O'Neill, to bully him, disappoint him, torment him, subject him to all the pressures he would inevitably come under in the course of the next few months, trying to see how far O'Neill could be pushed before reaching the limit. He had not a moment longer to wait as the Irishman hit his limit and burst through it with volcanic passion.

'Francis, you promised! That was part of the deal! You gave your word, and now you're telling me it's not on. No job. No knighthood. Not now, not soon, not ever! You've got what you wanted and now you think you can get rid of me. Well, think again! I've lied, I've cheated, I've forged and I've stolen for you. Now you treat me just like all the rest. I'm not going to have people laughing at me behind my back any more and looking down their noses as if I were some smelly Irish peasant. I deserve that knighthood and I demand it!'

The tumbler was emptied and O'Neill, shaking with emotion, refilled it from the decanter, spilling the malt whisky as it flowed over the edge of the glass. He slurped a huge mouthful down before resuming his avalanche of anger.

'We've been through this all together, as a team. Everything I've done has been for you, and you wouldn't have been able to get into Downing Street without me. We succeed together – or we fail together. If I'm going to end up on the compost heap, Francis, I'm damned if I'm going to be there alone. You can't afford to let me tell what I know. You owe me!'

The words had been spoken, the threat made. Urquhart had offered O'Neill a gauntlet of provocation, which almost without pause had been picked up and slapped back into Urquhart's face. It was clear it was no longer a matter of whether O'Neill would lose control, but how quickly, and it had taken no time at all.

There was no point in continuing to test him, and Urquhart brought it to a rapid conclusion with a broad smile and shake of the head.

'Roger, my dear friend. You misunderstand me entirely. I am only saying that it will be difficult this time around, in the New Year's Honours List. But there's another one in the Spring, for the Queen's Birthday. Just a few weeks away, really. I'm only asking you to wait until then. And if you want a job in Downing Street, then we shall find one. We work as a team, you and I. You have deserved it, and on my word of honour I will not forget what I owe you.'

O'Neill could not respond above a murmur. His passion had been spent, the alcohol burrowing its way into his nervous system, his emotions torn asunder and now pasted back together. He sat there drained, ashen, exhausted.

'Look, have a sleep before lunch. We can sort out precisely what you want later,' suggested Urquhart.

Without another word, O'Neill slumped in his chair and closed his eyes. Within seconds his breathing had slowed as he found sleep, but his fingers kept twitching with little spasms of energy as his eyes flickered beneath their lids in constant turmoil. Wherever O'Neill's mind was wandering, it had not found peace.

Urquhart sat looking at the shrunken figure. O'Neill was drooling, with mucus dripping from his nose. It was a sight which would have left some men feeling pity, but Urquhart felt a chilling emptiness. As a youth he had wandered the moors and hills on his family's estates with a labrador which had earned his tolerance through years of faithful service as a gun dog and constant companion. Yet the dog had grown old and less capable, and one day the gillie had come and explained with great sorrow that the dog had suffered a stroke, and must be put down. Urquhart had visited the dog in the stable where it slept, and was greeted with the pitiful sight of an animal which had lost control of itself. The rear legs were paralysed, it had fouled itself and its nose and mouth, like O'Neill's, were dribbling uncontrollably. It was as much as it could do to raise a whimper of greeting as the tail swung laboriously back and forth. There was a tear in the old gillie's eye as he fondled its ear to bring it some comfort.

'There'll be no more chasing o' rabbits for you, old fella,' he had whispered.

Urquhart had dispatched the animal with a single blow of his rifle butt, instructing the gillie to bury the body well away from the house. As he stared now at O'Neill, he remembered the dog, and wondered why some men deserved less pity than dumb animals.

He left O'Neill in the library, and made his way quietly towards the kitchen. Under the sink he found a pair of rubber kitchen gloves, and stuffed them along with a teaspoon into his pocket before proceeding through the back door towards the outhouses which served as garage, workshop and storage. The old wooden door groaned open on its rusty hinges as he entered the potting shed, and the mustiness hit him immediately. He used this place rarely, but he knew precisely what he was looking for. High on the far wall stood an ancient, battered kitchen cupboard which had been thrown out of the old scullery many years before, and which now served as a home for half-used tins of paint, stray cans of oil and a vigorous army of woodworm. The door opened with a protesting creak, and he immediately found the tightly sealed can. He put on the rubber gloves before taking it from its shelf and walking back towards the house, holding the can well away from him as if he were carrying a flaming torch.

Once back in the house, he made his way quietly upstairs after checking that O'Neill was still soundly asleep. As soon as he had reached the guest room, he entered and turned the key in the door, securing it behind him. He was relieved to discover that O'Neill had not locked his overnight case, and taking great care not to leave any signs of interference he began methodically to search through its contents. He found what he was looking for in the toilet bag, crammed alongside the toothpaste and shaving gear. It was a tin of men's talcum powder, the head of which came away from the shoulders when he gave it a slight wrench. Inside there was no talcum powder but a small self-sealing polythene bag, with the equivalent of a tablespoon full of white powder nestling in one corner.

He took the bag over to the polished mahogany writing desk which stood by the window, and extracted three large sheets of blue writing paper from the drawer before slowly pouring the contents of the bag into a small mound on top of one of the blue sheets. Gingerly he opened the tin he had brought from the potting shed and out of it spooned another similarly sized pile of white powder onto a second sheet. Using the flat end of the spoon as a spatula he proceeded with the greatest care to divide both mounds of white powder into two equal halves, scraping one half of each onto the third page of writing paper. With relief he could see that they were of an almost identical colour and consistency, the white grains standing out against the smooth blue background, and he mixed the two halves quickly together to hide the fact that they had ever been anything but one and the same. He made a single crease along the middle of the paper, and prepared to pour the mixture back into the polythene bag.

At that moment it hit him. The conviction which had filled his veins turned to burning acid, the certainty which had guided his hand suddenly deserted him, and the composure in which he took so much pride vanished. His will had become a battleground. The morality and restraint which the system had tried to beat into him from birth screamed at him to stop, to change his mind, even now to turn back, while his guts told him that morality was weakness. What mattered was reality. And the reality was that he was about to become the most powerful man in the country – so long as his nerve held.

It was clarity of purpose which he needed now, which the Government needed. All too often Administrations had been brought to their knees as leaders listened to the siren voices, confronting the harsh realities of power only to withdraw into weakness and compromise. Didn't they say that once they were elected, all politicians were the same? Most politicians *were* the same – weak, irresolute, insignificant characters, who fouled the nest and got in the way of those who had the resolve to move forward.

Great men had an inner strength, and he was furious with himself now for having doubts. Whether they wished to recognise it or not, all politicians played with other men's lives, and all lives had a price – not just in war, but in placing limits on the care of the sick and the elderly, in setting punishment for crime, in sending men down coal mines or out to the angry fishing grounds of the Arctic Circle. The national interest required sacrifice from many, and often of the few.

He looked out at the mists which still clung tenaciously to the tree tops of the New Forest, blotting out the horizon and transporting his thoughts. He felt as Caesar must have done when faced with the Rubicon, uncertain of what lay on the opposite shore, knowing that he could never retrace his footsteps. Few men were favoured enough to take control of the great decisions of life; most simply suffered the consequences of decisions taken by others. He thought of his brother in the hedgerows of Dunkirk, a pawn like a million others in the games of the great. Urquhart could be one of the great, *should* be one of them, and O'Neill was as insignificant a pawn as he could imagine.

Once more he picked up the paper with its load of white powder. His hand was still trembling, but less than before. He was glad he was not looking down the sights of a shotgun at some deer; he would have missed. Or building a house of cards. The powder slipped unprotesting into the polythene bag, which he then quickly resealed. It looked as if it had never been touched.

Five minutes later he had flushed all the remaining powder down the toilet, following that with the torn-up pieces of writing paper. The writing table was carefully wiped with a damp rag and polished with a towel to hide any trace that he had sat there, and he replaced the polythene bag in the talcum tin, the tin in the toilet bag and the bag back where he had found it. He was absolutely satisfied that O'Neill would never know his case had been tampered with.

He returned to the bathroom where he ran the taps at

full flow. He washed the spoon meticulously and as the gushing water swirled down the drain, he poured the remaining contents of the tin into the water and watched it disappear.

Finally, he left the house once more by the kitchen door, walking across the carefully manicured lawns to a far corner behind the weeping willow tree, where his gardener always had a small pile of garden rubbish ready to burn. It was soon ablaze, with the empty tin and rubber gloves buried deep in its midst. When he was satisfied the fire was burning thoroughly, he returned to the house, poured himself a large whisky which he swallowed as greedily as O'Neill, and at last relaxed.

It was done.

O'Neill had been asleep for three hours when he was roused by someone shaking him fiercely by the shoulder. Slowly he focused his eyes, and saw Urquhart leaning over him, instructing him to wake up.

'Roger. There's had to be a change of plan. I've just had a call from the BBC asking if they can send a film crew over here to shoot some domestic footage for their news coverage on Tuesday. Samuel has apparently already agreed, so I felt I had little choice but to say yes. They will be here in about an hour and will be staying all afternoon. It's just what we didn't want. If they find you here it will start all sorts of speculation about how party headquarters is interfering in the leadership race. We must avoid any confusion at this late stage. I'm sorry. I think it best that you leave right away.'

O'Neill was still trying to find second gear on his tongue as Urquhart poured some coffee past it, explaining once again how sorry he was about the weekend but how glad he was they had cleared up any confusion between them.

'Remember, Roger. A knighthood next Whitsun, and we can sort out the job you want next week. I'm so happy you were able to come. I really am so grateful,' Urquhart was saying as he tipped O'Neill into his car.

He watched as O'Neill's car edged its way carefully and

311

with practised caution down the driveway and out through the gates.

'Goodbye, Roger,' he whispered.

SUNDAY 28TH NOVEMBER

True to the information their editors had given him the previous day, the quality Sunday newspapers made good reading for the Chief Whip and his supporters.

'Urquhart ahead', announced the *Sunday Times*, adding the endorsement of its editorial columns to boost the Chief Whip's campaign still further. Both the *Sunday Telegraph* and the *Express* openly backed Urquhart, while the *Mail on Sunday* tried uncomfortably to straddle the fence. Only the *Observer* gave editorial backing to Samuel, but even this was deeply qualified by its front page report of Urquhart's clear lead in the opinion polls.

It took one of the more scurrilous Sunday papers to give the campaign a real shake. 'Samuel was a commie!' it screamed over half its front page, declaring it had discovered that Samuel had been an active left-winger while at university. Indeed, when contacted by a friendly sounding reporter from the newspaper who said he was 'doing a feature on the early days' of both Samuel and Urquhart and had discovered some youthful indulgence in radical politics, Samuel had rather reluctantly admitted to a passing involvement in many different university clubs, saying that until the age of twenty he had been a sympathiser with a number of fashionable causes which, thirty years later, seemed naive and misplaced.

'But we have documentary evidence to suggest that they included CND and gay rights, Mr Samuel,' the reporter pressed.

'Not that old nonsense again,' responded Samuel testily. He thought he had finished with those wild charges twenty years ago when he had first stood for Parliament. An opponent had sent a letter of accusation to party headquarters; the allegations had been fully investigated by the

313

Party's Standing Committee on Candidates and he had been given a clean bill of health. But here they were again, risen from the dead after all these years, just a few days before the final ballot.

'I did all the things that an eighteen-year-old college student in those days did. I went on two CND marches, and was even persuaded to take out a regular subscription to a student newspaper which I later found was run by the gay rights movement.' He tried to raise a chuckle at the memory, determined not to give any impression that he had something to hide.

'I was also quite a strong supporter of the anti-apartheid movement, and to this day I actively oppose apartheid, although I intensely dislike the violent methods used by some of the self-proclaimed leaders of the movement,' he had told the journalist. 'Regrets? No, I have no real regrets about those early involvements; they weren't so much youthful mistakes as an excellent testing ground for the opinions I now hold. I know how foolish CND is – I've been there!'

Samuel could scarcely believe the manner in which his remarks had been interpreted in the newspaper. It was ludicrous to suggest he had ever been a Communist; he wondered for a moment whether it was actually libellous. Yet underneath the headline, the article got even worse.

'I marched for the Russians', admitted Samuel last night, recalling those days of the 1960s when ban-the-bomb marches frequently ended in violence and disruption.

He also acknowledged that he had been a financial supporter of homosexual rights groups, making regular monthly payments to the Cambridge Gay Charter Movement which was amongst the earliest organisations pushing for a change in the laws on homosexuality.

Samuel's early left-wing involvement has long been a source of concern to party leaders. In 1970 when the twenty-seven-year-old Samuel applied to party headquarters to fight as an official party candidate in

314

the general election of that year, the Party Chairman wrote to demand an explanation of 'the frequency with which your name was associated at university with causes which have no sympathy for our Party'.

He seemed to satisfy the Party then, and won his way into the House of Commons at that election. However, last night Samuel was still defiant about those early involvements.

'I have no regrets', he said, acknowledging that he still sympathised strongly with some of those left-wing movements he used to support.

For the rest of the day there was fluster and commotion amongst the political reporters and in the Samuel house hold. Nobody really believed that he was a closet Communist; it was another of those silly, sensationalist pieces intended to raise circulation rather than the public's consciousness, but it had to be checked out, causing confusion and disruption at a time when Samuel was trying desperately to reassure his supporters and refocus attention on the serious issues of the campaign.

By midday Lord Williams had issued a stinging denunciation of the newspaper for using confidential documents which had been stolen from a security cabinet by forcing the lock. The newspaper immediately responded that, while the Party itself seemed to be unforgivably incompetent with safeguarding their confidential material, the newspaper was happy to fulfil its public obligations and return the folder on Samuel to its rightful owners at party headquarters – which they did later that day in time to catch the television news and give the story yet another lease of life.

Most observers, after discussing the story at some length, dismissed it as a passing misfortune for Samuel brought about by the typical incompetence of party headquarters. But Samuel's campaign had run into a lot of misfortune since it began. It was not reassuring for someone who claimed to be on top of events, and it was definitely not the way to spend the final weekend of the leadership race.

*   *   *

The phone call upset Krajewski. He had been trying hard to keep a grip on his wayward emotions about Mattie, being alternately eaten away by frustration at her inconsistency and consumed with hunger for her body. He was also discovering that he simply downright missed her, and only occasionally did he succeed in forcing his thoughts about her to the back of his mind. When one of his colleagues telephoned to say that he had met Mattie and that she looked tired and unwell, he hadn't needed a second to realise how concerned he still was.

She had agreed to see him, but rejected his suggestion that he should come straight round. She didn't want him to see the apartment this way, with the dirty plates, the empty cartons which seemed to infest every available table top, and the worn clothes which had simply been dumped in the corner. The last few days had been hell. Unable to sleep, her mind and her emotions snarled up in one immense knot, her bed like a slab of ice, she was no longer sure which way to turn. The walls closed in around her, squeezing out her ability to think straight or feel anything other than growing depression.

So when Krajewski called she had shown little enthusiasm even though she knew she needed support from someone. Reluctantly she had been cajoled into meeting him at the coffee shop on the eastern edge of the Serpentine, the winding duck-strewn lake which dominates the centre of Hyde Park. He cursed as he hurried towards it. The bitter November wind was raising foam-topped waves as it sliced across the water, and as he approached the empty, lifeless coffee shop he realised that it must have closed for the winter. He found the small, forlorn figure of Mattie sheltering under the eaves, wrapped in a thin anorak which suddenly seemed too large for her. She appeared to have shrunk since they had last met. There were uncharacteristic dark rings under her eyes, and the vitality which normally lit her face was missing. She looked awful.

'What a bloody silly place for us to meet,' he apologised.

'Don't worry, Johnnie. I guess I needed the fresh air.'

He wanted to put his arms around her and squeeze the

316

chill out of her bones, but instead he tried to smile cheerfully.

'What's new with Britain's top female journalist?' he enquired. Immediately he wanted to bite his tongue off. He hadn't intended sarcasm, not at all, but it was a clumsy choice of words. She shivered before she replied.

'Perhaps you're right to laugh. A few days ago I thought I had the world at my feet.'

'And now?'

'Now it's all gone wrong. The job . . . The story . . .' – a slight pause – '. . . You. I thought I could do it all on my own. I was wrong. Sorry.'

This was a new Mattie, all full of self-doubt and insecurity. He didn't know what to say, so said nothing.

'When I was a young girl my grandfather used to take me out onto the Yorkshire dales. He said it was a lot like parts of Norway. The weather could get bitter and inhospitable up there but I never had any fears. Grandpa was always there with a helping hand and a smile. He always carried a flask of hot soup and I never felt better or warmer than when I was out with him, no matter how hard it blew. Then one day I thought I was grown up, didn't need Grandpa any more, so I slipped away on my own. I left the track and the ground started getting softer. Soon I was sinking up to my ankles and then slipping deeper and deeper.' She was shivering again. 'I couldn't get out. The more I struggled the deeper I became stuck. I thought I would never get out. It was the first time in my life that I had known what real fear was. But then Grandpa found me and plucked me out, and hugged me while I cried and dried my tears and made everything better.' Johnnie noted how frail and vulnerable she looked now inside the voluminous folds of her anorak, as if she was reliving the experience all over again.

'It's just like that now, Johnnie. I'm desperately trying to find some firm ground, something I can stand on and believe in, both about the story and in my own life. But I'm just sinking deeper and deeper, Grandpa's no longer around and I'm afraid. Do you understand? I feel as if I shall never step on solid ground again.'

317

'But haven't you seen the Sunday newspapers?' he encouraged. 'Someone filched Samuel's personal papers. Another bombshell hits the leadership race from party headquarters. Even more evidence pointing directly at Teddy Williams. Isn't that firm ground?'

She shook her head sadly. 'If only it were that simple.'

'I don't understand,' he said. 'We've got the deliberate theft of personal files. We've got the tampering with the central computer file – that's deliberate too. We've had the leaking of all sorts of damaging material out of party headquarters to you, to Kendrick, seemingly to anyone who was passing in the neighbourhood. We've got party officials opening accommodation addresses in false names, and politicians' corpses lying around like hedgehogs on a motorway. What more do you need? And it all leads back to party headquarters – which must mean Williams. He can't make Prime Minister himself, so he's making sure he controls whoever does.'

'You're missing the point, Johnnie. Why on earth should Williams need to steal his own documents? He could simply have copied the vital information without breaking in and stealing the whole bloody file. And he doesn't need to force locks – he's got all the keys. He is supposed to be Samuel's strongest ally, yet Samuel's campaign has been pedalling backwards ever since the election began.'

Her eyes were burning with disappointment. 'Can you really imagine an elder statesman like Williams framing the Prime Minister for fraud? Or leaking so much material from party headquarters that it has made him look like a doddering imbecile? No, Johnnie. It's not Williams.'

'Then who the hell is it? Samuel? Urquhart? Some other Cabinet Minister? Landless?'

'I don't know,' she cried. 'That's why I feel as if I am drowning! The more I struggle, the deeper I get stuck. Professionally. Emotionally. It's like a great quagmire sucking me under. I'm just not sure about anything any more.'

'I'd like to help you, Mattie. Please don't turn me away.'

'Like Grandpa, you're always there when I need you. Thanks, Johnnie. But I've got to find my own path now or

I never will. There's all this confusion inside me; I've got to sort these things out for myself.'

'I can wait,' he said gently.

'But I can't. I've got only two more days to come up with the answer and only one strong lead – Roger O'Neill.'

MONDAY 29TH NOVEMBER

The janitor found the body just after he had clocked on at 4.30 on Monday morning. He was beginning his morning duties at the Rownhams motorway service area just outside Southampton on the M27, starting with cleaning out the toilets, when he discovered that one of the cubicle doors would not open. He was nearing his sixty-eighth birthday, and he cursed as he lowered his old bones gently onto their hands and knees so that he could peer under the door. He had great difficulty getting all the way down, but he didn't need to. He saw the two shoes quite clearly, and that was enough to satisfy his curiosity. There was a man in there, and whether he was drunk, diseased or dying meant nothing to him except that it was going to put him way behind his cleaning schedule, and he cursed again as he staggered off to call his supervisor.

The supervisor was in no better temper when he arrived, and used a screwdriver to open the lock from the outside. But the man's knees were wedged firmly up against the door, and push as hard as they might the two of them could not force it open more than a few inches. The supervisor put his hand around the door, trying to shift the man's knees, but instead grabbed a dangling hand which was as cold as ice. He recoiled in horror and gave a wail of anguish, insisting on washing his hands meticulously before he stumbled off to call the police and an ambulance.

The police arrived shortly after 5 a.m. and, with rather more experience in such matters than the janitor and supervisor, had the cubicle door lifted off its hinges in seconds.

O'Neill's body was sitting there, fully clothed and slumped against the wall. His face, drained of all colour, was stretched into a leering death mask exposing his teeth and with his eyes staring wide open. In his lap they found two halves of an empty tin of talc, and on the floor beside him they discovered a small polythene bag containing a few grains of white powder and a briefcase stuffed with political pamphlets. They found other small white granules of powder still clinging to the leather cover of the briefcase, which had clearly been placed on O'Neill's lap to provide a flat surface. From one clenched fist they managed to prise a twisted £20 note which had been fashioned into a tube before being crumpled by O'Neill's death fit. His other arm was stretched aloft over his head, as if the grinning corpse was giving one final, hideous salute of farewell.

'Another junkie taking his last fix,' muttered the police sergeant, who had seen more than a few such sights in his time. 'It's more usual to find them with a needle up their arm,' he explained to his young colleague who lacked the relevant experience. 'But this one looks as if he was doing cocaine, and either it was too much for his heart or he's got hold of some adulterated stuff. There's quite a lot of drug pushing goes on around these motorway service stations, and the junkies never know what they're buying from whom. You often get impure drugs being peddled, either diluted with anything from castor sugar to baking powder, or mixed with something rather more lethal. The pushers will sell anything for money and the junkies will pay anything for a fix, whatever it is. This is just one of the unlucky ones.'

He started rummaging through O'Neill's pockets for clues to his identity. 'Funny way the body and face have contorted, though. Well, we can let the police surgeon and the coroner's office sort that one out. Let's get on with it, laddie, and call the ruddy photographers to record this sordid little scene. No use us standing here guessing about . . . Mr Roger O'Neill,' he announced as he found a wallet bearing a few credit cards. 'Wonder who he is?'

'There's a car outside in the car park, been here all night by the looks of it,' volunteered the janitor. 'Probably his.'

'Well, let's take the details and check it out then,' instructed the sergeant.

It was 7.20 by the time the coroner's representative had

authorised the removal of the body. The sergeant was making sure the junior officer had finished with the required procedures and the ambulancemen were man-handling the rigid, contorted body out from its seat and onto their stretcher when the call came over the radio.

'Sod it,' the sergeant told the radio controller. 'That'll set the cat amongst the pigeons. I'd better make double sure we've done everything this end before we have CID inspectors, superintendents and chief constables floating in for a look.'

He turned to the fresh-faced constable. 'Got yourself a prize one there, you have. Seems the car is registered to the Government's party headquarters, and our Mr Roger O'Neill is – rather was – a senior party official with his fingers in Downing Street and everywhere else, no doubt. Better make sure you write a full report, lad, or we'll both be for the high jump.'

It had been another sleepless night. Her physical reserves of stamina had just about run out and she was on the point of surrendering to her growing mood of depression when the phone call threw her the lifeline she needed. It was Johnnie, calling from the *Telegraph* news room.

'How's this for another one of your coincidences?' he enquired. 'Just come over on the tape. It seems the South-ampton police found your Roger O'Neill dead in a public lavatory just a few hours ago.'

'Tell me this is simply your tasteless way of saying good morning,' she said without humour.

'Sorry. It's for real. I've already sent a reporter down to the scene, but it appears the local police have called in the Drug Squad. Seems he may have overdosed.'

Mattie gasped as one of the pieces fell into place with a noise like a coffin lid slamming closed.

'So that was it. An addict. No wonder he was all over the place . . .' As she spoke she nudged in her excitement the large stack of dirty crockery which had built up beside the kitchen telephone, sending them crashing to the floor.

'Mattie, what on earth . . .'

322

'Don't you see, Johnnie. He was the key man, the only man we knew for certain was involved in all the dirty tricks. Our Number One lead has just very conveniently disappeared from the scene, the day before they elect a new Prime Minister, leaving us with a big fat zero. Don't you see, Johnnie.'

'What?'

'There's not a moment to waste!' she gasped, as he heard the phone go dead.

Mattie almost didn't find Penny Guy. She had rung the bell of the mansion block continuously for several minutes, and was just about to give up when the latch was released by the electronic buzzer and the door swung open. The door to Penny's flat on the first floor was also ajar, and Mattie walked in. She found Penny sitting quietly on the sofa, curtains drawn, staring at nothing.

Mattie did not speak, but sat down beside her and held her. Slowly Penny's fingers tightened around Mattie's hand, acknowledging her presence, begging her to stay.

'He didn't deserve to die,' Penny said in a hushed, faltering voice. 'He was a weak man, but not an evil one. He was very kind.'

'What was he doing in Southampton?'

'He was spending the weekend with someone. Wouldn't say who. It was one of his silly secrets.'

'Any idea who?'

Penny shook her head with painful slowness.

'Do you know why he died?' Mattie asked.

Penny turned to face her with round, dark eyes which had a faraway look and from which the shock had squeezed any trace of emotion.

'You're not interested in him, are you? Only in his death.' It was not an accusation, simply a statement of fact.

'I'm sorry he died, Penny. I'm also sorry because I think Roger will be blamed for a lot of bad things that have happened recently. And I don't think he's the one who should be blamed.'

Penny blinked for the first time, as if the question had

at last disturbed the emptiness which had taken hold of her.

'Why would they . . . blame Roger?' The words were formed slowly, as if half of her were elsewhere, in a world where O'Neill was still alive and where Penny could still save him.

'Because he's a victim who has been set up to take the blame. Someone has been using Roger, has been twisting him and bending him in a dirty little political game – until Roger snapped.'

Penny considered this for several long moments. 'He's not the only one,' she said.

'What do you mean?'

'Patrick. Patrick was sent a tape, of him with me. He thought I'd done it.'

'Patrick who, Penny?'

'Woolton. He thought I had made the tape of us in bed together to blackmail him. But it was someone else. It wasn't me.'

'So that's why he quit,' exclaimed Mattie. 'Who could have made the tape, Penny?'

'Don't know. Almost anybody at the party conference I suppose. Anyone in Bournemouth, anyone at the hotel.'

'But Penny, I don't understand! Who could have blackmailed Patrick Woolton? Who could have known you were sleeping with him?'

'Roger knew. But Roger would never . . .'

'Don't you see, Penny. Someone was blackmailing Roger, too. Someone who must have known he was on drugs. Someone who forced him to leak opinion polls and alter computer files. Someone who . . .'

'Killed him!' The words unlocked the misery which Penny had been trying to hide since they had telephoned her earlier that morning. But now the barriers burst and tears were flooding from her eyes, forced out by the cries of anguish which racked her body. Further discussion with her was clearly impossible, and Mattie helped the sobbing girl into bed, making her as comfortable as she could. She stayed with her until the tears had emptied her soul and she was fast asleep.

Mattie walked down the street in confusion. The first snow of winter was beginning to fall gently around her, but she did not notice it. She was lost in her own misery of doubt. All the firm evidence she had led back to O'Neill. Now he was dead and the door at which she had been pushing, behind which she knew she would find the answer, had suddenly slammed shut on her. It was not the first time that the frustrated ambition of men had led to blackmail and violence — the appeal of political power had fascinated, seduced and corrupted men and women throughout the ages – but none had daubed blood on the door of 10 Downing Street. Until now. It had to be washed clean. She had a day to do it – and no idea where to go next.

'Come on, come on, come on, come on!' she shouted, beating her hands on the desk in frustration. As the day had turned to evening and she had tossed the facts around fruitlessly in her mind she had become more tense, unable to find any new direction. The clock had ticked remorselessly on, and she found her mind crossing the same old ground, travelling up the same blind alleys and discovering the same dead ends. The harder she tried, the more elusive any new insight became. Perhaps a change of scene might fire her imagination. So she had gone for a walk, driven around, taken a bath and was now sitting at home, crying for enlightenment. But it was to no avail. Her inspiration and intuition had failed her as the sleepless nights took their toll, and the one man who could answer all her burning questions was dead, taking his secrets with him. She buried her head in her hands, reduced to praying for a miracle in a world which God seemed to have deserted.

Something sparked. Later she could never recall what aroused it, but among the dying embers of her confidence a small flame began to glow and lick itself back to life. Perhaps it was not all over yet.

Two hours later Krajewski arrived clutching a large box of hot pizza. He had telephoned but got no answer. He was concerned, and was attempting to hide his concern beneath the pepperoni and extra cheese. He found Mattie sitting on the floor in the dark, huddled in the corner with her knees drawn up under her chin, clenching her arms around her tightly. She had been crying.

He said nothing but knelt beside her, and this time she allowed him to hug the tears away. It was some time before she could say anything.

'Johnnie, you told me that if I couldn't offer commitment I could never make it as a journalist, that I would be no better than a butterfly. I realise now that you were right. Until today I was simply chasing a story – oh, a big one, for sure, but what really mattered was ending up with my name at the top of the page one lead. Like a film – rooting out the wrongdoers from their hiding places, never giving a damn about the cost. I've been acting a role, the intrepid journalist struggling to unravel the lies in the face of over-whelming odds. But it's no longer a game, Johnnie . . .'

She looked into his eyes, and he saw that her tears were not tears of fear or pain, but tears of release, as if she had at last struggled from the clutches of the bog onto solid ground.

'All I wanted was a story, a great one. I threw away my job and I even trampled over your feelings just in case you got in the way. Now I would give anything for the whole story to disappear, but it's too late.'

She gripped his hand, needing someone now. 'You see, Johnnie, none of it was coincidence. Woolton was deliber-ately blackmailed out of the leadership race. Somebody got rid of him, just as they got rid of Collingridge, of McKenzie, of Earle. And of O'Neill.'

'Do you realise what you're saying?'

'O'Neill's death was suicide or murder. And how many people have you ever heard of committing suicide in a public lavatory!'

'Mattie, this isn't the KGB we are dealing with.'

'As far as O'Neill is concerned, it may just as well have been.'

'Jesus!'

'Johnnie, there is someone out there who will stop at nothing to fix the election of the man who in a few hours' time will become the most powerful individual in the country.'

'That's terrifying. But who . . . ?'

She pounded the floor in anger.

'That's the bloody trouble. I don't know! I've been sitting here in the dark knowing that there is a man, a name, some clue which will reveal it all, but I just can't find it. Everything leads back to O'Neill, and now he's gone . . .'

'You are certain that it couldn't have been O'Neill, perhaps, who got so deeply involved . . . got scared. Lost control and killed himself?'

'No! Of course it wasn't O'Neill. It couldn't have been . . .'

The flame spluttered once more, warming her, its heat dispelling a little more of the mists of confusion which clung to her mind.

'Johnnie, while O'Neill played his part with most and possibly all of the leaks, he couldn't have done it by himself. Some of those leaks were from Government, not from the Party. Highly confidential information which would not have been available to all members of the Cabinet, let alone a party official.'

She took a deep breath, as deep as if it were the first breath of fresh air she had taken in days.

'Do you see what that means, Johnnie. There must be a common link. There must be, if only we could find it . . .'

'Mattie, we can't give up now. There has to be a way. Look, have you got a list of Cabinet Ministers?'

'In the drawer of my work table.'

He leapt to his feet and scrabbled about in the drawer before coming up with the list. With a broad sweep of his arm he cleared all the papers, books and assorted debris off the top of her large work table, exposing its smooth, laminated white work surface. The whiteness of the desk was like an open page waiting to be filled. He grabbed an artist's pen and began scrawling down on the laminate all the twenty-two names from the sheet.

'OK. Who could have been responsible for the leaks? Come on, Mattie. Think!' The fire had caught inside him now.

Mattie did not move. She was frozen in the corner, all her last reserves of energy concentrated on sorting out the jumble in her mind.

'There were at least three leaks which had to come from inside the Cabinet,' she said at last. 'There were the Territorial Army cuts, the cancellation of the hospital expansion scheme, and the Renox drug approval. O'Neill would never have known about those first-hand. But who in Government would have?'

Slowly, she began reciting the Cabinet members who would have had early knowledge of the decisions. As she did so, Krajewski feverishly began ticking off the names on his list.

Who was on the Cabinet Committee which dealt with major military matters and would have made the decision on the TA cuts? Concentrate, Mattie, even though every part of your mind wants to go to sleep. Slowly the thoughts began to focus and take form. The Defence Secretary, the Financial Secretary, the Chancellor possibly, and of course the Prime Minister. Damn it, who else? Right, the Employment Secretary and the Foreign Secretary, too.

Then the hospital scheme which would have been considered by another Committee including the Health Secretary and the Treasury Ministers, the Trade and Industry Secretary, Education Secretary and Environment Secretary also. She prayed she hadn't missed any names. The membership and even existence of these committees were supposed to be a state secret, which meant the information was never formally published and was left to become yet another part of the Westminster system of lobby gossip. But the system was so effective she felt sure she had missed no names.

Was she getting closer? The Renox drug approval – damn, that wouldn't have been considered by any Cabinet Committee; it was a Department of Health decision and known solely to the Health Secretary and his Ministers. And of course the Prime Minister would have been informed in advance, but who else?

She leapt up to join Krajewski, who was staring at his handiwork.

'We seem to have screwed up rather badly, I'm afraid,' he muttered quietly.

She looked at the list. There was only one name with three ticks beside it, one man with access to all three bits of leaked information, one man whom her detective work could pronounce guilty. And that was the victim himself – the Prime Minister, Henry Collingridge! Her efforts had left them with the most absurd conclusion of all. The little flame of hope gave one last splutter and prepared to die.

She stood there staring. Something was wrong.

'Johnnie, this list of names. Why isn't Urquhart on it?'

She snorted in ridicule at herself as she provided her own answer. 'Because I'm a silly bitch and forgot that the Chief Whip is not technically a full member of Cabinet and so doesn't appear on my Cabinet list. But it makes no difference. He's not on the Defence Committee, nor could he have known about Renox.'

But she stopped with a gasp. The flame had suddenly sprung into life once again and was burning at her from deep inside.

'But of course . . . He's not formally a member, but if I remember correctly he does sit in on the committee which dealt with the hospital programme. He wouldn't have attended the defence committee, yet as he is responsible for parliamentary discipline they would have been sure to consult him well in advance about a decision which was going to cause uproar on the backbenches.'

'But he couldn't have known about Renox,' interjected Krajewski.

She was gripping his arm so tightly now that the nails were digging into the flesh.

'Johnnie, every Government Department has a Junior Whip attached to it, one of Urquhart's men, to make sure there is proper liaison about Government business. Every week most Secretaries of State hold a business meeting amongst their departmental Ministers to discuss the activities of the week ahead, and the Junior Whip usually attends. He then goes back and reports to the Chief Whip to ensure that Ministers don't trip over each other's feet. It *is* possible, Johnnie. Urquhart could have known . . .'

329

'But what about the rest of it. How would he have known about O'Neill's drug taking? Or Woolton's sex life? Or any of the other pieces?'

'Because he's Chief Whip. It's his job to know about those things. He had the means, and hell did he have a motive. From nowhere to Prime Minister in a couple of months! How on earth did we miss it?'

'But it's all still circumstantial, Mattie. You don't have a single shred of proof.'

'Then let's see if we can get it!'

She grabbed the phone and began punching a number.

'Penny? It's Mattie Storin. I'm sorry it's so late, but I need some answers. It's very important. I think I know who got Roger into all the trouble. Where did you meet Patrick Woolton?'

'At the Bournemouth party conference,' a sad voice replied.

'But in what circumstances? Please try to remember. Who introduced you?'

'Roger said he wanted to meet me, and took me along to a party to introduce us.'

'Where was the party?'

'At Mr Urquhart's. He had the bungalow right next door to Patrick's, and it was he who actually took me over to say hello to Patrick.'

'Did Roger know Francis Urquhart particularly well?'

'No, not really. At least not until recently. As far as I know they had scarcely spoken to each other before the election, but they have talked with each other a couple of times on the phone since then, and they met for dinner. I don't think even now they are – were – very close, though. Last time they spoke Roger was very upset. Something about a computer file which got Roger very angry.'

At last the pieces began to fit.

'One more question, Penny. I presume Francis Urquhart has a country residence as well as his house in Pimlico. Do you happen to know where that is?'

'No, I don't I'm afraid. I've only got a list of Cabinet weekend telephone numbers which I keep for Roger.'

'Can I have the Urquhart number?'

'I can't, Mattie, they are absolutely confidential. You must remember there have been terrorist attacks at Ministers' homes, and it would be totally wrong for me to give them out to the press, even to you. I am sorry, Mattie, truly.'

'Can you tell me the area in which he lives? Not the address, just the town or even the county?'

'I don't know it. I've only got the telephone number.'

'Give me the dialling code, then. Just the dialling code,' she pleaded.

There was the sound of a slight shuffling of paper at the other end of the phone.

'Mattie, I'm not sure why you want it, but it is to help Roger, isn't it?'

'I promise you, Penny.'

'042128.'

'Thanks. You won't regret it.'

Mattie flicked the receiver and got a new line. She punched the area code into the telephone, followed by a random set of numbers. A connection was made, and a phone started ringing at the other end.

'Lyndhurst 37428,' a drowsy voice announced.

'Good evening. I'm sorry to bother you so late. Is that Lyndhurst, Surrey, 37428?'

'No. It's Lyndhurst in Hampshire 37428. And it's very late for you to be telephoning wrong numbers!' an irritated voice snapped before the phone was disconnected.

The fire inside Mattie was roaring brightly now as she threw herself across the room towards her bookcase, where she ripped a road atlas from its place. She scrabbled through the maps until she found the South Coast section, jabbed a finger at the page and whooped with triumph.

'It's him, Johnnie. It's him!'

He looked over her shoulder at where the finger was placed. It was pointing directly at the Rownhams service area on the M27 where O'Neill had died. It was the first service station on the motorway back to London from Lyndhurst. O'Neill had died less than eight miles from Urquhart's country home.

331

TUESDAY 30TH NOVEMBER

The morning newspapers fell onto the doormats of a million homes like a death knell for Samuel's candidacy. One by one, editor by editor, they began to line up behind Urquhart. It was not surprising to the Chief Whip that all the newspapers in the Telegraph and United Newspapers groups came to the same conclusion – some with more enthusiasm than others, to be sure, but to the same conclusion nonetheless – but it was of even greater satisfaction that many of the others had also decided to throw their weight behind him. Editorial offices tend to provide little comfort for politicians who trail their consciences; and some still remembered how badly their papers had got their fingers burnt with Neville Chamberlain's pious bits of paper. Others had reached the same cynical conclusion as Woolton about the drawbacks of creating another 'era' so soon after Thatcher which, with Samuel's youth, could last another fifteen years or more. Phrases such as 'experience', 'maturity' and 'balance' were peppered freely around the columns. Still others wanted simply to play safe, wishing to swim with the tide which was flooding strongly in Urquhart's favour.

Only two newspapers stood out amongst the quality press, the *Guardian* for its habit of deliberately swimming against the tide, requiring it to support Samuel, and the *Independent* which stood proud and isolated like a rock withstanding the battering of storms and tide, refusing to endorse either.

The mood was reflected in the two camps, with Urquhart's supporters finding it difficult to hide their air of quiet confidence, and Samuel's finding it impossible in private to disguise their sense of looming disappointment.

As the tall doors of Committee Room 14 swung open at

10 a.m. to accept the first batch of MPs waiting outside to vote, neither Sir Humphrey nor others present expected any disappointments.

In best traditional style it would be an orderly and gentlemanly ballot; the loser would be gracious and the winner even more so. The covering of snow which was beginning steadily to blanket Westminster gave the proceedings a surrealistic calm. It would be Christmas soon, it reminded them, and the lights had already long been switched on in Oxford Street. Time soon for the winter break, for family reunions and peace on earth. The long period of indecision would be over in a few hours and ordinary folk could return to their normal lives. In public there would be handshakes and congratulations all the way round when the result was announced, even as in private the victors planned their recriminations and the losers plotted their revenge.

When Mattie walked towards the office of Benjamin Landless just off Charterhouse Square, the snow was several inches thick. Outside the capital the snow had settled much more deeply, making travel difficult and persuading many commuters simply to stay at home. The streets of the City of London were strangely quiet in their white cocoon as the falling flakes muffled all sound and the few cars crept quietly about their business. She felt unreal, as if she were on a film set acting out a role, hoping she would wake up in the morning and discover that the script had been changed. Even now she was tempted to turn around and forget all about it, to let others concern themselves about the great affairs of state while she concentrated on paying her mortgage and whether she could afford a holiday next year.

Then a flurry of snow blew into her face, blinding her and transporting her back many years before she was born to an isolated Norwegian fjord and her grandfather setting off in a leaking fishing boat to risk his life on the tides of war. He could have collaborated, turned a blind eye, left it to others to sort out the world while he got on with his own life. But something had driven him on, just as she was being driven now.

When at first she had realised the necessity of confronting Landless, she had discovered all the many reasons why it would be futile – she wouldn't even get to see him; if she did he would ruthlessly ensure that she would never work as a journalist again, and she wouldn't be the first such victim. She had seen him bully and intimidate so many, how could she expect to succeed where so many other more experienced and powerful hands had failed? She had to confront him yet she desperately needed his help. And how was she supposed to squeeze support from a man who instinctively would prefer to throttle her with his own huge hands?

It was only when she realised that she had run out of time and alternatives that she summoned up the courage to unravel her excuses and deal with them one by one. Her first problem was access to the heavily protected businessman. He may depict himself as a man of the people, but he took elaborate and expensive precautions to ensure that he did not have to rub shoulders with them.

So she had phoned the writer of the *Telegraph*'s diary column, the keeper of society's gossip and scandal. Had Landless recently had any close female friends, women of whom he was known to be particularly fond? Fine! A lady twenty years younger than him, now safely ensconced in Wiltshire with a new husband and brood, but known to have been the favoured recipient of a large measure of the magnate's hugely expensive overtime. Mrs Susannah Richards. Yes, she hoped that would do nicely.

But nothing seemed easy as she walked along the strange, empty streets. She arrived at her destination and shook the snow from her boots and hair. She was surprised to see how small were the offices from which Landless ran his many empires, and how opulently the East-Ender had learned to live. The place reeked of British tradition. The small foyer and reception area was cloaked almost entirely in English carved oak panelling, on which were hung several fine oil paintings of old London scenes and a vast portrait of the Queen. The carpeting was thick, the electronics sophisticated and the commissionaire very ex-military.

'Can I help you, Miss?' he asked from beneath his pencil-line moustache.

'My name is Mrs Susannah Richards. I am a personal friend of Mr Landless, you understand,' she explained with a hint of intrigue, 'and I was passing in the vicinity. He's not expecting me, but could you see if he has five minutes free? I have an important personal message for him.'

The commissionaire was all discretion and efficiency – it was so rare that one of the boss's 'personal friends' came to the office, and he was eager to make a good impression. He relayed the message to Landless's secretary precisely and with just the right degree of enthusiasm. No doubt the secretary passed on the message in similar fashion, for within a few seconds Mattie was being ushered into the lift with instructions to proceed to the top floor.

As she stood in the doorway of the penthouse suite, Landless was seated behind his desk in the middle of a vast office which had been designed to accommodate his own huge bulk. She had time to take in none of the detail before an animal growl of rage began erupting from his throat.

'You miserable bloody cow . . .'

She had to cut him short. Before he had time to make up his mind, let alone utter the angry words of dismissal, she had to take control. It was her only slender chance.

'It's your takeover of United.'

'The takeover? What about it?' he shouted, betraying only the slightest edge of interest.

'It's finished.'

'What on earth do you mean?' he snarled, but a little less loudly this time.

She stood there, silent, challenging him to decide whether his curiosity would overcome his anger. It took a moment before she knew she had won the first round. With a snort, he waved a fleshy hand in the direction of a chair. It was a good six inches lower than his own, down onto which he could glower from beneath his huge, eruptive eyebrows and stare its occupant into submission. She moved slowly into the room, but away from the chair. She wasn't going to give him the advantage of physically intimidating her on the low, uncomfortable perch. Anyway, she felt better moving around.

'You've backed the wrong horse. Francis Urquhart has cheated and lied his way to the party leadership, and possibly much worse. By the time that all gets out, his endorsement of the takeover won't be worth a bean.'

'But he hasn't endorsed the takeover. He said he wouldn't decide until after the leadership election.'

'But you and I know that is only part of the deal you did with him – the support of your newspapers in return for his approval of the takeover after he had won.'

'What the hell are you talking about? You listen to me, you little bitch . . .'

'No, Mr Landless. It's you who's going to have to listen to me!' She was smiling now, trying to display the quiet confidence of a poker player intent on persuading her opponent that the cards she held were of much higher value than his own. She had no proof, of course, only the coincidence of timing to suggest a deal had been done, but now she understood about Urquhart it was the only scenario which made sense. Anyway, she had to keep raising the stakes, she had to force him to show his hand.

'You see, you are not the first proprietor to put puppets into their newspapers as editors, but you made a great mistake when you chose Greville Preston. The man is so weak that every time you pulled the strings he started jerking around totally out of control. He couldn't possibly pretend that he was his own boss. So when you, Mr Landless, decided to go gunning for Henry Collingridge at the party conference, there was no chance that Preston could pretend it was his own decision or hide the fact that he was acting under your direct instructions. And when *you*, Mr Landless, decided to propel Francis Urquhart into the leadership race at the last, dramatic minute through the editorial columns of the *Telegraph*, there was no chance that Preston could justify it to the staff. He had to slip it into the edition on a Sunday evening without any consultation, skulking around his own newspaper like a thief in the night. You see, he's very good at doing what he's told, but he simply doesn't understand half the time why he's been told to do it. If you like to put it that way, Mr Landless, in spite of all his university education you're too good for him.'

Landless did not respond to the backhanded compliment. His fleshy features were set uncharacteristically rigid.

'You made Urquhart's candidacy. Put quite simply – as I am sure you have put it to him yourself – he could not be on the point of becoming Prime Minister without your help. And for that you would have got something in return – his agreement to turn the Government's competition policy on its head and to endorse your takeover of United Newspapers.'

At last Landless came to life, calling her bluff.

'What proof do you have of this extraordinary tale, Miss Storin?'

'That's the beauty of it. I don't need proof. I need just enough to stir up the most awful public row and you will find the politicians deserting your camp and heading for the hills, no matter what they have been saying during the leadership contest. You will find yourself without a single friend.'

'But according to your weird and wonderful hypothesis, Francis Urquhart is my friend, and he will be in 10 Downing Street,' Landless smiled mockingly.

'But not for long, Mr Landless, not for long. I'm afraid you know less about him than you think. Did you know, when you instructed Preston to use the opinion poll to undermine the Prime Minister, that it was Urquhart who had leaked it in the first place? He set you up.'

There was a sufficient look of surprise on Landless's face to let Mattie know that she was right and he resented being used like that.

'But all politicians leak,' Landless responded. 'It's not criminal, certainly not enough to throw him out of Downing Street.'

'No, but insider share dealing, fraud, blackmail and theft are!' She delighted in the look of concern spreading across his fat jowls.

'I can show beyond a reasonable doubt that it was

337

Urquhart who set up Charles Collingridge by buying Renox shares in his name in a deliberate and very successful attempt to implicate the Prime Minister. That Urquhart blackmailed Patrick Woolton into standing down by bugging his room at Bournemouth. And ordered the theft of confidential personal files on Michael Samuel from party headquarters.' She was bluffing on the Samuel file, she had no proof only inner certainty, but she knew her bluff would not be called from the way in which Landless had by now lost his air of confidence. Yet he was one of nature's fighters. He hadn't given in yet.

'What makes you think anyone is going to believe you? By tonight Francis Urquhart will be Prime Minister, and who do you think is going to want to see the Prime Minister and the country dragged down by a political scandal of that sort? I think you underestimate the Establishment and its powers of self-protection, Miss Storin. If the Prime Minister is dragged down, confidence in the whole system suffers. It's not justice which wins, but the radicals and the revolutionaries. Not even the Opposition would welcome that. So you'll find it damned difficult to get any newspaper to print your allegations, and next to impossible to get a law officer to proceed on them.'

He was beginning to relish his own argument now, regaining his confidence.

'Why, it took them seven years before they were forced to indict Jeremy Thorpe who was only Leader of the Liberal Party, not even the Prime Minister. And he was arrested for attempted murder, which makes your charges of petty theft and blackmail look really rather pathetic. You don't even have a body on which to build your case!'

'Oh, but I do, Mr Landless,' she said softly. 'I believe he killed Roger O'Neill to silence him, and although I'm not sure I can prove it yet, I can raise such a storm as will blow down the shutters of Downing Street and will quite overwhelm your little business venture. Someone in the Thorpe case shot a dog. Here we are talking about murder. Do you really think your Establishment is going to keep quiet about that?'

Landless levered his great girth out of his chair and

walked across to the large picture window. From it he could see the chimneys, steeples and hideous tower blocks of Bethnal Green less than two miles away where he had been born and where in the slums of his childhood he had learnt all he needed to know about survival. He had never wanted to move far away from the area even with all his wealth; his roots were there, and if he screwed it all up that was where he knew he would have to return.

When he turned around to face her once more, she thought she could detect the signs of defeat etched deep into his features.

'What are you going to do, Miss Storin?'

'I am too late to stop Urquhart getting elected. But I intend to make sure he stays in office for as short a time as possible. And for that I want your help '

'My help! I . . . I don't understand. You accuse me of causing all this bleedin' chaos and then you ask for my help. Christ all bloody Mighty!' he spluttered in broadest cockney, his defences in tatters.

'Let me explain. You may be a rogue, Mr Landless, and you may run a rotten newspaper, but I suspect that deep down you care for the idea of a man like Urquhart running this country as little as I do. You have worked very hard to develop the reputation of a working class patriot. Corny to some people, perhaps, but I suspect you mean it – and if I'm right, you would never dream of conspiring to put a murderer in Downing Street.'

She paused but he said nothing.

'In any event, I think I can persuade you to help on straightforward commercial grounds. Whatever happens, your takeover of United Newspapers is dead. You can either watch it be swept away in the storm which will undoubtedly engulf Urquhart, which means the Establishment will turn on you and you will never be able to raise money in the City of London for a business deal ever again – or you can kill it yourself, help me nail Urquhart, save your business and become the hero of the hour.'

'Why should I trust you?'

'Because I need you.'

'Need me?' his jowls fluttered in surprise.

'I need you to be a good newspaper man and publish the full story. If it's published with the backing of the *Telegraph* rather than dribbling out over the next few months in bits and pieces, nobody can ignore it. I will give you an exclusive which will blow your patriotic socks off. And once I've done that, I am scarcely going to be able to turn on you.'

'And if I say no?'

'Then I shall find an army of Opposition backbenchers who would like nothing more than to take all the ammunition I can provide them with, stand up in the House of Commons where they are protected from the laws of slander, and make accusations against both you and Urquhart which will bring you crashing down together.'

All her cards were on the table now. The game was nearly over. Had he any cards left up his sleeve?

'Urquhart will fall, Mr Landless, one way or the other. The only thing you have to decide is whether you fall with him or help me push him . . .'

It was early afternoon before Mattie returned to Westminster. The snow had stopped falling and the skies were clearing, leaving the capital looking like a scene from a traditional Christmas card. The Houses of Parliament looked particularly resplendent, like some wondrous Christmas cake covered in brilliant white icing beneath a crystal blue sky. Opposite in the churchyard of St Margaret's, nestling under the wing of the great medieval Abbey, carol singers brought an air of tranquillity and Victorian charm to the passers-by, wishing goodwill to all men.

Celebrations were already under way in various parts of the House of Commons. One of Mattie's colleagues in the press gallery rushed over to explain.

'About 80 per cent of Government MPs have already voted. They think Urquhart's home and dry. It looks like a landslide.'

Big Ben tolled; to Mattie it had a new and awesome ring. She felt as if an icicle had dislodged itself from the Palace walls and pierced straight into her heart. But she had to press on.

Urquhart was not in his room, nor in any of the bars or restaurants in the Palace of Westminster. She asked in vain around the corridors after him and was just about to conclude that he had left the premises entirely, for lunch or interviews, when one of the Palace policemen told her that he had seen Urquhart not ten minutes earlier headed in the direction of the roof garden. She had no idea that any roof garden existed, or even where it was.

'Yes, miss. Not many people do know about our roof garden, and those that do like to keep quiet about it in case everybody rushes up there and spoils the charm. It's directly above the House of Commons, all around the great central skylights which light up the Chamber itself. It's a flat roof terrace, and we've put some tables and chairs up there so that in summer the staff can enjoy the sunshine, take some sandwiches and a flask of coffee. Not many Members know about it and even fewer ever go up there, but I've seen Mr Urquhart up there a couple of times before. Likes the view, I imagine. But it'll be damned cold and lonely today, if you don't mind my saying so.'

She followed his directions, up the stairs past the Strangers Gallery and up again until she had passed the panelled dressing room reserved for the Palace door-keepers. Then she saw a fire door which was slightly ajar. As she stepped through it she emerged onto the roof, and drew in her breath sharply. The view was magnificent. Right in front of her, towering into the cloudless sky, made brilliant in the sunshine and snow, was the tower of Big Ben, closer than she had ever seen it before. Every little detail of the beautifully crafted stone stood out with stunning clarity, and she could see the tremor of the great clock hands as the ancient but splendid mechanism pursued its remorseless course.

To the left she could see the great tiled roof of Westminster Hall, the oldest part of the Palace, which had survived the assault of fire, war, bomb and revolution and which had witnessed so much human achievement and misery. To her right she could see the River Thames, ebbing and flowing in its own irresistible fashion even as the tides of history swept capriciously along its banks. And in front of her she could see fresh footsteps in the snow.

He was there, standing by the balustrade at the far end of the terrace, looking out beyond the rooftops of Whitehall, north to where he knew the moors of his childhood still beckoned. He had never seen the view like this before, blanketed in snow. The sky was as clear as the air in the Scottish valleys he had deserted; the rooftops carpeted in white he imagined to be the rolling moors on which he had spent so many enthralling hours hunting with the gillie; the steeples became the copses of spruce in which they had hidden while they watched the progress of the deer. On a day such as this, he felt as if he could see right to the heart of his old Perthshire home, and beyond even to the heart of eternity. It was all his now.

He could see the white stone walls of the Home Office, behind which lay Buckingham Palace where, later that evening, he would be driven in triumph. There stood the Foreign Office, and next to it the Treasury at the entrance to Whitehall which he would shortly command more effectively than any hereditary king. Before him were spread the great offices of state which he would soon dispense and dominate in a way which would at last lay to rest his father's haunting accusations and recompense for all the bitterness and loneliness to which he had so long condemned himself.

He was startled as he realised that someone was at his elbow.

'Miss Storin!' he exclaimed. 'This is a surprise. I didn't think anyone would find me here – but you seem to have a habit of tracking me down. What is it this time – another exclusive interview?'

'I hope it will be very exclusive, Mr Urquhart.'

'You know, I remember you were right in on the start. You were the first person ever to ask if I were going to stand for the leadership.'

'Perhaps it is appropriate that I should also be in on the end . . .'

'What do you mean?'

The time had come.

'Perhaps you should read this. It's the Press Association copy I have just taken from the printer.'

She pulled out of her shoulder bag a short piece of news agency copy which she handed to him.

LONDON – 30.11.91.

In a surprise development, Mr Benjamin Landless has announced that he has withdrawn his takeover offer for the United Newspapers Group.

In a brief statement, Landless indicated that he had been approached by senior political figures asking for editorial and financial support in exchange for their approval of the merger.

'In such circumstances,' he said, 'I think it to be in the national interest that the deal be suspended. I do not wish the reputation of my company in any way to be impugned by the reprehensible and possibly corrupt activity which has begun to infect this transaction.'

Landless announced that he hoped to be able to release further details after he had consulted with his lawyers.

'I don't understand. What does this mean?' asked Urquhart in a calm voice. But Mattie noticed that he had crumpled the news release up in his clenched fist.

'It means, Mr Urquhart, that I know the full story. Now so does Benjamin Landless. And in a few days so will every newspaper reader in the country.'

A frown crossed his brow. There was no anger or anguish in his face yet, like a soldier who had been shot but whose nervous system had still to allow the pain to prize away the blanket of numbness which the shock had wrapped about him. But Mattie could have no mercy. She reached into her shoulder bag yet again, extracting a small tape recorder, and pressed a button. The tape which Landless had given Mattie began to turn and in the quiet, snow-clad air they could hear very distinctly the voices of the newspaper proprietor and the Chief Whip as they

343

conspired together. The conversation was unambiguous, the recording of remarkable clarity and the contents unmistakably criminal as the two plotted to exchange editorial endorsement for political endorsement.

Mattie pressed another button, and the voices stopped.

'I don't know whether you make a habit of taping all your colleagues' bedrooms, or just Patrick Woolton's, but I can assure you that Benjamin Landless tapes all of his telephone conversations,' she said.

Urquhart's face had frozen in the winter's air. He was beginning to feel the pain now.

'Tell me, Mr Urquhart. I know you blackmailed Roger O'Neill into opening the false address in Paddington for Charles Collingridge, but when the police investigate will they find his or your signature on the bank account?'

There was silence.

'Come now, as soon as I go to the authorities you will have to tell them everything, so why not tell me first?'

More silence.

'I know you and O'Neill between you leaked opinion polls and the news about the Territorial Army cuts. I know you also got him to enter a false computer file on Charles Collingridge into the Party's central computer – he didn't care for that, did he? I suspect he was even less excited about stealing the Party's confidential files on Michael Samuel. But one thing I'm not sure about. Was it you or Roger who concocted that silly tale about the cancelled publicity campaign on the hospital expansion scheme to feed to Stephen Kendrick?'

At last Urquhart managed to speak. He was breathing deeply, trying to hide the tension inside.

'You have a vivid imagination.'

'Oh, if only I did, Mr Urquhart, I would have caught you much earlier. No, it's not imagination which is going to expose you. It's this tape,' she said, patting the recorder she held in her hand. 'And the report which Mr Landless is going to publish at great length in the *Telegraph*.'

Now Urquhart visibly flinched.

'But Landless wouldn't . . . couldn't!'

'Oh, you don't think Mr Landless is going to take any

344

of the blame, do you? No. He's going to make you the fall
guy, Mr Urquhart. Don't you realise? They are never going
to let you be Prime Minister. I will write it, he will publish
it, and you will never get to Downing Street.'

He shook his head in disbelief. A thin, cruel smile began
to cross his lips. He couldn't tell whether it was the freezing weather or the frost he felt inside him, but he had
that cold, tingling sensation up his spine once more. His
breathing was steadier now, his hunter's instincts restoring
his sense of physical control.

'I don't suppose you would be willing to . . . ?' He let
out a low, chilling laugh. 'No, of course not. Silly of me.
You seem to have thought of almost everything, Miss
Storin.'

'Not quite everything. How did you kill Roger O'Neill?'

So she had that, too. The frost finally gripped his heart.
His ice-blue hunter's eyes did not flicker. His body was
motionless, tense, ready for action. At last he knew how
his brother had felt, yet this was no iron-clad enemy which
confronted him but a stupid, vulnerable, defenceless
young woman. Only one of them could survive, and it
must be him!

His voice was soft, almost a whisper, melting into the
snow around them. 'Rat poison. It was so simple. I mixed
it with his cocaine.' His piercing eyes were fixed on Mattie;
she was no longer hunter, but prey. 'He was so weak, he
deserved to die.'

'No one deserves to die, Mr Urquhart.'

But he was no longer listening. He was hunting, in a
game of life or death whose rules allowed no respect for
moral clichés. When he gazed down the gun sights at a
deer he did not debate whether the deer deserved to die,
nature decreed that some must die in order for others to
survive and triumph. No one, particularly now, was going
to deprive him of his triumph.

With surprising energy for a man of his age, he picked
up one of the heavy wooden chairs from the terrace and
held it aloft, poised to strike down at her head. But she
did not cower as he had expected. She stood her ground,

defiant in front of him, even as she tried to comprehend her own danger.

'In cold blood, Mr Urquhart? Face to face, in cold blood?'

This was like no prey he had ever hunted. Here, face to face, not a thousand impersonal yards away down a rifle sight but staring right back into his eyes! As her words pierced home, the moment was broken. The look of doubt crept into his eyes, and in a single bound his stag and his courage had disappeared. He gave a whimper as the chair had dropped from his hands and the awful truth of his own cowardice dawned upon him. He had faced his challenge, a fight to the death, confronted the truth, and had failed. He sank to his knees in the deep snow.

'You can't prove a thing. It's your word against mine,' he whispered.

Mattie said nothing at first, but pressed the rewind button on her recorder. As the tape spun round, she looked down upon Urquhart, who was shivering violently.

'Your final mistake, Mr Urquhart. You thought I switched it off.' She punched yet another button. As she did so, the clearly recorded words of their conversation filled the air, damning him in every syllable, the proof which would condemn him.

As she walked slowly away, leaving him wretched in the snow, the silence in his head was filled with the ghostly, mocking laughter of his father.

The setting sun pierced through the frosty sky. As it did so, it glanced off the snow-covered tower of Big Ben and cascaded into a thousand tiny streams of light, blinding the American tourist who was trying to capture the scene on video.

He was quite clear later in his description of what had happened.

'The Parliament building had suddenly become like a great torch, set alight by the sun. It was really a beautiful sight, as if the whole building were ablaze. And then from way up under Big Ben, something seemed to fall. As if a moth had flown into the heart of an immense candle, and its blackened and charred body was falling all the way to

346

the ground. It's difficult to believe it was a man, one of your politicians. What did you say his name was?'

She was tired, desperately tired, yet she felt an unaccustomed peace. The struggle with her memories was over, the pain purged. She could stop running now.

He sensed the change and could see it reflected in her exhausted but triumphant eyes. 'You know,' he mused, 'I think you might make a halfway decent journalist after all.'

'Johnnie, I think you may just be right,' she said softly. 'Let's go home.'

THE END

TO PLAY THE KING

Prologue

It was the day they would put him to death.

They led him through the park, penned in by two companies of infantrymen. The crowd was thick and he had spent much of the night wondering how they would react when they saw him. With tears? Jeers? Try to snatch him to safety or spit on him in contempt? It depended who had paid them best. But there was no outburst; they stood in silence, dejected, cowed, still not believing what was about to take place in their name. A young woman cried out and fell in a dead faint as he passed, but nobody tried to impede his progress across the frost-hard ground. The guards were hurrying him on.

Within minutes they were in Whitehall, where he was lodged in a small room. It was just after ten o'clock on a January morning, and he expected at any moment to hear the knock on the door that would summon him. But something had delayed them; they didn't come until nearly two. Four hours of waiting, of demons gnawing at his courage, of feeling himself fall to pieces inside. During the night he had achieved a serenity and sense of inner peace, almost a state of grace, but with the heavy passage of unexpected minutes, growing into hours, the calm was replaced by a sickening sense of panic which began somewhere in his brain and stretched right through his body to pour into his bladder and his bowels. His thoughts became scrambled and the considered words, crafted with such care to illuminate the justice of his cause and impeach their twisted logic, were suddenly gone. He dug his finger nails deep into his palms; somehow he would find the words, when the time came.

The door opened. The captain stood in the dark entrance and gave a curt, sombre nod of his helmeted head. No need for words. They took him and within seconds he was in the Banqueting Hall, a place he cherished with its Rubens ceiling and magnificent oaken doors, but he had difficulty in making out the details through the unnatural gloom. The tall windows had been partially bricked up and boarded during the war to provide better defensive positions. Only at one of the farther windows was there light where the masonry and barricades had been torn down and a harsh grey glow surrounded the hole, like the entrance to another world. The corridor formed by the line of soldiers led directly to it.

My God, but it was cold. He'd had nothing to eat since yesterday, he'd refused the meal they had offered, and he was grateful for the second shirt he had asked for, to prevent him shivering. It wouldn't do to be seen to shiver. They would think it was fear.

He climbed up two rough wooden steps and bowed his head as he crossed the threshold of the window, onto a platform they had erected immediately outside. There were half a dozen other men on the freshly built wooden stage while every point around was crammed by teeming thousands, on foot, on carriages, on roofs, leaning from windows and other vantage points. Surely now there would be some response? But as he stepped out into the harsh light and their view, their restlessness froze in the icy wind and the huddled figures stood silent and sullen, ever incredulous. It still could not be.

Driven into the stage on which he stood were four iron staples. They would rope him down, spread-eagled between the staples, if he struggled, yet it was but one more sign of how little they understood him. He would not struggle. He had been born to a better end than that. He would but speak his few words to the throng and that would be sufficient. He prayed that the weakness he felt in his knees would not betray him; surely he had been betrayed enough. They handed him a small cap into which with great care he tucked his hair, as if preparing for nothing more than a walk through the park with his wife and children. He must make a fine show of it. He dropped his cloak to the ground so that he might be better seen.

Heavens! The cold cut through him as if the frost were reaching for his racing heart and turning it straightway to stone. He took a deep, searing breath to recover from the shock. He must not tremble! And there was the captain of his guard, already in front of him, beads of sweat on his brow despite the weather.

'Just a few words, Captain. I would say a few words.' He racked his mind in search of them.

The captain shook his head.

'For the love of God, the commonest man in all the world has the right to a few words.'

'Your few words would be more than my life is worth, Sir.'

'As my words and thoughts are more than my life to me. It is my beliefs that have brought me to this place, Captain. I will share them one last time.'

'I cannot let you. Truly, I am sorry. But I cannot.'

'Will you deny me even now?' The composure in his voice had been supplanted by the heat of indignation and a fresh wave of panic. It was all going wrong.

'Sir, it is not in my hands. Forgive me.'

The captain reached out to touch him on the arm but the prisoner stepped back and his eyes burned in rebuke. 'You may silence me, but you will never make me what I am not. I am no coward, Captain. I have no need of your arm!'

The captain withdrew, chided.

The time had come. There would be no more words, no more delay. No hiding place. This was the moment when both they and he would peer deep inside and discover what sort of man he truly was. He took another searing lungful of air, clinging to it as long as he could as he looked to the heavens. The priest had intoned that death was the ultimate triumph over worldly evil and pain but he discovered no inspiration, no shaft of sunlight to mark his way, no celestial salvation, only the hard steel sky of an English winter. He realized his fists remained clenched with the nails biting into the flesh of his palms; he forced his palms open and down the side of his trousers. A quiet prayer. Another breath. Then he bent, thanking God that his knees still had sufficient strength to guide him, lowering himself slowly and gracefully as he had practised in his room during the night, and lay stretched out on the rough wooden platform.

Still from the crowd there came no sound. His words might not have lifted or inspired them, but at least they would have vindicated. He was drenched in fury as the overwhelming injustice of it all hit him. Not even a chance to explain. He looked despairingly once more into the faces of the people, the men and women in whose name both sides had fought the war and who stood there now with blank stare, ever uncomprehending pawns. Yet, dullards all, they were his people, for whose salvation he was bound to fight against those who would corrupt the law for their own benefit. He had lost, but the justice of his cause would surely be known in the end. In the end. He would do it all again, if he had another chance, another life. It was his duty, he would have no choice. No more choice than he had now on this bare wooden stage, which still smelt of resin and fresh sawdust. And they would understand, wouldn't they? In the end . . . ?

A plank creaked beside his left ear. The faces of the crowd seemed frozen in time, like a vast mural in which no one moved. His bladder was going – was it the cold or sheer terror? How much longer . . . ? Concentrate, a prayer perhaps? Concentrate! He set on a small boy, no more than eight years old, in rags, with a dribble of crumbs on his dirt-smeared chin, who had stopped chewing his hunk of loaf and whose innocent brown eyes had grown wide with expectation and were focused on a point about a foot above his head. By God, but it was cold, colder than he had ever known! And suddenly the words he had fought so hard to remember came rushing back to him, as though someone had unlocked his soul.

And in the year sixteen hundred and forty-nine, they took their liege lord King Charles Stuart, Defender of the Faith and by hereditary right King of Great Britain and Ireland, and they cut off his head.

In the early hours of a winter's day, in a bedroom overlooking the forty-acre garden of a palace which hadn't existed at the time Charles Stuart took his walk into the next life, his descendant awoke with a start. The collar of his pyjama shirt clung damply and he lay face-down on a block-hard pillow stained with sweat, yet he felt as cold as . . . As cold as death. He believed in the power of dreams and their ability to unravel the mysteries of the inner being, and it was his custom on waking to write down everything he could remember, reaching for the notebook he kept for the purpose beside his bed. But not this time. There was no need. He would never forget the smell of the crowd mixed with resin and sawdust nor the heavy metallic colour of the sky on that frost-ridden afternoon. Nor the innocent, expectant brown eyes of a boy with a dirty chin smeared with crumbs. Nor that feeling of terrible despair that they had kept him from speaking out, rendering his sacrifice pointless and his death utterly in vain. He would never forget it. No matter how hard he tried.

PART ONE

December: The First Week

It had not been a casual invitation, he never did anything casually. It had been an insistent, almost peremptory call from a man more used to command than to cajolement. He expected her for breakfast and it would not have crossed his mind that she might refuse. Particularly today, when they were changing Prime Ministers, one out and another in and long live the will of the people. It would be a day of great reckoning and few could doubt that by evening he would have still more trophies to adorn his many mansions. She wondered if she were intended to be one of them.

Benjamin Landless opened the door himself, which struck her as strange. It was an apartment for making impressions, overdesigned and impersonal, the sort of apartment where you'd expect if not a doorman then at least a secretary or a PA to be on hand, to fix the coffee, to flatter the guests while ensuring they didn't run off with any of the Impressionist paintings enriching the walls. There was a Pissarro, a Monet and at least two Wilson Steers, all displayed ostentatiously at the whim of some interior designer rather than hung for the discerning pleasure of a true collector. Landless was no work of art himself. He had a broad, plum-red face which was fleshy and beginning to sag like a candle held too near the flame. His bulk was huge and his hands rough, like a labourer's, with a reputation to match. His *Telegraph* newspaper empire had been built by breaking strikes as well as careers; it had been as much he as anyone who had broken the career of the man who was, even now, waiting to drive to the Palace to relinquish the power and prestige of the office of Prime Minister.

'Miss Quine. Sally. I'm so glad you could come. I've wanted to meet you for a long time.'

She knew that to be a lie. Had he wanted to meet her before he would most certainly have arranged it. Something had happened to make him want to meet her now, and alone. He escorted her into the main room around which the penthouse apartment was built. Its external walls were fashioned entirely of toughened glass, which offered a magnificent panorama of the parliament buildings across the Thames, and half a rain forest seemed to have been sacrificed to cover the floor in intricate wooden patterns. Not bad for a boy from the back streets of Bethnal Green, he occasionally admitted, but the description was redundant. They had all been back streets where he was born.

With so much light the apartment seemed to hover in the air, suspended halfway between street and sky, gazing down upon the politicians and law-makers on the other side of the river and thereby diminishing them to the scale and significance of punctuation marks in one of his editorials, an effect she felt sure was intentional. It was Olympus, an eyrie which seemed to cut them off from reality, and Sally off from any means of escape. But that was why she had come, the challenge of meeting a man of power face-to-face, the opportunity to test herself, to prove she was as good or better than any of them, perhaps to beat them at their own game and to get her own back. It might end in disaster, of course, in a crass attempt at physical flattery and seduction or even coercion, but it was a risk she had to take if she were to stand any chance of getting what she wanted. Risk was all part of the exhilaration.

He ushered her towards an oversized leather sofa in front of which stood a coffee table laden with trays of piping-hot breakfast food. There was no sign of the hidden helper who must only recently have prepared the dishes and laid out the crisp linen napkins. She declined any of the food but he was not offended. He took off his jacket and fussed about his own plate while she took a cup of black coffee and waited.

He ate his breakfast in single-minded fashion; etiquette and table manners were not his strong points. He offered little small talk, his attention focused on the eggs rather than on her, and for a while she wondered if he might have decided he'd made a mistake in inviting her. He was already making her feel vulnerable. Eggs finished, he wiped his mouth and pushed his plate away.

'Sally Quine. Born in Dorchester, Massachusetts. Aged thirty-two, and a girl who's already made quite a reputation for herself as an opinion pollster. In Boston, too, which is no easy city for a woman amongst all those thick-headed Micks.' She knew all about that; she'd married one. Landless had done his homework; he wanted to make that clear, and to know what she felt about her past being pawed over by him. His eyes searched for her reaction from beneath huge eyebrows tangled like rope. 'It's a lovely city, Boston, know it well. Tell me, why did you leave everything you'd built there and come to England to start all over again? From nothing?'

He paused, but got no reply. 'It was the divorce, wasn't it? And the death of the baby?'

He saw her jaw stiffen and wondered whether it was the start of a storm of outrage or a move for the door. But he knew there would be no tears. She wasn't the type, you could see that from her eyes. She was not unnaturally slim and pinched as the current fashion demanded, her beauty was more classical, the hips perhaps a half-inch too wide but all the curves well defined. She was immaculately presented. The skin of her face was smooth, darker and with more lustre than any English rose, the features carefully drawn as though by a sculptor's knife. The lips were full and expressive, the chin flat and the cheekbones high, her long hair thick and of such a deep shade of black that he thought she might be Italian or Jewish. It was a face full of strength and passion, capable of defying the world or captivating it as she chose. Yet her most exceptional feature was her nose, straight and a fraction long with a flattened end which twitched as she talked and nostrils which dilated with emphasis and emotion. It was the most provocative and sensuous nose he had ever seen; he couldn't

361

help but imagine it on a pillow. Yet the eyes disturbed him, didn't belong on this face. They were shaped like almonds, uplifted, full of autumnal russets and greens, translucent like a cat's, yet, while the nose was prominent and almost public in its emotion, the eyes hid behind over-sized spectacles. They didn't sparkle like a woman's should, like they probably once had, he thought. They had an edge of mistrust, as if holding something back, and when she concentrated her mouth turned down puckishly but defiantly at the corners. She was a woman who would not easily lose control, nor readily give of herself.

She looked out of the window, ignoring him. Christmas was but a couple of weeks away, yet there was no seasonal cheer in the air. It was a typical December scene for London, wet and dreary as if the day had not properly woken. Low clouds scudded across the sky, seemingly only feet above their heads. It was a day when Waterloo Bridge would be tap-tap-tapping to the sound of umbrella points as pedestrians hid inside their raincoats and tried to make it across to the other side before the next squall hit. Street traders would be cursing as they struggled to keep their Christmas stock from getting soaked while try-ing to entice customers out of the warm coffee shops and pubs. Another couple of pounds would be added to the fare of every mini-cab and to hell with the punter who argued. The festive spirit lay discarded in the running gut-ters, and somehow it didn't seem a propitious day for changing Prime Ministers.

A seagull beaten inland by North Sea storms cart-wheeled outside the window, its shrieks and insults pen-etrating the double-glazing while it made repeated attacks on their position, envying them their breakfast and beating up against the window before finally tumbling away through the blustery sky. She watched it disappear into the greyness.

'Don't expect me to be upset or offended, Mr Landless. The fact that you have enough money and clout to do your homework doesn't impress me. Neither does it flatter me. I'm used to being chatted up by middle-aged busi-nessmen.' The insult was intended; she wanted him to know he wasn't going to get away with one-way traffic. 'You want something from me. I've no idea what but I'll listen. So long as it's business.'

She crossed her legs slowly and deliberately so that he would notice. From her days as a child she had had no doubts that men found her body appealing and their excessive attention meant she had never had the opportunity to treat her sex as something to treasure, only as a tool to carve a path through a difficult and ungenerous world. She had decided long ago that if sex were to be the currency of life then she would turn it into a business asset, to open the doors which would otherwise be barred. While captains of industry drooled and got a tight sensation in their pants, she would put a contract under their noses and get them to sign. Men could be such dickheads. She saw Landless's eyes following her ankles. So, he was just like the rest of them and she had dressed for the part. A meanly cut black cashmere sweater which hugged those parts of her figure it didn't reveal and a Donna Karan skirt straight from Fifth Avenue which was tight and shorter than most professional women would dare to wear but not so short as to make her seem a tart. Anyway, she had the legs for it. And she wore a fashionable and expensive silk-cotton jacket from Harvey Nicks which hung loosely over her shoulders. She could shift around inside it and either expose her cashmere-covered breasts or hide them, as she chose. It was all part of the risk, of the tension of dealing with men and exploiting their weaknesses. She dressed to dominate and to be in control. Power dressing. And in the tight-assed business circles of London it seemed to work all the more effectively.

'You're very direct, Miss Quine.'

'I prefer to cut through it rather than spread it. And I can play your game.' She sat back into the sofa and began counting off the carefully manicured fingers of her left hand. 'Ben Landless. Age . . . well, for your well-known vanity's sake, let's say not quite menopausal. A rough son-of-a-bitch who was born to nothing and now controls one of the largest press operations in this country.'

'Soon to be the largest,' he interrupted quietly.

'Soon to take over United Newspapers,' she nodded, 'when the Prime Minister you nominated, backed and got elected virtually single-handed takes over in a couple of hours' time and waves aside the minor inconvenience of his predecessor's mergers and monopolies policy. You must've been celebrating all night, I'm surprised you had the appetite for breakfast. But you have the reputation of being a man with insatiable appetites. Of all kinds. So what's on your mind, Ben?' She spoke almost seductively in an accent that had been smoothed and carefully softened but not obliterated. She wanted people to take notice and to remember, to pick her out from the crowd. So the vowels were still New England, a shade too long and lazy for London, and the sentiments often rough as if they had been fashioned straight from the dole queues of Dorchester.

A smile played around the publisher's rubbery lips as he contemplated his good fortune and her defiance, but his eyes remained unmoved, watching her closely. His humour seemed confined to the lower half of his face, not touching his eyes nor penetrating beneath the skin. 'There is no deal. I backed him because I thought he was the best man for the job, but there's no private pay-off. I shall take my chances, just like all the rest.'

She suspected that was the second lie of the conversation, but let it pass.

'Whatever else happens, it's a new era. A change of Prime Minister means fresh challenges. And opportunities. I suspect he'll be more relaxed about getting the wheels of business turning and letting people make money than was Henry Collingridge. That's good news for me. And potentially for you.'

'With all the economic indicators scooting downhill?'

'That's just the point. Your opinion-research company has been in business for . . . what, twenty months? You've made a good start, you're well respected. But you're small, and small boats like yours could be swamped if the economy gets rough over the next couple of years. Anyway, you've no more patience than I do in running a shoestring operation. You want to make it big, to be on top. And for that you need cash.'

'Not your cash. If I had newspaper money poured into my operation it would ruin every shred of credibility I've built. My business is supposed to be objective analysis, not smears and scares with a few naked starlets thrown in to boost circulation.'

He ran his thick tongue around his mouth as if trying absent-mindedly to dislodge a piece of breakfast. 'You underestimate yourself,' he muttered. He produced a toothpick, which he used like a sword-swallower to probe into a far corner of his jaw. 'Opinion polls are not objective analysis. They're news. If an editor wants to get an issue rolling he commissions people like you to carry out some research. He knows what answers he wants and what headline he's going to run, he just needs a few statistics to give the whole thing the smack of authenticity. Opinion polls are the weapons of civil war. Kill off a government, show the nation's morals are shot to hell, establish that we all love Palestinians or hate apple pie. You don't need facts, just the blessing of an opinion poll.'

He grew more animated as he warmed to his theme. His hands had come down from his mouth and were grasped in front of him as if throttling an incompetent editor. There was no sign of the toothpick; perhaps he had simply swallowed it, as he did most things which got in his way.

'Information is power,' he continued. 'And money. A lot of your work is done in the City, for instance, with companies involved in takeover bids. Your little polls tell them how shareholders and the financial institutions might react, whether they'll be supportive or simply dump the company for a bit of quick cash. You can discover how opinion is running amongst the analysts and financial journalists, not over some wine-sodden lunch at the Savoy Grill with a company chairman but back at their desks, where it matters. Takeover bids are wars, life or death for the companies concerned, and your job is to tell them whose guts are most likely to be spread over the floor at the end of the day. That information has great value.'

'And we charge a very good fee for such work.'

'I'm not talking thousands or tens of thousands,' he barked dismissively. 'That's petty cash in the City. The sort of information we're talking about allows you to name your own figure, if you make it work for you.' He paused to see if there would be a squawk of impugned professional integrity; instead she reached behind her to pull down her jacket, which had ridden up against the back of the sofa. As she did so she exposed and accentuated the rounded curves at the top of her breasts. He took it as a sign of encouragement.

'You need money. To expand. To grab the polling industry by the balls and to become its undisputed queen. Otherwise you go belly-up in the recession. Be a great waste.'

'I'm flattered by your avuncular interest.'

'You're not here to be flattered. You're here to listen to a proposition.'

'I've known that from the moment I got your invitation. Although for a moment there I thought we'd wound up on the lecture circuit.'

Instead of responding he levered himself out of his chair and crossed to the window. The gun-grey clouds had descended still lower and it had begun to rain. A barge was battling to make headway through the ebbing tide beneath Westminster Bridge where the December winds had turned the usually tranquil river into a muddy, ill-tempered soup of urban debris and bilge oil. He gazed in the direction of the Houses of Parliament, his hands stuffed firmly into the folds of his tent-like trousers, scratching himself.

'Our leaders over there, the fearless guardians of the nation's welfare. Government is necessarily a secretive business, full of shared confidences, of information which is restricted because its public release would be sensationalized or abused. And every single one of those bastards would leak the lot if it served their purposes. There's not a political editor in town who doesn't know every word of what's gone on within an hour of a Cabinet meeting finishing, nor a general who hasn't leaked a confidential report about the nation's security before doing battle with the Treasury over the defence budget. And you find me the politician who hasn't tried to undermine a rival by starting gossip about his sex life.' His hands flapped in his trouser pockets like the sails of a great ship trying to catch the wind. 'Prime Ministers are the worst,' he snorted contemptuously. 'If they want to rid themselves of a troublesome Minister, they'll assassinate him in the press beforehand with tales of drunkenness or disloyalty. Inside information. It's what makes the world go round. And it's not a matter to our masters of *if* you use it, but when.'

'Perhaps that's why I never went into politics,' she mused.

He turned towards her, to discover her seemingly engrossed in removing a stray hair from her sweater. When she was sure she had his full attention she stopped toying with him and hid once again inside the folds of her jacket. 'So what is it you are going to suggest I do?'

Once again his tongue rolled distractedly around his mouth, this time in search not of the elusive piece of breakfast but of inspiration and the appropriate words. He sat down beside her on the sofa and the proximity of his shirt-clad bulk squeezed any suggestion of levity from the air. His physical presence was, surprisingly to her fashion-conscious eye, indeed impressive.

'I'm going to suggest you stop being an also-ran, a woman who may strive for years to make it to the top yet never succeed. I'm suggesting a partnership. With me. Your expertise' – they both knew he meant inside information – 'backed by my financial clout. It would be a formidable combination.'

'But what's in it for me?'

'A guarantee of survival. A chance to make a lot of money, to get where you want to go, to the top of the pile. To show your former husband that not only can you survive without him but even succeed. That's what you want, isn't it?'

'And how is all this supposed to happen?'

'We pool our resources. Your information and my money. If there's any action going on in the City I want to be part of it. Get in there ahead of the pack and the

367

potential rewards are huge. You and I split any profit right down the middle.'

She brought her forefinger and thumb together in front of her face. Her nose offered an emphatic bob. 'Excuse me, but if I understand you right, isn't that just the tiniest bit illegal?'

He responded with silence and a look of unquenchable boredom.

'And it sounds as if you would be taking all the risk,' she continued.

'Risk is a fact of life. I don't mind taking the risk with a partner I know and trust. I'm sure we could get to trust each other very closely; it would be vital.'

He reached out and brushed the back of her hand; there was no mistaking the glaze of distrust which flashed into her eyes.

'Before you ask, getting you into bed is not an essential part of the deal – no, don't look so damned innocent and offended. You've been flashing your tits at me from the moment you sat down so let us, as you say, cut through it all and get down to basics. Getting you on your back would be a pleasure, but this is business and in my book business comes first. I've no intention of cocking up what could be a first-class deal by letting my brains slip between my legs. You've got a body which I've no doubt you know how and when to use, but I can buy all the beauty and bum I want at very much less of a price than potentially I'm offering you. We're here to screw the competition, not each other. So . . . what's it to be? Are you interested?'

As if on cue a phone began to warble in a distant part of the room. With a grunt of exasperation he levered himself up, but as he crossed the room to answer the call there was also anticipation; his office had the strictest instruction not to bother him unless . . . He barked briefly into the phone before returning to his guest, his hands spread wide as though approaching a table laden with fine food.

'Extraordinary. My cup runs over. That was a message from Downing Street. Apparently our new Prime Minister wishes me to call on him as soon as he's back from the Palace, so I'm afraid I must rush off. Wouldn't do to keep him waiting.' His candle-wax face was contorted in what passed for a grin. She would be the focus of his attention for only a few moments longer: another place, another partner beckoned. He was already climbing into his coat. 'So make it a very special day for me. Accept.'

She stretched for her handbag on the sofa but he was there also, his huge labourer's hand completely encasing her own. They were very close and she could feel the heat from his body, smell him, sense the power beneath the bulk which was capable of crushing her instantly if he so chose. But there was no threat in his manner, his touch was surprisingly gentle. For a moment she caught herself feeling disarmed, almost aroused. Her nose twitched.

'You go sort out the nation's balance of payments. I'll think about mine.'

'Think carefully, Sally, and not too long.'

'I'll consult my horoscope. I'll be in touch.'

At that moment the seagull made another screeching attack, hurling insults as it pounded against the window, leaving it dripping with guano. He cursed.

'It's supposed to be a lucky omen,' she laughed lightly.

'Lucky?' he growled as he led her out of the door. 'Tell that to the bloody window cleaner!'

It hadn't been as he had expected. The crowds had been much thinner than in years gone by; indeed, fewer than two dozen people standing outside the Palace gates, skulking tortoise-like beneath umbrellas and plastic raincoats, could scarcely be counted as a crowd at all. Perhaps it was the approach of Christmas and the foul weather which had kept them away. Maybe the great British public simply didn't give a damn anymore who their Prime Minister was.

He sat back in the car, a man of bearing and distinction amidst the leather, his tired smile implying a casual, almost reluctant acceptance of his lot. He had a long face which led from a high and distinguished forehead to thin lips, the skin ageing but still taut beneath the chin, austere like a Roman bust with lank silver-sandy hair carefully combed away from the face. He was dressed in his habitual charcoal-grey suit with two buttons and a brightly coloured, almost foppish silk handkerchief which erupted out of the breast pocket, an affectation he had adopted to distance himself from the Westminster hordes in their banal Christmas-stocking ties and Marks & Spencer suits. Every few seconds he would bend low, stretching down behind the seat to suck at the cigarette he kept hidden below the window line, the only outward show of the tension and excitement which bubbled within. He took a deep lungful of nicotine and for a while didn't move, feeling his throat go dry as he waited for his heart to slow, pondering, only the small blue eyes moving sharply, never resting. They seemed perpetually strained, agitated, slightly damp and raw at the rims as if they had spent too long poring late into the night over official papers. The eyes attracted many women, stimulating their protective maternal instincts, while in men they aroused only anxiety. They suggested tension, an impatience, a man quick to ire and slow to forget.

The Right Honourable Francis Ewan Urquhart, MP, since six o'clock the previous evening the leader of his party and within minutes to be asked to accept the leadership of a new government, gave a perfunctory wave to the huddled group of onlookers from the rear seat of his new ministerial Jaguar as it passed into the forecourt of Buckingham Palace. His wife had wanted to lower the window in order for the assorted cameramen lurking nearby to obtain a better view of them both, but discovered that the windows on the official car were more than an inch thick and cemented in place. She had been assured by the driver that nothing less than a direct hit from a mortar with armour-piercing shells would open them.

The last few hours had seemed all but comic. After the result of the leadership ballot had been announced and with victory confirmed, he had rushed back to his house in Cambridge Street and waited with his wife. For what, they hadn't quite known. What was he supposed to do now? There had been no one to tell him. He had waited beside the phone but it stubbornly refused to ring. He'd rather expected a call of congratulation from some of his parliamentary colleagues, perhaps from the President of the United States or at the very least his sister, but already the new caution of his colleagues towards a man formerly their equal and now their master was beginning to exert itself; the President wouldn't call until he'd been confirmed as Prime Minister and his sister apparently thought his telephone would be permanently engaged for days. In desperation for someone with whom to share their joy they took to posing for photo-calls at the front door and chatting with the journalists assembled on the pavement outside.

He was not naturally gregarious, a childhood spent roaming alone with no more than a dog and a satchelful of books across the heathers of the family estates in Scotland had attuned him well to his own company, but it was never enough. He needed others, not simply to mix with but against whom to measure himself. It was what had driven him South, that and the financial despair of the Scottish moorlands. A grandfather who had died with no thought of how to avoid the venality of the Exchequer; a father whose painful sentimentality and attachment towards tradition had brought the estate's finances to their knees. He had watched his parents' fortunes and their social position wither like apple blossom in snow. Urquhart had got out while there was still something to extract from the heavily mortgaged moors, ignoring his father's entreaties on family honour which in despair had turned to tearful denunciation. It had been scarcely better at Oxford. His childhood companionship with books had led to a brilliant academic career and to a readership in Economics, but he had not taken to the life. He had grown to despise the crumpled corduroy uniforms and fuzzy moralizing which so many of his colleagues seemed to dress and die in, and found himself losing patience with the dank river mists which swept off the Cherwell and the petty political posturings of the dons' dinner table. One evening the Senior Common Room had indulged in mass intellectual orgasm as they had flayed a junior Treasury Minister within an inch of his composure; for most of those present it had merely confirmed their views of the inadequacies of Westminster, for Urquhart it had reeked only of the opportunities. So he had turned his back on both the teeming moors and dreaming spires and had risen fast, while taking great care all the while to preserve his reputation as an academic. It made other men feel inferior, and in politics that was half the game.

It was only after his second photo-call, about eight thirty p.m., that the telephone jumped back to life. A call from the Palace, the Private Secretary. Would he find it convenient to come by at about nine tomorrow morning? Yes, he would find that most convenient, thank you. Then the other calls began to flow in. Parliamentary colleagues unable any longer to control their anxieties about what job he might in the morning either offer to or strip from them. Newspaper editors uncertain whether to fawn or threaten their way to that exclusive first interview they all wanted. Solicitous mandarins of the civil service anxious to leave none of the administrative details to chance. The chairman of the party's advertising agency who had been drinking and couldn't stop gushing. And Ben Landless. There had been no real conversation, simply coarse laughter down the phone line and the unmistakable sound of a champagne cork popping. Urquhart thought he might have heard at least one woman giggling in the background. Landless was celebrating, as he had every right to. He had been Urquhart's first and most forthright supporter, and between them they had manoeuvred, twisted and tormented Henry Collingridge into premature retirement. Urquhart owed him, more than he could measure, while characteristically the newspaper proprietor had not been coy in identifying an appropriate yardstick.

He was still thinking about Landless as the Jaguar shot the right-hand arch at the front of the Palace and pulled into the central courtyard. The driver applied the brakes cautiously, aware not only of his regal surroundings but also of the fact that you cannot stop more than four tons of reinforced Jaguar in a hurry without making life very uncomfortable for the occupants and running the risk of triggering the automatic panic device which transmitted a priority distress alert to the Information Room at Scotland Yard. The car drew to a halt not beneath the Doric columns of the Grand Entrance used by most visitors but beside a

372

much smaller door to the side of the courtyard, where, smiling in welcome, the Private Secretary stood. With great speed yet with no apparent hurry he had opened the door and ushered forward an equerry to spirit Elizabeth Urquhart off for coffee and polite conversation while he led Urquhart up a small but exquisitely gilded staircase to a waiting room scarcely broader than it was high. For a minute they hovered, surrounded by oils of Victorian horse-racing scenes and admiring a small yet revealingly uninhibited marble statue of Renaissance lovers until the Private Secretary, without any apparent consultation of his watch, announced that it was time. He stepped towards a pair of towering doors, knocked gently three times and swung them open, motioning Urquhart forward.

'Mr Urquhart. Welcome!'

Against the backdrop of a heavy crimson damask drape which dressed one of the full-length windows of his sitting room stood the King. He offered a nod of respect in exchange for Urquhart's deferential bow and motioned him forward. The politician paced across the room and not until he had almost reached the Monarch did the other take a small step forward and extend his hand. Behind Urquhart the doors had already closed; the two men, one ruler by hereditary right and the other by political conquest, were alone.

Urquhart remarked to himself how cold the room was, a good two or three degrees below what others would regard as comfortable, and how surprisingly limp the regal handshake. As they stood facing each other neither man seemed to know quite how to start. The King tugged at his cuffs nervously and gave a tight laugh.

'Worry not, Mr Urquhart. Remember, this is the first time for me, too.' The King, heir for half a lifetime and Monarch for less than four months, guided him towards two chairs which stood either side of a finely crafted white stone chimneypiece. Along the walls, polished marble columns soared to support a canopied ceiling covered in elaborate classical reliefs of Muses and celestial paraphernalia, while in the alcoves formed between the stone columns were hung oversized and heavily oiled portraits of royal ancestors painted by some of the greatest artists of their age. Hand-carved pieces of furniture stood around a huge Axminster, patterned with ornate red and gold flowers and stretching from one end of the vast room to the other. This was a sitting room, but only for a king or emperor, and it might not have changed in a hundred years. The sole note of informality was struck by a desk, placed in a distant corner to catch the light cast by one of the garden windows and completely covered by an eruption of papers, pamphlets and books which all but submerged the single telephone. The King had a reputation for conscientious reading; from the state of his desk it seemed a reputation well earned.

'I'm not quite sure where to start, Mr Urquhart,' the King began as they settled in the chairs. 'We are supposed to be making history but it appears there is no form for these occasions. I have nothing to give you, no rich words of advice, not even a seal of office to hand over. I don't have to invite you to kiss my hand or take any oath. All I have to do is ask you to form a Government. You will, won't you?'

The obvious earnestness of his Sovereign caused the guest to smile. Urquhart was in his early sixties, ten years older than the King, although the difference appeared less; the younger man's face was stretched and drawn beyond its years with a hairline in rapid retreat and the beginnings of a stoop. It was said that the King had replaced his complete lack of material concerns with a lifetime of tortured spiritual questioning, and the strain was evident. While Urquhart had the easy smile and small talk of the politician, the intellectual aloofness of an academic and the ability to relax of a man trained to dissemble and if necessary to deceive, the King had none of this. Urquhart felt no nervousness, only the cold; indeed, he began to pity the younger man's gravity. He leaned forward.

'Yes, Your Majesty. It will be my honour to attempt to form a Government on your behalf. I can only hope that my colleagues won't have changed their minds since yesterday.'

The King missed the mild humour as he struggled with

his own thoughts, a deep furrow slicing across the fore-head of a face which had launched a million commemorative mugs, plates, tea trays, T-shirts, towels, ashtrays and even the occasional chamber pot, most of them made in the Far East. 'You know, I do hope it's auspicious, a new King and new Prime Minister. There's so much to be done. Here we are on the very brink of a new millennium, new horizons. Tell me, what are your plans?'

Urquhart spread his hands wide. 'I scarcely . . . there's been so little time, Sir. I shall need a week or so, to reshuffle the Government, set out some priorities . . .' He was waffling. He knew the dangers of being too prescriptive and his leadership campaign had offered years of experience rather than comprehensive solutions. He treated all dogma with a detached academic disdain and had watched with grim satisfaction while younger opponents tried to make up for their lack of seniority with detailed plans and promises, only to discover they had advanced too far and exposed vulnerable ideological flanks. Urquhart's strategy for dealing with aggressive questioning from journalists had been to offer a platitude about the national interest and to phone their editors; it had got him through the twelve tumultuous days of the leadership race, but he had doubts how long such a game plan would last. 'Above all I shall want to listen.'

Why was it that politicians uttered such appalling clichés which their audiences nevertheless seemed so blithe to accept? The Monarch was nodding his head in silent agreement, his tense body rocking gently to and fro as he sat on the edge of his chair. 'During your campaign you said that we were at a crossroads, facing the challenges of a new century while building on the best from the old. "Encouraging change while preserving continuity".'

Urquhart acknowledged the phrase.

'Bravo, Mr Urquhart, more power to your hand. It's an admirable summation of what I believe my own job to be, too.' He grasped his hands together to form a cathedral of bony knuckles, his frown unremitting. 'I hope I shall be able to find – that you will allow me – some way, however small, of helping you in your task.' There was an edge of apprehension in his voice, like a man accustomed to disappointment.

'But of course, Sir, I would be only too delighted . . . did you have anything specific in mind?'

The King's fingers shifted to the knot of his unfashionably narrow tie and twisted it awkwardly. 'Mr Urquhart, the specifics are the stuff of party politics, and that's your province. It cannot be mine.'

'Sir, I would be most grateful for any thoughts you have . . .' Urquhart heard himself saying.

'Would you? Would you really?' There was a rising note of eagerness in his voice which he tried to dispel, too late, with a chuckle. 'But I must be careful. While I was merely heir to the Throne I was allowed the luxury of having my own opinions and was even granted the occasional privilege of expressing them, but Kings cannot let themselves be dragged into partisan debate. My advisers lecture me daily on the point.'

'Sir,' Urquhart interjected, 'we are alone. I would welcome any advice.'

'No, not for the moment. You have much to do and I must not delay you.' He rose to indicate that the audience was at an end, but he made no move towards the door, steepling his fingers to the point of his bony, uneven nose and remaining deep in thought, like a man at prayer. 'Perhaps – if you will allow me? – there is just one point. I've been reading the papers.' He waved towards the chaos of his desk. 'The old Department of Industry buildings on Victoria Street which are to be demolished. The current buildings are hideous, such a bad advertisement for the twentieth century, they deserve to go. I'd love to drive the bulldozer myself. But the site is one of the most important in Westminster, near the parliament buildings and cheek by jowl with the Abbey itself, one of our greatest ecclesiastical monuments. A rare opportunity for us to grasp, don't you think, to create something worthy of our era, something we can pass on to future generations with pride? I do so hope that you, your Government, will ensure the site is developed . . . how shall I put it?' The clipped boarding school tones searched for an appropriately diplomatic phrase. 'Sympathetically.' He nodded in self-approval and seemed emboldened by Urquhart's intent stare. 'Encouraging change while preserving continuity, as one wise fellow put it? I know the Environment Secretary is considering several different proposals and, frankly, some of them are so outlandish they would disgrace a penal colony. Can't we for once in our parsimonious lives make a choice in keeping with the existing character of Westminster Abbey, create something which will respect the achievements of our forefathers, not insult them by allowing some misguided modernist to construct a stainless-steel monolith which crams people on the inside and has its mechanical entrails displayed without?' Passion had begun to overtake the diffidence and a flush had risen to colour his cheeks.

Urquhart smiled in reassurance, an expression which came as easily as oxygen. 'Sir, I can assure you that the Government' – he wanted to say 'my Government' but the words still seemed to dry behind his dentures – 'will have environmental concerns at the forefront of their considerations.' More platitudes, but what else was he supposed to say?

'Oh, I do hope so. Perhaps I should apologize for raising the matter, but I understand the Environment Secretary is to make a final decision at any time.'

For a moment Urquhart felt like reminding the King that it was a quasi-judicial matter, that many months and more millions had been poured into an official planning inquiry which now awaited the Solomon-like deliberation of the relevant Minister. Urquhart might have suggested that, to some, the King's intervention would look no better than jury-nobbling. But he didn't. 'I'll look into it. You have my word, Sir.'

The King's pale blue eyes had a permanent downward cast which made him appear always sincere and frequently mournful as though burdened by some sense of guilt, yet now they sparkled with unmistakable enthusiasm. He reached out for the other man's hand. 'Mr Urquhart, I believe we are going to get along famously.'

Seemingly unbidden, the King's Private Secretary was once more at the open doors and with a bow of respect

377

Urquhart made his way towards them. He had all but crossed the threshold when he heard the words thrown after him. 'Thank you once again, Prime Minister!'

Prime Minister. There it was, for the first time. He'd done it. My Government. *My* Government. It had all seemed so improbable, but there had been so many improbable Prime Ministers. Pitt, a mere youth of twenty-four. Disraeli, a Jew. Lloyd George, an outrageous adulterer who sold peerages for hard cash. Churchill, son of a syphilitic. Macmillan, a cuckold who honoured his wife's lover with a peerage. The Earl of Home, the Tory Party's noble ruin. And Margaret Thatcher, housewife. Lord Home was a thoroughgoing gentleman whereas she was unrepentantly ruthless, yet she had won every election she fought while he led his Government to instant defeat. It took ruthlessness and even a little sin to understand power and its uses. He had learnt the lesson. Never repent. For most the art of politics was all about survival, but that alone had never been enough for him. What was the use of engaging in the battle of ideas and egos if all one was left with was survival? Political success required sacrifices, preferably of others, and he had sacrificed enough in his time. Friends, colleagues, those closest to him. Pushed, prodded, thrown from the rooftops and beneath the wheels of public opinion. And he had never repented. Leadership brought with it the awesome and inescapable responsibilities of life and death, and he knew he was worthy of such decisions.

'So . . . what did he say?' They were in the car on the way to Downing Street before his wife roused him from his reverie.

'What? Oh, not a lot. Wished me well. Talked about the great opportunities ahead. Went on about a building site near Westminster Abbey. Wants me to ensure it's built in mock Tudor or some such nonsense.'

'Will you humour him?'

'Elizabeth, if sincerity could build temples then the whole of England would be covered in his follies, but this is no longer the Dark Ages. The King's job is to give garden parties and to save us the bother of electing someone else president, not to go round interfering in the business of government.'

Elizabeth snorted her agreement as she fumbled impatiently through her bag in search of lipstick. She was a Colquhoun by birth, a family which could trace its descent in direct line from the ancient kings of Scotland. They had long since lost the feudal estates and heirlooms to the confiscations of early cross-border raiding parties and the latter-day ravages of taxmen and inflation, but she had never lost her sense of social positioning or her belief that most modern aristocracy were interlopers – including 'the current Royal Family', as she would frequently put it. Royalty was merely an accident of birth, and of marriage and of death and the occasional execution or bloody murder; it could just as easily have been a Colquhoun as a Windsor, and all the more pure stock for that. At times she became distinctly tedious on the subject, and Urquhart decided to head her off.

'Of course I shall humour him. Better a King with a conscience than not, I suspect, and the last thing I need is sour grapes growing all over the Palace. Anyway, there are other battles to be fought and I want him and his popularity firmly behind me. I shall need it.' His tone was serious and his eyes set upon a future of perceived challenges. 'But at the end of the day, Elizabeth, *I* am the Prime Minister and he is the King. He does what I tell him to, not the other way around. The job's ceremonial, that's all it is and that's all it's got to be. He's the Monarch, not a bloody architect.'

They were driving past the Banqueting Hall in Whitehall, slowing down as they approached the barriers at the head of Downing Street, and Urquhart was relieved to see there were rather more people here to wave and cheer him on for the benefit of the cameras than at the Palace. He thought he recognized a couple of young faces, perhaps party headquarters had turned out their rent-a-crowd. His wife idly slicked down a stray lock of his hair while his mind turned to the reshuffle and the remarks he would make on the doorstep, which would be televised around the world.

'So what are you going to do?' Elizabeth pressed.

'It really doesn't matter,' Urquhart muttered out of the corner of his mouth as he smiled for the cameras which were thrusting their lenses towards him as the car turned into Downing Street. 'As a new King the man is inexperienced, and as constitutional Monarch he is impotent. He has all the menace and bite of a rubber duck. But fortunately on this matter I happen to agree with him. Away with modernism!' He waved as a policeman came forward to open the heavy car door. 'So it really can't be of any consequence . . .'

'Put the papers down, David. For God's sake take your nose out of them for just a minute of our day together.' The voice was tense, more nervous than aggressive.

The grey eyes remained impassive, not moving from the sheaf of documents upon which they had been fixed ever since he had sat down at the breakfast table. The only facial reaction was an irascible twitch of the neatly trimmed moustache. 'I'm off in ten minutes, Fiona, I simply have to finish them. Today of all days.'

'There's something else we have to finish. So put the bloody papers down!'

With reluctance David Mycroft raised his eyes in time to see his wife's hand shaking so vigorously that the coffee splashed over the edge of her cup. 'What on earth's the matter?'

'You. And me. That's the matter.' She was struggling to control herself. 'There's nothing left to our marriage and I want out.'

The King's press aide and principal public spokesman switched automatically into diplomatic gear. 'Look, let's not have a row, not now, I'm in a hurry and . . .'

'Don't you realize, we never have rows. That's the problem!' The cup smashed down into the saucer, overturning and spreading a menacing brown stain across the tablecloth. For the first time he lowered his sheaf of papers, every movement careful and deliberate, as was every aspect of his life.

'Perhaps I could get some time off. Not today, but . . .

380

We could go away together. I know it's been a long time since we had any real chance to talk . . .'

'It's not lack of time, David! We could have all the time in the world and it would make no difference. It's you, and me. The reason we don't have any rows is because we have nothing to argue about. Nothing at all. There's no passion, nothing. All we have is a shell. I used to dream that once the children were off our hands it might all change.' She shook her head. 'But I'm tired of deluding myself. It will never change. You will never change. And I don't suppose I will.' There was pain and she was dabbing her eyes, yet held her control. This was no flash of temper.

'Are you . . . feeling all right, Fiona? You know, women at your time of life . . .'

She smarted at his patronizing idiocy. 'Women in their forties, David, have their needs, their feelings. But how would you know? When did you last look at me as a woman? When did you last look at any woman?' She returned the insult, meaning it to hurt. She knew that to break through she was going to have to batter down the walls he had built around himself. He had always been so closed, private, a man of diminutive stature who had sought to cope with his perceived physical inadequacies by being utterly formal and punctilious in everything he did. Never a hair on his small and rather boyish head out of place, even the streaks of grey beginning to appear around his dark temples looking elegant rather than ageing. He always ate breakfast with his jacket on and buttoned.

'Look, can't this wait? You know I have to be at the Palace any—'

'The bloody Palace again. It's your home, your life, your lover. The only emotion you ever show nowadays is about your ridiculous job and your wretched King.'

'Fiona! That's uncalled-for. Leave him out of this.' The moustache with its hint of red bristled in indignation.

'How can I? You serve him, not me. His needs come before mine. He's helped ruin our marriage far more effectively than any mistress, so don't expect me to bow and fawn like the rest.'

He glanced anxiously at his watch. 'Look, for goodness sake can we talk about this tonight? Perhaps I can get back early.'

She was dabbing at the coffee stain with her napkin, trying to delay meeting his gaze. Her voice was calmer, resolved. 'No, David. Tonight I shall be with somebody else.'

'There's someone else?' There was a catch in his throat, he had clearly never considered the possibility. 'Since when?'

She looked up from the mess on the table with eyes which were now defiant and steady, no longer trying to evade. This had been coming for so long, she couldn't hide from it anymore. 'Since two years after we got married, David, there has been someone else. A succession of "someone elses". You never had it in you to satisfy me – I never blamed you for that, really I didn't, it was just the luck of the draw. What I bitterly resent is that you never even tried. I was never that important to you, not as a woman. I have never been more than a housekeeper, a laundress, your twenty-four-hour skivvy, an object to parade around the dinner circuit. Someone to give you respectability at Court. Even the children were only for show.'

'Not true.' But there was no real passion in his protest, any more than there had been passion in their marriage. She had always known they were sexually incompatible; he seemed all too willing to pour his physical drive into his job while at first she had contented herself with the social cachet his work at the Palace brought them. But not for long. In truth she couldn't even be sure who the father of her second child was, while if he had doubts on the matter he didn't seem to care. He had 'done his duty', as he once put it, and that had been an end of it. Even now as she poured scorn on him as a cuckold she couldn't get him to respond. There should be self-righteous rage somewhere, surely, wasn't that what his blessed code of chivalry called for? But he seemed so empty, hollow inside.

Their marriage had been nothing but a rat's maze within which both led unrelated lives, meeting only as if by accident before passing on their separate ways. Now she was leaping for the exit.

'Fiona, can't we—'

'No, David. We can't.'

The telephone had started ringing in its insistent, irresistible manner, summoning him to his duty, a task to which he had dedicated his life and to which he was now asked to surrender his marriage. We've had some great times, haven't we, he wanted to argue, but he could only remember times which were good rather than great and those were long, long ago. She had always come a distant second, not consciously but now, in their new mood of truth, undeniably. He looked at Fiona through watery eyes which expressed sorrow and begged forgiveness; there was no spite. But there was fear. Marriage had been like a great sheet anchor in strong emotional seas, preventing him from being tossed about by tempestuous winds and blown in directions which were reckless and lacking in restraint. Wedlock. It had worked precisely because it had been form without substance, like the repetitive chanting of psalms that had been forced on him during his miserable school years at Ampleforth. Marriage had been a burden but, for him, a necessary one, a distraction, a diversion. Self-denial, but also self-protection. And now the anchor chains were being cut.

Fiona sat motionless across a table littered with toast and fragments of eggshell and bone china, the household clutter and crumbs which represented the total sum of their life together. The telephone still demanded him. Without a further word he rose to answer it.

'Come in, Tim, and close the door.'

Urquhart was sitting in the Cabinet Room, alone except for the new arrival, occupying the only chair around the coffin-shaped table which had arms. Before him was a simple leather folder and a telephone. The rest of the table stood bare.

'Not exactly luxurious, is it? But I'm beginning to like it.' Urquhart chuckled.

Tim Stamper looked around, surprised to discover no one else present. He was – or had been until half an hour ago when Urquhart had exchanged the commission of Chief Whip for that of Prime Minister – the other man's loyal deputy. The role of Chief Whip is mysterious, that of his deputy invisible, but together they had combined into a force of incalculable influence, since the Whips Office is the base from where discipline within the parliamentary party is maintained through a judicious mixture of team spirit, arm twisting and outright thuggery. Stamper had ideal qualities for the job – a lean, pinched face with protruding nose and dark eyes of exceptional brightness which served to give him the appearance of a ferret, and a capacity for rummaging about in the dark corners of his colleagues' private lives to uncover their personal and political weaknesses. It was a job of vulnerabilities, guarding one's own while exploiting others'. He had long been Urquhart's protégé; fifteen years younger, a former estate agent from Essex, it was an attraction of opposites. Urquhart was sophisticated, elegant, academic, highly polished; Stamper was none of these and wore off-the-peg suits from British Home Stores. Yet what they shared was perhaps more important – ambition, an arrogance that for one was intellectual and for the other instinctive, and an understanding of power. The combination had proved stunningly effective in plotting Urquhart's path to the premiership. Stamper's turn would come, that had been the implicit promise to the younger man. Now he was here to collect.

'Prime Minister.' He offered a theatrical bow of respect. 'Prime Minister,' Stamper repeated, practising a different intonation as if trying to sell him the freehold. He had a familiar, almost camp manner which hid the steel beneath, and the two colleagues began to laugh in a fashion which managed to be both mocking and conspiratorial, like two burglars after a successful night out. Stamper was careful to ensure he stopped laughing first; it wouldn't do to out-mock a Prime Minister. They had shared so much over recent months but he was aware that Prime Ministers have a tendency to hold back from their colleagues, even their fellow conspirators, and Urquhart didn't continue laughing for long.

'Tim, I wanted to see you entirely *à deux.*'

'Probably means I'm due to get a bollocking. What've I done, anyway?' His tone was light, yet Urquhart noticed the anxious downward cast at the corner of Stamper's mouth and discovered he was enjoying the feeling of mastery implied by his colleague's discomfort.

'Sit down, Tim. Opposite me.'

Stamper took the chair and looked across at his old friend. The sight confirmed just how much their relationship had changed. Urquhart sat before a large oil portrait of Robert Walpole, the first modern and arguably greatest Prime Minister who had watched for two centuries over the deliberations in this room of the mighty and mendacious, the woeful and miserably weak. Urquhart was his successor, elevated by his peers, anointed by his Monarch and now installed. The telephone beside him could summon statesmen to their fate or command the country to war. It was a power shared with no other man in the realm; indeed, he was no longer just a man but, for better or worse, was now the stuff of history. Whether in that history he would rate a footnote or an entire chapter only time would tell.

Urquhart sensed the swirling emotions of the other man. 'Different, isn't it, Tim? And we shall never be able to turn back the clock. It didn't hit me until a moment ago, not while I was at the Palace, not with the media at the front door here, not even when I walked inside. It all seemed like a great theatre piece and I'd simply been assigned one of the roles. Yet as I stepped across the threshold every worker in Downing Street was assembled in the hallway, from the highest civil servant in the land to the cleaners and telephonists, perhaps two hundred of them. They greeted me with such enthusiasm that I almost expected bouquets to be thrown. The exhilaration of applause,' he sighed. 'It was beginning to go to my head, until I remembered that scarcely an hour beforehand they'd gone through the same routine with my predecessor as he drove off to oblivion. That lot'll probably applaud at their own funerals.' He moistened his thin lips, as was his habit when reflecting. 'Then they brought me here, to the Cabinet Room, and left me on my own. It was completely silent, as though I'd fallen into a time capsule. Everything in order, meticulous, except for the Prime Minister's chair which had been drawn back. For me! It was only when I touched it, ran my finger across its back, realized no one was going to shout at me if I sat down, that finally it dawned on me. It isn't just another chair or another job, but the only one of its kind. You know I'm not by nature a humble man yet, dammit, for a moment it got to me.' There was a moment of prolonged silence, before his palm smacked down on the table. 'But don't worry. I've recovered!'

Urquhart laughed that conspiratorial laugh once more, while Stamper could only manage a tight smile as he waited for the reminiscing to stop and for his fate to be pronounced.

'To business, Tim. There's much to be done and I shall want you, as always, right by my side.'

Stamper's smile broadened.

'You're going to be my Party Chairman.'

The smile rapidly disappeared. Stamper couldn't hide his confusion and disappointment.

'Don't worry, we'll find you some ministerial sinecure to get you a seat around the Cabinet table – Chancellor of the Duchy of Lancaster or some such nonsense. But for the moment I want your mittens firmly on the Party machine.'

Stamper's jaw was working furiously, trying to marshal his arguments. 'But it's been scarcely six months since the last election, and a long haul before the next one. Three, maybe four years. Counting paper clips and sorting out squabbles amongst local constituency chairmen is scarcely my strong suit, Francis. You should know that after what we've been through together.' It was an appeal to their old friendship.

'Think it through, Tim. We've a parliamentary majority of twenty-two and a party that's been torn apart by the recent leadership battle. And we are just about to get a beating from a swine of a recession. We're no better than even in the opinion polls and our majority won't last three or four years. We'll be shot to pieces at every by-election we face and we've only to lose fewer than a dozen seats before this Government is dead. Unless, that is, you can guarantee me no by-elections, that you've found some magic means of ensuring none of our esteemed colleagues will be caught canvassing in a brothel, misappropriating church funds or simply succumbing to senility and excessive old age?'

'Doesn't sound like a lot of fun for a Party Chairman, either.'

'Tim, the next couple of years are going to be hell, and we probably don't have a sufficient majority to survive long enough for us to get through the recession. If it's painful for the Party Chairman it'll be bloody agony for the Prime Minister.'

Stamper was silent, unconvinced, unsure what to say. His excitement and dreams of a few moments before had suddenly frayed.

'Our futures can be measured almost in moments,' Urquhart continued. 'We'll get a small boost in popularity because of my honeymoon period while people give me the benefit of their doubt. That will last no longer than March.'

'You're very precise about that.'

'Indeed I am. For in March there has to be a Budget. It'll be a bastard. We let everything rip in the markets to get us through the last election campaign and the day of judgement for that little lot is just around the corner. We borrowed off Peter to buy off Paul, now we have to go back to pick the pockets of them both. They're not going to care for it.' He paused, blinking rapidly as he ordered his thoughts. 'That's not all. We'll take a beating from Brunei.'

'What?'

'The Sultan of that tiny oil-infested state is a great Anglophile and one of the world's most substantial holders of sterling. A loyal friend. Unfortunately not only does he know what a mess we're in but he's also got his own problems. So he's going to unload some of his sterling – at least three billion worth sloshing around the markets like orphans in search of a home. That'll crucify the currency and stretch the recession on for probably another year. For old time's sake he says he'll sell only as and when we suggest. So long as it's before the next Budget.'

Stamper found difficulty in swallowing, his mouth had run dry.

Urquhart began to laugh but without the slightest hint of humour. 'And there's more, Tim, there's more! To top it all the Attorney General's office has quietly let it be known that the trial of Sir Jasper Harrod will begin immediately after Easter. Which is March the twenty-fourth, to save you looking it up. What do you know of Sir Jasper?'

'Only what most people know, I guess. Self-made megamillionaire, chairman of the country's biggest computer-leasing operation. Does a lot of work with Government departments and local authorities, and has got himself accused of paying substantial backhanders all over the place to keep hold of his contracts. Big into charities, I seem to remember, which is why he got his "K".'

'He got his knighthood, Tim, because he was one of the party's biggest contributors. Loyally and discreetly over many years.'

'So what's the problem?'

'Having come to our aid whenever we asked for it, he now expects us to come equally loyally to his. To pull a few strings with the Director of Public Prosecutions. Which of course we can't, but he refuses to understand that.'

'There's more, I know there's more . . .'

'And he insists that if the case comes to trial he will have to reveal his substantial party donations.'

'So?'

'Which were paid all in cash. Delivered in suitcases.'

'Oh, shit.'

'Enough of it to give us all acute haemorrhoids. He not only gave to the central Party but supported the constituency election campaigns of almost every member of the Cabinet.'

'Don't tell me. All spent on things which weren't reported as election expenses.'

'In my case everything was recorded religiously and will bear full public scrutiny. In other cases . . .' He arched an eyebrow. 'I'm told the Trade Secretary, later this afternoon to reinforce our glorious backbenches, used the money to pay off a troublesome mistress who was threatening to release certain compromising letters. It was made over to her, and Harrod still has the cancelled cheque.'

Stamper pushed his chair back from the table until it was balancing on its rear legs, as if trying to distance himself from such absurdity. 'Christ, Francis, we've got all this crap about to hit us at a hundred miles an hour and you want me to be Party Chairman? If it's all the same to you, I'd rather seek asylum in Libya. By Easter, you say? It'll take more than a bloody resurrection to save anybody caught in the middle of that lot.'

His waved his arms forlornly, drained of energy and resistance, but Urquhart was straining forward in great earnest, tension stiffening his body.

'By Easter. Precisely. Which means we have to move before then, Tim. Use the honeymoon period, beat up the Opposition, get in ahead of the recession and get a majority which will last until all the flak has been left well behind us.'

Stamper's voice was breathless. 'An election, you mean?'

'By the middle of March. Which gives us exactly fourteen weeks, only ten weeks before I have to announce it, and in that time I want you as Party Chairman getting the election machine as tight as it can be. There are plans to be made, money to be raised, opponents to be embarrassed. And all without anyone having the slightest idea what we're about to spring on them.'

Stamper's chair rocked back with a clatter as he endeavoured to recover his wits. 'Bloody Party Chairman.'

'Don't worry. It's only for fourteen weeks. If all goes well you can have the pick of any Government department you want. And if not . . . Well, neither of us will have to worry about a political job ever again.'

'This is truly appalling.' Elizabeth Urquhart screwed up her nose with considerable violence as she surveyed the

room. It had been several days since the Collingridges
removed the last of their personal effects from the small
apartment above 10 Downing Street reserved for the use
of Prime Ministers, and the sitting room now had the ambi-
ence of a three star hotel. It lacked any individual character,
that had already been transported in the packing cases,
and what was left was in good order but carried the aes-
thetic touch of a British Rail waiting room. 'Simply revolt-
ing. It won't do,' she repeated, gazing at the wallpaper,
where she half expected to find the faded impressions of
a row of flying china ducks. She was momentarily distracted as she passed by a long wall mirror, surreptitiously
checking the conspicuous red tint her hairdresser had
applied earlier in the week as she had waited for the final
leadership ballot. A celebratory highlight, the stylist had
called it, but no one could any longer mistake it for a natural hue and it had left her constantly fiddling with the
colour balance on the remote control, wondering whether
it was time to change the television or her hair salon.

'What extraordinary people they must have been,' she
muttered, brushing some imagined speck of dust from the
front of her Chanel suit while her husband's House of
Commons secretary, who was accompanying her on the
tour of inspection, buried herself in her notebook. She
thought she rather liked the Collingridges; she was more
definite in her views of Elizabeth Urquhart, whose cold
eyes gave her a predatory look and whose constant diets
to fend off the advance of cellulite around her expensively
clad body seemed to leave her in a state of unremitting
impatience, at least with other women, particularly those
younger than herself.

'Find out how we get rid of all this and see what the
budget is for refurbishment,' Mrs Urquhart snapped as she
led the way briskly down the short corridor leading to the
dark entrails of the apartment, fingertips tapping in rebuke
the flesh beneath her chin as she walked. She gave a
squawk of alarm as she passed a door on her left, behind
which she discovered a tiny galley kitchen with a stainless-
steel sink, red and black plastic floor tiles and no micro-
wave. Her gloom was complete by the time she had

inspected the claustrophobic dining room with the atmosphere of a locked coffin and a view directly onto a grubby
attic and roof. She was back in the sitting room, seated in
one of the armchairs covered in printed roses the size of
elephants' feet and shaking her head in disappointment,
when there came a knock from the entrance hall.

'Come in!' she commanded forlornly, remembering that
the front door didn't even have a lock on it – for security
reasons she had been told, but more for the convenience
of civil servants as they came to and fro bearing papers
and dispatches, she suspected. 'And they call this home,'
she wailed, burying her head theatrically in her hands.

She brightened as she looked up to examine her visitor.
He was in his late thirties, lean with razor-cropped hair.

'Mrs Urquhart. I'm Inspector Robert Insall, Special
Branch,' he announced in a thick London accent. 'I've been
in charge of your husband's protection detail during the
leadership election and now they've been mug enough to
make me responsible for security here in Downing Street.'
He had a grin and natural charm to which Elizabeth
Urquhart warmed, and a build she couldn't help but
admire.

'I'm sure we shall be in safe hands, Inspector.'

'We'll do our best. But things are going to be a bit different for you, now you're here,' he continued. 'There are a
few things I need to explain, if you've got a moment.'

'Come and cover up some of this hideous furniture,
Inspector, and tell me all about it   .'

Landless waved as the crowd applauded. The onlookers
had no idea who sat behind the darkened glass of the Silver
Spur, but it was an historic day and they wanted a share
in it. The heavy metal gates guarding the entrance to
Downing Street drew back in respect and the duty
policemen offered a smart salute. Landless felt good, even
better when he saw the pavement opposite his destination
crowded with cameras and reporters.

'Is he going to offer you a job, Ben?' a chorus of voices
sang out as he prised himself from the back seat of the car.

'Already got a job,' he growled, showing off his well-known proprietorial glare and enjoying every minute of it. He buttoned up the jacket flapping at his sides.

'A peerage, perhaps? Seat in the House of Lords?'

'Baron Ben of Bethnal Green?' His fleshy face sagged in disapproval. 'Sounds more like a music hall act than an honour.'

There was much laughter, and Landless turned to walk through the glossy black door into the entrance hall but he was beaten to the step by a courier bearing a huge assortment of flowers. Inside, the hallway was covered with a profusion of bouquets and baskets, all still unwrapped, with more arriving by the minute. London's florists, at least temporarily, could forget the recession. Landless was directed along the deep red carpet leading straight from the front door to the Cabinet Room on the other side of the narrow building, and he caught himself hurrying. He slowed his step, relishing the sensation. He couldn't remember when he had last felt so excited. He was shown directly into the Cabinet Room by a solicitous and spotty civil servant who closed the door quietly behind him.

'Ben, welcome. Come in.' Urquhart waved a hand in greeting but didn't rise. The hand indicated a chair on the other side of the table.

'Great day, Francis. Great day for us all.' Landless nodded towards Stamper, who was leaning against a radiator, hovering like a Praetorian Guard, and Landless found himself resenting the other man's presence. All his previous dealings with Urquhart had been one-on-one; after all, they hadn't invited an audience as they'd laid their plans to exhaust and overwhelm the elected head of government. On those earlier occasions Urquhart had always been the supplicant, Landless the power, yet as he looked across the table he couldn't help but notice that things had changed, their roles reversed. Suddenly ill at ease, he stretched out a hand to offer Urquhart congratulation, but it was a clumsy gesture. Urquhart had to put down his pen, draw back his large chair, rise and stretch, only to discover that the table was too wide and all they could do was to brush fingers.

'Well done, Francis,' Landless muttered sheepishly, and

sat down. 'It means a lot to me, your inviting me here on your first morning as Prime Minister. Particularly the way you did. I thought I'd have to sneak in round the back by the dustbins, but I have to tell you I felt great as I passed all those cameras and TV lights. I appreciate the public sign of confidence, Francis.'

Urquhart spread his hands wide, a gesture meant to replace the words he couldn't quite find, while Stamper jumped in.

'*Prime Minister*,' he began, with emphasis. It was meant as a rebuke at the newspaperman's overfamiliarity, but it slid off the Landless hide without making a dent. 'My apologies, but the new Chancellor will be here in five minutes.'

'Forgive me, Ben. Already I'm discovering that a Prime Minister is not a master, only a slave. Of timetables, mostly. To business, if you don't mind.'

'That's how I like it.' Landless shuffled forward on his chair in expectation.

'You control the *Telegraph* group and have made a takeover bid for United Newspapers, and it falls to the Government to decide whether such a takeover would be in the public interest.' Urquhart was staring at his blotter as if reading from a script, rather like a judge delivering sentence. Landless didn't care for this sudden formality, so unlike their previous conversations on the matter.

Urquhart's hands were spread wide again as he sought for elusive words. Finally, he clenched his fists. 'Sorry, Ben. You can't have it.'

The three men turned to effigies as the words circled the room and settled like birds of prey.

'What the 'ell do you mean I can't bloody have it?' The pronunciation was straight off the streets, the veneer had slipped.

'The Government does not believe it would be in the national interest.'

'Crap, Francis. We agreed.'

'The Prime Minister was careful throughout the entire leadership campaign to offer no commitments on the takeover, his public record on that is clear,' Stamper interposed. Landless ignored him, his attention rigidly on Urquhart.

'We had a deal! *You* know it. *I* know it.'

'As I said, Ben, a Prime Minister is not always his own master. The arguments in favour of turning the bid down are irresistible. You already own more than thirty per cent of the national press; United would give you close on forty.'

'My thirty per cent supported you every step of the way, as will my forty. That was the deal.'

'Which still leaves just over sixty who would never forgive or forget. You see, Ben, the figures simply don't add up. Not in the national interest. Not for a new Government that believes in competition, in serving the consumer rather than the big corporations.'

'Bullshit. We had a deal!' His huge fists crashed down on the bare table.

'Ben, it's impossible. You must know that. I can't in my first act as Prime Minister let you carve up the British newspaper industry. It's not good business. It's not good politics. Frankly it would make pretty awful headlines on every other front page.'

'But carving me up will make bloody marvellous headlines, is that it?' Landless's head was thrust forward like a charging bull, his jowls shaking with anger. 'So that's why you asked me in by the front door, you bastard. They saw me coming in, and they'll see me going out. Feet first. You've set up a public execution in front of the world's cameras. Fat capitalist as sacrificial lamb. I warn you, Frankie. I'll fight you every step of the way, everything I've got.'

'Which only leaves seventy per cent of the newspapers plus every TV and radio programme applauding a publicly spirited Prime Minister,' Stamper interjected superciliously, examining his finger nails. 'Not afraid to turn away his closest friends if the national interest demands. Great stuff.'

Landless was getting it from both sides, both barrels. His crimson face darkened still further, his whole body shook with frustration. He could find no words with which

394

to haggle or persuade, he could neither barter nor brow-beat, and he was left with nothing but the physical argument of pounding the table with clenched fists. 'You miserable little sh—'

Suddenly the door opened and in walked Elizabeth Urquhart in full flow. 'Francis, it's impossible, completely impossible. The apartment's appalling, the decorations are quite disgusting and they tell me there's not enough money left in the budget . . .' She trailed off as she noted Landless's fists trembling six inches above the table.

'You see, Ben, a Prime Minister is not master even in his own house.'

'Spare me the sermon.'

'Ben, think it through. Put this one behind you. There will be other deals, other interests you will want to pursue, in which I can help. It would be useful to have a friend in Downing Street.'

'That's what I thought when I backed you for Prime Minister. My mistake.' Landless was once again in control of himself, his hands steady, his gaze glacial and fixed upon Urquhart, only the quivering of his jowls revealing the tension within.

'I'm sorry if I've interrupted,' Elizabeth said awkwardly.

'Mr Landless was just about to leave, I think,' Stamper cut in from his guard post beside the radiator.

'I am sorry,' Elizabeth repeated.

'Don't worry,' replied Landless, eyes still on her husband. 'I can't stay. I just learned of a funeral I have to attend.'

'Ben, seriously, if there's anything I can do . . .'

Landless offered no reply. He rose and buttoned his jacket purposefully, straightening his tie and drawing back his broad shoulders before striding out to face the cameras.

'I won't hear of it, David.'

It was ludicrous. Mycroft was in turmoil; there were so many unformed doubts, half-fears which he could not or dared not realize, which he needed to talk through with the King, for both their sakes. Yet he was reduced to snatching a few words along with mouthfuls of chlorinated water as they ploughed through the waves of the Palace swimming pool. The King's only concession to the interruption in his daily exercise schedule was to switch from the crawl to the breaststroke, enabling Mycroft more easily to match his pace. It was his rigid discipline that enabled the King to maintain his excellent physical shape, and kept all those who served him struggling to keep up.

The King was a fierce defender of the forms of marriage – it came with the job, he would say – and Mycroft had felt it necessary to make the offer. 'It's for the best, Sir,' he persisted. 'I can't afford to let you become embroiled in my personal difficulties. I need some time to sort myself out. Better for all of us if I resign.'

'I disagree.' The King spat out a mouthful of water, finally resolving to finish the conversation on dry land, and headed for the marbled poolside. 'We've been friends since university and I'm not going to throw away the last thirty years simply because some reptilian gossip columnist might hear of your private problems. I'm surprised you should think I would consider it.' He ducked his shiny head one last time beneath the water as he reached for the steps. 'You're part of the management board of this firm, and that's how it's going to stay.'

Mycroft shook his head like a dog, trying to clear his vision. It wasn't just the marriage, of course, it was all the other pressures he felt crowding in on him which made him feel so apprehensive and wretched. If he couldn't be completely honest even with himself, how could he expect the King to understand? But he had to try.

'Suddenly everything looks different. The house. The street. My friends. Even I look different, to myself. It's as if my marriage was a lens which gave the world a particular perspective over all these years, and now that it's gone nothing seems quite the same. It's a little frightening . . .'

'I'm sorry, truly, about Fiona. After all, I'm godfather to your eldest, I'm involved.' The King reached for his towel. 'But, dammit, women have their own extraordinary ways and I can't profess to understand them. What I do know,

David, is that it would make no sense for you to try to get through your problems on your own, to cut yourself off not only from your marriage but also from what you have here.' He placed a hand on Mycroft's dripping shoulder. The contact was very close, his voice concerned. 'You understand me, David, you always have. I am known by the whole world yet understood by so few. You do, you understand. I need you. I will not allow you to resign.'

Mycroft stared into his friend's angular face. He found himself thinking the King's leanness made him look drawn and older than his years, particularly with his hair grown so thin. It was as if a furnace inside was burning the King up too quickly. Perhaps he cared too much.

Care too much – was it possible? Fiona had tossed Mycroft back into the pool and he was struggling in the deep waters, unable to touch bottom. It dawned on him that he had never touched bottom, not once in his life. Far from caring too much, he realized he had never really cared at all and the sudden understanding made him panic, want to escape before he drowned. His emotional life had been shapeless, without substance or roots. Except here at the Palace, which now provided his only support. The man he had once tossed fully clothed through the ice of the college fountain and who had come up spitting bindweed and clutching a lavatory seat was saying, in the only way a lifetime of self-control allowed, that he cared. Suddenly it mattered, very much.

'Thank you, Sir.'

'I don't know a single marriage, Royal, common or just plain vulgar, which hasn't been through the wringer; it's so easy to think you're on your own, to forget that practically everyone you know has jumped through the same hoops.'

Mycroft remembered just how many nights of their marriage he and Fiona had spent apart, and imagined what she had been up to on every one of those nights. There really had been a lot of hoops. He didn't care, not even about that. So what did he care about?

'I need you, David. I've waited all my life to be where I am today. Don't you remember the endless nights at university when we would sit either side of a bottle of college port and discuss what we would do when we had the opportunity? *We*, David, you and me. Now the opportunity has arrived, we can't throw it away.' He paused while a liveried footman deposited a silver tray with two mugs of herbal tea on the poolside table. 'If it's really over with Fiona, try to put it behind you. Look ahead, with me. I can't start on the most important period of my life by losing one of my oldest and most trusted friends. There's so much to do, for us both.' He began towelling himself vigorously as though determined to start that very minute. 'Don't make any decisions now. Stick with it for a couple of months and, if you still feel you need a break, we'll sort it out. But trust me, stay with me. All will be fine, I promise.'

Mycroft was unconvinced. He wanted to run, but he had nowhere and no one he wanted to run to. And the thought of what he might find if he ran too far overwhelmed him. After so many years he was free, and he didn't know if he could handle freedom. He stood, water dripping from the end of his nose and through his moustache, weighing his doubts against the Sovereign's certainty. He could find no sense of direction, only his sense of duty.

'So, what do you feel, old friend?'

'Bloody cold, Sir.' He managed a weak smile. 'Let's go and have a shower.'

'Circulate, Francis. And smile. This is supposed to be a celebration, remember.'

Urquhart acknowledged his wife's instruction and began forcing his way slowly through the crowded room. He hated these occasions. It was supposed to be a party to thank those who had helped him into Downing Street, but inevitably Elizabeth had intervened and turned it into another of her evenings for rubbing shoulders with anyone from the pages of the social columns she wanted to meet. 'The voters love a little glamour,' she argued, and like any self-respecting Colquhoun she had always wanted to preside over her own Court. So instead of a small gathering of colleagues he had been thrust into a maelstrom of actresses, opera stars, editors, businessmen and assorted socialites, and he knew his small talk couldn't last the evening.

The guests had clattered through the dark December night into the narrow confines of Downing Street, where they found a large Christmas tree outside the door of Number Ten, placed at Elizabeth Urquhart's instructions to give TV-viewers the impression that this was simply another family eagerly waiting to celebrate Christmas. Inside Number Ten the glitterati had crossed the threshold, unaware they had already been scanned by hidden devices for weapons and explosives. They handed over their cloaks and overcoats in exchange for a smile and a cloakroom ticket, and waited patiently in line on the stairs which led to the Green Room where the Urquharts were receiving their guests. As they wound their way slowly up the stairs and past its walls covered in portraits of previous Prime Ministers, they tried not to stare too hard at the other guests or their surroundings. Staring implied you hadn't done this a hundred times before. Most had little to do with politics, some were not even supporters of the Government, but the enthusiasm with which they were greeted by Elizabeth Urquhart left them all impressed. The atmosphere was sucking them in, making them honorary members of the team. If power were a conspiracy, they wanted to be part of it too.

For ten minutes Urquhart struggled with the confusion of guests, his eyes never resting, darting rapidly from one fixed point to another as if always on guard, or on the attack, forced to listen to the complaints of businessmen and the half-baked social prescriptions of chat-show hosts. At last he reached gratefully for the arm of Tim Stamper and dragged him into a corner.

'Something on your mind, Francis?'

'I was just reflecting on how relieved Henry must be not to have to put up with all this any longer. Is it really worth it?'

'Ambition should be made of more solid stuff.'

'If you must quote Shakespeare, for God's sake get it right. And I'd prefer it if you chose some other play than

Julius Caesar. You'll remember they'd had him butchered well before the interval.'

'I am suitably reproached. In future in your presence I shall quote only from *Macbeth*.'

Urquhart smiled grimly at the cold humour, wishing he could spend the rest of the evening crossing swords with Stamper and plotting the next election. In less than a week the polls had already placed them three points ahead as the voters responded to the fresh faces, the renewed sense of urgency throughout Whitehall, the public dispatch of a few of the less acceptable faces of Government. 'They like the colour of the honeymoon bed linen,' Stamper had reported. 'Fresh, crisp, with just enough blood to show you're doing your job.' He had a style all his own, did Stamper.

Across the chatter of the crowded room they could hear Elizabeth Urquhart laughing. She was immersed in conversation with an Italian tenor, one of the more competent and certainly the most fashionable opera star to have arrived in London in recent years. She was persuading him through a mixture of flattery and feminine charm to give a rendition later in the evening. Elizabeth was nearing fifty yet she was well preserved and carefully presented, and already the Italian was acquiescing. She rushed off to enquire whether there was a piano in Downing Street.

'Ah, Dickie,' Urquhart chanted, reaching out for the arm of a short, undersized man with a disproportionately large head and serious eyes who had thrust purposefully through the crowd towards him. Dickie was the new Secretary of State for the Environment, the youngest member of the new Cabinet, a marathon runner, an enthusiast and an intervener, and he had been deeply impressed by Urquhart's admonition that he was to be the defender of the Government's green credentials. His appointment had already been greeted with acclaim from all but the most militant pressure groups, yet at this moment he was looking none too happy. There were beads of moisture on his brow; something was bothering him.

'Was hoping to have a word with you, Dickie,' said Urquhart before the other had a chance to unburden himself. 'What about this development site in Victoria Street? Had a chance to look into it yet? Are you going to cover it in concrete, or what?'

'Good heavens, no, Prime Minister. I've studied all the options carefully, and I really think it would be best if we dispense with the more extravagant options and go for something traditional. Not one of these steel and glass air-conditioning units.'

'Will it provide the most modern office environment?' Stamper intervened.

'It'll fit into the Westminster environment,' Dickie continued a little uneasily.

'Scarcely the same thing,' the Party Chairman responded.

'We'd get a howl of protest from the heritage groups if we tried to turn Westminster into downtown Chicago,' Dickie offered defensively.

'I see. Planning by pressure group.' Stamper gave a cynical smile.

The Environment Secretary looked flustered at the unexpected assault but Urquhart came quickly to his rescue. 'Don't worry about Stamper, Dickie. Only a week at party headquarters and already he can't come into contact with a pressure group without raising his kneecap in greeting.' He smiled, this was considerably greater fun than being preached at by the two large female charity workers who were hovering behind Dickie, waiting to pounce. He drew Dickie closer for protection. 'So what else was on your mind?'

'It's this mystery virus along the North Sea coast which has been killing off the seals. The scientific bods thought it had disappeared, but I've just had a report that seal carcasses are being washed up all around Norfolk. The virus is back. By morning there will be camera crews and newshounds crawling over the beaches with photos of dying seals splashed across the news.'

Urquhart grimaced. 'Newshounds!' He hadn't heard that term used in years. Dickie was an exceptionally serious and unamusing man, exactly the right choice for dealing with environmentalists. They could bore each other for

401

months with their mutual earnestness. As long as he kept them quiet until after March . . . 'Here's what you do, Dickie. By the time they reach the beaches in the morning, I want you there, too. Showing the Government's concern, being on hand to deal with the questions of the . . . news-hounds.' From the corner of his eye he could see Stamper smirking. 'I want your face on the midday news tomorrow. Alongside all those dead seals.' Stamper covered his mouth with a handkerchief to stifle the laugh, but Dickie was nodding earnestly.

'Do I have your permission to announce a Government inquiry, if I feel it necessary?'

'You do. Indeed you do, my dear Dickie. Give them whatever you like, as long as it's not money.'

'Then if I am to be there by daybreak, I'd better make tracks immediately. Will you excuse me, Prime Minister?'

As the Environment Secretary hustled self-importantly towards the door, Stamper could control himself no longer. His shoulders shook with mirth.

'Don't mock,' reproached Urquhart with an arched eye-brow. 'Seals are a serious matter. They eat all the damned salmon, you know.'

Both men burst into laughter, just as the two charity workers decided to draw breath and swoop. Urquhart spied their heaving bosoms and turned quickly away to find himself looking at a young woman, attractive and most elegantly presented with large, challenging eyes. She seemed a far more interesting contest than the elderly matrons. He extended a hand.

'Good evening. I'm Francis Urquhart.'

'Sally Quine.' She was cool, less gushing than most guests.

'I'm delighted you could come. And your hus-band . . . ?'

'Beneath a ton of concrete, I earnestly hope.'

Now he could detect the slightly nasal accent and he glanced discreetly but admiringly at the cut of her long Regency jacket. It was red with large cuffs, the only decor-ation provided by the small but ornate metal buttons which made the effect both striking and professional. The raven hair shimmered gloriously in the light of the chandeliers.

'It's a pleasure to meet you, Mrs . . . ? Miss Quine.' He was picking up her strong body language, her independence, and couldn't fail to notice the taut expression around her mouth; something was bothering her.

'I hope you are enjoying yourself.'

'To be frank, not a lot. I get very irritated when men try to grope and pick me up simply because I happen to be an unattached woman.'

So that's what was bothering her. 'I see. Which man?'

'Prime Minister, I'm a businesswoman. I don't get very far by being a blabbermouth.'

'Well, let me guess. He sounds as if he's here without a wife. Self-important. Probably political if he feels sufficiently at ease to chance his hand in this place. Something of a charmer, perhaps?'

'The creep had so little charm he didn't even have the decency to say please. I think that's what riled me as much as anything. He expected me to fall into his arms without even the basic courtesy of asking nicely. And I thought you English were gentlemen.'

'So . . . Without a wife here. Self-important. Political. Lacking in manners.' Urquhart glanced around the room, still trying to avoid the stares of the matrons who were growing increasingly irritated. 'That gentleman in the loud three-piece pinstripe, perhaps?' He indicated a fat man in early middle age who was mopping his brow with a spotted handkerchief as he perspired in the rapidly rising warmth of the crowded room.

She laughed in surprise and acknowledgement. 'You know him?'

'I ought to. He's my new Minister of Housing.'

'You seem to know your men well, Mr Urquhart.'

'It's my main political asset.'

'Then I hope you understand your women just as well, and much better than that oaf of a Housing Minister . . . In the political rather than the biblical sense,' she added as an afterthought, offering a slightly impertinent smile.

'I'm not sure I follow.'

'Women. You know, fifty-two per cent of the electorate?

Those strange creatures who are good enough to share your beds but not your clubs and who think your Government is about as supportive and up-to-the-mark as broken knicker elastic?'

In an Englishwoman her abruptness would have been viewed as bad manners, but it was normal to afford Americans somewhat greater licence. They talked, ate, dressed differently, were even different in bed so Urquhart had been told, although he had no first-hand experience. Perhaps he should ask the Housing Minister. 'It's surely not that bad . . .'

'For the last two months your Party has been pulling itself apart while it chose a new leader. Not one of the candidates was a woman. And according to women voters, none of the issues you discussed were of much relevance to them, either. Particularly to younger women. You treat them as if they were blind copies of their husbands. They don't like it and you're losing out. Badly.'

Urquhart realized he was relinquishing control of this conversation; she was working him over far more effectively than anything he could have expected from the charity representatives, who had now drifted off in bitter disappointment. He tried to remember the last time he had torn apart an opinion poll and examined its entrails, but couldn't. He'd cut his political teeth in an era when instinct and ideas rather than psephologists and their computers had ruled the political scene, and his instincts had served him very well. So far. Yet this woman was making him feel dated and out of touch. And he could see a piano being wheeled into a far corner of the huge reception room.

'Miss Quine, I'd like very much to hear more of your views, but I fear I'm about to be called to other duties.' His wife was already leading the tenor by the hand towards the piano, and Urquhart knew that at any moment she would be searching for him to offer a suitable introduction. 'Would you be free at some other time, perhaps? It seems I know a great deal less about women than I thought.'

'I appear to be in demand by Government Ministers this evening,' she mused. Her jacket had fallen open to reveal an elegantly cut but simple dress beneath, secured by an oversized belt buckle, which for the first time afforded him a glimpse of her figure. She saw he had noticed, and had appreciated. 'I hope at least you will be able to say please.'

'I'm sure I will,' he smiled, as his wife beckoned him forward.

DECEMBER: THE SECOND WEEK

The signs of festive celebration were muted this year. Mycroft, with the pressure of work easing as journalists forsook word processors for the crush of Hamley's toy counter and the karaoke bars, trudged aimlessly through the damp streets in search of . . . he knew not what. Something, anything, to keep him out of the tomb-like silence of his house. The sales had started early, even before Christmas, yet instead of customers the shop doorways seemed full of young people with northern accents and filthy hands asking for money. Or was it simply that he'd never had time to notice them before? He made a pretence at Christmas-shopping along the King's Road, but quickly became frustrated. He hadn't the slightest idea what his children might want, what they were interested in, and anyway they would be spending Christmas with their mother. 'Their mother', not 'Fiona'. He noticed how easily he slipped into the lexicon of the unloved. He was staring into the window of a shop offering provocative women's lingerie, wondering if that was really what his daughter wore, when his thoughts were interrupted by a young girl who, beneath the make-up and lipstick, looked not much older than sixteen. It was cold and drizzling, yet the front of her plastic raincoat was unbuttoned.

''Ullo, sunshine. Merry Christmas. Need anything to stick on top of your tree?' She tugged at her raincoat, revealing an ample portion of young, pale flesh. 'Christmas sale special. Only thirty quid.'

He gazed long, mentally stripping away the rest of the raincoat, discovering a woman who, beneath the plastic, imitation leather and foundation, retained all the vigour and appealing firmness of youth, with even white teeth and a smile he could almost mistake as genuine. He hadn't

talked to anyone about anything except business for more
than three days, and he knew he desperately missed companionship. Even bickering with his wife about the brand
of toothpaste had been better than silence, nothing. He
needed some human contact, a touch, and he would feel
no guilt, not after Fiona's performance. A chance to get
back at her in some way, to be something other than a
witless cuckold. He looked once again at the girl and even
as he thought of revenge he found himself overcome with
revulsion. The thought of her nakedness, her nipples, her
body hair, the scratchy bits under her armpits, the very
smell of her suddenly made him feel nauseous. He panicked, at the embarrassment of being propositioned – what
if someone saw? – but more in surprise at the strength of
his own feelings. He found her physically repellent – was
it simply because she was the same sex as Fiona? He found
a five-pound note in his hand, thrust it at her and spat,
'Go away! God sake . . . go away!' He then panicked more,
realizing that someone might have seen him give the tart
money, turned and ran. She followed, calling after him,
anxious not to forgo the chance of any trick, particularly
one who gave away free fivers. He'd run seventy yards
before he realized he was still making a fool of himself out
on the street and saw a door for a drinking club. He dashed
in, lungs and stomach heaving.

He ignored the sardonic look of the man who took his
coat and went straight to the bar, ordering himself a large
whisky. It took a while before he had recovered his breath
and his composure sufficiently to look around and run the
risk of catching someone's eye. The club itself was nothing
more than a revamped pub with black walls, lots of mirrors
and plentiful disco lights. There was a raised dance floor
at one end, but neither the lights nor juke box were working. It was still early, there was scarcely a handful of customers who gazed distractedly at one of the plentiful
television monitors on which an old Marlon Brando film
was playing, the sound turned off so as not to clash with
the piped Christmas music the staff had turned on for their
own entertainment. There were large photos of Brando on
the walls, in motorcycle leathers from one of his early films,

along with posters of Presley, Jack Nicholson, and a couple of other younger film stars he didn't recognize. It was odd, different, a total contrast to the gentlemen's clubs of Pall Mall to which Mycroft was accustomed. There were no seats; this was a watering hole designed for standing and moving, not for spending all evening mooning over a half pint. He rather liked it.

'You entered in something of a hurry.' A man, in his thirties and well presented, a Brummie by his accent, was standing next to him. 'Mind if I join you?'

Mycroft shrugged. He was still dazed from his encounter and lacked the self-confidence to be rude and turn away a friendly voice. The stranger was casually but very neatly dressed, his stone-washed jeans immaculately pressed, as was his white shirt, sleeves rolled up narrow and high and with great care. He was obviously fit, the muscles showed prominently.

'You looked as if you were running from something.'

The whisky was making Mycroft feel warmer, he needed to ease up a little. He laughed. 'A woman actually. Tried to pick me up!'

They were both laughing, and Mycroft noted the stranger inspecting him carefully. He didn't object; the eyes were warm, concerned, interested. And interesting. A golden shade of brown.

'It's usually the other way round. Women running from me,' he continued.

'Makes you sound like something of a stud.'

'No, that's not what I meant . . .' Mycroft bit his lip, suddenly feeling the pain and the humiliation of being alone at Christmas. 'My wife walked out on me. After twenty-three years.'

'I'm sorry.'

'Why should you be? You don't know her, or me . . .' Once more the confusion flooded over him. 'My apologies. Churlish of me.'

'Don't worry. Shout if it helps. I don't mind.'

'Thanks. I might just do that.' He extended a hand. 'David.'

'Kenny. Just remember, David, that you're not on your

own. Believe me, there are thousands of people just like you. Feeling alone at Christmas, when there's no need. One door closes, another opens. Think of it as a new beginning.'

'Somebody else I know said something like that.'

'Which must make it right.' He had a broad, easy smile which had a lot of life to it, and was drinking straight from a bottle of exotic Mexican beer with a lime slice stuffed in the neck. Mycroft looked at his whisky, and wondered whether he should try something new, but decided he was probably too old to change his habits. He tried to remember how long it had been since he had tried anything or met anyone new, outside of work.

'What do you do, Kenny?'

'Cabin crew. Fly the fag BA. And you?'

'Civil servant.'

'Sounds horribly dull. Then my job sounds horribly glamorous, but it's not. You get bored fending off movie queens in first class. You travel a lot?'

Mycroft was just about to answer when the piped strains of 'Jingle Bells' was replaced by the heavy thumping of the juke box. The evening was warming up. He had to bend close to hear what Kenny was saying and to be heard. Kenny had a freshly scrubbed smell with the slightest trace of aftershave. He was bawling into Mycroft's ear to make himself heard, suggesting they might find a place to eat, out of the din.

Mycroft was trembling once again. It wasn't just the prospect of going back out alone onto the cold streets again, perhaps finding the tart waiting to accost him, or returning home to an empty house. It wasn't just the fact that this was the first time for years someone had been interested in him as a person, rather than as someone who was close to the King. It wasn't even that he felt warmed by Kenny's easy smile and already felt better than he had done all week. It was the fact that, however much he tried to hide from it or explain it away, he wanted to get to know Kenny very much better. Very much better indeed.

The two men were walking around the lake, one dressed

409

warmly in hacking jacket and gumboots while the other shivered inside his cashmere overcoat and struggled to prevent his hand-stitched leather shoes slipping in the damp grass. Near at hand a domestic tractor was ploughing up a substantial section of plush lawn marked off inside guide ropes while, beyond, a pair of workmen manoeuvred saplings and young trees into holes which further disfigured the once gracious lawn, already scarred by the tyre marks of earth-moving equipment. The effect was to spread dark winter mud everywhere, and even the enthusiasm of the King couldn't persuade Urquhart that the gardens of Buckingham Palace would ever recover their former glories.

The King had suggested the walk. At the start of their first weekly audience to discuss matters of state, the King had clasped Urquhart with both hands and thanked him fervently for the decision on the Westminster Abbey site, announced that morning, which had been hailed as a triumph by heritage groups as vehemently as it had been attacked by the luminaries of the architects' profession. But as Urquhart had concluded at Cabinet Committee, how many votes had the architects? The King inclined to the view that his intervention had probably been helpful, perhaps even crucial, and Urquhart chose not to disillusion him. Prime Ministers were constantly surrounded by the complaints of the disappointed and it made a refreshing change to be greeted with genuine, unaffected enthusiasm.

The King was ebullient and, in the characteristically Spartan fashion that often made him oblivious to the discomfort of others, had insisted on showing Urquhart the work which had begun to transform the Palace gardens. 'So many acres of barren, closely cropped lawn, Mr Urquhart, with not a nesting-place in sight. I want this to be made a sanctuary right in the heart of the city, to recreate the natural habitat of London before we smothered it in concrete.'

Urquhart was picking his way carefully around the freshly ploughed turf, trying unsuccessfully to avoid the cloying earth and divots while the King enthused about the muddy tract. 'Here, this is where I want the wild-

410

flower garden. I'll sow it myself. You can't imagine what a sense of fulfilment it gives me, dragging around a bucket of earth or manhandling a tree.'

Urquhart decided it would be ill-mannered to mention that the last recorded instance of someone with such an upbringing manhandling a tree had been the King's distant ancestor, George III, who in a fit of clinical madness had descended from his coach in Windsor Great Park and knighted an oak. He also lost the American colonies, and had eventually been locked away.

'I want to bring more wildlife into the garden; there's so much that can be done, so simply. Choosing the right mix of trees, allowing some areas of grass to grow to their natural height so they can provide cover. Look, I'm putting up these nesting boxes.' He indicated a workman halfway up a ladder, fixing wooden boxes to the high brick wall which ran all the way around the gardens.

The King was walking, head down and fingers steepled, in the prayer posture he so often adopted when engrossed in thought. 'This could be done in every park and large garden in London, you know. It would transform the wild-life of our city, of cities all round the country. We've wasted so many opportunities in the past . . .' He turned towards Urquhart. 'I want to put an idea to you. I would like to make our weekly meetings an opportunity to discuss what the Government might do to promote such matters. And how I might help.'

'I see,' Urquhart mused, the creeping cold sending his left leg into spasm while a pair of ducks splashed their way into flight from the lake. Wonderful targets, he thought. 'That's a kind offer, of course, Sir. But I wouldn't want the Environment Secretary to feel in any way that we were undermining his authority. I have to keep a happy team around me . . .'

'You are absolutely right, I do agree. That's why I took the precaution of chatting about this with the Environment Secretary myself. I didn't want to put any proposal to you which might be an embarrassment. He said he would be delighted, offered to brief me himself.'

411

Bloody Dickie. He'd no sense of humour, that was clear, now it appeared as if he had no other sense either.

'Today this is just a muddy field,' the King continued. 'But in the years to come this could be a new way of life for us all. Don't you see?'

Urquhart couldn't. He could see only piles of mud spread around like newly turned graves. Damp was seeping through the welts of his shoes and he was beginning to feel miserably uncomfortable. 'You must take care, Sir. Environmental matters are becomingly increasingly the stuff of party politics. It's important that you remain above such sordid matters.'

The King laughed. 'Fear not, Prime Minister. If I were meant to become involved in party politics the Constitution would have allowed me a vote! No, such things are not for me; in public I shall stick strictly to matters of the broadest principle. Simply to encourage, to remind people that there is a better way ahead.'

Urquhart was growing increasingly irritable. His socks were sodden, and the thought of the public being told from on high that there was a better way ahead than the one presently being pursued, no matter how delicately phrased, smacked of grist to the Opposition's mill and filled him with unease, but he said nothing in the hope that his silence would bring an end to the conversation. He wanted a warm bath and a stiff whisky, not more regal thoughts on how to do his job.

'In fact, I thought I might pursue the point in a speech I have to make in ten days' time to the charitable foundations . . .'

'The environment?' The irritation and impatience were beginning to show in Urquhart's tone, but the King appeared not to have noticed.

'No, no, Mr Urquhart. An address intended to bring people together, to remind them how much we have achieved, and can continue to achieve, as a nation. Broad principles, no specifics.'

Urquhart felt relieved. An appeal to motherhood.

'The charitable foundations are making such prodigious efforts, when there are so many forces trying to divide

412

us,' the King continued. 'Successful from the less well-off. Prosperous South from the Celtic fringe. Suburbs from the inner cities. No harm in encouraging families secure in their own homes this Christmas to spare a thought for those forced to sleep rough in the streets. In the rush, so many seem to have been left behind, and at this time of year it's appropriate to reach out to the less fortunate, don't you think? To remind us all that we must work towards being one nation.'

'You're intending to say that?'

'Something on those lines.'

'Impossible!'

It was a mistake, a rash outburst brought on by frustration and the growing cold. Since there was no book of rules, no written Constitution to order their conduct, it was vital to maintain the fiction of agreement, of discussing but never disputing, no matter how great their differences, for in a house of cards which lean one upon the other each card has its place. A King must not be seen to disagree with a Prime Minister, nor a Prime Minister with a King. Yet it had happened. One impatient word had undermined the authority of one and threatened both.

The King's complexion coloured rapidly; he was not used to being contradicted. The scar on his left cheekbone inflicted in a fall from a horse showed suddenly prominent and purple while his eyes carried an undisguised look of annoyance. Urquhart sought refuge in justification.

'You can't talk of one nation as if it didn't exist. That implies there are two nations, two classes, a divide which runs between us, top dogs and the downtrodden. The term reeks of unfairness and injustice. It's not on! Sir.'

'Prime Minister, you exaggerate. I'm simply drawing attention to the principle – exactly the same principle as your Government has just endorsed in my Christmas address to the Commonwealth. North and South, First World and Third, the need to secure advancement for the poor, to bring the different parts of the world community closer together.'

'That's different.'

'How?'

'Because . . .'

'Because they're black? Live in distant corners of the world? Don't have votes, Prime Minister?'

'You underestimate the power of your words. It's not what the words mean, it's how others will interpret them.' He waved his arms in exasperation and sought to pummel life back into his frozen limbs. 'Your words would be used to attack the Government in every marginal constituency in the country.'

'To read criticism of the Government into a few gen-eralized Christmas-time sentiments would be ridiculous. Christmas isn't just for those with bank accounts. Every church in the country will be ringing to the stories of Good King Wenceslas. Would you have him banned as politically contentious? Anyway, marginal seats, indeed . . . We've only just had an election. It's not as if we have to worry about another just yet.'

Urquhart knew it was time to back down. He couldn't reveal his election plans – Palace officials were notoriously gossipy – and he had no taste for a personal dispute with the Monarch. He sensed that danger lay therein. 'Forgive me, Sir, perhaps the cold has made me a little too sensitive. Just let me say there are potential dangers with any subject as emotive and complex as this. Perhaps I could suggest you allow us to see a draft of the speech so that we can check the detail for you? Make sure the statistics are accu-rate, that the language is unlikely to be misinterpreted? I believe it is the custom.'

'Check my speech? Censorship, Mr Urquhart?'

'Heavens, no. I'm sure you would find our advice entirely helpful. We would take a positive attitude, I can guarantee.' His politician's smile was back, trying to thaw the atmosphere, but he knew it would take more than flattery. The King was a man of rigid principles; he'd worked hard for many years developing them, and he wasn't going to see them smothered by a smile and a poli-tician's promise.

'Let me put it another way,' Urquhart continued, his leg once more going into spasm. 'Very soon, within the next few weeks, the House of Commons must vote on the new

Civil List. You know how in recent years the amount of money provided for the Royal Family has become increasingly a subject of dispute. It would help neither you nor me if you were engaged in a matter of political controversy at a time when the House wanted to review your finances in a cool, constructive manner.'

'You're trying to buy my silence!' the King snapped. Neither man was renowned for his patience, and they were goading each other on.

'If you want a semantic debate then I put it to you that the whole concept of a constitutional monarchy and the Civil List is precisely that – we buy your silence and active cooperation. That's part of the job. But really . . .' The Prime Ministerial exasperation was undisguised. 'All I'm offering is a sensible means for us both to avoid a potential problem. You know it makes sense.'

The King turned away to gaze across the bedraggled lawns. His hands were behind his back, his fingers toying irritably with the signet ring on his little finger. 'What has happened to us, Mr Urquhart? Just a few moments ago we were talking of a bright new future, now we haggle over money and the meaning of words.' He looked back towards Urquhart, who could see the anguish in his eyes. 'I am a man of strong passion, and sometimes my passion runs ahead of what I know is sensible.' It was as close to an apology as Urquhart was going to get. 'Of course you shall see the speech, as Governments have always seen the Monarch's speeches. And of course I shall accept any suggestion you feel you must make. I suppose I have no choice. I would simply ask that you allow me to play some role, however small and discreet, in pushing forward those ideals I hold so deeply. Within the conventions. I hope that is not too much to ask.'

'Sir, I would hope that in many years to come you and I, as Monarch and Prime Minister, will be able to look back on today's misunderstanding and laugh.'

'Spoken like a true politician.'

Urquhart was uncertain whether the words implied compliment or rebuke. 'We have our principles, too.'

'And so do I. You may silence me, Prime Minister, that is

415

your right. But you will not get me to deny my principles.'

'Every man, even a monarch, is allowed his principles.'

The King smiled thinly. 'Sounds like an interesting new constitutional concept. I look forward to discussing it with you further.' The audience was over.

Urquhart sat in the back of his armoured Jaguar, trying vainly to scrape mud from his shoes. He remembered that George III, finished with the oak tree, had also made a general of his horse. His mind filled with visions of a countryside turned over once again to the yoke and plough and city streets smothered in decaying horse manure, By Royal Appointment. His feet were frozen, he thought he was developing a cold, his Environment Secretary was a complete dolt and it was scarcely nine weeks before he wanted to call an election. He could take no chances, there was no time for cock-ups. There could be no suggestion of a Two Nation debate with the Government inevitably on the receiving end. It was impossible; he couldn't take the risk. The King would have to be stopped.

The taxi picked her up from home seven minutes late, which made her furious. She decided it would be for the last time; they'd been late three times this week. Sally Quine didn't want to be mistaken for other women, the kind who arrive for client meetings habitually late, flash a leg in excuse and laugh a lot. She didn't mind showing off a leg but she hated having to offer excuses and always ensured she arrived anywhere five minutes before the rest so she would be fully prepared and in charge of proceedings. The early bird always hijacks the agenda. She would fire the taxi firm first thing in the morning.

She closed the door to her home behind her. It was a terraced house in a highly fashionable part of Islington with small rooms and reasonable overheads. It represented all that she'd been able to squeeze out of the wreckage she had left behind in Boston, but in the banks' view it was good collateral for the loans on her business and at the moment that was more important than running the sort of gin palace and entertainment lounge preferred by most of her larger competitors. It had two bedrooms, one of which had come set up as a nursery. It had been the first room to be ripped apart; she couldn't bear the sight of any more bears bouncing across the wallpaper and the memories they brought with them. The room was now covered in impersonal filing cabinets and shelves carrying thick piles of computer print-out rather than talcum powder and tubs of vaseline. She didn't think of her baby too often, she couldn't afford to. It hadn't been her fault, no one's fault really, but that hadn't dammed the flood of guilt. She had sat and watched the tiny hand clutching her little finger, the only part of her body small enough for him to cling to, his eyes closed, struggling for each breath, all but submerged beneath the impersonal tubes and anonymous surgical paraphernalia. She had sat and sat and watched, and watched, as the struggle was gradually lost and the strength and spirit of the tiny bundle had faded away, to nothing. Not her fault, everyone had said so. Everyone, that is, except that slimehound of a husband.

'Downing Street, you say,' commented the cab driver, ignoring a barbed rejoinder about his timing. 'You work there, do you?' He seemed relieved to discover she was simply another ordinary sufferer and began a steady monologue composed of complaints and observations about their political masters. It was not that he was ill-disposed towards the Government, which seemed one stage removed from his daily life since he took all his fares in cash and therefore paid practically no income tax. 'It's just the streets are looking grim, luv. A week before Christmas and it's not really happening. Shops half-empty, fewer people needing cabs and those what do're skimping on the tips. Dunno what your pals in Downing Street are saying, but tell 'em from me the tough times are right around the corner. Old Francis Urquhart better pull his socks up or he won't be long in following whatsisname . . . er, Collingridge.'

Less than a month out of office and already the memory was beginning to slip inexorably from the mind.

She ignored his chatter as they meandered through the dark, drizzly streets of Covent Garden, past the restored monument of Seven Dials which marked what had been

417

some of the worst slums of Dickensian London with its typhoid and footpads, and which now presided over the heart of London's theatreland. They passed a theatre that stood dark and empty; the show had closed, in what should have been the busiest time of year. Straws in the wind, she thought, remembering Landless's warning, or maybe great armfuls of hay.

The taxi dropped her off at the top of Downing Street and in spite of his blunt hints she refused to sign for a tip. The policeman at the wrought-iron gate consulted the personal radio tucked away beneath his rain cape, there was a crackle in response and he let her through. A hundred yards away loomed the black door, which swung open even before she had put her foot on the step. She signed a visitors book in the entrance hall, which was deserted except for a couple of policemen. There was none of the bustle and activity she had expected and none of the crowds of the evening she had met Urquhart. It seemed as if Christmas had arrived early.

Within three minutes she had passed through as many sets of hands, each civil servant contriving to appear more important than the last, as she was led up stairs, through corridors, past display cases full of porcelain until she was shown into an inner office and the door closed behind her. They were on their own.

'Miss Quine. So good of you to come.' Francis Urquhart stubbed out a cigarette and held out his hand, guiding her towards the comfortable leather chairs placed in the corner of his first-floor study. The room was dark, book-lined and very masculine, with no overhead light and the sole illumination coming from a desk lamp and two side lights. It was reminiscent of the timeless, smoky atmosphere of the gentlemen's club on Pall Mall she had visited one ladies' night.

As he offered her a drink she studied him carefully. The prominent temples, the tired but defiant eyes which never seemed to rest. He was thirty years older than she. Why had he brought her here? What sort of research was he truly interested in? As he busied himself with two glasses of whisky she noted he had soft hands, perfectly formed, with slender fingers and nails which were carefully manicured. So unlike those of her former husband. She couldn't imagine those hands clenched and balled, thrusting into her face or pounding her belly into miscarriage, the final act of their matrimonial madness. Damn all men!

Her memories bothered her as she took the proffered crystal tumbler and sipped the whisky. She spat in distaste. 'Do you have any ice and soda?'

'It's a single malt,' he protested.

'And I'm a single girl. My mother always told me never to take it neat.'

He seemed amused by her outspokenness. 'Of course. But let me ask you to persevere, just for a little. It really is a very special whisky distilled near my birthplace in Perthshire, and would be ruined by anything other than a little water. Try a few sips to acquire the taste and, if not, I'll drown you in as many club sodas and ice cubes as I can find.'

She sipped again, it was a little less fiery. She nodded. 'That's something I've learned this evening.'

'One of the many benefits of getting older is that I have learned a lot about men and whisky. About women, however, it seems I am still quite ignorant. According to you.'

'I've brought some figures . . .' She stretched down for her bag.

'Before we look at that, I have another topic.' He settled back in his chair, a reflective mood on his face as he held his glass in both hands, like a don quizzing one of his charges. 'Tell me, how much respect do you have for the Royal Family?'

Her nose wrinkled as she savoured the unexpected question. 'Professionally, I'm completely uncommitted. I'm not paid to respect anything, only to analyse it. And personally . . . ?' She shrugged her shoulders. 'I'm American, from Paul Revere country. Used to be when we saw one of the King's men, we shot him. Now it's just another kind of show business. Does that upset you?'

He ducked the question. 'The King is keen to make a speech about One Nation, about pulling together the divisions in the country. A popular theme, do you think?'

'Of course. It's a sentiment expected of a nation's leaders.'

'A powerful theme, too, then?'

'That depends. If you're running for Archbishop of Canterbury then it's bound to help. The nation's moral conscience and all that.' She paused, waiting for some sign that she was moving in the right direction. All she got was the arched eyebrow of a professor in his lair; she would have to fly this one entirely on instinct. 'But politics, that's a different matter. It's expected of politicians, but rather like background music is expected in a lift. What matters to the voters is not the music but whether the lift they're travelling in is going up or down – or more accurately, whether they *perceive* the lift to be going up or down.'

'Tell me about perceptions.' He studied her with more than academic interest. He liked what he heard, and what he saw. As she talked and particularly when she became animated, the point of her nose bobbed up and down as if she were conducting an orchestra of thoughts. He found it fascinating, almost hypnotic.

'If you were brought up on a street where no one could afford shoes, yet now you've got a sackful of shoes but are the only family in the street without a car and a continental holiday, you feel as if you've got poorer. You look back on your childhood as the good old days, the fun of running to school in bare feet, while you resent not being able to drive to work like all the rest.'

'And the Government gets the blame.'

'Certainly. But what matters politically is how many others in the street feel the same way. Once they're locked behind their front doors, or in a polling booth come to that, their conscience about their neighbour down the street matters much less than whether their own car is the latest model. You can't feed a family or fill up a gas tank on moral conscience.'

'I've never tried,' he mused. 'So what about the other divisions? Celtic fringe versus prosperous South. Home owners versus homeless.'

'Bluntly, you're down to less than twenty per cent support in Scotland anyway, you don't have many seats there left to lose. And as for the homeless, it's difficult to get onto the electoral register with an address like Box Three, Row D, Cardboard City. They're not a logical priority.'

'Some would say that's a little cynical.'

'If you want moral judgements, call a priest. I analyse, I don't judge. There are divisions in every society. You can't be all things to all men and it's a waste of time trying.' The nose wobbled aggressively. 'What's important is to be something to the majority, to make them believe that they, at least, are on the right side of the divide.'

'So, right now, and over the next few weeks, which side will the majority perceive themselves to be?'

She pondered, remembering her conversations with Landless and the taxi driver, the closed theatre. 'You're gaining a small lead in the polls, but it's finely balanced. Volatile. They don't really know you yet. The debate could go either way.'

He was staring at her directly across the rim of his glass. 'Forget debate. Let's talk about open warfare. Could your opinion polls tell who would win such a war?'

She leaned forward in her chair, as if to get closer to him in order to share a confidence. 'Opinion polls are like a cloudy crystal ball. They can help you look into the future, but it depends what questions you ask. And on how good a gypsy you are.'

His eyes fired with appreciation.

'I couldn't tell you who would win such a war. But I could help wage it. Opinion polls are weapons, mighty powerful weapons at times. Ask the right question at the right time, get the right answer, leak it to the press . . . If you plan a campaign with expertise, you can have your opponent pronounced dead before he realizes there's a war on.'

'Tell me, O Gypsy, why is it that I don't hear this from other opinion pollsters?'

'First, because most pollsters are concerned with what people are thinking right now, at this moment in time. What we are talking about is moving opinion from where it is now to where you want it to be in the future. That's called political leadership, and it's a rare quality.'

421

He knew he was being flattered, and liked it. 'And the second reason?'

She took a sip from her glass, recrossed her legs and took off her glasses, shaking her dark hair as she did so. 'Because I'm better than the rest.'

He smiled in return. He liked dealing with her, both as a professional and as a woman. Downing Street could be a lonely place. He had a Cabinet full of supposedly expert Ministers whose duty it was to take most of the decisions, leaving him only to pull the strings and carry the can if the rest of them got it horribly wrong. Few Government papers came to him unless he asked for them. He was protected from the outside world by a highly professional staff, a posse of security men, mortar-proof windows and huge iron gates. And Elizabeth was always off taking those damned evening classes . . . He needed someone to confide in, to gather his ideas and sort them into coherent order, who had self-confidence, who didn't owe their job to him, who looked good. Who believed she was the best.

'And I suspect you are.'

Their eyes enjoyed the moment.

'So you think there will be war, Francis? Over One Nation? With the Opposition?'

He rested back in his chair, staring into a distance, struggling to discern the future. This was no longer the energetic exchange of academic ideas, nor the intellectual masturbation of cynical old men around a Senior Common Room dining table. The horrid stench of reality clung to his nostrils. When he answered his words were slow, carefully considered. 'Not just with the Opposition. Maybe even with the King – if I let him make his speech.' He was pleased to see no trace of alarm in her eyes, only intense interest.

'War with the King . . . ?'

'No, no . . . Not if I can avoid it. I want to avoid any confrontation with the Palace, truly I do. I have enough people to fight without taking on the Royal Family and every blue-rinsed loyalist in the country. But . . .' He paused. 'Let us suppose. If it did come to that. I should need plenty of gypsy craft, Sally.'

Her lips were puckered, her words equally deliberate. 'If that's what you want, remember – you only have to say please. And anything else I can help you with.'

The gyrations of the end of her nose had become almost animalistic and, for Urquhart, exquisitely sensuous. They remained looking at each other in silence for a long moment, careful not to say a word in case either of them should destroy the magic of innuendo which both were relishing. He had only ever once – no, twice – combined tutorials with sex. He would have been drummed out had he been discovered, yet the risk was what had made it some of the best sex of his life, not only rising above the lithe bodies of his students but in the same act rising above the banality and pathetic pettiness of the university establishment. He was different, better, he had always known it, and no more clearly than on the huge overstuffed Chesterfield in his college rooms overlooking the Parks.

The sex had also helped him rise above the memory of his considerably older brother, Alistair, who had died defending some scrappy bit of France during the Second World War. Thereafter, Urquhart had lived in his dead brother's shadow. He had not only to fulfil his own substantial potential but, in the eyes of his mourning mother, to fulfil that of the lost first-born, whom time and grief had imbued with almost mythical powers. When Francis passed exams, his mother reminded him that Alistair had been Captain of the school. Where Francis became one of the fastest-travelling dons of his age, in his mother's eyes Alistair would already have arrived. As a small boy he would climb into his mother's bed, for comfort and warmth, but all he found were silent tears trickling down her cheeks. He could remember only the feeling of rejection, of being somehow inadequate. In later life he could never completely expel from his mind his mother's look of misery and incomprehension, which seemed to haunt any bedroom he entered. While a teenager he had never taken a girl to bed, it only served to remind him that for his mother he had always been second-born and second-best. There had been girls, of course, but never in bed – on floors, in tents, standing up against the walls of a deserted country house. And, eventually, on Chesterfields, during tutorials. Like this one.

'Thank you,' he said softly, breaking the moment and his lurid reminiscence by swirling the whisky around in his glass and downing it in a gulp. 'But I must deal with this speech.' He took a sheaf of papers from a coffee table and waved them at her. 'Head him off at the pass, or whatever it is you say.'

'Drafting speeches isn't exactly my line, Francis.'

'But it is mine. And I shall treat it with the greatest respect. Like a surgeon. It will remain a fine and upstanding text, full of high sentiment and ringing phrases. It simply won't have any balls left when I send it back . . .'

DECEMBER: THE THIRD WEEK

The Detective Constable squirmed in his seat as he tried to regain some of the feeling he had lost in his lower limbs. He'd been stuck in the car for four hours, the drizzle prevented him from taking a walk around the car, and his mouth felt like a mouse nest from sucking at the cigarettes. He'd give the weed up. Again. Tomorrow, he vowed, just as he always did. *Mañana.* He reached for a fresh thermos of coffee and poured a cup for himself and the driver beside him.

They sat gazing at the small house in the exotically named Adam and Eve Mews. It stood behind one of London's most fashionable shopping thoroughfares, but the mews was well protected from the capital's bustle and stood quiet, secluded and, for onlookers, unremittingly dull.

'Christ, I should think her Italian's perfect by now,' the driver muttered mindlessly. They had exchanged similar sentiments on all five trips to the mews over the last fortnight, and the Special Branch DC and driver found their conversation going round in circles.

The DC broke wind in response. The tide of coffee was getting to him and he desperately wanted to take a leak. His basic training had provided instruction in how to take an unobtrusive leak beside the car while pretending to make running repairs so that he never left his vehicle and its radio, but he would get soaked in the steady drizzle. Anyway, last time he'd tried it the driver had driven off, leaving him kneeling in full flow in the middle of the bloody street. Funny bastard.

He had been enthusiastic when they offered him a job as a Protection Officer in Downing Street. They hadn't told him it would be for Elizabeth Urquhart and her endless

425

round of shopping, entertaining, socializing. And Italian lessons. He lit another cigarette and cracked the window to allow in some fresh air, coughing as it hit his lungs. 'Naw,' he offered in reply. 'I reckon we've got weeks of this. I bet her teacher's one of the really slow, methodical types.'

They sat gazing at the mews house with the leafless ivy clinging to its walls, the dustbin in its neat little alcove and in the front window a miniature Christmas tree, complete with lights and decorations, £44.95 from Harrods. Inside, behind the drawn curtains, Elizabeth Urquhart was lying on a bed, naked and sweating, taking yet another slow, methodical lesson from her Italian opera star with the beautiful tenor voice.

It was still dark when Mycroft woke, stirred by the clatter of milk bottles being deposited on doorsteps. Outside a new day was beginning, dragging him back to some semblance of reality. He was a reluctant captive. Kenny was still asleep, one toy bear from his immense collection propped precariously beside his pillow, the rest tumbled to the floor beside the Kleenex, victims of a long night's loving. Every corner of Mycroft's body ached, and still cried out for more. And somehow he would ensure he would get it, before he returned to the real world waiting beyond Kenny's front door. The last few days had been like a new life for him, getting to know Kenny, getting to know himself, becoming lost in the mysteries and rites of a world he scarcely knew. There had been times at Eton and university, of course, during those days of the hash-smoking free-for-all do-everything-screw-anything sixties, but that had proved to be a limited voyage of self-discovery which had been all too self-indulgent and lacking in direction ever to be complete. He had never fallen in love, never had the chance, his affairs had been all too brief and hedonistic. With time he might have got to know himself better, but then had come the call from the Palace, a summons which did not allow for exhaustive and, at that time, illegal sexual experimentation. And so for more than twenty years he had pretended. Pretended he didn't look at men as anything other than colleagues. Pretended that he was happy with Fiona. Pretended that he wasn't who he knew he was. It had been a necessary sacrifice but now, for the first time in his life, he had begun to be completely honest with himself, to be his own person. At last his feet had touched bottom. He was in at the deep end, not knowing whether he had been pushed by Fiona or had jumped, but it didn't matter. He was there. He knew he might drown in the depths, but it was better than drowning in corrupt respectability.

He wished Fiona could see him now and hoped she would be hurt, disgusted even; it was like shitting all over their marriage and everything she stood for. But she prob ably wouldn't give a damn. He'd found more passion in the last few days than he had experienced during the entire course of his marriage, enough to last him a lifetime per- haps, though he hoped there would be more. Much more.

The real world was waiting for him outside and he knew he would have to return to it soon. Leave this Kenny- Come-Lately, perhaps for good. He had no illusions about his new lover, with a teddy in every port 'and a franky and a miguel too', he had bragged. Once the adrenaline of initiation had worn off Mycroft doubted whether he would have the physical stamina to keep hold of a man twenty years his junior with a velvet skin and a tongue which was both inexhaustible and utterly uninhibited, but it would be fun trying. Before he returned to the real world . . .

Could an incorrigible air steward with the inhibitions of a Calcuttan street dog coexist beside the duties and obliga- tions of his other world? He wanted it to be, but he knew others would not let him, not if they knew, not if they found him here amidst the clutter of teddy bears, underpants and dirty towels. They would say he was fail- ing the King. But if he ran away now, he would be failing himself, and wouldn't that be far worse?

He was still confused but happy, more elated than he could remember, and he would remain that way so long as he stayed beneath this duvet and didn't venture outside that front door. Kenny was stirring now, his long-haul tan stretching all the way from the stubble on his chin to the

trunk line just above his white buttocks. Damn it, let
Kenny decide. He leaned over, ran his lips across Kenny's
neck just where the vertebrae protruded, and started working his way down.

As he waited, Benjamin Landless gazed at the barrel-
vaulted ceiling, illuminated by six great chandeliers, where
Italianate plaster cherubs with pouting cheeks chased each
other through an abundance of clouds, gilded stars and
spectacular plasterwork squiggles. He hadn't been to a
carol service in more than thirty years and he'd never
before been inside St Martin-in-the-Fields but, as he
always mused, life is full of new experiences. Or at least
new victims.

She had a reputation for being late for everything except
meals, and this evening was no exception. The drive was
less than three miles, complete with police motorcycle
escort, from Kensington Palace to the fine Hanoverian
church overlooking Trafalgar Square, but presumably she
would make some asinine excuse like getting stuck in the
traffic. Or perhaps as a Royal Princess she no longer
bothered making excuses.

Landless did not know Her Royal Highness Princess
Charlotte well. They had only met twice before, at public
receptions, and he wanted to meet her more informally.
He was not a man who accepted delay or excuses, particularly from the chinless and indigent son of minor nobility
he paid twenty grand a year for 'consulting services' –
which meant fixing private lunches or soirées with whom-
ever he wanted to meet. Even Landless had to compromise
this time, however; the Princess's Christmas schedule was
so hectic as she prepared for seasonal festivities and the
Austrian piste that sharing a private box at a carol service
was as good as he was going to get, and even that had cost
him a hefty donation to the Princess's favourite children's
charity. Still, charitable donations came from a private trust
set up by his accountants to mitigate his tax position and
he had found that a few carefully targeted donations could
bring him, if not acceptability, then at least access and

invitations. And they were worth paying for, particularly for a boy from Bethnal Green.

At last she was there; the organist struck up the strains of Handel's 'Messiah' and the clergy, choristers and acolytes processed down the aisle. As they peeled off to occupy their allotted positions, in the Royal Box above their heads Landless nodded respectfully while she smiled from beneath the broad brim of a matador's hat, and the service began. Their seating was, indeed, private, at gallery level and beneath a finely carved eighteenth-century canopy affording them a view of the choir but keeping her at some distance from most of the congregation, who in any event were largely Christmas tourists or refugees from the cold streets. She leaned across to whisper as the choir struck up their interpretation of 'O Come O Come Emmanuel'.

'I'm dying for a pee. Had to rush here straight from lunch.'

Landless had no need to consult his watch to know that it was already past five thirty. Some lunch. He could smell stale wine on her breath. The Princess was renowned for her bluntness: putting people at their ease, as her defenders argued; displaying her basic coarseness and con- genital lack of authentic style, according to her rather greater number of detractors. She had married into the Royal Family, the daughter of an undistinguished family who counted more actuaries than aristocrats amongst their number, a fact of which the less respectful members of the press never ceased to remind their readers. Still, she had done her job, allowing her name to be used by endless charities, opening new hospital wings, cutting the ribbons, feeding the gossip columns and providing the nation with a daughter and two sons, the elder of whom would inherit the throne if some dozen of his more senior royal relatives all suddenly succumbed. 'A disaster waiting for a disaster,' as the *Daily Mail* had once ungraciously described her after a dinner during which she had been overheard suggesting that her son would make an excellent monarch.

She looked at Landless quizzically. There were small, fragile creases underneath and at the corners of her slate-green eyes which became more prominent when she

frowned, and the flesh at the bottom of her neck was beginning to lose its elasticity, as happened with women of her
age, but she still retained much of the good looks and
appeal for which the Prince had married her all those years
ago, ignoring the advice of his closest friends.

'You've not come here to write some scandalous nonsense about me, have you?' she demanded roughly.

'There are enough journalists in the gutter taking advantage of your family without my joining in.'

She nodded in agreement, the brim of her hat bobbing
up and down in front of her face. 'Occupational hazard.
But what can one do about it? You can't lock an entire
family away, even a Royal one, not in this day and age.
We've got to be allowed to participate like other people.'

It was her endless refrain of complaint and justification:
Let us be an ordinary family. Yet her desire to be ordinary
had never stopped her embracing the paparazzi, dragging
all the First Women of Fleet Street backstage behind the
royal footlights to write gushing tributes, being seen eating
at London's most fashionable restaurants and sedulously
ensuring she received more column inches than most other
members of the Royal Family, including her husband. With
each passing year her desire not to fade from the spotlight
had grown more apparent. It was part of being a modern
Monarchy, she had contended, not getting oneself cut off,
being able to join in. It was an argument borrowed from
the King before he ascended the throne, but it was one
she had never understood. He had been seeking to find a
concrete but constitutional role for the heir, while she saw
it in terms of being able to find some form of personal
fulfilment and excitement to take the place of a family life
which had largely ceased to exist.

They nodded deferentially through a prayer before picking up the conversation during the reading of the lesson
from Isaiah – 'For a boy has been born for us, a son given
to us, to bear the symbol of dominion on his shoulder; and
he shall be called . . .'

'That's what I wanted to talk to you about, the gutter
press.'

She leaned closer and he tried to shift his bulk around

in the narrow chair, but it was an unequal struggle.

'There's a story going round which I'm afraid could do you harm.'

'Not counting the empty liquor bottles in my dustbin again?'

'A story that you're getting designer clothes worth thousands of pounds from leading fashion houses and somehow forgetting to pay for them.'

'That old rubbish! Been floating around for years. Look, I'm the best advertisement those designers have. Why else would they still keep sending me clothes. They get so much free publicity it's me who ought to be charging them.'

'As they offered gifts most rare, At Thy cradle rude and bare,' the choir rang out

'That's only part of it, Ma'am. The story goes that you are then taking these clothes which have been . . . donated, shall we say, and selling them for cash to your friends.'

There was a moment of guilty silence before she responded, deeply irritated. 'What do they know? It's nonsense. Can't possibly have any evidence. Who, tell me who. Who's supposed to have these bloody clothes?'

'Amanda Braithwaite. Your former flatmate, Serena Chiselhurst. Lady Olga Wickham-Furness. The Honourable Mrs Pamela Orpington. To name but four. The last lady received an exclusive Oldfield evening dress and an Yves St Laurent suit, complete with accessories. You received one thousand pounds. According to the report.'

'There's no evidence for these allegations,' the Princess snapped in a strangulated whisper. 'Those girls would never—'

'They don't need to. Those clothes are bought to wear, to show off. The evidence is all in a series of photographs of you and these other ladies taken over the last few months, quite properly, in public places.' He paused. 'And there's a cheque stub.'

She considered in silence for a moment, finding reassurance lacking as the choir sang sentiments of bleak midwinter and frosty winds.

'Won't look too good, will it. There'll be a bloody stink.' She sounded deflated, the self-confidence waning. She studied her gloves intently for a moment, distractedly smoothing out the creases. 'I'm expected to be in five different places a day, never wearing the same outfit twice. I work damned hard to make other people happy, to bring a little Royal pleasure into their lives. I help to raise millions, literally millions, every year for charity. For others. Yet I am expected to do it all on the pittance I get from the Civil List. It's impossible.' Her voice had become a whisper as she took in the inevitability of what Landless had said. 'Oh, stuff it all,' she sighed.

'Don't worry, Ma'am. I think I'm in a position to acquire these photographs and ensure they never see the light of day.'

She looked up from the gloves, relief and gratitude swelling in her eyes. Not for a moment did she realize that Landless already had the photographs, that they had been taken on his explicit instructions after a tip-off from one of the women's disgruntled Spanish au pair who had overheard a telephone conversation and stolen the cheque stub.

'But that's not really the point, is it,' Landless continued. 'We need to find some way of ensuring you don't run into this sort of trouble ever again. I know what it's like to be the victim of constant press sneering. I feel we're in this together. I'm British, born and bred and proud of it, and I've no time for those foreign creeps who own half our national press yet who don't understand or care a fig about what makes this country great.'

Her shoulders stiffened under the impact of his bombastic flattery as the vicar began an appeal for help to the homeless built heavily around images of insensitive innkeepers and quotations from the annual report of a housing action charity.

'I'd like to offer you a consultancy with one of my companies. Entirely confidential, only you and me to know about it. I provide you with a suitable retainer, and in return you give me a few days of your time. Open one or two of our new offices. Meet some of my important foreign business contacts over lunch. Perhaps host an occasional dinner at the Palace. And I'd love to do something like that on the Royal Yacht, if that's possible. But you tell me.'

'How much?'

'A dozen times a year, perhaps.'

'No. How much money?'

'A hundred thousand. Plus a guarantee of favourable coverage and exclusive interviews in my newspapers.'

'What's in it for you?'

'The chance to get to know you. Meet the King. Get some great PR support for me and my business. Get the sort of exclusive Royal coverage which sells newspapers. Do you need more?'

'No, Mr Landless. I don't particularly care for my job, it's brought me no great personal happiness, but if I do something I like to do it properly. Without making too much of the matter, I need more money than the Civil List makes available. In the circumstances, so long as it remains an entirely private arrangement and requires nothing which will demean the Family, I'd be delighted to accept. And thank you.'

There was more, of course. Had she known Landless better she would have known there was always more. A Royal connection would have its uses, filling the gap left by his withered line to Downing Street, a tool to impress those who still thought majesty mattered. But this was a particularly versatile connection. He knew the Princess was usually indiscreet, occasionally unwise, frequently uninhibited – and unfaithful. She was despair waiting to be exposed at the heart of the Royal Family and when at last the despair became too large to contain, as eventually he was sure it would, his newspapers would be at the front of the jackal pack, armed with their exclusive insights, as they tore her to pieces.

The room had a hushed, almost reverential atmosphere. It was a place of contemplation, of escape from the outside world with its persistent telephones and interruptions, a haven where businessmen could repair after a heavy lunch to collect their thoughts. At least, that was what they told their secretaries, unless, of course, their secretaries were waiting in one of the simple bedrooms upstairs. The Turkish Bath of the Royal Automobile Club on Pall Mall is one of those many London institutions which never advertise their blessings. It is not a case of English modesty, simply that if the institution is good enough its reputation will circulate sufficiently without causing an influx of what is called 'the wrong type of people'. It is impossible to define what is the wrong type of people, but gentlemen's clubs have generations of experience in spotting it as soon as it walks through the door, and assisting it straight back out. Such people do not normally include politicians or newspaper editors.

The politician, Tim Stamper, and the editor, Bryan Brynford-Jones, sat in a corner of the steam room. It was still morning and the after-lunch crush had not yet developed; in any event, the denseness of the steamy atmosphere made it impossible to see further than five feet. It clouded the dim wall lights like a London fog and muffled any sound. They would be neither seen, nor overheard. A good place to share confidences. The two men leaned forward on their wooden bench, working up a sweat, the perspiration dripping off their noses and trickling down their bodies. Stamper had draped a small crimson towel across himself while BBJ, as he liked to be known, sat completely naked. He was as overweight and fleshy as Stamper was gaunt, his stomach practically covering his private parts as he leaned forward. He was extrovert, opinionated, insecure, mid-forties and very menopausal, beginning to turn that delicate corner between maturity and physical decrepitude. He was also deeply disgruntled. Stamper had just given him a flavour of the New Year's Honours list soon to be announced, and he wasn't on it. What was worse, one of his fiercest rivals amongst the national editors' club was to get a knighthood, joining two other Fleet Street 'K's.

'It's not so much I feel I deserve one, of course,' he had explained. 'But when all your competitors are in on the act it makes people point their fingers at you, as if you're second rate. I don't know what the hell I have to do to establish my credentials with this Government. After all, I've turned *The Times* into your biggest supporter amongst the quality press. You might not have scraped home at the last election had I turned on you, like some of the rest.'

'I sympathize, really I do,' the Party Chairman responded, looking less than sincere as he offered condolence while perusing a copy of the *Independent*. 'But you know these things aren't entirely in our hands.'

'Bullshit.'

'We have to be even-handed, you know . . .'

'The day a Government starts being even-handed between its friends and its enemies is the day it no longer has any friends.'

'All the recommendations have to go before the Scrutiny Committee. You know, checks and balances, to keep the system smelling sweet. We don't control their deliberations. They often recommend against . . .'

'Not that ancient crap again, Tim.' Brynford-Jones was beginning to feel increasingly indignant as his ambitions were brushed aside without Stamper even lifting his eyes from the newspaper. 'How many times do I have to explain. It was years ago. A minor offence. I only pleaded guilty to get rid of it. If I'd fought it the whole thing would have been dragged out in court and my reputation smeared much more badly.'

Stamper looked up slowly from his newspaper. 'Pleading guilty to a charge of flashing your private parts at a woman in a public place is not designed to recommend you to the good and the great of the Scrutiny Committee, Bryan.'

'For Chrissake, it wasn't a public place. I was standing at the window of my bathroom. I didn't know I could be seen from the street. The woman was lying when she said I made lewd gestures. It was all a disgusting stitch-up, Tim.'

'You pleaded guilty.'

'My lawyers told me to. My word against hers. I could've fought the case for a year and still lost with every newspaper in the country having a field day at my expense. As it was it only got a couple of column inches in some local rag. Christ, a couple of column inches is probably all that prying old bag wanted. Maybe I should have given it to her.'

Stamper was struggling to fold the pages of the *Independent*, which had become flaccid in the damp atmosphere, his apparent lack of concern infuriating Brynford-Jones further.

'I'm being victimized! I'm paying for the lies of some shrivelled old woman almost fifteen years ago. I've worked my balls off trying to make up for all that, to put it behind me. Yet it seems I can't even rely on the support of my friends. Maybe I should wake up and realize they're not my friends after all. Not the people I thought they were.'

The bitterness, and the implied threat to withdraw his editorial support, were impossible to misunderstand, but Stamper did not respond immediately, first carefully attempting to refold his newspaper, but it was pointless: the *Independent* was beginning to disintegrate amidst the clouds of steam, and Stamper finally thrust it soggily to one side.

'It's not a matter of just friends, Bryan. To override the objections of the Scrutiny Committee and be willing to put up with the resulting flak would require a very good friend. To be quite honest, Henry Collingridge was never that sort of friend for you, he'd never stick his neck out.' He paused. 'Francis Urquhart, however, is a very different sort of dog. Much more of a terrier. And right now, with a recession around the corner, he's a strong believer in friendship.'

They paused as, through the murk, the door opened and a shadowy figure appeared, but the cloying atmosphere was evidently too much and after two deep breaths he coughed and left.

'Go on.'

'Let's not beat about the bush, Bryan. You don't have a cat in hell's chance of getting your gong unless you find a Prime Minister willing to fight in the last ditch for you. A Prime Minister isn't going to do that unless you're willing to reciprocate.' He wiped a hand over his forehead to clear his line of vision. 'Your unstinting support and cooperation all the way up to the next election. In exchange for informed briefings, exclusive insights, first shot at the best stories. And a knighthood at the end of it. It's a chance to wipe the slate clean, Bryan, and put the past behind you. No one argues with a "K".'

Brynford-Jones sat, his elbows on his knees and the folds of his belly piled one upon the other, staring straight ahead. A smile began to etch its way across his damp face like a beam of light through this murky, misting world of fallen chests and sagging scrota.

'You know what I think, Tim?'

'What?'

'I think you may have just rekindled my faith.'

Buckingham Palace
16 December

My dear Son,
You will soon be back with us for Christmas, but I felt I needed someone with whom to share. There are so few people to trust.

My life, and yours to come, are beset by frustration. We are expected to be examples – but of what? Apparently of servility. At times I despair.

As we discussed when last you came down from Eton, I had planned to make a speech drawing the country's attention to the growing divisions within the country. Yet the politicians have 'redrafted' some of my thoughts, so I no longer recognize them as my own. They are trying to make me a eunuch and force me to deny my own manhood.

Is the role of the King to reign mute over a nation being led to dissolution and division? There seem to me to be few clear rules, except that of caution. My anger at the Government's treatment of my speech must remain private. But I cannot be a Monarch without also retaining my self-respect as a man – as you will find when your time comes.

If we have not the freedom to defend those things in which we believe passionately, then at least we can avoid colluding in those actions we oppose and feel dangerously inappropriate. Never let them put words into your mouth. I have simply

437

omitted large chunks of the Government's draft.

My task, and yours to come, is a heavy burden. We are meant to be figureheads, to symbolize the virtues of the nation. To do so grows increasingly difficult in a modern world which surrounds us with many temptations but so few occupations. But if our role is to mean anything, then it must at very least allow us our conscience. I would sign a bill proclaiming a republic tomorrow if it were put to me approved by Lords and Commons, but I will not speak politicians' nonsense and bless it as my own.

Everything I do, every blunder I make, every morsel of respect I gather, will in time be passed on to you. I have not always been able to be the sort of father I would want. Formality, convention, distance too often come between a King and his son – me and you, as they did between me and my own father. But I will not betray you and your inheritance, on that you have my word. In previous times they have taken our forefathers to a public place and chopped off their heads! At least they had the dignity of dying with their conscience intact.

The world seems dark to me at the moment. I eagerly await the light which your return for the seasonal holiday will bring.

With my warmest affection to you, my son.
Father.

Mycroft had spent the evening pacing disconsolately around his cold, empty house, searching for distraction. It had been a miserable day. Kenny had been called off at short notice for a ten-day tour to the Far East which would keep him away over the holiday. Mycroft had been with the King when Kenny called, so all he got was a message left with his secretary wishing him Happy Christmas. As Mycroft gazed at the four walls, he imagined Kenny already cavorting along some sun-kissed beach, laughing, enjoying himself, enjoying others.

The King hadn't helped, either, spitting incandescence at the Government's redraft of his speech. For some reason Mycroft blamed himself. Wasn't it his job to ensure that the King's views got across? He felt as if he had failed. It was another pang of the guilt which plagued him whenever he was away from Kenny and out from under his spell.

The house was so neat, orderly, impersonal, he even longed for the sight of some of Fiona's clutter but there wasn't even a dirty dish in the sink. He'd paced all evening, unable to settle, feeling ever more alone, drinking too much in a vain attempt to forget, drowning once again. Thoughts of Kenny only made him jealous. When he tried to distract himself by thinking of his other life, all he could feel was the force of the King's passion and his bitterness at the Prime Minister. 'If only I hadn't been so open with him, thought he might be different from the rest. It's my fault,' he had said. But Mycroft held himself to blame.

He sat at his desk, the King's emasculated draft in front of him, the photo of Fiona in the silver frame still not removed, his diary open with a ring around the date of Kenny's return, his refilled glass leaving rings of dampness on the leather top. God, but he needed someone to talk with, to remind himself there was a world out there, to break the oppressive silence around him and to distract from his feeling of guilt and failure. He felt confused and vulnerable, and the drink wasn't helping. He was still feeling confused and vulnerable when the phone rang.

'Hello, Trevor,' he greeted the *Telegraph*'s Court Correspondent. 'I was hoping someone would ring. How can I help? Good God, you've heard what . . . ?'

'I am not an 'appy man. I am not an 'appy bloody man.' The editor of the *Sun*, an undersized and wiry man from the dales of Yorkshire, began swearing quietly to himself as he read the lead item in the *Telegraph* first edition. The profanity became louder as he read down the copy until he could contain his frustration no longer. 'Sally. Get me that bastard Incest.'

'He's in hospital. Just had his appendix out,' a female voice floated through his open door.

'I don't care if he's in his bloody coffin. Dig him up and get him on the phone.'

439

Roderick Motherup, known as Incest throughout the newspaper world, was the paper's Royal Correspondent, the man paid to know who was doing what to whom behind the discreet facades of any of the Royal residences. Even while he lay flat on his back.

'Incest? Why the hell did we miss this story?'

'What story?' a weak voice sounded down the line.

'I pay you a whole truckful of money to spread around enough Palace servants, chauffeurs and snitches so we know what's going on. Yet you've bloody gone and missed it.'

'What story?' the voice chimed in again, more weakly.

The editor began reading the salient facts. The extracts from the King's draft speech excised by the Government. The replacement sections suggested by the Government, full of economics and optimism, which the King had refused to use. The conclusion that behind the King's recent address to the National Society of Charitable Foundations lay one hell of a row.

'So I want the story, Incest. Who's screwing who. And I want it for our next edition in forty minutes.' He was already scribbling draft headlines.

'But I haven't even seen the story,' the correspondent protested.

'Have you got a fax?'

'I'm in hospital!' came the plaintive protest.

'I'll bike it round. In the meantime get on the phone and get back to me with something in ten.'

'Are you sure it's true?'

'I don't care if the damned thing's true. It's a fantastic ball-breaking story and I want it on our front page in forty minutes!'

In editorial offices all around London similar words of motivation were being relayed to harassed Royal-watchers. There was the sniff of a downturn in the air, advertising revenues were beginning to fall, and that meant nervous proprietors who would more happily sacrifice their editors than their bottom lines. Fleet Street needed a good circulation-boosting story. This would put many tens of thousands on tomorrow's sales figures, and had the promise of being a story which would run and run.

A long time ago, at a point lost in the mists of time, an incident took place during a war fought in Canada between the British and the French. At least, it was probably in Canada, although it could have taken place at almost any point on the globe where the two fiercely imperialist nations challenged each other, if indeed it took place at all. According to the reports two armies, one British and the other French, marched up opposite sides of the same hill, discovering unexpected confrontation on the brow. Heavily packed ranks of infantrymen faced each other, readying themselves for battle, hastily preparing their muskets in a deadly race to shed first blood.

But the troops were led by officers who were also gentlemen. The English officer, seeing his counterpart but a few feet away, was quick to see the demands of courtesy and, taking off his hat with a low sweep, invited the French to shoot first.

The Frenchman could be no less gallant than his English enemy and, with a still deeper bow, offered: 'No, sir. I insist. After you.'

At which the English infantrymen fired and blew the French apart.

Prime Minister's Question Time in the House of Commons is much like that confrontation in Canada. All MPs are addressed as 'honourable' and all in trousers as 'gentlemen', even by their fiercest enemy. They are drawn up facing each other in ranks only two sword lengths apart and, in spite of the apparent purpose of asking questions and seeking information, the real intent is to leave as many of your opponents' bodies as you can manage bleeding on the floor of the Chamber. But there are two crucial differences with the confrontation on the hilltop. It is the one who strikes second, the Prime Minister with the last word, who normally has the advantage. And MPs on all sides have learnt the lesson that the midst of battle is no place for being a gentleman.

The news of the dispute over the King's speech hit the

newspapers on the last full day of business before the Christmas recess. There was little seasonal goodwill to be found anywhere as His Majesty's Loyal Opposition sensed its first good opportunity of testing the mettle of the new Prime Minister. At three fifteen p.m., the hour appointed for the Prime Minister to take questions, the Chamber of the House of Commons was packed. Opposition benches were strewn with copies of that morning's newspapers and their graphic front-page headlines. During the course of the previous night editors had worked hard to outbid each other, and headlines such as 'A Right Royal Rumpus' had given way to 'King's Draft Daft Says PM', eventually becoming simply 'King of Cardboard City'. It was all richly amusing and luridly speculative.

The Leader of the Opposition, Gordon McKillin, rose to put his question amidst a rustle of expectation on all sides. Like Urquhart he had been born north of the border but there the resemblance ceased. He was considerably younger, his waistline thicker, his hair darker, his politics more ideological and his accent much broader. He was not noted for his charm but had a barrister's mind, which made his words always precise, and he had spent the morning with his advisers wondering how best to circumvent the rules of the House which forbid any controversial mention of the Royal Family. How to raise the topic of the King's speech, without touching on the King?

He was smiling as he reached out to lean on the polished wooden Dispatch Box which separated him from his adversary by less than six feet. 'Will the Prime Minister tell us whether he agrees . . .' – he looked theatrically at his notes – 'it is time to recognize that more people than ever are disaffected in our society, and that the growing sense of division is a matter for grave concern?'

Everyone recognized the direct quote from the King's forbidden draft.

'Since the question is a very simple one, which even he should be able to understand, a simple yes or no will suffice.' Very simple indeed. No room for wriggling away from this one.

He sat down amidst a chorus of approval from his own

backbenchers and a waving of newspaper headlines. When Urquhart rose from his seat to respond he, too, wore an easy smile, but some thought they saw a distinct reddening of his ears. No wriggling. The only sensible course of action was direct avoidance, not to risk a cacophony of questions about the King's views, yet he didn't like to be seen running away from it. But what else could he do?

'As the Right Honourable Gentleman is aware, it is not the custom of this House to discuss matters relating to the Monarch, and I do not intend to make it my custom to comment on leaked documents.'

He sat down, and as he did so a roar of mock anger arose from the benches in front of him. The bastards were enjoying this one. The Opposition Leader was already back on his feet, his smile broader still.

'The Prime Minister must have thought I asked a different question. I don't recall mentioning His Majesty. It is entirely a matter between him and the Palace if the Prime Minister chooses to censor and cut to ribbons His Majesty's remarks. I wouldn't dream of raising such matters in this place.' A howl of mockery was hurled towards Urquhart from along the Opposition benches. Beneath her long judicial wig Madam Speaker shook her head in disapproval at such obvious circumvention of the rules of the House, but decided not to intervene. 'So can the Prime Minister get back to the question which was actually asked, rather than the one he wishes had been asked, and give a straight question a straight answer?'

Opposition MPs were pointing fingers at Urquhart, trying to get under his skin. 'He's chicken, running away!' exclaimed one. 'Can't face up to it,' said another. 'Happy Christmas, Francis,' mocked a third. Most simply rocked back and forth on the leather benches in delight at the Prime Minister's discomfort. Urquhart glanced at the Speaker, hoping she might slap down such conduct and with it the entire discussion, but she had suddenly found something of great interest to study on her Order Paper. Urquhart was on his own.

'The purpose of the question is clear. My answer remains the same.'

There was pandemonium now as the Opposition Leader rose for the third time. He leaned with one elbow on the Dispatch Box for many long moments without speaking, savouring the state of passion of his audience, waiting for the din to die, enjoying the sight of Urquhart impaled on his hook.

'I have no way of knowing what passed between the Prime Minister and the Palace. I know only what I read in the newspapers' – he waved a copy of the *Sun* for the benefit of the television cameras – 'and I have long ceased to believe anything I read there. But the question is simple. Such concerns about the growth of division within our society are shared by millions of ordinary people, whether or not they are held by those, shall we say, somewhat less than ordinary. But if the Prime Minister is having trouble with the question, let me rephrase it. Does he agree' – McKillin glanced down, a copy of the *Telegraph* now in his hand – 'with the sentiment that we cannot rest content while tens of thousands of our fellow citizens sleep rough on our streets, through no fault of their own? Does he accept that in a truly United Kingdom the sense of belonging of unemployed crofters in the Scottish Highlands is just as vital as that of home-owners in the southern suburbs? Would he support the view that it is a sign for concern rather than congratulation if more people drive our streets in Rolls-Royces while the disabled in their wheelchairs are left in the gutters, still unable to catch a Number 57 bus?' Everyone recognized the words which had been hijacked from the censored speech. 'And if he doesn't like those questions, I've got lots more.'

They were baiting Urquhart now. They didn't want answers, just blood, and in parliamentary terms they were getting it. Yet Urquhart knew that once he responded to any point concerning the King's speech he would lose all control of the matter, that he would be open to attack without restraint.

'I will not be drawn. Particularly by a pack of jackals.' From the Government backbenches, which had grown increasingly quiet during the exchanges, came a growl of support. This was more like the exchanges they were used to handling, and insults began to fly freely across the Chamber as Urquhart continued, shouting to make himself heard above the din. 'Before he takes his pretence of interest in the plight of the homeless and unemployed too far, perhaps the Right Honourable Gentleman should have a word with his trade union paymasters and tell them to stop pushing through inflationary pay claims which only force decent citizens out of their jobs and out of their homes.' The roar was almost deafening. 'He greets the problems of others with all the relish of a grave digger!'

It was an adept attempt at self-preservation. The insults had at last dragged attention away from the question and a tide of protest swept across the Chamber creating waves of heaving arms and invective which crashed like surf on either side. The Opposition Leader was back on his feet for a fourth attempt but Madam Speaker, conscious that perhaps she should have done more to curtail the questioning and protect the Prime Minister, decided that enough was enough and handed the floor over to Tony Marples, a prison officer elected to represent the marginal constituency of Dagenham at the last election who regarded himself as a saviour of 'the ordinary chap' and who made no secret of his ambition to get a Ministerial job. He wouldn't get one, of course, not simply because he probably wouldn't last long in the House nor because he was homosexual, but because an estranged boyfriend had recently retaliated by wrecking the MP's Westminster flat before being carted away by the police. Disaffected lovers had dragged down many finer men than Marples, and no Prime Minister was going to give him the chance to follow in their footsteps, no matter how well trodden. But in Madam Speaker's eyes his ambition made Marples just the man to lob the PM an easy ball to hit and so provide the House with an opportunity to regain its composure.

'Wouldn't the Prime Minister agree with me,' Marples began in strong Cockney tones; he hadn't prepared a question in advance, but he thought he knew how to help his beleaguered leader, 'that this Party stands second to none in its respect for the institutions of this country, and in particular in its respect, love and devotion to our wonderful Royals?' He paused for a second. Once on his feet he was suddenly uncertain how to finish. He coughed, hesitated, too long, exposing a gap like a chink in medieval armour. The Opposition lunged. Interventions were hurled at him from across the Chamber, throwing him even further off-stride until his mind jammed in second and stalled. His jaw sagged and his eyes grew wide with the terror of those who wake from a dream to find that nightmare has become reality and they are naked in a public place. 'Our wonderful Royals,' he was left repeating, ever more feebly.

It was left to an Opposition MP to deliver the final blow, putting him out of his misery with a stage whisper which carried to all parts of the House.

'Particularly our queens!'

Even many on Marples' own side failed to restrain their smug grins. Marples saw an Opposition member blow a silent kiss of mockery in his direction, his confidence drained from him for all to see, and he sank miserably back into his seat as the Opposition once more reached a state of euphoria.

Urquhart closed his eyes in despair. He had hoped he'd staunched the flow of blood; now he would need a tourniquet. He thought he would apply it to Marples' neck.

The King was standing, as was his custom, near the window of his sitting room. He was toying self-consciously with the crested signet ring on his left hand, and made no move towards Urquhart. The Prime Minister had been kept waiting outside for a period which was not actually discourteous but was noticeably longer than usual, now he was forced to pace across the full length of the room before the King extended his hand. Once again Urquhart was surprised at the limp handshake, remarkable for someone who took such pride in his physical fitness. A sign of inner weakness? Or an occupational injury? At the King's silent direction they sat in the two chairs by the fireplace.

'Your Majesty, we must put an end to this open sore.'

'I do so agree, Prime Minister.'

The informality of their earlier meetings had been

replaced by an almost theatrical precision, like two chess players taking patient turns with the pieces. They sat just a few feet apart, knees together, waiting for the other to begin. Eventually Urquhart was forced to make his move.

'I must ask that this never happens again. Such material emanating from the Palace makes my task impossible. And if the leak came from a Palace servant, then he should be disciplined as an example to others for the future—'

'Confound your insolence!'

'I beg—?'

'You come here to impugn my integrity, to suggest that I or one of my staff leaked these wretched documents!'

'You don't for one moment think that I leaked them, not for all the damage they have done . . .'

'That, Mr Urquhart, is politics, which is your game and *not* mine. Downing Street is notorious for leaking documents when it serves their purpose. I am not in that game!'

The King's head was thrust forward, his balding temples glowing with indignation and the bony bridge of his long and much broken nose showing prominently, like a bull about to charge. The limp handshake had been deceptive. Urquhart couldn't fail to mistake the sincerity of the other man's anger, and knew he had misjudged the situation. He flushed and swallowed hard.

'I . . . apologize, Sir. I can assure you I played no part in the leaking of these documents, and I had assumed that, perhaps, a Palace servant . . . ? I misconstrued.' The knuckles of his tightly clenched hands were cracking with frustration, while the King snorted through his nose several times, banging a hand down upon his right knee as if to expend his anger and to regain control of his temper. They both sat silent for several moments, gathering their wits.

'Sir, I am at a loss as to which devil is responsible for the leak and our misunderstanding.'

'Prime Minister, I am well aware of my constitutional duties and restraints. I have made a deep study of them. Open warfare with my Prime Minister is not within my prerogative and it is not my desire. Such a course of action can only be damaging, perhaps disastrous, for us both.'

'The damage has already been inflicted for the Government. After this afternoon's Question Time, I have no doubt that tomorrow's newspapers will be full of coverage supporting what they believe to be your view and attacking what they will describe as an insensitive and heavy-handed Government. They will say it is censorship.'

The King smiled grimly at Urquhart's recognition of the balance of popular sentiment.

'Such coverage will only do us both harm, Sir. Drive a wedge between us, expose those parts of our Constitution which are best left in the privacy of darkness. It would be a grave error.'

'On whose part?'

'On all our parts. We must do whatever we can to avoid that.' Urquhart left the statement hanging in the air while he tried to judge the other man's reaction, but all he could see was the continuing puffiness of exasperation around the eyes. 'We must try to prevent the newspapers ruining our relationship.'

'Well, what do you expect that I can do? I didn't start this public row, you know.'

Urquhart took a deep breath to blunt the edge of his tongue. 'I know, Sir. I know you didn't start it. But you can stop it.'

'Me? How?'

'You can stop it, or at least minimize the damage, here from the Palace. Your press secretary must phone round the editors' offices this evening to tell them that there is no dispute between us.'

The King nodded as he considered the proposal. 'Maintain the constitutional fiction that the King and his Government are as one, eh?'

'Precisely. And he must suggest that the press leaks have got it wrong, that the draft does not represent your views. Perhaps implying that it was prepared for you by some adviser or other?'

'Deny my words?'

'Deny that there is any difference between us.'

'Let me be clear about this. You want me to disown my own beliefs.' A pause. 'You want me to lie.'

'It's more a smoothing over the cracks. Repairing the damage . . .'

'Damage which I did not cause. I have said nothing in public to dispute your position and I shall not. My views are entirely private.'

'They are not private when they are spread all over the front pages of the newspapers!' Urquhart could not control his exasperation; winning this argument was crucial.

'That is your problem, not mine. I discussed my ideas only with a small circle of my own family, around the dinner table. No Palace servants. No journalists. Certainly no politicians.'

'Then you did discuss it.'

'In private. As I must, if my advice to my Government is to be of any use.'

'There are some types of advice the Government can do without. We are elected to run this country, after all.'

'Mr Urquhart!' The blue eyes were ablaze with indignation, his hands white as they gripped the arm of his chair. 'May I remind you that you have not been elected as Prime Minister, not by the people. You have no mandate. Until the next election you are no better than a constitutional caretaker. Meanwhile I am the Monarch with the right accorded by tradition and all the constitutional law books ever damn well written to be consulted by you and to offer advice.'

'In private.'

'There is no constitutional duty on me to lie publicly to save the Government's skin.'

'You must help with the editors.'

'Why?'

'Because . . .' Because if he didn't, Urquhart would be stranded and done to death by a dribble of by-elections. 'Because you cannot be seen to dispute matters of policy with the Government.'

'I will not repudiate my own beliefs. It would be offensive to me not only as a Monarch, but as a man. And you have no damned right to ask!'

'In your capacity as Monarch you have no right to personal beliefs, not on politically sensitive matters.'

449

'You deny me my rights as a man? As a father? How can you look your children in the eye—'

'On such matters you are not a man, you are a constitutional tool . . .'

'A rubber stamp for your folly? Never!'

'. . . who must support the duly elected Government on all matters in public.'

'Then I suggest, Mr Urquhart, that you go get yourself elected, by the people. Tell them you have no care for their future. Tell them that you are content to see the Scots drift away in discontent and despair. That you don't find it obscene for thousands of Englishmen to have no concept of home other than a cardboard box in some pestilential urban underpass. That large swathes of our inner cities are no-go areas for either police or social workers. Tell them you don't give a damn about anything except trying to line the pockets of your own supporters. Tell them all that, get yourself elected, and then you come back here and issue me with your orders. But until then, I will not lie for you!'

The King was on his feet, propelled upwards more by the energy of his uncontrollable rage than any conscious desire to finish the audience. But Urquhart knew there was no point in continuing. The King was unshakable, he would not agree to bend, not, at least, until after Urquhart had won an election in his own right as Prime Minister. And as Urquhart strode slowly out of the room, he knew the King's intransigence had torn to shreds any chance of holding that early election, and winning.

The telephone rang in the private apartments of Kensington Palace. It was past eight o'clock in the evening and Landless hadn't expected to find the Princess at home. Her husband was away in Birkenhead opening a gas terminal and he thought she would either be with him or out on the town celebrating her freedom, but she answered the phone herself.

'Good evening, Your Royal Highness. I'm delighted to find you in.'

'Benjamin, this is a pleasant surprise.' She sounded reserved, slightly distracted, as though she was holding

450

something back. 'I'm recuperating from the rigours of a day spent with two thousand members of the Women's Institute. You can't imagine how tired one gets after shaking all those hands and listening to all that sincerity. I'm in the middle of a massage.'

'Then I apologize for disturbing you, but I have some good news.'

He had spent the afternoon pondering how she might react to the furore caused by the speech she had passed to him as the first fruit of their new arrangement. Her intention had been to illustrate the integrity and deep concerns of the private King; she'd less than half an idea it would be published and no idea of the storm it would cause. There might even be an inquiry. Had she now taken fright?

'I just wanted you to know that the newspapers tomorrow will be overflowing with articles in praise of the King. It's remarkable, done him a huge amount of good. And all because we handled matters the right way. You've done a fine job.'

She stretched out on the massage table in search of a glass of champagne. 'Great team, eh, Benjamin?'

'Yes, Ma'am. A great team.' She was still standing off; had he ruined it already? 'And I've been thinking, doing some recalculation. You know, now I've had the chance to meet you and see how capably you handle yourself, I think the value of your help is going to be even greater than I originally thought. Another fifty thousand pounds. How does that sound?'

'Benjamin, you serious? Sounds brillig.'

He winced at the garble of slang, the cultural product of an endless diet of gossip columns, fashion magazines and adult comics. He'd left school at fifteen and had fought his way through life burdened with all his uncut edges, his rough tongue and even rougher accent. It had given him a sense of self-esteem yet it was a brutal road, not one he had wanted for his three daughters who had found their own paths littered with the finest in educational opportunities. As he listened to the Princess he could neither understand nor abide those who, having been born with every advantage, proceeded to disgrace them. Still, he knew he

451

had found his woman. He chuckled amiably down the phone.

After she replaced the receiver she took another sip from her glass. She wondered if she were getting herself in too deep. She had long ago learned that there was no such thing as a free lunch for any member of the Royal Firm, let alone a free fifty thousand pounds. There were strings to everything, and she suspected that Ben Landless would pull hard.

'You're tensing up, Ma'am.'

She rolled over, the towel slipping from her body as she examined her newly tightened breasts.

'Forget the shoulder muscles, Brent. Time to take care of the inner woman.'

Lieutenant Brentwood Albery-Hunt, a six foot three Guards Officer on secondment to the Palace as the Princess's personal equerry, gave a sharp salute and stood to attention as his own towel fell to the floor and the Princess cast a critical eye over him in mock inspection. He knew from past form that she was a demanding Colonel of the regiment, and that night-duty under her supervision would be arduous.

December: Christmas Week

'It can't be done, Francis.'

I don't appoint Ministers to tell me things can't be done, Urquhart raged inside. But the Chancellor of the Exchequer was insistent, and Urquhart knew he was right.

They were huddled in the corner of a reception room at party headquarters where the good and the great of the party had gathered to save money and time by celebrating Christmas and bidding farewell to a long-serving official. The pay of such officials was appalling, their working conditions usually pitiable and they were expected to show independence neither of mind nor manner. In return they expected, after the passage of many years, recognition, in the form either of an invitation to a Buckingham Palace Garden Party, a modest mention in the Honours List, or a farewell reception at which busy Ministers gathered to drink sweet German wine and nibble cocktail sausages while the retiring and frequently unrecognizable servant was fêted. But Urquhart had been pleased to attend this function, for an elderly but ebullient tea lady named Mrs Stagg. No one else was sufficiently senior to remember how long she had been there. Her tea was poisonous and her coffee indistinguishable from her tea, but her sense of fun had cut through the pomposity which so frequently befogs politicians and her bustling presence in a room usually managed to defuse even the most sombre of occasions. Urquhart had fallen for her when, as an aspiring MP more than thirty years ago, he had watched transfixed as she had spotted a button loose on Ted Heath's jacket and had insisted on stripping the bachelor party leader to his shirt sleeves while she repaired the damage on the spot. Urquhart was aware that this was her third attempt at retirement but, at the age of seventy-two, it seemed likely

453

to be her very last and he had looked forward to the escape from official business. But it was not to last.

'It simply cannot be done,' the Chancellor repeated. 'Christmas has scarcely happened in the shops and the recession is going to be here earlier than we expected. We can massage the statistics a bit, explain them away for a month or two as rogues, but we won't be able to massage away the school leavers who'll be flooding into the work-force at Easter. Most of them are going to go straight from the classroom to the dole queue, and there's sod all you or I can do about it.'

The four men standing with heads bowed in their huddle drew closer together, as if to protect a great secret. Urquhart had asked the Chancellor what he thought of the chances of putting off the impact of recession for a month or two, squeezing out a little more time. But the Treasury Minister only confirmed what he already knew.

Stamper was next to speak, very briefly. There was no use in making a feast of bad news. 'Four points, Francis.'

'In front?'

'Behind. This aggravation with the King has shot our lead to hell. Four points and moving in the wrong direction.'

Urquhart ran his tongue along thin lips. 'And what of you, Algy? What bucketful of sorrows do you bring to drench me?'

As Urquhart turned to the Party Treasurer they had to huddle still closer, for the financier was scarcely more than five feet tall and listening to him in a room full of the buzz of conversation was an effort. Unlike the Chancellor and Stamper, he'd not been told of the plans for an early election, but he was no fool. When a Treasurer is asked how a party living on an overdraft might raise ten million pounds in a hurry, he knows that mischief is afoot. His well-lunched face was flushed as he craned his neck to look at the others.

'Can't be done. So soon after an election, immediately after Christmas and just about to go into recession . . . I couldn't raise ten million pounds this year, let alone this month. Let's be realistic, why would anyone want to lend that sort of money to a party with a slim majority about to get slimmer.'

'What do you mean?' Urquhart demanded.

'Sorry, Francis,' Stamper explained. 'The message must be waiting on your desk. Freddie Bancroft died this morning.'

Urquhart contemplated the news about one of his back-benchers from the shires. It was not entirely unexpected. Bancroft had been a political corpse for many years, and it was time the rest of him caught up. 'That's a pity, what's his majority?' Urquhart had to struggle to provide any form of punctuation or pause between the two thoughts. They were all too aware of his concern, how the lurid headlines of a by-election campaign had a habit of creating a new national mood, usually at the Government's expense as their candidate was put to ritual slaughter.

'Not enough.'

'Bollocks.'

'We'll lose it. And the longer we delay the worse it will be.'

'The first by-election with me as Prime Minister. Not a great advertisement, eh? I was rather hoping I'd be riding the bandwagon, not being shoved under its wheels.'

Their deliberations were interrupted by a sallow-faced youth in much-creased suit and crooked tie, whose reluctance to invade what was clearly a very private confabulation had been overcome by the Liebfraumilch and a bet made with one of the lissom secretaries, who had wagered her bed against his bashfulness. 'Excuse me, I've just joined the party's research department. Can I have your autographs?' He thrust a piece of paper and grubby pen into their midst.

The others waited for Urquhart to move, to instruct that the youth be keelhauled for impudence and dismissed for ill-judgement. But Urquhart smiled, welcoming the interruption. 'You see, Tim, somebody wants me!' He scribbled on the paper. 'And what are your ambitions, young man?'

'I want to be Chancellor, Mr Urquhart.'

'No vacancy!' the Chancellor insisted.

'Yet . . .' the Prime Minister warned.

'Try Brunei,' Stamper added, in less frivolous tones.

There was more merriment as the piece of paper did its round, but as the banter died away and the youth retreated in the direction of a deeply blushing secretary, Urquhart found himself staring into the humourless, uncompromising eyes of Stamper. Unlike the others they both knew how important was an early election. If recession and overdraft were the brush of the noose around their necks, then the news of the by-election had come as the sound of the trapdoor-bolt beginning its final slide. There had to be a way out, or else.

'Merry Christmas, Tim?'

Stamper's words sighed with the edge of perpetual Arctic night. 'Not this year, Francis. It can't be done. You must recognize the fact. Not now, not after the King. It simply cannot be done.'

PART TWO

New Year

Buckingham Palace
31 December

My dearest Son,

Today I begin my first full year as the King, and I am filled with *foreboding*.

Last night I had a *dream*. I was in a room, all white, in soft focus as things sometimes are in dreams, a *hospital* I think. I was standing beside a bath, white like everything else, in which two nurses were bathing my father, old and wasted, as he was before he died. They were treating him with such tenderness and care, floating him in the warm water, he was *at peace*, and so was I. I felt a calm, a serenity I have not felt for *many* months.

Then there appeared another nurse. She was carrying a bundle. A baby. *You!* Wrapped in a white shawl. But even as I reached so eagerly for you the nurse, and the two others attending my father, were *gone*. I held on to you but without support my father was no longer floating but suddenly submerged in the bath, water washing over his face, his eyes closed. I reached for him with one arm, but you began to fall. To help *him*, save him, I had to allow *you* to fall. I *could not* save you both. I had not a moment longer to decide, he was drowning, you were falling from my arms . . . Then I awoke.

It is all *too clear* to me. The Royal Family is intended to symbolize the continuity between the past and the future; I *no longer* think this possible. A King can cling to the past, the traditions, the decay. Or choose to reach out for the future, with all its uncertainties, its dangers, and its hopes. We *must* choose.

I am at a *crossroads*, both as a man and as a Monarch. I know I am *well loved*, but I take no pleasure in the fact.

When that popularity is claimed in part at the expense of the Prime Minister, it can bring <u>neither</u> any good. Mr Urquhart is a man of <u>great</u> resolution and, I believe, <u>little</u> <u>scruple</u>. He lays exclusive claim to the future – perhaps any Prime Minister would – but he does so with an unstinting lack of reserve. Yet if I can have no part in building that future, either as man or Monarch, then I have no manhood, no soul, <u>nothing</u>.

I shall not seek confrontation, because in the end I will lose. But I will not become merely a silent cipher for an unscrupulous and unwise Government. <u>Watch carefully</u> how this great dispute develops. And <u>learn</u>, for your own time will come.

 Your devoted,
  Father.

It was supposed to be a masked ball to welcome in the New Year, but Stamper had refused to cooperate. For the first time in his political career people had begun to recognize him, to make all those fawning motions which suggested he was important and to blame only themselves if they became bored talking to him. He was damned if he were going to wrap it all up behind some ludicrous headgear just to please his hostess. Lady Susan 'Deccy' Kassar was the wife of the governing chairman of the BBC. He spent his year trying to ensure that the Corporation's increasingly meagre budget eked out sufficiently to cover his commitments, while she spent it planning how to destroy half his salary in one go at her renowned and monumental New Year's Eve bash. The extravagance of the hospitality was matched by that of the guest list, compiled on computer over the course of the year to ensure none but the most powerful and notorious were included. It was said to be insufficient simply to be a spy master or bank robber in order to gain inclusion, you had to be caught and very publicly identified as such, preferably by the BBC. Stamper had been included only after a second recount. 'Deccy' – named after the décolleté for which she had been justifiably famed ever since passing from her teens to the first of three husbands – had decided the invitation was a mistake as soon as she saw Stamper arrive in nothing more elaborate than a dinner jacket. She had a passion for masked balls, which hid her eyes and enabled her to be on constant lookout for still more glittering victims while concentrating the guests' attention undistractedly upon her neckline. She didn't care for mutineers at her parties, particularly ones who greased their hair. Deliberately and as publicly as possible she had mistaken Stamper for a television soap star who had recently emerged from a drying-out clinic, while privately vowing not to invite him next year unless he was by then at least Home Secretary. She was soon off in search of more cooperative prey, fluttering her mask aggressively to carve a passage through the crowd.

It was shortly before midnight when Stamper spied the ample figure of Bryan Brynford-Jones holding forth from within the folds of a Laughing Cavalier's uniform, and passed in front of him.

'Tim! Great to see you!'

'Hello, BBJ. Didn't see you there.'

'This is one for the Diary. Chairman of the Party come disguised as a human being.'

'Should be worth at least a mention on the front page.'

'Not unless you leak the information, old chap. Sorry, forgot. Leaks not the favourite vocabulary in Government circles at the moment.'

The other guests enjoyed the banter, although Stamper had the distinct feeling he'd come off second best. It was not a sensation he relished. He drew the editor to one side.

'Talking of leaks, old friend, tell me. Who was the bastard who leaked the King's speech? Always wondered.'

'And wonder you shall. You know I couldn't possibly reveal journalistic sources.' Brynford-Jones chuckled mischievously, but there was a nervous corner to his smile.

'Yes, of course. But our informal inquiry ran into the sand, bound to over Christmas, never had a chance. This would be just between friends. Very close friends, remember. Who was it?'

'Never! Trade secret, you know.'

'I'm very good with trade secrets. Or had you forgotten?'

The editor looked perplexed. 'Look, Tim, I'll support you in every way I can, you know that. But sources . . . They're the crown jewels. Journalistic integrity, and all that.'

Stamper's dark eyes burned bright. The pupils were small, almost unnaturally so, which gave Brynford-Jones the impression they were carving at him.

'Just so we don't misunderstand each other, BBJ . . .' The hubbub around them had fallen to an expectant hush as a voice over the radio announced the chimes of Big Ben were about to strike. Stamper had to lower his voice to a whisper, but not so low that Brynford-Jones could be sure others would not hear. 'Integrity comes in many shapes and sizes, but not in your size and not through an open bathroom window. Don't go coy on me now.'

There was dead silence as the wheels of the great clock began to turn and engage. The editor wriggled in discomfort.

'Truth is, I can't be sure. Seriously. *Telegraph* got it first. We only followed up in the later editions.'

'But.'

Brynford-Jones' eyes darted nervously around the room, not settling. The introductory peal of the bells had begun giving him a little cover. The bastard wasn't going to let go. 'But. The story was written by their Court Correspondent, good contacts with the Palace. When we enquired in Downing Street and other Government departments, all we got were squawks of outrage and confusion.'

'And from the Palace?'

'Nothing. No denial, no outrage. No confirmation, either. I spoke to the King's press man, Mycroft, myself. Said he'd check it out and get back if he could, but he never did. He knew we'd have to print without a pretty authoritative denial.'

'So.'

'It came from the Palace. The King, or one of his merry men. Must've been. They could have stopped it. They didn't.' He was sweating, wiping his pink brow with a handkerchief he had lodged beneath the lace ruffles of his cavalier's sleeve. 'Christ, Tim. I don't know for certain.'

462

Big Ben struck and the room echoed with the sound of renewed revelry. Stamper leaned close, forced to shout into the other's ear. 'So you've told me nothing but gossip and your integrity's intact. See how easy it was, old friend?' Stamper squeezed the editor's arm tightly, with surprising force for one whose frame seemed so narrow and pinched.

'Peace and goodwill to all men, eh, Tim?'

'Don't be a bloody fool.'

In a bar not more than two miles from Lady Susan's party, Mycroft was also welcoming in the New Year. It would have been easy, too easy, to have moped. At this time of year, alone. Kenny away. An empty, cheerless house. But Mycroft didn't feel sorry for himself. To the contrary, he felt better, more at ease with himself, cleaner than he could remember ever feeling. His feelings had surprised him, but there could be nothing grubbier than going through the motions of sex while pretending it was love, when in truth there was no love to be shared, and he realized he had felt grubby all his married life. Yet with Kenny, Mycroft felt surprised, astonished at some of the things he had been asked to do, but totally untainted. He had wandered around Kenny's flat all afternoon, reading his postcards, playing his records, flopping about in Kenny's slippers and one of his favourite jumpers, trying to touch him in any way he could. He'd never been in love and he was far too old to be misty eyed, but he felt about Kenny as he had done for no other person. He didn't know if it was love but what the hell, at very least it was immense gratitude for Kenny's sharing, his understanding, for putting him straight. Straight! Mycroft smiled as he enjoyed his own joke.

The desire to share something of Kenny's on New Year's Eve had driven him back to the place where they had first met. This time the club was packed, with lights flashing and a DJ with moustache dyed party purple keeping up a steady patter on the disco. He had propped himself quietly in the corner, enjoying the spectacle. Three very athletic young men provided a floor show, doing something with balloons which necessitated their taking off most of their clothing, with 'more to come' as the DJ eagerly promised. Mycroft had been anxious that someone would bother him, try to pick him up – 'those queers are such tarts,' Kenny had once teased. He didn't know if he would be able to handle it, but no one tried. He was clearly at ease with himself and his bottle of Mexican beer with lime twist and, anyway, Mycroft mused, he was probably ten years older than anyone else in the bar. Grandfather deserved his bit of peace.

As the evening progressed the noise level had grown and the company became more boisterous. Men were queuing to have provocative photographs taken with one of the floor-show artistes, a drag queen who was promised for the after-midnight cabaret. Almost out of sight on the far side of the room, men disappeared into the scrum of the dance floor, to reappear many minutes later glowing with heat and often with rumpled clothing. He suspected he would not care for all he might find going on beneath the pulsating lights of the disco's laser system, deciding he was content with his ignorance. There were some doors he wasn't yet ready to pass through.

Midnight approached. The crush grew. Everyone else was jostling, dancing, stealing kisses, waiting. The radio was on. Big Ben. One man was already overcome, the tears cascading down his cheeks and onto his T-shirt, but they were obviously tears of happiness. The atmosphere was warm and emotional as all around couples held hands. He imagined Kenny's. Then the hour struck, a cheer went up and the whole bar became a confusion of balloons, streamers, 'Auld Lang Syne' and passionate embraces. He smiled in contentment. Quickly the embraces became less passionate and more free-wheeling as everyone in the room seemed to be kissing each other in a game of musical lips. One or two tried it on with Mycroft but with a smile he waved them coyly away. There was another shadow beside him, bending for a kiss, a portly man in a leather waistcoat with one hand on Mycroft's shoulder and the other attached to an unhealthy looking youth with a bad case of barber's rash.

464

'Don't I know you?'

Mycroft froze. Who the hell could know him in here?

'Don't worry, old man. No need to look so alarmed. Name's Marples, Tony Marples. Lady Clarissa to my friends. We met at the Garden Party during the summer. You obviously don't recognize me in my party frock.'

It began to come back. The face. The bristles at the top of the cheek he habitually missed while shaving. The thick lips and crooked front tooth, the sweat gathered along the crease in his chin. Now he remembered. 'Aren't you . . . ?'

'MP for Dagenham. And you're Mycroft, the King's press secretary. Didn't know you were one of the girls.'

The youth with pimples looked scarcely sixteen with unpleasant yellow stains between his teeth. Mycroft felt sick.

'Don't worry, old love. I'm not from the News of the Screws or anything. If you want to lock it away, your dark and dreadful secret's safe with me. All girls together now, aren't we? Happy New Year!' A gurgle began in the back of Marples' throat which passed as a chuckle and he leaned to kiss Mycroft. As two thick wet lips extended towards him Mycroft knew he was on the verge of vomiting and gave a lunge of desperation, pushing the MP away as he made a dash for the door.

Outside it was pouring with rain and he'd left his mohair overcoat inside. He was freezing and would soon be soaked. It didn't matter. As he fought to rid himself of the taste of bile and to cleanse his lungs with fresh air, he decided the overcoat was the least of his concerns. With creatures like Marples inside, he would rather die of pneumonia than go back to collect it.

She studied his face meticulously. It had lost its brightness and energy. The eyes sagged, looked older, the high forehead was rutted, the lips dry and inelastic, the jaw set. The atmosphere was heavy with cigarette smoke.

'You arrive in this place, believing you'll remould the world to your will. And all it does is to close in around you until you feel there's no way out. Reminds you how mortal you are.'

He was no longer a Prime Minister, an elevated figure above the rest. All she saw was a man, like any other, with troubles piled high upon his shoulders.

'Mrs Urquhart not here . . . ?'

'No,' he responded, brooding, until he seemed to realize he might have given the wrong impression. He looked up at her from his glass of whisky. 'No, Sally. It's not that. It's never quite like that.'

'Then what?'

He shrugged slowly, as if his muscles ached from the unseen burden. 'Normally I'm not prone to self-doubt. But there are times when all you've planned seems to slip like sand between your fingers, the more you scrabble for it the more elusive and intangible it becomes.' He lit another cigarette, sucking the harsh smoke down hungrily. 'It has, as they say, been one of those fortnights.'

He looked at her silently for a long moment through the fresh blue haze which hung like incense in a cathedral. They were seated in the two leather armchairs of his study, it was past ten and the room was dark except for the light of two standard lamps which seemed to reach out and embrace them, forming a little world of their own and cutting them off from what lay in darkness beyond the door. She could tell he'd already had a couple of whiskies.

'I'm grateful for the distraction.'

'Distraction from what?'

'Ever the businesswoman!'

'Or gypsy. What's bothering you, Francis?'

His eyes, rims red, held her, wondering how far he should trust her, trying to burrow inside to discover what thoughts hid behind the coyness. He found not pools of feminine sentimentality but resilience, toughness. She was good, very good, at hiding the inner core. They were two of a kind. He took another deep lungful of nicotine; after all, what did he have to lose? 'I was thinking of holding an election in March. Now I'm not. I can't. It will all probably end in disaster. And God save the King.'

There was no hiding the bitterness, or the genuine anguish of his appraisal. He had expected her to be taken aback, surprised by the revelation of his plans, but she

466

seemed to show no more emotion than if she were studying a new recipe.

'The King's not standing for election, Francis.'

'No, but the Opposition are walking in his shadow, which is proving to be exceptionally long. What are we . . . eight points behind? And all because of one naive ribbon cutter.'

'And you can't deal with the Opposition without dealing with the King?'

He nodded.

'Then what's the problem? You were willing to have a crack at him before Christmas.'

His gaze was rueful. 'I was trying to silence him, not slaughter him. And I lost. Remember? Over a simple, silly speech. Now his words have become weapons on the field of parliamentary battle and I can't discredit them without discrediting the King.'

'You don't have to kill him, just kill off his popularity. A public figure is only as popular as his opinion-poll ratings, and they can be fixed. At least temporarily. Wouldn't that do?'

He swilled another mouthful of whisky, staring hard at her body. 'O Gypsy, there is fire in your breast. But I have already taken him on once, and lost. I couldn't afford to lose a second time.'

'If what you say about the election is true, it seems to me you can't afford not to take him on. He's only a man,' she persisted.

'You don't understand. In an hereditary system the man is everything. You are all George Washingtons, you Americans.' He was dismissive, deep into his glass.

She ignored the sarcasm. 'You mean the same George Washington who grew to be old, powerful, rich – and died in his bed?'

'A Monarch is like a great oak beneath which we all shelter . . .'

'Washington was cutting down trees when he was a boy.'

'An attack on the Monarchy would turn the electorate

into a lynch mob. Bodies – my body – swinging from the highest branches.'

'Unless you lopped off the branches.'

They were engaged in a verbal duel, thrust and parry, parry and thrust, automatic responses, using the honed edges of their intellects. Only now did Urquhart pause to reflect, and as his eyes ran over her she could feel the tension begin to drain from him, the malt beginning to dissolve the shards of glass grating inside. She felt his gaze wandering up from her ankles, over her knees, admiring the waist. Then he was lingering at her breasts, oh, and how he lingered, peeling off layer after layer, and she knew the mellowness had already been replaced by a renewed tightening inside. He was changing from victim to hunter. It brought back a sense of boldness, of command, as the energy of fresh ideas began to flow through his veins and wipe away the lines of despondency which had crowded in around his eyes. In their small world of the armchairs, he began to rise above his troubles and to feel once more in control. As if he were back on his Chesterfield. When, finally, his thoughts had travelled up her body and their eyes met, she was smiling, slightly mocking, reproachful but not discouraging. Her body had been massaged by his imagination, and responded. He brightened.

'To do battle with the Monarch would be . . .'

'Constitutionally improper?' She was goading.

'Bad politics. As I have already learned, to my cost. The King's speech gave him the high ground and I cannot afford to be seen once again in public dispute with him . . .' He arched an eyebrow, exquisitely. She had never known an eyebrow to express such passion. 'But perhaps you are right. If I am denied the high ground, then there is always the low ground.' Once more he was alive, tingling, she could feel the energy and renewed hope. 'An hereditary Monarchy is an institution which defies all logic. An opiate we sprinkle on the masses from time to time to reassure them, to fill them full of pride and respect, to extract their allegiance without them asking too many questions.'

'Isn't that what tradition is all about?'

'Yet once they start asking questions about an hereditary system there is little logic left to sustain it. All inbreeding and isolation, palaces and princely privilege. It is not the stuff of a modern world. Or of a debate about the under-privileged. Of course, I couldn't possibly be seen to lead such an attack. But if such an attack were to be mounted . . .'

'The King is Dead, Long Live the Prime Minister!'

'No, you go too far! You're talking revolution. If you start hacking away at the greatest tree in the forest, there's no telling how many others will be brought down with it.'

'But maybe that's not necessary,' she continued, picking up his thought. 'Perhaps simply cut it down to size. No shadow for the Opposition to hide in.'

'No branches from which to lynch me.'

'No more Royal bark?' She smiled.

'You might say that.' He nodded in appreciation.

'Not so much off with his head as . . . off with his limbs?'

'*You* might say that, Sally. But as Prime Minister I couldn't possibly comment.'

He spread his hands wide and they both began to laugh. She thought she heard the sound of an axe being gently honed.

'Did you have any specific limbs in mind?'

'There are many branches to our beloved Royal Family. Some easier to reach than others.'

'The King and his kind embarrassed, harassed, and on the defensive. A public spotlight probing the darker corners of the Palace. The shine knocked off him and his words, his motives discredited. And all backed by an opinion poll or two? The right questions, eh?'

Suddenly his face went rigid. He leaned across and placed his hand firmly above her knee. Considerably higher above her knee than was necessary. The fingers were stiff with tension and she could smell the whisky on his breath. 'By God, but it would be dangerous. We would be taking on hundreds of years of history. A tussle behind the scenes over a simple speech left me humiliated. If this were to turn into a public battle, me and the King, there would be no going back. If I were to lose, it would be the end for me. And for all who were with me.'

'But unless you have your election in March, you're dead anyway.' She placed her own hand upon his, warming it gently, massaging away the tension with her palm and the caress of her own fingers, welcoming his closeness.

'You would take such risks? For me?'

'Just say please, Francis. I told you, anything you want. Anything. Just say please.' She turned his hand over so that it was palm up, and began to stroke it with the tips of her fingers. Her nose was quivering. 'And you know how to say please, don't you?'

He brought his other hand across to still the sensuousness of her fingers. Theirs couldn't be solely a professional relationship, not if he were to tilt full at the King. There was too much at stake. He knew he would have to make her commitment deeper, more personal, tie her to him.

'There are civil servants just beyond that door. And no lock . . .'

She took off her glasses and shook her hair. It glowed like midnight in the light of the lamps. 'Life is full of risks, Francis. I find risk makes it all the better.'

'Makes life better?'

'Certain parts of it. What risks are you willing to take, Francis?'

'With the King? As few as possible. With you . . . ?'

And already she was in his arms.

Urquhart didn't care for opera, but being Prime Minister involved him in so many things he had no liking for. Attending the Slaughter House twice a week for Question Time. Being affable to visiting presidents, smiling black faces who, calling themselves colonial freedom fighters, had brought their countries to impoverishment and dictatorship, and who Urquhart could remember in their youth having been nothing but murderous thugs. Listening to the front door of the so-called private apartment in Downing Street, the door with no lock, bounce on its hinges as civil servants cascaded still more red boxes and ministerial papers down upon him. As Prime Minister, he had discovered, there was no hiding place.

Elizabeth had insisted he come to the opening night of a new opera and had been so persistent he had been forced to succumb, even though he had no ear for Janáček or forty-member choruses who seemed intent on singing from forty different scores, all at the same time. Elizabeth sat transfixed, her attention upon the tenor who was battling to drag his beloved back from the dead. Rather like the leader of the Liberal Party, Urquhart mused.

Stamper had also encouraged him to come and had secured the private box. Anyone who can afford three hundred pounds a seat for the stalls, he had said, must be worth bumping into. He'd arranged with the management to swap the publicity of Urquhart's presence for the address list of the Opera House patrons, all of whom within a week would be hit with an invitation to a Downing Street reception, a vaguely worded letter about future support for the arts, and a telephone call asking for cash.

And there was Alfredo Mondelli, a man with a face like a light bulb, round, solid, all bone and no hair, with eyes which bulged as if the bow tie of his evening dress had been secured too tightly. The Italian businessman sat with his wife alongside Stamper and the Urquharts; judging by the fidgeting which could be heard coming from his direction, he was equally filled with tedium. For several endless minutes Urquhart tried to find distraction from the music in the procession of gilded female figures who chased plaster cherubs around the domed ceiling, while beside him the creaking of Mondelli's chair grew more persistent. When finally the interval came it was a release for them all; a clearly exulted Elizabeth and Signora Mondelli rushed off to the powder room, permitting the three men to take refuge in a bottle of vintage Bollinger.

'A pity to spoil business with so much pleasure, don't you think, Signor Mondelli?'

The Italian rubbed life back into his buttocks and thighs. 'When God was giving out 'is gifts, Prime Minister, 'e was a little short on musical appreciation when it came to my

471

turn.' His English was proficient, his pronunciation slow and distinctly Soho bistro.

'Then let us make sure we use the interval well before we get drenched in another dose of culture. Straight to it. How can I help you?'

The Italian nodded in gratitude. 'As I think Mr Stamper 'as told you, I am proud to be one of my country's leading manufacturers of environmentally friendly products. To 'alf of Europe I am Mr Green. I employ tens of thousands of people, 'ole communities depend upon my business. A big research institute in Bologna named after me . . .'

'Very commendable.' Urquhart recognized the Latin exaggeration. Mondelli ran a company which, though significant by Italian standards, was not in the same league as the far more powerful multinationals.

'But now, now it is all threatened, Your Excellency. Bureaucrats who understand nothing about business, about life. They terrorize everything I 'ave built.' Champagne washed over the side of his glass and spilt as the passion built in his voice. 'Those foolish *bambini* at the European Community and their draft regulations. You know, in two years' time they wish to change the 'ole way we dispose of chemical waste.'

'Why does that concern you?'

'Mr Akat . . .' He made it sound as if he were clearing his throat. 'These are the chemicals I spend my life taking out of my products. What you wrap your food in, wash in, dress in, the paper you write on. I make them environmentally friendly by taking the wretched . . .' – he gesticulated with his stubby fingers and screwed up his face as if performing on the stage – 'wretched chemicals out of them. What the 'ell am I supposed to do with them now? Governments, you run your nuclear power stations and you bury all your nuclear waste, but that's not good enough for businessmen. We shall no longer be allowed to bury the by-products, or simply burn them, or dispose of them deep in the ocean. Those *bastardi* in Brussels even want to stop me exporting them to store in the deserts of the Third World, no matter that the people of those countries are starving and are in desperate need for the income. Africans will starve, Italians will starve, my family will starve. It is madness!' He took a huge draught of champagne, emptying the glass.

'Forgive me, Signor Mondelli, but aren't all your competitors in the same position?'

'My competitors are mainly German. They 'ave the Deutsch marks for such 'uge investments to dispose of the chemicals 'ow the bureaucrats want. I do not. It is a conspiracy by the Germans to force the competition out of business.'

'So why come to me? Why not your own Government?'

'Oh, Mr Akat, do you not know Italian politics? My Government will not 'elp because they 'ave done a deal with the Germans over the wine lake. Italian farmers to carry on producing subsidized wine which nobody wants, in exchange for the new regulations on chemical dumping. There are three 'undred thousand Italian wine producers and only one Mondelli. You are a politician, you know 'ow such numbers add up.'

Mondelli refrained from adding that he had complicated matters notoriously by running off with a young television actress from Naples while still married to the sister of the Italian Minister of Finance. He was now greeted in Rome with as much warmth as a coachload of English soccer fans.

'Very sad, Signor Mondelli, I feel for you. But surely this is an Italian matter.'

'It is a European matter, Signor Akat. The bureaucrats act in the name of Europe. They overstretch themselves. And you and the British are well known for being the best and most strong opponents of interfering bureaucrats in Brussels. So I ask you, for consideration. For 'elp. Stop the directive. The Environment Commissioner in Brussels. 'E is English. Your friend, eh?'

'You might say that . . .'

'A nice man – a little weak, perhaps. Too easily led astray by 'is officials. But nice.'

'You might say that, too . . .'

'I understand 'e wishes you to reappoint 'im when 'is term of office expires. 'E will listen to you.'

It was true, of course, every word.

'You might conclude that, Signor Mondelli, but I couldn't possibly comment.'

'Prime Minister, I could not describe 'ow grateful I would be.'

This was not accurate. Urquhart knew from his Party Chairman that Mondelli had described precisely how grateful he wished to be. He had suggested one hundred thousand pounds, paid to party funds. 'In recognition of a great internationalist', as he had put it. Stamper had thought himself very skilful in bringing such a prize to the party; Urquhart was about to disillusion him.

'I'm afraid I cannot help you, Signor Mondelli.'

'Ah, your British sense of 'umour.' He did not sound as if he appreciated it.

Urquhart's expression suggested he'd been weaned on pickles. 'Your personal problems are really something for the Italian authorities to sort out. You must understand that.'

'I will be ruined . . .'

'A great pity.'

'But I thought . . .' The Italian threw a beseeching look at Stamper, who shrugged his shoulders. 'I thought you could 'elp me.'

'I cannot help you, Signor Mondelli, not as an Italian citizen. Not directly.'

Mondelli was tearing at his black tie and his eyes seemed to bulge still further in consternation.

'However, in the serious circumstances perhaps I can share something with you. The British Government, too, is unenthusiastic about the Brussels proposals. In our own interest, you understand. If it were left entirely up to me, I would veto the whole scheme.' The orchestra were beginning to reassemble in the pit, and a buzz of expectation began to rise around the opera house.

'Unfortunately,' Urquhart continued, 'this is one of but a number of issues we have to negotiate with our European partners and with the Commissioners, even the British ones. There will be give and take. And we have so many distractions on the home front. Times are likely to get tough, very distracting.'

'My entire business is at stake, Prime Minister. Either the regulations go under, or I do.'

'As serious as that?'

'Yes!'

'Well, it would be a happy coincidence if my Government's interests were to coincide with your own.'

'I would be so grateful . . .'

'If I were in your position, Signor Mondelli, facing ruin . . .' – he paused to sniff the air, like a prowling wolf – 'I think I should be ten-fold grateful.'

Urquhart gave a perfunctory laugh to suggest light-heartedness, but the Italian had understood. Urquhart had led him to the edge of the cliff and made him peer over; now he offered a lifeline. Mondelli stopped to consider for a few moments, and when he spoke there was no alarm left in his voice. They were no longer talking lifeline, but business. The sum represented around two per cent of his annual profit – significant, but affordable. And his accountants might find a way to write it off against tax as an overseas investment. He nodded his head slowly.

'As you say, Signor Akat, I would indeed be grateful. Ten- fold.'

Urquhart appeared not to have heard, as if he were pursuing his own idea quite separately from the Italian. 'You know, it's about time we had another shot at putting Brussels back in its box. I think this might be just the issue to do it on. There are several British companies who would suffer . . .'

'I would like to 'elp your campaigning activities.'

'Oh, really? Talk to Stamper, he's the man. Nothing to do with me.'

'I 'ave already told 'im that I think you are a great internationalist.'

'Most kind. It really has been a splendid evening.'

'Yes. But I am not a great lover of opera, Prime Minister.' He was massaging his thighs again. 'You would excuse me if I did not stay for the second 'alf?'

'But Stamper here has paid for the tickets . . .'

''E 'as paid for the tickets, but I believe I 'ave paid for my freedom.' The bow tie hung limply down his chest.

'Then goodnight to you, Signor Mondelli. It has been a pleasure.'

Stamper offered words of rueful admiration as the bulk of the Italian benefactor disappeared through the door, then Elizabeth Urquhart was with them once more, wafting perfume and muttering something about attending a reception for the cast after the opera was finished. Urquhart heard scarcely a word. His fighting fund had been opened and the wind had started blowing in his direction yet again. But even as he felt the satisfaction wash over him, he dared not forget that winds in politics rarely blow fair for long. He mustn't let this one blow out of control, if he did it would form a whirlwind of destruction, probably his own. But if they blew strong enough, and long enough, perhaps it was possible after all. By March. As the cymbals clashed to announce the commencement of the second act, he sat back in his seat and gazed at the ceiling. The cherub bottoms reminded him of someone, an undergraduate, on a Chesterfield. He couldn't recall her name.

The Leader of the Opposition was an earnest man, the son of a crofting family from the Western Isles of Scotland. He was not noted for his sense of humour, the peat moors of the Western Isles being too dour to encourage frivolity, but even his rivals acknowledged his dedication and hard work. Government Ministers privately acknowledged he made an excellent Leader of the Opposition, while in public providing every assistance to ensure he continued in this well-fitting job. At times it appeared as if the inevitable pressure on him came more from within his own ranks than from his political opponents; there had been several press stories in recent days suggesting that, following the narrow election defeat of the previous year and the arrival of a fresh face in Downing Street, his party was getting restless and his position coming under threat. The stories were vague and thin, tending to feed off each other as much as on hard views, but *The Times* seemed to have a particularly strong handle on it and had quoted one 'senior party source' as suggesting that 'the party leadership is not a retirement job for losers'. It was more a rumble than a revolution, the polls still pointed to the Opposition having a four-point lead, yet political parties always find difficulty in containing the swirling personal ambitions of its also-rans and, as one editorial had put it, there was no smoke without someone lighting a few matches. So Gordon McKillin had welcomed the opportunity to clear the air on a popular current affairs programme which pitted politician against three leading journalists.

For most of the forty minutes the programme had been uneventful, a little dull even, certainly unsuccessful from the point of view of the producer, whose own job security depended on the regular spillage of someone else's blood. McKillin had parried every thrust with skill and patience – none of the supposed opponents had been identified, he suggested, the real issue was not his leadership but the looming recession which threatened millions of jobs. It was the Prime Minister's job under threat, not his. The story of his troubles had been whipped up by the press, he argued, casting a baleful eye in the direction of Bryan Brynford-Jones, whose journal had published the first and most dramatic report. 'Are you able to name a single one of your sources for this story?' he challenged. The editor, unaccustomed to being in the firing line, quickly moved the discussion on.

Scarcely two minutes remained before the wrap and, much to the producer's despair, the discussion had become stranded in the marshy fields of the Opposition's environmental credentials. It was Brynford-Jones' turn once again. McKillin smiled generously, as a farmer might eye a prize hog on market day. He was enjoying it.

'Mr McKillin, let me turn in the short time we have left to a more personal question.' Brynford-Jones was toying with some form of brochure. 'You are an elder of the Wee Free Church of Scotland, are you not?'

The politician nodded sagely.

'Now the Church has just published a pamphlet – I have it here – which is entitled "Towards the Twenty First

Century: A Moral Guide for Youth". It's fairly wide-ranging and contains, in my view, some excellent prescriptions. But there is one section which intrigued me. On page . . . fourteen, it reaffirms its attitude to homosexuality, which it describes as "a pernicious sin". Do you, Mr McKillin, believe homosexuality is a pernicious sin?'

The politician swallowed. 'I'm not sure this is the right time to get into this sort of complex and difficult discussion. This is, after all, a programme on politics rather than the Church—'

'But it's a relevant question, nonetheless,' Brynford-Jones interrupted. 'A simple one, too. Do you hold homosexuality to be a sin?'

A small bead of sweat had begun to gather in the politician's sideburn, only just perceptible to the professional eye of the producer, who began to brighten.

'I find it difficult to imagine how to respond to such a broad-ranging question as that on a programme like this—'

'Let me help you, then. Imagine your dreams have been fulfilled and you are Prime Minister, at the Dispatch Box, and I'm the Leader of the Opposition. I'm asking you a direct question. Do you believe homosexuality to be evil, a sin? I think the accepted parliamentary phrase goes: "Since the question is a very simple one, which even he should be able to understand, a simple yes or no will suffice".'

All those present and several million viewers recognized the phrase, McKillin's own, which he had used so frequently in taunting Urquhart at Question Time. It was his own hook. The bead of sweat was beginning to trickle.

'Let me rephrase it, if you like,' the editor encouraged. 'Do you believe your kirk's moral guidance is wrong?'

McKillin struggled for his words. How could he explain, in an atmosphere like this, that it had been his kirk's guidance which since his earliest days had fuelled the desire to help others and to mount his own crusade, giving him a clear personal creed on which he had based his political beliefs and guiding him through the moral cesspits around Westminster, that as an elder he had to accept his kirk's

478

teachings with an open heart and without question or compromise. He understood sin and others' weaknesses and could accept them, but his faith would not permit him to deny them.

'I am an elder of the Kirk, Mr Brynford-Jones. Of course I accept my church's teachings, as an individual soul. But as a politician such matters can be more complicated—'

'Let me be clear, *absolutely* clear. You accept your church's edict on this matter?'

'As an individual, I must. But allow me to—'

It was too late. The end credits were already rolling and the signature music beginning to flood the studio. Several million viewers had to struggle to discern Brynford-Jones' sign-off. 'Thank you, Mr McKillin. I'm afraid that's all we have time for. It's been a fascinating forty minutes.' He smiled. 'We are grateful to you.'

Kenny and Mycroft had watched the evening news in silence. It had contained a factual report of McKillin's interview, and also of the volcanic response. The Opposition Leader's office was said to be in the process of issuing a statement of clarification, but it was inevitably too late. Leaders of rival church groups had already opined, gay campaigners had assailed, his own Front Bench transport spokesman had stated boldly that on this issue his leader was utterly, miserably and inexcusably wrong. 'Is there a leadership crisis?' he had been asked. 'There is now,' had been his response.

There was no need for the newspapers to keep their sources anonymous any longer, the protesters were tripping over themselves in the rush to denounce bigotry, medieval morality and cant. Even those who agreed with McKillin had been of no help, a leading anti-gay campaigner being dragged from obscurity to demand in venomous tones that McKillin sack all homosexual MPs in his party or be branded a hypocrite.

Kenny switched off the television. Mycroft sat silently for some time, slumped amongst bean bags piled in front of the screen, while Kenny quietly prepared two mugs of hot coffee, laced with brandy out of miniatures smuggled back from one of his trips. He had seen it all before, the outrage, the alarm, the invective, the inevitable suspicion it brought. He could also see how upset was Mycroft. The older man had seen none of this before, not from this angle.

'God, I'm confused,' Mycroft eventually muttered, biting his lip. He was still staring at the blank screen, unwilling to look directly into Kenny's eyes. 'All this fuss, this talk about rights. I just can't help remembering that odious man Marples dragging along the young boy. Didn't the boy have rights, too?'

'All queers tarred with the same brush, eh?'

'I sometimes ask myself what the hell I'm doing. What does it all mean for my job, for me. You know, I still can't identify, join the club, not when I see men like Marples and some of those militants jumping up and down on the screen.'

'I'm gay, David. A queer. A faggot. A fairy queen. Nancy boy. Poof. Call it what you like, that's what I am. You saying you can't identify with me?'

'I'm . . . not very good at this, am I? All my life I've been brought up to conform, to believe that such things are . . . Christ, Kenny, half of me agrees with McKillin. Being a queer is wrong! Yet, and yet . . .' He raised troubled eyes to look directly at his partner. 'I've had more happiness in the last few weeks than I ever thought possible.'

'That's gay, David.'

'Then I suppose I must be, Kenny. I must be. Gay. Because I think I love you.'

'Then forget about all that crap.' Kenny waved angrily in the direction of the television. 'Let the rest of the world go mount their own soap boxes and get splinters in their dicks, we don't have to join them in slagging off everybody else. Love's meant to be inside, private, not open bloody warfare on every street corner.' He looked earnestly at Mycroft. 'I don't want to lose you, David. Don't go getting guilty on me.'

'If McKillin is right, we may never get to heaven.'

'If heaven's full of people who are so utterly stinking miserable, who can't even accept what they are or what they feel, then I don't think I want to join. So why don't we just stick with what we've got here, you and me, and be happy.'

'For how long, Kenny?'

'For as long as we've got, old love.'

'For as long as they leave us alone, you mean.'

'Some people come to the edge of the cliff and they look over, then run away in fear. They never realize it's possible to fly, to soar away, to be free. They spend their lives crawling along cliff tops without ever finding the courage. Don't spend your life crawling, David.'

Mycroft gave a weak smile. 'I never knew you were poetic.'

'Until now I never knew I cared so much for you.'

Slowly, Mycroft lifted his coffee mug in salutation. 'A toast, Kenny. To jumping off cliff tops?'

Slowly and with agonizing care, the rifle sight lined up on its target exactly twenty-five yards away, the head of Gordon McKillin, embossed upon one of his old campaign posters. Slowly, steadily, the finger squeezed, and there was a sharp retort as the .22-calibre bullet sped on its way. A perfect hole appeared exactly where the Opposition Leader's mouth had been, before the badly peppered target disintegrated and fluttered like orphaned pieces of tissue to the floor.

'Don't make campaign posters like they used to.'

'Nor Leaders of the Opposition.'

Urquhart and Stamper enjoyed their joke. Directly beneath the dining room of the House of Lords in a low, wood-lined cellar strewn with the piping, conduits and other architectural entrails of the Palace of Westminster, the two men lay side by side in the narrow rifle range where parliamentarians retreat to vent their murderous instincts on paper targets rather than each other. It was where Churchill had practised his gunnery in preparation for the expected German invasion, vowing to fight it personally and to the last from behind the sandbags at the top of Downing Street. And it was where Urquhart practised for Question Time, freed from the inhibitions of Madam Speaker's censorious stare.

'A stroke of luck yours, coming up with that church pamphlet,' Stamper acknowledged somewhat grudgingly, adjusting the leather wrist sling which supported the heavy bolt-action target rifle. He was a much less experienced shot than Urquhart, and had never beaten him.

'The Colquhouns are a rather exotic tribe, members of which descend upon Elizabeth from time to time bearing all sorts of strange gifts. One of them thought I would be interested in the morality of youth, strange man. It wasn't luck, Tim. Simply good breeding.'

The former estate agent glowered. 'You want to shoot any more?' he enquired, placing another bullet in the chamber.

'Tim, I want a veritable war.' Urquhart raised the rifle to his well-padded shoulder once more, peering fixedly down the telescopic sight. 'I've decided. It's on again.'

'Another of your campus jokes.'

Urquhart obliterated a further paper portrait before turning to Stamper. His smile was withering.

'McKillin's in trouble. He went out on a limb, and it broke. So sad.'

'We're not ready, Francis. It's too soon,' Stamper objected, deeply unconvinced.

'The Opposition will be even less well prepared. Parties facing an election are like tourists being pursued by a man-eating lion. You don't have to outrun the lion – you can't. All you have to do is make sure you run faster than the other bastard.'

'The country might be buried under a foot of snow at this time of year.'

'Great! We've got more vehicles with four-wheel drive than they have.'

'But we're still four points behind in the polls,' the Party Chairman protested.

'Then there's no time to lose. Six weeks, Tim. Let's get a grip on them. A major policy announcement every week. A high profile foreign trip, the new PM taking Moscow or Washington by storm. Let's have a row in Europe, demand some money back. I want dinner with every friendly editor in Fleet Street, on his own, while you tickle the political correspondents. And, if we can get away with it, a cut in interest rates. Castrate a few criminals. Get a bandwagon rolling. We've got McKillin on the floor, let's be sure to kick hell out of him while he's down. No prisoners, Tim. Not for the next six weeks.'

'Let's hope His Majesty decides to cooperate this time.' Stamper couldn't hide his scepticism.

'You're right. I've been thinking we should take a new approach to the Palace. Build a few bridges. Put your ear to the ground, find out what the gossip is. What's going on in the dark places.'

Stamper cocked an ear, as if he heard the sound of prey lumbering through the forest.

'And we need foot soldiers, Tim. Loyal, dedicated. Not too bright. Men who would be happy to charge across those bridges, should the need arise.'

'That does sound like war.'

'Better win it, old boy. Or they'll be putting us up there as targets. And I'm not talking about paper images, either.'

The gravel of the long drive leading from the gate lodge to the front of the old manor house rattled against the bodywork of the car as it drew up alongside the other vehicles. The polished dark-blue Rolls-Royce seemed out of place alongside the battered Land-Rovers and muddy estate cars, and Landless already knew he would not fit in. He didn't mind, he was used to it. The manor house was the ancestral home of Mickey, Viscount Quillington, and commanded magnificent views over the rolling countryside of Oxfordshire, although a grey January afternoon was not the best of settings. The fabric of the building charted the chaotic progress of an ancient aristocratic family and was mostly William and Mary or Victorian with a hint of Tudor in the wing nearest the tiny chapel, but of the twentieth century there was little sign.

The damp seemed to follow him into the rough and tumble of the large entrance hall filled with tangled hunting dogs, mucky Wellington boots and a variety of anoraks and outer garments all struggling to dry. The floor tiles were badly chipped and there was not a hint of central-heating anywhere. It was the type of house which in many other parts had been rescued from decay by an expanding Japanese hotel group or golf-course consortium, but not here, not yet. He was glad he had declined the invitation to stay the night.

The Quillingtons traced their line back to the time when one of their ancestors had travelled to Ireland with Cromwell, collected his estates for bloody services rendered, and returned to England at the time of the Restoration to make a second fortune. It was a fine history, on which the current generation of Quillingtons, impoverished by time, misfortune and inadequate tax planning, reflected with awe. The estates had gradually been whittled away, the ties with Ireland finally broken, many of the paintings sold, the best pieces of furniture and silver auctioned, the large staff pared. This was old money, and it was growing increasingly short.

Meeting the other guests proved something of a trial for the businessman. They were all old friends, some dating from nursery days and displaying the type of public school clannishness boys from Bethnal Green find impossible to penetrate. His clothes hadn't helped. 'Country casual' he'd been told. He had turned up in a check two-piece with waistcoat and brown shoes; they were all wearing jeans. Not until Princess Charlotte greeted him warmly did he begin to feel less defensive.

The weekend had been built around the Princess Arranged by Quillington's younger brother, David, it was an opportunity for her to relax amongst old friends away from the petty intrigues of London's socialites and gossip columnists. Here they were almost all scions of old families, some older than the Windsors, and to them she was a friend with a job to do, still the 'Beany' of childhood squabbles in the swimming pool and fancy-dress parties organized by po-faced nannies. She had insisted on a private bedroom well away from other guests and David had seen to all the arrangements, tidying the two detectives and chauffeur of the Royal Protection Group well away at the back of the house. The Princess had the Chinese Room, not so much a suite but more a single vast room on the first floor of the East Wing, with David occupying the only other bedroom on the floor. Her privacy was ensured.

There was a certain sadness in surveying the house with its ancient wiring, frayed edges, dank corners and one wing almost completely closed down, yet it had character and a great sense of history, and the dining room was magnificent Fifty feet long, oak-panelled, lit by two fern-like chandeliers whose lights shone deep into a burnished table constructed from the timbers of an old Man o' War and crafted by prisoners from Napoleon's navy. The silver was old and monogrammed, the crystal assorted, the effect timeless. Old money, even in short supply, certainly knew

485

how to eat. Quillington presided at the head of the table, on his right the Princess and on his left Landless, with others further down, and they listened politely to the publisher's stories of City life as their ancestors might have listened to explorer's tales of the South Sea islands.

After dinner they took their port and cognac into the Old Library, where the ceiling was high and the winter air clung tenaciously to the far corners, where leather-clad books were piled along endless shelves and smoke-darkened oil paintings covered the one free wall. Landless thought he could see marks on the wall where paintings had been removed, presumably for auction, with the remainder spread around a little more thinly. The furniture seemed as old as any part of the house. One of the two large sofas crowding around the roaring log fire was covered in a car rug to hide the ravages of age, while the other stood battered and naked, its dark-green fabric torn by the insistent scratching of dogs, with its stuffing of horse hair dribbling out like candle wax from underneath one of the cushions. Within the embrace of the Library, dinner guests became almost family and the conversation grew more relaxed and uninhibited.

'Shame about today,' Quillington muttered, kicking the fire with the heel of his leather boot. The fire spat back, sending a shower of sparks up the broad chimney. He was a tall, streaky figure much used to wandering around in tightly tailored jeans, high boots and a broad kangaroo-skin fedora, which looked eccentric if not vaguely ridiculous on a fifty-year-old. Eccentricity was a useful cover for encroaching impoverishment. 'Damned hunt-saboteurs, buzz like flies around horse shit. There they are, on my land, and the police refuse to arrest them or even move them on. Not unless they actually attack someone. God knows what this country is coming to when you can't even prevent layabouts like that rampaging all over your own land. Home a man's damned castle, 'n'all that.'

It had not been a successful day's hunting. The animal-rights protesters had waved their banners and spread their pepper and aniseed, unsettling the horses, confusing the hounds and outraging the huntsmen. It had been a soggy morning overflowing with drizzle, not good for picking up trails, and they had lumbered through the heavy clay of the countryside to find nothing more enthralling than the carcass of a dead cat.

'You can't throw them off your own land?' enquired Landless.

'Not bloody likely. Trespass isn't criminal, police'll do damn-all about it. You can ask them politely to move on, they tell you to piss off. You so much as lay a finger on them and you find yourself in court on assault charges. For protecting your own bloody property.'

'Chalked up one of the yobs, I did,' the Princess intervened gaily. 'Saw him hovering close behind my horse so I backed the beast up. Scared all hell out of him when he saw sixteen hands shunting straight towards him. He jumped back, stumbled, and fell straight into a pile of fresh crap!'

'Bravo, Beany. Filled his pants, I hope,' David Quillington interjected. 'You hunt, Mr Landless?'

'Only in the City.'

'You should try it sometime. See the countryside at its best.'

Landless doubted that. He had arrived in time to find the stragglers returning from the hunt, faces red and blotched, covered in mud and thoroughly soaked. Mix in the sight of a fox being torn apart, its entrails smeared over the ground and squelched beneath horses' hooves, and he thought he could well do without such pleasures. Anyway, boys born and brought up in concrete tower-blocks surrounded by broken street lamps and derelict cars tend to have a naive empathy for the countryside and the things that live in it. He hadn't seen any of England's green and pleasant pastures until a school day-trip when he was thirteen and, in truth, he held an undemanding admiration for the fox.

'Foxes are vermin,' the younger Quillington continued. 'Attack chickens, ducks, new-born lambs, even sick calves. Scrounge off city rubbish dumps and spread disease. It's too easy to knock the landowners but, I tell you, without their work in protecting the countryside, keeping it clear of pests like foxes, rebuilding the walls and hedgerows, planting woodlands for fox and pheasant cover – all at their own expense – those protesters would have a lot less countryside to protest about.'

Landless noticed that the younger Quillington, seated on the sofa next to the Princess, was moderate both in his language and his drinking. That could not be said of his brother, leaning against the Adam fireplace, glass in hand. 'Under threat. Everything under threat, you know. They trample over your land, shouting, screaming like Dervishes, waving their banners and blowing their bloody horns, trying to pull the hounds onto busy roads and railway lines. Even when they manage to get themselves arrested some damned fool magistrate takes pity on them. And me, because I've got land, because my family have worked it for generations, devoted themselves to the local community, done their bit for the country in the House of Lords, because I've tried so hard and got no bloody money left and nothing but bills and bank letters to read, I'm supposed to be a parasite!'

'There's no sense of proportion anymore,' the Princess agreed. 'Take my family. Used to be held in respect. Nowadays journalists are more interested in what goes on in the bedroom than the State Room.'

Landless noticed the exchange of looks between the Princess and the younger Quillington. It was not their first. They had begun the evening sitting well apart at opposite ends of the sofa, but they seemed to have drawn ever closer, like magnets.

'Absolutely, Beany. They know you can't defend yourself so they lay into you without pity,' Mickey continued from his position by the fire. 'We've all worked damned hard for what little we have. Yet they get at the fox-hunting, they attack the landowners, they undermine the hereditary principle, and the next thing you know we're a sodding republic. It's about time we started sticking up for ourselves, stopped taking it on the chin and turning the other cheek.'

Charlotte had finished her glass and was holding it out towards the younger Quillington for a refill. 'But, Mickey,

I can't, none of my lot can. The Family's supposed to be
the silent service.' She turned to Landless. 'What do you
think, Benjamin?'

'I'm a businessman, not a politician,' he protested coyly,
but checked himself. She had offered him a chance to break
into their tight circle of concerns, there was no point in
turning it down. 'Very well, take a lesson from the politician's book. If a Minister wants something said but finds
it injudicious to say it himself, he gets somebody else to
do the talking. A fellow MP, a business leader, a newspaper editor even. You have friends, influential friends.
Like Lord Quillington here, with a voice and seat in the
House of Lords.'

'Slave labour, rowing the Government's galley, that's all
they reckon we are,' Quillington sniffed.

'And so you shall remain if you don't speak up for yourselves,' Landless warned.

'Sounds like mutiny,' his brother said from the drinks
table, 'taking on the Government.'

'So what? You've got nothing to lose. Better than staying
silent simply in order to be abused. Remember what they
tried with the King's speech? You're in the same firing
line.'

'Never did have any time for that Urquhart,' Quillington
muttered into his brandy balloon.

'The press wouldn't report it anyway,' his brother commented, handing a full glass back to the Princess. When
he sat down, Landless noticed he had drawn even closer
to her. Their hands were side by side on the car rug.

'Some press would,' Landless interjected.

'Benjamin, of course, *you're* a darling,' Charlotte said
soothingly, 'but all the rest of them are interested in is a
photograph of me with my dress blown up around my ears
so they can gossip about where I buy my knickers.'

It was not an entirely accurate picture, mused Landless.
The press were mostly interested in where she left her
underwear, not where she bought it.

'Shouldn't give honours to press men,' Mickey continued. 'Particularly peerages. Clouds their objectivity.
Makes them too damned self-important.'

Landless didn't feel insulted; rather, he felt as if slowly they were beginning to offer him acceptance, setting aside the fact that he was born to a different world.

'You know, perhaps you're right,' Quillington continued. 'Hell, about the only right they allow us nowadays is to get on our hind legs in the Lords, and it's about time we started using it properly. You know, making the Lords and the hereditary principle the first line of defence for you and yours, Beany.'

'If you've anything you want to say, I'll make sure it gets an outing,' Landless offered. 'Just like we did with the Christmas speech.'

'I think we've hit on a damned fine idea, Beany,' Quillington said. Already he was beginning to expropriate the idea for his own. 'Anything you want said, I'll say it for you. If the King can't make a public speech, then I'll make it for him. Into the public record on the floor of the Lords. We mustn't let them gag us.' He nodded in self-approval. 'Sorry you can't stay the night, Landless,' he continued. 'Plenty of other ideas I'd like to try on you.' The conversion was complete. 'Some other time, eh?'

Landless understood the hint and glanced at his watch. 'Time I was going,' he offered, and rose to his feet to make his rounds of farewell.

He would be glad to get out into the fresh air. He didn't belong here, not with these people: no matter how polite they were and no matter how successful he became, he would never belong. They wouldn't allow it. He might have purchased a ticket to the dinner table, but he could never buy his way into the club. He didn't mind, he didn't care to join. This was yesterday, not tomorrow. Anyway, he'd look ridiculous on a horse. But he had no regrets. As he glanced behind him from the door, he could see his host standing by his fireplace, dreaming of chivalrous battles yet to come on the floor of the House of Lords. And he could see the Princess and the younger Quillington, already anticipating the disappearance of the outsider, holding hands on the sofa. There were stories here aplenty, with patience. It had been worth it.

490

The House of Commons attendant entered the gentlemen's lavatory in search of his quarry. He had an urgent message for Tom Worthington, a Labour MP from what used to be a mining constituency in Derbyshire before they closed the mines, who prided himself on his working-class origins in spite of the fact that it had been more than twenty years since anything other than ink and ketchup had stained his hands. The lavatory was inescapably Victorian with fine antique tiles and porcelain, sullied only by an electric hot-air drier at which Jeremy Colthorpe, an ageing and notoriously pompous Member from the pretentious shires, was drying his hands.

'By chance seen Mr Worthington, sir?' the attendant enquired.

'Can only handle one shit at a time in here, my man,' Colthorpe responded through his nose. 'Try one of the bars. In some corner under a table, most likely.'

The attendant scurried off as Colthorpe was joined at the wash basins by the only other man in the room, Tim Stamper.

'Timothy, dear boy. Enjoying party headquarters? Making an excellent job of it, if you don't mind my saying.'

Stamper turned from the basin and lowered his head in appreciation, but there was no warmth. Colthorpe was known for his airs, purporting to be a leader of local society, yet he'd married into every penny, which only made him still more condescending towards former estate agents. Classlessness was a concept Colthorpe would never support, having spent most of his life trying to escape from its clutches.

'Glad for a chance to speak with you actually, old chap,' Colthorpe was saying, his smile more a simper as he searched keenly in the corners of the mirror for reassurance that he and Stamper were alone in the echoing room. 'Confidentially, man to man,' he continued, trying to glance surreptitiously beneath the doors of the cubicles.

'What's on your mind, Jeremy?' Stamper responded, mindful that during all of his years in the House Colthorpe had never done more than pass the time of day with him.

'Lady wife. Getting on a bit, seventy next year. And not

in the best of health. Brave gal, but finding it more than ever difficult to help in the constituency – it's damned large, forty-three villages, don't you know, takes some getting round, I can tell you.' He moved over towards Stamper at the basins and started washing his hands for the second time, trying to evince confidentiality but clearly ill at ease. 'Owe it to her to take off some of the pressure, spend a little more time together. No way of telling how long she may have.' He paused while he worked up a considerable lather as if he were always meticulous about hygiene and to emphasize the depth of his concern for his wife. Both effects were wasted on Stamper who, when Deputy Chief Whip, had seen Colthorpe's private file, which included reference to the regular payments he made to a single mother who used to tend bar in his local pub.

'To be frank, I'm thinking of giving up my seat at the next election. For her sake, of course. But it'd be a damnable pity to see all that experience I've gained over the years go to waste. Would love to find some way of . . . still being able to contribute, don't you know. To go on doing my bit for the country. And the party, of course.'

'What did you have in mind, Jeremy?' Stamper already knew precisely where the conversation was headed.

'Open to suggestion. But obviously the Lords would seem a sensible option. Not for me, so much, but for the little lady. Mean a lot to her after all these years. Particularly when . . . you know, she might not have very long to enjoy it.'

Colthorpe was still splashing water around to make a pretence at casualness and had succeeded in drenching the front of his trousers. He realized he was beginning to make a fool of himself and turned the taps off with a savage twist, turning directly towards Stamper, hands by his side, water dripping from his soaked cuffs. 'Would I have your support, Tim? The backing of the party machine?'

Stamper turned away and headed for the electric hand dryer, its harsh noise forcing Colthorpe to follow him across the room, and them both to raise their voices.

'There will be quite a few colleagues retiring at the next

election, Jeremy. I expect a number of them will want a seat in the Lords.'

'Wouldn't press my own case, but for the wife. I'd work hard at the job, wouldn't skive off like so many of the others.'

'Ultimately, of course, it's up to Francis. He'll have a tough job deciding between the various claims.'

'I voted for Francis . . .' – that was a lie – 'I'd be loyal.'

'Would you?' Stamper threw over his shoulder. 'Francis does value loyalty above everything.'

'Absolutely. Anything the two of you want, rely on me!'

The hand drier suddenly ceased its raucous huffing and in a moment the atmosphere had grown hushed, almost confessional. Stamper turned to stare at Colthorpe from only a few inches away.

'Can we really rely on you, Jeremy? Loyalty first?'

Colthorpe was nodding.

'Even as far as the King is concerned?'

'The King . . . ?' Confusion crept in.

'Yes, Jeremy, the King. You've already seen how he's rocked the boat. And Francis fears it's going to get worse. The Palace needs reminding, very firmly, who's in charge.'

'But I'm not sure . . .'

'Loyalty, Jeremy. That's what will make the difference between those who get what they want out of this Government, and those who don't. It's an unpleasant business, this thing with the Palace, but somebody has to stand up and defend the important constitutional principles at stake. Francis can't, you see, not formally and publicly as Prime Minister. That would create a constitutional crisis, which he absolutely does not want. The only way to avoid that may be to get someone other than a Minister, someone with great seniority and authority – someone like you, Jeremy – to remind the Palace and the public what's at stake. It's the least Francis has a right to expect from his loyal supporters.'

'Yes, but . . . Get into the House of Lords by attacking the King?'

'Not attacking. Reminding him of the highest constitutional principles.'

'But it's the King who creates new peers—'

'Solely and exclusively on the advice of the Prime Minister. The King cannot refuse his recommendations.'

'It's a little like *Alice In Wonderland*—'

'So's a lot of what the Palace has been saying.'

'I'd like to think about it a little.'

'You need to think about loyalty?' Stamper's tone was harsh, accusatory. His lip curled in contempt and there was fire in the sepulchral eyes. Without a further word the Party Chairman turned on his heel and made his way towards the door. His hand was already on the shiny brass door knob, and Colthorpe realized his ambitions were ruined if the door closed on this conversation.

'I'll do it!' he squealed. 'Tim, I know where my loyalties lie. I'll do it.' He was breathing heavily with the tension and confusion, trying to regain his self-control, wiping his hands on his trousers. 'You can rely on me, old chap.'

Stamper held his stare, spreading his lips in the coldest of smiles. Then he closed the door behind him.

The lunch had started excellently. Both Mickey Quillington and his first cousin, Lord Chesholm of Kinsale, appreciated a good claret and the cellar of the House of Lords dining room had a large number from which to choose. They had chosen to drink Leoville-Barton but were unable to decide between the '82 and '85 vintage. So they had ordered a bottle of both and slipped gently into mid-afternoon in the warm embrace of the elegant mahogany panelling and attentive staff. Chesholm was a good twenty years older than Quillington and substantially more wealthy, and the impecunious younger peer had hoped to use the lunch for the launch of an appeal to family solidarity which would involve his relative in leasing several hundred of Quillington's Oxfordshire acres at a generous rate, but sadly his tactics had gone awry. The claret proved too much for the elderly peer to manage and he couldn't concentrate, repeatedly exclaiming that he didn't live in Oxfordshire. The bill, although heavily subsidized, still reflected the exceptional nature of the wine and Quillington felt bruised. Maybe the old bugger would regain his wits by teatime.

494

They were attending the House to voice objection to a Bill which sought a total ban on fox-hunting, and the debate was well underway by the time they took their places on the deep-red morocco benches in the Gothic chamber. Within minutes Chesholm was asleep while Quillington slouched with his knees tucked beneath his chin as he listened with growing resentment to a former polytechnic lecturer, recently elevated to the life-peerage for his diligence in the study of trade union matters, expounding his belief in the decay and corruption of those who still believed they owned the countryside as if by divine right. Debates in the Lords are conducted in far less pompous and vitriolic style than in the Lower Chamber, as befits its aristocratic and almost familial atmosphere, but the lack of outright rudeness did not prevent the peer from putting across his point of view forcefully and effectively. From around the Chamber, uncharacteristically packed for the occasion by hereditary peers and noble backwoodsmen from distant rural parts, came a growl of wounded pride, like a stuck boar at bay. Such displays of emotion are not commonplace in the Upper Chamber, but such a concentration of hereditary peers was also unusual outside the circumstance of state funeral or Royal wedding. It may not have been the Lords at their norm, nor even at their best, but it was certainly their Lordships at their most decorous.

Quillington cleared his throat; the debate was threatening to spoil the warm glow left by the claret. The poly-peer had broadened his attack from fox-hunting itself to those who hunted, and Quillington took great exception. He was not the type of person who rode roughshod over others' rights; he'd never forced any farm labourer out of a tied cottage, and any damage inadvertently caused while hunting was always paid for. Blast the man, the Quillingtons had been dedicated custodians. It had cost them their fortune and his father's health and had left his mother with little but years of tearful widowhood. Yet here was an oaf who had spent all his working life in some overheated lecture room living off an inflation-proofed salary, accusing him of being no better than a scrounger. It was too much, really too bloody much. This sort of wheedling and insolent insinuation had gone on for too long, harking back to a style of class warfare which was fifty years out of date.

''Bout time we put them in their place, don't you think, Chesy?' Almost before he realized it, Quillington was on his feet.

'This debate is only nominally about fox-hunting, that is merely the excuse. Behind it lies an insidious attack on the traditions and values which have not only held our countryside together, not only held this House together, but have held the whole of society together. There are wreckers in the land, some maybe even amongst our number here' – he deliberately avoided looking at the previous speaker, so that everyone would know precisely whom he meant – 'who in the name of democracy would force their own narrow, militant opinions upon the rest, the silent majority which is the true and glorious backbone of Britain.'

He licked his lips, there was a flush in his cheeks, a mixture of Leoville-Barton and real emotion that succeeded in engulfing the unease he customarily felt in public, which on more than one occasion had left him tongue-tied and floundering at the opening of the annual village fête. 'They want revolution, no less. They would abandon our traditions, abolish this Chamber, stamp on our rights.' Quillington waved a finger at the canopied Throne which dominated one end of the hall and stood empty and forlorn. 'They even seek to reduce to silence and insignificance our own Royal Family.'

Several of Their Lordships raised a collective eyebrow. The rules about discussion of the Royal Family were very restrictive, particularly in a debate on blood sports. 'To the point, my Lord,' one growled in warning.

'But, noble Lords, this *is* the point,' protested Quillington. 'We are not here to rubber-stamp what comes from the Lower House. We are here to offer counsel, advice, warning. And we do so, just as the Monarch does, because we represent the true long-term interests of this country. We represent the values which have made our nation great over previous centuries and which will continue to guide her well into the next century. We are not here to be swayed by every passing fashion and fad. We do not suffer from the corruption of having to get ourselves elected, of having to pretend that we are all things to all men, of making promises we know we cannot keep. We are here to represent what is immutable and constant in society.'

Mutters of 'Hear, hear' could be heard from the crowded benches around Quillington. The Lord Chancellor drummed his fingers as he concentrated in bewigged and ermined splendour from his seat on the Woolsack; the speech was most unusual, but really rather a splendid entertainment.

'It may seem a long way from the plottings of hunt-saboteurs to assaults on Buckingham Palace, but what we have seen of both recently should encourage us to stand firm in our beliefs, not to run for the cover of undergrowth like terrified vermin.' His long, thin arms were extended theatrically away from his body, as if trying to haul in their sympathy. He needn't have bothered, peers were beginning to nod and tap their knees to indicate support. 'Both this House and the Royal Family are here to defend those timeless aspects of the national interest, unfettered by the selfishness of The Other Place. There is no need for this House to kowtow to the muscle and money of commercial interests!' The poly-peer was sitting upright, ready to try and intervene. He was sure Quillington was about to go too far. 'Not for us the temptations of bribing the public with their own money, we are here to defend the public against shortsightedness and falsehood. And at no time is that duty more pressing upon us than when we have a new Cabinet and a Prime Minister who have not even been elected by the people. Let him go to the country promising to castrate the Monarch and abolish the House of Lords if he dare, but until he has won that right and power at an election, let us not allow him to do quietly and privately what he has not yet been able to do publicly.'

The poly-peer had had enough. He was not quite sure what transgression Quillington was making, but the emotional temperature in the Chamber had soared, shouts of support for Quillington were coming from all sides, and the poly-peer suddenly felt the Chamber close in around him like a courtroom dock. 'Order! The noble Lord must restrain himself,' he interjected.

'Why . . . ?' 'No, let him go on . . .' 'Allow him to finish . . .' On all sides Quillington was being offered advice and encouragement, while the poly-peer sprang to his feet, shouting across the Chamber and wagging his finger in vain. Quillington had won, and knew it.

'I have finished, my Lords. Do not forget your duty, nor your allegiance to the King, nor the sacrifices which you and your forefathers accepted in order to make this nation great. Use this wretched Bill to remind others that you have not forgotten, and let the lion roar once more!'

He sat down as peers took their Order Papers and rapped them sharply on the leather benches in front of them to show their approbation.

As Order Papers beat down either side of his head, the elderly Chesholm woke with a start. 'What? What was that? Did I miss something, Mickey?'

'On a Point of Order, Madam Speaker.'

'Point of Order, Mr Jeremy Colthorpe.'

Madam Speaker's shrill voice cut through the din of the House of Commons as MPs milled around preparing to vote after an Opposition debate on sub-standard housing, which had just wound its way through three turbid hours. Normally Madam Speaker was caustic about points of order raised during divisions and, indeed, the ancient rules of the House made such interruptions problematic by requiring the MP to have his head covered – in order better to be seen amidst the confusion, so said the rule book; to deflect idle time-wasters, according to common sense. But Colthorpe was a Member of long standing and not a renowned trouble-maker; he stood defiantly if somewhat absurdly attired in a collapsible opera hat kept in the Chamber for the purpose. Points of order often had an element of comedy to them, and the bustle in the Chamber subsided as MPs strained to hear what was upsetting the old man.

'Madam Speaker, on rare occasions a question of such importance and urgency arises that it is of overriding importance to the business of the House, and you decide it is necessary for the appropriate Minister to be summoned before us to answer for it. I believe this matter is just that.' It was more than that. News of Quillington's speech had drifted through the tea rooms and bars of the House of Commons even as Colthorpe was still chiding himself for making such a nonsense of his exchange with Stamper; he didn't have much practice in grovelling to estate agents, he told himself, and he knew he'd made a hash of it. He had listened to reports of the peer's words like a drowning man greets the sound of an approaching rescue ship, and had bustled off to find Stamper, terrified that someone else would find him first. Within forty minutes he was back in the Chamber, and on his feet.

'Earlier this afternoon, in Another Place, a noble Lord accused this House of political corruption, of seeking to deprive both their Lordships and His Majesty the King of their constitutional rights, and claiming that His Majesty had been improperly silenced. Such a challenge to the actions of this House and to the office of the Prime Minister is such as to—'

'Hold on a minute!' Madam Speaker enjoined Colthorpe to silence in a broad Lancashire accent. 'I've heard nothing about this. Most improper. You know it's against the rules of this House to discuss personal matters relating to the King.'

'This is not a personal matter but a constitutional matter of the highest importance, Madam Speaker. The rights of this House are enshrined in custom and established over the course of many years. When they are challenged, they must be defended.'

'Nevertheless, I want to see what was said before I allow this one to run.' The Speaker waved Colthorpe down but he was not to be deflected.

'We tarry and delay at our peril, Madam Speaker. This is just another example of the interfering, interventionist tendencies of the mod-Monarchy—'

'That's enough!' She was on her feet now, staring furiously over half-moon glasses, demanding Colthorpe subside.

'But Madam Speaker, we must be allowed to respond to attacks made on us, no matter from what source those attacks emanate. The debate in Another Place, ostensibly about fox-hunting, has been turned into a direct assault on this Chamber. Now, Madam Speaker, I don't wish to impugn the integrity of anyone wishing to make such attacks . . .'

She liked the sound of that, and hesitated.

'It is possible, I suppose,' Colthorpe continued, 'to care passionately for the welfare of the nation from the back of a horse while out pursuing foxes.' There was an amused growl of support from the benches around. 'It may even be possible to identify with the plight of the homeless from within the luxury of a palace – indeed, several palaces. It may even be possible, I could not deny it, that being driven around the country in chauffeured limousines and private trains with forty carriages affords a unique insight into the problems of those confined to wheelchairs . . .'

'Forty coaches?' a voice queried. 'What on earth does he need with forty coaches?'

Madam Speaker was on her feet again, lifting onto her toes, trying to give herself added height and authority and angrily pointing her glasses in his direction, but Colthorpe, voice rising in turn, ignored her.

'It may also be possible for those who live entirely off the backs of taxpayers and who pay no tax at all to accuse those who do of greed and selfishness. It is possible, Madam Speaker, but isn't it more likely that this is just another load of the organic fertilizer which gets spread all over the Palace Gardens?'

The Speaker's cries of 'Order! Order!' were lost amidst the instant hubbub. 'If the Honourable Gentleman doesn't resume his seat immediately I shall be forced to name him,' she mouthed, threatening Colthorpe with the procedure that would eject him from Parliament for the rest of the week's business. But already it was too late. As Colthorpe looked towards the press gallery he could see scribes furiously tearing at their notebooks. There would be a posse of them waiting as he left the Chamber. His point had already been made; he would be named in every morning newspaper. 'Order! O-o-o-order!' cried the Speaker. With what he hoped was a bow of great dignity, which caused the opera hat to tumble from his head and roll across the floor, Colthorpe resumed his seat.

Landless was having his hair trimmed when the call came through, and he didn't care for being disturbed at such moments. His secretary thought his reluctance arose from embarrassment because his hairdresser, who visited the businessman once a fortnight at his office, was what she called 'delicate', but Landless didn't mind. Quentin was the only barber he'd ever found who could manage to keep his rope-like hair under control without larding it in hair cream and, besides, the Landless reputation with women was sufficiently beyond dispute to survive contact with an affected queen. In truth the hairdresser was a disgraceful gossip who had a fund of stories about his other fashion-able clients, all of whom seemed to regard him as a father-confessor for their sex lives. Landless never ceased to be intrigued by what others would admit to or fantasize about under the influence of nothing more potent than shampoo and an expert scalp massage. He kept his own mouth shut, and listened. He was engrossed in a fascinating report of what other parts of his body the country's leading romantic soap star shaved, and in what designs, when the whine of the telephone dragged him away.

It was his editor-in-chief, seeking guidance, covering his ass as usual. But Landless didn't object, not on this occasion. This was his story, after all.

'How are the others going to play it?' he growled.

'No one's quite sure. This story's so out of the ordinary.' The issue involved King, Prime Minister, Lords and Commons – the Archbishop wasn't in there yet, but doubtless the *Sun* or *Mirror* would find some connection. Yet it had been raised by two such nonentities – few had heard of Colthorpe, none of Quillington. It was a sensitive issue, perhaps an item on the parliamentary page?

'Any guidance from Downing Street?'

'They're cautious. Clean hands, so they insist. Serious issues which they understand must be reported and all that, but suggest Quillington's a fool and Colthorpe went over the top. They don't want a repeat of what happened before Christmas.'

'But they didn't request we spike it, either?'

'No.'

'Colthorpe tried to shift the argument away from a divided nation to hard cash. Clever – too clever for him on his own. They're flying kites. Trying it out with Colthorpe to see if it gets a fair wind.'

'So what do we do?'

It was not so much that he had promised Quillington, it was more instinct – the instinct of a man who had been used to street-fighting all his life, used to recognizing the difference between shadows that provided cover and those that hid the enemy. He trusted his instincts, and they told him that amongst these shadows there lurked the figure of Francis Urquhart. If Landless threw a little light around, who knows what he might flush out. Anyway, he had a lot of money invested in the Royal Family and there was no dividend in it unless the Royal Family was news. Good, bad, indifferent news, he didn't mind – so long as it was news.

'Splash it. Page One lead.'

'You think it's that big?'

'We make it that big.'

There was agitated breathing on the end of the phone as the editor tried to catch up and comprehend his proprietor's flow of logic. 'Peers Attack Urquhart?' he suggested, practising a few headlines. 'PM Unelected and Unelectable, Say King's Allies?'

'No, you bloody idiot. Six weeks ago we were telling the world what a fine, noble creature he was. From Roger Rabbit to Rasputin in one bound is more than even our readers will swallow. You make it balanced, fair, authoritative. Just make it big.'

'You want to catch the others standing on this one.' It was an assumption, not a question: this was going to be a front page like none of the competition.

'No, not on this one,' Landless responded thoughtfully. 'Spread word around the news room.'

'But that'll mean it will be all through Fleet Street in under an hour.' They both knew there were journalists in the news room taking backhanders for alerting their rivals to what was going on, just as they paid for whispers in the other direction. 'They'll all follow. Think we're up to something, know something they don't. No one will want to be caught out, it'll be used on every front page . . . ?'

'Precisely. This one is going to be a runner, because we're going to make it run. Freely, fairly, in the national interest. Until the time comes for us to climb down off the fence, by which time the noise we make will give our Mr Urquhart nightmares for months. That's when we make sure he's not only unelected, but unelectable.'

He dropped the phone back into its cradle and turned to Quentin, who was propping himself up against a far wall of the huge marble-covered private bathroom, seemingly engrossed in pursuit of a stray eyelash.

'Quentin, do you remember King Edward the Second?'

'You mean the one they did for with the red-hot poker?' He puckered his lips in distaste at the legend of sordid butchery.

'If I hear a word of this conversation breathed outside these walls, you're going to become Quentin the First. And I personally am going to administer the poker. Get it?'

Quentin tried hard, very hard, to imagine the newspaper man was joking. He smiled encouragingly, but all he received in return was a sustained glare which left no room for doubt. Quentin remembered that Landless had never joked. He went back to cutting the hair, and said not another word.

She had taken the first editions up herself. She'd bumped into the messenger on the stairs.

'Nice to see you again, Miss.'

'Again' – Sally thought she detected undue inflexion on the word. Perhaps it was her imagination – or her guilt? No, not guilt. She had long ago decided not to run her life by codes and rules which others so blithely ignored. She owed no one, and there was no sense in being the only impoverished virgin in the cemetery.

He laid the newspapers side by side on the floor, and stood over them for a considerable time, lost in thought.

'It's started, Sally,' he said at last. She noted an edge of apprehension. 'Soon we shall be beyond the point of no return.'

'To victory.'

'Or to hell.'

'Come on, Francis, it's what you wanted. People beginning to ask questions.'

'Don't misunderstand. I'm not despondent, only a little cautious. I'm an Englishman, after all, and he is my King. And it appears we are not alone in asking questions. Who is this Quillington, this unknown peer with a mission?'

'Don't you know? He's the brother of the man who is, as it is said, close enough to Princess Charlotte to catch her colds. Always in the gossip columns.'

'You read gossip columns?' He was surprised; it was one of Elizabeth's least attractive breakfast traits. He eyed Sally closely, wondering if he would ever get the chance to eat breakfast with her.

'Many of my clients live in them. Pretend to be upset when they appear, are mortified when they don't.'

'So Quillington's a King's man, is he? And the King's men are already answering the call to battle.' He was still standing over the papers.

'Talking of clients, Francis, you said you'd introduce me to some new contacts, but I've not met anyone apart from the occasional messenger and tea lady. For some reason we seem to spend all our time alone.'

'We're never truly alone. It's impossible in this place.'

She came behind him and slid her hands around his chest, burying her face in the crisp, clean cotton of his shirt. She could smell him, the male smell, its muskiness mixed with the pine starch and the faint tang of cologne, and she could feel the body heat already rising. She knew it was the danger he enjoyed, which made him feel he was conquering not only her but, through her, the entire world. The fact that at any moment a messenger or civil servant might blunder in only heightened his sense of awareness and drive; while he was having her he felt invincible. The time would come when he would feel like that all the time, would dispense with caution and recognize no rules other than his own, and even as he reached the height of his powers he would begin the downward slide to defeat. It happened to them all. They begin to convince themselves that each new challenge is no longer new but is simply a repeat of old battles already fought and won. Their minds begin to close, they lose touch and flexibility, are no longer attuned to the dangers they confront. Vision becomes stale repetition. Not Urquhart, not yet, but sometime. She didn't mind being used, so long as she could use him, too, and so long as she remembered that this, like all things, couldn't last forever. She ran her hands down his chest, poking her fingers between his shirt buttons. Prime Ministers are always pushed, initially by their own vanity and sense of impregnability, and eventually by the electorate or their own colleagues and political friends. Although not by a King, not for many years.

'Don't worry about your clients, Sally. I'll fix it.'

'Thank you, Francis.' She kissed the back of his neck, the fingers still descending on his buttons as though she were practising a piano scale.

'You understand your job exceptionally well,' he breathed.

'Mrs Urquhart not around?'

'She's visiting her sister. In Fife.'

'Sounds a long way away.'

'It is.'

'I see.'

She had run out of buttons. He was still standing, newspapers at his feet, facing the door like Horatius at the bridge, ready to take on any intruders, feeling omnipotent. When he was like this, with her, she knew that nothing else mattered for him. Part of him yearned for the door to burst open and for all of Downing Street to see him with this much younger, desirable woman and to understand what a true man he was. Perhaps he hadn't realized that they had stopped barging in with their interminable messages and Cabinet papers while she was here, always finding an excuse to telephone ahead first, or simply not bothering to come at all. They knew, of course they knew. But maybe he didn't know they knew. Maybe he was already losing touch.

'Francis,' she whispered in his ear. 'I know it's late. It will be in darkness, but . . . You always promised to show me the Cabinet Room. Your special chair.'

He couldn't answer. Her fingers held him speechless.

'Francis? Please . . .'

He hadn't slept again. And he knew he was beginning to get things out of proportion. Ridiculous things like his tooth mug. The valet had changed it, just like that, assuming as they all did that they knew best what was good for him. It had caused an unholy, spitting row, and now he felt ashamed. He'd got his mug back, but in the process lost his equilibrium and dignity. Yet somehow knowing what was happening to him only seemed to make it worse.

The face in the bathroom mirror looked haggard, aged, the crow's feet around the eyes like great talons of revenge, the fire within damped and exhausted. As he studied his own image he saw reflected the face of his father, fierce, intemperate, unyielding. He shivered. He was growing old even before his life had properly started, a lifetime spent waiting for his parents to die just as now his own children waited for him. If he died today there would be a huge state funeral at which millions would mourn. But how many would remember him? Not him the figurehead, but him, the man?

As a child there had been some compensations. He remembered his favourite game dashing back and forth in front of the Palace guard, all the time being greeted with the satisfying clatter of boots being scraped and arms being presented until both he and the guard were breathless. But it had never been a proper childhood, alone and unable to reach out and touch like other children, and now they were intent on depriving him of his manhood, too. He would watch television yet couldn't understand half the commercials. A stream of messages about mortgages, savings plans, money dispensers, new liquids for washing whiter and gadgets which got the paint into those difficult corners and out of the bristles of the brush. It was as though the messages came from another planet. He already had the softest brand of toilet tissue, but hadn't the slightest idea where to buy it. He didn't even have to take the top off his toothpaste in the morning or change a razor blade. It was all done for him, everything. His life was unreal, somehow so irrelevant, a gilded cage of miseries. Even the girls they'd found to help with some of the basics had called him 'Sir', not only when they first met and in public, but later when they were alone, in bed, with nothing else between them other than an enthusiastic sweat while showing him how the rest of the world spent their time.

He'd done his best, everything that was expected of him and more. He'd learned Welsh, walked the Highlands, captained his own ship, flown helicopters and jumped out of planes at five thousand feet, presided over charity committees, opened the hospital wings and unveiled their plaques, laughed at the humiliations and lamentable impersonations, ignored the insults, bitten his lip at the vicious untruths about his family and turned the other cheek, crawled on his belly through the mud and slime of military training grounds just as he was expected to crawl through the mud and slime of Fleet Street. He'd done everything they had asked of him, yet still it was not enough. The harder he strived, the more cruel their jests and barbs became. The job, the expectations, had grown too much for any man.

He looked at the bony, balding head, so like his father's, and the sagging eyes. He'd already seen the morning newspapers, the reports of the debates, the speculation and innuendo, the pontification of the leader-writers who either discussed him as if he were known so intimately to them they could peer deep into his soul, or treated him as if he, the man, simply didn't exist. He was their chattel, a possession brought out on display at their convenience to sign their legislation, cut their ribbons and help sell their newspapers. They wouldn't allow him to join the rest of the world yet deprived him of the simple solace of being alone.

The once clear blue eyes were bloodshot with fatigue

and doubt. Somehow he had to find courage, a way out, before they broke him. But there was no way out for a King. Slowly his hand began to tremble, uncontrollably, as his thoughts began to tangle in confusion, and the tooth mug started to shake. His damp fingers gripped white around the porcelain, struggling to regain control, yet it was all slipping away and the mug flew off as though possessed, grazed the edge of the bath and bounced onto the tiled floor. He stared after it, captivated, as if watching the performance of a tragic ballet. The mug gave several tiny skips, the handle bouncing this way and that, waving at him, taunting him until, with a final extravagant leap of despair, it twisted over and smashed into a hundred angry, savage teeth. His favourite tooth mug was gone after all. And it was their fault.

'Couldn't I have done this at the Cup Final, Tim? You know how I hate football.' Urquhart was already having to raise his voice to make himself heard above the crowd, and the match hadn't even started.

'Final's not until May, and we don't have time.' Stamper's bright eyes darted around the ground. His pleasure was not going to be diluted by the whingeing of his boss; he had been a keen fan since the days he was no bigger than a football. Anyway, it was part of his programme to make Urquhart appear a man amongst the people, a Prime Minister out enjoying himself and keeping in touch. The media would get bored eventually with such spoon-feeding but not, Stamper had reasoned, before March. This was an ideal occasion, a floodlit European Championship qualifying match against arch rivals Germany with passions of victorious wars and World Cup defeats being rekindled on the terraces and in front of televisions throughout every constituency. As he had reminded the recalcitrant Urquhart several times, soccer fans may not have as much money as the crowd at the Opera House, but they have many more votes and Urquhart was there to be seen helping them defend the nation's honour.

A roar engulfed them as a Mexican wave rippled around the ground, the fans throwing themselves from their seats in the image of their forefathers going over the top at the Somme, Verdun, Vimy Ridge and countless other bloody encounters with the Hun. The VIPs' box was littered with an assortment of half-consumed drinks, overweight football bureaucrats and magazines carrying the latest news of twisted ligaments and even more distorted dressing-room gossip. None of it was to the Prime Minister's taste and he sat hunched over, seeming to have withdrawn inside the folds of his overcoat, yet as Stamper leaned over Urquhart's shoulder from his seat in the row behind he discovered his leader engrossed in the screen of a miniature television, less than three inches across. He was watching the evening news.

'She's getting too old for a bikini, if you want my opinion,' Stamper bantered.

The liquid-crystal display shone bright with the image of a paparazzi photograph, slightly shaky with the effect of a gentle Caribbean swell on the long-distance lens, but unmistakably showing Princess Charlotte cavorting on a secluded beach. The tropical colours were brilliant.

'You don't do our Royal Family justice, Tim. She is doing nothing improper. It is not a crime, after all, for a princess to be seen on a beach with a tanned companion, even if he happens to be considerably younger and slimmer than she. Nor does it matter that only last week she was skiing in Gstaad. You simply have no appreciation of how hard the Royal Family works. And I do deprecate the unpleasant British characteristic of envy, that simply because we are sitting here freezing our balls off in January while the country is slipping into recession, we should criticize those who happen to be more fortunate than ourselves.'

'I fear others won't see it in quite the same noble light as you.'

Urquhart wrapped the car rug more tightly around his knees and fortified himself from a thermos of hot coffee amply laced with whisky. He might feign being a young man while astride Sally, but the cold night air stripped away such pretences with little mercy. His breath was condensing in clouds. 'I fear you are right, Tim. More lurid stories about how many holidays she's had in the last year, how many nights she's spent in different parts of the country from the Prince, when she last saw the children. The gutter press will read anything into one harmless holiday snap.'

'OK, Francis. What the hell are you up to?'

Urquhart turned in his seat so that Stamper could hear him better above the noise around the stadium. He took another sip of coffee. 'I've been thinking. The agreement

on the Civil List expires shortly and we've just begun
renegotiating the Royal Family's income for the next ten
years. The Palace have put in a pretty tall bid based on
what some would say was an unreasonably high forecast
of inflation over the coming years. It's only an opening
position, of course, something to bargain with, to make
sure we are not too mean with them. It would be all too
easy at a time of general belt-tightening to squeeze them,
to argue that they should share the burdens along with the
rest of us.' He arched an eyebrow, and smiled. 'But I think
that would be shortsighted, don't you?'

'Give it to me, Francis. Unravel the workings of that
devious mind of yours, because you're way ahead of me
and I don't think I'm going to catch up.'

'I take that as a compliment. Listen, and learn, Timothy.'
Urquhart was enjoying this. Stamper was good, very good,
yet he didn't have the magnificent view of the political
lowlands afforded from the window of Number Ten. And
he didn't have Sally, either. 'I keep reading in the press
that we are moving to a position of constitutional . . . competition, shall we say, between King and Prime Minister, in
which the King appears to have considerable if uninformed
popular support. If I squeeze him on the Civil List I shall
simply be accused of churlishness. On the other hand if I
choose to be generous, it will prove I am fair-minded and
responsible.'

'As always,' the Party Chairman mocked.

'Unfortunately, the press and public have a simplistic
way of looking at the Civil List as rather like a Royal salary.
The going rate for the job. And I'm afraid the media will
not take kindly to a family which celebrates a huge pay
increase by dashing off from ski-slope to sun-blanched
beach while the rest of us shiver. Even responsible editors
like our friend Brynford-Jones are likely to misunderstand.'

'I shall insist on it!' Stamper shouted above the loud-
speaker system introducing the players.

'If it appears the Royal Family is abusing the Government's generosity, I fear that would be more of a problem
for the King than the Prime Minister. Little I can do about
it. Hope he doesn't find it too much of a distraction.'

The pitch was in brilliant floodlight, the teams lined up, the referee ready, the official photographs taken, the stadium noisy with the clamour of sixty thousand fans. Suddenly the chorus of raucous shouts subsided to a conspiratorial rustle.

'God Save The King, Tim!'

As Urquhart stood with Stamper for the playing of the national anthem, he felt warmer. He thought, above the perfunctory singing of the crowd, he could hear the sound of falling branches.

The King's desk was a mess. Books and copies of *Hansard* were piled along the front edge with pieces of paper sticking out like weeds to mark passages for future reference, the telephone had become submerged beneath a tide of computer print-out bearing the accounts of the Duchy of Lancaster, and an empty plate, which had earlier carried his lunch of a single round of wholemeal bread and smoked salmon, floated aimlessly around. Only the photograph of the children in its plain silver mount seemed immune from the encroachment, standing alone like a desert island amidst stormy seas. Typically, his brow was furrowed as he read the report on the Civil List.

'A little surprising, don't you think, David?'

'Frankly astonishing. We seem to be enjoying the spoils of victory without my being aware we've yet been engaged in combat. It's not what I expected.'

'Could it be a peace signal? There's been far too much gossip about the Palace and Downing Street. Maybe this a chance for a new start. Eh, David?' The voice sounded tired, lacking in conviction.

'Maybe,' Mycroft responded.

'It's certainly generous.'

'More generous than I realized he could be.'

The eyes shot a look of reproach across the jumbled desk. He was not a cynic, he liked to think of himself as a builder who found the best in people. It was one of his most infuriating characteristics, Mycroft had always thought. Yet the King did not disagree.

'It enables us to be generous in return.' The King had

risen from his chair and moved to gaze out of the window across the gardens, slowly twisting his signet ring. The new gardens were beginning to show definitive and distinctive form, and he found great solace as his mind filled in the many gaps and created a vista of beauty in front of him. 'You know, David, I've always thought it anomalous, embarrassing even, that our private income from the properties and interests owned by the Duchy of Lancaster and elsewhere remains free of tax. I'm the richest man in the country, yet I pay no income tax, no capital gains tax, no inheritance tax, nothing. And still in addition I get a Civil List allowance of several millions which is just about to be substantially increased.' He turned and clapped his hands. 'It's time for us to join the rest of the world. In exchange for the new Civil List, we should agree to pay tax on the rest of our incomes.'

'You mean a token payment?'

'No, no gestures. The full going-rate on it all.'

'But there's no need,' Mycroft protested. 'There's no real pressure on you, no controversy about it. Once you agree to it you'll never be able to renege. You will be binding your children and your children's children, no matter what Government is in power and no matter how punitive the taxes might be.'

'I have no intention of reneging!' His tone was sharp, a flush in his cheeks. 'I'm doing it because I think it is right. I've been over the Duchy accounts in great detail. Heavens, those assets should provide enough income for half a dozen Royal families.'

'Very well, Sir. If you insist.' Mycroft felt chided. It was his duty to offer advice and sound cautionary notes, and he did not care for being scolded. Even after the long years of friendship he was still not comfortable with the Monarch's flashes of impatience; it's what came of waiting a lifetime yet being in such a hurry, he told himself. And the outbursts were growing more frequent in the few short months since he had been on the Throne. 'What of the rest of the Family? You expect them also to volunteer tax?'

'I do. It would be a nonsense if the King were to pay tax yet more junior members of the Firm were not. People wouldn't understand. *I* wouldn't understand. Particularly not after the sort of press they've managed to organize for themselves recently. I know the media are vultures, but do we really have to offer ourselves up on plates ready to be devoured? A lot more clothing and a little more common sense wouldn't go amiss at times.' It was as close as he would come to personal criticism of his own family, but it had been no secret in the sculleries and laundry rooms of the Palace how incensed he'd been, both with Princess Charlotte's lack of discretion and the media's lack of restraint.

'If you are to . . . persuade them to forgo substantial income, the word needs to come directly from you. You can't expect them to take that sort of idea from me or any other aide.' Mycroft sounded restless. He had been sent before on similar errands to members of the Royal Family. He found that the more junior the rank, the more hostile grew their reception.

The King managed a rueful smile which turned his face down at one corner. 'You're right to be squeamish. I suspect any messenger sent on such a delicate task would return with his turban nailed firmly to his head. Don't worry, David, this one's for me. Brief them, if you will, on the new Civil List arrangements. Then prepare a short paper for me setting out the arguments and arrange for them to come and see me. Separately rather than in a gang. I don't want to be subjected to yet another collective family mugging around the dinner table, not on this one.'

'Some are abroad at the moment. It may take several days.'

'It has already taken several lifetimes, David.' The King sighed. 'I don't think a few more days can matter very much . . .'

The British Airways 747–400 from Kingston arrived ten minutes behind schedule on the approach to Heathrow, unable to make up the delay caused by a picket line of striking passport officers which had stretched around the departure terminal and spilled onto parts of the tropical runway. The flight had missed the pre-arranged landing slot and normally might have had to circle for another fifteen or twenty minutes before air-traffic control found a suitable gap in the queue, but this was not a normal flight and the captain was given immediate permission to land as twelve other flights which had arrived on schedule were shuffled back into the pack. The Princess was waiting to disembark the moment the wheels touched down.

The Boeing had taxied to a terminal in one of the quieter corners of the airport and normally the Princess and her escorts would be driven directly out of Heathrow through a private perimeter gateway. She would be back at Kensington Palace even before her fellow passengers had struggled to the head of the taxi rank. Today, however, the Princess did not drive directly away. First she had to collect the keys of her new car.

It had been a foul few months for all manufacturers of luxury cars and the prospects for the rest of the year looked worse. Trade was tough; sales – and sales promotions – were at a premium. So it had seemed an excellent idea for Maserati UK to offer the Princess a free edition of their latest and most sporty model in the expectation of considerable and on-going publicity. She had accepted with alacrity. As the aircraft drew alongside its arrival gate the managing director of Maserati waited anxiously on the tarmac, keys tied with an extravagant pink bow dangling from nervous fingers, eyeing the clouds. He could have wished for a kinder day, the intermittent drizzle had necessitated copious attention to the bodywork to keep it shining, but there were compensations. The media coverage afforded the Princess in recent days had considerably increased both the size and the enthusiasm of the press contingent lined up beside his car. The publicity value of his shares in the Princess had already increased considerably.

She breezed onto the damp tarmac with a polished white smile and tan which defied the elements. It would take less than ten minutes, a few words of greeting and thanks with the anxious little man in the shiny mohair suit waving the keys, a brief photo-call as the cameras compared her bodywork with that of the fierce red Maserati, and a couple of minutes spent driving slowly round in circles as she discovered the location of the gears and they squeezed off a few feet of promotional video. A breeze, and fair exchange of her time for a growling new £95,000 four-and-a-half litre turbocharged mechanical Italian beast.

The press, of course, had other ideas, wanting to enquire after her holiday and the whereabouts of her husband and holiday companion, but she was having none of it. 'The Princess will entertain questions only about the car, gentlemen,' an aide had announced. Why not a Jaguar – because it was American owned. How many other cars did she have – none like this wicked brute. What's the top speed – seventy miles an hour while I'm driving. Hadn't she recently been clocked at over a hundred on the M1 – a sweet smile and a grab for the next question. Would she lean a little lower over the bonnet for the benefit of the cameras – you guys must be joking. The next shower of rain looked imminent and already it was time for a few quick revolutions around the cameras before departing. She climbed in as gracefully as the low-slung bodywork would allow and wound down the window for a final smile at the jackal pack as they closed in.

'Isn't it a bit demeaning for a Princess to flog foreign cars?' a sharp voice asked bluntly.

Bloody typical. They were always at it. Her cheeks coloured beneath her tan. 'I spend my entire life "flogging", as you so snidely put it. I flog British exports wherever I go. I flog overpriced tickets for charity dinners to help the starving in Africa. I flog lottery tickets so we can build retirement homes for pensioners. I never stop flogging.'

'But flogging flash foreign sports cars?' the voice continued.

'It's you lot who demand the flash. If I turned up in second-hand clothes or third-hand cars, you'd be the first to complain. I have to earn my living the same as everybody else.' The smile had disappeared.

'What about the Civil List?'

'If you knew how difficult it was to do everything that's

expected of you on a Princess's allowance, you wouldn't ask such bloody fool questions!'

That was enough. They were goading her, she was losing her temper, it was time to go. She slipped the clutch, a fraction impatiently, for the car began to perform inelegant kangaroo hops towards the cameramen who scattered in alarm. Serve the bastards right. The V-8 engine stalled, the man in the shiny suit looked dismayed and the cameras snapped angrily. She restarted, selected a gear and was off. Damn their impertinence. Back at the Palace after only a week away she would be greeted with a small hillock of paperwork which would contain countless invitations, more requests and begging letters from charities and the underprivileged. She would show them. She would answer all the invitations, accept as many as possible, go on eating the dinners and raising the monies, smiling at the old and the young, the sick and the infirm, comforting those who were just plain unlucky. She would ignore the jibes and go on working hard, as she always did, grinding away through the hillock. She had no way of knowing that on top of the unopened pile lay a brief telling her about arrangements for the new Civil List, and that already copy was being prepared for the morning editions attacking a pouting princess in a brand new foreign sports car who complained she was not paid enough.

Misery in a Maserati.

The image of the Princess's glowing brake lights faded from the television as Urquhart hit the red button. His attention stayed fixed on the blank screen for a long time, his half-knotted tie hanging limply around his neck.

'Am I not old enough for you, Francis? You prefer middle-aged nymphomaniacs to good, clean-living young girls like me, is that it?'

He gave her a doleful look. 'I couldn't possibly comment.'

Sally dug him playfully in the ribs; distractedly he pushed her away. 'Stop that or I'll revoke your visa.' But the warning served only to redouble her efforts. 'Sally! We've got to talk.'

'God, not another of those serious, meaningful relationships. And just when I was beginning to have some fun.' She sat on the sofa opposite him, smoothing down her dress. She put her underwear in her handbag, she'd sort that tangled mess out later.

'There will be a storm about those pictures tomorrow. The headlines will be savage. Alas, it is also the day I've chosen to make the public announcement about the new Civil List. Unfortunate, the announcement sitting alongside those sort of pictures, but . . .' – he smiled a huge, theatrical smile like Macbeth welcoming dinner guests – 'it can't be helped. What I find most distressing is that it will focus attention not only on our hapless and witless Princess but on the whole Royal Family. And that's where I need your help, O Gypsy. Please.'

'I am a stranger in your land, Suh, and my campfire is small,' she mocked in a deep Southern drawl.

'But you have magic on your side. Magic that can take a family so royal, and make it so common.'

'How common?'

'So far as the lesser Royals are concerned? As common as gigolos on a beach. But not the King, though. This isn't all-out war. Just make sure he's not above criticism. Reflect a degree of disappointment. It can be done?'

She nodded. 'Depends on the questions, how you set it up.'

'How would you set it up?'

'Can I go to the bathroom first?' Her dress was now immaculately smoothed, but somewhere underneath she was still a mess.

'Tell me first, Sally. It's important.'

'Pig. OK, off the top of my head. You start with something like: "Have you seen any news about the Royal Family in the last few days, and if so, what?" Just to get them thinking about the photographs without, of course, being seen to lead them on. That would be unprofessional! If they're such bozos that they've not heard a damn thing about the Royals, you can exclude them as dickheads and deadbeats. Then something like: "Do you think it is important that the Royals set a good public example in their private lives?" Of course people will say yes, so you follow up with: "Do you think the Royal Family is setting a better or worse public example in their private lives than in previous years?" I'll bet my next month's income that eight out of every ten will answer worse, much worse or unprintable.'

'The Princess's bikini could yet prove to be as powerful as the sling of David.'

'If somewhat larger,' she added testily.

'Continue with the tutorial.'

'Then perhaps: "Do you think the Royal Family deserves its recent pay increase or do you think, in the current economic circumstances, it should be setting an example of restraint?" Words like that.'

'Perhaps even: "Do you think the number of members of the Royal Family supported by the taxpayer should remain the same, get larger, or be reduced?"'

'You're learning, Francis. If you put in a question immediately before that to ask whether they feel they get good value for money from the work of Princess Charlotte and a couple of other disreputable or unknown Royals, they'll be warmed up for it and you'll get an even fiercer response.'

His eyes were glittering.

'Only then do you come to the killer. "Is the Royal Family more or less popular, or doing a better or worse job for the country, than five years ago?" Top of the mind the public will say they are still great fans. So you have to bring out their deeper feelings, the concerns they hide away, the sort of things they're not always aware of themselves. Put that question up front, first off, and you'll probably discover that the Royals are only marginally less popular than they were. But ask away after you've given them a chance to think about sand, sex and Civil Lists, and your devoted and loyal citizens will have become a rebellious mob who will string up their beloved Princess Charlotte by her bikini straps. Is that enough?'

'More than enough.'

'Then if you don't mind I'm going to disappear for a little repair work.' Her hand was on the door handle when she turned around. 'You don't like the King, do you. Man to man, I mean.'

'No.' The reply was dry, blunt, reluctant. It only fuelled her curiosity.

'Why? Tell me.' She was pushing at doors he had not chosen to open freely, but she had to broaden the relationship if it were not to descend into empty habit and boredom. It had to be more than simply screwing each other, and the Opposition between times. Anyway, she was naturally curious.

'He's sanctimonious, naive,' came the low reply. 'A pathetic idealist who's getting in the way.'

'There's more, isn't there?'

'What do you mean?' he asked, irritation undisguised.

'Francis, you're halfway to raising a rebellion. You're not planning that just because he's sanctimonious.'

'He's trying to interfere.'

'Every editor in Fleet Street tries to interfere yet you invite them to lunch, not to their own lynching.'

'Why must you press it? All this twaddle about his children and the future!' His face revealed anguish, the tone had sharpened and his characteristic control had disappeared. 'He lectures me constantly about how passionate he is to build a better world, for his children. About how we shouldn't build a gas pipeline or nuclear power station without thinking first, about his children. How his first duty as a future King and Monarch was to produce an heir to the Throne – his children!' The flesh around his eyes had grown grey and his lips were spittled with saliva as he grew rapidly more animated. 'The man is possessed about his children. Forever talking about them whenever I meet him. Nagging. Harassing. Whining. As if children were some form of miracle which he alone could perform. Yet isn't it the commonest, most covetous and selfish act of all, to want to recreate your own image?'

She stood her ground. 'No, I don't think it is,' she said softly. She was suddenly frightened by the eyes which were red with fire, looking directly at her yet at the same time staring through her to some torment hidden beyond. 'No, it's not. Not selfish.'

'It's sheer egoism and self-love, I tell you. A pathetic attempt to grab at immortality.'

'It's called love, Francis.'

'Love! Was your child born out of love? Damned funny kind of love that leaves you in hospital with broken ribs and the child in a cemetery plot!'

She slapped him with the full force of an open palm, and knew at once it was a mistake. She should have recognized the danger signs in the throbbing veins at his temples. She should have remembered that he had no children, had never had children. She should have shown pity. Understanding came with a cry of pain as his hand lashed in return across her face.

Immediately he drew back, despairing at what he had done. He collapsed into a chair, the energy and hate draining from him like an hour-glass shedding its last grains of sand. 'My God, Sally, forgive me. I am so very sorry.'

By contrast, she retained a supreme calm. She'd had so much practice. 'Me too, Francis.'

He was panting, the leanness that often gave him the appearance of vigour and youth now turning him into a shrivelled, ageing man. He had breached his own defences. 'I have no children,' he said, gasping for breath, 'because I cannot. I have tried all my life to convince myself that it never mattered, but every time I see that damned man and listen to his taunts, it's as if I am stripped naked and humiliated simply by being in his presence.'

'You think he does it deliberately . . . ?'

'Of course it's deliberate! He uses his talk of love like weapons of war. Are you so blind you can't see?' His anger gave way to contrition. 'Oh, Sally, believe me, I'm sorry. I have never hit a woman before.'

'It happens, Francis.'

Sally stared at this new image of the man she had thought she knew, then closed the door quietly behind her.

A buzz of expectation grew as Urquhart walked into the House from behind the Speaker's Chair, red leather folder tucked beneath his arm, civil servants filing like ducklings into the officials' box at the back of the Chamber. They were there to provide him with instant information should the need arise, but it wouldn't. He had briefed himself very carefully for this one; he knew exactly what he wanted.

'Madam Speaker, with permission, I would like to make a statement . . .'

Urquhart looked slowly across the packed benches. McKillin sat on the other side of the Dispatch Box, double-checking the statement which Urquhart's office had made available to him an hour beforehand. He would be supportive. Such matters were supposed to be non-controversial and, in any event, as Urquhart's personal relations with the King had become the subject of press controversy, so the Opposition Leader's identification with the Monarch had grown. Your enemy, my friend. It's what Opposition was about. The Leader of the small Liberal Party, sitting with his band of eternal optimists towards the far end of the Chamber, was likely to be less enthusiastic. He had seventeen MPs in his party and an ego greater than all the others combined. As a precocious back-bencher he had made a name for himself by introducing a private bill to restrict the scope of the Civil List to only five members of the Royal Family and, furthermore, to batter home the message of equality by passing Royal succession down through the eldest child of either sex, and not exclusively the eldest son. It had given him ten minutes of parliamentary time before the bill was thrown out, but several hours of prime time on television and coverage in newspapers which he measured in feet. He had a record to defend; doubtless he would seek to do so with decorum but, as Urquhart glanced further around the House, the Prime Minister noted that decorum had a short shelf-life in politics.

His eyes alighted on 'The Beast of Bradford'. Dressed in his habitual shapeless sports jacket, the colourful and eccentric Member for Bradford Central was already leaning forward in anticipation, lank hair falling over his eyes, wringing his hands and waiting to leap to his feet at the first opportunity. The Opposition MP was a street-fighter who saw every issue as a chance to pursue the class war against capitalism, which he fought with considerable venom sustained by the scars of a factory accident as a working student which had left him with two short fingers on his left hand. An ardent republican, he was primed to self-ignite on issues involving hereditary rights. He was also utterly predictable, which is why Urquhart had ensured that one of his own members, a Knight of the Leafy Suburbs renowned for his bucolic complexion and pugnacious temper, was stationed directly opposite. The Knight had been deputed to 'take care' of The Beast during the statement; what this might involve had been left to The Knight's discretion, which was notoriously fragile, but he was anxious 'to get back into the fray', as he put it, after treatment for a mild heart complaint. He was already glowering across the floor at the Honourable Member for Bradford Central, seated barely six feet away.

'I would like to make a statement on arrangements for future financial support for His Majesty the King during the ten-year period ahead,' Urquhart continued. He paused to look directly at The Beast and smiled condescendingly. The other responded with an audible growl, which only served to broaden the Prime Minister's smile. The Beast's cage was already being rattled.

'The settlement is a considerable and I hope generous one, but is for a full ten-year period during which the vagaries of inflation must be accounted for. Should inflation prove to be less than predicted, the surplus will be carried forward . . .'

''Ow much is the Princess getting?' The Beast snapped.

Urquhart ignored him and continued with his explanation.

'Come on, then. Tell us. 'Ow much are we paying Charlotte to screw around in the Caribbean next year?'

'Order! Order!' Madam Speaker demanded shrilly.

'I was only asking,   '

'Shut up, you fool!' snapped The Knight, a comment heard by everyone in the Chamber with the exception of the official record takers of *Hansard*.

'Carry on, Prime Minister.'

The atmosphere was already tangled, the temperature

rising as Urquhart continued to the end of his short announcement. He had to struggle through growing noise as The Knight continued his private tussle across the floor of the Chamber. The Beast muttered away throughout the brief and supportive response of the Leader of the Opposition who, in a modest attempt to get under Urquhart's skin, was fulsome in his praise of the King's environmental work and social perceptiveness.

'Tell that to this bloody man!' the Knight stormed, waving an accusing finger at The Beast who had just impugned his wife's fidelity. He got a crude gesture involving two amputated fingers in response.

The Liberal leader, when it came to his turn, was less supportive. 'Will the Prime Minister recognize that, although we fully support the valuable work of the Royal Family, its financial affairs leave much to be desired? The Civil List represents but a fraction of the expense to the taxpayer of the Royal Family when you take into account the aeroplanes of the Royal Flight, the Royal Yacht, the Royal Train . . .'

'The Royal Racing Pigeons,' interrupted The Beast.

'. . . the costs of which are buried in the budgets of various Government departments. Wouldn't it be better, more open and honest, to consolidate all these expenditures into one budget so that we know exactly what the true figures are?'

'It's a sham. What're you 'iding?'

'I resent the Right Honourable Gentleman's insinuation that I am being neither open nor honest . . .' Urquhart began.

''Ow much is it, then?'

'There is no secret conspiracy on these matters. The Royal Family gives us excellent value for money—'

''Ow much money?'

A handful of others were joining in the interruptions from the Opposition benches. It seemed they might have found a weakness in the Prime Minister's defences and could not resist the temptation to exploit it.

'The figures vary greatly from year to year because of exceptional items . . .'

'Like what?'

'. . . such as refits and modernization of the Royal Trains. Also the Royal Palaces require extensive upkeep which in some years is unduly heavy. It is often very difficult to extract the exact cost out of large departmental budgets.' Urquhart appeared to be suffering from the interruptions. He was noticeably under pressure, reluctant to give details, which only excited his hecklers further. The more he prevaricated the louder became the calls for him to 'come clean'; even the Liberal leader was joining in.

'The House must understand that the statement I am making today covers the Civil List only. On other items of expenditure I am bound by custom, and it would be most improper of me to make announcements about such matters without first consulting His Majesty. We must preserve the dignity of the Crown and recognize the esteem and affection in which the Royal Family is held.'

As Urquhart paused to consider his words the noise levels around him rose sharply. His brow clouded.

'It was only the other day that the Opposition benches were accusing me of treating His Majesty with contempt, yet now they insist that is precisely what I do.' This antagonized his hecklers; the language swilling around the floor became increasingly unparliamentary. 'They are a shambolic lot, Mr Speaker.' Urquhart waved a menacing finger at the benches opposite. 'They don't want information, they just want a row!' He appeared to have lost his temper in the face of the constant baiting, and Madam Speaker knew that it would mark the end of any sensible dialogue. She was just about to curtail discussion and call the next business when an explosion erupted in the vicinity of The Knight, who was on his feet.

'On a Point of Order, Madam Speaker!'

'No points of order, please. We've already wasted enough time . . .'

'But that wretched man just told me to go and have another heart attack!'

Accusatory fingers pointed towards The Beast and the pandemonium grew worse.

'Really!' snapped the Speaker in exasperation.

''E's got it wrong, as always,' The Beast was protesting innocently. 'I told 'im 'e would have another 'eart attack, if he found out 'ow much the bloody Monarchy cost. It's millions and millions . . .'

The rest was lost in the storm of outrage from all sides.

Urquhart picked up his folder and started to leave. He looked at the parliamentary benches in turmoil. Great pressure would undoubtedly be brought to bear on him to reveal the full cost of the Royal Family, and he might have to give it. In any event, prompted by the row, every newspaper in Fleet Street would be setting journalists to dig and make inspired guesses, and reasonably accurate figures wouldn't be too difficult to find. A pity, he thought to himself, that last year the King's Flight replaced both their ageing aeroplanes, and modern jets don't come cheap. A still greater pity that it happened to coincide with an extensive refit for the Royal Yacht *Britannia*. The figures even the dimmest journalist would arrive at would be well in excess of one hundred and fifty million pounds, and that was too large a chunk of red meat for even the most loyal editor to ignore. Yet nobody could accuse Urquhart of being unfair or inconsiderate to the King, not personally. Hadn't he done his best to defend the King, even while under considerable pressure? By tomorrow morning's headlines it would be the King himself experiencing the pressure. Then for Sally's opinion poll.

Even for a Prime Minister it had been an exceptional day's work, he told himself.

'Mr Stamper would like a word, Prime Minister.'

'In his capacity as Privy Councillor, Chairman of the Party, Chief Bottle Washer or honorary president of his football club?' Urquhart swung his feet down from the green leather sofa on which he had been propped reading Cabinet papers as he waited in his House of Commons office for a series of late-night divisions. He couldn't remember what they were voting for next. Was it to increase punishment for offenders, or reduce subventions to the United Nations? Something, anyway, which would get the tabloids going and reveal the Opposition in the worst possible light.

'Mr Stamper didn't say,' responded the humourless private secretary, who had still put no more than his head and left shoulder around the door.

'Wheel him in!' the Prime Minister instructed.

Stamper appeared, offered no word of greeting, and made straight for the drinks cupboard where he poured himself a large whisky.

'Looks like bad news, Tim.'

'Oh, it is. Some of the worst I've heard for ages.'

'Not another selfish swine in a marginal seat gone and died?'

'Worse, much worse, Francis. Our latest private polls put us three points ahead. What's even more worrying, for some reason people seem to like you, you're ten points ahead of McKillin. Your vanity will be uncontrollable. Your ridiculous plan for an early election looks as if it could work after all!'

'Praise the Lord.'

'There's something even more fascinating, Francis,' Stamper continued in more serious demeanour. Unbidden he had filled a glass for Urquhart and handed it to him before continuing. 'I've just been having a quiet chat with the Home Secretary. The cock-up theory of politics rules supreme. Seems that little shit Marples has at last got himself caught with his trousers down, late the other night on the towpath at Putney.'

'In January?' Urquhart asked incredulously.

'Absolutely *in flagrante*. With a fourteen-year-old. Apparently he's into little boys.' He made himself comfortable behind Urquhart's desk, his feet up on the Prime Ministerial blotter. He was deliberately pushing his luck, teasing. His news must be particularly weighty, mused Urquhart.

'But lucky. The police were going to charge him so he broke down and told them everything in the hope they'd go easy on him. Lots of names, addresses, gossip, suggestions of where to look if they wanted to find an organized prostitution ring.'

'Castration's too good —'

'And it appears he came up with a very interesting name. David Mycroft.'

Urquhart took a deep swig.

'So all of a sudden our boys in blue have gone coy and are asking for a little informal guidance. If Marples gets prosecuted, he'll implicate Mycroft and all hell will break loose. The Home Secretary's given a nod and a wink that prosecuting the Honourable and Upright Member for Dagenham would not be in the public interest. So we're saved a by-election.'

Urquhart swung his legs down from the sofa. 'What do they have on Mycroft?'

'Not a lot. Just his name and the fact that Marples was tangling with him at some gay club on New Year's Eve. Who knows where that could lead? But they haven't interviewed him.'

'Maybe they should.'

'They can't, Francis. If they go after Mycroft they've got to do for Marples as well, which in turn will do for us all. Anyway, if spending time at a gay club were a crime we'd have to lock up half the House of Lords.'

'Listen to me, Tim. They can have Marples kebabbed on a rusty skewer for all I care. But he wouldn't be charged for weeks, not until after the election, by which time it won't matter a bent farthing. Yet if they can put pressure on Mycroft now, it may be just the insurance policy we need. Don't you see? Pieces for position. Capture the low ground today, in exchange for giving up a player later, when it no longer matters. I think they call it a queen sacrifice.'

'I think I need another drink. Problems like that, so close to the heart of the Palace. If this were to come out . . .'

'How long's Mycroft been with the King?'

'Known each other since they were both spotty youths. One of his longest-serving aides. And closest friends.'

'Sounds distressingly serious. It would be awful if the King knew.'

'And were covering up for Mycroft, in spite of the sensitivity of the work he does. Must know half the nation's secrets in his job.'

'Be even worse if His Majesty didn't know. Fooled, bamboozled, defrauded for thirty years by one of his closest friends, a man he has put into a position of trust.'

'A knave or a fool. A monarch who didn't fulfil his responsibilities, or couldn't. What will the press make of all this, if it gets out?'

'Terrible news, Tim. This is terrible.'

'Worst I've heard in ages.'

There was a long moment of silence. Then, coming from inside the Prime Minister's room, the private secretary heard a sustained, almost uncontrollable bout of gut wrenching laughter.

'Damn them! Damn them all, David! How could they be so cretinous?' The King hurled one newspaper after another into the air as Mycroft watched the pages flutter down to lay strewn across the floor. 'I didn't want the Civil List increase, but now I'm attacked for greed. And how can it be that only a few days after informing the Prime Minister that I wished the Royal Family to pay full taxes on our income, they report it as if it's his idea?'

'Downing Street's unattributable briefing . . .' Mycroft muttered feebly.

'Of course it is!' snapped the King as if talking with a backward pupil. 'They even suggest I'm caving in to pressure in agreeing to pay tax, that I've been forced into it by the hostile press coverage. That man Urquhart is abominable! He can't help but twist everything to his advantage. If he even stumbled by accident upon the truth he would pick himself up and carry on as if nothing had happened. It's preposterous!'

A copy of *The Times* was hurled to the farthest corner of the room, settling like huge flakes of snow.

'Did any of them bother to enquire after the facts?'

Mycroft coughed awkwardly. 'The *Telegraph*. Their story is fair . . .'

The King snatched the paper from amongst the pile, scanning its columns. He seemed to calm a little. 'Urquhart is trying to humiliate me, David. To cut me to ribbons, piece by piece, without even a chance to explain myself.' He'd had the dream again last night. From the pages of every newspaper he could see staring at him the wide, expectant eyes of the grubby boy with the dribble of crumbs on his chin. It terrified him. 'I will not let them drag me like a lamb to the slaughter, David. I must not permit that. I've been thinking: I must find some way of explaining my views. Get my point across without Urquhart getting in the way. I shall give an interview.'

'But Kings don't give newspaper interviews,' Mycroft protested weakly.

'Not before they haven't. But this is the age of the new, open Monarchy. I'm going to do it, David. With the *Telegraph*, I think. An exclusive.'

Mycroft wanted to protest that if an interview were a bad idea, an exclusive could be even worse, giving all the other newspapers something to shoot at. But he didn't have the strength to argue. He hadn't been able to think clearly all day, ever since he had answered a knock at the door early in the morning to discover a DC and Inspector from the Vice Squad standing on his front step.

January: The Fourth Week

Landless had driven himself, simply telling his staff that he would be uncontactable. His secretary hated mysteries; when he presented excuses she always assumed he was off being grubby with some young woman who had a strong back and weak bank balance. She knew what he was like. Some fifteen years earlier she, too, had been young and grubby with Landless, before things like marriage, respectability and stretch marks had intervened. Such insights into the inner man had helped her become an efficient and outrageously overpaid personal assistant, yet hadn't stopped her being jealous. And today he had told no one, not even her; he didn't want the whole world knowing where he was even before he had arrived.

The reception desk was tiny and the waiting room dull, covered in mediocre early Victorian oils of horses and hunting scenes in imitation of Stubbs and Ben Marshall. One of them might have been an authentic John Herring; he couldn't be positive but he was beginning to develop an eye for such things; after all, he'd bought enough of the genuine article over the past few years. Almost immediately he was being summoned by a young footman in full livery, waisted tails, buckles and stockings, and ushered into a small but immaculately appointed lift where the mahogany shone as deep as the Palace servant's shoes. He wished his mother had been here: she would have loved it. She'd been born on the day Queen Alexandra died and had always believed it somehow tied her in, hinting at a mysterious 'special link', and in later life attending gatherings of spiritualists. Just before his dear old mum had taken her own trip to 'the other side' she had stood for three hours to catch a view through the crowd of Princess Di on her wedding day. She'd only seen the back of the coach, and that for no more than a few seconds, but she'd waved her flag and cheered and cried, and come home feeling she had done her bit. For her it was all patriotic pride and commemorative biscuit tins. She would be wetting herself if she were gazing down now.

'Your first time?' the footman enquired.

Landless nodded. Princess Charlotte had telephoned him. An exclusive interview with the *Telegraph*, implying she had set it up herself. Would he be sure to send someone reliable? And allow the Palace to check the article before it was printed? Perhaps they could have lunch again soon? He was being led along a broad corridor with windows overlooking the inner courtyard. The paintings were better here, portraits of long-forgotten Royal scions by masters whose names had endured rather better.

'You address him as "Your Majesty" when you first go in. Afterwards you can simply call him "Sir",' the footman muttered as they approached a solid but unpretentious door.

As the door swung quietly open, Landless remembered Charlotte's other question. Was the idea a good one? He had doubts, serious doubts, about whether an exclusive interview would be good for the King, but he knew it would be bloody marvellous for his newspaper.

'Sally? Sorry to telephone so early. You haven't been in contact for a day or two. Everything all right?'

In fact it had been nearly a week, and although Urquhart had sent along flowers and two major potential clients, he hadn't found the right moment to call. He shrugged. They'd had a spat, she would get over it. She would have to if she wanted to retain an inside track. In any event, this was urgent.

'How's the opinion poll coming along? Ready yet?' He tried to judge her mood down the phone. Perhaps a little cool and formal, almost as if he'd woken her up. Anyway this was business. 'Something's come up. Word is His Royal Conscience has given an exclusive interview to the *Telegraph* and they're hoping to get it cleared for publication in a couple of days. I haven't any idea what's in it,

Landless is sitting on it as though he were hatching an egg, but I can't help feeling that in the public interest there should be a bit of balance. Don't you think? Perhaps an opinion poll, published beforehand, reflecting the growing public disaffection with the Royal Family? To put the interview in context?' He looked out of the window across St James's Park, where, beside the pelican pool, two women were struggling in the grubby morning light to pull their squabbling dogs apart. 'I suspect some newspapers like the *Times* might even infer that the King's interview was a hurried and somewhat desperate attempt to respond to the opinion poll.' He winced as one of the women, her smaller pet lodged firmly between the jaws of a large black mongrel, gave the other dog a firm kick in the testicles. The dogs separated, only for the two owners to begin snarling at each other. 'It would be really superb if the poll were ready for release by, say . . . this afternoon?'

As Sally rolled over to place the phone back in its cradle, she stretched the aches of the night out of her bones. She lay staring at the ceiling for a few moments, allowing the mental instructions to seep from her brain down through her body. Her nose was twitching like a periscope above the sheets, tasting the news she had just received. She sat up in bed, alive and alert, and turned to the form beside her.

'Got to go, lover. Mischief afoot and work to be done.'

Guardian, Page One, 27 January

NEW STORM HITS KING
'IS HE A CHRISTIAN?'

A new storm of controversy surrounded the Royal Family last night when the Bishop of Durham, from the pulpit of his cathedral, questioned the King's religious motives. Quoting the King's much-criticised newspaper interview earlier this week in which he revealed a deep interest in Eastern religions and did not discount the possibility of physical resurrection, the fundamentalist Bishop attacked such 'fashionable dalliance with mysticism'.

'The King is the Defender of the Faith and anointed head of our Church of England. But is he a Christian?'

Buckingham Palace indicated last night that the King had simply been trying to emphasize, as King of a country with a large number of racial and religious minorities, that he felt it his duty not to take a narrow and restrictive view of his religious role. But the Bishop's attack seems set to fuel further controversy in the wake of the recent critical opinion poll which showed dramatically falling support for some members of the Royal Family such as Princess Charlotte, and a growing demand to restrict the number of members of the Royal Family who receive their income from the Civil List.

Supporters of the King rallied to his defence last night. 'We shouldn't be enticed into a constitutional supermarket, shopping around for the cheapest form of government,' Viscount Quillington said.

In contrast, critics were quick to point out that the King, in spite of his own personal popularity, was failing to set a clear lead in many areas. 'The Crown should stand for the highest standards of public morality,' one senior Government backbencher said, 'but his leadership of his own family leaves much to be desired. They are letting down both him and us. They are overpaid, overtanned, underworked, and overly numerous.'

'The Royal oak is being shaken,' said another critic. 'It would do no harm if one or two members of the Family were to fall out of the branches . . .'

News began trickling through shortly before four in the afternoon, and by the time it was confirmed the short winter's day had finished and all London was dark. It was a wretched day; a warm front had passed across the capital bringing in its wake a deluge of relentless rain which would continue well into the night. It was a day for staying home.

Staying home had been the mistake, fatally so, of three women and their children who called 14 Queensgate Crescent, a tenement block in the middle of Notting Hill, home. It was the heart of old slumland, which in the sixties had housed streetwalkers and tides of immigrants under the stern eye of racketeers. 'Rachmanism' they had called it then, after the most notorious of the landlord-racketeers. 'Bed and breakfast' it was called in the modern parlance, where the local council housed one-parent and problem families while they searched around listlessly for somewhere or someone else to take over the responsibility. Much of the temporary accommodation provided in Number 14 had changed little in the thirty-odd years since it had been a brothel. Single rooms, shared bathrooms, inadequate heating, noise, rotting woodwork and unremitting depression. When it rained, they would watch the windowsills trickle and the damp brown stains creep even lower as the wallpaper peeled from the walls. But it was better than sitting in the middle of the downpour outside, or so they had thought.

Institutional housing breeds indifference, and no one had bothered to report the smell of gas which had been lingering for days. That was up to the caretaker, and so what if he only turned up when he felt like it. It was somebody else's problem. Or so they had thought.

As dusk had gathered the automatic timer had turned another gear and switched on the light in the communal hallways. They were only sixty-watt bulbs, one per landing, scarcely adequate, but the small spark caused by the electrical contact had been sufficient to ignite the gas and blow the five-storey building right out of the ground, taking much of the neighbouring building with it. Fortunately there had been no one in next door, it was derelict, but remnants of five families were inside Number 14 and of the twenty-one women, children and babies only eight would be pulled out of the rubble alive. By the time His Majesty reached the scene it consisted of little more than a huge pile of bricks, fractured door frames and twisted fragments of furniture over which firemen crawled beneath harsh arc lights. Several persons were believed to have been inside for whom there was still no account. A double bed teetered precariously on a ledge of splintered wood many feet above the heads of the rescuers, its sheets flapping in the squally wind. It should have been pulled down before it had a chance to fall on those below, but the mobile crane was having trouble getting through the rain and rush-hour traffic and they couldn't afford to wait. Someone thought they had heard a noise from the rubble directly beneath and although the infra-red image enhancer showed nothing, many willing hands were tearing at the ruins, lashed by the rain and the fear they would be too late.

As soon as the King had heard the news he had asked to visit the scene. 'Not to interfere, to gawk. But a word to the bereaved at a time such as this can speak louder than a thousand epitaphs later.' The request had gone through to the Met Police Control Room at Scotland Yard just as they were briefing the Home Secretary, who had immediately passed the news on to Downing Street. The King arrived on site only to discover he had unwittingly been involved in a race he had already lost. Urquhart was already there, holding hands, comforting the injured, consoling the distressed, giving interviews, searching for the television cameras, being seen. It made the Monarch look like a man sent onto the field from the substitutes' bench, no better than an able reserve, following in others' footsteps, but what did it matter? This wasn't a contest, or, at least, shouldn't be. Or so the King struggled to convince himself.

For some time the Monarch and his Prime Minister succeeded in avoiding each other as one took briefing and quietly sought out survivors while the other concentrated on finding a dry spot from which to give interviews. But both knew a meeting would have to come. Avoiding each other would be news in itself and would serve only to turn tragedy into farce. The King stood like a sentinel gazing at the devastation from atop a mound of rubble surrounded by a rapidly enlarging lake of slime and mud, through which Urquhart had to trudge to meet him.

'Your Majesty.'

'Mr Urquhart.'

Their greeting had the warmth of a collision of icebergs.

Neither looked directly at the other, but chose to examine the scene around them.

'Not a word, Sir. There has already been too much damage done, too much controversy stirred. See, but do not speak. I must insist.'

'No perfunctory expression of grief, Mr Urquhart? Not even to one of your own scripts?'

'Not a wink or a nod, no sideways expressions or exaggerated lowering of the eyes. Not even to an agreed formula, since you seem to delight in untangling every knot we weave.'

The King waved the charge away with a dismissive gesture.

The Prime Minister spoke slowly, with great deliberation, returning to his theme. 'I must insist.'

'Silence, you think?'

'Absolutely. For some considerable period.'

The King turned from the carnage and for the first time looked directly at the Prime Minister, his face frozen in condescension, his hands thrust deep into the pockets of his raincoat. 'I think not.'

Urquhart struggled to avoid rising to the challenge and losing his self-control. He wasn't willing to let the King escape with even a trace of satisfaction.

'As you have seen, your views have been widely misunderstood.'

'Or manipulated.'

Urquhart ignored the innuendo.

'Silence, you say,' the King continued, turning his face into the wind and spray, his nose jutting forward like the prow of some great sailing ship. 'I wonder what you would do, Mr Urquhart, if some damn fool bishop made you the target of such ludicrous misrepresentation. Shut up? Or stand up? Wouldn't you think it even more important to speak out, to give those willing to listen the opportunity to hear, to understand?'

'But I am not the King.'

'No. A fact for which both you and I should be grateful.'

Urquhart rode the insult. Beneath the burning arc lights a tiny hand was spotted beneath the rubble. Brief seconds

537

of confusion and hope, much scrabbling, only for the flicker of anticipation to die amidst the mud. It was nothing but a doll.

'I must make sure, Sir, that I am also heard and understood. By you.' To one side there was a crash of falling masonry but neither stirred. 'Any further public outpourings by you would be regarded as deeply provocative by your Government. A declaration of constitutional war. And no Monarch has taken on a Prime Minister and won in nearly two hundred years.'

'An interesting point. I had forgotten you were a scholar.'

'Politics is about the attainment and use of power. It is a rough, indeed ruthless arena. No place for a King.'

The rain ran in rivulets down their faces, dripping from their noses, creeping behind their collars. They were both soaking and chilled. Neither was young, they should have sought shelter but neither would be the first to move. At a distance onlookers could hear nothing beyond the rattle of jackhammers and the urgent shouts of command, they could see only two men staring face to face, rulers and rivals, silhouetted against the harsh glow of the rescue lights in a monochrome scene washed by rain. They could not distinguish the insolence on the face of Urquhart nor the ageless expression of regal defiance that suffused the cheeks of the other. Perhaps an astute observer might have seen the King brace his shoulders, but surely only against the elements and the harsh fortune that had brought him to this place?

'Did I miss a mention of morality in there, Prime Minister?'

'Morality, Sir, is the monologue of the unexcited and the unexcitable, the revenge of the unsuccessful, the punishment of those who tried and failed, or who never had the courage to try at all.'

It was Urquhart's turn to attempt to provoke the other. A silence hung between them for many moments.

'Prime Minister, may I congratulate you? You have succeeded in making me understand you with absolute clarity.'

'I didn't wish to leave you in any doubt.'

'You haven't.'

'We are agreed, then? No more words?'

When finally the King spoke, his voice had grown soft so that Urquhart had to strain to hear it. 'You may rest assured that I shall guard my words as carefully as you aim yours. Those you have used today I shall never forget.'

The moment was broken as a shout of warning rose above the scene and men scurried from the rock pile as the wooden ledge shivered, jarred and finally collapsed, propelling the bed into a slow, graceful somersault of death before it was reduced to nothing more than another pile of matchwood on the ruins below. A solitary pillow sagged drunken in the wind, skewered upon the pointed shard of what that morning had been a baby's cot, its plastic rattle still singing in the wind. Without another word Urquhart began the trudge back through the slime.

Mycroft joined the King in the back of his car for the return drive to the Palace. For much of the trip the Monarch was silent, lost in thought and his emotions, eyes closed – affected by what he had witnessed, thought Mycroft. When he spoke, his words were soft, almost whispered, as though they were in a church or visiting a condemned cell.

'No more words, David. I am commanded to silence, or must accept the consequences.' His eyes were still closed.

'No more interviews?'

'Not unless I want open warfare.'

The thought hung between them for several moments which dragged into silent minutes. His eyes were still closed. Mycroft thought it might be his opportunity to speak.

'Perhaps it's not the right time . . . it's never really the right time. But it would be helpful for me to take a few days away. If you're not doing much in public. For a while. There are a few personal things I need to sort out.'

The King's head was still back, eyes shut, words coming in a monotone and squeezed of emotion. 'I must apologize, David. I've rather taken you for granted, I'm afraid. Lost in my own problems.' He sighed. 'With all this confusion I should still have found time to enquire. Christmas without Fiona must have been hell. Of course. Of course you must have a little time off. But there's one small thing I want your help with beforehand, if you can bear it. I want to arrange a small trip.'

'To where?'

'Three days, David. Just three days, and not far. I was thinking of Brixton, Handsworth, perhaps Moss Side and the Gorbals. Work my way up the country. Dine at a soup kitchen in Cardboard City one day, have breakfast at the Salvation Army the next. Take tea with a family living off benefit and share their one-bar fire. Meet the youngsters sleeping rough. You get the idea.'

'You can't!'

The head remained back, sightless, the tone still cold. 'I can. And I want cameras to accompany me everywhere. Maybe I shall live off a pensioner's diet for three days and challenge the press travelling with me to do the same.'

'That's bigger headlines than any speech!'

'I shall say not a word.' He started laughing, as if cold humour were the only way to suppress the feelings that battered him within, so forcefully they had left him a little in fear of himself.

'You don't have to. Those pictures will be top of the news every night.'

'If only every Royal engagement could get such coverage.' The tone was almost whimsical.

'Don't you know what you're doing? It's a declaration of war on the Government. Urquhart will retaliate . . .'

Mention of the Prime Minister's name had a galvanizing effect on the King. His head came up, red eyes open and burning bright, the jaw tightened as if a burst of electricity had passed through him. There was fire in his belly. 'We retaliate first! Urquhart cannot stop me. He may object to my speeches, he may bully and threaten me, but this is my kingdom, and I have every right to go wherever and whenever I bloody well please!'

'When did you have in mind for starting this civil war?'

The grim humour settled on him once more. 'Oh, I was thinking . . . next week.'

540

'Now I know you're not serious. It would take months to organize.'

'Wherever and whenever I please, David. It needs no organization. I'm not going to meet anyone in particular. No advance notice need be given. Anyway, if I give them time to prepare all I will see is some anaesthetized version of Britain which has been swept and whitewashed just for my visit. No, David. No preparation, no warning. I'm bored with playing the King; time to play the man! Let's see if I can take for three days what so many others have to take for a lifetime. Let's see if I can lose the silk-covered shackles and look my subjects in the eye.'

'Security! What of security?' Mycroft urged desperately.

'The best form of security is surprise, when no one expects me. If I have to get in my car and drive myself, by God I'm doing it.'

'You must be absolutely clear. Such a tour would be war, right out in front of the cameras, with no hiding place and no diplomatic compromise later on to smooth everything over. It would be a direct public challenge to the Prime Minister.'

'No, David, that's not the way I see it. Urquhart is a public menace, to be sure, but this is more about me. I need to find myself, respond to those things I feel deep inside, see whether I am up to the task not just of being a King, but of being a man. I can't go on running away from what I am, David, what I believe. This is not just a challenge to Urquhart. It's more of a challenge to myself. Can you understand?'

As the words hit him, Mycroft's shoulders sagged, the weight of several worlds seeming to bear down upon his shoulders. He felt exhausted from his own lifetime of running, he had no resources left. The man sitting beside him was not just a King, he was more, a man who insisted on being his own man. Mycroft knew exactly how he felt, and marvelled at his courage. He nodded. 'Of course I do,' he responded softly.

'Elizabeth. The toast is burnt again!'

Urquhart contemplated the ruins of his breakfast which

541

had crumbled at the first touch of his knife and showered into his lap. His wife was still in her dressing gown; she had been out late again – 'working hard, telling the world how wonderful you are, darling' – and was only half awake.

'I cannot think in that ridiculous little kitchen, Francis, let alone cook your toast. Sort out the refurbishment and then you can have a proper breakfast.'

That again. He'd forgotten about it, pushed it to one side. There were other things on his mind.

'Francis, what's wrong?' She had known him too long not to catch the signs.

He gestured to the newspapers, announcing plans for the King's visit. 'He's called my bluff, Elizabeth.'

'Will it be bad?'

'Could it be worse? Just when everything was beginning to come right. The opinion polls turning in our favour, an election about to be called. It will change everything.' He dusted the crumbs off his lap. 'I can't go to the country with everyone talking about nothing but poverty and freezing pensioners. We'd be out of Downing Street before you had time to choose new wallpaper let alone get your paste bucket out.'

'Out of Downing Street?' She sounded alarmed. 'It may sound churlish, but haven't we only just got here?'

He looked at her pointedly. 'You'd miss it? You surprise me, Elizabeth. You seem to spend so much time away.' But she usually came back before daybreak, and as she sat there he understood why. She wasn't at her best first thing in the morning.

'Can't you fight him?'

'With time, yes. And beat him. But I don't have time, Elizabeth, only two weeks. The pathetic thing is that the King doesn't even realize what he's done.'

'You mustn't give in, Francis. You owe it to me as well as yourself.' She was struggling with her own toast as if to emphasize what weak, useless creatures men were. She was no more successful than he, and it irritated her. 'I've shared in all the sacrifices and the hard work, remember. And I have a life, too. I enjoy being the Prime Minister's

542

wife. And one day I'm going to be a former Prime Minister's widow. I'll need some support, a little social respectability for when I'm on my own.' It sounded selfish, uncaring. And as she did when she couldn't help herself, she used her most potent weapon, his guilt. 'If we had children to support me, it would be different.'

He stared at the ruins of his breakfast. That's what it had come to. Dickering over his coffin.

'Fight him, Francis.'

'I intend to, but don't underestimate him. I chop off a leg, yet he keeps bouncing back up again.'

'Then fight him harder.'

'You mean like George Washington?'

'I mean like bloody Cromwell. It's us or him, Francis.'

'I've struggled so hard to avoid that, Elizabeth, truly I have. It would not simply be destroying one man but several hundred years of history. There are limits.'

'Think about it, Francis. Is it possible?'

'It would certainly be a distraction from bellyaching about the underprivileged.'

'Governments don't solve people's concerns, they simply try to rearrange them in their favour. Can't you rearrange them in your favour?'

'Inside two weeks?' He examined the determined look in her eyes. She was in earnest. Deadly earnest. 'That's what I've spent all night thinking about.' He nodded gently. 'It might just be. With a little luck. And witchcraft. Make him the issue, the people versus the King. But this would not simply be an election, it would be a revolution. If we won, the Royal Family would never recover.'

'Spare me the pity. I'm a Colquhoun.'

'But am I a Cromwell?'

'You'll do.'

He suddenly remembered they had dug up Cromwell and stuck his rotting skull on a gibbet. He looked at the remnants of charred toast, and was very much afraid she might be right.

PART THREE

FEBRUARY: THE FIRST WEEK

The ringing of the telephone startled him, intruding into the quiet of the apartment. It was late, well after ten, and Kenny had already retired to leave Mycroft working on some last-minute arrangements for the King's tour. Kenny was on stand-by; Mycroft wondered whether the telephone was summoning him to fill a last-minute vacancy on some flight crew, but surely not at this time of night?

Kenny appeared at the bedroom door, rubbing wearily at his eyes. 'It's for you.'

'For me? But who . . . ?'

'Dunno.' Kenny was still half asleep.

With considerable trepidation Mycroft lifted the extension. 'Hello.'

'David Mycroft?' the voice enquired.

'Who's speaking?'

'David, this is Ken Rochester from the *Mirror*. I'm sorry to bother you so late. It's not too inconvenient, is it, David?'

Mycroft had never heard of the man before. His nasal tones were unpleasant, his informality insolent and unwelcome, his concern patently insincere. Mycroft made no reply.

'It's something of an emergency; my editor's asked if I can come on the tour tomorrow, along with our Royal correspondent. I'm a special features writer myself. You moved, have you, David? Not your old number, this.'

'How did you get this number?' Mycroft asked, forcing out every word through suddenly leaden lips.

'It is David Mycroft, isn't it? From the Palace? I'd feel a total fool talking about this to anyone else. David?'

'How did you get this number?' he asked again, the constriction in his throat drying his words. He had supplied it to the Palace switchboard for use only in an emergency.

'Oh, we usually get whatever we want, David. So I'll turn up tomorrow to join the rest of the reptiles, if you'll make the necessary arrangements. My editor would be furious if I couldn't find some way of persuading you. Was that your son I spoke to on the phone? Sorry, silly question. Your son's at university, isn't he, David?'

Mycroft's throat was now desiccated, unable to pass any words.

'Or a colleague, perhaps? One of your high-flyers? Sounded as if I'd woken him from bed. Sorry to have disturbed you both so very late at night, but you know how editors are. My apologies to your wife . . .'

The journalist prattled on with his confection of innuendo and enquiry. Slowly Mycroft withdrew the telephone from his ear and dropped it back into its cradle. So they knew where he was. And they would know who he was with, and why. After the visit of the Vice Squad he had known it would happen sooner or later. He'd prayed it would be much later. And he knew the press. They wouldn't be satisfied with just himself. They'd go for Kenny, too, his job, his family, his private life, his friends, everybody and anybody he'd ever known, even through his dustbins in search of all the mistakes he had ever made. And who hadn't made mistakes? They would be remorseless, unstinting, uncompromising, unspeakable. Mycroft wasn't sure he could take that sort of pressure; he was even less sure he had the right to ask Kenny to take it. He wandered over to the window and glanced up and down the darkened street, searching the shadows for any hint of prying eyes. There was nothing, nothing that he could see at least, but it wouldn't be long, maybe as soon as tomorrow.

Kenny had fallen asleep again, innocent and unaware, his body twisted in the sheets as only young people can manage. All they had wanted was to be left alone, yet it was only a matter of time before others came to tear them apart. As he lay beside Kenny, trying to share his warmth, he shivered, already feeling the exposure. The real world no longer lay beyond Kenny's doorstep, it was forcing itself right inside the room.

Urquhart had arrived back late from the diplomatic reception to find Sally waiting for him, chatting over a plastic cup of coffee with a couple of Protection Squad officers in what passed as their office: a cramped closet-sized room just off the entrance hall. She was perched on the corner of their desk, supported by her long and elegant legs, which the seated detectives were admiring with little sign of reticence.

'My apologies for disturbing you at your work, gentlemen,' he muttered tetchily. He realized he was jealous, but felt better as the detectives sprang to their feet in evident confusion, one of them spilling the coffee in his haste.

'Good evening, Prime Minister.' Her smile was broad, warm, showing no after-effects of their previous meeting's misunderstanding.

'Ah, Miss Quine. I was forgetting. More opinion polls?' He attempted an air of distraction.

'Who do you think you're kidding?' Sally muttered from the corner of her mouth as they made their way from the room.

He arched an eyebrow.

'If they thought you'd really forgotten about a late-night meeting with a woman who had a figure like mine, they'd send for the men in white coats.'

'They are not paid to think but to do as I tell them,' he responded waspishly. He sounded as if he meant every word, and Sally felt alarmed. She decided to change the subject.

'Talking of opinion polls, you're six points ahead. But before you start congratulating yourself, I have to tell you that the King's tour will blow that lead right out of the water. It's going to be one heck of a circus – lots of hand-wringing and talk of compassion. Frankly, not a game where your side fields a strong team.'

'I'm afraid His Majesty is going to have distractions of his own before the week is out.'

'Meaning?'

'His press officer and close friend, Mycroft, is a homosexual. Shacked up with an air steward.'

'So what? It's no crime.'

'But sadly the story is just dribbling out to the press, and
in their usual disreputable fashion they will be bound to
make him wish he were a simple criminal. There's not only
the deceit of his family – apparently his poor wife has been
forced to leave the marital home after more than twenty
years of marriage in disgust at what he's been up to.
There's also the security angle. A man who has access to
all sorts of sensitive information, state secrets, at the heart
of our Royal Family, has lied his way right through the
regular vetting procedures. Laid himself wide open to
blackmail and pressure.' Urquhart was leaning on the wall
button which would summon the private lift to the top-
floor apartment. 'And then, most serious of all, is deceit
of the King. A lifelong friend, whom he has betrayed.
Unless, of course, you wish to be uncharitable and conclude that the King knew all along and has been covering
up to help an old friend. Messy.'

'You're not implying that the King, too—'

'I imply nothing. That's the job of the press,' he
responded, 'who, I confidently predict, by the end of the
week will be wading in it.'

The lift doors were open, beckoning. 'Then why wait,
Francis? Why not strike now, before the King sets off and
does all that damage?'

'Because Mycroft is no more than a dunghill. The King
needs to be pushed not from a dunghill but from a mountain top, and by the end of his tour he will have climbed
about as high as he's going to get. I can wait.'

They stepped into the lift, a small, insalubrious affair
which had been squeezed into a recess of the old house
during refurbishment earlier in the century. The narrow-
ness of its bare metal walls forced them together and, as
the doors closed, she could see the way his eyes lit up,
sense the confidence, arrogance even, like a lion in his lair.
She could be either his prey, or his lioness; she had to keep
pace with him or find herself devoured.

'Some things you shouldn't wait for, Francis.' Match him

step for step, hold on to him, even as he slithered towards his own mountain top. She leaned across him to the control panel, and as her groping fingers found the key the lift stopped quietly between floors. Already her blouse was unbuttoned and he was kneading the firm flesh of her breasts. She winced, he was getting rougher, more bruising, his thrust for domination more insistent. He still had on his overcoat. She had to allow it, to encourage and indulge him. He was changing, no longer bothering with self-restraint, perhaps no longer able. But as she wedged herself uncomfortably in the corner of the lift, bracing her legs against the walls, feeling cold metal on her buttocks, she knew she had to go with him as far as she could and as far as he wanted to go; it was the type of opportunity that would not present itself again. It was once in a lifetime and she had to grab it, whether or not he any longer said please.

It was four a.m. and pitch dark when Mycroft crept slowly from the bedroom and began to dress quietly outside. Kenny still slept, his body innocently engaged in a tumbling match with the bed linen, an arm wrapped around a toy bear. Mycroft felt more father than lover, driven by a deep and innate sense of protectiveness towards the younger man. He had to believe that what he was doing was right.

When he had finished dressing he sat down at the table and switched on a small lamp. He needed light to write the note. He made several hopeless attempts, all of which he tore into small pieces and placed atop a mounting pile beside him. How could he explain that he was fractured between his feelings of love and duty towards two men, the King and Kenny, both of whom were now threatened through him? That he was running away because that is what he had done all his life and he knew no other answer? That he would continue running as soon as the King's tour was over – for surely he had three days left before disaster struck?

The pile of torn paper mounted, and in the end he was

left with nothing more than: 'I love you, believe me. I'm sorry.' It sounded so pathetic, so insufficient.

He placed the scraps of paper back inside his briefcase, snapping the locks as quietly as he was able, and put on his overcoat. He glanced out of the window to check the street, which he found silent and cold, as he felt inside. As carefully as he could he crept back to place the note on the table where Kenny would find it. As he placed it against the vase of flowers, he saw Kenny sitting up in bed, staring at the case, the overcoat, the note, understanding flooding into his sleep-filled eyes.

'Why, David? Why?' he whispered. He raised no shout, shed no tears, he had seen too many departures in his life and with his job, but accusation filled every syllable.

Mycroft had no answer. He had nothing but a sense of imminent despair from which he wanted to save all those he loved. He fled, away from the sight of Kenny clutching a favourite bear to his chest as he sat forlornly amidst his throne of sheets, he ran out of the apartment and back into the real world, into the dark, past the empty milk bottles, his footsteps on the pavement stones echoing down the empty street. And as he ran, for the first time in his adult life Mycroft discovered he was crying.

Later that day there were tears elsewhere. Tears that hung in the damp night air of winter, that dripped down the mould-covered walls and into the overflowing gullies of the concrete underpass, and clung around the eyes of the old derelict as he stared into the face of his King. The dirt of weeks beneath his finger nails he no longer noticed and the stench of stale urine he no longer smelled, but the King had been aware from several yards away and even more so as he knelt beside the sum of all the old man's possessions – a hand grip tied with sisal, a torn and stain-covered sleeping bag, and a large cardboard box stuffed with newspapers, which would probably be gone by the time he returned the following night.

'How on earth did he get like this?' the King enquired of a charity worker at his elbow.

'Ask him,' suggested the charity worker, who over the

years had lost patience with the high and mighty who came bearing their hearts on their sleeves, to express their deeply felt concerns yet who always, without exception, did so in front of accompanying cameramen, who treated the down-and-outs as impersonal objects rather than as people, who peered and passed on.

The King flushed. At least he had the decency to recognize his own crassness. He knelt on one knee, ignoring the damp and the debris which seemed to be everywhere, to listen and to attempt understanding. And in the distance, at the end of the underpass where they had been shepherded by Mycroft, the cameras turned and recorded the image of a sad, tearful man, bent low amidst the filth, listening to the tale of a tramp.

It was said later by those accompanying members of the media that never had a royal press aide worked more tirelessly and imaginatively to give them the stories and pictures they needed. Without interfering with the King or intruding too savagely on the pathetic scenes of personal misery and deprivation, they were faced with abundance. Mycroft listened, understood, cajoled, wheeled and dealed, encouraged, advised and facilitated. At one point he intervened to delay the King a moment while a camera crew found their ideal position and changed their tape, at another he whispered in the Royal ear and got the King to repeat a scene, steam rising from the drains and beautifully backlit for effect by a street light, with a mother cradling a young baby. He argued with police and remonstrated with local officials who tried to insinuate themselves into the picture. This was not to be a caravan of officialdom who would pass by on the other side as soon as the obligatory photographs were taken; this was a man, out discovering his Kingdom, alone with a few derelicts and his conscience. Or so Mycroft explained, and was believed. If during those three days the King slept fitfully, then Mycroft slept not at all. But whereas the King's cheeks became more sallow and his eyes more sunken and full of remorse as the tour passed from day to night and back to freezing day, Mycroft's blazed with the fire of a conqueror who saw justification in every scene of deprivation and triumph in every click of the shutter.

As the King stooped beside the derelict's cardboard hovel to listen, he knew his suit was being ruined by the damp slime which covered everything, but he did not move. He was only kneeling in it, the old man lived in it. He forced himself to stay, to ignore the odours and the chill wind, to nod and smile encouragement as the old man, through the bubbling of his lungs, told his tale, of university degrees, of a faithless marriage which shattered his career and confidence, of dropping out, only to find no way back. Not without the basic respectability of an address. It was no one's fault, there was no blame, no complaints, except for the cold. He had once lived in the sewers, it was drier and warmer down there and no hassle from policemen, but the Water Board had found out and put a lock on the entrance. It took a moment to take in. They had locked this man out of the sewers . . .

The derelict stretched out his arm, revealing a bandage through which some bodily fluid had escaped and solidified. The bandage was filthy, and the King felt his flesh crawl. The old man drew closer, the misshapen fingers trembling and blackened with filth, thick and broken finger nails like talons, a hand not fit even for the sewers. The King held it very tightly and very long.

When at last he rose to move on, there was foul smear on the leg of his suit and his eyes were damp. From the bite of the wind, probably, because his jaw was set firm and angry, but from tears of compassion the press would say. 'King of Conscience' the headlines would shout. The King walked slowly and stained out of the dripping underpass and onto the front page of every newspaper in the country.

Gordon McKillin's advisers had argued the matter through for a full day. The original idea had been to call a press conference, the full works, and deliver as strong a message as possible to ensure that no journalist left with any question unanswered. But the Opposition Leader had his doubts. If the purpose of the exercise was to identify himself as closely as possible with the King's tour, shouldn't he match it in style? Wouldn't a formalized press conference seem too heavy, too intrusive, as if he were trying to hijack the King for party political purposes? His doubt grew into a flood of uncertainty and the plans were changed. The word was circulated. McKillin would be found on his doorstep immediately after breakfast time, bidding his wife farewell in a touching family scene which complemented the informal fashion of the King's tour, and if any cameras or press men happened to be passing . . .

The scrum outside the front door in Chapel Street was appalling and it took several minutes before McKillin's communications adviser nodded that the multitude of cameras was in position and organized. It had to be right; after all, Breakfast TV was carrying it live.

'Good morning, ladies and gentlemen,' he began as his wife hovered shyly in the background. 'I'm delighted to see you all, for what I assume is an early look at our forthcoming announcements on transport policy.'

'Not unless it includes the abolition of the Royal Trains.'

'Hardly.'

'Mr McKillin, do you think the King is right to take such a high-profile tour?' The questioner was young, blonde, aggressive, thrusting a microphone at him as though it were a weapon. Which, of course, it was.

'The King is high profile, in that he has no choice. Of course he is right to see for himself how the underprivileged live. I believe what he is doing is admirable and I applaud it.'

'But Downing Street is said to be very upset; they say that such matters should be left to the politicians,' another voice chimed in.

'When did Mr Urquhart last visit such places himself, for goodness sake? Just because he doesn't have the *nerve*' – in his Highland tongue the word sounded like a military drum roll calling troops to the advance – 'to face the victims of his policies, that is no reason why others should also run away.'

'You wouldn't criticize the King's tour in any respect?'

McKillin paused. Keep the vultures waiting, guessing,

anticipating. His chin came up to make him look more statesmanlike, less fleshy around the jowls, as he had rehearsed a thousand times. 'I identify myself entirely with what the King has done. I've always been a firm supporter of the Royal Family, and I believe we should be thanking fortune we have a King who is as concerned and involved as he is.'

'So you're one hundred per cent behind him?'

The voice was slow, emphatic, very dour. 'One hundred per cent.'

'Will you be raising the matter in the House?'

'Och, no. I cannot. The rules of the House of Commons are quite clear in excluding any controversial discussion of the Monarch, but, even if the rules permitted, I would not. I believe very firmly that our Royal Family should not be used by politicians for narrow partisan purposes. So I'm not planning to raise the matter or hold any press conferences. I will go no further than simply expressing my view that the King has every right to do what he is doing, and I join in his concern for the underprivileged, who form such a large part of modern Britain . . .'

The communications man was waving his hands about his head, drawing one arm across his throat. Time to wrap up. Enough said to grab a headline, not enough to be accused of exploiting the situation. Always keep the vultures underfed, wanting more.

McKillin was making his final self-deprecating plea to the cameras when from the street came the noisy rapping of a car horn. He looked up to see a green Range-Rover shuffling past. Wretched man! It was a Liberal MP, a neighbour from farther down Chapel Street who took delight whenever he could in disrupting the Opposition Leader's doorstep interviews. The more McKillin protested about fair play, the louder and more sustained became his neighbour's efforts. He knew it would mark the end of interest in the interview from the Breakfast TV producer, he had perhaps only a second or two of live television left. McKillin's eyes lit up with pleasure, he offered a broad smile and cast an extravagant wave in the direction of the retreating Range-Rover. Eight million viewers saw a politician at his best, for all the world as if he were responding graciously and enthusiastically to the unexpected greeting of one of his most ardent supporters. Serve the bugger right. McKillin wasn't going to allow anything to spoil what was turning out to be an excellent day.

As the producer brought the programme back to the studio, Elizabeth Urquhart dragged her attention away from the flickering screen to look at her husband. He was playing with pieces of blackened toast, and he was smiling.

The coach taking the party of journalists from the Gorbals to the airport on the outskirts of Glasgow swayed as it turned the sharp corner into the car park. Mycroft, standing in the aisle, clung tightly as he surveyed the results of his handiwork. Throughout most of the coach sat journalists who were exhausted but content, their work having dominated the front pages for three full days, their expenses justified for at least another month. Plaudits were offered in abundance to Mycroft for his Herculean efforts on their behalf. Goodwill expressed itself in face after face, genuine and wholehearted, until his eyes reached the back rows of the coach. There, like truculent schoolboys, sat Ken Rochester and his photographer, alongside another pair from a rival newspaper who had also joined the tour at the last minute. They weren't accredited Royal correspondents but sailed under a flag of journalistic convenience which described them as feature writers. The attention they had been paying him, and the cameras that had been turned in his direction when they should have been pointed at the King, left Mycroft in no doubt as to whom they intended to feature in their next reports. The word was clearly spreading, the vultures were circling overhead, and the presence of competitors would make them all the more anxious to pounce. He had less time than he had realized.

His thoughts returned to the words which had inspired him and others over the last few days, words he had taken directly from the King. Words about the need to find himself, to respond to those things he felt deep inside, to see whether he was up to the task not just of doing his job, but of being a man. The need to stop running. He thought of Kenny. They wouldn't leave him alone, he was sure of that, the Rochesters of this world weren't the type. Even if Mycroft never saw Kenny again, they would treat Kenny as fuel to feed the pyre, destroy Kenny in order to get at him, destroying him in order to get at the King. He felt no anger, there was no point. That was the way the system worked. Defend the free press and damn the weak. He felt numb, almost clinical, distanced even from his own plight, as if he had stepped outside himself and could regard this other man with the objective detachment of a professional. After all, that's what he was.

At the rear of the coach Rochester was talking conspiratorially in the ear of his photographer, who proceeded to squeeze off yet another series of shots as Mycroft stood above the heads of the journalists, like an actor before his audience playing out some great drama of the doomed. By the weekend, Mycroft reasoned. That was all the time he had left. Such a pity it was excrement like Rochester who would get the credit for the story rather than the court correspondents he had worked with and grown to respect over all these years. As the camera shutter clicked away, he began to find his calmness being steadily eaten away by his acid dislike of Rochester with his curled lip and ingratiating whine. He could feel himself beginning to tremble and he held on more tightly. Don't lose control, he shouted at himself, or the Rochesters will win, tear you to pieces. For God's sake be professional, go out on your own terms!

They were well inside the car park now, heading for the bustle of the departures building. Through his lens, Rochester's photographer saw Mycroft tap the driver on the shoulder and say something which caused the coach to turn aside and park in a quiet lay-by some considerable distance from the terminal. As the coach stopped, Mycroft squeezed out a tight smile for the throng around him. He was right in their midst.

'Before you finish this tour, there's one part of the story you haven't yet got. It might surprise you. It might even surprise the King . . .'

Urquhart sat on the Government Front Bench, shielded only in part by the Dispatch Box, surveying the army of waving hands and wagging tongues before him. George Washington? He felt more like General Custer. The restraint of Opposition shown on McKillin's doorstep had gone as the backbench hounds scented blood. It needed nerve, this job, to withstand the slings and arrows and all the vile taunts of which a parliamentary enemy could think. He had to believe in himself, utterly, to force out any room for doubt which his enemies might exploit. Perfect, absolute, uncompromising certainty in his cause. They were a rabble, not only lacking in principle but also in imagination; he wouldn't be surprised if in their new-found royalist fervour they descended to singing the national anthem, right here and now, in the Chamber of the House of Commons, the one place in all the Kingdom to which the Monarch was denied entry. His eyes lit on The Beast and he smiled grimly. The Beast was, after all, a man true to himself. While others around him roared and waved and stirred themselves to heights of manufactured passion, The Beast sat there looking simply embarrassed. The cause was, to him, more important than victory. He wouldn't cast it aside simply to grasp the opportunity of humiliating his opponent. Bloody idiot.

They were such petty, unworthy specimens. They called themselves politicians, leaders, but none of them understood power. He would show them. And his mother. Show her that he was better than Alistair, had always been better, would always be better than them all. No doubts.

As the first backbencher was called, Urquhart knew what he would say, regardless of the question. But they always asked such predictable questions. It would be the King. And Madam Speaker would object, but he would answer it anyway. Emphasize the principle of keeping the Monarch out of politics. Deprecate their ill-concealed attempt to drag him into partisan warfare. Insinuate that any damned fool could identify problems, the responsible looked for solutions. Encourage them to make as much noise as possible, even if it meant an afternoon of prime ministerial humiliation, to tie themselves as tightly as they could to the King so that they could never unravel the knots. Then, and only then, would it be time to push His Majesty off the mountain top.

'Damn! Damn! Damn!!!' The expletives ricocheted off the walls as Stamper gave vent to his fury, for a moment drowning the television commentary.

Sally and Urquhart were not alone. Stamper sat in one of the large leather armchairs of the Prime Minister's study, agitatedly devouring the news report and his finger nails. For the first time since their relationship had started, she was being shared with someone else. Perhaps Urquhart wanted others to know, maybe she had become a status symbol, another prop for his virility and ego. Or maybe he had simply wanted an audience to witness another of his triumphs. If so, he must be sorely chagrined at the scenes unfolding in front of their eyes.

'In an astonishing finale to the Royal tour this afternoon, the King's press secretary, David Mycroft, announced his resignation,' the reporter intoned.

'I am a homosexual.' The pictures of Mycroft were not particularly clear, there was too much backlighting coming from the windows of the coach, but they were good enough. Surrounded by seated colleagues, sharing news with them as he had done for many years, a player plucking at his audience. This was no fugitive with shifting eyes and sweaty brow, cornered, back to the wall. This was a man in control.

'I had hoped that my private life would remain just that, and not interfere with my responsibilities to the King, but I can no longer be sure of this. So I am resigning.'

'What was the King's response?' a reporter was heard to challenge.

'I don't know. I haven't told him. When last I asked to resign, he refused my resignation. As you all know, he is a man of the utmost compassion and understanding. But the task of the Monarch is more important than any one man, particularly a press aide, and so I have taken it upon myself to relieve him of any responsibility by announcing my resignation publicly, to you. I only hope that His Majesty will understand.'

'But why on earth is being a homosexual a bar to your job?'

Mycroft bent his face into an expression of wry amusement. 'You ask *me* that question?' He laughed as if someone had made a modestly good joke. No animosity, no snarl of an animal at bay. God, it was a fine performance. 'A press officer is meant to be a channel for news, not the target of it. Speculation about my private life would have made my professional duties impossible.'

'Why have you hidden it all these years?' It was Rochester from the back of the bus.

'Hidden it? I haven't. My marriage broke up recently after many years. I was always faithful to my wife, and I am deeply grateful to her for the years of happiness we spent together. But with that break-up came a new understanding and possibly a final opportunity, to be the man that perhaps I always wanted to be. I have made that choice. I have no regrets.'

With apparent utter frankness he had turned the attack. Anyway, most of the people here were old colleagues, friends, nothing could disguise the atmosphere of sympathy and goodwill. Mycroft had chosen his moment, and his interrogators, well.

Urquhart turned off as the TV reporter continued the saga of the Royal aide, whom he described as 'much respected and well liked', against a background of footage from the just-completed tour.

'Selfish bastard,' Stamper muttered.

'I thought you wanted him out,' Sally interjected.

'We wanted him hung, not walking into the sunset with the applause of the crowd ringing in his ears,' snapped Stamper. Sally suspected he was irritated by her presence in what had formerly been an all-male preserve.

'Don't fret, Tim,' Urquhart responded. 'Our target was not Mycroft, but the King. And even as he surveys his realm from the mountain top, the ground beneath his feet is beginning to crumble. Almost time to give him a helping hand. In the small of the back, I think.'

561

'But you only have a week before . . . Those images of the tour are killing you, Francis,' she said softly, marvelling at his composure.

He looked at her with narrowed, hard eyes, as if scolding her for lacking faith. 'But there are images, dear Sally, and there are images.' A dark smile split his face but his eyes remained like rock. He crossed to his desk, extracting a small key from his wallet before slowly unlocking a top drawer. He extracted a large manila envelope and spilled its contents across the desk. Every action was meticulous, like a craftsman jeweller displaying his most precious stones. There were photographs, perhaps a dozen of them, all in colour, which he sorted through to select two, holding them up so that Sally and Stamper could clearly see.

'What do you think of them?'

She was uncertain whether he meant the photographs or the pair of breasts they prominently displayed. The two photographs, as all the others, revealed the uninhibited charms of Princess Charlotte. The only variation on the central theme was the precise position of her body and the contortions of the young man with her.

'Oh, I say,' breathed Stamper.

'One of the more onerous burdens of being Prime Minister is that one is entrusted with a variety of secrets. Stories that are never told. Such as the tale of a young military equerry to the Princess who, fearing that his favoured position at the side and on top of the Princess was in jeopardy, took out an insurance policy in the form of these photographs.'

'Oh, I say,' Stamper said once more as he rifled through the other shots.

'It was the equerry's bad luck,' Urquhart continued, 'that he should try to encash the policy with the wrong man, an investigative journalist who also happens to be a former operative for the security services. And so the photographs finished up in my drawer while the unfortunate lovesick boy has been told in no uncertain terms that his testicles will be ripped from his body should any copies find their way around Fleet Street.' He took back the photographs, which Stamper had been clinging to perhaps a moment too long. 'Something tells me, Timothy, that I wouldn't wish to be in his predicament in a few days' time.'

The two men laughed bawdily, but Urquhart noticed that Sally seemed not to be enjoying the moment.

'Something bothering you, Sally?'

'It doesn't feel right. It's the King who is doing the damage to you, not Mycroft or the Princess.'

'The limbs first . . .'

'But she's done nothing. She's not involved.'

'Bloody soon will be,' snorted Stamper.

'Call it an occupational hazard,' Urquhart added. His smile was stretching more thinly.

'I can't help thinking of her family. The effect on her children.' An edge of stubbornness was beginning to creep into her voice and her full, expressive lips pouted in defiance.

His response was slow and stonily firm. 'War breeds misery. There are many unfortunate victims.'

'Her only sin, Francis, is to be saddled with a healthy sex drive and an inbred English wimp for a husband.'

'Her sin is getting caught.'

'Only because she's a woman!'

'Spare me the collective feminism,' Urquhart snapped in exasperation. 'She's spent a lifetime living off the fat served at the Royal table, and the time has come for her to pay the bill.'

She was about to respond but she saw his eyes flare and pulled herself back. She wasn't going to win this argument and, in pursuing it, she might lose much more. She told herself not to be so naive. Hadn't she always known that a woman's sex was no more than a tool, a weapon, which as often as not fell into the hands of men? She turned away, conceding.

'Tim, make sure these get a good airing, will you? Just a couple for the moment. Leave the rest.'

Stamper nodded and took the opportunity to bend over the desk and rifle once more through the photographs.

'Now, Tim. There's a good fellow.'

Stamper's head came up sharply, his eyes flickering as he looked first at Urquhart, then at Sally, then back to

Urquhart. The ember of understanding began to glow in his eyes, and with it rivalry. She was muscling in on his relationship with the boss, and had an advantage not even Stamper with all his guile and gamescraft could match.

'I'll get right to it, Francis.' He gathered up two of the images and looked sharply at Sally. 'Night, one and all.' Then he was gone.

Neither of them spoke for some time. Urquhart tried to appear nonchalant, taking great care to adjust the razor-sharp creases of his trousers, but the softness of the words when eventually they came belied their menace.

'Don't go coy on me now, O Gypsy.'

'She's going to get a very raw deal out of this one.'

'It's them or me.'

'I know.'

'Still on side?'

In answer, she crossed slowly to him and kissed him passionately, forcing her body up against his and her tongue into his mouth. Within seconds his hands were fondling, bruising. She knew his instincts were angry, animal. Roughly he bent her forward across his desk, sweeping his pen tray and telephone to one side and knocking over a framed photograph of his wife. Her skirt was lifted over her back and he was at her, tearing at her underwear, forcing himself inside, kneading the flesh of her buttocks with such intensity that she winced at the bite of his nails. She was prostrate across the desk, her nose and cheek forced flat into the leather top. And she remembered. As a young girl of perhaps thirteen she had taken a short cut through the back alleys of Dorchester on her way to the cinema and there had come face to face with a woman, bent low across the hood of a car. She was black, with bright crimson lips and gaudy eyes which were hard, impatient, bored. The man behind her was fat and white and had sworn at Sally, foul, disgusting words, but he had not stopped. The memory crowded back in all its chilling clarity, as Urquhart's nails dug ever more deeply into her skin and her face was pressed painfully into the scattering of photographs across the desktop. She felt like crying, not in ecstasy but in pain and degradation. Instead, she simply bit her lip.

Mycroft found him on the moors above Balmoral, where he often went when troubled and wanting to be alone, even in the middle of winter with snow on the ground and an easterly wind which had found nothing to obstruct or deflect it since it had gathered strength in the shadows of the Urals two thousand miles away. There were ageless spirits up there, he had once said, which lurked in the crannies of the granite outcrops and sang as they ran with the wind through the rough heather, long after the deer had sought the shelter of lower pastures. The King had seen him coming, but had not offered any greeting.

'I had no choice. We had no choice.'

'We? Since when was I consulted?' The regal tone betrayed a sense of insult and personal hurt. The anger – or was it solely the wind? – brought a bucolic flush to his cheeks and his words came slowly. 'I would have stuck by you.'

'You think I didn't realize that?' It was Mycroft's turn for exasperation. 'That's why I had to take the decision out of your hands. It's time to start following your head rather than your heart.'

'You have committed no offence, David, broken no law.'

'Since when did such things matter? I would have become a monumental distraction. Instead of listening to you they would have been sniggering behind their hands at me. You've taken such personal risks to carry your message across without interference and I would simply have got in the way, another excuse for them to sidetrack and confuse. Don't you see? I didn't resign in spite of you. I resigned because of you.' He paused, searching the mists which clung to the moorland around them and burying himself deeper inside the borrowed ski jacket. 'And, of course, there's someone else. I had to think of him, too. Protect him.'

'I feel almost jealous.'

'That I could love two men in such different ways I never thought possible.' Mycroft's hand reached out to touch the other man on the arm, an unforgivable action between man and Monarch, but the words and the freezing wind seemed to have stripped the formality away.

'What's his name?'

'Kenny.'

'He will always be welcome. With you. At the Palace.'

The King placed his hand to cover that of Mycroft, who lowered his head, weighed down by gratitude and emotion.

'Ours was a very private matter, not something for headlines and the baying of hounds, of having his private life turned inside out,' Mycroft explained.

'Such plants rarely grow when showered in innuendo and the manure of publicity.'

'I'm very much afraid this may all have been too much for him. But thank you.'

The wind sighed through the heather, a low, mournful sound as the light began to fade, like demons of the night come to reclaim their land.

'It has all been such an unhappy accident, David.'

'Funny, but I feel almost relieved, released. No regrets. But no accident, either.'

'Meaning?'

'I'm not a great believer in coincidence. It was timed to detract from your tour, meant to damage you as much as me.'

'By whom?'

'By whoever had a motive to get at you. And by whoever had the opportunity. By someone who knows the Member for Dagenham and who has the resources to track down a private phone number.'

'It would require someone who could sink very low.'

'The lowest. And he will continue his pursuit of you, have no doubts. There will be more.'

'Then I hope I can find your courage.'

'You already have. All you need is the courage to face up to yourself, that's what you said. To play the man – your own words. Facing up to others holds fewer torments, believe me. But I think you already know that.'

'I shall need your advice, David, more than ever if, as you say, it is all to get worse.'

Slowly at first, then with gathering force, drops of cold-hardened rain began to fall across the two lonely figures. Darkness was encroaching fast.

'Then the best advice I have for you, Sir, is for us to get off this bloody moor before we both freeze to death and save Francis Urquhart the bother.'

FEBRUARY: THE SECOND WEEK

It took less than a second for the phone to be answered in the foreign-currency dealing room at one of the City's leading finance houses which squatted alongside the Thames, in a site near to where the Great Fire that had destroyed half of London more than three centuries earlier had started. It wouldn't take another fire to ruin the City again, they joked, just another Japanese takeover.

The phones never took long to be answered. The difference between disaster and success could often be measured in seconds, and the chief currency dealer couldn't afford to be caught napping by either the markets or any of the seventeen other currency dealers, all of whom envied his job and the commissions that went with it. He dragged his thoughts away from the ruinously fashionable forty-foot cruiser he had just agreed to purchase to concentrate on the voice at the end of the phone. It was not, however, a deal, but an enquiry from one of his many press contacts.

'Heard any rumours about some scandal at the Palace, Jim?'

'What rumours?'

'Oh, nothing very specific. Simply a buzz that there's something brewing which is just about to blow the Royal Yacht out of the water.' He didn't see the dealer wince. 'My editor's asking us all to check around, bit of a dragnet, really. But something's smelling pretty ripe.'

The dealer's eyes flashed up to his screen yet again, checking the mixture of red, black and yellow figures. Sterling seemed to be fine, all the attention today was on the rouble following news of a fresh outbreak of food riots in Moscow. A cripplingly severe winter seemed to have frozen both the capacity of its leaders and the nerve of its foreign exchanges. The dealer rubbed his eyes to make sure; his eyes ached from the constant strain, yet he didn't dare wear his prescription glasses in the office. His position was all about maintaining confidence and at thirty-seven he couldn't afford the slightest sign of age or physical decline; there were too many waiting eagerly to push him off his seat.

'Heard nothing this end, Pete. There's no activity in the markets.'

'I can tell you, the flies are definitely beginning to buzz at this end.'

'Maybe it's just another load of Royal bullshit being spread about the Royal parks.'

'Yeah, maybe,' responded the journalist, sounding unconvinced. 'Let me know if you hear anything, will you?'

The dealer punched the button to disconnect the line and returned to massaging his eyeballs while trying to figure out how he was going to stretch his already crippling mortgage to cover his latest material indulgence. He was dreaming of naked girls covered in smiles and coconut oil and laid out across glass-fibre reinforced with kevlar when the phone rang again. It was a client who had heard similar rumours and who wanted to know whether to make a quick switch into dollars or yen. More flies. And as the dealer looked once again at the screen, the sterling figures began to flash red. A fall. Not much of one, only a few pips, but it was another hint. Could he afford to ignore them? Hell, he was getting too old for this, maybe he should pack it all in and spend a year sailing around the Caribbean before getting himself a proper job. But not yet, not before he had made one last big hit, to cover the boat and the bloody mortgage. He tuned in his aching brain to the box that connected him to the brokers and their constant dangling of buy and sell prices, pressing the button which put him through.

'Cable?' he enquired. It was dealers' kvetch for the price of sterling, harking back to the days when the two great financial empires of London and New York were connected only by unquenchable avarice and a submarine cable.

'Twenty, twenty-five. Five by ten,' came the crackling response. Even in this age of space travel they still couldn't fix the lines connecting them with the brokers' rooms less than a sparrow's fart away. Or were his ears going, too?

He sighed. In for a penny, in for five million. 'Yours. Five.'

The selling had begun.

The door to the editor's office had been slammed shut. It wouldn't make any difference; everybody in the building would hear about it within minutes. The deputy, news and picture editors stood around the chief editor's desk in a formation which gave the impression of Sioux circling a wagon train, but he wasn't giving up without a fight.

'I'm not holding the front page for this. They're disgusting. An invasion of privacy.'

'They're news,' responded his deputy through clenched teeth.

'You know the proprietor's breakfast rule. Nothing on the front page that would offend two old ladies reading the paper over breakfast,' the editor countered.

'That's why there's no one other than old women who read our paper nowadays!'

The editor wanted to shove the words straight back down his pushy deputy's throat, but since they were precisely those he had used in his increasingly frequent rows with the ageing proprietor, he couldn't. He stared once again at the two plate-sized photographs which had already been cropped in red pencil to concentrate the attention away from extraneous features such as the bed, the disarranged pillows and entangled legs, and onto the body and face of the Princess.

'We can't. It's simply obscene.'

Without a word the picture editor leaned across the desk and, with red pencil and ruler, drew two neat lines cutting both photographs just above the nipple. What was left had all been seen before in countless beach photographs of the Princess, but it made no fundamental difference; the expression on her face, the arched back and the tongue in her ear told the whole story.

'What does the Palace have to say?' the editor enquired wearily.

'Sweet bugger all. Since Mycroft publicly deflowered himself they're in something of a mess.'

'First Mycroft, now this . . .' The editor shook his head, conscious that he would be hounded off the society dinner circuit if these went out under his name. He found another burst of resistance. 'Look, this isn't the bloody French Revolution. I will not be the one to drag the Royal Family to the guillotine.'

'There's a real public issue here,' the news editor interjected, somewhat more quietly than the deputy. 'The King involves himself in all sorts of matters, stirring up political controversy, while quite clearly he is ignoring what's going on under his own palace roof. He's supposed to be the personal embodiment of the nation's morality, not running a knocking shop. He's turned out to have more blind eyes than Nelson.'

The editor lowered his head. Sterling had already dipped nearly two cents on the rumours; it was inflicting real harm.

'No one's asking you to lead a revolution, just keep step with the others.' The deputy took up the cudgels once more. 'These piccies are all over town. By morning we might be the only paper not carrying them.'

'I disagree. I don't give a damn about the foreign rags. This is a British affair. Every editor in this town knows the consequences of using these photos. No one's going to rush, not in British newspapers. No.' He braced his shoulders with patriotic pride and shook his head in determined fashion. 'We are not going to use them unless we know for certain that someone else has. It may be throwing away a scoop, but it's the kind of scoop I don't want etched on my gravestone.'

The deputy was about to make some comment that the accountants were already chiselling the circulation figures on his gravestone when the door burst open and the gossip columnist rushed in. He was too excited and breathless to make any sense, his words wrapping themselves in impenetrable knots, until in exasperation he threw his hands in the air and made a dive for the TV remote control on the editor's desk. He punched the button to call up one of the satellite news channels. It was German-owned, run out of Luxembourg and had a footprint that covered half of Europe, including most of Southern England. As the screen came to life they were greeted with the images of an ecstatic Princess Charlotte, nipples and all. Without a further word the deputy grabbed the pictures and rushed off to save the front page.

'Oh, I like this, Elizabeth. I like this a lot.'

It was after one in the morning, the early editions had arrived, and Elizabeth with them. He seemed not to mind, chuckling as he glanced through the reports.

'"This morning the King stands accused of dereliction of duty",' Urquhart read out from the pages of *The Times*. '"In pursuit of personal popularity and his own political scruples he has laid open not only himself but the institution of the Monarchy to frontal attack. The politicians and press lords who have jumped on his bandwagon in the last few weeks have revealed themselves as opportunistic and unprincipled. It has taken courage to stand firm for constitutional principle, to remind the nation that the Monarch should be neither showbiz nor social conscience, but an impartial and politically uninvolved head of state. Francis Urquhart has shown that courage; he is to be applauded".' Urquhart chuckled again. 'Yes, I do like that. But then I should, my dear. I wrote most of it myself.'

'I prefer *Today*,' Elizabeth responded. '"An end to Royal tittle and tattle. It's time for them all to belt up and button up!"'

'"Crackpot King",' Urquhart announced, reading from another. '"HRH should have an urgent word in the Princess's ear, even if he has to jump to the front of the queue to do so . . ."'

Elizabeth was in fits of laughter. She had just picked up the *Sun* with its blaring headline: 'King of Cock-Up'. 'Oh, my dear,' she struggled to respond through convulsions of mirth, 'you really have won this battle.'

He grew suddenly serious, as though someone had

thrown a switch. 'Elizabeth, I've scarcely even started to fight.' He picked up the phone, an operator answered. 'See if the Chancellor of the Exchequer is still in the land of the living,' he instructed, replacing the phone very carefully. It rang less than half a minute later.

'How are you, Francis?' a weary and just-woken voice enquired down the line.

'Well, and about to get considerably better. Listen carefully. We have a particularly difficult crisis on our hands which has already set the doves fluttering in the dovecote. We need to take action before they all fly away for good. I believe sterling is about to take yet another precipitous fall. In the circumstances it would be uncivil and unworthy if we were to ask our friends in Brunei to hold on any longer. It would place an important international alliance at risk. You are to call the Sultan's officials and suggest they sell their three billion pound tranche immediately.'

'Christ Almighty, Francis, that will do for the currency completely.' There was not a trace of tiredness now.

'The markets must have their way. It is a matter of great misfortune that the consequences will strike terror into the hearts of ordinary voters as they see the pound plummet and their mortgage rates about to soar. It will be an even greater misfortune that the whole debacle will be blamed on the King's conscience and those who support him.'

There was silence on the end of the phone.

'I make myself clear?'

'Absolutely,' came the quiet answer.

Urquhart looked attentively at the receiver before softly replacing it. Elizabeth was looking at him with unconcealed admiration.

'We must all make sacrifices in battle, Elizabeth.' He placed the tips of his fingers to the point of his nose. Unconsciously he was beginning to mimic the King in some of his mannerisms, Elizabeth thought. 'I'm not quite sure how to put this delicately,' he continued, 'so perhaps I shall have to crave your understanding and be blunt. It does not pay to fight a battle from within glass houses. It would be helpful if you would stop taking such an ardent interest in Italian arias. Your new-found operatic interests

573

could be so easily . . . misconstrued. It might confuse the troops.'

Elizabeth, who had been sipping a glass of wine, replaced the glass gently on the table.

'Government drivers are such a gossipy bunch,' he added, as if by way of explanation and excuse.

'I see.'

'No hard feelings?'

'After all these years?' She inclined her head. 'Of course not.'

'You are very understanding, my dear.'

'I have to be.' She reached for her purse and extracted an earring. It was bold, fashionable, enamelled, costume jewellery from Butler & Wilson in the Fulham Road. One of Sally's. 'The cleaner gave me this the other day. Found it jammed down the side of the Chesterfield. Thought it was one of mine. I'm not sure how to put this delicately, Francis . . .'

He flushed, lowered his eyes, said nothing.

'Sauce for the goose? Even a Canadian goose?'

'She's . . . American,' he responded haltingly.

'Nevertheless.'

'Elizabeth, she is important to me; she has more vital work to do.'

'But not on her back, Francis. Not in a glass house.'

He looked directly at his wife. It had been a long time since anyone had put him in such a corner. He wasn't used to it. He sighed, he had no choice.

'All you have to do, Elizabeth, is to say please. You remember how to say please, don't you?'

'It's getting very messy.'

'It'll get worse.'

'You sure?'

'Never been more certain.'

'How so?'

'Because he can't yet be certain about winning an election; there's more to be done. He needs a few more points on the polls. He can't stop now. Risk a Royal comeback. And . . .' She hesitated. 'And because he's an axeman. His target isn't the Princess, it's the King himself. I'm not sure if he knows any longer when to stop hacking.'

He was silent, pondering. 'Sally, you're absolutely certain about this?'

'About his plans? Yes. About him . . . ?' She could still feel the mangled flesh of her buttocks where his finger nails had dug deep. 'I'm certain.'

'Then I have work to do.'

He rolled out of bed and reached for his trousers. Moments later he was gone.

The currency dealer turned over and lay in the luminous blue glow of his digital alarm. Four thirteen a.m. Crap. He wouldn't get back to sleep again now. He'd been unsettled all night, his thoughts jarring between the yacht and the young nurse he'd tried and failed to pull a few hours previously. They had shared a ludicrously indulgent meal at Nikita's; she'd drunk too much cherry vodka and been sick. *Tant pis.*

He flicked on his palm-sized Pocketwatch and checked the miniature screen for the latest state of the markets. Perhaps that's what had been eating away at him. Christ! Sterling was down almost another two hundred points in the Far East and he was beginning to wish he, too, had drunk a little less vodka. He was holding twenty million pounds overnight, and he suddenly felt very exposed. He punched one of the memory buttons on his bedside phone which connected with his branch in Singapore, eight hours ahead. 'What's up?'

'Negara's been selling steadily since the market opened,' an accented voice told him. So the Malaysian central bank was in on the act . . .

'What's Cable in forty?' he demanded.

'Sixty-five seventy.'

Selling at sixty-five, buying at seventy. But no one was buying. Time to join the herd. 'Shit, let's move it. At sixty-five.' He put the phone down, having just sold forty million pounds sterling in the belief the price would continue falling. If it did he would have covered his overnight position, and more. He'd better get into the office early, in case the entire bloody world woke up with a headache and the herd started to stampede. And maybe he would call that very special client who helped with all those unofficial deals on the side. The client wouldn't mind being woken at this hour, not for the size of stakes he played with. And if they got it right, he could stop worrying about the yacht. And that silly nurse.

Evening Standard, City Edition, 9 February

POUND AND PRINCESS EXPOSED

Sterling continued to come under heavy pressure as the London market followed the lead set overnight in the Far East. Dealers expressed concern that the stream of sexual scandal enveloping the Royal Family could cause a full-blown constitutional and political crisis, following the resignation of the King's press secretary last week and lurid photographs of Princess Charlotte published in many of this morning's newspapers.

The Bank of England and other European banks moved to support sterling as soon as the markets opened but could not prevent further speculative selling driving the currency down hard against the bottom of its EC limits. There were reports of a major holder of sterling in the Far East dumping significant quantities of the currency. It is feared that interest rates may have to be raised substantially to prop up the ailing pound.

'This sort of situation is a new one for us,' one dealer commented. 'The markets hate the uncertainty, at times this morning they were in turmoil. The sheiks are saying if Buckingham Palace crumbles, how safe is the Bank of England? The City has the atmosphere of a farmyard before Christmas . . .'

It was a good day for a hanging, McKillin thought. The Chamber was packed beyond capacity with many Members, deprived of a seat on the benches, standing at the Bar, crouching in gangways or crowding around the sides of the Speaker's Chair. The pressure of so many mostly male bodies crushed together gave rise to a heady, boisterous atmosphere, overflowing with expectation. It was said there had been similar scenes at Tyburn when they came to hang some wretch from the three-legged gallows, and that they even paid for the privilege of watching the poor bastard swing.

There had already been a long queue of victims today. The waves of panic rippling through the currency markets had washed over into the Stock Exchange and by lunchtime share prices were off, badly. The cries of pain emanating from those with exposed positions could be heard from all over the City and it was going to spread faster than a lassie's legs at the Edinburgh Festival. The building societies were meeting in emergency session; mortgages would have to be raised, the only question was by how much. It wasn't the King's fault, of course, but people had lost their innocent belief in bad fortune, in catastrophes simply happening, they had to have someone to blame. And that meant that McKillin, too, was in the firing line, reflecting ruefully on his recent public displays of indulgence on behalf of the Royal Family, wincing at one hundred per cent. He had thought all morning of defence through aggression, making a full-scale charge in support of the King, but decided that the King's position was too well covered by hostile guns. The troops behind him were no Light Brigade, and he wasn't Errol Flynn. No point in getting shot in the Trossachs for nothing, much better to fight another day. Some question about human rights, perhaps, high-ground stuff, related to the PM's lightning trip to Moscow which had been announced for the coming week. That would do, give him some distance from the sound of battle, get him out from under the gibbet . . . As he waited, he began to feel sticky with the heat and pressure from the bodies of overfed men crowding around.

He saw Urquhart appear just in time for the three-fifteen p.m. start, forcing his way through the scrum which surrounded the Speaker's Chair and squeezing past the outstretched limbs of other Cabinet Ministers perched untidily along the Front Bench. Urquhart smiled across the Dispatch Box at McKillin, a fleeting parting of thin lips to expose the incisors, the first warning shot of the afternoon's campaign. Behind Urquhart's position sat the Honourable Lady Member for Dorset North, bobbing obsequiously as her master took his seat, wearing a garishly crimson outfit which stood out like a traffic beacon amidst the gloom of grey suits and which would show well on the television screens. She had been practising her expressions of support all morning in front of a mirror. She was a handsome and well-presented woman, early forties, with a voice like a hyena, which rumour had it could reach top C in bed, as even some members of the Opposition claimed to know. She'd never make Ministerial office, but her memoirs would probably outsell the rest.

McKillin leaned back, giving the impression of a relaxed demeanour while he studied the press gallery above his head; over the finely carved balustrade he could see the heads of the scribblers, faces strained in expectation, their pencils and prejudices sharpened. He wouldn't keep them waiting, he would get in there at the first opportunity, show his colours and retire from the field before the real battle started and it all got out of control. Human rights, that was it. Damned good idea.

Already Madam Speaker had called the first question, to ask the Prime Minister his engagements for the day, and Urquhart was giving his standard and calculatedly unhelpful response, detailing a few of his official appointments 'in addition to answering questions in the House'.

'It'd be the first bloody time.' It was The Beast, from his seat below the gangway which he claimed by right of constant occupation. He looked dyspeptic; perhaps his sandwiches and pint of bitter had disagreed with him.

Urquhart gave short shrift to the first question, about a local by-pass, posed by a conscientious constituency member with a small majority, and it was McKillin's opportunity. He leaned forward and inclined his head towards Madam Speaker.

'The Leader of the Opposition.' Madam Speaker's voice summoned him to the Dispatch Box. He hadn't even finished rising to his feet before another voice cut through the bustle.

'You couldn't mistake him for a Leader of the Opposition, the grovelling little shit.'

McKillin felt his cheeks flush with anger, then astonishment. It was The Beast. His own side!

'Order! Order!' trilled Madam Speaker. In an atmosphere charged like this, with so many hot MPs rubbing shoulders and jostling elbows, she knew it was vital to stamp her authority on proceedings from the first moment of disruption. 'I heard that. The Honourable Member will withdraw that remark immediately!'

'What else would you call someone who threw away all his principles and got caught licking the boots of the Royal Family. He's made a complete balls of it.'

Opposition Members sat largely silent, stunned. Government backbenchers, too, were uncertain, not knowing whether to agree with The Beast or to denounce his vulgarity, but knowing it was essential to make as much noise as possible and stir the pot. In the midst of the growing uproar The Beast, his tangled forelock tumbling across his face and his baggy sports jacket unbuttoned and open, was on his feet and ignoring the repeated demands of Madam Speaker.

'But isn't it an undeniable fact—'

'No more!' shrieked the Speaker, her half-moon glasses slipping down her nose as she flushed uncomfortably hot beneath her wig. 'I shall have no hesitation in naming the Honourable Member unless he withdraws his remarks immediately!'

'But . . .'

'Withdraw!' Cries demanding his retraction grew from all sides. The Serjeant at Arms, the parliamentary constable, dressed for the part in executioner's garb of black cloth court dress, complete with silk stockings and ceremonial sword, was standing to attention at the Bar, waiting on Madam Speaker's instructions.

'But . . .' began The Beast once again.

'Withdra-a-a-a-w!'

There was pandemonium. The Beast looked around,

seeming unperturbed, as if he could hear none of the noise nor see the flailing hands and Order Papers. He smiled, then at last seemed to appreciate that his game was up for he started nodding his head in agreement. The din subsided, allowing him to be heard.

'OK.' He looked towards the Speaker's Chair. 'Which words do you want me to withdraw? Grovelling? Little? Or Shit?'

The tidal wave of outrage all but drowned Madam Speaker's cries. 'All of it! I want it all withdrawn!' Eventually she was heard.

'The lot? You want me to withdraw the lot?'

'Immediately!' The wig had been shaken askew and she was attempting to readjust herself, desperately struggling to maintain her temper and sense of dignity.

'All right. All right.' The Beast held up his hands to silence the tumult. 'You all know my views about grovelling to their Royal Mightinesses but . . .' – he stared around fiercely at the pack of parliamentary hounds snapping at his heels – 'if you rule I can't say such things, that I've got to retract it, then I shall.'

'Now. This instant!'

There was a baying of approval from all sides. The Beast was now pointing at McKillin.

'Yes, I was wrong. You obviously *can* mistake him for a Leader of the Opposition. The grovelling little shit!'

In the cacophony of shouts from all sides there was not the slightest chance for Madam Speaker to make herself heard, but The Beast didn't wait to be named, gathering up his papers from the floor and throwing a lingering look of insolence in the direction of his party leader before withdrawing himself from the Chamber. The Serjeant at Arms, who could lip-read the Speaker's instructions, fell in beside The Beast to ensure he remained withdrawn from the premises of the Palace of Westminster for the next five working days.

As The Beast's back passed through the doors and beyond, some semblance of order began to be restored to the Chamber. From beneath her wig, still slightly askew, Madam Speaker gazed in the direction of McKillin, her eyes enquiring after his intentions. He shook his head. He didn't want any longer to ask some fool question about human rights. What about his own human rights? All he wanted was for this cruel and exceptional punishment to come to an end, for someone to come and gently cut him down from the parliamentary gallows on which he was swinging, and hope they might give him a decent burial.

'How do you do it, Francis?' Stamper demanded as he strode into the Prime Minister's office in the House of Commons.

'Do what?'

'Get The Beast so wound up that on his own he's more effective at stuffing McKillin than a dozen Barnsley butchers.'

'My dear Tim, you've become such a sad old cynic. You look for conspiracies everywhere. The truth – if you could ever recognize it as such – is that I don't have to wind him up. He comes ready wound. No, my contribution to the fun is more along these lines.' He indicated the television with its display of the latest teletext news. The building societies had finished their emergency meeting and the result of their deliberations was flashing up on the screen.

'Christ. Two per cent on mortgages? That'll go down like a shovel of shit in drinking water.'

'Precisely. See how much concern the average punter has for the homeless when the mortgage on his own semi-detached roof starts burning its way through his beer money. By closing time tonight the King's conscience will seem an irrelevant and unaffordable luxury.'

'My apologies for ever having uttered a cynical remark in your presence.'

'Accepted. Voters appreciate clear choices, Tim, it helps them concentrate. I am presenting them with a choice which is practically transparent. The King may be a rare orchid to my common cabbage, but when the buggers start starving, they'll grab for the cabbage every time.'

'Enough cabbage to give the King chronic wind.'

'My dear Tim, you might say that. On such matters I couldn't possibly comment.'

The King was also seated before his television screen, where he had remained silently watching events since the televising of Prime Minister's Question Time had begun. He had left instructions not to be disturbed but eventually his Private Secretary could restrain his sense of unease no longer. He knocked and entered with a deferential bow.

'Sir, my apologies, but you must know that we are being inundated with calls from the media, wanting some reaction, some guidance as to your feelings about events in the House of Commons. They will not take silence as an answer, and without a press officer . . .'

The King seemed not to have noticed the intrusion, staring fixedly at the screen, unblinking, his body taut, the veins at his temple a vivid blue against the parchment skin of his skull. He looked ashen – not with anger, the Private Secretary was well used to the flashes of fire which sparked from the King. The stillness suggested more a man on a different plane, driven deep within himself, the strain indicating that the search to find equilibrium had proved futile.

The Private Secretary stood motionless, watching the other man's agony, embarrassed at his intrusion yet not knowing how to dismiss himself.

Eventually the King spoke, in a whisper, but not to the Secretary. 'It is no use, David.' The voice was parched and hoarse. 'It cannot be. They will no more let a King be a man than they would any man be King. It cannot be done – you know that, don't you, old friend . . . ?'

Then there was silence. The King had not moved, still staring, unseeing, at the screen. The Private Secretary waited for several seemingly endless seconds and then left, pulling the door gently behind him as if he were closing the lid on a coffin.

Sally rushed across to the House of Commons as soon as she received the summons. She had been in the middle of a pitch to a potential new client, one of the country's leading manufacturers of processed beans, but he had been most understanding, impressed even, and had assured her of the business. With contacts like that he seemed uninterested in further credentials.

A secretary was waiting for her at St Stephen's entrance to escort her like a VIP past the long queues of visitors and through the security gates, rushing her past several hundred years of history. It was her first time; one day, she promised herself, she would be back and take a calmer look at the glories of Old England, when she had the patience to queue for several hours with all the rest. But for the moment she preferred the preferential treatment.

They showed her straight into his office. He was on the phone, pacing around the room in his shirtsleeves, trailing the cord of the telephone behind him, animated, issuing orders.

'Yes, Bryan, I am well and my wife is well. Thank you very much, now shut up and listen. This is important. You will be receiving details of a new poll tomorrow afternoon. A telephone poll following the panic in the markets. It will be a startling one. It will show the Government in a ten-point lead over the Opposition, and my personal lead over McKillin having doubled.' He listened for a moment. 'Of course it's bloody front-page news, why on earth do you think I'm giving it to you? That front-page poll will be supported by an editorial inside your newspaper, something along the lines of "Mortgages and the Monarchy". It will blame the problem with sterling and international confidence four-square on the King and his flawed personality, and those opportunistic politicians who have sought to encourage him in what you will conclude are his grave errors of judgement for seeking to take on the elected Government. Are you listening?'

There was a mild squawking on the end of the phone and Urquhart rolled his eyes in impatience.

'You are to suggest that their unprincipled support for the King has shattered the Opposition and ruined the credibility of McKillin, and even more seriously has cast the country into a constitutional mess which is causing deep economic anguish. Reluctantly you will call for a thoroughgoing review of the Monarchy – restricting its powers, its influence, its size, its income. Take it all down

583

carefully. Yes, I've got time . . .' He paused. 'Now we come to the important bit, Bryan. Pay great attention. Your editorial will finish by concluding that so much economic, political and constitutional uncertainty has been created that it requires an immediate solution. No time for extended debates, parliamentary commissions of inquiry – not while every shareholder and mortgage-payer in the country is swinging on the hook. The matter needs to be dealt with decisively. Once and for all, in the national interest. You are to suggest that the only established means of deciding who governs Britain is to hold an election. Do you understand? An election.' He looked across at Sally and winked.

'My dear Bryan, of course this is something of a shock, that's why I'm giving you the opportunity to prepare. But just between the two of us, until tomorrow. No running down to the bookies to put a couple of quid on an early election, now. Another of our little secrets, eh? You call me, only me, Bryan, day or night, if you have any questions. OK? Bye.'

He turned with an expectant expression towards Sally. She offered back a serious, hard look, almost a scowl.

'So who's supposed to be producing this magical overnight poll of yours, Francis?'

'Why, you are, my dear. You are.'

Her bug eyes sank back into their sockets as if trying to hide. It was after midnight and she had been sitting in front of the computer terminal ever since the last of her staff had departed for the night and left her on her own. She needed space to think.

Preparing a questionnaire had been simple. Nothing fancy or out of the ordinary. And she had on the shelf any number of computer disks with their random digit dialling facilities which would give a spin to the sample and so to the results, to drive the survey upmarket or downmarket, give added weight to council-house tenants or the substantial leafy glades of suburbia, question only company directors or the unemployed. The trouble was she had no idea how much the sample needed to be leant on to get the desired result – Urquhart was clearly ahead, but by how much? By however much, it would be more after *The Times* had sounded off. There was so much unease and anxiety around, it was a perfect time to hotwire the bandwagon.

She wandered around her scruffy premises. The over-heads were kept low, all the flash was up front in the reception area, all the quality poured into the strategy and the thinking. The mechanical side was low life. She walked alongside rows of open booths, covered in cloth for sound-proofing, where tomorrow the motley collection of part-time staff would gather to sit in front of their individual computer screens, phoning the randomly chosen telephone numbers thrown out by the mainframe, mindlessly reading out the required questions and equally mindlessly tapping in the answers. They would not suspect. They were junkies in torn jeans, off-duty New Zealand nurses worrying about missed periods, failed businessmen who had suffered from the mistakes of others and fresh-faced students eagerly waiting to make their own. All that mattered was they were vaguely computer-literate and could turn up at two hours' notice. They had no means of knowing what was happening to the information they gathered, and wouldn't care. She paced along the carpet worn with time and well trodden with gum, examining the polystyrene tiles missing from the corner where the gutter had blocked and backed up, running a finger along the open metal shelves overflowing with computer manuals and telephone directories, and dispatch dockets cast around like sweet wrappers on a windy day. Little natural light penetrated in here to expose the workings of the opinion-research industry. She told clients it was for security, in reality it was simply because the place was a dump. A pot plant had struggled and withered and eventually died, and now doubled as an ashtray. This was her empire.

It had its advantages, this air conditioned, computerized, paperless empire. A few years ago she would have needed to shift a ton of paper to do what she had been asked to do; now she had to lift no more than a couple of fingers, tap a few keys – the right keys, mind you – and

there you had it. Your result. Urquhart's result. But there
was the rub. He had been uncompromisingly specific
about the figures he wanted, had already given them to
Brynford-Jones. No matter how much she toyed with the
specs or put a wobble into the weighting of the sample,
what was required was more than a little spin. She would
have to end up doing what she had never done before,
and fiddle the result. Take two figures, one Government,
the other Opposition, and work backwards. Not so much
massaging as beating them to pulp. If she were found out
she would never work again, might even be put away for
criminal deception. To lie, to cheat, to steal the opinions
of ordinary men and women and abuse them. For Francis
Urquhart. Is that what her dreams were all about?

She gazed once more around the room, its walls painted
black to disguise the cracks, its mustiness which even
the lavatory deodorizers couldn't disguise, its tired-out
percolators and second-hand furniture, its corners which
overflowed with plastic cups and discarded cigarette pack-
ets, its fire alarm system, brick-red amidst the gloom, a
relic of the 1970s, which probably wouldn't work even if
tossed into Vesuvius. She picked up the pot plant, plucked
off its withered leaves, swept away the stub ends, tidied
it as if it were an old and rather disreputable friend, then
she dropped the whole thing, container and all, into the
nearest waste bin. This was her empire. And it was not
enough.

The lack of sleep showed in Sally's eyes, and she had
hidden them behind spectacles with a slight tint, which
only served to emphasize the fullness of her mouth and
the exceptional animation of her nose. As she walked in
through the doorway of Downing Street one of the door-
men nudged a colleague; they had heard talk of her, of
course, but this was the first time she had appeared during
daylight. And Elizabeth Urquhart was at home, too. They
smiled at her encouragingly, both wishing they could find
some excuse to frisk her for weapons.

He was in the Cabinet Room. It was different from the
last occasion they had been here, in the dark, with nothing

but the distant glow of street lamps and the tips of their fingers and tongues to guide them. He still sat in his special chair, but this time a civil servant drew back a chair on the opposite side of the table for her. It felt as though she were a million miles away from him.

'Good afternoon, Miss Quine.'

'Prime Minister.' She nodded coyly while the civil servant made herself scarce.

He waved his arms a little awkwardly. 'Excuse the, er . . . working formality. A busy day.'

'Your poll, Francis.' She opened her briefcase and extracted a single sheet of paper which she thrust across the table. He had to stretch to retrieve it. He studied it briefly.

'Of course, I know these are the figures I asked for. But where are the real figures, Sally?'

'You're holding them, Francis. Ludicrous, isn't it? You didn't have to get me to cheat and fiddle. Ten points ahead, just as you asked. You're home and dry.'

His eyelids blinked rapidly as he took the information in. A smile began, like the fingers of a new dawn creeping across his face. He started nodding in pleasure, as if he had known all along.

'I could have kept my virginity after all.'

He looked up from the piece of paper, a crease across his brow. She was making a point of sorts but damned if he could figure out what. Over a set of figures, one poll amongst the thousands? Selective statistics, the sort of thing Government departments did by instinct? He took out a colourful handkerchief and wiped his nose with meticulous, almost exaggerated care. He wanted to celebrate yet she seemed intent on puncturing his euphoria. That, and the distance between them across the table, would make the next bit easier.

'How are those new clients I sent you?'

She raised her eyebrows in surprise; it seemed such a tangent. 'Fine. Really fine. Thanks.'

'I'm the one who should be grateful, Sally. There will be more in the future . . . clients, that is. I want to go on helping.' He was looking at the figures again, not at her.

He was evidently uncomfortable, unsnapping his watch strap and massaging his wrist, easing his collar as if he felt claustrophobic. Claustrophobic? When she was the only other person in the room?

'What is it, Francis?' She pronounced his name in a more nasal manner than usual; less attractive, he thought.

'We have to stop seeing each other.'

'Why?'

'Too many people know.'

'It never bothered you before.'

'Elizabeth knows.'

'I see.'

'And there's the election. It's all very difficult.'

'It wasn't exactly easy fiddling your goddamned figures.'

There was a silence. He was still trying to find something in the sheet of paper on which to concentrate.

'For how long? How long do we have to stop seeing each other?'

He looked up, a flicker of unease in his eyes, his lips stretched awkwardly. 'I'm . . . afraid it must be for good. Elizabeth insists.'

'And if Elizabeth insists . . .' Her tone was scornful.

'Elizabeth and I have a very solid relationship, mature. We understand each other. We don't cheat on that understanding.'

'My God, Francis, what the hell do you think we've been doing here, there, everywhere in this building, even in that chair you're sitting in, if it wasn't cheating on your wife? Or wasn't it personal for you? Just business?'

He couldn't hold her stare. He began fiddling with his pencil, wondering if she were going to burst into hysterics. Not that, anything but that. He couldn't handle hysterical women.

'Not even after the election, Francis?'

'I've never cheated on her, not like that. Not when she has made her wishes clear.'

'But she need never know. Our work together, it's been fantastic, historic.'

'And I'm grateful . . .'

'It's been much more than that, Francis. At least for me.

You are like none of the other men I've ever been with. I'd hate to lose that. You're better than the rest. You know that, don't you?'

Her nose was bobbing sensuously, full of sexual sema-phore, and he felt himself torn. His relationship with Eliza-beth was his bedrock; through the years, it had made up for his sense of guilt and sexual inadequacy, provided a foundation from which he had withstood all the storms of political ambition and had conquered. It had made him a man. By God, he owed her. She had sacrificed as much as he for his career, in some ways more, but it was all begin-ning to blur as he stared at Sally. She leant forward, her full breasts enticing, offered up still more fully by the sup-port of the Cabinet table.

'I'd be happy to wait, Francis. It would be worth waiting for.'

And wasn't she right. He owed Elizabeth but with her it had never been like this, not raw, uninhibited, dominating lust.

'And there's our work together. We're lucky for each other, Francis. It's got to go on.'

He had never betrayed his wife before, never! But he could feel that irresistible tightness growing within him once more and somehow Elizabeth seemed to belong to another world, the sort of world they had inhabited before he became Prime Minister. Things had changed; the job imposed different rules and responsibilities. He had given Elizabeth what she wanted, the chance to run her own court in Downing Street, did she have a right to ask still more of him? And somehow he knew he would never be able to find another Sally, would have neither the time nor the opportunity. He might be able to replace her mind, but not her body and what it did for him. She had made him feel so supreme, a young man once again. And he could always explain to Elizabeth that it was in nobody's interest to have Sally roaming free, discontented, perhaps venge-ful, not now.

'It would be difficult, Sally.' He swallowed. 'But I'd like to try.'

'First time? Give up your virginity, Francis?'

589

'If you would have it that way.'

He was staring at her breasts, which held him like a rabbit in the beam of a lamp. She smiled, closed the lid of her briefcase and snapped the locks shut as if inside it she had trapped his innocence. Then she rose and walked slowly around the long table. She wore a tight black body stocking in an oversized silk-cotton jacket from Harvey Nicks, an arrangement he hadn't seen before, and as she approached him the jacket was drawn back to expose her full physical charms. He knew he had made the right decision. It was good for the cause, would ensure continued support and security, Elizabeth would understand that – if she ever found out.

Sally was there, beside him. She extended a hand. 'I can't wait. Partner.'

He stood up, they shook hands. He felt triumphant, all-powerful, as though there were no challenge, no dilemma, to which he could not rise.

She was a remarkable woman, this American, practically a true British sport, his smile suggested.

What an utter English prick, she thought.

Brian Redhead's beard had grown longer and wispier with the years, but his Geordie bite remained formidably sharp. Why else would he have survived so long as the doyen of early morning radio and continued to attract an endless stream of politicians to be mangled and torn even before their first cup of coffee had time to grow cold? He sat in his studio within Broadcasting House like a hermit in his cave, searching for some intangible truth, the table strewn with dirty cups, disused notes and soiled reputations, glowering at his producer through the murky window of the control room. A huge old-fashioned wall clock with a burnished oak surround hung on the wall, like a British Rail waiting room, the second hand ticking remorselessly onward.

'It's time once more for our review of the morning papers and we have our regular Thursday reviewer, Matthew Parris, to do just that for us. The Royal robes seem to be in something of a twist again, Matthew.'

'Yes, Brian. Our home-bred answer to all those Austra-
lian soaps begins another tangle-filled episode this morning, but perhaps there are signs that some sort of ending
may be in sight. There are suggestions that we could be
losing at least one of the key players, because the latest
straw poll carried in *The Times* puts the Opposition ten
points behind and it could be the straw that breaks the
Opposition camel's back. Not that Gordon McKillin will
take kindly to being compared to a camel, or a tramp for
that matter, but he must be wondering how soon it will be
before he's sent off to live in a Royal underpass. He might
find it a lot more comfortable than the House of Commons
this afternoon. But it's *The Times* editorial comment which
has galvanized the rest of Fleet Street in their late editions.
Time for an election to clear the air? it asks. No one doubts
that it would not only be Mr McKillin's leadership under
public scrutiny, but also the King's. The *Mirror* goes back to
basics. "Under the present system he could be the biggest
twerp in the kingdom yet still get to reign. To use his own
words, something has got to be done." And not all the
other papers show as much respect. Have you forgotten
the *Sun* headline of just a few days ago which shouted
"King of Conscience"? The *Sun*'s editor obviously has,
because he's reused the same headline today – except it's
been abbreviated to read simply: "King Con". It seems a
week is a long time in Royal politics. There's more in the
rest . . .'

In a City office a few miles away from Broadcasting
House, Landless switched off the radio. Dawn was still a
brushstroke in the sky but already he was at his desk. His
first job had been delivering newspapers as an eight-year-
old, running all the way through the dark streets because
his parents couldn't afford a bike, stuffing letter boxes and
catching glimpses of negligée and bare flesh through the
badly drawn curtains. He'd put on a bit of weight since
then, and a few millions, but the habit of rising early to
catch the others at it had stuck. There was only one other
person in the office, the oldest of his three secretaries who
took the early turn. The silence and her greying hair helped
him think. He stood lingering over his copy of *The Times*,

laid open on his desk. He read it again, cracking the knuckles of each of his fingers in turn as he tried to figure out what – and who – lay behind the words. When he had run out of knuckles he leaned across his desk and tapped the intercom.

'I know it's early, Miss Macmunn, and they'll still be pouring the milk over their wholemeal cornflakes and scratching their Royal rumps. But see if you can get the Palace on the phone . . .'

He had wondered, very briefly and privately, whether he should consult them, take their advice. But only very briefly. As he gazed around the Cabinet table at his colleagues, he could find no patience within himself for their endless debates and dithering, their fruitless searches for the easy way ahead, the constant resort to compromise. They had all arrived with their red Cabinet folders containing the formal Cabinet papers and the notes which civil servants felt might be necessary to support their individual positions or gently undermine those of rival colleagues. Colleagues! It was only his leadership, his authority which prevented them from indulging in the sort of petty squabbles that would disgrace a kindergarten. Anyway, the civil servants' notes were irrelevant, because the civil servants had not known that he was about to hijack the agenda.

There had been no point in seeking opinions; they would have been so pathetically predictable. Too soon, too precipitate, too uncertain, too much damage to the institution of the Monarchy, they would have said. Too much chance they would lose their Ministerial chauffeurs sooner than necessary. Oh, ye of little faith! They needed some backbone, some spunk. They needed terrifying out of their political wits.

He had waited until they finished smiling and congratulating each other at their favourable showing in the opinion polls – *their* favourable showing! He had called on the Chancellor of the Exchequer to recite for them just how wretched it was all going to be, particularly after the chaos in the markets had knocked the stuffing out of business confidence. A tunnel which had been dug deeper and longer than anyone could have expected, the Chancellor recited, with not a flicker of light to be seen and a Budget in the middle of next month which would blow holes in their socks. If they had any socks left.

While they were chewing nauseously on those bones he had asked the Employment Secretary about the figures. School holidays beginning on March 15, some three hundred thousand school leavers flooding onto the market, and employment prospects which looked as welcoming as a witch's armpit. The jobless total would rise above two million. Another election pledge out of the window. And then he had turned to the Attorney General's report about the prospect for Sir Jasper Harrod's trial. From the ague which crossed one or two of the faces he suspected there were other individual donations which had not yet come to light amongst the high and, for the moment, mighty. Thursday March 28 was the trial date. No, no postponements likely, the dirty linen being hung out to dry within days of the first rap of the judge's gavel. Sir Jasper had made it clear he did not wish to suffer on his own.

The colleagues had begun to look as though they were sailing in an overcrowded dinghy through a Force Nine before he put his own twist to their discomfort. A strong rumour that McKillin was considering resignation at Easter. Only that twerp of an Environment Secretary Dickie thought it good news; the rest had recognized it immediately for what it was – the Opposition's best hope of salvation, a new start, a clean break with McKillin's fooleries and failures, a leap for firm new ground. Even the other dunderheads had seen that – all except Dickie. He would have to go, after the election.

Only after silence had hung in the air for many seconds did he thrown them a lifeline, a chance to be hauled towards dry land. An election. On Thursday March 14. Just enough time if they hurried and scuttled to tidy up the parliamentary loose ends and a dissolution which would squeeze them through before the next storms hit and overwhelmed them. Not a suggestion, not a request for opinions, simply an indication of his mastery of tactics and why he was Prime Minister, and not any of the rest of them. A strong opinion poll lead. An Opposition in disarray. A Royal scapegoat. A timetable. And an audience with the King in under an hour to issue the Royal Proclamation. What more could they want. Yes, he knew it was tight, but there was time enough. Just.

'Your Majesty.'

'Urquhart.'

They did not bother sitting. The King showed no signs of offering a chair, and Urquhart needed only seconds to deliver his message.

'There is only one piece of business I wish to raise. I want an immediate election. For March 14.'

The King stared at him, but said nothing.

'I suppose in fairness I must tell you that part of the Government's manifesto will be a proposal to establish a parliamentary committee of inquiry into the Monarchy, its duties and responsibilities. I shall propose to that commission a series of radical restrictions on the activities, role and financing of both you and your relatives. There has been too much scandal and confusion. It is time for the people to decide.'

When he replied the King's voice was remarkably soft and controlled. 'It never ceases to amaze me how politicians can always pontificate in the name of the people, even as they utter the most absurd falsehoods. Yet if I, an hereditary Monarch, were to read from the Testaments my words would still be regarded with suspicion.'

The insult was delivered slowly so that it sank deep. Urquhart smiled patronizingly but offered no response.

'So it is to be outright war, is it? You and me. The King and his Cromwell. Whatever happened to that ancient English virtue of compromise?'

'I am a Scot.'

'So you would destroy me, and with me the Constitution which has served this country so well for generations.'

'A constitutional Monarchy is built on the mistaken concept of dignity and perfect breeding. It is scarcely my fault

594

that you have all turned out to have the appetites and sexual preferences of goats!'

The King flinched as if he had been slapped and Urquhart realized he may have gone a step too far. After all, what was the point?

'I will bother you no longer, Sir. I merely came to inform you of the dissolution. March 14.'

'So you say. But I don't think you shall have it.'

There was no alarm in Urquhart's demeanour; he knew his rights. 'What nonsense is this?'

'You expect me to issue a Royal Proclamation today, this instant.'

'As I have every right to do.'

'Possibly. And then again, possibly not. An interesting point, don't you think? Because I also have rights accorded by the same constitutional precedents, rights to be consulted, to advise and to warn.'

'I am consulting you. Give me as much advice as you want. Warn me, threaten me for all I care. But that cannot prevent you from granting the dissolution I demand. That is the right of the Prime Minister.'

'Be reasonable, Prime Minister. This is my first time at this, I am new to the job. I need to take advice myself, talk to a few people, make sure I am taking the correct constitutional action. I'm sure I could be in a position to grant your request by, say, next week? Not unreasonable, is it? Just a few days?'

'That cannot be!'

'And why not?'

'You cannot expect me to hold an election on Maundy Thursday when those who are not on their knees are flat on their backs for the Easter holidays. No delay. I will not have it, d'you hear!'

The composure had been peeled away; Urquhart's fists were clenched in consternation and his legs braced as if he were about to launch a direct physical attack against the Monarch. Instead of flinching or drawing back, the King began to laugh, a frosty, hollow noise which echoed around the high ceiling.

'You must forgive me, Urquhart. My little joke. Of

course I cannot delay your demand. I merely wanted to see how you would react.' The muscles continued to pull his face into the expression of a smile, but behind it there was no sense of warmth. The eyes were like frost. 'You seem to be in something of a hurry. And so, I have to tell you, am I, for your eagerness has helped prompt a decision of my own. You see, Urquhart, I despise you and all that you stand for. The ruthless, relentless, utterly soulless way you pursue your ends. I feel bound to do everything within my power to stop you.'

Urquhart was shaking his head. 'But you cannot delay an election.'

'No. But neither can I accept what I know to be a fact, that you have destroyed my friends, and my family, and now you attempt to destroy me and along with me, the Crown. You know, Charlotte may be a foolish woman but she is basically a kind soul. She didn't deserve what you did to her. But then, neither did Mycroft.' He waited for a second or two. 'I see you don't even feel the need to deny it.'

'I make no comment. You can prove nothing.'

'I don't need to. Only to myself, at least. You see, Urquhart, you have used those I love as a doormat on which to wipe your boots as you wade your way through the sewers. Now you wish to trample on me. I won't allow it.'

'There's nothing you can do. After this election the Crown will never be in a position to play politics again.'

'On that, Prime Minister, we are agreed. It's taken me much anguish to face up to the fact that what I have been doing these last months, the ideals I have been trying to cherish, the interests I wish to propagate, are politics. Sadly, there is no clear dividing line anymore. If I hold a view in public, even about the weather, then it is politics.'

'At last we are making progress.'

'I am. I'm not so sure about you. I have a duty, a divine duty almost, to do everything within my powers to protect the Crown. I have an equally strong commitment to myself and those things in which I believe. But conscience sits uneasily beneath a modern Crown. You have made certain of that.'

'The people will make certain of that.'

'Perhaps. But not on March 14.'

Urquhart wiped a hand across his mouth in exasperation. 'You are wearing my patience thin. It shall be March 14.'

'But it cannot be. Because you must delay the dissolution of Parliament for an unexpected piece of business.'

'What business?'

'For a Bill of Abdication.'

'Another of your silly jokes!'

'I am not noted for my sense of humour.'

'You will abdicate?' For the first time Urquhart began to feel he was losing his grip. His jaw betrayed the slightest quiver

'In order to protect the Crown and my conscience. And in order to fight you and your kind by every means possible. It is the only way.'

There was no mistaking the earnestness, that had always been the man's weakness, a complete inability to hide his honesty. Urquhart's eyes flickered rapidly as he tried to calculate the political fall-out, and how much damage any delay might inflict on his plans. He would still win, surely? The People's Parliament before the Crown. He would have to squeeze another week's grace out of the calendar, even if it meant Maundy Thursday – a propitious day for giving Kings their comeuppance. Unless . . . my God, he wasn't going to replace McKillin as Leader of the Opposition, was he? No, it was too ludicrous.

'What role do you expect to play in the campaign?' The words were hesitant.

'A modest one. Highlighting the issues of concern to me – of poverty, the lack of opportunities for the young. Urban and environmental squalor. I shall ask David Mycroft for his help. He has a flair for publicity, don't you think?' The King had changed, the habitual tension in his face seemed to have eased, grown softer, no longer plagued by nightmares and self-inflicted guilt. He seemed almost to be enjoying himself. 'But whatever I shall do shall be done entirely properly. I will not engage in personal confrontation or debate with you. Although others, I suspect, will be less fastidious.' He moved to a button hidden behind one of the window drapes and pushed it. Almost immediately the door opened, and in walked Benjamin Landless.

'You!'

'Me.' He nodded. 'It's been a long time, Francis. Seems like a lifetime ago, almost a different world.'

'Bizarre bedfellows, a King and a low-born thug like you.'

'Needs must.'

'I suppose you intend to publish and promote the Royal witterings.'

'Possibly, Francis. But not to the exclusion of other important news.'

For the first time Urquhart noticed that Landless held something in his hand . . . a clutch of papers?

'Photos, Francis. You know about photos, don't you?'

Landless held them out towards Urquhart, who took them as though offered a goblet of hemlock. He studied them in complete silence, unable to engage his tongue even if he had found the words.

'There seems to have been an outbreak of this sort of thing recently, don't you think, Sir?' Landless offered.

'Regrettably,' the King responded.

'Francis, you'll recognize your wife, of course. The other person, the one underneath – sorry, on top in the one you're looking at now – is an Italian. Possibly you've met him. Sings, or some such nonsense. And doesn't draw his curtains properly.'

Urquhart's hands were trembling such that the photographs were in danger of falling from his grasp. With an angry cry he crushed them within his fist and hurled them across the room. 'I'll disown her. People will understand, sympathize. That's not politics!'

The King could not restrain his snort of contempt.

'I sincerely hope you're right, Frankie,' Landless continued. 'But I have my doubts. People will find it very lumpy porridge when they find out about your own outside interests.'

'Meaning?' A haunted edge was creeping into Urquhart's eyes.

'Meaning a particular young and very attractive lady who has not only been seen a lot in Downing Street since you got there, but who has also recently made a huge killing on the foreign exchanges. Anyone might think she knew something – or someone – on the inside. Or will you try to disown her, too?'

The cheeks were suddenly drained, the words tumbling between trembling lips. 'How on earth . . . ? You couldn't possibly know . . .'

A huge bearlike arm was placed around Urquhart's shoulders and Landless lowered his voice to a conspiratorial whisper. As if on cue, the King walked over to a window and turned his back on them, preoccupying himself with the view of his garden.

'Let you in on a little secret, old chum. You see, she's been my partner as well as yours. I have to thank you. Did very nicely out of the currency wobbles, switched out of sterling just in time.'

'This isn't necessary,' he gasped, bewildered. 'You could have done just as well with me . . .'

Landless looked the other man carefully up and down. 'Nope. 'Fraid you're not my type, Francis.'

'Why, Ben? Why are you doing this to me?'

'How many reasons do you want?' He raised his hand to count off the pudgy fingers. 'Because you so obviously enjoyed treating me like shit. Because Prime Ministers come and go, as you'll soon be gone, while the Royal Family endures.' He nodded his huge head in the direction of the King's back. 'And perhaps mostly because he welcomed me, just as I am, Big Bad Benjamin from Bethnal Green, without looking down his nose, when I was never good enough for you or your high and mighty wife.' He twisted over his hand so that it became an upturned claw. 'So I'm squeezing your balls, as hard as I can.'

'Why? Oh, why?' Urquhart continued to moan.

Landless's fist closed tight. 'Because they're there, Francis. Because they're there.' He chuckled. 'Talking of which, I have good news of Sally.'

Urquhart could only raise mournful eyes in enquiry.

'She's pregnant.'

'Not by me!' Urquhart gasped.

'No, not by you.' The voice, which had patronized, now sneered. 'Seems you're not man enough for anything.'

So he knew about that, too. Urquhart turned away from his antagonist, trying to hide the humiliation, but Landless was in full pursuit.

'She's played you for the fool you are, Frankie. In politics, and in bed – or wherever it was. You shouldn't have used her. All that brains and beauty, and you threw it away.'

Urquhart was shaking his head, like a dog trying to rid itself of an unwanted collar.

'She's got new business, new clients, new capital. And a new man. It's a different life for her, Frankie. And being pregnant, too . . . well, you know what women are like about things like that. Or rather you don't, but take it from me. She's an exceptional and very happy lady.'

'Who? Who did she . . . ?' He seemed unable to finish.

'Who did she prefer to you?' Landless chuckled. 'You idiot. You still can't see it, can you.'

Urquhart's whole body had shrunk, his shoulders sagged and his mouth gaped open. He couldn't, wouldn't, take it in.

A look of triumph suffused the publisher's rubbery face. 'I've beat you at everything, Frankie. Even with Sally.'

Urquhart had an overwhelming, primal desire to crawl away, to find a dark place, any place, to bury his humiliation as quickly and as deeply as he could manage, but he couldn't depart, not yet. There was one more thing he had to do first. A final chance, perhaps, to buy a little time. He made an attempt at straightening his shoulders and walked stiffly across the room until he was facing the King's back. His face was contorted with the effort and he drew a deep, gulping breath. 'Sir, I have changed my mind. I withdraw my request for a dissolution.'

The King spun round on his heel, like an officer on parade. 'Oh, do you, Prime Minister? Damned difficult that, I've already set the wheels in motion, you see. Prime

Minister's right to demand an election, of course, the Constitution's clear about that. Can't for the life of me remember the bit where it says he's allowed to call one off. Anyway, I'm the one who dissolves Parliament and signs the Royal Proclamation, and that's just what I'm going to do. If you find my actions objectionable on constitutional or personal grounds, I'm sure I can rely on your vote during the abdication debate.'

'I shall withdraw my proposals for constitutional reform,' Urquhart uttered in exhaustion. 'If necessary, I shall make a public apology for any . . . misunderstanding.'

'Decent of you to offer, Urquhart. Saves me and Mr Landless here insisting on it. I would like the apology made when you introduce the Abdication Bill.'

'But there's no need. You win. We can turn the clock back . . .'

'You still don't understand, do you? I am going to abdicate, whether you want that or not. I am not the right man for this task I was born to, I don't have the self-restraint required of a King. I've come to terms with that. My abdication will protect the Crown and all it stands for much more effectively than if I try to muddle my impatient way through the murky constitutional waters. My son has already been sent for and the regency papers are being drawn up. He is more patient than I, younger, more flexible. He will have a better chance of growing into the great King I shall never be.' He prodded his own chest. 'It's the best thing for me, the man.' The finger turned on Urquhart. 'And it is also the best damned way I can devise of destroying you and everything you stand for.'

Urquhart's lip trembled. 'You used to be an idealist.'

'And you, Mr Urquhart, used to be a politician.'

EPILOGUE

There was a knock on the front door, a soft, tentative sort of rapping. Kenny put down his book and went to answer it. The door opened and there, on the darkened doorstep, wrapped in a new overcoat against the blustery rain, stood Mycroft.

Mycroft had prepared his explanations and apologies carefully. With the announcement of the abdication and election, things had changed. The press had new fish to gut and fry and would leave them alone, if Kenny could understand. And forgive. But as he looked up at the other man he could see the pain deep within the startled eyes, and his words deserted him.

They stood facing each other, each afraid of what the other might say, not wanting to expose once again the scarcely healed wounds. It seemed to Mycroft several lifetimes before Kenny finally spoke.

'Are you going to stand out there all sodding night, David? The bears' tea will be getting cold.'